Printed in the USA
10to2childrensbooks.com

Meet the Author

www.darylcobb.com

Daryl Cobb lives in New Jersey with his wife and two children. Daryl's writing began in college as a Theatre Arts major at Virginia Commonwealth University. He found a freshman writing class inspiring and, combined with his love for music and the guitar, he discovered a passion for songwriting. This talent would motivate him for years to come and the rhythm he created with his music also found its way into the bedtime stories he later created for his children. The story "Boy on the Hill," about a boy who turns the clouds into animals, was his first bedtime story/song and was inspired by his son and an infatuation with the shapes of clouds. Through the years his son and daughter have inspired much of his work, including "Daniel Dinosaur" and "Daddy Did I Ever Say? I Love You, Love You, Every Day."

Daryl spends a lot of his time these days visiting schools promoting literacy with his interactive educational assemblies "Teaching Through Creative Arts." These performance programs teach children about the writing and creative process and allow Daryl to do what he feels is most important -- inspire children to read and write. He also performs at benefits and libraries with his "Music & Storytime" shows.

He is a member of the SCBWI.

Meet the Illustrator

www.piedenero.com

Manuela Pentangelo lives in Busnago, Italy, near Milan, with her flowers, family and friends. She was born in Holland, but has lived all of her life in Italy. A student of architectural design, Manuela discovered that her dreams and goals lay elsewhere. She likes to say that she was born with a pencil in her hand, but it took a while before she realized that her path was to illustrate for children. Manuela often visits London, where she likes to sketch at the British Museum, and likes traveling to different places to find inspiration.

She is a member of the SCBWI.

One cow can produce up to 46,000 cups of milk in a year.

There are approximately 175 different kinds of chickens.

Roosters will almost always start crowing before they are 4 months old.

Pigs are intelligent and can be trained to perform simple tricks.

Texas has the most sheep in the United States.

Cows can live up to 25 years.

A male chicken is called a rooster and a female is a hen.

A runt is an unusually small and weak piglet.

Cows don't sweat.

Sheep move around in large groups called flocks.

A group of pigs is called a herd.

A lamb will know its mother by her bleat, which is the sound she makes.

Chicken eggs come in different colors like white, brown, blue or bluish green and pink.

A baby horse is called a foal. A young boy horse is a colt and a female is a filly.

In the United States there are two types of cows that are used "most" of the time for milk: Holsteins and Jerseys.

The female sheep is called an ewe. The young are called lambs and the male is called a ram.

A chicken takes about 21 days to hatch from its egg.

A rooster says, "Cock-a-doodle-doo," a hen goes, "Cluck-cluck" and a chick says, "Chick-chick."

An adult male cow is called a bull. An adult female is called a cow. A young one is called a calf.

A hen can lay about 300 eggs per year.

Male pigs are called boars. The females are called sows and the babies are called piglets.

Cows have a keen sense of smell and can smell things up to 5 miles away.

An adult horse can eat more than 24 pounds of food a day.

Written by
Daryl K. Cobb

Illustrated by
Manuela Pentagelo

"Barnyard Buddies: Perry Parrot Finds a Purpose"

10 To 2 Children's Books / Clinton

Book design by Daryl K. Cobb.
10 To 2 Children's Book logo was created by Manuela Pentangelo.

ISBN 978-0-578-06391-1

Written by Daryl K. Cobb
Illustrated by Manuela Pentangelo

10to2childrensbooks.com

First Printing 2010

To Joanne, Cameron & Kayley

Through the years I have often wondered, "What am I meant to do, what is my purpose?" Then one day I looked at my family and I realized that this is it, what is more special than this? I am Dad and that is all I need to be.

Daryl K. Cobb

To me and to all the children who will follow their dreams.

Manuela Pentangelo

Perry the parrot
grew up on a farm

with all of his friends
who lived near the barn.

He lived in a home
that was hung from a wall,
in a room full of windows
with a view of it all.

He'd wake up each day
to "Cock-a-doodle-doo,"
sung in the morning
when the sun was new.

Rory the rooster
sang once every day.
He'd sing and he'd sing
till you heard what he'd say.

Perry saw from his perch
all his friends start to rise
and only the piglets
ignored Rory's cries.

Their mom said, "Get up,
you can't stay in bed."
The littlest piglet
just covered her head.

All his friends now awake
with a stretch and a yawn,
made their way to the food
before it was all gone.

Then Perry sat down
with tea and some toast.
It was the time of day
that he loved the most.

He watched all of his friends
get on with their day.
"We all have a purpose,"
he heard someone say.

Perry thought for a second,
"They're right, this is true.
But what is *my* purpose?
Really, what do I do?"

A chicken lays eggs
to scramble and fry.

A cow gives us milk
and cheeses to try.

A sheep gives us wool
for clothes that we wear.

They do so much work.
Is that really fair?

The rooster sounds off
to start out the day.

The cat and the mouse
are always at play.

I hear there's a place
where a dog pulls a sled.
But the one I see
just lays there in bed.

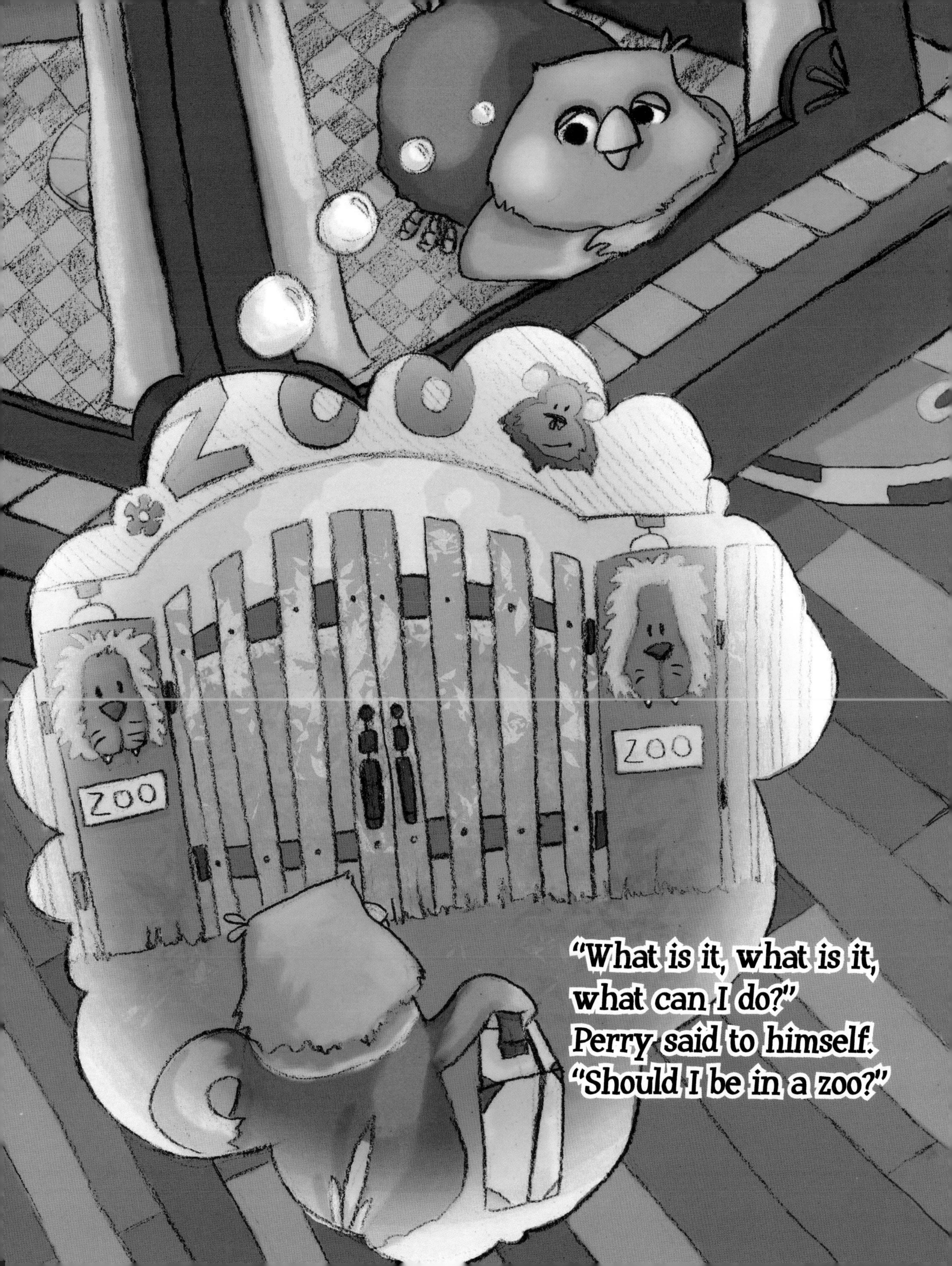

"What is it, what is it,
what can I do?"
Perry said to himself.
"Should I be in a zoo?"

The little boy
who lived in the house
snuck up on Perry,
quiet as a mouse.

Perry was startled
when Jim said, "Hello."
He said, "Jim, Jim,
you scared me you know."

The little boy's laugh
left Perry confused.

"What did I say?
What did I do?"

What happened next
he can't quite explain.
Perry mooed like a cow.
"He'll think I'm insane."

But that only made
Jim laugh even more.
He called to his sister
who walked in the door.

Perry thought, "Hey,
if Jim liked the cow,
I could neigh like a horse.
I can do it somehow."

So he curled his tongue
and gave it a try.
They laughed and they laughed
till they started to cry.

Perry followed that up
with the cluck of a hen.
Then the oink of a pig
as he plays in his pen.

Now Perry's purpose
became very clear.
"I can make people laugh!
I can make people cheer!"

He thought to himself,
"What a beautiful day!"

With a smile on his face
and one last thing to say,

"Cock-a-doodle-doo!"

PROSE PIECES

PROSE PIECES

ESSAYS AND STORIES

SIXTEEN MODERN WRITERS

PAT C. HOY II
U.S. Military Academy, West Point

ROBERT DIYANNI
Pace University, New York

Random House  New York

Copyright acknowledgments can be found at the back of the book, following the Appendix.

First Edition

987654321

Library of Congress Cataloging-in-Publication Data

Prose pieces.

1. College readers. 2. English language—Rhetoric.
I. Hoy, Pat C. II. DiYanni, Robert.
PE1417.P755 1988 808'.0427 87–23426
ISBN 0–394–36888–6

Cover design: Sandra Josephson

Manufactured in the United States of America

For Mothers
and
Other Muses

PREFACE

We begin our composition courses by reading a good, short essay with our students, sometimes a student essay, sometimes one by a professional writer. If that essay is imaginative and if it contains striking dialogue, vivid images, and a memorable scene or two, most students will hesitate to call it an essay; instead, they will suggest that it is a story. They reason that essays must have a standard introductory paragraph with a thesis statement somewhere near its end; that the body ought to have three or four paragraphs with clearly identifiable topic sentences; and that the concluding paragraph ought to restate the essay's main points and thesis, ending with a generalization that relates the essay somehow to the world at large. They respond this way, they tell us later, because they have been conditioned to limit the way they think about essays. They are generally delighted when we open the door to more imaginative possibilities.

In our courses, we turn back and forth between good student essays and good published ones, listening to the sounds of language making sense. We work our way toward more meaningful definitions and more meaningful essays. But as we read published essays with our students, we look for more than a definition. We mine those essays for techniques, for attitudes about writing. We look, ultimately, for an open-ended notion of the essay that does not violate our experience of reading and writing.

The essays in this anthology repeatedly surprise and delight us. Why? Largely because for the modern essayists whose work we anthologize, no idea seems too trivial to be treated seriously or too serious to rule out deeply personal revelations. As these writers think about an astonishing variety of subjects, including seeing, family relationships, politics, culture, gods, identity, and maturation, they create essays as different as their personalities and as variable as their experiences. Though polished and perfected, these essays nevertheless reflect minds in the act of thinking. After the revising and the editing, something nonetheless remains of the writer's original sense of exploration, a delight in the developing idea. We are drawn into these essays because they are dynamic; they move us round a subject, sometimes round and round, giving us intellectual and emotional experiences we may not have had before, making connections we may have overlooked in our own explorations. At the end of each, we sense that we have been in the writer's world.

At the outset in our classes, we proceed from T. S. Eliot's mature discovery: we encourage a "greater expression of personality." For twenty years Eliot called for an "extinction of personality," considering the writer a "medium and not a personality," his mind a "shred of platinum," a voice separate from the "man who suffers." Later, reading Yeats, Eliot discovered "a unique personality which makes one sit up in excitement and eagerness to learn more about the author's mind and feelings." In the face of that discovery, he tempered his earlier judgments and called for a poet "who, out of intense and personal experience, is able to express a general truth;

retaining all the particularity of his experience, to make of it a general symbol." The essays in this book show students how to make of their experiences something significant, how to turn experience—both the experience of life and the experience of reading—into persuasive, evocative essays.

The sixteen American, British, and Canadian writers in this anthology represent men and women whose distinguished work has already earned for them critical recognition. They are among the finest writers of this century. By offering no fewer than four selections for each of them, we give readers an opportunity to study style, personality, and vision, to see each writer's mind working over a variety of experiences, transforming them as they make use of traditional rhetorical modes as well as techniques often considered the province of fiction. When possible, we have included a short story or a chapter from a novel for each of these writers so that teachers can explore with students the appropriate use of such techniques in the essay. Our aim is to open up possibilities for student writers but to do so in the context of tried-and-true methods that appear throughout the essays in this anthology. To that end we offer long and short essays, essays that are easy to read and some that are more difficult. Perhaps most important we offer either complete essays or complete chapters so that every piece in the anthology affords glimpses into the art of composition and into the product that is art.

In the "Introduction" we demonstrate that the reciprocal acts of reading and writing feed and engender one another. And we give students, in jargon-free language, some sense of how to go about reading and writing as well as some sense of the joyous work that goes into the making of memorable prose. We help them understand the writing process by examining evidence from many of the essays that actually focus on writing. Finally, we read carefully and deliberatively Annie Dillard's essay, "Living Like Weasels" so that students can see how to consider stylistic nuances as well as meaning when they read.

For each writer in the anthology, we provide a headnote that focuses primarily on rhetorical considerations, always pointing students to the writing itself. Questions following each selection ask students to do what we did in the "Introduction," to look closely at thought and structure as well as style and strategy. These questions guide reading and provide the occasion for more deliberate second readings. Many can also serve as short writing requirements, assigned along with the essay to focus class discussion. For longer more imaginative writing assignments, we also provide "Suggestions for Writing" that call for additional reading within the anthology, for library research, and for a variety of interpretive exercises—all designed to combine those reciprocal, regenerative acts of reading and writing. The thematic and rhetorical tables suggest other ways to use this text; the possibilities are endless, limited in no way by our own suggested methods. The anthology, like the essays, creates infinite potentialities, sets before us uncharted territory, and allows us to embark on new, exciting journeys with our students.

Pat C. Hoy

Robert DiYanni

EDITORS' ACKNOWLEDGMENTS

For assistance during the preparation of our book, we would like to thank our friends and colleagues who listened to our ideas, occasionally read our work, and gave us sound advice. We would also like to thank our reviewers: Amy Doerr, State University of New York at Buffalo; Helen Ewald, Iowa State University; Patricia Ferrara, Georgia State University; Phyllis Frus, Vanderbilt University; and Dennis Rygiel, Auburn University.

We have been fortunate in working with a fine professional staff at Random House. We would like to thank especially Steve Pensinger and Cynthia Ward who saw promise in our work from the beginning and whose valuable suggestions helped us shape this anthology. Beena Kamlani edited the manuscript with great care and showed genuine concern for the book, concern that went far beyond her professional obligations. Rose Arlia set the wheels in motion at the beginning by bringing us from the field into the editorial chambers. These supporters made our work more pleasurable.

Finally we would like to thank our wives, Ann and Mary, whose generous encouragement sustained us, but whose patience rarely outlasted our enthusiasm. Fellowship among the four of us afforded one of the book's unexpected pleasures. The younger Hoys inspired from afar as the DiYanni children provided musical interludes and spirited conversation at home, restoring us to our senses.

CONTENTS

*Fiction

ONE

Introduction

Writing—Thought, Voice, and Style

Command of grammar, intense reading, and spirited thinking will not of themselves create good essays. Grammar, reading, thinking feed the process, but making good essays is a matter of practice and experimentation, arranging and rearranging words in repeated attempts to discover and create meaning. Although good writers seem to write naturally, influenced perhaps by the subconscious, they develop their craft over time through reading, study, and experimentation. Good essays do not just come into being. Essayists, as the word implies, must try and try and try again, reconsidering, revising, reshaping as they go along. But while they are experimenting, they must also be able to let go, must write without thinking too much about the rules. They must think with pens in hand, almost as if the pen (or the keyboard) is an extension of their minds. Later, they can revise for clarity of thought and expression.

We begin to write alone, finding a personal style in much the same way Joan Didion says we find self-respect, by lying down alone in that "notoriously uncomfortable bed, the one we make ourselves." What we find there in that bed is some sense of our own worth as thinkers, some sense of whether we have something to say. Lying there alone, we discover that E. B. White, Loren Eiseley, and their predecessors, beginning with Montaigne, are right: the self is interesting. The essays in this anthology show us that good writers never venture far away from that bed; neither do they abandon self, trying to disappear entirely from their essays.

Good writing depends, of course, on intellectual growth, on inner debate followed by choice. As we become educated—reading and thinking and writing—we begin to hear competing voices in our heads, conflicting points of view. When we let our readers hear snatches of the debate going on among our inner voices, our writing becomes more interesting, and we become more convincing. We're looking for a way to rouse our readers, to let them know that we are capable of looking round a subject, capable of examining it from many angles even as we present our own conclusions. We want to reach those readers, and we cannot do that if we appear to be single-minded, if we appear to have drawn our conclusions without careful consideration of the subject. We try to give those readers, in the most interesting and convincing ways we know, our view of things, and we try to express that view in an appealing and convincing written voice that is personal and distinctive.

One way, paradoxically, to find this voice is to learn to hear the distinctive voices of other writers, not so much to mimic them, but to recognize what an authentic voice sounds like. In his essay "What I Believe," E. M. Forster tells us what he believes and doesn't. "I do not believe in Belief," Forster writes. He challenges the foundation of Western culture, dares to fly in the face of Christianity, and before he finishes his first paragraph, we know that cultural self-righteousness—reflected in a misapplication of Faith and Belief—is, in Forster's imagination in 1939, associated with the sound of jackboots on pavement. In that first sentence, he wastes not a word getting to his point. There are no cushioning sentences that lead to a thesis near the terminal position in the introductory paragraph; indeed there is no thesis statement. What we have instead is a statement of unbelief, followed by an exploration of wrongheaded Belief. Here is Forster's opening paragraph:

> I do not believe in Belief. But this is an Age of Faith, and there are so many militant creeds that, in self-defence, one has to formulate a creed of one's own. Tolerance, good temper and sympathy are no longer enough in a world which is rent by religious and racial persecution, in a world where ignorance rules, and Science, who ought to have ruled, plays the subservient pimp. Tolerance, good temper and sympathy—they are what matter really, and if the human race is not to collapse they must come to the front before long. But for the moment they are not enough, their action is no stronger than a flower, battered beneath a military jackboot. They want stiffening, even if the process coarsens them. Faith, to my mind, is a stiffening process, a sort of mental starch, which ought to be applied as sparingly as possible. I dislike the stuff. I do not believe in it, for its own sake, at all. Herein I probably differ from most people, who believe in Belief, and are only sorry they cannot swallow even more than they do. My law-givers are Erasmus and Montaigne, not Moses and St Paul. My temple stands not upon Mount Moriah but in that Elysian Field where even the immoral are admitted. My motto is: "Lord, I disbelieve—help thou my unbelief."

Not every writer can be so bold. Forster can because his is such a reasonable, nonthreatening voice. He does not attack Christianity; he argues against a misapplication of its principles, a misapplication that fed the war. When he finally tells us somewhere near the middle of his essay that he believes in "an aristocracy of the sensitive, the considerate and the plucky," we are comforted, perhaps pleased. He has taken away our belief in Belief, but he has replaced it with an idea that offers hope. Forster's provocative exploration ends with a Jobian echo: "Naked I came into the world, naked I shall go out of it! And a very good thing too, for it reminds me that I am naked under my shirt, whatever its colour." Forster says in this essay, without actually saying it: here I sit with my nation on the brink of war, being tested, being tried. I will not despair. I will not hide my good head in the sand. I will tell you that I do not believe in Belief as you seem to understand it. I do, however, believe in my fellowman. I believe in you, whatever the color of your uniform, if you act out of consideration for others. I believe especially in an aristocracy of the sensitive, the considerate, and the plucky. If we stick together, we might just prevail, present trials and tribulations notwithstanding. Yes, he says all of that directly or indirectly, and in the process turns the Bible to his own good use even as he shows us how we devalue it. In examining his own beliefs, he makes us reexamine ours, not because he hammers away at us but because he takes us round an old idea, teaches us to be reflective and discriminating, teaches us to think. No rules. Few admonitions. Just clear, unmuddled exploration.

But there is more to this essay than Forster's reasonable, nonthreatening voice and his sensible exploration of belief and unbelief. The word *voice* suggests part of it, but even voice is a metaphor; it points to a quality in Forster's text that we can't define precisely. As we have indicated, voice has something to do with tone, with the writer's expressed attitude about his material. It also suggests that written words might have a spoken quality, that the text might give us the sense that the writer is actually talking to us as we read the words. We decide whether we want to listen based on whether we like the sound of the voice, whether we find it grating, appealing, insistent, convincing, dramatic. Forster's voice is appealing because it seems to be conversational. We continue to listen to him because he seems willing to change his mind even as he writes; he makes us smile even as he admonishes us; and he enjoins us to laugh together even as he mulls over the most serious matters. Let's listen to him as he tells us one of the things he believes in; he has just told us that he does not believe in Great Men:

> I believe in aristocracy, though—if that is the right word, and if a democrat may use it. Not an aristocracy of power, based upon rank and influence, but an aristocracy of the sensitive, the considerate and the plucky. Its members are to be found in all nations and classes, and all through the ages, and there is a secret understanding between them when they meet. They represent the true human tradition, the one permanent victory of our queer race over cruelty and chaos. Thousands of them perish in obscurity, a few are great names. They are sensitive for others as well as for themselves, they are considerate without being fussy, their pluck is not swankiness but the power to endure, and they can take a joke. I give no examples—it is risky to do that—but the reader may as well consider whether this is the type of person he would like to meet and to be, and whether (going further with me) he would prefer that this type should *not* be an ascetic one. I am against asceticism myself. I am with the old Scotsman who wanted less chastity and more delicacy. I do not feel that my aristocrats are a real aristocracy if they thwart their bodies, since bodies are the instruments through which we register and enjoy the world. Still, I do not insist. This is not a major point. It is clearly possible to be sensitive, considerate and plucky and yet be an ascetic too, and if anyone possesses the first three qualities, I will let him in!

We could look through all of Forster's writing and not find a passage that more nearly captures his essence. Voice is a part of this representative passage, but something else also makes it Forster's.

John Henry Newman, one of the most distinguished nineteenth century educators, would call that other quality style, and he would argue that one's style is like one's shadow. Newman believes, and we do too, that a writer's "thought and feeling are personal, and so his language is personal." Newman also observes the close connection between the written word and the spoken, and if he were alive to examine the essays in this book, he would call them literature because they express "not objective truth, as it is called, but subjective; not things, but thoughts."

Scientific writing, on the other hand, would contain no "colouring derived from [the writer's] mind" and would instead try to express some general, objective truth, using words as symbols. Style, for the essayist, is a "thinking out into language," and literature, the product of that thinking, is "not . . . mere *words;* but thoughts expressed in language." This special sense of the word *style* suggests more than the shape of one's sentences or one's penchant for various writing strategies; it suggests as well a writer's intimate relationship with the words themselves—the inseparable connection between a writer and thought itself. Certainly, over time, good writers become familiar with the way other men and women have used language effectively—with their methods of expression, with their forms, with their turns of phrase—but good writers will not simply mimic or copy what others have done. Their use of language will be as personal as their thoughts are personal.

In Forster's essay, we sense that he is there, present in the text. We can hear him talking directly to us. And if we read several of his essays, we discover that he talks in much the same way in each of them. As we read more of his work, we start to think of him as a person; we start to draw conclusions about his special concerns, his personality, his way of seeing the world. So overwhelming is our sense of him that we may even wish we could meet him, because we think we already know him. Could we meet, we might find that he turns out to be a little bit different from what we expected. We might discover that he was creating another "Forster" for us in those essays, different in some ways from the so-called "real" one. Writers can indeed put on masks, play roles, but they generally do so for a particular reason. It's part of their strategy on occasion. But even then, they do not disappear altogether.

We can gain insight into this problem if we examine an essay in which the writer does not make a personal appearance in the essay. She does not speak directly to us; she does not identify herself as I; she does not play over her thoughts as Forster does. But she is there nevertheless. In her very short essay "Old Mrs. Grey," Virginia Woolf teases us into thought from behind the scene. The focus is on a ninety-two-year-old woman, confined to her room in old age. When she tries to look beyond her open door, she sees only "a zizgag of pain wriggling across the door." Nowhere in the eleven paragraphs do we catch a direct glimpse of Woolf, but her unmistakable sensibility is there from the beginning shaping her idea, creating the form of the argument. Her values—her concern about the old woman, her own personal preoccupation with death, her fanciful imagination—come into play as she creates her compelling conclusion that "we—humanity" are doing Mrs. Grey a disservice by keeping her alive with "a bottle of medicine, a cup of tea, a dying fire." We "pinion" her body to the "wire" that jerks her around, pulls her painfully into awareness of herself. We pinion her body in this world "like a rook on a barn door; but a rook that still lives, even with a nail through it." These are Woolf's images, Woolf's words. It is her argument and no one else's, an argument developed as only she could develop it. Should Forster write about Mrs. Grey, he would undoubtedly do it differently. Were Woolf to write about Belief, she would certainly not replicate Forster's essay. Because they are good writers, their work bears their personal stamp; it is their own, following them about as their very shadows.

At the back of Newman's idea and ours is the suggestion that one's style, the character of one's thoughts, will change over time, reflecting experience gained through study, contemplation, reading, and writing. Neither of these activities is sufficient unto itself; neither can be pursued at the expense of the others. But together they lead to important discoveries; they lead finally to texts that are unmistakably ours—personal, exploratory, authentic.

Reading and Writing—Seeing, Rendering, Shaping

Perhaps the most important goal in reading and writing essays is to learn how to observe. Seeing is a basic and primary aim of education whether we are learning to see ourselves, our culture, our nation, or the world at large. We all know that seeing is important, but it's nice to be told by someone like Annie Dillard whose essay "Seeing" opens windows on the world. Dillard explores two ways of seeing. She tells us that we can learn to see the way the "lover . . . and the knowledgeable" see; that is, we might see as the scrupulous observer sees, from a base of knowledge with an intimate concern for our subject. If we know enough and if we go out looking, consciously searching, we can see things that others miss. Dillard reminds us that "Seeing [this way] is . . . very much a matter of verbalization." She wants us to know that we have to become conscious of what passes before our eyes, have to remind ourselves of what we have seen, find words to account for the experience. We have to keep in our heads "a running description of the present." But we might also see another way, if we are lucky. We might just let go by returning to our senses, by opening up to the world around us. We let the world act on us in whatever way it will. Seeing as the "unscrupulous observer" sees, we too might "[fill] up like a new wineskin," just as Dillard claims to do. She even tells us what happened to her when she opened up: "I breathed an air like light; I saw a light like water. I was the lip of a fountain the creek filled forever; I was ether, the leaf in the zephyr; I was flesh-flake, feather, bone." While that poetic language may not make things perfectly clear, it creates in our minds new possibilities, both for seeing and for writing.

By verbalizing our observations, we move together beneath the surface of our subjects. We notice surfaces, of course, but we discover depths of significance beneath them. We notice, for example, in "Goodbye to All That" that Didion focuses on the cockroach on the tile floor of the White Rose bar in New York and diverts us away from the space shot on the TV screen above the bar; we notice how, through that diversionary move, she makes an indirect statement about her own state of mind. That kind of discovery leads us to considerations of technique and matters of form. If two or three days later, we read E. B. White's "Good-bye to Forty-eighth Street," we might see that White would choose the "orbiting of trotting horses" and the "wild look in the whites of a cow's eyes" over the "the first little moon" that the government put into orbit. At the Fryeburg fair where White spent the day the Russians launched the first satellite, he turned from the "Russian moon" to life: "The wheels wheeled, the chairs spun, the cotton candy tinted the faces of children, the bright leaves tinted the woods and hills." Reading White and Didion together, we suspect that the older man and the younger woman have more in common than their interest in writing. They both turn away from space to the more immediate things of this earth; they have an interest in the particular, concrete details of the life around them. Over time, we discover that reading is a cumulative experience; the more we do it, the better we get. The more we do it, the more we know, the more we have to write about, the more connections we can make. We learn too about writing itself.

Those other teachers—the essayists, our fellow collaborators—teach us on occasion something explicit about writing, about the craft itself. White, who is fond of tongue-in-cheek observations, reminds us that essay writers must be "congenitally self-centered"; they have to sustain themselves "by the childhood belief that everything [they] think about, everything that happens to [them], is of general interest." He uses humor to make the truth palpable. When he's in a more serious mood, he feels quite responsible as the "writing man, or secretary" who is "charged with the safekeeping of all unexpected items of worldly or unworldly enchantment, as though [he] might be held personally responsible if even a small one were to be lost." In "The Ring of Time" he claims that he failed to "describe what is indescribable"—the enchantment of the circus and the bareback horse rider—but he has, he believes, "discharged [his] duty to [his] society." White reminds all of us who aspire to be good writers that we are like acrobats, that we "must occasionally try a stunt that is too much for [us]." He teaches us about self-centered responsibility and reminds us that we ought to experiment and take risks as we fulfill our responsibilities. We ought to jump on the rhetorical trampoline even if we fall off on occasion. Because White's main business is not to teach us how to write, his hints come to us, Dillard might say, as "unwrapped gifts and free surprises."

On occasion, good writers are even more explicit about writing than White; they actually write essays about writing. And when they do, they provide the occasion for stimulating insights into the writing process. Joan Didion, echoing White, reminds us that "writing is the act of saying *I,* of imposing oneself upon other people, of saying *listen to me, see it my way, change your mind.*" But, she goes on to tell us so much more about the necessity for writing. "I write entirely to find out what I'm thinking, what I'm looking at, what I see and what it means." What Didion wants eventually to do is come to grips with those special images in her mind, the "images that shimmer around the edges." Those are the charged images that seem to come to her and to us out of the blue; they come, she argues, with a "grammar" of their own, "the grammar in the picture." She explains:

> Just as I meant "shimmer" literally I mean "grammar" literally. Grammar is a piano I play by ear, since I seem to have been out of school the year the rules were mentioned. All I know about grammar is its infinite power. To shift the structure of a sentence alters the meaning of that sentence, as definitely and inflexibly as the position of a camera alters the meaning of the object photographed. Many people know about camera angles now, but not so many know about sentences. The arrangement of the words matters, and the arrangement you want can be found in the picture in your mind. The picture dictates the arrangement. The picture dictates whether this will be a sentence with or without clauses, a sentence that ends hard or a dying-fall sentence, long or short, active or passive. The picture tells you how to arrange the words and the arrangement of the words tells you, or tells me, what's going on in the picture. *Nota bene:*
>
> It tells you.
> You don't tell it.

Didion quite simply gives all of us a new way to think about our work of writing.

Loren Eiseley offers us another way. In his essay "Willy," he describes the pictures in his mind, what they're like, how they get there, how they accumulate over the years, how he remembers them, and what they mean. He is acutely aware of his own peculiar angle of vision, informed as it is by his anthropological leanings. But he is also aware that scientific articles tend to report facts, make careful assertions, and present findings. In his autobiography, Eiseley tells us how he came to write "the concealed essay, in which personal anecdote was allowed gently to bring under observation thoughts of a more purely scientific nature." In the midst of a personal crisis when he had temporarily lost his hearing, Eiseley received a second blow. A scientific journal turned down an article he had written on evolution. Rejected, he "turned aside from the straitly defined scientific article" to another form:

> That the self and its minute adventures may be interesting every essayist from Montaigne to Emerson has intimated, but only if one is utterly, nakedly honest and does not pontificate. In a silence upon which nothing could impinge, I shifted from the article as originally intended. A personal anecdote introduced it, personal material lay scattered through it, personal philosophy concluded it, and yet I had done no harm to the scientific data. . . . Out of the ghost world of my journeys through the silent station arose by degrees the prose world with which, it is true, I first toyed long ago, but which had been largely submerged by departmental discipline. *The Immense Journey,* perhaps my most widely read and translated book, was born on that little kitchen table where my wife had to write me notes to save her voice.

And so we move from White's call for self-centeredness to Didion's pictorial grammar to Eiseley's concealed essay. Moving so quickly, we move past a host of other essayists in this collection who also have much to say that can improve our vision as well as our notions about writing. But the idea is clear: reading informs good writing, takes us closer to our primary task: making meaning out of words, making sense of experience.

Reading also serves a complementary purpose. Reading actively, we learn to respond not only to what an essay says but also to how someone else makes meaning. Over time, we become aware of the essay's literary qualities, the various stylistic devices that good writers use. Tom Wolfe believes that journalists in the 1960s borrowed "techniques of realism" from the novelists. These writers used "scene-by-scene construction," moving away from "sheer historical narrative." They rendered a number of scenes to move the reader along through a time sequence, obviating the need for explanations. Witnessing the scenes and hearing the conversations, the writers could "record the dialogue in full." They could also present the scene through the eyes of another character, taking us closer to the "emotional reality of the scene." Finally, the writer might note gestures, furniture, styles, modes of behavior, what Wolfe calls "people's *status life*": "the entire pattern of behavior and possessions through which people express their position in the world or what they think it is or what they hope it to be." The immediate effect of these techniques in nonfiction is to give the reader a sense of being involved, of being at the scene. Such immediacy convinces; it creates interest. Wolfe knew, of course, that essayists as well as novelists were using these and other literary techniques long before the New Journalists came along, but these reporters for whom Wolfe served as spokesman may have sparked a new interest in the kind of personal essays we see in this collection.

That is not to say that all of our essayists are New Journalists; many are not. But many are fiction writers, and like New Journalists, they too use literary devices to enrich their essays. We can do the same thing, keeping in mind that essayists, like journalists, are responsible for the points they make; they do not fabricate evidence. Neither do they create fictional situations and characters, trying to pass them off as real in the nonfiction essay. But they are free to use the techniques of the literary artist, free to shape everyday experience to make their points in interesting ways.

As we learn to give voice to our individual visions of experience, to explore and enrich our ways of perceiving the world, and to verbalize those perceptions, we begin to care about our writing. As a result we take time to invest ourselves honestly, thoroughly in what we write. We take time to shape and revise our work once it is composed. As our written voice becomes more authentic, we can learn more complicated writing strategies. But those more complicated strategies will not make our writing exciting for us or engaging to our readers unless it reflects our personal vision, unless it is natural, and honest. Technique, style, and conviction are all helpful; they are necessary elements of good writing. But they are not enough. Powerful, convincing essays—essays that reflect minds' thinking, essays that account for a writer's personal vision, essays that speak to us directly in an enticing personal voice—evolve over a period of time. They are the products of reading, writing, thinking, collaborating, and revising. They come into being only when writers have something to say and care strongly about saying it well.

Reading toward Writing—An Exploration

Reading fiction and nonfiction alerts us to nuances, to things rendered but not explained. Active, deliberative reading involves both intellectual comprehension and emotional apprehension, a consideration of the feelings essays generate as well as the thinking they stimulate. This reading process requires that we make sense of gaps in texts; that we recognize linguistic, literary, and cultural conventions; that we abstract and generalize on the basis of textual details; that we bring our values to bear on the text. We do these things simultaneously. And as we do, patterns of meaning emerge in repeated acts of observation and inference, with readjustments and interpretive realignments occurring throughout the reading process. When, for example, we practice *active reading* with Annie Dillard's "Living Like Weasels," we learn about much more than her momentary, expansive love affair with the weasel.

Let's begin an experiment in reading with Dillard's opening paragraph; our aim is to see what Dillard is saying and how she says it, to discover what we think about it and why:

> 1 A weasel is wild. Who knows what he thinks? He sleeps in his underground den, his tail draped over his nose. Sometimes he lives in his den for two days without leaving.

> Outside, he stalks rabbits, mice, muskrats, and birds, killing more bodies than he can eat warm, and often dragging the carcasses home. Obedient to instinct, he bites prey at the neck, either splitting the jugular vein at the throat or crunching the brain at the base of the skull, and he does not let go. One naturalist refused to kill a weasel who was socketed into his hand deeply as a rattlesnake. The man could in no way pry the tiny weasel off, and he had to walk half a mile to water, the weasel dangling from his palm, and soak him off like a stubborn label.

A few questions:

What strikes us most about this passage? What do we notice on first reading it? What observations would we most like to make about it? What questions do we have? What feelings does the text inspire? What expectations do we have about where the essay is heading? About what the writer is up to?

And some observations:

The first sentence is abrupt. It announces directly and forcefully an important point: a weasel is wild. But what does it imply? What do we understand by *wild?* How wild? In what way is the weasel wild? The second sentence is a question, one that invites us to consider what a weasel thinks about. (Or perhaps it suggests that we shouldn't bother because we simply cannot know.) "Who knows what he thinks?" How we take this sentence depends on how we hear it, which in turn, affects how we say it. Here's one way: Who knows what he *thinks?* Another: Who knows *what* he thinks? Still another: Who *knows* what he thinks? Whichever we prefer, we recognize the possibility of alternative readings.

The third and fourth sentences provide information—that weasels sleep in dens where they can remain for up to two days at a time. There's nothing really surprising there. But what about that other little bit—*how* the weasel sleeps: with his tail draped over his nose. Whether factual or fanciful, that draped tail is lovely and surprising, an image gratuitously offered to engage, amuse, surprise.

Sentences five and six reveal the weasel as hunter—stalking prey, killing it, dragging it to his den where he'll eat and then, presumably sleep. When we are told that the weasel is obedient to instinct and are shown how he kills—by splitting the jugular vein or by crunching his victim's brain—we remember the opening sentence: "A weasel is wild." And we begin to understand what that means. Although we "understood" before, that knowledge was vague, obscure, distantly intellectual. Now, we know.

It is here, in the middle of the paragraph, that we perhaps register our strongest emotional response. How do we respond to Dillard's details about the killing? Are we amazed? Engaged? Appalled? Or what? That question about response is directed at our experience of the essay. We can also ask a writerly, technical question: Does Dillard need that degree of detail? Suppose she had diluted it or perhaps even omitted concrete detail almost entirely. Or suppose, conversely, that she had provided an even more elaborate rendering of the killing. How would such alterations affect our response?

Dillard's opening paragraph concludes with an anecdote about a naturalist bitten by the tenacious weasel. The anecdote makes a point. But it does more. The image impresses itself on our minds in language worth noting: the verb, "socketed"; the comparison with the rattlesnake; the image of the stubborn label. To make sense of the opening paragraph, even preliminary sense, is to make such observations and to wonder about their significance. And it is to wonder also where the essay is heading, where the writer is taking us. What do we expect? Why?

Once we read Dillard's second paragraph, we can consider how it affects our understanding of and response to the first. How does it follow from the first? What does it do rhetorically—or, how does it affect us as readers?

> 2 And once, says Ernest Thompson Seton—once, a man shot an eagle out of the sky. He examined the eagle and found the dry skull of a weasel fixed by the jaws to his throat. The supposition is that the eagle had pounced on the weasel and the weasel swiveled and bit as instinct taught him, tooth to neck, and nearly won. I would like to have seen that eagle from the air a few weeks or months before he was shot: was the whole weasel still attached to his feathered throat, a fur pendant? Or did the eagle eat what he could reach, gutting the living weasel with his talons before his breast, bending his beak, cleaning the beautiful airborne bones?

Our questions at the beginning of this second paragraph necessarily invite our responses, both intellectual and emotional. In asking what strikes us about the details or the language of the second paragraph, we move from those subjective responses to more objective considerations. On the basis of the details we notice and relate, we form inferences. We move backward, in a way, from our initial response to a set of observations about the essay's rhetoric. We might observe, for example, that the second paragraph begins with an image very much like the one at the end of the opening paragraph: the tenacious weasel fiercely holds on, in one instance to a man's hand, in another, to an eagle's throat. And we might register the justness of this pair of images, the more striking image of the eagle following the image of the weasel, man, and hand. We might observe also that the paragraph begins with statements and ends with questions, that it includes a reference to another written text (did we notice this in the opening paragraph also?), and that the writer speaks personally ("I"), revealing her desire to have seen the amazing thing she had read about.

In addition, we note Dillard's use of precise, vivid, strong verbs; we notice too their preponderance, their exactness, and their differing grammatical forms. We might consider particularly apt the image of the eagle gutting the living weasel, bending his own beak, cleaning the weasel's bones—an image brought forward and elaborated from the previous sentence where it exists only as a pair of adjectives and corresponding nouns: "his feathered throat, a fur pendant." Dillard actually brings the dormant image to life with that string of participles: *gutting, living, bending,* and *cleaning.*

The repeated words in the paragraph create a litany of eagle and weasel, their rhyming sound echoed again in "*ea*t," "*rea*ch," "*bea*k," and "*clea*ning." We could notice as well the alliterative b's of the final sentence: "his talons *b*efore his *b*reast, *b*ending his *b*eak, cleaning the *b*eautiful air*b*orne *b*ones." And further, we might see how the paragraph's monosyllabic diction is counterpointed against both the polysyllabic name of the naturalist, Ernest Thompson Seton, and the continual yoking and reyoking of the animals: eagle and weasel always coming together. Moreover, to hear the remarkable sound play of Dillard's second paragraph, especially its subtle yet muscular rhythms, we must read it aloud.

Here is the rest of the essay without interruption. Further observations and questions follow the text:

3 I have been reading about weasels because I saw one last week. I startled a weasel who startled me, and we exchanged a long glance.

4 Twenty minutes from my house, through the woods by the quarry and across the highway, is Hollins Pond, a remarkable piece of shallowness, where I like to go at sunset and sit on a tree trunk. Hollins Pond is also called Murray's Pond; it covers two acres of bottomland near Tinker Creek with six inches of water and six thousand lily pads. In winter, brown-and-white steers stand in the middle of it, merely dampening their hooves; from the distant shore they look like miracle itself, complete with miracle's nonchalance. Now, in summer, the steers are gone. The water lilies have blossomed and spread to a green horizontal plane that is terra firma to plodding blackbirds, and tremulous ceiling to black leeches, crayfish, and carp.

5 This is, mind you, suburbia. It is a five-minute walk in three directions to rows of houses, though none is visible here. There's a 55 mph highway at one end of the pond, and a nesting pair of wood ducks at the other. Under every bush is a muskrat hole or a beer can. The far end is an alternating series of fields and woods, fields and woods, threaded everywhere with motorcycle tracks—in whose bare clay wild turtles lay eggs.

6 So. I had crossed the highway, stepped over two low barbed-wire fences, and traced the motorcycle path in all gratitude through the wild rose and poison ivy of the pond's shoreline up into high grassy fields. Then I cut down through the woods to the mossy fallen tree where I sit. This tree is excellent. It makes a dry, upholstered bench at the upper, marshy end of the pond, a plush jetty raised from the thorny shore between a shallow blue body of water and a deep blue body of sky.

7 The sun had just set. I was relaxed on the tree trunk, ensconced in the lap of lichen, watching the lily pads at my feet tremble and part dreamily over the thrusting path of a carp. A yellow bird appeared to my right and flew behind me. It caught my eye; I swiveled around—and the next instant, inexplicably, I was looking down at a weasel, who was looking up at me.

8 Weasel! I'd never seen one wild before. He was ten inches long, thin as a curve, a muscled ribbon, brown as fruitwood, soft-furred, alert. His face was fierce, small and pointed as a lizard's; he would have made a good arrowhead. There was just a dot of chin, maybe two brown hairs' worth, and then the pure white fur began that spread down his underside. He had two black eyes I didn't see, any more than you see a window.

9 The weasel was stunned into stillness as he was emerging from beneath an enormous shaggy wild rose bush four feet away. I was stunned into stillness twisted backward on the tree trunk. Our eyes locked, and someone threw away the key.

10 Our look was as if two lovers, or deadly enemies, met unexpectedly on an overgrown path when each had been thinking of something else: a clearing blow to the gut. It was also a bright blow to the brain, or a sudden beating of brains, with all the charge and intimate grate of rubbed balloons. It emptied our lungs. It felled the forest, moved the fields, and drained the pond; the world dismantled and tumbled into that black hole of eyes. If you and I looked at each other that way,

our skulls would split and drop to our shoulders. But we don't. We keep our skulls. So.

11 He disappeared. This was only last week, and already I don't remember what shattered the enchantment. I think I blinked, I think I retrieved my brain from the weasel's brain, and tried to memorize what I was seeing, and the weasel felt the yank of separation, the careening splashdown into real life and the urgent current of instinct. He vanished under the wild rose. I waited motionless, my mind suddenly full of data and my spirit with pleadings, but he didn't return.

12 Please do not tell me about "approach-avoidance conflicts." I tell you I've been in that weasel's brain for sixty seconds, and he was in mine. Brains are private places, muttering through unique and secret tapes—but the weasel and I both plugged into another tape simultaneously, for a sweet and shocking time. Can I help it if it was a blank?

13 What goes on in his brain the rest of the time? What does a weasel think about? He won't say. His journal is tracks in clay, a spray of feathers, mouse blood and bone: uncollected, unconnected, loose-leaf, and blown.

14 I would like to learn, or remember, how to live. I come to Hollins Pond not so much to learn how to live as, frankly, to forget about it. That is, I don't think I can learn from a wild animal how to live in particular—shall I suck warm blood, hold my tail high, walk with my footprints precisely over the prints of my hands?—but I might learn something of mindlessness, something of the purity of living in the physical senses and the dignity of living without bias or motive. The weasel lives in necessity and we live in choice, hating necessity and dying at the last ignobly in its talons. I would like to live as I should, as the weasel lives as he should. And I suspect that for me the way is like the weasel's: open to time and death painlessly, noticing everything, remembering nothing, choosing the given with a fierce and pointed will.

15 I missed my chance. I should have gone for the throat. I should have lunged for that streak of white under the weasel's chin and held on, held on through mud and into the wild rose, held on for a dearer life. We could live under the wild rose wild as weasels, mute and uncomprehending. I could very calmly go wild. I could live two days in the den, curled, leaning on mouse fur, sniffing bird bones, blinking, licking, breathing musk, my hair tangled in the roots of grasses. Down is a good place to go, where the mind is single. Down is out, out of your ever-loving mind and back to your careless senses. I remember muteness as a prolonged and giddy fast, where every moment is a feast of utterance received. Time and events are merely poured, unremarked, and ingested directly, like blood pulsed into my gut through a jugular vein. Could two live that way? Could two live under the wild rose, and explore by the pond, so that the smooth mind of each is as everywhere present to the other, and as received and as unchallenged, as falling snow?

16 We could, you know. We can live any way we want. People take vows of poverty, chastity, and obedience—even of silence—by choice. The thing is to stalk your calling in a certain skilled and supple way, to locate the most tender and live spot and plug into that pulse. This is yielding, not fighting. A weasel doesn't "attack" anything; a weasel lives as he's meant to, yielding at every moment to the perfect freedom of single necessity.

17 I think it would be well, and proper, and obedient, and pure, to grasp your one necessity and not let it go, to dangle from it limp wherever it takes you. Then

even death, where you're going no matter how you live, cannot you part. Seize it and let it seize you up aloft even, till your eyes burn out and drop; let your musky flesh fall off in shreds, and let your very bones unhinge and scatter, loosened over fields, over fields and woods, lightly, thoughtless, from any height at all, from as high as eagles.

Interpreting "Living Like Weasels," coming to terms with its meaning, requires analysis of its formal characteristics. We've singled out four: voice, style, structure, and thought.

Voice

Dillard's voice is personal. She speaks to us in the first person, casually, directly: "I tell you I've been in that weasel's brain for sixty seconds. . . ." In advancing the proposal that we live like weasels, Dillard reassures us with "we could, you know." She is thus both confident and authoritative while being personal, almost but not quite informal. As a result we feel obliged to hear her out, to respond to her passionate insistence; we feel obliged to try to understand even when her explanation grazes mystery.

Style

Dillard's voice is part of her style. Her sentences are short—they speak to the point whether that point is factual or mystical. There are few connectives, almost no coordinating *ands, buts,* and *fors;* and there is no subordination through the use of *because, although, if,* and *whenever.* The lack of formal syntactic links contributes to the authority of Dillard's style. "A weasel is wild," she tells us, announcing her theme. And before long, as we have seen, we know just how wild. Later she notes that "a weasel lives as he's meant to," concisely summing up both the weasel and the essay.

Dillard seems fond of questions. Her questions engage us, stimulate our responses, spur our thinking: "What goes on in his brain the rest of the time? What does a weasel think about?" Like her assertions, Dillard's questions are clear, direct, cryptic. Some of her questions are simultaneously speculative and provocative: "Could two live that way? Could two live under the wild rose, and explore by the pond?" These questions she answers: "We could, you know," giving us a somewhat frightening kind of assurance. Beyond her authoritative declarations and her startling questions is a single exclamation: "Weasel!" which catches us by surprise and captures Dillard's surprise in encountering the little animal. We shouldn't miss her imperative final sentence that startles as much by its commanding tone as by its astonishing advice.

A further stylistic observation: Dillard leans heavily on verbs, especially verbs of action, often violent action. She stacks verbs up, creating on occasion driving, relentless prose. Here are two examples:

> Obedient to instinct, he bites prey at the neck, either splitting the jugular vein at the throat or crunching the brain at the base of the skull, and he does not let go.

> It emptied our lungs. It felled the forest, moved the fields, and drained the pond; the world dismantled and tumbled into that black hole of eyes.

We should also note her fondness for and skill in using figures of comparison. Describing the weasel, Dillard compares him to "a muscled ribbon," and an "arrowhead" with a color "brown as fruitwood." Describing the impact of her encounter she reaches even further into analogy: "Our look was as if two lovers, or deadly enemies, met unexpectedly." The effect of this look, which she describes in another place as eyes locked together, is "a clearing blow to the gut." Moreover, the energy of Dillard's style is captured in the physical imagery and the taut syntax of this last phrase.

Structure

The structure of the essay can be mapped this way:

1. Paragraphs 1–2: facts about weasels, especially their wildness and their ability to hang on and not let go; two stunning examples (the naturalist and the eagle), one for each of the first two paragraphs.

2. Paragraphs 3–7: The second, longer section of the essay depicts Dillard encountering the weasel, exchanging glances with it. The middle paragraphs (4–6) set the scene, with paragraphs 3 and 7 framing the section with the repeated mention of Dillard and the weasel's locked glances. Paragraph 5 mixes details as it contrasts wilderness and civilization. The two exist side-by-side, one within the other: beer cans coexist with muskrat holes; turtle eggs sit in motorcycle tracks; a highway runs alongside a duck pond.

3. Paragraphs 8–13: The crescendo and climax of the essay. Here Dillard describes in detail the weasel (paragraph 8); the shock of their locked looks (9 and 10); and the shattering of the spell (11). She also laments her unsuccessful attempt to reforge the link with the weasel after the spell had been snapped. The section ends with Dillard (and us) pondering the mystery she has experienced.

4. Paragraphs 14–17: Dillard speculates about the meaning of the encounter with the weasel. She contemplates living like a weasel—what it means, why it appeals to her and perhaps appalls us. She explores the implications of what a weasel's life is like—how it relates to human life, especially her own. She concludes with an image from the opening: an eagle carrying something that is clinging fiercely to it, not letting go, holding on into and beyond death. The image brings the essay full circle—but with one significant difference: we have taken the weasel's place.

Thought

What begins as an expository essay, outlining facts about wildness and the tenacity of weasels, turns into a meditation on the value and necessity of wildness, instinct, and tenacity in human life. By the end of the essay Dillard has made the weasel a symbol, a model of how we should live. Her tone changes from factual declaration to speculative wonder, and, finally, to admonition.

But what does she mean? How can we live like weasels? How can we imitate and appropriate the weasel's wildness and tenacity? Dillard doesn't say exactly. She only exhorts us to seize necessity, to lock on to what is essential and not let go for anything. She invites us to decide for ourselves what our necessity is and then relentlessly to catch and hold it.

Another idea develops in the essay: that man and animal can indeed communicate and understand one another. Dillard opts for a mystical communion between man and beast, by necessity a brief communion, one beyond the power of words to describe (though Dillard comes very close). The experience for woman and weasel "stuns into stillness," stops time, empties one consciousness into another. In linking her mind even momentarily with the weasel, Dillard undergoes an extraordinary transforming experience. It's something she would like to repeat. The experience prompts her to read up on weasels, reading she turns to good account as she uses those memorable details to launch her essay. She wants not just to learn more about weasels but to know a weasel in this mystical way again. But she can't because her own consciousness, the distinctive human quality of her thinking mind, prevents her from being at one and staying at one with an animal.

There seems to be, thus, in Dillard's essay, a pull in two directions. On one hand, there is the suggestion that we can link ourselves with the weasel and, like him, live in necessity instinctively, opening ourselves to time and death, noticing everything and remembering nothing. On the other hand sits an opposing idea: we cannot stay linked with the weasel or with any animal, primarily because our minds prohibit it. We are creatures for whom remembering is necessary, vital. Dillard, in fact, could never have savored her experience and shared it with us without her capacity for remembering. The weasel's mindlessness, its purity of living, cannot be wholly hers or ours, for we are mindful creatures, not mindless ones. Our living as we should is necessarily different from the weasel's living as it should. Although we can learn from the weasel's instinct, its pure living, its tenacity, we can follow it only so far on the way to wildness.

Our consideration of the thought of "Living Like Weasels" brings us to its values. Dillard privileges wildness over civilization, mystical communion over separateness, instinct and tenacity over intellectuality. She prizes the majesty and mystery of nature, and she values the weasel's relentlessness, along with its consistency, predictability, and reliance on instinct. She implies that the simplicity, purity, and elementary fierceness of nature have been lost to man with the advent and development of civilization. We might agree—or we might not, choosing instead to value the laws and directives of spiritual and mental life over the instincts and appetites. Whereas Dillard seems to lament her and our inability to keep ourselves joined to nature/weasel in the intense manner of her encounter, some readers may find such a disjunction not only necessary but happier far for human beings. Those readers might see Dillard's mystical union as a dangerous drifting away from human responsibility and obligation. Our reactions both to what Dillard describes directly—the weasel's and eagle's instinct to kill for survival—and what she implies about the relationship between the human and natural worlds will differ markedly depending on our own moral and cultural attitudes. Dillard's essay opens up questions about our relationship to nature, and it leads to questions about our own human nature. It strikes to the heart of our values, inviting us by implication to consider what, for us, is necessary and essential. What we decide about this may be very different from what Dillard has decided for herself. And the attitude we take toward our "necessity" as she calls it may also differ. We may believe, for example, that nothing has to be held with the weasel's tenaciousness, that it is better sometimes to let go rather than hang on.

In raising such questions, we move beyond interpreting Dillard's essay to evaluating it. Our evaluation of its implied and expressed values is an act of judgment or criticism. This judgment extends beyond the moral and cultural values the essay displays to our appraisal of it as a literary work. In making any such appraisal, of course, we rely on our experience of the work, on its power to move us. We judge it also according to its power to make us think, to instruct us. And finally, we consider whether or not it pleases us. But all of these considerations cause us to bring our minds to bear on Dillard's essay: on its images, on her style and her literary techniques, on her voice, her values and her attitudes, on the essay's subtle, internal connections, on meaning. Finally, we must consider our own ideas and values against Dillard's. We must make our own judgments, formulate our own beliefs.

Learning to read actively and with critical judgment, we learn indirectly to write. We learn about suggestiveness, about allusion, about economy, about richness. In short, we learn to figure out what goes on around the words. But we learn more directly too, from what the writers tell us about seeing, about writing to find out what we're thinking, about the importance of personal anecdote in our essays. We learn that we collaborate with good essayists in discovering the world. We learn to see the world not only as they see it, but to discover ourselves and our connection with that world.

We read so that we can write well, but we also write to enhance our reading. Reading prose and writing it, alternatively experiencing and creating the written word, we improve our perceptions, develop our minds, and refine our writing, learning to write and speak in our own voices.

TWO

E. M. Forster

(1879–1970)

E. M. Forster lived a full, rich productive life, leaving us six fine novels, three collections of short stories, three volumes of essays, and a small critical text—*Aspects of the Novel*—that many regard as a classic. His reputation in our time continues to grow; three of the novels—*A Room with a View, A Passage to India,* and *Maurice*—have been made into movies; his letters have been published; and the Abinger Edition of his collected works is well underway. The legacy is established.

Forster appeals to us precisely because he writes about critical human issues that remain especially important today in the face of cultural forces that threaten our security and our peace of mind. He writes against the grain of two World Wars, but he does not confine himself to topics related to conflict. In *Howards End* (1910) he gives us a fine sense of the changes being wrought on the English countryside and on London by modern technology. The exodus from the country into the city and the resulting destruction and rebuilding that accompanied those moves appealed no more to him than the petrol smells and the dust in the air from motorcars. Behind those changes he sensed a fundamental flaw in the English character—on the one hand, a lassitude that kept the common man stuck in the confines of a fairly rigid class structure where he was acted on and shoved about within the country, and on the other hand a governing class bent on the extension of Empire. Forster saw more clearly than the nineteenth-century reformers who preceded him how difficult reform is under such conditions. Nevertheless, in both his essays and in his novels, he examines the consequences of behaving too rigidly, of living too much under the influence of accepted social patterns, of surrendering spirit to dogma, and of the well-intentioned but wrongheaded involvement of one class in the life of another. Always, Forster champions moderation, sanity, commonsense, and the intimacy of personal relations, but he never does so with his eyes shut to the reality of things, to the difficulty of living in the modern world.

Forster was on the side of intuition, feeling, imagination, and the unconscious, and he delighted in playing his mind against too much rationality. So in his written work we find a playful voice that is appealing because it seems to talk directly to us, teasing us into new considerations, criticizing without offending, teaching without preaching, searching always for the spirit of life. Two volumes of his essays—*Abinger Harvest* and *Two Cheers for Democracy*—reflect the range and depth of his inquiry into modern culture.

Much of the uplifting spirit that informs Forster's vision and his writing found its clearest manifestation in other cultures. Italy and Greece unleashed his imagination after his undergraduate days at Cambridge, and he found confirmation in those two cultures of his own interest in a life free of too much restraint, a more open and spontaneous life. Later, in India, he found evidence of his own nation's excesses, but he also found a culture so diverse that it could not be contained even by English power. And so when he came to write *A Passage to India* (1924), he asked not for a simple unity, but for a unity that could contain diversity, multiplicity. He sought in the imaginative world of that novel not so much a reconciliation of opposites as an informed tolerant coexistence between East and West, a dynamic and evolving marriage of opposites.

Aspects of the Novel suggests that Forster was as uneasy about patterns in the novel as he was about patterns in English culture. He argued for flexibility in the novel, for an opening out into life. He did not want the aesthetic demands of form to close the novel to the spontaneity of life, and so he was willing to experiment even if it meant sacrificing artistic control to the life of his characters. One critic thinks that, fascinating as *The Longest Journey* is, it seems to fly apart at the seams. But *Journey* was Forster's favorite even though he considered it the most problematic. The essays in this anthology show evidence of the same kind of experimenting, but instead of characters being given free reign to develop and round out, Forster gives vent to his own imagination as he explores an idea. So in some cases, we find perfection subordinated to the association of ideas. An essay such as "English Prose" will open out to include as many subordinate and supporting ideas and as many writers as Forster can muster to illustrate his sense of the evolving character of the English language between 1918 and 1939, but near the end of the essay, when he has done his best to hold all of his ideas together, he remembers D. H. Lawrence, who doesn't quite fit the theory. A more careful writer would leave Lawrence out. Forster doesn't; he pulls him in and tries to place him even though he's hard to classify. Forster cares more about the exploration of the idea than he does about having a neat, tidy theory within a perfect structure.

Forster's own prose invites us because it is so charming and so free of rant. There is nothing stuffy about it, nothing to close us out, or exclude us. P. N. Furbank, his official biographer, tells us "there is a teasing refusal of the high road" of Victorian prose. In fact, Forster and his Bloomsbury friends (Virginia Woolf, Lytton Strachey) were trying to dismantle that prose, so sonorous, so powerfully strident—so certain. Bloomsbury prose, argues Furbank, "aims at a beautiful amusingness." Forster's style, his "ease and informality," gives him "a new flexibility," and his use of metaphor and his shifting angle of vision give us pause and suggest a direction for our own writing. He "trusted metaphor to lead him where it would because he believed 'things' contained the truth, albeit a truth probably very different from men's presuppositions" and so by following the logic of his metaphor he sometimes got "extreme originality." The angle of Forster's vision, the perspective from which he chooses to view things, is continually shifting, causing us to go round an object with him as he examines it thoroughly. He was, as Furbank reminds us, "the master of *angle,*" and he shows us in innumerable ways how to add depth and variety to our own inquiries.

What I Believe

1 I do not believe in Belief. But this is an Age of Faith, and there are so many militant creeds that, in self-defence, one has to formulate a creed of one's own.

Tolerance, good temper and sympathy are no longer enough in a world which is rent by religious and racial persecution, in a world where ignorance rules, and Science, who ought to have ruled, plays the subservient pimp. Tolerance, good temper and sympathy—they are what matter really, and if the human race is not to collapse they must come to the front before long. But for the moment they are not enough, their action is no stronger than a flower, battered beneath a military jackboot. They want stiffening, even if the process coarsens them. Faith, to my mind, is a stiffening process, a sort of mental starch, which ought to be applied as sparingly as possible. I dislike the stuff. I do not believe in it, for its own sake, at all. Herein I probably differ from most people, who believe in Belief, and are only sorry they cannot swallow even more than they do. My law-givers are Erasmus and Montaigne, not Moses and St Paul. My temple stands not upon Mount Moriah but in that Elysian Field where even the immoral are admitted. My motto is: "Lord, I disbelieve—help thou my unbelief."

2 I have, however, to live in an Age of Faith—the sort of epoch I used to hear praised when I was a boy. It is extremely unpleasant really. It is bloody in every sense of the word. And I have to keep my end up in it. Where do I start?

3 With personal relationships. Here is something comparatively solid in a world full of violence and cruelty. Not absolutely solid, for Psychology has split and shattered the idea of a "Person", and has shown that there is something incalculable in each of us, which may at any moment rise to the surface and destroy our normal balance. We don't know what we are like. We can't know what other people are like. How, then, can we put any trust in personal relationships, or cling to them in the gathering political storm? In theory we cannot. But in practice we can and do. Though A is not unchangeably A, or B unchangeably B, there can still be love and loyalty between the two. For the purpose of living one has to assume that the personality is solid, and the "self" is an entity, and to ignore all contrary evidence. And since to ignore evidence is one of the characteristics of faith, I certainly can proclaim that I believe in personal relationships.

4 Starting from them, I get a little order into the contemporary chaos. One must be fond of people and trust them if one is not to make a mess of life, and it is therefore essential that they should not let one down. They often do. The moral of which is that I must, myself, be as reliable as possible, and this I try to be. But reliability is not a matter of contract—that is the main difference between the world of personal relationships and the world of business relationships. It is a matter for the heart, which signs no documents. In other words, reliability is impossible unless there is a natural warmth. Most men possess this warmth, though they often have bad luck and get chilled. Most of them, even when they are politicians, *want* to keep faith. And one can, at all events, show one's own little light here, one's own poor little trembling flame, with the knowledge that it is not the only light that is shining in the darkness, and not the only one which the darkness does not comprehend. Personal relations are despised today. They are regarded as bourgeois luxuries, as products of a time of fair weather which is now past, and we are urged to get rid of them, and to dedicate ourselves to some movement or cause instead. I hate the idea of causes, and if I had to choose between betraying my country and betraying my friend I hope I should have the guts to betray my country. Such a choice may scandalize the modern reader, and he may stretch out his patriotic hand to the

telephone at once and ring up the police. It would not have shocked Dante, though. Dante places Brutus and Cassius in the lowest circle of Hell because they had chosen to betray their friend Julius Caesar rather than their country Rome. Probably one will not be asked to make such an agonizing choice. Still, there lies at the back of every creed something terrible and hard for which the worshipper may one day be required to suffer, and there is even a terror and a hardness in this creed of personal relationships, urbane and mild though it sounds. Love and loyalty to an individual can run counter to the claims of the State. When they do—down with the State, say I, which means that the State would down me.

5 This brings me along to Democracy, "Even love, the beloved Republic, That feeds upon freedom and lives". Democracy is not a beloved Republic really, and never will be. But it is less hateful than other contemporary forms of government, and to that extent it deserves our support. It does start from the assumption that the individual is important, and that all types are needed to make a civilization. It does not divide its citizens into the bossers and the bossed—as an efficiency-regime tends to do. The people I admire most are those who are sensitive and want to create something or discover something, and do not see life in terms of power, and such people get more of a chance under a democracy than elsewhere. They found religions, great or small, or they produce literature and art, or they do disinterested scientific research, or they may be what is called "ordinary people", who are creative in their private lives, bring up their children decently, for instance, or help their neighbours. All these people need to express themselves; they cannot do so unless society allows them liberty to do so, and the society which allows them most liberty is a democracy.

6 Democracy has another merit. It allows criticism, and if there is not public criticism there are bound to be hushed-up scandals. That is why I believe in the press, despite all its lies and vulgarity, and why I believe in Parliament. Parliament is often sneered at because it is a Talking Shop. I believe in it *because* it is a talking shop. I believe in the Private Member who makes himself a nuisance. He gets snubbed and is told that he is cranky or ill-informed, but he does expose abuses which would otherwise never have been mentioned, and very often an abuse gets put right just by being mentioned. Occasionally, too, a well-meaning public official starts losing his head in the cause of efficiency, and thinks himself God Almighty. Such officials are particularly frequent in the Home Office. Well, there will be questions about them in Parliament sooner or later, and then they will have to mind their steps. Whether Parliament is either a representative body or an efficient one is questionable, but I value it because it criticizes and talks, and because its chatter gets widely reported.

7 So two cheers for Democracy: one because it admits variety and two because it permits criticism. Two cheers are quite enough: there is no occasion to give three. Only Love the Beloved Republic deserves that.

8 What about Force, though? While we are trying to be sensitive and advanced and affectionate and tolerant, an unpleasant question pops up: does not all society rest upon force? If a government cannot count upon the police and the army, how can it hope to rule? And if an individual gets knocked on the head or sent to a labour camp, of what significance are his opinions?

9 This dilemma does not worry me as much as it does some. I realize that all society rests upon force. But all the great creative actions, all the decent human relations, occur during the intervals when force has not managed to come to the front. These intervals are what matter. I want them to be as frequent and as lengthy as possible, and I call them "civilization". Some people idealize force and pull it into the foreground and worship it, instead of keeping it in the background as long as possible. I think they make a mistake, and I think that their opposites, the mystics, err even more when they declare that force does not exist. I believe that it exists, and that one of our jobs is to prevent it from getting out of its box. It gets out sooner or later, and then it destroys us and all the lovely things which we have made. But it is not out all the time, for the fortunate reason that the strong are so stupid. Consider their conduct for a moment in *The Nibelung's Ring.* The giants there have the guns, or in other words the gold; but they do nothing with it, they do not realize that they are all-powerful, with the result that the catastrophe is delayed and the castle of Valhalla, insecure but glorious, fronts the storms. Fafnir, coiled round his hoard, grumbles and grunts; we can hear him under Europe today; the leaves of the wood already tremble, and the Bird calls its warnings uselessly. Fafnir will destroy us, but by a blessed dispensation he is stupid and slow, and creation goes on just outside the poisonous blast of his breath. The Nietzschean would hurry the monster up, the mystic would say he did not exist, but Wotan, wiser than either, hastens to create warriors before doom declares itself. The Valkyries are symbols not only of courage but of intelligence; they represent the human spirit snatching its opportunity while the going is good, and one of them even finds time to love. Brünnhilde's last song hymns the recurrence of love, and since it is the privilege of art to exaggerate she goes even further, and proclaims the love which is eternally triumphant, and feeds upon freedom and lives.

10 So that is what I feel about force and violence. It is, alas! the ultimate reality on this earth, but it does not always get to the front. Some people call its absences "decadence"; I call them "civilization" and find in such interludes the chief justification for the human experiment. I look the other way until fate strikes me. Whether this is due to courage or to cowardice in my own case I cannot be sure. But I know that, if men had not looked the other way in the past, nothing of any value would survive. The people I respect most behave as if they were immortal and as if society was eternal. Both assumptions are false: both of them must be accepted as true if we are to go on eating and working and loving, and are to keep open a few breathing-holes for the human spirit. No millennium seems likely to descend upon humanity; no better and stronger League of Nations will be instituted; no form of Christianity and no alternative to Christianity will bring peace to the world or integrity to the individual; no "change of heart" will occur. And yet we need not despair, indeed, we cannot despair; the evidence of history shows us that men have always insisted on behaving creatively under the shadow of the sword; that they have done their artistic and scientific and domestic stuff for the sake of doing it, and that we had better follow their example under the shadow of the aeroplanes. Others, with more vision or courage than myself, see the salvation of humanity ahead, and will dismiss my conception of civilization as paltry, a sort of tip-and-run game. Certainly it is presumptuous to say that we *cannot* improve, and that Man, who has only been

in power for a few thousand years, will never learn to make use of his power. All I mean is that, if people continue to kill one another as they do, the world cannot get better than it is, and that, since there are more people than formerly, and their means for destroying one another superior, the world may well get worse. What is good in people—and consequently in the world—is their insistence on creation, their belief in friendship and loyalty for their own sakes; and, though Violence remains and is, indeed, the major partner in this muddled establishment, I believe that creativeness remains too, and will always assume direction when violence sleeps. So, though I am not an optimist, I cannot agree with Sophocles that it were better never to have been born. And although, like Horace, I see no evidence that each batch of births is superior to the last, I leave the field open for the more complacent view. This is such a difficult moment to live in, one cannot help getting gloomy and also a bit rattled, and perhaps short-sighted.

11 In search of a refuge, we may perhaps turn to hero-worship. But here we shall get no help, in my opinion. Hero-worship is a dangerous vice, and one of the minor merits of a democracy is that it does not encourage it, or produce that unmanageable type of citizen known as the Great Man. It produces instead different kinds of small men—a much finer achievement. But people who cannot get interested in the variety of life, and cannot make up their own minds, get discontented over this, and they long for a hero to bow down before and to follow blindly. It is significant that a hero is an integral part of the authoritarian stock-in-trade today. An efficiency-regime cannot be run without a few heroes stuck about it to carry off the dullness—much as plums have to be put into a bad pudding to make it palatable. One hero at the top and a smaller one each side of him is a favourite arrangement, and the timid and the bored are comforted by the trinity, and, bowing down, feel exalted and strengthened.

12 No, I distrust Great Men. They produce a desert of uniformity around them and often a pool of blood too, and I always feel a little man's pleasure when they come a cropper. Every now and then one reads in the newspapers some such statement as: "The *coup d'état* appears to have failed, and Admiral Toma's whereabouts is at present unknown." Admiral Toma had probably every qualification for being a Great Man—an iron will, personal magnetism, dash, flair, sexlessness—but fate was against him, so he retires to unknown whereabouts instead of parading history with his peers. He fails with a completeness which no artist and no lover can experience, because with them the process of creation is itself an achievement, whereas with him the only possible achievement is success.

13 I believe in aristocracy, though—if that is the right word, and if a democrat may use it. Not an aristocracy of power, based upon rank and influence, but an aristocracy of the sensitive, the considerate and the plucky. Its members are to be found in all nations and classes, and all through the ages, and there is a secret understanding between them when they meet. They represent the true human tradition, the one permanent victory of our queer race over cruelty and chaos. Thousands of them perish in obscurity, a few are great names. They are sensitive for others as well as for themselves, they are considerate without being fussy, their pluck is not swankiness but the power to endure, and they can take a joke. I give no examples—it is risky to do that—but the reader may as well consider whether

this is the type of person he would like to meet and to be, and whether (going further with me) he would prefer that this type should *not* be an ascetic one. I am against asceticism myself. I am with the old Scotsman who wanted less chastity and more delicacy. I do not feel that my aristocrats are a real aristocracy if they thwart their bodies, since bodies are the instruments through which we register and enjoy the world. Still, I do not insist. This is not a major point. It is clearly possible to be sensitive, considerate and plucky and yet be an ascetic too, and if anyone possesses the first three qualities I will let him in! On they go—an invincible army, yet not a victorious one. The aristocrats, the elect, the chosen, the Best People—all the words that describe them are false, and all attempts to organize them fail. Again and again Authority, seeing their value, has tried to net them and to utilize them as the Egyptian Priesthood or the Christian Church or the Chinese Civil Service or the Group Movement, or some other worthy stunt. But they slip through the net and are gone; when the door is shut, they are no longer in the room; their temple, as one of them remarked, is the holiness of the Heart's affections, and their kingdom, though they never possess it, is the wide-open world.

14 With this type of person knocking about, and constantly crossing one's path if one has eyes to see or hands to feel, the experiment of earthly life cannot be dismissed as a failure. But it may well be hailed as a tragedy, the tragedy being that no device has been found by which these private decencies can be transmitted to public affairs. As soon as people have power they go crooked and sometimes dotty as well, because the possession of power lifts them into a region where normal honesty never pays. For instance, the man who is selling newspapers outside the Houses of Parliament can safely leave his papers to go for a drink, and his cap beside them: anyone who takes a paper is sure to drop a copper into the cap. But the men who are inside the Houses of Parliament—they cannot trust one another like that, still less can the Government they compose trust other governments. No caps upon the pavement here, but suspicion, treachery and armaments. The more highly public life is organized the lower does its morality sink; the nations of today behave to each other worse than they ever did in the past, they cheat, rob, bully and bluff, make war without notice, and kill as many women and children as possible; whereas primitive tribes were at all events restrained by taboos. It is a humiliating outlook—though the greater the darkness, the brighter shine the little lights, reassuring one another, signalling: "Well, at all events, I'm still here. I don't like it very much, but how are you?" Unquenchable lights of my aristocracy! Signals of the invincible army! "Come along—anyway, let's have a good time while we can." I think they signal that too.

15 The Saviour of the future—if ever he comes—will not preach a new Gospel. He will merely utilize my aristocracy, he will make effective the goodwill and the good temper which are already existing. In other words, he will introduce a new technique. In economics, we are told that if there was a new technique of distribution there need be no poverty, and people would not starve in one place while crops were being ploughed under in another. A similar change is needed in the sphere of morals and politics. The desire for it is by no means new; it was expressed, for example, in theological terms by Jacopone da Todi over six hundred years ago. "Ordena questo amore, tu che m'ami," he said; "O thou who lovest me—set this

love in order." His prayer was not granted, and I do not myself believe that it ever will be, but here, and not through a change of heart, is our probable route. Not by becoming better, but by ordering and distributing his native goodness, will Man shut up Force into its box, and so gain time to explore the universe and to set his mark upon it worthily. At present he only explores it at odd moments, when Force is looking the other way, and his divine creativeness appears as a trivial by-product, to be scrapped as soon as the drums beat and the bombers hum.

16 Such a change, claim the orthodox, can only be made by Christianity, and will be made by it in God's good time: man always has failed and always will fail to organize his own goodness, and it is presumptuous of him to try. This claim—solemn as it is—leaves me cold. I cannot believe that Christianity will ever cope with the present world-wide mess, and I think that such influence as it retains in modern society is due to the money behind it, rather than to its spiritual appeal. It was a spiritual force once, but the indwelling spirit will have to be restated if it is to calm the waters again, and probably restated in a non-Christian form. Naturally a lot of people, and people who are not only good but able and intelligent, will disagree here; they will vehemently deny that Christianity has failed, or they will argue that its failure proceeds from the wickedness of men, and really proves its ultimate success. They have Faith, with a large F. My faith has a very small one, and I only intrude it because these are strenuous and serious days, and one likes to say what one thinks while speech is comparatively free; it may not be free much longer.

17 The above are the reflections of an individualist and a liberal who has found liberalism crumbling beneath him and at first felt ashamed. Then, looking around, he decided there was no special reason for shame, since other people, whatever they felt, were equally insecure. And as for individualism—there seems no way of getting off this, even if one wanted to. The dictator-hero can grind down his citizens till they are all alike, but he cannot melt them into a single man. That is beyond his power. He can order them to merge, he can incite them to mass-antics, but they are obliged to be born separately, and to die separately, and, owing to these unavoidable termini, will always be running off the totalitarian rails. The memory of birth and the expectation of death always lurk within the human being, making him separate from his fellows and consequently capable of intercourse with them. Naked I came into the world, naked I shall go out of it! And a very good thing too, for it reminds me that I am naked under my shirt, whatever its colour.

(1938)

QUESTIONS

Thought and Structure

1. Does it help, even in the first paragraph, to know when this essay was written? Why? Why do you suppose Forster capitalizes Belief, Age of Faith, Tolerance, Science, and Faith? Look for evidence within the body of the essay to support your opinion.

2. Why does Forster capitalize Psychology in paragraph 3? What has been going on in intellectual circles that would cause him to highlight psychological notions so early in this essay? Freud? Adler? Jung? Is it ironic that "Psychology has split and shattered the idea of a 'Person' "? What is Forster's response to this new knowledge?
3. If we consider that the middle of this essay is divided into two parts—paragraphs 3–7 and 8–16—what can we learn about Forster's argument? What does he accomplish by looking first at personal relations, friendship, and Democracy in the first section before he turns to Force, hero-worship, and his special aristocracy in the second section?
4. Is paragraph 17 an adequate conclusion for this essay? Why? Pay particular attention to the way Forster develops his definitions of individualism and liberalism, the way he plays with meaning.

Style and Strategy

5. Forster begins his essay talking about Belief and Faith. He says a great deal about his own beliefs as he develops his argument, but very little about Belief. He virtually ignores Faith until paragraph 16. Why do you suppose he waits so long to turn directly to the related question of Christianity?
6. How would you characterize the tone of this essay? Cite some specific examples where Forster tries to achieve balance, where he seems to be particularly reasonable.
7. Forster seems to have a delightful time with words and images in this essay. What do you think he gains from the following associations in the first paragraph: "Science" playing the "subservient pimp"; "Tolerance, good temper and sympathy" whose action in 1939 is "no stronger than a flower, battered beneath a military jackboot"? Look too at "Talking Shop" (paragraph 6); "breathing-holes for the human spirit," and "under the shadow of aeroplanes" (paragraph 10); and "authoritarian stock-in-trade" and "efficiency-regime" (paragraph 11). What does Forster gain from this use of figurative language?
8. Why does Forster introduce "primitive tribes" at the end of paragraph 14?

SUGGESTIONS FOR WRITING

A. In a well-developed paragraph explain why Forster would not give Democracy a third cheer.

B. Look very carefully at paragraph 4. Assume that you are the head of an American institution such as a college, church, or corporation. Assume too that Forster is still alive. As the head of the institution, write Forster an epistolary essay (an essay in the form of a letter), reacting to paragraph 4. Be as reasonable in laying out your argument as Forster is in developing his.

C. In a well-developed paragraph explain what Forster means in his essay by "creativeness." In a second paragraph, explain why the notion is so important to him in light of his argument against Force.

D. Write your own essay entitled "What I Believe." Make it more than a mere listing of your beliefs. Instead, like Forster, develop a thoughtful exploration of two or three of your central convictions.

Not Looking at Pictures

1 Pictures are not easy to look at. They generate private fantasies, they furnish material for jokes, they recall scraps of historical knowledge, they show landscapes where one would like to wander and human beings whom one would like to resemble or adore, but looking at them is another matter, yet they must have been painted to be looked at. They were intended to appeal to the eye, but, almost as if it were gazing at the sun itself, the eye often reacts by closing as soon as it catches sight of them. The mind takes charge instead and goes off on some alien vision. The mind has such a congenial time that it forgets what set it going. Van Gogh and Corot and Michelangelo are three different painters, but if the mind is indisciplined and uncontrolled by the eye they may all three induce the same mood, we may take just the same course through dreamland or funland from them, each time, and never experience anything new.

2 I am bad at looking at pictures myself, and the late Roger Fry enjoyed going to a gallery with me now and then, for this very reason. He found it an amusing change to be with someone who scarcely ever saw what the painter had painted. "Tell me, why do you like this, why do you prefer it to that?" he would ask, and listen agape for the ridiculous answer. One day we looked at a fifteenth-century Italian predella, where a St George was engaged in spearing a dragon of the plesiosaurus type. I laughed. "Now, *what* is there funny in this?" pounced Fry. I readily explained. The fun was to be found in the expression upon the dragon's face. The spear had gone through its hooped-up neck once, and now startled it by arriving at a second thickness. "Oh dear, here it comes again, I hoped that was all," it was thinking. Fry laughed too, but not at the misfortunes of the dragon. He was amazed that anyone could go so completely off the lines. There was no harm in it—but really, really! He was even more amazed when our enthusiasms coincided: "I fancy we are talking about different things," he would say, and we always were; I liked the mountain-back because it reminded me of a peacock, he because it had some structural significance, though not as much as the sack of potatoes in the foreground.

3 Long years of wandering down miles of galleries have convinced me that there must be something rare in those coloured slabs called "pictures", something which I am incapable of detecting for myself, though glimpses of it are to be had through the eyes of others. How much am I missing? And what? And are other modern sightseers in the same fix? Ours is an aural rather than a visual age, we do not get so lost in the concert-hall, we seem able to hear music for ourselves, and to hear it as music, but in galleries so many of us go off at once into a laugh or a sigh or an amorous day dream. In vain does the picture recall us. "What have your obsessions got to do with me?" it complains. "I am neither a theatre of varieties nor a spring-mattress, but paint. Look at my paint." Back we go—the picture kindly standing still meanwhile, and being to that extent more obliging than music—and resume the looking business. But something is sure to intervene—a tress of hair, the half-open door of a summerhouse, a Crivelli dessert, a Bosch fish-and-fiend salad—and to draw us away.

4 One of the things that helps us to keep looking is composition. For many years now I have associated composition with a diagonal line, and when I find such a line I imagine I have gutted the picture's secret. Giorgione's *Castelfranco Madonna* has such a line in the lance of the warrior-saint, and Titian's *Entombment* at Venice has a very good one indeed. Five figures contribute to make up the diagonal: beginning high on the left with the statue of Moses, it passes through the heads of the Magdalene, Mary and the dead Christ, and plunges through the body of Joseph of Arimathea into the ground. Making a right angle to it, flits the winged Genius of Burial. And to the right, apart from it, and perpendicular, balancing the Moses, towers the statue of Faith. Titian's *Entombment* is one of my easiest pictures. I look at photographs of it intelligently, and encourage the diagonal and the pathos to reinforce one another. I see, with more than usual vividness, the grim alcove at the back and the sinister tusked pedestals upon which the two statues stand. Stone shuts in flesh; the whole picture is a tomb. I hear sounds of lamentation, though not to the extent of shattering the general scheme; that is held together by the emphatic diagonal, which no emotion breaks. Titian was a very old man when he achieved this masterpiece; that too I realize, but not immoderately. Composition here really has been a help, and it is a composition which no one can miss: the diagonal slopes as obviously as the band on a threshing-machine, and vibrates with power.

5 Unfortunately, having no natural aesthetic aptitude, I look for diagonals everywhere, and if I cannot find one think the composition must be at fault. It is a word which I have learnt—a solitary word in a foreign language. For instance, I was completely baffled by Velasquez's *Las Meninas.* Where ever was the diagonal? Then the friend I was with—Charles Mauron, the friend who, after Roger Fry, has helped me with pictures most—set to work on my behalf, and cautiously underlined the themes. There is a wave. There is a half-wave. The wave starts up on the left, with the head of the painter, and curves down and up through the heads of the three girls. The half-wave starts with the head of Isabel de Velasco, and sinks out of the canvas through the dwarfs. Responding to these great curves, or inverting them, are smaller ones on the women's dresses or elsewhere. All these waves are not merely pattern; they are doing other work too—e.g. helping to bring out the effect of depth in the room, and the effect of air. Important too is the pushing forward of objects in the extreme left and right foregrounds, the easel of the painter in the one case, the paws of a placid dog in the other. From these, the composition curves back to the central figure, the lovely child-princess. I put it more crudely than did Charles Mauron, nor do I suppose that his account would have been Velasquez's, or that Velasquez would have given any account at all. But it is an example of the way in which pictures should be tackled for the benefit of us outsiders: coolly and patiently, as if they were designs, so that we are helped at last to the appreciation of something non-mathematical. Here again, as in the case of the *Entombment,* the composition and the action reinforced one another. I viewed with increasing joy that adorable party, which had been surprised not only by myself but by the King and Queen of Spain. There they were in the looking-glass! *Las Meninas* has a snapshot quality. The party might have been taken by Philip IV, if Philip IV had had a Kodak. It is all so casual—and yet it is all so elaborate and sophisticated, and I suppose those curves and the rest of it help to bring this out, and to evoke a vanished civilization.

6 Besides composition there is colour. I look for that, too, but with even less success. Colour is visible when thrown in my face—like the two cherries in the great gray Michael Sweerts group in the National Gallery. But as a rule it is only material for dream.

7 On the whole, I am improving, and after all these years I am learning to get myself out of the way a little, and to be more receptive, and my appreciation of pictures does increase. If I can make any progress at all, the average outsider should do better still. A combination of courage and modesty is what he wants. It is so unenterprising to annihilate everything that's made to a green thought, even when the thought is an exquisite one. Not-looking at art leads to one goal only. Looking at it leads to so many.

(1939)

QUESTIONS

Thought and Structure

1. Look carefully at Forster's second sentence in the first paragraph:

   They generate private fantasies,
   they furnish material for jokes,
   they recall scraps of historical knowledge,
   they show landscapes where one would like to wander,
   and human beings whom one would like to resemble or adore,
   but looking at them is another matter,
   yet they must have been painted to be looked at.

   Explain how this complicated sentence gives us a clue to the organization of Forster's essay. (Would you punctuate it the way Forster does?)
2. How does Forster make use of his friend Roger Fry, the art critic, in paragraph 2? What does Forster stand for, what Fry?
3. Paragraphs 4–6 concentrate on the language of painting: "composition," and "colour." What does Forster manage to get you to think about in these three paragraphs? Is he effective? Can you judge his effectiveness without looking at the paintings he describes?
4. Unravel the meaning in the essay's last two sentences. What is the "one goal"? What are the "many"?

Style and Strategy

5. Why do you think Forster shifts from an impersonal and general perspective in the first paragraph to a very personal and specific perspective in the following paragraphs?
6. What does Forster gain by comparing an "aural" and a "visual" age in paragraph 3? Translate the last sentence of the paragraph. Can you tell what the sentence means without knowing who Crivelli and Bosch are? What is a "fish-and-fiend salad"?
7. Throughout this essay, Forster makes fun of himself. In paragraph 5, he claims to have "no natural aesthetic aptitude." Can we believe him? Do we trust him more because he is self-deprecating or less? Do you think Forster's playful tone makes this a more serious essay?

SUGGESTIONS FOR WRITING

A. Assume that you are Annie Dillard and that you have just finished writing "Seeing." That evening a friend of yours asks you to read "Not Looking at Pictures." Write a short note to Forster reacting to his essay, especially to his thoughts about the difficulty of seeing.

B. Go to the library and find one of the following paintings: Giorgione's *Castelfranco Madonna,* Titian's *Entombment,* or Velasquez's *Las Meninas.* In one well-developed paragraph evaluate how well Forster describes the selected painting in his essay; in a second paragraph, account for what you see that Forster did not see. Is the painting "not easy to look at"? That is, do you find your mind wandering when you look at the picture? Write another paragraph about the fantasy your mind creates, the fantasy that turns your mind away from the painting itself.

English Prose between 1918 and 1939

1 This is a period between two wars—the Long Weekend it has been called—and some of the books published in it look backward—like Siegfried Sassoon's *Memoirs of an Infantry Officer*—and try to record the tragedy of the past; others look forward and try to avert or explain the disaster which overtook Europe in the thirties. And even when they are not directly about a war—like the works of Lytton Strachey or Joyce or Virginia Woolf—they still display unrest or disillusionment or anxiety, they are still the products of a civilization which feels itself insecure. The French lady, Madame de Sévigné, writing letters during the wars of the late seventeenth century, can feel tranquil. The English lady, Jane Austen, writing novels in the Napoleonic wars, can feel tranquil. Those wars were not total. But no one can write during or between our wars and escape their influence. There, then, is one obvious characteristic of our prose. It is the product of people who have war on their mind. They need not be gloomy or hysterical—often they are gay and sane and brave—but if they have any sensitiveness they must realize what a mess the world is in, and if they have no sensitiveness they will not be worth reading.

2 We can conveniently divide the long weekend into two periods—the 1920s and the 1930s. The division is not hard-and-fast, still it is helpful. The twenties react after a war and recede from it, the thirties are apprehensive of a war and are carried towards it. The twenties want to enjoy life and to understand it; the thirties also want to understand but for a special purpose: to preserve civilization. They are less detached. In *Life among the English* Rose Macaulay contrasts the two periods neatly:

> The twenties were, as decades go, a good decade; gay, decorative, intelligent, extravagant, cultured. There were booms in photography, Sunday film and theatre clubs, surrealism, steel furniture, faintly obscure poetry, Proust, James Joyce, dancing, rink-skating, large paintings on walls of rooms.
>
> The next decade was more serious, less cultured, less aesthetic, more political. The slump blew like a cold draught at its birth, war stormed like forest fire at its close; between these two catastrophes Communists and Fascists battled and preached, and eyes turned apprehensively across the North Sea towards the alarming menace which had leaped up like a strident jack-in-the-box from a beer-cellar to more than a throne.

Rose Macaulay is a wise guide, tolerant, generous-minded, liberal, courageous, cheerful, and her judgements of society and social values are always sound. She sums up the two decades very well.

3 But of course there is more to say. There are influences in this world more powerful than either peace or war. And we cannot get a true idea of our period and the books it produces until we look deeper than fashions or politics or the achievements and failures of generals. For one thing, there is a huge economic movement which has been taking the whole world, Great Britain included, from agriculture towards industrialism. That began about a hundred and fifty years ago, but since 1918 it has accelerated to an enormous speed, bringing all sorts of changes into national and personal life. It has meant organization and plans and the boosting of the community. It has meant the destruction of feudalism and relationships based on the land, it has meant the transference of power from the aristocrat to the bureaucrat and the manager and the technician. Perhaps it will mean democracy, but it has not meant it yet, and personally I hate it. So I imagine do most writers, however loyally they try to sing its praises and to hymn the machine. But however much we detest this economic shift we have to recognize it as an important influence, more important than any local peace or war, which is going on all the time and transforming our outlooks. It rests on applied science, and as long as science is applied it will continue. Even when a writer seems to escape it, like T. E. Lawrence, he is conditioned by it. T. E. Lawrence hated the progress of industrialism, he hated what your city of Glasgow and my city of London stand for. He fled from it into the deserts of Arabia and the last of the romantic wars, in the search of old-time adventure, and later on into the deserts of his own heart. I think he was right to fly, because I believe that a writer's duty often exceeds any duty he owes to society, and that he often ought to lead a forlorn retreat. But of course the flight failed. Industrialism did T. E. Lawrence in in the long run, and it was not by the spear of an Arab but by a high-power motor-bike that he came to his death. We must face the unpleasant truths that normal life today is a life in factories and offices, that even war has evolved from an adventure into a business, that even farming has become scientific, that insurance has taken the place of charity, that status has given way to contract. You will see how disquieting all this is to writers, who love, and ought to love, beauty and charm and the passage of the seasons, and generous impulses, and the tradition of their craft. And you will appreciate how lost some of them have been feeling during the last quarter of a century, and how they have been tempted to nostalgia like Siegfried Sassoon, or to disgust like Evelyn Waugh and Graham Greene.

4 But this economic movement, from the land to the factory, is not the only great movement which has gathered strength during our period. There has been a psychological movement, about which I am more enthusiastic. Man is beginning to understand himself better and to explore his own contradictions. This exploration is conveniently connected with the awful name of Freud, but it is not so much in Freud as in the air. It has brought a great enrichment to the art of fiction. It has given subtleties and depths to the portrayal of human nature. The presence in all of us of the subconscious, the occasional existence of the split personality, the persistence of the irrational, especially in people who pride themselves on their

reasonableness, the importance of dreams and the prevalence of day-dreaming—here are some of the points which novelists have seized on and which have not been ignored by historians. This psychology is not new, but it has newly risen to the surface. Shakespeare was subconsciously aware of the subconscious, so were Emily Brontë, Herman Melville and others. But conscious knowledge of it only comes at the beginning of the century, with Samuel Butler's *The Way of All Flesh,* and only becomes general after 1918—partly owing to Freud. It gathers strength now, like the economic movement, and, like it, is independent of war or peace. Of course, writers can be stupid about it, as about anything else, they can apply it as a formula instead of feeling it as a possibility; the stupid psychologist who applies his (or her) formula in season or out and is always saying "You think you don't but you do" or "You think you do but you don't" can be absolutely maddening. But the better minds of our age—what a rich harvest they have reaped! Proust in France to begin with; Gertrude Stein and her experiments in uninhibited talk—not too successful in her own case but influential; Dorothy Richardson's novels, another pioneer in this country; the later work of D. H. Lawrence, the novels of Virginia Woolf, Joyce, de la Mare, Elizabeth Bowen. History too has profited. This new method of examining the human individual has helped to reinterpret the past. Aldous Huxley's *Grey Eminence* is one example—it gives a fresh view of Cardinal Richelieu and his adviser Father Joseph—a fresh view of their insides. Livingston Lowes's *The Road to Xanadu* is another example: a fresh view of the genius and make-up of Coleridge. And then there is the great work of a Christian historian, Arnold Toynbee, *A Study of History,* which regards history as a record of what men think and feel as well as of what they assert and achieve, and tries, with this extra material, to account for the rise and fall of civilizations. Professor Toynbee comes to the conclusion that they rise and fall in accord with a religious law, and that except the Lord build the house their labour is but lost that build it; or, if you prefer the language of Freud to that of the Old Testament, that the conscious must be satisfactorily based on the subconscious.

5 So, though we are justified in thinking of our period as an interval between two wars, we must remember that it forms part of larger movements where wars become insignificant: part of an economic movement from agriculture to industrialism, and of a psychological movement which is reinterpreting human nature. Both these movements have been speeded up, and writers have in my judgement been worried by the economic shift but stimulated by the psychological. Remember too, in passing, another factor, and that is the shift in physics exemplified by the work of Einstein. Can literary men understand Einstein? Of course they cannot—even less than they can understand Freud. But the idea of relativity has got into the air and has favoured certain tendencies in novels. Absolute good and evil, as in Dickens, are seldom presented. A character becomes good or evil in relation to some other character or to a situation which may itself change. You can't measure people up, because the yard-measure itself keeps altering its length. The best exponent of relativity in literature known to me is Proust, though there are instances in English too. Most of Proust's people are odious, yet you cannot have the comfort of writing any of them off as bad. Given the circumstances, even the most odious of them all, Madame Verdurin, can behave nobly. Proust and others have this attitude—not because they know anything about science, but because

the idea of relativity, like the idea of the subconscious self, has got about and tinged their outlook.

6 A word must now be said on the special character of prose. Prose, unlike poetry, does two things. It serves us in daily life and it creates works of art. For instance, I travelled from Euston to Glasgow on prose, I am talking prose now, and, like Monsieur Jourdain, I am astonished at finding myself doing so. For prose, besides serving our practical ends, also makes great literature.

7 Now, one of the problems which a critic has to tackle is that these two uses of prose are not watertight, and one of them is as it were constantly slopping over into the other. The practical popular prose is always getting into the deliberate artistic prose which makes books. Indeed, if it didn't, the artistic prose couldn't live very long, as it would get stale and stuffy. It has to be replenished by contemporary speech. And in this period of ours there has been a great deal of this replenishment. New words and phrases—and, what is more important, the new habits of thought expressed by them—are rapidly absorbed by authors and put into books. That is one tendency of our period, and it may be called, for want of a better word, the popular tendency. The writer feels himself part of his people. He enters or wants to enter into their ways. And he wants to be understood by them, and so he tries to be informal and clear. I'll give several examples of it. Here is a little example, taken from letter-writing. In 1918, if I had had a letter from a stranger it would certainly have begun "Dear Sir". Today, if I have a letter from a stranger, it will probably begin "Dear Mr Forster". One form of address doesn't mean more than another, but the convention is a more friendly one. I expect it came in, like other speak-easies, from America. It shows which way the wind of words is blowing. Another sign is the speeches of public men. Public men are becoming less formal—some of them because of the influence of the radio, for they know if they broadcast too pompously listeners will switch off. Others are informal by instinct, like Winston Churchill, whose speeches sound and read more democratic than those of the Prime Ministers of the last war. Novelists too—they practise the friendly unpatronizing tone; Christopher Isherwood's *Mr Norris Changes Trains* is an example of this. Isherwood—who is extremely intelligent—always writes as if the reader were equally intelligent. He is an example of democratic good manners. He trusts his public. Another novelist—Ernest Hemingway—introduces a new technique of conversation. Another straw which shows which way this wind is blowing is the tendency of official notices and proclamations to become more intelligible. They do so reluctantly, for the bureaucrat who gives his meaning clearly is afraid he may be giving something else away too. Still, they do it. They tend to issue orders which we understand. And since we live under orders this is a good thing.

8 I could continue this list of the popular tendencies in prose. We have had an example in the demand from high quarters for Basic English—and I expect it is a useful commercial idea, though I cannot see what it has to do with literature, or what it can do to literature, except impoverish it. I'll conclude with an example of another kind, a reference to the English of the Authorized Version of the Bible. This, the great monument of our seventeenth-century speech, has constantly influenced our talk and writing for the last three hundred years. Its rhythm, its atmosphere, its turns

of phrase, belonged to our people and overflowed into our books. Bunyan, Johnson, Blake, George Eliot, all echo it. About ten years ago an edition of the Bible came out called *The Bible Designed to be Read as Literature.* Its publication gave some of us a shock and caused us to realize that the English of the Authorized Version had at last become remote from popular English. This was well put in a review by Somerset Maugham. The English of the Bible, he agreed, is part of our national heritage, but it is so alien to our present idiom that no writer can study it profitably. I shall soon be quoting from a writer who has studied it, still Somerset Maugham is right on the whole, and there is now an unbridgeable gulf between ourselves and the Authorized Version as regards style, and the gulf widened about 1920, when those other influences we have discussed became strong. Quotations from the Bible still occur, but they support my contention: they are usually conventional and insensitive, introduced because the author or speaker wants to be impressive without taking trouble. Listen to the following advertisement of Cable and Wireless in *The Times* of 28 July 1943. The advertisement is reporting a speech made by a cabinet minister, Colonel Oliver Stanley, at a Cable and Wireless staff lunch:

> When the end comes, when victory is won, then history will begin to assess merit. We shall all of us be searching our conscience. . . . We shall be discussing who succeeded and who failed. . . . I have no doubt at all, when we come to discuss the part that Cable and Wireless has played, what the verdict of the nation will be—"Well done thou good and faithful servant!"

No doubt Cable and Wireless has done and deserved well, but I do not feel it can be suitably congratulated in the words of St Matthew's Gospel, and if the English of the Bible had been in Colonel Stanley's blood instead of in his cliché-box I do not think he would have used such words. It is an example of insensitiveness to the Authorized Version and of the complete divorce between Biblical and popular English. (A similar example, this time of insensitiveness to Milton, was the slogan "They also serve" on a war-workers' poster.)

9 So much for this popular tendency in prose. I have suggested that it takes various forms, bringing freshness and informality and new usages and democratic good manners into literature, but also bringing vulgarity and flatness. Now for the other tendency to which I will attach the name esoteric: the desire on the part of writers—generally the more distinguished writers—to create something better than the bloodshed and dullness which have been creeping together over the world. Such writers are often censured. You may complain that Lytton Strachey, Virginia Woolf, James Joyce, D. H. Lawrence and T. E. Lawrence have done little to hearten us up. But you must admit they were the leading writers of our age. It is an age that could not produce a Shakespeare or even a Madame de Sévigné or a Jane Austen: an age in which sensitive people could not feel comfortable, and were driven to seek inner compensation: an age similar in some ways to that which caused St Augustine to write *The City of God.* St Augustine, though he looked outside him, worked within. He too was esoteric. These writers look outside them and find their material lying about in the world. But they arrange it and re-create it within, temporarily sheltered from the pitiless blasts and the fog.

10 A further word on T. E. Lawrence. The *Seven Pillars of Wisdom* is a most enigmatic book. Lawrence made good in the world of action and was what most of us regard as a hero—brave, selfless, modest and kind by nature yet ruthless at need, loyal and the inspirer of loyalty, magnetic, a born leader of men, and victorious at Damascus in the last of the picturesque wars. Such a man, even if not happy, will surely be true to type. He will remain the man of action, the extrovert. But when we read the *Seven Pillars* we find beneath the gallant fighting and the brilliant description of scenery—sensitiveness, introspection, doubt, disgust at the material world. It is the book of a man who cannot fit in with twentieth-century civilization, and loves the half-savage Arabs because they challenge it. This comes out in the following quotation; note in the final sentence the hit at "vested things": at the innate commercialism of the West which ruined the peace of Versailles.

> Their mind [the Arabs'] was strange and dark, full of depressions and exaltations, lacking in rule, but with more of ardour and more fertile in belief than any other in the world. They were a people of starts, for whom the abstract was the strongest motive, the process of infinite courage and variety, and the end nothing. They were as unstable as water, and like water would perhaps finally prevail. Since the dawn of life, in successive waves they had been dashing themselves against the coasts of flesh. Each wave was broken, but, like the sea, wore away ever so little of the granite on which it failed, and some day, ages yet, might roll unchecked over the place where the material world had been, and God would move upon the face of those waters. One such wave (and not the least) I raised and rolled before the breath of an idea, till it reached its crest, and toppled over and fell at Damascus. The wash of that wave, thrown back by the resistance of vested things, will provide the matter of the following wave, when in fullness of time the sea shall be raised once more.

11 The *Seven Pillars* for all its greatness is too strange a book to be typical of the period, and the same applies to another curious masterpiece, James Joyce's *Ulysses.* For a typical example I'd take Lytton Strachey's *Queen Victoria.* This is important for several reasons. It came out at the beginning of our period, it is an achievement of genius, and it has revolutionized the art of biography. Strachey did debunk of course: he hated pomposity, hypocrisy and muddle-headedness, he mistrusted inflated reputations, and was clever at puncturing them, and he found in the Victorian age, which had taken itself very, very seriously, a tempting target for his barbed arrows. But he was much more than a debunker. He did what no biographer had done before: he managed to get inside his subject. Earlier biographers, like Macaulay and Carlyle, had produced fine and convincing pictures of people; Lytton Strachey makes his people move; they are alive, like characters in a novel: he constructs or rather reconstructs them from within. Sometimes he got them wrong: his presentation of General Gordon has been questioned, so has his brilliant later work on Elizabeth and Essex. But even when they are wrong they seem alive, and in the *Queen Victoria* his facts have not been seriously challenged; and, based on dry documents, a whole society and its inhabitants rise from the grave, and walk about. That was his great contribution. He was a historian who worked from within, and constructed out of the bones of the past something more real and more satisfactory than the chaos surrounding him. He is typical of our period, and particularly of the

twenties—throughout them his influence is enormous; today it has declined, partly because people are again taking themselves very, very seriously, and don't like the human race to be laughed at, partly because Strachey had some tiresome imitators, who have brought his method into discredit. However, that doesn't matter. Reputations always will go up and down. What matters is good work, and *Queen Victoria* is a masterpiece. It is a pageant of the historical type, but as the grand procession passes we—you and I, we little readers—are somehow inside the procession, we mingle unobserved with royalty and statesmen and courtiers and underlings, and hear their unspoken thoughts.

12 Even a frivolous passage, like the one about the boy Jones, has its historical function. Lytton Strachey was a gay person who loved fun and nonsense, and he knew how to make use of them in his work. Through the episode of the enigmatic boy Jones, an undersized youth who repeatedly entered Buckingham Palace and hid there in the year 1840, was discovered under sofas, and confessed "that he had 'helped himself to soup and other eatables . . . sat upon the throne, seen the Queen, and heard the Princess Royal squall' ", Strachey re-creates the domestic confusion existing there, and makes the period come alive. Then he passes on to more serious topics.

13 What was he serious about? Not about political ideals or social reform. Like T. E. Lawrence, he was disillusioned, though in another way. He believed, however, in wit and aristocratic good manners, and he was implacable in his pursuit of truth. He believed, furthermore, in fidelity between human beings. There, and there only, the warmth of his heart comes out. He is always moved by constant affection, and the Queen's love for the Prince Consort, and for his memory, makes the book glow and preserves it from frigidity. Strachey's belief in affection, like his fondness for fun, is too often forgotten. Here is the famous passage describing the Queen's death, with which the book closes. He begins by being the dignified historian; then he dismisses his subject tenderly, and launches the Queen as it were on an ebbing tide, carrying her backwards through the manifold joys of life till she vanishes in the mists of her birth.

> By the end of the year the last remains of her ebbing strength had almost deserted her; and through the early days of the opening century it was clear that her dwindling forces were kept together only by an effort of will. On January 14, she had at Osborne an hour's interview with Lord Roberts, who had returned victorious from South Africa a few days before. She inquired with acute anxiety into all the details of the war; she appeared to sustain the exertion successfully; but, when the audience was over, there was a collapse. On the following day her medical attendants recognized that her state was hopeless; and yet, for two days more, the indomitable spirit fought on; for two days more she discharged the duties of a Queen of England. But after that there was an end of working; and then, and not till then, did the last optimism of those about her break down. The brain was failing, and life was gently slipping away. Her family gathered round her; for a little more she lingered, speechless and apparently insensible; and, on January 22, 1901, she died.
>
> When, two days previously, the news of the approaching end had been made public, astonished grief had swept over the country. It appeared as if some monstrous reversal of the course of nature was about to take place. The vast majority of her

> subjects had never known a time when Queen Victoria had not been reigning over them. She had become an indissoluble part of their whole scheme of things, and that they were about to lose her appeared a scarcely possible thought. She herself, as she lay blind and silent, seemed to those who watched her to be divested of all thinking—to have glided already, unawares, into oblivion. Yet, perhaps, in the secret chambers of consciousness, she had her thoughts, too. Perhaps her fading mind called up once more the shadows of the past to float before it, and retraced, for the last time, the vanished visions of that long history—passing back and back, through the cloud of years, to older and ever older memories—to the spring woods at Osborne, so full of primroses for Lord Beaconsfield—to Lord Palmerston's queer clothes and high demeanour, and Albert's face under the green lamp, and Albert's first stag at Balmoral, and Albert in his blue and silver uniform, and the Baron coming in through a doorway, and Lord M. dreaming at Windsor with the rooks cawing in the elm-trees, and the Archbishop of Canterbury on his knees in the dawn, and the old King's turkey-cock ejaculations, and Uncle Leopold's soft voice at Claremont, and Lehzen with the globes, and her mother's feathers sweeping down towards her, and a great old repeater-watch of her father's in its tortoiseshell case, and a yellow rug, and some friendly flounces of sprigged muslin, and the trees and the grass at Kensington.

You'll remember what I said before about the new psychology being in the air, and this last long lovely drifting sentence, with its imaginings of the subconscious, could not have been created at an earlier date.

14 A word on the authors whom I have mentioned. I have kept to those who may be said to belong to our period, who were formed by it, and received its peculiar stamp. Authors like Arnold Bennett, Galsworthy, Wells, Belloc, Chesterton, Frank Swinnerton, Norman Douglas, Bertrand Russell, Lowes Dickinson, George Moore, Max Beerbohm, did good work after 1920, and some of them are still active. But they got their impressions and formed their attitudes in an earlier period, before the first of the two world wars. D. H. Lawrence presents a special difficulty. Does he come in or not? His finest novels, *The White Peacock* and *Sons and Lovers,* were published round about 1912, and he displays all his life a blend of vision and vituperation which seem to date him further back still—right back to Carlyle. On the other hand, he was alive to the new economics and the new psychology, and well aware, when he died in 1930, that the war to end war had ended nothing but the Victorian peace. My own feeling is that he does come into our survey.

15 To sum up my remarks. Our period: a long weekend between two wars. Economic and psychological changes already in existence intensify. Writers are intimidated by the economic changes but stimulated by the psychological. Prose, because it is a medium for daily life as well as for literature, is particularly sensitive to what is going on, and two tendencies can be noted: the popular, which absorbs what is passing, and the esoteric, which rejects it, and tries to create through art something more valuable than monotony and bloodshed. The best work of the period has this esoteric tendency. T. E. Lawrence, though heroic in action, retreats into the desert to act. Lytton Strachey is disillusioned, except about truth and human affection.

16 As for assessing the value of our period, I am disposed to place it high, and I do not agree with those numerous critics who condemn it as a failure, and scold

mankind for enjoying itself too much in the twenties and for theorizing too much in the thirties. We are plunged in a terrific war, and our literary judgements are not at their best. All our criticism is or ought to be tentative. And tentatively I suggest that the long weekend did valuable work, and I ask you to pause before you yield to the prevalent tendency to censure it.

(1944)

QUESTIONS

Thought and Structure

1. What general relationship between language and culture is Forster trying to establish in his two-paragraph introduction? Why do you suppose he quotes Rose Macaulay so extensively?
2. What are the three great "movements" that Forster identifies in paragraphs 3–5? What measurable impact do those movements have on English prose?
3. Read carefully paragraphs 7–8 and paragraphs 9–13; those groupings constitute sections of Forster's argument. See if you can figure out two things about each section: what idea is Forster developing; what is the relationship between that idea and the larger idea that controls the essay?
4. Look at paragraphs 5 and 9. Each of those paragraphs begins with a summary of material that has just been covered. But paragraph 5 also constitutes what seems to be the final paragraph of a three-paragraph section of the argument. Why then does Forster summarize at this particular point? The beginning of paragraph 9 seems a more logical place to summarize an argument in progress. Why?
5. Look at paragraphs 15–16 (the conclusion) in terms of paragraphs 1–2 (the introduction). How do those two sections comment on one another? Does the conclusion add a slightly different dimension to the essay, a dimension not easily detected in the introduction?

Style and Strategy

6. Think about the general organizational pattern of paragraphs 3–13; each of those paragraphs seems to be very much alike, with a few exceptions. There are several sentences at the beginning of each paragraph that lay out an idea, followed by information about selected writers and their literary texts. Forster explains those texts for his own purposes. How effective do you find this general pattern? Does Forster tell you enough to keep you informed and to push you helpfully through the essay, or is this argument too tough for you?
7. Keeping question 6 in mind, turn to paragraph 12. When Forster calls our attention to Lytton Strachey's allusion to "boy Jones," how does Forster deal with and explain that allusion so that those of us who have not read *Queen Victoria* will still be included in the discussion? In other words, how does Forster demonstrate a concern for his own "intelligent" reader? In answering that question, do we get a better sense of Forster's judgment about Isherwood who "always writes as if the reader were equally intelligent" (paragraph 7)?

SUGGESTIONS FOR WRITING

A. In paragraph 7, Forster claims that during the historical period he is discussing, official notices and proclamations became "more intelligible" and that the speeches of public men became "less formal," "more democratic." Write a short essay about such proclamations and speeches in our time. Examine evidence that is available to you in the newspaper or in government documents. Just to enliven your mind, you might imagine what Forster would say about those documents were he still alive to read them.

B. Write a short paragraph about Forster's last sentence in paragraph 13. How does that sentence pull the entire essay together? Do you think his judgment about Strachey's sentence is reliable? See if you can write a sentence of your own that resembles Strachey's "last long lovely drifting sentence, with its imaginings of the subconscious."

The Point of It

I

1 "I don't see the point of it," said Micky, through much imbecile laughter.

2 Harold went on rowing. They had spent too long on the sand-dunes, and now the tide was running out of the estuary strongly. The sun was setting, the fields on the opposite bank shone bright, and the farm-house where they were stopping glowed from its upper windows as though filled to the brim with fire.

3 "We're going to be carried out to sea," Micky continued. "You'll never win unless you bust yourself a bit, and you a poor invalid, too. I back the sea."

4 They were reaching the central channel, the backbone, as it were, of the retreating waters. Once past it, the force of the tide would slacken, and they would have easy going until they beached under the farm. It was a glorious evening. It had been a most glorious day. They had rowed out to the dunes at the slack, bathed, raced, eaten, slept, bathed and raced and eaten again. Micky was in roaring spirits. God had never thwarted him hitherto, and he could not suppose that they would really be made late for supper by an ebbing tide. When they came to the channel, and the boat, which had been slowly edging upstream, hung motionless among the moving waters, he lost all semblance of sanity, and shouted:

"It may be that the gulfs will wash us down,
It may be we shall touch the Happy Isles,
And see the great Achilles, whom we knew."

5 Harold, who did not care for poetry, only shouted. His spirits also were roaring, and he neither looked nor felt a poor invalid. Science had talked to him seriously of late, shaking her head at his sunburnt body. What should Science know? She had sent him down to the sea to recruit, and Micky to see that he did not tire himself. Micky had been a nuisance at first, but common sense had prevailed, as it always

does among the young. A fortnight ago, he would not let the patient handle an oar. Now he bid him "bust" himself, and Harold took him at his word and did so. He made himself all will and muscle. He began not to know where he was. The thrill of the stretcher against his feet, and of the tide up his arms, merged with his friend's voice towards one nameless sensation; he was approaching the mystic state that is the athlete's true though unacknowledged goal: he was beginning to *be.*

6 Micky chanted, "One, two—one, two," and tried to help by twitching the rudder. But Micky had imagination. He looked at the flaming windows and fancied that the farm was a star and the boat its attendant satellite. Then the tide was the rushing ether stream of the universe, the interstellar surge that beats for ever. How jolly! He did not formulate his joys, after the weary fashion of older people. He was far too happy to be thankful. "Remember now thy Creator in the days of thy youth," are the words of one who has left his youth behind, and all that Micky sang was "One, two."

7 Harold laughed without hearing. Sweat poured off his forehead. He put on a spurt, as did the tide.

8 "Wish the doctor could see you," cried Micky.

9 No answer. Setting his teeth, he went berserk. His ancestors called to him that it was better to die than to be beaten by the sea. He rowed with gasps and angry little cries, while the voice of the helmsman lashed him to fury.

10 "That's right—one, two—plug it in harder. . . . Oh, I say, this is a bit stiff, though. Let's give it up, old man, perhaps."

11 The gulls were about them now. Some wheeled overhead, others bobbed past on the furrowed waters. The song of a lark came faintly from the land, and Micky saw the doctor's trap driving along the road that led to the farm. He felt ashamed.

12 "Look here, Harold, you oughtn't to—I oughtn't to have let you. I—I don't see the point of it."

13 "Don't you?" said Harold with curious distinctness. "Well, you will some day," and so saying dropped both oars. The boat spun round at this, the farm, the trap, the song of the lark vanished, and he fell heavily against the rowlock. Micky caught at him. He had strained his heart. Half in the boat and half out of it, he died, a rotten business.

II

14 A rotten business. It happened when Michael was twenty-two, and he expected never to be happy again. The sound of his own voice shouting as he was carried out, the doctor's voice saying, "I consider you responsible," the coming of Harold's parents, the voice of the curate summarizing Harold's relations with the unseen—all these things affected him so deeply that he supposed they would affect him for ever. They did not, because he lived to be over seventy, and with the best will in the world, it is impossible to remember clearly for so long. The mind, however sensitive and affectionate, is coated with new experiences daily; it cannot clear itself of the steady accretion, and is forced either to forget the past or to distort it. So it was with Michael. In time only the more dramatic incidents survived. He remem-

bered Harold's final gesture (one hand grasping his own, the other plunged deep into the sea), because there was a certain æsthetic quality about it, not because it was the last of his friend. He remembered the final words for the same reason. "Don't you see the point of it? Well, you will some day." The phrase struck his fancy, and passed into his own stock; after thirty or forty years he forgot its origin. He is not to blame; the business of life snowed him under.

15 There is also this to say: he and Harold had nothing in common except youth. No spiritual bond could survive. They had never discussed theology or social reform, or any of the problems that were thronging Michael's brain, and consequently, though they had been intimate enough, there was nothing to remember. Harold melted the more one thought of him. Robbed of his body, he was so shadowy. Nor could one imagine him as a departed spirit, for the world beyond death is surely august. Neither in heaven nor hell is there place for athletics and aimless good temper, and if these were taken from Harold, what was left? Even if the unseen life should prove an archetype of this, even if it should contain a sun and stars of its own, the sunburn of earth must fade off our faces as we look at it, the muscles of earth must wither before we can go rowing on its infinite sea. Michael sadly resigned his friend to God's mercy. He himself could do nothing, for men can only immortalize those who leave behind them some strong impression of poetry or wisdom.

16 For himself he expected another fate. With all humility, he knew that he was not as Harold. It was no merit of his own, but he had been born of a more intellectual stock, and had inherited powers that rendered him worthier of life, and of whatever may come after it. He cared for the universe, for the tiny tangle in it that we call civilisation, for his fellow-men who had made the tangle and who transcended it. Love, the love of humanity, warmed him; and even when he was thinking of other matters, was looking at Orion perhaps in the cold winter evenings, a pang of joy, too sweet for description, would thrill him, and he would feel sure that our highest impulses have some eternal value, and will be completed hereafter. So full a nature could not brood over death.

17 To summarize his career.

Soon after the tragedy, when he in his turn was recruiting, he met the woman who was to become his helpmate through life. He had met her once before, and had not liked her; she had seemed uncharitable and hard. Now he saw that her hardness sprang from a morality that he himself lacked. If he believed in love, Janet believed in truth. She tested all men and all things. She had no patience with the sentimentalist who shelters from the world's rough and tumble. Engaged at that time to another man, she spoke more freely to Michael than she would otherwise have done, and told him that it is not enough to feel good and to feel that others are good; one's business is to make others better, and she urged him to adopt a profession. The beauty of honest work dawned upon the youth as she spoke. Mentally and physically, he came to full manhood, and, after due preparation, he entered the Home Civil Service—the British Museum.

18 Here began a career that was rather notable, and wholly beneficial to humanity. With his ideals of conduct and culture, Michael was not content with the official routine. He desired to help others, and, since he was gifted with tact, they consented to the operation. Before long he became a conciliatory force in his department. He

could mollify his superiors, encourage his inferiors, soothe foreign scholars, and show that there is something to be said for all sides. Janet, who watched his rise, taxed him again with instability. But now she was wrong. The young man was not a mere opportunist. He always had a sincere opinion of his own, or he could not have retained the respect of his colleagues. It was really the inherent sweetness of his nature at work, turned by a woman's influence towards fruitful ends.

19 At the end of a ten years' acquaintance the two married. In the interval Janet had suffered much pain, for the man to whom she had been engaged had proved unworthy of her. Her character was set when she came to Michael, and, as he knew, strongly contrasted with his own; and perhaps they had already interchanged all the good they could. But the marriage proved durable and sufficiently happy. He, in particular, made endless allowances, for toleration and sympathy were becoming the cardinal points of his nature. If his wife was unfair to the official mind, or if his brother-in-law, an atheist, denounced religion, he would say to himself, "They cannot help it; they are made thus, and have the qualities of their defects. Let me rather think of my own, and strive for a wider outlook ceaselessly." He grew sweeter every day.

20 It was partly this desire for a wider outlook that turned him to literature. As he was crossing the forties it occurred to him to write a few essays, somewhat retrospective in tone, and thoughtful rather than profound in content. They had some success. Their good taste, their lucid style, the tempered Christianity of their ethics, whetted the half-educated public, and made it think and feel. They were not, and were not intended to be, great literature, but they opened the doors to it, and were indubitably a power for good. The first volume was followed by "The Confessions of a Middle-aged Man." In it Michael paid melodious tribute to youth, but showed that ripeness is all. Experience, he taught, is the only humanizer; sympathy, balance and many-sidedness cannot come to a man until he is elderly. It is always pleasant to be told that the best is yet to be, and the sale of the book was large. Perhaps he would have become a popular author, but his wife's influence restrained him from writing anything that he did not sincerely feel. She had borne him three children by now—Henry, Catherine, and Adam. On the whole they were a happy family. Henry never gave any trouble. Catherine took after her mother. Adam, who was wild and uncouth, caused his father some anxiety. He could not understand him, in spite of careful observation, and they never became real friends. Still, it was but a little cloud in a large horizon. At home, as in his work, Michael was more successful than most men.

21 Thus he slipped into the fifties. On the death of his father he inherited a house in the Surrey hills, and Janet, whose real interests were horticultural, settled down there. After all, she had not proved an intellectual woman. Her fierce manner had misled him and perhaps herself into believing it. She was efficient enough in London society, but it bored her, for she lacked her husband's pliancy, and aged more rapidly than he did. Nor did the country suit her. She grew querulous, disputing with other ladies about the names of flowers. And, of course, the years were not without their effect on him, too. By now he was somewhat of a valetudinarian. He had given up all outdoor sports, and, though his health remained good, grew bald, and rather stout and timid. He was against late hours, violent exercise, night walks, swimming when

hot, muddling about in open boats, and he often had to check himself from fidgeting the children. Henry, a charming sympathetic lad, would squeeze his hand and say, "All right, father." But Catherine and Adam sometimes frowned. He thought of the children more and more. Now that his wife was declining, they were the future, and he was determined to keep in touch with them, remembering how his own father had failed with him. He believed in gentleness, and often stood between them and their mother. When the boys grew up he let them choose their own friends. When Catherine, at the age of nineteen, asked if she might go away and earn some money as a lady gardener, he let her go. In this case he had his reward, for Catherine, having killed the flowers, returned. She was a restless, scowling young woman, a trial to her mother, who could not imagine what girls were coming to. Then she married and improved greatly; indeed, she proved his chief support in the coming years.

22 For, soon after her marriage, a great trouble fell on him. Janet became bedridden, and, after a protracted illness, passed into the unknown. Sir Michael—for he had been knighted—declared that he should not survive her. They were so accustomed to each other, so mutually necessary, that he fully expected to pass away after her. In this he was mistaken. She died when he was sixty, and he lived to be over seventy. His character had passed beyond the clutch of circumstance and he still retained his old interests and his unconquerable benignity.

23 A second trouble followed hard on the first. It transpired that Adam was devoted to his mother, and had only tolerated home life for her sake. After a brutal scene he left. He wrote from the Argentine that he was sorry, but wanted to start for himself. "I don't see the point of it," quavered Sir Michael. "Have I ever stopped him or any of you from starting?" Henry and Catherine agreed with him. Yet he felt that they understood their brother better than he did. "I have given him freedom all his life," he continued. "I have given him freedom, what more does he want?" Henry, after hesitation, said, "There are some people who feel that freedom cannot be given. At least I have heard so. Perhaps Adam is like that. Unless he took freedom he might not feel free." Sir Michael disagreed. "I have now studied adolescence for many years," he replied, "and your conclusions, my dear boy, are ridiculous."

24 The two rallied to their father gallantly; and, after all, he spent a dignified old age. Having retired from the British Museum, he produced a little aftermath of literature. The great public had forgotten him, but the courtliness of his "Musings of a Pensioner" procured him some circulation among elderly and educated audiences. And he found a new spiritual consolation. *Anima naturaliter Anglicana,* he had never been hostile to the Established Church; and, when he criticized her worldliness and occasional inhumanity, had spoken as one who was outside her rather than against her. After his wife's death and the flight of his son he lost any lingering taste for speculation. The experience of years disposed him to accept the experience of centuries, and to merge his feeble personal note in the great voice of tradition. Yes; a serene and dignified old age. Few grudged it to him. Of course, he had enemies, who professed to see through him, and said that Adam had seen through him too; but no impartial observer agreed. No ulterior motive had ever biased Sir Michael. The purity of his record was not due to luck, but to purity within, and his conciliatory manner sprang from a conciliated soul. He could look back on

failures and mistakes, and he had not carried out the ideals of his youth. Who has? But he had succeeded better than most men in modifying those ideals to fit the world of facts, and if love had been modified into sympathy and sympathy into compromise, let one of his contemporaries cast the first stone.

25 One fact remained—the fact of death. Hitherto, Sir Michael had never died, and at times he was bestially afraid. But more often death appeared as a prolongation of his present career. He saw himself quietly and tactfully organizing some corner in infinity with his wife's assistance; Janet would be greatly improved. He saw himself passing from a sphere in which he had been efficient into a sphere which combined the familiar with the eternal, and in which he would be equally efficient—passing into it with dignity and without pain. This life is a preparation for the next. Those who live longest are consequently the best prepared. Experience is the great teacher; blessed are the experienced, for they need not further modify their ideals.

26 The manner of his death was as follows. He, too, met with an accident. He was walking from his town house to Catherine's by a short cut through a slum; some women were quarrelling about a fish, and as he passed they appealed to him. Always courteous, the old man stopped, said that he had not sufficient data to judge on, and advised them to lay the fish aside for twenty-four hours. This chanced to annoy them, and they grew more angry with him than with one another. They accused him of "doing them," of "getting round them," and one, who was the worse for drink, said, "See if he gets round that," and slapped him with the fish in the face. He fell. When he came to himself he was lying in bed with one of his headaches.

27 He could hear Catherine's voice. She annoyed him. If he did not open his eyes, it was only because he did not choose.

28 "He has been like this for nearly two years," said Henry's voice.

29 It was, at the most, ten minutes since he had fallen in the slum. But he did not choose to argue.

30 "Yes, he's pretty well played out," said a third voice—actually the voice of Adam; how and when had Adam returned? "But, then, he's been that for the last thirty years."

31 "Gently, old boy," said Henry.

32 "Well, he has," said Adam. "I don't believe in cant. He never did anything since Mother died, and damned little before. They've forgotten his books because they aren't first-hand; they're rearranging the cases he arranged in the British Museum. That's the lot. What else has he done except tell people to dress warmly, but not too warm?"

33 "Adam, you really mustn't—"

34 "It's because nobody speaks up that men of the old man's type get famous. It's a sign of your sloppy civilisation. You're all afraid—afraid of originality, afraid of work, afraid of hurting one another's feelings. You let any one come to the top who doesn't frighten you, and as soon as he dies you forget him and knight some other figurehead instead."

35 An unknown voice said, "Shocking, Mr. Adam, shocking. Such a dear old man, and quite celebrated, too."

36 "You'll soon get used to me, nurse."

37 The nurse laughed.

38 "Adam, it is a relief to have you," said Catherine after a pause. "I want you and your boy to help me with mine." Her voice sounded dimmer; she had turned from her father without a word of farewell. "One must profit by the mistakes of others . . . after all, more heroism. . . . I am determined to keep in touch with my boy—"

39 "Larrup him," said Adam. "That's the secret." He followed his sister out of the room.

40 Then Henry's delightful laugh sounded for the last time. "You make us all feel twenty years younger," he said; "more like when—"

41 The door shut.

42 Sir Michael grew cold with rage. This was life, this was what the younger generation had been thinking. Adam he ignored, but at the recollection of Henry and Catherine he determined to die. If he chose, he could have risen from bed and driven the whole pack into the street. But he did not choose. He chose rather to leave this shoddy and ungrateful world. The immense and superhuman cynicism that is latent in all of us came at last to the top and transformed him. He saw the absurdity of love, and the vision so tickled him that he began to laugh. The nurse, who had called him a dear old man, bent over him, and at the same moment two boys came into the sick-room.

43 "How's grandpapa?" asked one of them—Catherine's boy.

44 "Not so well," the nurse answered.

45 There was a silence. Then the other boy said, "Come along, let's cut."

46 "But they told us not to."

47 "Why should we do what old people tell us! Dad's pretty well played out, and so's your mother."

48 "Shocking; be off with you both," said the nurse; and, with a little croon of admiration, Catherine's boy followed his cousin out of the room. Their grandfather's mirth increased. He rolled about in the bed; and, just as he was grasping the full irony of the situation, he died, and pursued it into the unknown.

III

49 Micky was still in bed. He was aware of so much through long melancholy dreams. But when he opened his mouth to laugh, it filled with dust. Choosing to open his eyes, he found that he had swollen enormously, and lay sunk in the sand of an illimitable plain. As he expected, he had no occasion greatly to modify his ideals; infinity had merely taken the place of his bedroom and of London. Nothing moved on its surface except a few sand-pillars, which would sometimes merge into each other as though confabulating; and then fall with a slight hiss. Save for these, there was no motion, no noise, nor could he feel any wind.

50 How long had he lain here? Perhaps for years, long before death perhaps, while his body seemed to be walking among men. Life is so short and trivial, that who knows whether we arrive for it entirely, whether more than a fraction of the soul is aroused to put on flesh? The bud and the blossom perish in a moment, the husk endures, and may not the soul be a husk? It seemed to Micky that he had lain in

the dust for ever, suffering and sneering, and that the essence of all things, the primal power that lies behind the stars, is senility. Age, toothless, dropsical age; ungenerous to age and to youth; born before all ages, and outlasting them; the universe as old age.

51 The place degraded while it tortured. It was vast, yet ignoble. It sloped downward into darkness and upward into cloud, but into what darkness, what clouds! No tragic splendour glorified them. When he looked at them he understood why he was so unhappy, for they were looking at him, sneering at him while he sneered. Their dirtiness was more ancient than the hues of day and night, their irony more profound; he was part of their jest, even as youth was part of his, and slowly he realized that he was, and had for some years been, in Hell.

52 All around him lay other figures, huge and fungous. It was as if the plain had festered. Some of them could sit up, others scarcely protruded from the sand, and he knew that they had made the same mistake in life as himself, though he did not know yet what the mistake had been; probably some little slip, easily avoided had one but been told.

53 Speech was permissible. Presently a voice said, "Is not ours a heavenly sky? Is it not beautiful?"

54 "Most beautiful," answered Micky, and found each word a stab of pain. Then he knew that one of the sins here punished was appreciation; he was suffering for all the praise that he had given to the bad and mediocre upon earth; when he had praised out of idleness, or to please people, or to encourage people; for all the praise that had not been winged with passion. He repeated "Most beautiful," and the sky quivered, for he was entering into fuller torments now. One ray of happiness survived: his wife could not be in this place. She had not sinned with the people of the plain, and could not suffer their distortion. Her view of life had proved right after all; and, in his utter misery, this comforted him. Janet should again be his religion, and as eternity dragged forward and returned upon itself and dragged forward she would show him that old age, if rightly managed, can be beautiful; that experience, if rightly received, can lead the soul of man to bliss. Then he turned to his neighbour, who was continuing his hymn of praise.

55 "I could lie here for ever," he was saying. "When I think of my restlessness during life—that is to say, during what men miscall life, for it is death really—this is life—when I think of my restlessness on earth, I am overcome by so much goodness and mercy, I could lie here for ever."

56 "And will you?" asked Micky.

57 "Ah, that is the crowning blessing—I shall, and so will you."

58 Here a pillar of sand passed between them. It was long before they could speak or see. Then Micky took up the song, chafed by the particles that were working into his soul.

59 "I, too, regret my wasted hours," he said, "especially the hours of my youth. I regret all the time I spent in the sun. In later years I did repent, and that is why I am admitted here where there is no sun; yes, and no wind and none of the stars that drove me almost mad at night once. It would be appalling, would it not, to see Orion again, the central star of whose sword is not a star but a nebula, the golden seed of worlds to be. How I dreaded the autumn on earth when Orion rises, for he

recalled adventure and my youth. It was appalling. How thankful I am to see him no more."

60 "Ah, but it was worse," cried the other, "to look high leftward from Orion and see the Twins. Castor and Pollux were brothers, one human, the other divine; and Castor died. But Pollux went down to Hell that he might be with him."

61 "Yes; that is so. Pollux went into Hell."

62 "Then the gods had pity on both, and raised them aloft to be stars whom sailors worship, and all who love and are young. Zeus was their father, Helen their sister, who brought the Greeks against Troy. I dreaded them more than Orion."

63 They were silent, watching their own sky. It approved. They had been cultivated men on earth, and these are capable of the nicer torments hereafter. Their memories will strike exquisite images to enhance their pain. "I will speak no more," said Micky to himself. "I will be silent through eternity." But the darkness prised open his lips, and immediately he was speaking.

64 "Tell me more about this abode of bliss," he asked. "Are there grades in it? Are there ranks in our heaven?"

65 "There are two heavens," the other replied, "the heaven of the hard and of the soft. We here lie in the heaven of the soft. It is a sufficient arrangement, for all men grow either hard or soft as they grow old."

66 As he spoke the clouds lifted, and, looking up the slope of the plain, Micky saw that in the distance it was bounded by mountains of stone, and he knew, without being told, that among those mountains Janet lay, rigid, and that he should never see her. She had not been saved. The darkness would mock her, too, for ever. With him lay the sentimentalists, the conciliators, the peacemakers, the humanists, and all who have trusted the warmer vision; with his wife were the reformers and ascetics and all sword-like souls. By different paths they had come to Hell, and Micky now saw what the bustle of life conceals: that the years are bound either to liquefy a man or to stiffen him, and that Love and Truth, who seem to contend for our souls like angels, hold each the seeds of our decay.

67 "It is, indeed, a sufficient arrangement," he said; "both sufficient and simple. But answer one question more that my bliss may be perfected; in which of these two heavens are the young?"

68 His neighbour answered, "In neither; there are no young."

69 He spoke no more, and settled himself more deeply in the dust. Micky did the same. He had vague memories of men and women who had died before reaching maturity, of boys and unwedded maidens and youths lowered into the grave before their parents' eyes. Whither had they gone, that undeveloped minority? What was the point of their brief existence? Had they vanished utterly, or were they given another chance of accreting experiences until they became like Janet or himself? One thing was certain: there were no young, either in the mountains or the plain, and perhaps the very memory of such creatures was an illusion fostered by cloud.

70 The time was now ripe for a review of his life on earth. He traced his decomposition—his work had been soft, his books soft, he had softened his relations with other men. He had seen good in everything, and this is itself a sign of decay. Whatever occurred he had been appreciative, tolerant, pliant. Consequently he had

been a success; Adam was right; it was the moment in civilisation for his type. He had mistaken self-criticism for self-discipline, he had muffled in himself and others the keen, heroic edge. Yet the luxury of repentance was denied him. The fault was his, but the fate humanity's, for every one grows hard or soft as he grows old.

71 "This is my life," thought Micky; "my books forgotten, my work superseded. This is the whole of my life." And his agony increased, because all the same there had been in that life an elusive joy which, if only he could have distilled it, would have sweetened infinity. It was part of the jest that he should try, and should eternally oscillate between disgust and desire. For there is nothing ultimate in Hell; men will not lay aside all hope on entering it, or they would attain to the splendour of despair. To have made a poem about Hell is to mistake its very essence; it is the imagination of men, who will have beauty, that fashions it as ice or flame. Old, but capable of growing older, Micky lay in the sandy country, remembering that once he had remembered a country—a country that had not been sand. . . .

72 He was aroused by the mutterings of the spirits round him. An uneasiness such as he had not noted in them before had arisen. "A pillar of sand," said one. Another said, "It is not; it comes from the river."

73 He asked, "What river?"

74 "The spirits of the damned dwell over it; we never speak of that river."

75 "Is it a broad river?"

76 "Swift, and very broad."

77 "Do the damned ever cross it?"

78 "They are permitted, we know not why, to cross it now and again."

79 And in these answers he caught a new tone, as if his companions were frightened, and were finding means to express their fear. When he said, "With permission, they can do us no harm," he was answered, "They harm us with light and a song." And again, "They harm us because they remember and try to remind."

80 "Of what would they remind us?"

81 "Of the hour when we were as they."

82 As he questioned a whisper arose from the low-lying verges. The spirits were crying to each other faintly. He heard, "It is coming; drive it back over the river, shatter it, compel it to be old." And then the darkness was cloven, and a star of pain broke in his soul. He understood now; a torment greater than any was at hand.

83 "I was before choice," came the song. "I was before hardness and softness were divided. I was in the days when truth was love. And I am."

84 All the plain was convulsed. But the invader could not be shattered. When it pressed the air parted and the sand-pillars fell, and its path was filled with senile weeping.

85 "I have been all men, but all men have forgotten me. I transfigured the world for them until they preferred the world. They came to me as children, afraid; I taught them, and they despised me. Childhood is a dream about me, experience a slow forgetting: I govern the magic years between them, and am."

86 "Why trouble us?" moaned the shades. "We could bear our torment, just bear it, until there was light and a song. Go back again over the river. This is Heaven, we were saying, that darkness is God; we could praise them till you came. The book of our deeds is closed; why open it? We were damned from our birth; leave it there.

O supreme jester, leave us. We have sinned, we know it, and this place is death and Hell."

87 "Death comes," the voice pealed, "and death is not a dream or a forgetting. Death is real. But I, too, am real, and whom I will I save. I see the scheme of things, and in it no place for me, the brain and the body against me. Therefore I rend the scheme in two, and make a place, and under countless names have harrowed Hell. Come." Then, in tones of inexpressible sweetness, "Come to me all who remember. Come out of your eternity into mine. It is easy, for I am still at your eyes, waiting to look out of them; still in your hearts, waiting to beat. The years that I dwelt with you seemed short, but they were magical, and they outrun time."

88 The shades were silent. They could not remember.

89 "Who desires to remember? Desire is enough. There is no abiding home for strength and beauty among men. The flower fades, the seas dry up in the sun, the sun and all the stars fade as a flower. But the desire for such things, that is eternal, that can abide, and he who desires me is I."

90 Then Micky died a second death. This time he dissolved through terrible pain, scorched by the glare, pierced by the voice. But as he died he said, "I do desire," and immediately the invader vanished, and he was standing alone on the sandy plain. It had been merely a dream. But he was standing. How was that? Why had he not thought to stand before? He had been unhappy in Hell, and all that he had to do was to go elsewhere. He passed downwards, pained no longer by the mockery of its cloud. The pillars brushed against him and fell, the nether darkness went over his head. On he went till he came to the banks of the infernal stream, and there he stumbled—stumbled over a piece of wood, no vague substance, but a piece of wood that had once belonged to a tree. At his impact it moved, and water gurgled against it. He had embarked. Some one was rowing. He could see the blades of oars moving towards him through the foam, but the rower was invisible in cloud. As they neared mid-channel the boat went more slowly, for the tide was ebbing, and Micky knew that once carried out he would be lost eternally; there was no second hope of salvation. He could not speak, but his heart beat time to the oars—one, two. Hell made her last effort, and all that is evil in creation, all the distortions of love and truth by which we are vexed, came surging down the estuary, and the boat hung motionless. Micky heard the pant of breath through the roaring, the crack of angelic muscles; then he heard a voice say, "The point of it . . ." and a weight fell off his body and he crossed midstream.

91 It was a glorious evening. The boat had sped without prelude into sunshine. The sky was cloudless, the earth gold, and gulls were riding up and down on the furrowed waters. On the bank they had left were some sand-dunes rising to majestic hills; on the bank in front was a farm, full to the brim with fire.

(1911)

QUESTIONS

1. "The Point of It" is a short story, yet its very title suggests one of the features of the essay. Does this short story make a point? If so, what is the point? If so, should this piece

be called a fictive essay? Tom Wolfe has called "The Angels" a nonfiction short story. How does that judgment confuse our ability to make distinctions? Is it important to make such distinctions? Why?

2. So that you can get a better sense of Forster's organizing principles, outline what he is doing in each of the story's three sections. See if you can classify what is going on in each of those sections. Do they resemble in any way the beginning, the middle, and the end of an essay?
3. Do you think the characters in this story are people Forster actually knew, or do you think he made them up? What makes you think so?
4. Forster relies on some of the trappings of Christianity, such as Heaven and Hell. He also refers quite frequently to attitudes that we have come to associate with what is right and acceptable. How does Forster confuse our traditional sense of this material? How does he keep surprising us as we go along—putting us off guard, depriving us of what we expect, confusing us—about what might be "The Point of It"?
5. Why do you think this story relies so much on death? Can we separate Forster's notions about death from those of the narrator? Do you think Forster and the narrator might be one and the same, or can you distinguish them?
6. Can you tell as you go along how the narrator actually feels about Michael and his life-style? What are your clues? Why is Michael Micky in Part I and Part III?

SUGGESTIONS FOR WRITING

A. Write a short essay about what you think the invalid Harold knows about life that Michael does not know. Cite evidence from the story to support your argument.

B. Write a well-developed paragraph about what we can tell about Michael by examining his relationship with his children.

C. In a short paragraph tell your friends in your class what you think the narrator means by this comment: "He [Micky] had seen good in everything, and this is itself a sign of decay." Cite evidence from the story to support your analysis.

THREE

Virginia Woolf

(1882–1941)

To do justice to Virginia Woolf's work in a short note is not possible; the range of her mind, the sheer quantity of her work, its remarkable quality, the intensity of her perceptions, and her extraordinary experiments with form in the novel, in the essay, in the memoir, in biography, all argue against a neat summing up. The major novels alone—*Jacob's Room* (1922), *Mrs. Dalloway* (1925), *To The Lighthouse* (1927), *The Waves* (1931)—set her apart, distinguish her. There are also five volumes of collected essays that do not begin to represent her output in that genre. *Roger Fry: A Biography* (1940), *Moments of Being* (1976), a collection of autobiographical writings, and *A Room of One's Own* (1938), an expansive exploration about women, writing, and dire circumstance, attest to her interests in other genres and confirm her genius.

That Woolf educated herself in her famous father's library and did not attend formal schools is a well-known fact, as is her lifelong struggle against the Victorian fathers, including her own. But her bitterness has been overstated at the expense of her balance and her astonishing subtlety. Few escaped her acerbic wit, few satisfied her sense of perfection, but her friends were important to her, both for the conversation they provided and the support they gave her. Those friends, who gathered in her home in a section of London called Bloomsbury, included her brother Thoby, her sister Vanessa, Clive Bell, Lytton Strachey, E. M. Forster, Maynard Keynes, Roger Fry, Desmond McCarthy, and Leonard Woolf—the leading intellectuals of her time. The Bloomsbury Group turned aside from convention and provided a milieu in which sexuality, philosophy, writing, art, and psychology could be discussed freely and openly, an atmosphere in which experimentation and exploration were the watchwords. Woolf's genius flourished in this new order; her imagination took flight, producing a body of work so distinguished that critics are still trying to sum her up. The pieces in this anthology hint at her range and diversity and provide a sense of her style.

"Women and Fiction" from *Granite and Rainbow,* "Montaigne" from *The Common Reader,* and "Craftsmanship" from the *Collected Essays* touch on themes of recurring interest to Woolf: women writers' perpetual battle against the established male tradition; the necessity for courage in the battle; the emerging signs of success reflected in new forms and in a healthy impersonality that shifts concerns away from personal complaints to the larger culture; the importance nevertheless of writing always as woman, writing always from one's very personal center; the importance of words and the life they live in the mind, their playfulness, their independence, their power, and their suggestiveness. As Woolf develops these ideas in these three essays, we are privileged to watch her experiment with language, flash her wit, go on intellectual rambles, examine her many selves. We can see her change her style, change her tactics as she meets the demands of different audiences.

"Kew Gardens," an early experiment with form, affords glimpses of the brilliant novelist at work. The story opens with a dazzling impressionist scene of a flower bed, and we get to see her impart color, elicit movement, and create a play of light as she sets our minds in motion and moves us through a series of overlapping scenes. We are left at the end not so much concerned about meaning as we are spellbound by the power of the images themselves and of Woolf's pictorial imagination.

Central to all of Woolf's work is the importance of the image, and so she is in league with Eiseley and Dillard and Didion who came after her. But hers is, if not a unique view, a very special one as she expresses it in one of her autobiographical pieces. She believes that much of life is made up of routine, uneventful moments that she calls "non-being," but in the midst of life there come to us moments of such intensity that they seem to be accompanied by a "sledge-hammer force." Those "moments of being" embed themselves in memory; they last. And for her, the shock is always accompanied "by the desire to explain it":

> I feel that I have had a blow; but it is not, as I thought as a child, simply a blow from an enemy hidden behind the cotton wool of daily life; it is or will become a revelation of some order; it is a token of some real thing behind appearances; and I make it real by putting it into words. It is only by putting it into words that I make it whole; this wholeness means that it has lost its power to hurt me; it gives me, perhaps because by doing so I take away the pain, a great delight to put the severed parts together. Perhaps this is the strongest pleasure known to me. It is the rapture I get when in writing I seem to be discovering what belongs to what; making a scene come right; making a character come together.

What Woolf discovers is a pattern behind the appearance of things, a pattern that binds the whole world together: "we are the words; we are the music; we are the thing itself." And she tells us, "I see this when I have a shock."

So for Woolf, writing is therapy, writing is insight, writing is rapture. Writing takes her momentarily from the realm of terror into the land of peace. But sometimes, in an essay like "Old Mrs. Grey", she takes us into the land of terror, and gives us glimpses of the possibility of peace in death.

Ultimately, even her writing could not sustain her against the onslaught of forces over which she had no control; it could not provide a stay against the world outside her—or perhaps she could not put the severed parts together fast enough to attenuate the pain. And so she took her life. Nevertheless, she gives us pause because she had the courage to face her many-sided self and turn it into the most astonishing art in modern prose. She showed us how to write ourselves. She showed us indirectly what Didion later set before us: "Style is character."

Women and Fiction

1 The title of this article can be read in two ways: it may allude to women and the fiction that they write, or to women and the fiction that is written about

them. The ambiguity is intentional, for in dealing with women as writers, as much elasticity as possible is desirable; it is necessary to leave oneself room to deal with other things besides their work, so much has that work been influenced by conditions that have nothing whatever to do with art.

2 The most superficial inquiry into women's writing instantly raises a host of questions. Why, we ask at once, was there no continuous writing done by women before the eighteenth century? Why did they then write almost as habitually as men, and in the course of that writing produce, one after another, some of the classics of English fiction? And why did their art then, and why to some extent does their art still, take the form of fiction?

3 A little thought will show us that we are asking questions to which we shall get, as answer, only further fiction. The answer lies at present locked in old diaries, stuffed away in old drawers, half-obliterated in the memories of the aged. It is to be found in the lives of the obscure—in those almost unlit corridors of history where the figures of generations of women are so dimly, so fitfully perceived. For very little is known about women. The history of England is the history of the male line, not of the female. Of our fathers we know always some fact, some distinction. They were soldiers or they were sailors; they filled that office or they made that law. But of our mothers, our grandmothers, our great-grandmothers, what remains? Nothing but a tradition. One was beautiful; one was red-haired; one was kissed by a Queen. We know nothing of them except their names and the dates of their marriages and the number of children they bore.

4 Thus, if we wish to know why at any particular time women did this or that, why they wrote nothing, why on the other hand they wrote masterpieces, it is extremely difficult to tell. Anyone who should seek among those old papers, who should turn history wrong side out and so construct a faithful picture of the daily life of the ordinary women in Shakespeare's time, in Milton's time, in Johnson's time, would not only write a book of astonishing interest, but would furnish the critic with a weapon which he now lacks. The extraordinary woman depends on the ordinary woman. It is only when we know what were the conditions of the average woman's life—the number of her children, whether she had money of her own, if she had a room to herself, whether she had help in bringing up her family, if she had servants, whether part of the housework was her task—it is only when we can measure the way of life and the experience of life made possible to the ordinary woman that we can account for the success or failure of the extraordinary woman as a writer.

5 Strange spaces of silence seem to separate one period of activity from another. There was Sappho and a little group of women all writing poetry on a Greek island six hundred years before the birth of Christ. They fall silent. Then about the year 1000 we find a certain court lady, the Lady Murasaki, writing a very long and beautiful novel in Japan. But in England in the sixteenth century, when the dramatists and poets were most active, the women were dumb. Elizabethan literature is exclusively masculine. Then, at the end of the eighteenth century and in the beginning of the nineteenth, we find women again writing—this time in England—with extraordinary frequency and success.

6 Law and custom were of course largely responsible for these strange intermissions of silence and speech. When a woman was liable, as she was in the fifteenth

century, to be beaten and flung about the room if she did not marry the man of her parents' choice, the spiritual atmosphere was not favourable to the production of works of art. When she was married without her own consent to a man who thereupon became her lord and master, 'so far at least as law and custom could make him', as she was in the time of the Stuarts, it is likely she had little time for writing, and less encouragement. The immense effect of environment and suggestion upon the mind, we in our psychoanalytical age are beginning to realize. Again, with memoirs and letters to help us, we are beginning to understand how abnormal is the effort needed to produce a work of art, and what shelter and what support the mind of the artist requires. Of those facts the lives and letters of men like Keats and Carlyle and Flaubert assure us.

7 Thus it is clear that the extraordinary outburst of fiction in the beginning of the nineteenth century in England was heralded by innumerable slight changes in law and customs and manners. And women of the nineteenth century had some leisure; they had some education. It was no longer the exception for women of the middle and upper classes to choose their own husbands. And it is significant that of the four great women novelists—Jane Austen, Emily Brontë, Charlotte Brontë, and George Eliot—not one had a child, and two were unmarried.

8 Yet, though it is clear that the ban upon writing had been removed, there was still, it would seem, considerable pressure upon women to write novels. No four women can have been more unlike in genius and character than these four. Jane Austen can have had nothing in common with George Eliot; George Eliot was the direct opposite of Emily Brontë. Yet all were trained for the same profession; all, when they wrote, wrote novels.

9 Fiction was, as fiction still is, the easiest thing for a woman to write. Nor is it difficult to find the reason. A novel is the least concentrated form of art. A novel can be taken up or put down more easily than a play or a poem. George Eliot left her work to nurse her father. Charlotte Brontë put down her pen to pick the eyes out of the potatoes. And living as she did in the common sitting-room, surrounded by people, a woman was trained to use her mind in observation and upon the analysis of character. She was trained to be a novelist and not to be a poet.

10 Even in the nineteenth century, a woman lived almost solely in her home and her emotions. And those nineteenth-century novels, remarkable as they were, were profoundly influenced by the fact that the women who wrote them were excluded by their sex from certain kinds of experience. That experience has a great influence upon fiction is indisputable. The best part of Conrad's novels, for instance, would be destroyed if it had been impossible for him to be a sailor. Take away all that Tolstoi knew of war as a soldier, of life and society as a rich young man whose education admitted him to all sorts of experience, and *War and Peace* would be incredibly impoverished.

11 Yet *Pride and Prejudice*, *Wuthering Heights*, *Villette*, and *Middlemarch* were written by women from whom was forcibly withheld all experience save that which could be met with in a middle-class drawing-room. No first-hand experience of war or seafaring or politics or business was possible for them. Even their emotional life was strictly regulated by law and custom. When George Eliot ventured to live with Mr Lewes without being his wife, public opinion was scandalized. Under its pressure

she withdrew into a suburban seclusion which, inevitably, had the worst possible effects upon her work. She wrote that unless people asked of their own accord to come and see her, she never invited them. At the same time, on the other side of Europe, Tolstoi was living a free life as a soldier, with men and women of all classes, for which nobody censured him and from which his novels drew much of their astonishing breadth and vigour.

12 But the novels of women were not affected only by the necessarily narrow range of the writer's experience. They showed, at least in the nineteenth century, another characteristic which may be traced to the writer's sex. In *Middlemarch* and in *Jane Eyre* we are conscious not merely of the writer's character, as we are conscious of the character of Charles Dickens, but we are conscious of a woman's presence—of someone resenting the treatment of her sex and pleading for its rights. This brings into women's writing an element which is entirely absent from a man's, unless, indeed, he happens to be a working-man, a Negro, or one who for some other reason is conscious of disability. It introduces a distortion and is frequently the cause of weakness. The desire to plead some personal cause or to make a character the mouthpiece of some personal discontent or grievance always has a distressing effect, as if the spot at which the reader's attention is directed were suddenly twofold instead of single.

13 The genius of Jane Austen and Emily Brontë is never more convincing than in their power to ignore such claims and solicitations and to hold on their way unperturbed by scorn or censure. But it needed a very serene or a very powerful mind to resist the temptation to anger. The ridicule, the censure, the assurance of inferiority in one form or another which were lavished upon women who practised an art, provoked such reactions naturally enough. One sees the effect in Charlotte Brontë's indignation, in George Eliot's resignation. Again and again one finds it in the work of the lesser women writers—in their choice of a subject, in their unnatural self-assertiveness, in their unnatural docility. Moreover, insincerity leaks in almost unconsciously. They adopt a view in deference to authority. The vision becomes too masculine or it becomes too feminine; it loses its perfect integrity and, with that, its most essential quality as a work of art.

14 The great change that has crept into women's writing is, it would seem, a change of attitude. The woman writer is no longer bitter. She is no longer angry. She is no longer pleading and protesting as she writes. We are approaching, if we have not yet reached, the time when her writing will have little or no foreign influence to disturb it. She will be able to concentrate upon her vision without distraction from outside. The aloofness that was once within the reach of genius and originality is only now coming within reach of ordinary women. Therefore the average novel by a woman is far more genuine and far more interesting today than it was a hundred or even fifty years ago.

15 But it is still true that before a woman can write exactly as she wishes to write, she has many difficulties to face. To begin with, there is the technical difficulty—so simple, apparently; in reality, so baffling—that the very form of the sentence does not fit her. It is a sentence made by men; it is too loose, too heavy, too pompous for a woman's use. Yet in a novel, which covers so wide a stretch of ground, an ordinary and usual type of sentence has to be found to carry the reader on easily

and naturally from one end of the book to the other. And this a woman must make for herself, altering and adapting the current sentence until she writes one that takes the natural shape of her thought without crushing or distorting it.

16 But that, after all, is only a means to an end, and the end is still to be reached only when a woman has the courage to surmount opposition and the determination to be true to herself. For a novel, after all, is a statement about a thousand different objects—human, natural, divine; it is an attempt to relate them to each other. In every novel of merit these different elements are held in place by the force of the writer's vision. But they have another order also, which is the order imposed upon them by convention. And as men are the arbiters of that convention, as they have established an order of values in life, so too, since fiction is largely based on life, these values prevail there also to a very great extent.

17 It is probable, however, that both in life and in art the values of a woman are not the values of a man. Thus, when a woman comes to write a novel, she will find that she is perpetually wishing to alter the established values—to make serious what appears insignificant to a man, and trivial what is to him important. And for that, of course, she will be criticized; for the critic of the opposite sex will be genuinely puzzled and surprised by an attempt to alter the current scale of values, and will see in it not merely a difference of view, but a view that is weak, or trivial, or sentimental, because it differs from his own.

18 But here, too, women are coming to be more independent of opinion. They are beginning to respect their own sense of values. And for this reason the subject matter of their novels begins to show certain changes. They are less interested, it would seem, in themselves; on the other hand, they are more interested in other women. In the early nineteenth century, women's novels were largely autobiographical. One of the motives that led them to write was the desire to expose their own suffering, to plead their own cause. Now that this desire is no longer so urgent, women are beginning to explore their own sex, to write of women as women have never been written of before; for of course, until very lately, women in literature were the creation of men.

19 Here again there are difficulties to overcome, for, if one may generalize, not only do women submit less readily to observation than men, but their lives are far less tested and examined by the ordinary processes of life. Often nothing tangible remains of a woman's day. The food that has been cooked is eaten; the children that have been nursed have gone out into the world. Where does the accent fall? What is the salient point for the novelist to seize upon? It is difficult to say. Her life has an anonymous character which is baffling and puzzling in the extreme. For the first time, this dark country is beginning to be explored in fiction; and at the same moment a woman has also to record the changes in women's minds and habits which the opening of the professions has introduced. She has to observe how their lives are ceasing to run underground; she has to discover what new colours and shadows are showing in them now that they are exposed to the outer world.

20 If, then, one should try to sum up the character of women's fiction at the present moment, one would say that it is courageous; it is sincere; it keeps closely to what women feel. It is not bitter. It does not insist upon its femininity. But at the same time, a woman's book is not written as a man would write it. These qualities

are much commoner than they were, and they give even to second- and third-rate work the value of truth and the interest of sincerity.

21 But in addition to these good qualities, there are two that call for a word more of discussion. The change which has turned the English woman from a nondescript influence, fluctuating and vague, to a voter, a wage-earner, a responsible citizen, has given her both in her life and in her art a turn towards the impersonal. Her relations now are not only emotional; they are intellectual, they are political. The old system which condemned her to squint askance at things through the eyes or through the interests of husband or brother, has given place to the direct and practical interests of one who must act for herself, and not merely influence the acts of others. Hence her attention is being directed away from the personal centre which engaged it exclusively in the past to the impersonal, and her novels naturally become more critical of society, and less analytical of individual lives.

22 We may expect that the office of gadfly to the state, which has been so far a male prerogative, will now be discharged by women also. Their novels will deal with social evils and remedies. Their men and women will not be observed wholly in relation to each other emotionally, but as they cohere and clash in groups and classes and races. That is one change of some importance. But there is another more interesting to those who prefer the butterfly to the gadfly—that is to say, the artist to the reformer. The greater impersonality of women's lives will encourage the poetic spirit, and it is in poetry that women's fiction is still weakest. It will lead them to be less absorbed in facts and no longer content to record with astonishing acuteness the minute details which fall under their own observation. They will look beyond the personal and political relationships to the wider questions which the poet tries to solve—of our destiny and the meaning of life.

23 The basis of the poetic attitude is of course largely founded upon material things. It depends upon leisure, and a little money, and the chance which money and leisure give to observe impersonally and dispassionately. With money and leisure at their service, women will naturally occupy themselves more than has hitherto been possible with the craft of letters. They will make a fuller and a more subtle use of the instrument of writing. Their technique will become bolder and richer.

24 In the past, the virtue of women's writing often lay in its divine spontaneity, like that of the blackbird's song or the thrush's. It was untaught; it was from the heart. But it was also, and much more often, chattering and garrulous—mere talk spilt over paper and left to dry in pools and blots. In future, granted time and books and a little space in the house for herself, literature will become for women, as for men, an art to be studied. Women's gift will be trained and strengthened. The novel will cease to be the dumping-ground for the personal emotions. It will become, more than at present, a work of art like any other, and its resources and its limitations will be explored.

25 From this it is a short step to the practice of the sophisticated arts, hitherto so little practised by women—to the writing of essays and criticism, of history and biography. And that, too, if we are considering the novel, will be of advantage; for besides improving the quality of the novel itself, it will draw off the aliens who have been attracted to fiction by its accessibility while their hearts lay elsewhere. Thus

will the novel be rid of those excrescences of history and fact which, in our time, have made it so shapeless.

26 So, if we may prophesy, women in time to come will write fewer novels, but better novels; and not novels only, but poetry and criticism and history. But in this, to be sure, one is looking ahead to that golden, that perhaps fabulous, age when women will have what has so long been denied them—leisure, and money, and a room to themselves.

(1929)

QUESTIONS

Thought and Structure

1. What do you think of the conclusion Woolf reaches at the end of paragraph 4? Has she convinced you? Why? How? (Take a close look at the structure of that concluding sentence; break it down into its component elements; dissect it.)
2. Examine the argument about writing and experience that Woolf makes in the first 11 paragraphs of the essay. What is her point? How does she bring male novelists into her discussion to strengthen her case?
3. What do you think Woolf means by "woman's presence" in fiction (paragraphs 12 and 13)? How could she have made her point more clearly and her case more convincingly? What do her assertions depend on?
4. Why is "aloofness" so important for a writer (paragraph 14)?
5. Why is it necessary, according to Woolf, for a woman writer to have "the courage to surmount opposition and the determination to be true to herself"?
6. What does Woolf mean by "impersonality," and what is likely to result from impersonality in women's writing (paragraphs 21–24)?

Style and Strategy

7. As a writer, what kind of latitude is Woolf creating for herself in the first paragraph: "it is necessary to leave oneself room to deal with other things besides their work, so much has that work been influenced by conditions that have nothing whatever to do with art"?
8. Consider Woolf's thoughts about the "sentence" (paragraph 15). If a man's sentence is "too loose, too heavy, too pompous for a woman's use," what kind of sentence is suitable for a woman? Derive your answer by looking at Woolf's sentences. How would you describe them?
9. What is the purpose of paragraph 20? How well does the paragraph serve its purpose?

SUGGESTIONS FOR WRITING

A. Look at Woolf's "prophesy" in paragraph 26. Go to the library, if you have not already done so, and look at the shelves that contain women's books, look in the card catalog, call up the computer menu, read selectively, and record some of the details of what you find. Prepare a short report that assesses Woolf's prophecy against the facts.

B. Compare and contrast an essay of Woolf's and an essay of Lawrence's; then compare and contrast an essay of Didion's and of Tom Wolfe's. Examine those comparisons in terms of Woolf's argument in "Women and Writing." Can you see differences between women's writing and men's? Do those differences seem to change over time? Jot down notes as you consider all of these questions, and be prepared to present your point of view to the class.

C. Identify what you consider to be a fine woman's sentence. Imitate it in a sentence of your own. Change it into a man's sentence.

D. Read Margaret Atwood's essay "On Being a 'Woman Writer': Paradoxes and Dilemmas" (pp. 494–503). Imagine how Atwood would respond to Woolf or how Woolf would respond to Atwood. Write an exchange of letters between Woolf and Atwood.

Montaigne

1 Once at Bar-le-Duc Montaigne saw a portrait which René, King of Sicily, had painted of himself, and asked, "Why is it not, in like manner, lawful for every one to draw himself with a pen, as he did with a crayon?" Offhand one might reply, Not only is it lawful, but nothing could be easier. Other people may evade us, but our own features are almost too familiar. Let us begin. And then, when we attempt the task, the pen falls from our fingers; it is a matter of profound, mysterious, and overwhelming difficulty.

2 After all, in the whole of literature, how many people have succeeded in drawing themselves with a pen? Only Montaigne and Pepys and Rousseau perhaps. The *Religio Medici* is a coloured glass through which darkly one sees racing stars and a strange and turbulent soul. A bright polished mirror reflects the face of Boswell peeping between other people's shoulders in the famous biography. But this talking of oneself, following one's own vagaries, giving the whole map, weight, colour, and circumference of the soul in its confusion, its variety, its imperfection—this art belonged to one man only: to Montaigne. As the centuries go by, there is always a crowd before that picture, gazing into its depths, seeing their own faces reflected in it, seeing more the longer they look, never being able to say quite what it is that they see. New editions testify to the perennial fascination. Here is the Navarre Society in England reprinting in five fine volumes* Cotton's translation; while in France the firm of Louis Conard is issuing the complete works of Montaigne with the various readings in an edition to which Dr. Armaingaud has devoted a long lifetime of research.

3 To tell the truth about oneself, to discover oneself near at hand, is not easy.

> We hear of but two or three of the ancients who have beaten this road [said Montaigne]. No one since has followed the track; 'tis a rugged road, more so than it seems, to follow a pace so rambling and uncertain, as that of the soul; to penetrate the dark profundities of its intricate internal windings; to choose and lay hold of so many

---

**Essays of Montaigne,* translated by Charles Cotton, five volumes.

> little nimble motions; 'tis a new and extraordinary undertaking, and that withdraws us from the common and most recommended employments of the world.

There is, in the first place, the difficulty of expression. We all indulge in the strange, pleasant process called thinking, but when it comes to saying, even to some one opposite, what we think, then how little we are able to convey! The phantom is through the mind and out of the window before we can lay salt on its tail, or slowly sinking and returning to the profound darkness which it has lit up momentarily with a wandering light. Face, voice, and accent eke out our words and impress their feebleness with character in speech. But the pen is a rigid instrument; it can say very little; it has all kinds of habits and ceremonies of its own. It is dictatorial too: it is always making ordinary men into prophets, and changing the natural stumbling trip of human speech into the solemn and stately march of pens. It is for this reason that Montaigne stands out from the legions of the dead with such irrepressible vivacity. We can never doubt for an instant that his book was himself. He refused to teach; he refused to preach; he kept on saying that he was just like other people. All his effort was to write himself down, to communicate, to tell the truth, and that is a "rugged road, more than it seems."

4 For beyond the difficulty of communicating oneself, there is the supreme difficulty of being oneself. This soul, or life within us, by no means agrees with the life outside us. If one has the courage to ask her what she thinks, she is always saying the very opposite to what other people say. Other people, for instance, long ago made up their minds that old invalidish gentlemen ought to stay at home and edify the rest of us by the spectacle of their connubial fidelity. The soul of Montaigne said, on the contrary, that it is in old age that one ought to travel, and marriage, which, rightly, is very seldom founded on love, is apt to become, towards the end of life, a formal tie better broken up. Again with politics, statesmen are always praising the greatness of Empire, and preaching the moral duty of civilising the savage. But look at the Spanish in Mexico, cried Montaigne in a burst of rage. "So many cities levelled with the ground, so many nations exterminated . . . and the richest and most beautiful part of the world turned upside down for the traffic of pearl and pepper! Mechanic victories!" And then when the peasants came and told him that they had found a man dying of wounds and deserted him for fear lest justice might incriminate them, Montaigne asked:

> What could I have said to these people? 'Tis certain that this office of humanity would have brought them into trouble. . . . There is nothing so much, nor so grossly, nor so ordinarily faulty as the laws.

5 Here the soul, getting restive, is lashing out at the more palpable forms of Montaigne's great bugbears, convention and ceremony. But watch her as she broods over the fire in the inner room of that tower which, though detached from the main building, has so wide a view over the estate. Really she is the strangest creature in the world, far from heroic, variable as a weathercock, "bashful, insolent; chaste, lustful; prating, silent; laborious, delicate; ingenious, heavy; melancholic, pleasant; lying, true; knowing, ignorant; liberal, covetous, and prodigal"—in short, so com-

plex, so indefinite, corresponding so little to the version which does duty for her in public, that a man might spend his life merely in trying to run her to earth. The pleasure of the pursuit more than rewards one for any damage that it may inflict upon one's worldly prospects. The man who is aware of himself is henceforward independent; and he is never bored, and life is only too short, and he is steeped through and through with a profound yet temperate happiness. He alone lives, while other people, slaves of ceremony, let life slip past them in a kind of dream. Once conform, once do what other people do because they do it, and a lethargy steals over all the finer nerves and faculties of the soul. She becomes all outer show and inward emptiness; dull, callous, and indifferent.

6 Surely then, if we ask this great master of the art of life to tell us his secret, he will advise us to withdraw to the inner room of our tower and there turn the pages of books, pursue fancy after fancy as they chase each other up the chimney, and leave the government of the world to others. Retirement and contemplation—these must be the main elements of his prescription. But no; Montaigne is by no means explicit. It is impossible to extract a plain answer from that subtle, half smiling, half melancholy man, with the heavy-lidded eyes and the dreamy, quizzical expression. The truth is that life in the country, with one's books and vegetables and flowers, is often extremely dull. He could never see that his own green peas were so much better than other people's. Paris was the place he loved best in the whole world—*"jusques à ses verrues et à ses taches."* As for reading, he could seldom read any book for more than an hour at a time, and his memory was so bad that he forgot what was in his mind as he walked from one room to another. Book learning is nothing to be proud of, and as for the achievements of science, what do they amount to? He had always mixed with clever men, and his father had a positive veneration for them, but he had observed that, though they have their fine moments, their rhapsodies, their visions, the cleverest tremble on the verge of folly. Observe yourself: one moment you are exalted; the next a broken glass puts your nerves on edge. All extremes are dangerous. It is best to keep in the middle of the road, in the common ruts, however muddy. In writing choose the common words; avoid rhapsody and eloquence—yet, it is true, poetry is delicious; the best prose is that which is most full of poetry.

7 It appears, then, that we are to aim at a democratic simplicity. We may enjoy our room in the tower, with the painted walls and the commodious bookcases, but down in the garden there is a man digging who buried his father this morning, and it is he and his like who live the real life and speak the real language. There is certainly an element of truth in that. Things are said very finely at the lower end of the table. There are perhaps more of the qualities that matter among the ignorant than among the learned. But again, what a vile thing the rabble is! "the mother of ignorance, injustice, and inconstancy. Is it reasonable that the life of a wise man should depend upon the judgment of fools?" Their minds are weak, soft and without power of resistance. They must be told what it is expedient for them to know. It is not for them to face facts as they are. The truth can only be known by the well-born soul—*"l'âme bien née."* Who, then, are these well-born souls, whom we would imitate, if only Montaigne would enlighten us more precisely?

8 But no. *"Je n'enseigne poinct; je raconte."* After all, how could he explain other people's souls when he could say nothing "entirely simply and solidly, without

confusion or mixture, in one word," about his own, when indeed it became daily more and more in the dark to him? One quality or principle there is perhaps—that one must not lay down rules. The souls whom one would wish to resemble, like Etienne de La Boétie, for example, are always the supplest. *"C'est estre, mais ce n'est pas vivre, que de se tenir attaché et obligé par necessité a un seul train."* The laws are mere conventions, utterly unable to keep touch with the vast variety and turmoil of human impulses; habits and customs are a convenience devised for the support of timid natures who dare not allow their souls free play. But we, who have a private life and hold it infinitely the dearest of our possessions, suspect nothing so much as an attitude. Directly we begin to protest, to attitudinise, to lay down laws, we perish. We are living for others, not for ourselves. We must respect those who sacrifice themselves in the public service, load them with honours, and pity them for allowing, as they must, the inevitable compromise; but for ourselves let us fly fame, honour, and all offices that put us under an obligation to others. Let us simmer over our incalculable cauldron, our enthralling confusion, our hotch-potch of impulses, our perpetual miracle—for the soul throws up wonders every second. Movement and change are the essence of our being; rigidity is death; conformity is death: let us say what comes into our heads, repeat ourselves, contradict ourselves, fling out the wildest nonsense, and follow the most fantastic fancies without caring what the world does or thinks or says. For nothing matters except life; and, of course, order.

9 This freedom, then, which is the essence of our being, has to be controlled. But it is difficult to see what power we are to invoke to help us, since every restraint of private opinion or public law has been derided, and Montaigne never ceases to pour scorn upon the misery, the weakness, the vanity of human nature. Perhaps, then, it will be well to turn to religion to guide us? "Perhaps" is one of his favourite expressions; "perhaps" and "I think" and all those words which qualify the rash assumptions of human ignorance. Such words help one to muffle up opinions which it would be highly impolitic to speak outright. For one does not say everything; there are some things which at present it is advisable only to hint. One writes for a very few people, who understand. Certainly, seek the Divine guidance by all means, but meanwhile there is, for those who live a private life, another monitor, an invisible censor within, *"un patron au dedans,"* whose blame is much more to be dreaded than any other because he knows the truth; nor is there anything sweeter than the chime of his approval. This is the judge to whom we must submit; this is the censor who will help us to achieve that order which is the grace of a well-born soul. For *"C'est une vie exquise, celle qui se maintient en ordre jusques en son privé."* But he will act by his own light; by some internal balance will achieve that precarious and ever changing poise which, while it controls, in no way impedes the soul's freedom to explore and experiment. Without other guide, and without precedent, undoubtedly it is far more difficult to live well the private life than the public. It is an art which each must learn separately, though there are, perhaps, two or three men, like Homer, Alexander the Great, and Epaminondas among the ancients, and Etienne de La Boétie among the moderns, whose example may help us. But it is an art; and the very material in which it works is variable and complex and infinitely mysterious—human nature. To human nature we must keep close. *". . . il faut vivre entre les vivants."* We must dread any eccentricity or refinement which cuts us off from

our fellow-beings. Blessed are those who chat easily with their neighbours about their sport or their buildings or their quarrels, and honestly enjoy the talk of carpenters and gardeners. To communicate is our chief business; society and friendship our chief delights; and reading, not to acquire knowledge, not to earn a living, but to extend our intercourse beyond our own time and province. Such wonders there are in the world; halcyons and undiscovered lands, men with dogs' heads and eyes in their chests, and laws and customs, it may well be, far superior to our own. Possibly we are asleep in this world; possibly there is some other which is apparent to beings with a sense which we now lack.

10 Here then, in spite of all contradictions and of all qualifications, is something definite. These essays are an attempt to communicate a soul. On this point at least he is explicit. It is not fame that he wants; it is not that men shall quote him in years to come; he is setting up no statue in the market-place; he wishes only to communicate his soul. Communication is health; communication is truth; communication is happiness. To share is our duty; to go down boldly and bring to light those hidden thoughts which are the most diseased; to conceal nothing; to pretend nothing; if we are ignorant to say so; if we love our friends to let them know it.

> *. . . car, comme je scay par une trop certaine expérience, il n'est aucune si douce consolation en la perte de nos amis que celle que nous aporte la science de n'avoir rien oublié a leur dire et d'avoir eu avec eux une parfaite et entière communication.*

11 There are people who, when they travel, wrap themselves up *"se défendans de la contagion d'un air incogneu"* in silence and suspicion. When they dine they must have the same food they get at home. Every sight and custom is bad unless it resembles those of their own village. They travel only to return. That is entirely the wrong way to set about it. We should start without any fixed idea where we are going to spend the night, or when we propose to come back; the journey is everything. Most necessary of all, but rarest good fortune, we should try to find before we start some man of our own sort who will go with us and to whom we can say the first thing that comes into our heads. For pleasure has no relish unless we share it. As for the risks—that we may catch cold or get a headache—it is always worth while to risk a little illness for the sake of pleasure. *"Le plaisir est des principales espèces du profit."* Besides if we do what we like, we always do what is good for us. Doctors and wise men may object, but let us leave doctors and wise men to their own dismal philosophy. For ourselves, who are ordinary men and women, let us return thanks to Nature for her bounty by using every one of the senses she has given us; vary our state as much as possible; turn now this side, now that, to the warmth, and relish to the full before the sun goes down the kisses of youth and the echoes of a beautiful voice singing Catullus. Every season is likeable, and wet days and fine, red wine and white, company and solitude. Even sleep, that deplorable curtailment of the joy of life, can be full of dreams; and the most common actions—a walk, a talk, solitude in one's own orchard—can be enhanced and lit up by the association of the mind. Beauty is everywhere, and beauty is only two fingers' breadth from goodness. So, in the name of health and sanity, let us not dwell on the end of the journey. Let death come upon us planting our cabbages, or on horseback, or let us

steal away to some cottage and there let strangers close our eyes, for a servant sobbing or the touch of a hand would break us down. Best of all, let death find us at our usual occupations, among girls and good fellows who make no protests, no lamentations; let him find us *"parmy les jeux, les festins, faceties, entretiens communs et populaires, et la musique, et des vers amoureux."* But enough of death; it is life that matters.

12 It is life that emerges more and more clearly as these essays reach not their end, but their suspension in full career. It is life that becomes more and more absorbing as death draws near, one's self, one's soul, every fact of existence: that one wears silk stockings summer and winter; puts water in one's wine; has one's hair cut after dinner; must have glass to drink from; has never worn spectacles; has a loud voice; carries a switch in one's hand; bites one's tongue; fidgets with one's feet; is apt to scratch one's ears; likes meat to be high; rubs one's teeth with a napkin (thank God, they are good!); must have curtains to one's bed; and, what is rather curious, began by liking radishes, then disliked them, and now likes them again. No fact is too little to let it slip through one's fingers and besides the interest of facts themselves, there is the strange power we have of changing facts by the force of the imagination. Observe how the soul is always casting her own lights and shadows; makes the substantial hollow and the frail substantial; fills broad daylight with dreams; is as much excited by phantoms as by reality; and in the moment of death sports with a trifle. Observe, too, her duplicity, her complexity. She hears of a friend's loss and sympathises, and yet has a bitter-sweet malicious pleasure in the sorrows of others. She believes; at the same time she does not believe. Observe her extraordinary susceptibility to impressions, especially in youth. A rich man steals because his father kept him short of money as a boy. This wall one builds not for oneself, but because one's father loved building. In short the soul is all laced about with nerves and sympathies which affect her every action, and yet, even now in 1580, no one has any clear knowledge—such cowards we are, such lovers of the smooth conventional ways—how she works or what she is except that of all things she is the most mysterious, and one's self the greatest monster and miracle in the world. *". . . plus je me hante et connois, plus ma difformité m'estonne, moins je m'entens en moy."* Observe, observe perpetually, and, so long as ink and paper exist, *"sans cesse et sans travail"* Montaigne will write.

13 But there remains one final question which, if we could make him look up from his enthralling occupation, we should like to put to this great master of the art of life. In these extraordinary volumes of short and broken, long and learned, logical and contradictory statements, we have heard the very pulse and rhythm of the soul, beating day after day, year after year through a veil which, as time goes on, fines itself almost to transparency. Here is some one who succeeded in the hazardous enterprise of living; who served his country and lived retired; was landlord, husband, father; entertained kings, loved women, and mused for hours alone over old books. By means of perpetual experiment and observation of the subtlest he achieved at last a miraculous adjustment of all these wayward parts that constitute the human soul. He laid hold of the beauty of the world with all his fingers. He achieved happiness. If he had had to live again, he said, he would have lived the same life over. But, as we watch with absorbed interest the enthralling spectacle of a soul

living openly beneath our eyes, the question frames itself, Is pleasure the end of all? Whence this overwhelming interest in the nature of the soul? Why this overmastering desire to communicate with others? Is the beauty of this world enough, or is there, elsewhere, some explanation of the mystery? To this what answer can there be? There is none. There is only one more question: *"Que scais-je?"*

(1925)

QUESTIONS

Thought and Structure

1. What do you think Montaigne means by "drawing oneself with a pen"?
2. What does Montaigne mean by soul? What are the two chief difficulties of presenting the soul in writing? Do you think a modern reader would be interested in having you present your soul in an essay? Why?
3. What are the dangers inherent in retiring to the "tower" to do one's writing? What does Woolf mean by "democratic simplicity" (paragraph 7)?
4. What, according to Montaigne, is the problem that results from establishing rules to govern either life or writing? But then what about freedom, which is the "essence of our being" but has to be controlled?
5. What is the relationship between one's life (or life itself) and writing?

Style and Strategy

6. Woolf seems to be trying to give us Montaigne's thoughts on writing and living rather than her own. If her aim is to reveal Montaigne, how well do you think she does it, and how does she do it? She quotes him directly only on occasion and then often in French, but what is her primary method for presenting his view of things?
7. How would you guess Montaigne's essays might develop, linearly or roundabout? Might the following clause have anything to do with your answer: "the journey is everything" (paragraph 11)? Explain.
8. What do those "facts of existence" in paragraph 12 have to do with essay writing? What do you think of the list Woolf provides? Does it make sense to you? What do those facts represent? Can you identify another list in that paragraph that arises out of repetition? Hint: "Observe."

SUGGESTIONS FOR WRITING

A. Prepare a short paper for class comparing and contrasting the methods that Woolf and Didion use to create character sketches of Montaigne and O'Keeffe. Which of the characters do you think you know better? Why?

B. Compare the ideas in this essay with those in Didion's "On Keeping a Notebook." Jot down a list of the similarities you find in the two texts.

C. Read an essay of Forster's or of Eiseley's and prepare a short report about why you think one or the other of these men claimed Montaigne as his teacher. Forster called him one of his "law-givers." Eiseley simply referred to him as the first in a line of essayists who found "the self and its minute adventures" interesting. Go beyond these claims to the text of the essay you select; find the relationships there.

D. Read this essay carefully, making notes as you go along, notes that will help you formulate what you think Montaigne would consider a good essay. After you have made these notes, consider the essay printed below, and render a short written judgment about the essay in terms of the criteria outlined in your notes:

MONTAIGNE: OF SMELLS

It is said of some, as of Alexander the Great, that their sweat emitted a sweet odor, owing to some rare and extraordinary constitution of theirs, of which Plutarch and others seek the cause. But the common make-up of bodies is the opposite, and the best condition they may have is to be free of smell. The sweetness even of the purest breath has nothing more excellent about it than to be without any odor that offends us, as is that of very healthy children. That is why, says Plautus,

> A woman smells good when she does not smell.

The most perfect smell for a woman is to smell of nothing, as they say that her actions smell best when they are imperceptible and mute. And perfumes are rightly considered suspicious in those who use them, and thought to be used to cover up some natural defect in that quarter. Whence arise these nice sayings of the ancient poets: To smell good is to stink:

> You laugh at us because we do not smell.
> I'd rather smell of nothing than smell sweet.
>
> MARTIAL

And elsewhere:

> Men who smell always sweet, Posthumus, don't smell good.
>
> MARTIAL

However, I like very much to be surrounded with good smells, and I hate bad ones beyond measure, and detect them from further off than anyone else:

> My scent will sooner be aware
> Where goat-smells, Polypus, in hairy arm-pits lurk,
> Than keen hounds scent a wild boar's lair.
>
> HORACE

The simplest and most natural smells seem to me the most agreeable. And this concern chiefly affects the ladies. Amid the densest barbarism, the Scythian women, after washing, powder and plaster their whole body and face with a certain odoriferous drug that is native to their soil; and having removed this paint to approach the men, they find themselves both sleek and perfumed.

Whatever the odor is, it is a marvel how it clings to me and how apt my skin is to imbibe it. He who complains of nature that she has left man without an instrument to convey smells to his nose is wrong, for they convey themselves. But in my particular case my mustache, which is thick, performs that service. If I bring my gloves or my handkerchief near it, the smell will stay there a whole day. It betrays the place I come from. The close kisses of youth, savory, greedy, and sticky, once used to adhere to it and stay there for several hours after. And yet, for all that, I find myself little subject to epidemics, which are caught by communication and bred by the contagion of the air; and I have escaped those of my time, of which there have been many sorts in our cities and our armies. We read of Socrates that though he never left Athens during many recurrences of the plague which so many times tormented that city, he alone never found himself the worse for it.

The doctors might, I believe, derive more use from odors than they do; for I have often noticed that they make a change in me and work upon my spirits according to their properties; which makes me approve of the idea that the use of incense and perfumes in churches, so ancient and widespread in all nations and religions, was intended to delight us and arouse and purify our senses to make us more fit for contemplation.

I should like, in order to judge of it, to have shared the art of those cooks who know how to add a seasoning of foreign odors to the savor of foods, as was particularly remarked in the service of the king of Tunis, who in our time landed at Naples to confer with the Emperor Charles. They stuffed his foods with aromatic substances, so sumptuously that one peacock and two pheasants came to a hundred ducats to dress them in that manner; and when they were carved, they filled not only the dining hall but all the rooms in his palace, and even the neighboring houses, with sweet fumes which did not vanish for some time.

The principal care I take in my lodgings is to avoid heavy, stinking air. Those beautiful cities Venice and Paris weaken my fondness for them by the acrid smell of the marshes of the one and of the mud of the other.

Old Mrs. Grey

1 There are moments even in England, now, when even the busiest, most contented suddenly let fall what they hold—it may be the week's washing. Sheets and pyjamas crumble and dissolve in their hands, because, though they do not state this in so many words, it seems silly to take the washing round to Mrs. Peel when out there over the fields over the hills, there is no washing; no pinning of clothes-lines; mangling and ironing; no work at all, but boundless rest. Stainless and boundless rest; space unlimited; untrodden grass; wild birds flying; hills whose smooth uprise continues that wild flight.

2 Of all this however only seven foot by four could be seen from Mrs. Grey's corner. That was the size of her front door which stood wide open, though there was a fire burning in the grate. The fire looked like a small spot of dusty light feebly trying to escape from the embarrassing pressure of the pouring sunshine.

3 Mrs. Grey sat on a hard chair in the corner looking—but at what? Apparently at nothing. She did not change the focus of her eyes when visitors came in. Her eyes had ceased to focus themselves; it may be that they had lost the power. They were aged eyes, blue, unspectacled. They could see, but without looking. She had never used her eyes on anything minute and difficult; merely upon faces, and dishes and fields. And now at the age of ninety-two they saw nothing but a zigzag of pain wriggling across the door, pain that twisted her legs as it wriggled; jerked her body to and fro like a marionette. Her body was wrapped round the pain as a damp sheet is folded over a wire. The wire was spasmodically jerked by a cruel invisible hand. She flung out a foot, a hand. Then it stopped. She sat still for a moment.

4 In that pause she saw herself in the past at ten, at twenty, at twenty-five. She was running in and out of a cottage with eleven brothers and sisters. The line jerked. She was thrown forward in her chair.

5 'All dead. All dead,' she mumbled. 'My brothers and sisters. And my husband gone. My daughter too. But I go on. Every morning I pray God to let me pass.'

6 The morning spread seven foot by four green and sunny. Like a fling of grain the birds settled on the land. She was jerked again by another tweak of the tormenting hand.

7 'I'm an ignorant old woman. I can't read or write, and every morning when I crawls downstairs, I say I wish it were night; and every night, when I crawls up to bed, I say I wish it were day. I'm only an ignorant old woman. But I prays to God: O let me pass. I'm an ignorant old woman—I can't read or write.'

8 So when the colour went out of the doorway, she could not see the other page which is then lit up; or hear the voices that have argued, sung, talked for hundreds of years.

9 The jerked limbs were still again.

10 'The doctor comes every week. The parish doctor now. Since my daughter went, we can't afford Dr. Nicholls. But he's a good man. He says he wonders I don't go. He says my heart's nothing but wind and water. Yet I don't seem able to die.'

11 So we—humanity—insist that the body shall still cling to the wire. We put out the eyes and the ears; but we pinion it there, with a bottle of medicine, a cup of tea, a dying fire, like a rook on a barn door; but a rook that still lives, even with a nail through it.

(1942)

QUESTIONS

Thought and Structure

1. Read the opening paragraph without reading the rest of the essay. What do you think Woolf describes in that paragraph? How do your views change when you consider the paragraph in the context of the entire essay? What is "out there over the fields over the hills"?
2. How does paragraph 5 help us come to terms with the meaning of the essay, with the point that Woolf is trying to make? How does that paragraph change our sense of the first four paragraphs?
3. What is the meaning of this sentence from paragraph 6: "The morning spread seven foot by four green and sunny"?
4. What is "the other page" (paragraph 8)? What is Woolf suggesting in that paragraph about the limitations of Mrs. Grey's life, her entire life?
5. How is it that "we—humanity . . . put out the eyes and the ears" in that body (paragraph 11)?

Style and Strategy

6. Why does Woolf take us inside Mrs. Grey's house in the second paragraph? How does Woolf use the door frame? What is the significance of the "fire burning in the grate"?
7. Why does Woolf focus on Mrs. Grey's vision and her pain in the third paragraph. Identify the most effective language that Woolf uses to make her point about the vision and the pain. Why does she use comparisons—similes—near the end of the paragraph? What is their effect on you as a reader? How do they alter your perception of Mrs. Grey?

8. Paragraph 4 points back to a particular sentence in paragraph 3. Identify that sentence and explain its importance. Why does Woolf put it there in the middle of the paragraph?
9. What is the most important phrase in paragraph 5?
10. Paragraphs 7 and 10 consist entirely of dialogue. What is the effect of that dialogue? Why does Woolf separate those paragraphs with two different kinds of paragraphs? Would the essay be just as effective if the paragraphs were reordered this way: 7, 10, 8, 9, 11? Explain.
11. In the final paragraph, why does Woolf use the collective pronoun "we"? Think of some other words Woolf might have used instead of "pinion." Would one of them be more effective? Explain. How apt is her choice of the "rook"? Explain.

SUGGESTIONS FOR WRITING

A. Take away paragraph 11 from Woolf's essay, and write your own conclusion. Compare the two endings, listing the strengths and weaknesses of each.

B. In one paragraph, describe Mrs. Grey's condition. Summarize Woolf's entire essay in another paragraph. Does the shorter account of the essay shortchange the reader in any way? Explain.

C. Write a short, speculative account of what you think Woolf would have "us" do about the Mrs. Greys of the world.

D. Write an essay in which you argue for or against euthanasia. You might read Aldous Huxley's *Brave New World* as part of your preparation for writing the essay.

E. Go to the library and find a reproduction of René Magritte's *The Human Condition I.* Write a paragraph explaining how that painting helps us understand Mrs. Grey's condition.

F. Visit someone in a nursing home. Write an essay about that person's predicament.

G. Look at Mrs. Grey's language throughout this essay. Compare it with the language in the following letter written by Walt Whitman's mother. Rewrite the language in the two selections, correcting all of the grammar errors. Which version do you find more effective? Explain why.

> o Walt aint it sad to think the poor soul hadent a friend near him in his last moments and to think he had a paupers grave i know it makes no difference but if he could have been buried decently. . . . i was thinking of him more lately than common i wish Walter you would write to Jeff and hanna that he is dead i will write to george i feel very sad of course if he has done ever so wrong he was my first born but gods will be done good bie Walter dear

Craftsmanship

1 The title of this series is 'Words Fail Me,' and this particular talk is called 'Craftsmanship'. We must suppose, therefore, that the talker is meant to discuss the craft of words—the craftsmanship of the writer. But there is something incongruous, unfitting, about the term 'craftsmanship' when applied to words. The English dictionary, to which we always turn in moments of dilemma, confirms us

in our doubts. It says that the word 'craft' has two meanings; it means in the first place making useful objects out of solid matter—for example, a pot, a chair, a table. In the second place, the word 'craft' means cajolery, cunning, deceit. Now we know little that is certain about words, but this we do know—words never make anything that is useful; and words are the only things that tell the truth and nothing but the truth. Therefore, to talk of craft in connexion with words is to bring together two incongruous ideas, which if they mate can only give birth to some monster fit for a glass case in a museum. Instantly, therefore, the title of the talk must be changed, and for it substituted another—A Ramble round Words, perhaps. For when you cut off the head of a talk it behaves like a hen that has been decapitated. It runs round in a circle till it drops dead—so people say who have killed hens. And that must be the course, or circle, of this decapitated talk. Let us then take for our starting point the statement that words are not useful. This happily needs little proving, for we are all aware of it. When we travel on the Tube, for example, when we wait on the platform for a train, there, hung up in front of us, on an illuminated signboard, are the words 'Passing Russell Square'. We look at those words; we repeat them; we try to impress that useful fact upon our minds; the next train will pass Russell Square. We say over and over again as we pace. 'Passing Russell Square, passing Russell Square'. And then as we say them, the words shuffle and change, and we find ourselves saying 'Passing away saith the world, passing away . . . The leaves decay and fall, the vapours weep their burthen to the ground. Man comes . . .' And then we wake up and find ourselves at King's Cross.

2 Take another example. Written up opposite us in the railway carriage are the words: 'Do not lean out of the window'. At the first reading the useful meaning, the surface meaning, is conveyed; but soon, as we sit looking at the words, they shuffle, they change; and we begin saying, 'Windows, yes windows—casements opening on the foam of perilous seas in faery lands forlorn.' And before we know what we are doing, we have leant out of the window; we are looking for Ruth in tears amid the alien corn. The penalty for that is twenty pounds or a broken neck.

3 This proves, if it needs proving, how very little natural gift words have for being useful. If we insist on forcing them against their nature to be useful, we see to our cost how they mislead us, how they fool us, how they land us a crack on the head. We have been so often fooled in this way by words, they have so often proved that they hate being useful, that it is their nature not to express one simple statement but a thousand possibilities—they have done this so often that at last, happily, we are beginning to face the fact. We are beginning to invent another language—a language perfectly and beautifully adapted to express useful statements, a language of signs. There is one great living master of this language to whom we are all indebted, that anonymous writer—whether man, woman or disembodied spirit nobody knows—who describes hotels in the Michelin Guide. He wants to tell us that one hotel is moderate, another good, and a third the best in the place. How does he do it? Not with words; words would at once bring into being shrubberies and billiard tables, men and women, the moon rising and the long splash of the summer sea—all good things, but all here beside the point. He sticks to signs; one gable; two gables; three gables. That is all he says and all he needs to say. Baedeker carries the sign language still further into the sublime realms of art. When he wishes

to say that a picture is good, he uses one star; if very good, two stars; when, in his opinion, it is a work of transcendent genius, three black stars shine on the page, and that is all. So with a handful of stars and daggers the whole of art criticism, the whole of literary criticism could be reduced to the size of a sixpenny bit—there are moments when one could wish it. But this suggests that in time to come writers will have two languages at their service; one for fact, one for fiction. When the biographer has to convey a useful and necessary fact, as, for example, that Oliver Smith went to college and took a third in the year 1892, he will say so with a hollow O on top of the figure five. When the novelist is forced to inform us that John rang the bell; after a pause the door was opened by a parlourmaid who said, 'Mrs. Jones is not at home,' he will to our great gain and his own comfort convey that repulsive statement not in words, but in signs—say, a capital H on top of the figure three. Thus we may look forward to the day when our biographies and novels will be slim and muscular; and a railway company that says: 'Do not lean out of the window' in words will be fined a penalty not exceeding five pounds for the improper use of language.

4 Words, then, are not useful. Let us now inquire into their other quality, their positive quality, that is, their power to tell the truth. According once more to the dictionary there are at least three kinds of truth: God's or gospel truth; literary truth; and home truth (generally unflattering). But to consider each separately would take too long. Let us then simplify and assert that since the only test of truth is length of life, and since words survive the chops and changes of time longer than any other substance, therefore they are the truest. Buildings fall; even the earth perishes. What was yesterday a cornfield is today a bungalow. But words, if properly used, seem able to live for ever. What, then, we may ask next, is the proper use of words? Not, so we have said, to make a useful statement; for a useful statement is a statement that can mean only one thing. And it is the nature of words to mean many things. Take the simple sentence 'Passing Russell Square'. That proved useless because besides the surface meaning it contained so many sunken meanings. The word 'passing' suggested the transiency of things, the passing of time and the changes of human life. Then the word 'Russell' suggested the rustling of leaves and the skirt on a polished floor; also the ducal house of Bedford and half the history of England. Finally the word 'Square' brings in the sight, the shape of an actual square combined with some visual suggestion of the stark angularity of stucco. Thus one sentence of the simplest kind rouses the imagination, the memory, the eye and the ear—all combine in reading it.

5 But they combine—they combine unconsciously together. The moment we single out and emphasize the suggestions as we have done here they become unreal; and we, too, become unreal—specialists, word mongers, phrase finders, not readers. In reading we have to allow the sunken meanings to remain sunken, suggested, not stated; lapsing and flowing into each other like reeds on the bed of a river. But the words in that sentence—Passing Russell Square—are of course very rudimentary words. They show no trace of the strange, of the diabolical power which words possess when they are not tapped out by a typewriter but come fresh from a human brain—the power that is to suggest the writer; his character, his appearance, his wife, his family, his house—even the cat on the hearthrug. Why words do this, how they

do it, how to prevent them from doing it nobody knows. They do it without the writer's will; often against his will. No writer presumably wishes to impose his own miserable character, his own private secrets and vices upon the reader. But has any writer, who is not a typewriter, succeeded in being wholly impersonal? Always, inevitably, we know them as well as their books. Such is the suggestive power of words that they will often make a bad book into a very lovable human being, and a good book into a man whom we can hardly tolerate in the room. Even words that are hundreds of years old have this power; when they are new they have it so strongly that they deafen us to the writer's meaning—it is them we see, them we hear. That is one reason why our judgments of living writers are so wildly erratic. Only after the writer is dead do his words to some extent become disinfected, purified of the accidents of the living body.

6 Now, this power of suggestion is one of the most mysterious properties of words. Everyone who has ever written a sentence must be conscious or half-conscious of it. Words, English words, are full of echoes, of memories, of associations—naturally. They have been out and about, on people's lips, in their houses, in the streets, in the fields, for so many centuries. And that is one of the chief difficulties in writing them to-day—that they are so stored with meanings, with memories, that they have contracted so many famous marriages. The splendid word 'incarnadine', for example—who can use it without remembering also 'multitudinous seas'? In the old days, of course, when English was a new language, writers could invent new words and use them. Nowadays it is easy enough to invent new words—they spring to the lips whenever we see a new sight or feel a new sensation—but we cannot use them because the language is old. You cannot use a brand new word in an old language because of the very obvious yet mysterious fact that a word is not a single and separate entity, but part of other words. It is not a word indeed until it is part of a sentence. Words belong to each other, although, of course, only a great writer knows that the word 'incarnadine' belongs to 'multitudinous seas'. To combine new words with old words is fatal to the constitution of the sentence. In order to use new words properly you would have to invent a new language; and that, though no doubt we shall come to it, is not at the moment our business. Our business is to see what we can do with the English language as it is. How can we combine the old words in new orders so that they survive, so that they create beauty, so that they tell the truth? That is the question.

7 And the person who could answer that question would deserve whatever crown of glory the world has to offer. Think what it would mean if you could teach, if you could learn, the art of writing. Why, every book, every newspaper would tell the truth, would create beauty. But there is, it would appear, some obstacle in the way, some hindrance to the teaching of words. For though at this moment at least a hundred professors are lecturing upon the literature of the past, at least a thousand critics are reviewing the literature of the present, and hundreds upon hundreds of young men and women are passing examinations in English literature with the utmost credit, still—do we write better, do we read better than we read and wrote four hundred years ago when we were unlectured, uncriticized, untaught? Is our Georgian literature a patch on the Elizabethan? Where then are we to lay the blame? Not on our professors; not on our reviewers; not on our writers; but on words.

It is words that are to blame. They are the wildest, freest, most irresponsible, most unteachable of all things. Of course, you can catch them and sort them and place them in alphabetical order in dictionaries. But words do not live in dictionaries; they live in the mind. If you want proof of this, consider how often in moments of emotion when we most need words we find none. Yet there is the dictionary; there at our disposal are some half a million words all in alphabetical order. But can we use them? No, because words do not live in dictionaries; they live in the mind. Look again at the dictionary. There beyond a doubt lie plays more splendid than *Antony and Cleopatra;* poems more lovely than the *Ode to a Nightingale;* novels beside which *Pride and Prejudice* or *David Copperfield* are the crude bunglings of amateurs. It is only a question of finding the right words and putting them in the right order. But we cannot do it because they do not live in dictionaries; they live in the mind. And how do they live in the mind? Variously and strangely, much as human beings live, by ranging hither and thither, by falling in love, and mating together. It is true that they are much less bound by ceremony and convention than we are. Royal words mate with commoners. English words marry French words, German words, Indian words, Negro words, if they have a fancy. Indeed, the less we inquire into the past of our dear Mother English the better it will be for that lady's reputation. For she has gone a-roving, a-roving fair maid.

8 Thus to lay down any laws for such irreclaimable vagabonds is worse than useless. A few trifling rules of grammar and spelling are all the constraint we can put on them. All we can say about them, as we peer at them over the edge of that deep, dark and fitfully illuminated cavern in which they live—the mind—all we can say about them is that they seem to like people to think and to feel before they use them, but to think and to feel not about them, but about something different. They are highly sensitive, easily made self-conscious. They do not like to have their purity or their impurity discussed. If you start a Society for Pure English, they will show their resentment by starting another for impure English—hence the unnatural violence of much modern speech; it is a protest against the puritans. They are highly democratic, too; they believe that one word is as good as another; uneducated words are as good as educated words, uncultivated words as cultivated words, there are no ranks or titles in their society. Nor do they like being lifted out on the point of a pen and examined separately. They hang together, in sentences, in paragraphs, sometimes for whole pages at a time. They hate being useful; they hate making money; they hate being lectured about in public. In short, they hate anything that stamps them with one meaning or confines them to one attitude, for it is their nature to change.

9 Perhaps that is their most striking peculiarity—their need of change. It is because the truth they try to catch is many-sided, and they convey it by being themselves many-sided, flashing this way, then that. Thus they mean one thing to one person, another thing to another person; they are unintelligible to one generation, plain as a pikestaff to the next. And it is because of this complexity that they survive. Perhaps then one reason why we have no great poet, novelist, or critic writing today is that we refuse words their liberty. We pin them down to one meaning, their useful meaning, the meaning which makes us catch the train, the meaning which makes us pass the examination. And when words are pinned down

they fold their wings and die. Finally, and most emphatically, words, like ourselves, in order to live at their ease, need privacy. Undoubtedly they like us to think, and they like us to feel, before we use them; but they also like us to pause; to become unconscious. Our unconsciousness is their privacy; our darkness is their light . . . That pause was made, that veil of darkness was dropped, to tempt words to come together in one of those swift marriages which are perfect images and create everlasting beauty. But no—nothing of that sort is going to happen tonight. The little wretches are out of temper; disobliging; disobedient; dumb. What is it that they are muttering? 'Time's up! Silence!'

(1937)

QUESTIONS

Thought and Structure

1. In your own words, explain why Woolf changed the title of her talk from "Craftsmanship" to "A Ramble round Words." Do you think Woolf is telling the truth, or do you think she's just charming her listeners? Why?
2. What is the difference between "the useful meaning, the surface meaning" and those other meanings Woolf teases us with, what she later calls "sunken meanings"? (paragraphs 1–2, 4)?
3. What does Woolf mean by a "language of signs" that will replace the misleading language of words (paragraph 3)?
4. "What, then, we may ask next, is the proper use of words?"
5. What do you think is Woolf's attitude about the "power of suggestion" that words have? Show us how that attitude is reflected in her own words.
6. What lessons can you as a writer learn from Woolf's playful discussion about the life that words live in the mind? What do you make of Woolf's final consideration of "unconsciousness"? What do we as writers have to give up momentarily to let words have their play in the unconscious?

Style and Strategy

7. How effective is the hen anecdote in paragraph 1? Why?
8. Does Woolf "prove" in the first two paragraphs that "words are not useful"? Does she need to? Why?
9. Identify some of Woolf's subtle jokes in her ramble round words. How effectively does she use humor to advance her argument? Does she just let go and give words free reign in this piece, or does she bring her words under control while giving them a certain amount of latitude? Explain and illustrate with examples from the text.

SUGGESTIONS FOR WRITING

A. "Craftsmanship" was written to be read aloud, over the radio. Read one of her other selections in this anthology to see how that selection differs from "Craftsmanship." Prepare a short report for the class accounting for your findings.

B. Write a short paragraph about the relationship between Woolf's ideas in paragraphs 4 and 5 and the idea Didion expresses in "O'Keeffe": "Style is character." Write another paragraph about the relationship between Woolf's ideas and those she attributes to Montaigne in "Montaigne." Finally, compare Woolf's use of "impersonal" in "Women and Writing" and her use of the term in paragraph 4 of this essay.

Kew Gardens

1 From the oval-shaped flower-bed there rose perhaps a hundred stalks spreading into heart-shaped or tongue-shaped leaves half-way up and unfurling at the tip red or blue or yellow petals marked with spots of colour raised upon the surface; and from the red, blue or yellow gloom of the throat emerged a straight bar, rough with gold dust and slightly clubbed at the end. The petals were voluminous enough to be stirred by the summer breeze, and when they moved, the red, blue and yellow lights passed one over the other, staining an inch of the brown earth beneath with a spot of the most intricate colour. The light fell either upon the smooth, grey back of a pebble, or, the shell of a snail with its brown, circular veins, or falling into a raindrop, it expanded with such intensity of red, blue and yellow the thin walls of water that one expected them to burst and disappear. Instead, the drop was left in a second silver grey once more, and the light now settled upon the flesh of a leaf, revealing the branching thread of fibre beneath the surface, and again it moved on and spread its illumination in the vast green spaces beneath the dome of the heart-shaped and tongue-shaped leaves. Then the breeze stirred rather more briskly overhead and the colour was flashed into the air above, into the eyes of the men and women who walk in Kew Gardens in July.

2 The figures of these men and women straggled past the flower-bed with a curiously irregular movement not unlike that of the white and blue butterflies who crossed the turf in zig-zag flights from bed to bed. The man was about six inches in front of the woman, strolling carelessly, while she bore on with greater purpose, only turning her head now and then to see that the children were not too far behind. The man kept this distance in front of the woman purposely, though perhaps unconsciously, for he wished to go on with his thoughts.

3 "Fifteen years ago I came here with Lily," he thought. "We sat somewhere over there by a lake and I begged her to marry me all through the hot afternoon. How the dragonfly kept circling round us: how clearly I see the dragonfly and her shoe with the square silver buckle at the toe. All the time I spoke I saw her shoe and when it moved impatiently I knew without looking up what she was going to say: the whole of her seemed to be in her shoe. And my love, my desire, were in the dragonfly; for some reason I thought that if it settled there, on that leaf, the broad one with the red flower in the middle of it, if the dragonfly settled on the leaf she would say 'Yes' at once. But the dragonfly went round and round: it never settled anywhere—of course not, happily not, or I shouldn't be walking here with Eleanor and the children. Tell me, Eleanor. D'you ever think of the past?"

4 "Why do you ask, Simon?"

5 "Because I've been thinking of the past. I've been thinking of Lily, the woman

I might have married. . . . Well, why are you silent? Do you mind my thinking of the past?"

6 "Why should I mind, Simon? Doesn't one always think of the past, in a garden with men and women lying under the trees? Aren't they one's past, all that remains of it, those men and women, those ghosts lying under the trees, . . . one's happiness, one's reality?"

7 "For me, a square silver shoe buckle and a dragonfly—"

8 "For me, a kiss. Imagine six little girls sitting before their easels twenty years ago, down by the side of a lake, painting the water-lilies, the first red water-lilies I'd ever seen. And suddenly a kiss, there on the back of my neck. And my hand shook all the afternoon so that I couldn't paint. I took out my watch and marked the hour when I would allow myself to think of the kiss for five minutes only—it was so precious—the kiss of an old grey-haired woman with a wart on her nose, the mother of all my kisses all my life. Come, Caroline, come, Hubert."

9 They walked on past the flower-bed, now walking four abreast, and soon diminished in size among the trees and looked half transparent as the sunlight and shade swam over their backs in large trembling irregular patches.

10 In the oval flower-bed the snail, whose shell had been stained red, blue and yellow for the space of two minutes or so, now appeared to be moving very slightly in its shell, and next began to labour over the crumbs of loose earth which broke away and rolled down as it passed over them. It appeared to have a definite goal in front of it, differing in this respect from the singular high stepping angular green insect who attempted to cross in front of it, and waited for a second with its antennae trembling as if in deliberation, and then stepped off as rapidly and strangely in the opposite direction. Brown cliffs with deep green lakes in the hollows, flat, blade-like trees that waved from root to tip, round boulders of grey stone, vast crumpled surfaces of a thin crackling texture—all these objects lay across the snail's progress between one stalk and another to his goal. Before he had decided whether to circumvent the arched tent of a dead leaf or to breast it there came past the bed the feet of other human beings.

11 This time they were both men. The younger of the two wore an expression of perhaps unnatural calm; he raised his eyes and fixed them very steadily in front of him while his companion spoke, and directly his companion had done speaking he looked on the ground again and sometimes opened his lips only after a long pause and sometimes did not open them at all. The elder man had a curiously uneven and shaky method of walking, jerking his hand forward and throwing up his head abruptly, rather in the manner of an impatient carriage horse tired of waiting outside a house; but in the man these gestures were irresolute and pointless. He talked almost incessantly; he smiled to himself and again began to talk, as if the smile had been an answer. He was talking about spirits—the spirits of the dead, who, according to him, were even now telling him all sorts of odd things about their experiences in Heaven.

12 "Heaven was known to the ancients as Thessaly, William, and now, with this war, the spirit matter is rolling between the hills like thunder." He paused, seemed to listen, smiled, jerked his head and continued:

13 "You have a small electric battery and a piece of rubber to insulate the

wire—isolate?—insulate?—well, we'll skip the details, no good going into details that wouldn't be understood—and in short the little machine stands in any convenient position by the head of the bed, we will say, on a neat mahogany stand. All arrangements being properly fixed by workmen under my direction, the widow applies her ear and summons the spirit by sign as agreed. Women! Widows! Women in black—"

14 Here he seemed to have caught sight of a woman's dress in the distance, which in the shade looked a purple black. He took off his hat, placed his hand upon his heart, and hurried towards her muttering and gesticulating feverishly. But William caught him by the sleeve and touched a flower with the tip of his walking-stick in order to divert the old man's attention. After looking at it for a moment in some confusion the old man bent his ear to it and seemed to answer a voice speaking from it, for he began talking about the forests of Uruguay which he had visited hundreds of years ago in company with the most beautiful young woman in Europe. He could be heard murmuring about forests of Uruguay blanketed with the wax petals of tropical roses, nightingales, sea beaches, mermaids, and women drowned at sea, as he suffered himself to be moved on by William, upon whose face the look of stoical patience grew slowly deeper and deeper.

15 Following his steps so closely as to be slightly puzzled by his gestures came two elderly women of the lower middle class, one stout and ponderous, the other rosy cheeked and nimble. Like most people of their station they were frankly fascinated by any signs of eccentricity betokening a disordered brain, especially in the well-to-do; but they were too far off to be certain whether the gestures were merely eccentric or genuinely mad. After they had scrutinized the old man's back in silence for a moment and given each other a queer, sly look, they went on energetically piecing together their very complicated dialogue:

16 "Nell, Bert, Lot, Cess, Phil, Pa, he says, I says, she says, I says, I says—"

17 "My Bert, Sis, Bill, Grandad, the old man, sugar,
Sugar, flour, kippers, greens,
Sugar, sugar, sugar."

18 The ponderous woman looked through the pattern of falling words at the flowers standing cool, firm, and upright in the earth, with a curious expression. She saw them as a sleeper waking from a heavy sleep sees a brass candlestick reflecting the light in an unfamiliar way, and closes his eyes and opens them, and seeing the brass candlestick again, finally starts broad awake and stares at the candlestick with all his powers. So the heavy woman came to a standstill opposite the oval-shaped flower-bed, and ceased even to pretend to listen to what the other woman was saying. She stood there letting the words fall over her, swaying the top part of her body slowly backwards and forwards, looking at the flowers. Then she suggested that they should find a seat and have their tea.

19 The snail had now considered every possible method of reaching his goal without going round the dead leaf or climbing over it. Let alone the effort needed for climbing a leaf, he was doubtful whether the thin texture which vibrated with such an alarming crackle when touched even by the tips of his horns would bear his weight; and this determined him finally to creep beneath it, for there was a point where the leaf curved high enough from the ground to admit him. He had just

inserted his head in the opening and was taking stock of the high brown roof and was getting used to the cool brown light when two other people came past outside on the turf. This time they were both young, a young man and a young woman. They were both in the prime of youth, or even in that season which precedes the prime of youth, the season before the smooth pink folds of the flower have burst their gummy case, when the wings of the butterfly, though fully grown, are motionless in the sun.

20 "Lucky it isn't Friday," he observed.

21 "Why? D'you believe in luck?"

22 "They make you pay sixpence on Friday."

23 "What's sixpence anyway? Isn't it worth sixpence?"

24 "What's 'it'—what do you mean by 'it'?"

25 "O, anything—I mean—you know what I mean."

26 Long pauses came between each of these remarks; they were uttered in toneless and monotonous voices. The couple stood still on the edge of the flower-bed, and together pressed the end of her parasol deep down into the soft earth. The action and the fact that his hand rested on the top of hers expressed their feelings in a strange way, as these short insignificant words also expressed something, words with short wings for their heavy body of meaning, inadequate to carry them far and thus alighting awkwardly upon the very common objects that surrounded them, and were to their inexperienced touch so massive; but who knows (so they thought as they pressed the parasol into the earth) what precipices aren't concealed in them, or what slopes of ice don't shine in the sun on the other side? Who knows? Who has ever seen this before? Even when she wondered what sort of tea they gave you at Kew, he felt that something loomed up behind her words, and stood vast and solid behind them; and the mist very slowly rose and uncovered—O, Heavens, what were those shapes?—little white tables, and waitresses who looked first at her and then at him; and there was a bill that he would pay with a real two shilling piece, and it was real, all real, he assured himself, fingering the coin in his pocket, real to everyone except to him and to her; even to him it began to seem real; and then—but it was too exciting to stand and think any longer, and he pulled the parasol out of the earth with a jerk and was impatient to find the place where one had tea with other people, like other people.

27 "Come along, Trissie; it's time we had our tea."

28 "Wherever *does* one have one's tea?" she asked with the oddest thrill of excitement in her voice, looking vaguely round and letting herself be drawn on down the grass path, trailing her parasol; turning her head this way and that way forgetting her tea, wishing to go down there and then down there, remembering orchids and cranes among wild flowers, a Chinese pagoda and a crimson crested bird; but he bore her on.

29 Thus one couple after another with much the same irregular and aimless movement passed the flower-bed and were enveloped in layer after layer of green blue vapour, in which at first their bodies had substance and a dash of colour, but later both substance and colour dissolved in the green-blue atmosphere. How hot it was! So hot that even the thrush chose to hop, like a mechanical bird, in the shadow of the flowers, with long pauses between one movement and the next; instead of rambling vaguely the white butterflies danced one above another, making

with their white shifting flakes the outline of a shattered marble column above the tallest flowers; the glass roofs of the palm house shone as if a whole market full of shiny green umbrellas had opened in the sun; and in the drone of the aeroplane the voice of the summer sky murmured its fierce soul. Yellow and black, pink and snow white, shapes of all these colours, men, women, and children were spotted for a second upon the horizon, and then, seeing the breadth of yellow that lay upon the grass, they wavered and sought shade beneath the trees, dissolving like drops of water in the yellow and green atmosphere, staining it faintly with red and blue. It seemed as if all gross and heavy bodies had sunk down in the heat motionless and lay huddled upon the ground, but their voices went wavering from them as if they were flames lolling from the thick waxen bodies of candles. Voices. Yes, voices. Wordless voices, breaking the silence suddenly with such depth of contentment, such passion of desire, or, in the voices of children, such freshness of surprise; breaking the silence? But there was no silence; all the time the motor omnibuses were turning their wheels and changing their gear; like a vast nest of Chinese boxes all of wrought steel turning ceaselessly one within another the city murmured; on the top of which the voices cried aloud and the petals of myriads of flowers flashed their colours into the air.

(1949)

QUESTIONS

1. Identify the point in the first paragraph where Woolf introduces the idea of movement. Then identify the ways she keeps that movement in our minds. Think too about her use of color.
2. In what form do Simon's and Eleanor's memories of the past take shape?
3. Woolf seems to move as effortlessly from narration to human action to animals' struggles as her characters move from interior monologue to dialogue. Is there some hidden point, some suggestion, in this effortlessness, that is as intriguing as the movement of the flowers and their colors in the wind?
4. At what point does the narrator become obtrusive, making us take notice of her presence? Or is it his presence? Can you tell about gender? Does it matter in this story?
5. In this story four different pairs of people pass by the "oval-shaped flower-bed." Study their differing reactions to one another and to the flowers. Consider gender. Consider age. Consider what they do to the flowers. Consider their bodies and their voices. Consider too their relationship to the earth. What do those considerations seem to suggest to you, and perhaps to the narrator?
6. What is the snail's function in this story?
7. Do you think this story means anything or do you consider it a prose poem—a series of images, related in texture and circumstance but free of any necessity to mean anything? Defend your choice or suggest another possibility.

SUGGESTIONS FOR WRITING

A. Try to do some pictorial writing. Describe a scene in such a way that we can actually see it. Bring it to life as Woolf does her opening scene.

B. In their own ways each of the stories in this anthology by Woolf and Lawrence and Forster are experimental. Reread them in the company of one another, and try to account for their differences. Make notes as your mind works its way through the stories; at the end of your reading and musing and notetaking, try to draw some conclusions that will be helpful to you and to the class.

C. Imagine one more pair of people visiting the "oval-shaped flower-bed," and create another scene complete with dialogue. Try to make it fit within the structure of the story. If you would rather deal with the snail than with people that will be fine. Create another scene with the snail.

D. Compare Lawrence's description of the rabbit "Adolph" with Woolf's description of the snail. If you prefer, compare White's "Geese" with the snail. Or better, look at the geese and the rabbit in relation to Woolf's snail.

FOUR

D. H. Lawrence

(1885–1930)

D. H. Lawrence is perhaps known best for his novels, whose titles reveal their center of interest: *Sons and Lovers, Women in Love, Lady Chatterley's Lover, The Virgin and the Gypsy*—among many others. Of these, *Lady Chatterley's Lover* achieved the greatest notoriety if not the greatest critical acclaim when it was made the occasion of a court obscenity battle. Like much of Lawrence's work, it explores the relations between the sexes, contrasting an impotent and debilitating relationship (that between Lady Chatterley and her husband) with a vital and vibrant one (that between Lady Chatterley and the gamekeeper). The book is also a compendium of Lawrence's major thematic preoccupations: the importance of instinctual life, the celebration of the natural world, the condemnation of the conventional, the mechanical, and the artificial, and the power of sexual surrender.

David Herbert Lawrence was born in 1885 in Nottinghamshire, an English mining town. He was educated there, taking a teaching certificate from Nottingham College. He taught school from 1902 to 1912, with a one-year hiatus, before becoming a full-time writer. Between 1911, when he published his first novel, *The White Peacock,* and 1930, when he died of tuberculosis, he published more than sixty volumes, including novels, collections of stories, poems, essays, plays, travel books, social criticism, and translations from Russian and Italian literature.

Lawrence derived his penchant for learning and his impulse to write from his mother, who was better educated than her miner husband. She encouraged her son's intellectual pursuits, recognizing that his frail constitution made him unsuitable for the physical rigors of life as a miner. Affecting a somewhat self-conscious gentility, she considered herself the intellectual superior of her husband, whose semiliteracy and coarse working-class habits contrasted sharply with her sense of refinement. Lawrence himself favored his mother, but later in life came to see his father's virtues as well—especially his instinctive love of life, his naturalness, his devotion to hard labor, and his respect for the natural world.

Characteristics of both parents emerge in Lawrence's essay, "Adolf," which describes how the family took in an injured wild rabbit, temporarily making it a pet. Aside from its biographical interest, the essay displays Lawrence's respect for nature and his sympathy with the instinctual life of animals. This respect for the instinctual appears in a different way in his short story, "The Horse Dealer's Daughter." The story concerns the lives of a young man and woman who, very much alone, simultaneously desire and fear close physical and emotional contact with one another.

Lawrence portrays the emotional and psychological consequences of their sexual confrontation with great intensity.

The other selections by Lawrence included in this anthology are a bit different. Although one of them, "Cocksure Women and Hensure Men," centers on the relations between the sexes, the essay is primarily an argument about the psychology and behavior of women. It mixes fable and argument in about equal measure, establishing its point obliquely and humorously. At first glance, Lawrence's essay on Benjamin Franklin seems cut from a different bolt of cloth. And in one sense it has been, since it comes from a book of literary criticism: *Studies in Classic American Literature.* But this selection, like the others, displays Lawrence's passionate criticism of customs, behavior, habits, and attitudes that he considers unnatural and therefore dangerous. For Lawrence, Franklin is more villain than cultural hero. Lawrence sees him as embodying an excessive rationalism, a too-reasonable, overly mentalistic approach to life. Franklin suffers from the same disease as Dr. Fergusson in "The Horse Dealer's Daughter." But while Fergusson harms no one but himself, Franklin's fame and accomplishments make his ideas profoundly influential. And Lawrence simply tries to counter what he sees as their pernicious consequences. In the Franklin essay and throughout his work generally, Lawrence acts the social critic, condemning societal attitudes that run counter to his belief that human beings need to become less cerebral and analytical, and more instinctive and intuitive.

Lawrence's vision can be described as romanticist. And he renders this vision in prose at once urgent, passionate, and intense. Its vividness depends upon the repeated use of sensuous detail—the sights, sounds, smells, textures of life. His writing is direct to the point of challenge. In reading Lawrence we hear an insistent voice, urgently trying to convince us to accept what he says. His passion and intensity earn him, at least, a hearing, and at best, a favorable judgment.

Adolf

1 When we were children our father often worked on the night-shift. Once it was spring-time, and he used to arrive home, black and tired, just as we were downstairs in our nightdresses. Then night met morning face to face, and the contact was not always happy. Perhaps it was painful to my father to see us gaily entering upon the day into which he dragged himself soiled and weary. He didn't like going to bed in the spring morning sunshine.

2 But sometimes he was happy, because of his long walk through the dewy fields in the first daybreak. He loved the open morning, the crystal and the space, after a night down pit. He watched every bird, every stir in the trembling grass, answered the whinnying of the pewits and tweeted to the wrens. If he could, he also would have whinnied and tweeted and whistled in a native language that was not human. He liked non-human things best.

3 One sunny morning we were all sitting at table when we heard his heavy slurring walk up the entry. We became uneasy. His was always a disturbing presence, trammelling. He passed the window darkly, and we heard him go into the scullery and put down his tin bottle. But directly he came into the kitchen. We felt at once

that he had something to communicate. No one spoke. We watched his black face for a second.

4 "Give me a drink," he said.

5 My mother hastily poured out his tea. He went to pour it out into his saucer. But instead of drinking he suddenly put something on the table among the teacups. A tiny brown rabbit! A small rabbit, a mere morsel, sitting against the bread as still as if it were a made thing.

6 "A rabbit! A young one! Who gave it you, father?"

7 But he laughed enigmatically, with a sliding motion of his yellow-grey eyes, and went to take off his coat. We pounced on the rabbit.

8 "Is it alive? Can you feel its heart beat?"

9 My father came back and sat down heavily in his armchair. He dragged his saucer to him, and blew his tea, pushing out his red lips under his black moustache.

10 "Where did you get it, father?"

11 "I picked it up," he said, wiping his naked forearm over his mouth and beard.

12 "Where?"

13 "It is a wild one!" came my mother's quick voice.

14 "Yes, it is."

15 "Then why did you bring it?" cried my mother.

16 "Oh, we wanted it," came our cry.

17 "Yes, I've no doubt you did—" retorted my mother. But she was drowned in our clamour of questions.

18 On the field path my father had found a dead mother rabbit and three dead little ones—this one alive, but unmoving.

19 "But what had killed them, daddy?"

20 "I couldn't say, my child. I s'd think she'd aten something."

21 "Why did you bring it!" again my mother's voice of condemnation. "You know what it will be."

22 My father made no answer, but we were loud in protest.

23 "He must bring it. It's not big enough to live by itself. It would die," we shouted.

24 "Yes, and it will die now. And then there'll be *another* outcry."

25 My mother set her face against the tragedy of dead pets. Our hearts sank.

26 "It won't die, father, will it? Why will it? It won't."

27 "I s'd think not," said my father.

28 "You know well enough it will. Haven't we had it all before!" said my mother.

29 "They dunna always pine," replied my father testily.

30 But my mother reminded him of other little wild animals he had brought, which had sulked and refused to live, and brought storms of tears and trouble in our house of lunatics.

31 Trouble fell on us. The little rabbit sat on our lap, unmoving, its eye wide and dark. We brought it milk, warm milk, and held it to its nose. It sat as still as if it was far away, retreated down some deep burrow, hidden, oblivious. We wetted its mouth and whiskers with drops of milk. It gave no sign, did not even shake off the wet white drops. Somebody began to shed a few secret tears.

32 "What did I say?" cried my mother. "Take it and put it down in the field."

33 Her command was in vain. We were driven to get dressed for school. There sat the rabbit. It was like a tiny obscure cloud. Watching it, the emotions died out of our breast. Useless to love it, to yearn over it. Its little feelings were all ambushed. They must be circumvented. Love and affection were a trespass upon it. A little wild thing, it became more mute and asphyxiated still in its own arrest, when we approached with love. We must not love it. We must circumvent it, for its own existence.

34 So I passed the order to my sister and my mother. The rabbit was not to be spoken to, nor even looked at. Wrapping it in a piece of flannel I put it in an obscure corner of the cold parlour, and put a saucer of milk before its nose. My mother was forbidden to enter the parlour whilst we were at school.

35 "As if I should take any notice of your nonsense," she cried affronted. Yet I doubt if she ventured into the parlour.

36 At midday, after school, creeping into the front room, there we saw the rabbit still and unmoving in the piece of flannel. Strange grey-brown neutralization of life, still living! It was a sore problem to us.

37 "Why won't it drink its milk, mother?" we whispered. Our father was asleep.

38 "It prefers to sulk its life away, silly little thing." A profound problem. Prefers to sulk its life away! We put young dandelion leaves to its nose. The sphinx was not more oblivious. Yet its eye was bright.

39 At tea-time, however, it had hopped a few inches, out of its flannel, and there it sat again, uncovered, a little solid cloud of muteness, brown, with unmoving whiskers. Only its side palpitated slightly with life.

40 Darkness came; my father set off to work. The rabbit was still unmoving. Dumb despair was coming over the sisters, a threat of tears before bedtime. Clouds of my mother's anger gathered as she muttered against my father's wantonness.

41 Once more the rabbit was wrapped in the old pit-singlet. But now it was carried into the scullery and put under the copper fireplace, that it might imagine itself inside a burrow. The saucers were placed about, four or five, here and there on the floor, so that if the little creature *should* chance to hop abroad, it could not fail to come upon some food. After this my mother was allowed to take from the scullery what she wanted and then she was forbidden to open the door.

42 When morning came and it was light, I went downstairs. Opening the scullery door, I heard a slight scuffle. Then I saw dabbles of milk all over the floor and tiny rabbit-droppings in the saucers. And there the miscreant, the tips of his ears showing behind a pair of boots. I peeped at him. He sat bright-eyed and askance, twitching his nose and looking at me while not looking at me.

43 He was alive—very much alive. But still we were afraid to trespass much on his confidence.

44 "Father!" My father was arrested at the door. "Father, the rabbit's alive."

45 "Back your life it is," said my father.

46 "Mind how you go in."

47 By evening, however, the little creature was tame, quite tame. He was christened Adolf. We were enchanted by him. We couldn't really love him, because he was wild and loveless to the end. But he was an unmixed delight.

48 We decided he was too small to live in a hutch—he must live at large in the

house. My mother protested, but in vain. He was so tiny. So we had him upstairs, and he dropped his tiny pills on the bed and we were enchanted.

49 Adolf made himself instantly at home. He had the run of the house, and was perfectly happy, with his tunnels and his holes behind the furniture.

50 We loved him to take meals with us. He would sit on the table humping his back, sipping his milk, shaking his whiskers and his tender ears, hopping off and hobbling back to his saucer, with an air of supreme unconcern. Suddenly he was alert. He hobbled a few tiny paces, and reared himself up inquisitively at the sugar basin. He fluttered his tiny fore-paws, and then reached and laid them on the edge of the basin, whilst he craned his thin neck and peeped in. He trembled his whiskers at the sugar, then did his best to lift down a lump.

51 "*Do* you think I will have it! Animals in the sugar pot!" cried my mother, with a rap of her hand on the table.

52 Which so delighted the electric Adolf that he flung his hindquarters and knocked over a cup.

53 "It's your own fault, mother. If you left him alone—"

54 He continued to take tea with us. He rather liked warm tea. And he loved sugar. Having nibbled a lump, he would turn to the butter. There he was shooed off by our parent. He soon learned to treat her shooing with indifference. Still, she hated him to put his nose in the food. And he loved to do it. And one day between them they overturned the cream-jug. Adolf deluged his little chest, bounced back in terror, was seized by his little ears by my mother and bounced down on the hearth-rug. There he shivered in momentary discomfort, and suddenly set off in a wild flight to the parlour.

55 This last was his happy hunting ground. He had cultivated the bad habit of pensively nibbling certain bits of cloth in the hearth-rug. When chased from this pasture he would retreat under the sofa. There he would twinkle in Buddhist meditation until suddenly, no one knew why, he would go off like an alarm clock. With a sudden bumping scuffle he would whirl out of the room, going through the doorway with his little ears flying. Then we would hear his thunderbolt hurtling in the parlour, but before we could follow, the wild streak of Adolf would flash past us, on an electric wind that swept him round the scullery and carried him back, a little mad thing, flying possessed like a ball round the parlour. After which ebullition he would sit in a corner composed and distant, twitching his whiskers in abstract meditation. And it was in vain we questioned him about his outbursts. He just went off like a gun, and was as calm after it as a gun that smokes placidly.

56 Alas, he grew up rapidly. It was almost impossible to keep him from the outer door.

57 One day, as we were playing by the stile, I saw his brown shadow loiter across the road and pass into the field that faced the houses. Instantly a cry of "Adolf!"—a cry he knew full well. And instantly a wind swept him away down the sloping meadow, his tail twinkling and zigzagging through the grass. After him we pelted. It was a strange sight to see him, ears back, his little loins so powerful, flinging the world behind him. We ran ourselves out of breath, but could not catch him. Then somebody headed him off, and he sat with sudden unconcern, twitching his nose under a bunch of nettles.

58 His wanderings cost him a shock. One Sunday morning my father had just been quarrelling with a pedlar, and we were hearing the aftermath indoors, when there came a sudden unearthly scream from the yard. We flew out. There sat Adolf cowering under a bench, whilst a great black and white cat glowered intently at him, a few yards away. Sight not to be forgotten. Adolf rolling back his eyes and parting his strange muzzle in another scream, the cat stretching forward in a slow elongation.

59 Ha, how we hated that cat! How we pursued him over the chapel wall and across the neighbours' gardens.

60 Adolf was still only half grown.

61 "Cats!" said my mother. "Hideous detestable animals, why do people harbour them?"

62 But Adolf was becoming too much for her. He dropped too many pills. And suddenly to hear him clumping downstairs when she was alone in the house was startling. And to keep him from the door was impossible. Cats prowled outside. It was worse than having a child to look after.

63 Yet we would not have him shut up. He became more lusty, more callous than ever. He was a strong kicker, and many a scratch on face and arms did we owe to him. But he brought his own doom on himself. The lace curtains in the parlour—my mother was rather proud of them—fell on the floor very full. One of Adolf's joys was to scuffle wildly through them as though through some foamy undergrowth. He had already torn rents in them.

64 One day he entangled himself altogether. He kicked, he whirled round in a mad nebulous inferno. He screamed—and brought down the curtain-rod with a smash, right on the best beloved pelargonium, just as my mother rushed in. She extricated him, but she never forgave him. And he never forgave either. A heartless wildness had come over him.

65 Even we understood that he must go. It was decided, after a long deliberation, that my father should carry him back to the wildwoods. Once again he was stowed into the great pocket of the pit-jacket.

66 "Best pop him i' th' pot," said my father, who enjoyed raising the wind of indignation.

67 And so, next day, our father said that Adolf, set down on the edge of the coppice, had hopped away with utmost indifference, neither elated nor moved. We heard it and believed. But many, many were the heartsearchings. How would the other rabbits receive him? Would they smell his tameness, his humanized degradation, and rend him? My mother pooh-poohed the extravagant idea.

68 However, he was gone, and we were rather relieved. My father kept an eye open for him. He declared that several times passing the coppice in the early morning, he had seen Adolf peeping through the nettle-stalks. He had called him, in an odd, high-voiced, cajoling fashion. But Adolf had not responded. Wildness gains so soon upon its creatures. And they become so contemptuous then of our tame presence. So it seemed to me. I myself would go to the edge of the coppice, and call softly. I myself would imagine bright eyes between the nettle-stalks, flash of a white, scornful tail past the bracken. That insolent white tail, as Adolf turned his flank on us! It reminded me always of a certain rude gesture, and a certain unprintable phrase, which may not even be suggested.

69 But when naturalists discuss the meaning of the rabbit's white tail, that rude gesture and still ruder phrase always come to my mind. Naturalists say that the rabbit shows his white tail in order to guide his young safely after him, as a nursemaid's flying strings are the signal to her toddling charges to follow on. How nice and naïve! I only know that my Adolf wasn't naïve. He used to whisk his flank at me, push his white feather in my eye, and say *"Merde!"* It's a rude word—but one which Adolf was always semaphoring at me, flag-wagging it with all the derision of his narrow haunches.

70 That's a rabbit all over—insolence, and the white flag of spiteful derision. Yes, and he keeps his flag flying to the bitter end, sporting, insolent little devil that he is. See him running for his life. Oh, how his soul is fanned to an ecstasy of fright, a fugitive whirlwind of panic. Gone mad, he throws the world behind him, with astonishing hind legs. He puts back his head and lays his ears on his sides and rolls the white of his eyes in sheer ecstatic agony of speed. He knows the awful approach behind him; bullet or stoat. He knows! He knows, his eyes are turned back almost into his head. It is agony. But it is also ecstasy. Ecstasy! See the insolent white flag bobbing. He whirls on the magic wind of terror. All his pent-up soul rushes into agonized electric emotion of fear. He flings himself on, like a falling star swooping into extinction. White heat of the agony of fear. And at the same time, bob! bob! bob! goes the white tail, *merde! merde! merde!* it says to the pursuer. The rabbit can't help it. In his utmost extremity he still flings the insult at the pursuer. He is the inconquerable fugitive, the indomitable meek. No wonder the stoat becomes vindictive.

71 And if he escapes, this precious rabbit! Don't you see him sitting there, in his earthly nook, a little ball of silence and rabbit triumph? Don't you see the glint on his black eye? Don't you see, in his very immobility, how the whole world is *merde* to him? No conceit like the conceit of the meek. And if the avenging angel in the shape of the ghostly ferret steals down on him, there comes a shriek of terror out of that little hump of self-satisfaction sitting motionless in a corner. Falls the fugitive. But even fallen, his white feather floats. Even in death it seems to say: "I am the meek, I am the righteous, I am the rabbit. All you rest, you are evil doers, and you shall be *bien emmerdés!*"

(1920)

QUESTIONS

Thought and Structure

1. What picture of Lawrence's father emerges from this essay? Identify the details that contribute to the portrait. Do the same for his mother.
2. How does Lawrence engage our interest in the little rabbit? Does he succeed? Why or why not?
3. How is the essay organized? With what does it begin? How does it end? Where is the explanation heaviest and the dialogue and action lightest? Why?

4. What image of nature emerges in this essay? How is the human world related to the natural?

Style and Strategy

5. What words and phrases describing Adolf personify him? Is Lawrence justified in attributing human characteristics to an animal in this manner? Why or why not? What advantages does he gain from doing so?
6. Identify the comparisons Lawrence employs in paragraph 55. What do they have in common? What, cumulatively, do they reveal about Adolf?
7. Comment on the following word choices:

   every *stir* in the trembling grass (2)
   [he] *tweeted* to the wrens (2)
   his heavy *slurring* walk (3)
   retorted my mother (17)
   our *clamour* of questions (17)

8. Twice Lawrence uses inverted sentences:

   After him we pelted. (57)
   . . . and many a scratch on face and arms did we owe to him. (63)

   After reading both sentences in context consider these alternatives:

   We pelted after him.
   . . . and we owed him many a scratch on face and arms.

   Which version do you prefer, and why?

SUGGESTIONS FOR WRITING

A. Write an essay in which you characterize a pet you once had.
B. Analyze the way Lawrence characterizes the four figures of this essay: Adolf, the mother, the father, and the narrator.
C. Compare Lawrence's attitude toward Adolf with E. B. White's toward his animals in "The Geese."

Cocksure Women and Hensure Men

1 It seems to me there are two aspects to women. There is the demure and the dauntless. Men have loved to dwell, in fiction at least, on the demure maiden whose inevitable reply is: Oh, yes, if you please, kind sir! The demure maiden, the demure spouse, the demure mother—this is still the ideal. A few maidens, mistresses and mothers *are* demure. A few pretend to be. But the vast majority are not. And they don't pretend to be. We don't expect a girl skilfully driving her car to be demure, we expect her to be dauntless. What good would demure and maidenly Members of Parliament be, inevitably responding: Oh, yes, if you please, kind

sir!—Though of course there are masculine members of that kidney.—And a demure telephone girl? Or even a demure stenographer? Demureness, to be sure, is outwardly becoming, it is an outward mark of femininity, like bobbed hair. But it goes with inward dauntlessness. The girl who has got to make her way in life has got to be dauntless, and if she has a pretty, demure manner with it, then lucky girl. She kills two birds with two stones.

2 With the two kinds of femininity go two kinds of confidence: There are the women who are cocksure, and the women who are hensure. A really up-to-date woman is a cocksure woman. She doesn't have a doubt nor a qualm. She is the modern type. Whereas the old-fashioned demure woman was sure as a hen is sure, that is, without knowing anything about it. She went quietly and busily clucking around, laying the eggs and mothering the chickens in a kind of anxious dream that still was full of sureness. But not mental sureness. Her sureness was a physical condition, very soothing, but a condition out of which she could easily be startled or frightened.

3 It is quite amusing to see the two kinds of sureness in chickens. The cockerel is, naturally, cocksure. He crows because he is *certain* it is day. Then the hen peeps out from under her wing. He marches to the door of the hen-house and pokes out his head assertively: *Ah ha! daylight, of course, just as I said!*—and he majestically steps down the chicken ladder towards *terra firma,* knowing that the hens will step cautiously after him, drawn by his confidence. So after him, cautiously, step the hens. He crows again: *Ha-ha! here we are!*—It is indisputable, and the hens accept it entirely. He marches towards the house. From the house a person ought to appear, scattering corn. Why does the person not appear? The cock will see to it. He is cocksure. He gives a loud crow in the doorway, and the person appears. The hens are suitably impressed but immediately devote all their henny consciousness to the scattered corn, pecking absorbedly, while the cock runs and fusses, cocksure that he is responsible for it all.

4 So the day goes on. The cock finds a tit-bit, and loudly calls the hens. They scuffle up in henny surety, and gobble the tit-bit. But when they find a juicy morsel for themselves, they devour it in silence, hensure. Unless, of course, there are little chicks, when they most anxiously call the brood. But in her own dim surety, the hen is really much surer than the cock, in a different way. She marches off to lay her egg, she secures obstinately the nest she wants, she lays her egg at last, then steps forth again with prancing confidence, and gives that most assured of all sounds, the hensure cackle of a bird who has laid her egg. The cock, who is never so sure about anything as the hen is about the egg she has laid, immediately starts to cackle like the female of his species. He is pining to be hensure, for hensure is so much surer than cocksure.

5 Nevertheless, cocksure is boss. When the chicken-hawk appears in the sky, loud are the cockerel's calls of alarm. Then the hens scuffle under the verandah, the cock ruffles his feathers on guard. The hens are numb with fear, they say: Alas, there is no health in us! How wonderful to be a cock so bold!—And they huddle, numbed. But their very numbness is hensurety.

6 Just as the cock can cackle, however, as if he had laid the egg, so can the hen bird crow. She can more or less assume his cocksureness. And yet she is never so

easy, cocksure, as she used to be when she was hensure. Cocksure, she is cocksure, but uneasy. Hensure, she trembles, but is easy.

7 It seems to me just the same in the vast human farmyard. Only nowadays all the cocks are cackling and pretending to lay eggs, and all the hens are crowing and pretending to call the sun out of bed. If women today are cocksure, men are hensure. Men are timid, tremulous, rather soft and submissive, easy in their very henlike tremulousness. They only want to be spoken to gently. So the women step forth with a good loud *cock-a-doodle-do!*

8 The tragedy about cocksure women is that they are more cocky, in their assurance, than the cock himself. They never realize that when the cock gives his loud crow in the morning, he listens acutely afterwards, to hear if some other wretch of a cock dare crow defiance, challenge. To the cock, there is always defiance, challenge, danger and death on the clear air; or the possibility thereof.

9 But alas, when the hen crows, she listens for no defiance or challenge. When she says *cock-a-doodle-do!* then it is unanswerable. The cock listens for an answer, alert. But the hen knows she is unanswerable. *Cock-a-doodle-do!* and there it is, take it or leave it!

10 And it is this that makes the cocksureness of women so dangerous, so devastating. It is really out of scheme, it is not in relation to the rest of things. So we have the tragedy of cocksure women. They find, so often, that instead of having laid an egg, they have laid a vote, or an empty ink-bottle, or some other absolutely unhatchable object, which means nothing to them.

11 It is the tragedy of the modern woman. She becomes cocksure, she puts all her passion and energy and years of her life into some effort or assertion, without ever listening for the denial which she ought to take into count. She is cocksure, but she is a hen all the time. Frightened of her own henny self, she rushes to mad lengths about votes, or welfare, or sports, or business: she is marvellous, out-manning the man. But alas, it is all fundamentally disconnected. It is all an attitude, and one day the attitude will become a weird cramp, a pain, and then it will collapse. And when it has collapsed, and she looks at the eggs she has laid, votes, or miles of typewriting, years of business efficiency—suddenly, because she is a hen and not a cock, all she has done will turn into pure nothingness to her. Suddenly it all falls out of relation to her basic henny self, and she realizes she has lost her life. The lovely henny surety, the hensureness which is the real bliss of every female, has been denied her: she had never had it. Having lived her life with such utmost strenuousness and cocksureness, she has missed her life altogether. Nothingness!

(1929)

QUESTIONS

Thought and Structure

1. How would you formulate Lawrence's main point? Why doesn't he state his thesis explicitly?

2. In paragraph 1 Lawrence describes two kinds of women; in paragraph 2, two kinds of confidence. How are they different and how are they related?
3. The rest of the essay divides neatly into two parts: paragraphs 3–6, which focus on the cock, his hens, and their different kinds of sureness; paragraphs 7–11, which draw an analogy with human experience. How far do you think the analogy should be taken? Why?
4. What view of the relationship between men and women and the behavior of each does Lawrence argue for?

Style and Strategy

5. How many voices do you hear in the essay? Identify them and illustrate each.
6. Lawrence employs contrast both within and between sentences. Here is an example of each.

   Within: Just as the cock can cackle, however, as if he had laid the egg, so can the hen bird crow. (6)

   Between: Cocksure, she is cocksure, but uneasy. (6)
   Hensure, she trembles, but is easy. (6)

   Find other examples of these contrasting patterns.
7. Notice how often Lawrence begins a sentence with a coordinating conjunction. Paragraph 9 contains two examples and paragraph 10, one:

   But . . . But . . . And . . .

   What alternatives are available? Why do you think Lawrence begins so many sentences with "And" and "But"?
8. Describe the tone of the following sentences:
   a. It seems to me there are two aspects to women. (1)
      It seems to me just the same in the vast human farmyard. (7)
   b. The tragedy about cocksure women is that they are more cocky, in their assurance, than the cock himself. (8)
      It is the tragedy of the modern woman. (11)

SUGGESTIONS FOR WRITING

A. Imitate Lawrence by writing an essay in which you make an argument by means of a detailed analogy.

B. Refute or support Lawrence's argument in an essay of your own about modern women—or modern men.

Benjamin Franklin

1 The Perfectibility of Man! Ah heaven, what a dreary theme! The perfectibility of the Ford car! The perfectibility of which man? I am many men. Which of them are you going to perfect? I am not a mechanical contrivance.

2 Education! Which of the various me's do you propose to educate, and which do you propose to suppress?

3 Anyhow, I defy you. I defy you, oh society, to educate me or to suppress me, according to your dummy standards.

4 The ideal man! And which is he, if you please? Benjamin Franklin or Abraham Lincoln? The ideal man! Roosevelt or Porfirio Díaz?

5 There are other men in me, besides this patient ass who sits here in a tweed jacket. What am I doing, playing the patient ass in a tweed jacket? Who am I talking to? Who are you, at the other end of this patience?

6 Who are you? How many selves have you? And which of these selves do you want to be?

7 Is Yale College going to educate the self that is in the dark of you, or Harvard College?

8 The ideal self! Oh, but I have a strange and fugitive self shut out and howling like a wolf or a coyote under the ideal windows. See his red eyes in the dark? This is the self who is coming into his own.

9 The perfectibility of man, dear God! When every man as long as he remains alive is in himself a multitude of conflicting men. Which of these do you choose to perfect, at the expense of every other?

10 Old Daddy Franklin will tell you. He'll rig him up for you, the pattern American. Oh, Franklin was the first downright American. He knew what he was about, the sharp little man. He set up the first dummy American.

11 At the beginning of his career this cunning little Benjamin drew up for himself a creed that should "satisfy the professors of every religion, but shock none."

12 Now wasn't that a real American thing to do?

13 *"That there is One God, who made all things."*

14 (But Benjamin made Him.)

15 *"That He governs the world by His Providence."*

16 (Benjamin knowing all about Providence.)

17 *"That He ought to be worshipped with adoration, prayer, and thanksgiving."*

18 (Which cost nothing.)

19 *"But—"* But me no buts, Benjamin, saith the Lord.

20 *"But that the most acceptable service of God is doing good to men."*

21 (God having no choice in the matter.)

22 *"That the soul is immortal."*

23 (You'll see why, in the next clause.)

24 *"And that God will certainly reward virtue and punish vice, either here or hereafter."*

25 Now if Mr. Andrew Carnegie, or any other millionaire, had wished to invent a God to suit his ends, he could not have done better. Benjamin did it for him in the eighteenth century. God is the supreme servant of men who want to get on, to *produce.* Providence. The provider. The heavenly storekeeper. The everlasting Wanamaker.

26 And this is all the God the grandsons of the Pilgrim Fathers had left. Aloft on a pillar of dollars.

27 *"That the soul is immortal."*

28 The trite way Benjamin says it!

29 But man has a soul, though you can't locate it either in his purse or his pocket-book or his heart or his stomach or his head. The *wholeness* of a man is his soul. Not merely that nice little comfortable bit which Benjamin marks out.

30 It's a queer thing is a man's soul. It is the whole of him. Which means it is the unknown him, as well as the known. It seems to me just funny, professors and Benjamins fixing the functions of the soul. Why, the soul of man is a vast forest, and all Benjamin intended was a neat back garden. And we've all got to fit into his kitchen garden scheme of things. Hail Columbia!

31 The soul of man is a dark forest. The Hercynian Wood that scared the Romans so, and out of which came the white-skinned hordes of the next civilization.

32 Who knows what will come out of the soul of man? The soul of man is a dark vast forest, with wild life in it. Think of Benjamin fencing it off!

33 Oh, but Benjamin fenced a little tract that he called the soul of man, and proceeded to get it into cultivation. Providence, forsooth! And they think that bit of barbed wire is going to keep us in pound for ever? More fools they.

34 This is Benjamin's barbed wire fence. He made himself a list of virtues, which he trotted inside like a grey nag in a paddock.

1. TEMPERANCE

35 Eat not to fulness; drink not to elevation.

2. SILENCE

36 Speak not but what may benefit others or yourself; avoid trifling conversation.

3. ORDER

37 Let all your things have their places; let each part of your business have its time.

4. RESOLUTION

38 Resolve to perform what you ought; perform without fail what you resolve.

5. FRUGALITY

39 Make no expense but to do good to others or yourself—i.e., waste nothing.

6. INDUSTRY

40 Lose no time, be always employed in something useful; cut off all unnecessary action.

7. SINCERITY

41 Use no hurtful deceit; think innocently and justly, and, if you speak, speak accordingly.

8. JUSTICE

42 Wrong none by doing injuries, or omitting the benefits that are your duty.

9. MODERATION

43 Avoid extremes, forbear resenting injuries as much as you think they deserve.

10. CLEANLINESS

44 Tolerate no uncleanliness in body, clothes, or habitation.

11. TRANQUILLITY

45 Be not disturbed at trifles, or at accidents common or unavoidable.

12. CHASTITY

46 Rarely use venery but for health and offspring, never to dulness, weakness, or the injury of your own or another's peace or reputation.

13. HUMILITY

47 Imitate Jesus and Socrates.

48 A Quaker friend told Franklin that he, Benjamin, was generally considered proud, so Benjamin put in the Humility touch as an afterthought. The amusing part is the sort of humility it displays. "Imitate Jesus and Socrates," and mind you don't outshine either of these two. One can just imagine Socrates and Alcibiades roaring in their cups over Philadelphian Benjamin, and Jesus looking at him a little puzzled, and murmuring: "Aren't you wise in your own conceit, Ben?"

49 "Henceforth be masterless," retorts Ben. "Be ye each one his own master unto himself, and don't let even the Lord put His spoke in." "Each man his own master" is but a puffing up of masterlessness.

50 Well, the first of Americans practised this enticing list with assiduity, setting a national example. He had the virtues in columns, and gave himself good and bad marks according as he thought his behaviour deserved. Pity these conduct charts are lost to us. He only remarks that Order was his stumbling block. He could not learn to be neat and tidy.

51 Isn't it nice to have nothing worse to confess?

52 He was a little model, was Benjamin. Doctor Franklin. Snuff-coloured little man! Immortal soul and all!

53 The immortal soul part was a sort of cheap insurance policy.

54 Benjamin had no concern, really, with the immortal soul. He was too busy with social man.

1. He swept and lighted the streets of young Philadelphia.
2. He invented electrical appliances.
3. He was the centre of a moralizing club in Philadelphia, and he wrote the moral humorisms of Poor Richard.
4. He was a member of all the important councils of Philadelphia, and then of the American colonies.
5. He won the cause of American Independence at the French Court, and was the economic father of the United States.

55 Now what more can you want of a man? And yet he is *infra dig.*, even in Philadelphia.

56 I admire him. I admire his sturdy courage first of all, then his sagacity, then his glimpsing into the thunders of electricity, then his common-sense humour. All the qualities of a great man, and never more than a great citizen. Middle-sized, sturdy, snuff-coloured Doctor Franklin, one of the soundest citizens that ever trod or "used venery".

57 I do not like him.

58 And, by the way, I always thought books of Venery were about hunting deer.

59 There is a certain earnest naïveté about him. Like a child. And like a little old man. He has again become as a little child, always as wise as his grandfather, or wiser.

60 Perhaps, as I say, the most complete citizen that ever "used venery."

61 Printer, philosopher, scientist, author and patriot, impeccable husband and citizen, why isn't he an archetype?

62 Pioneer, Oh Pioneers! Benjamin was one of the greatest pioneers of the United States. Yet we just can't do with him.

63 What's wrong with him then? Or what's wrong with us?

64 I can remember, when I was a little boy, my father used to buy a scrubby yearly almanac with the sun and moon and stars on the cover. And it used to prophesy bloodshed and famine. But also crammed in corners it had little anecdotes and humorisms, with a moral tag. And I used to have my little priggish laugh at the woman who counted her chickens before they were hatched and so forth, and I was convinced that honesty was the best policy, also a little priggishly. The author of these bits was Poor Richard, and Poor Richard was Benjamin Franklin, writing in Philadelphia well over a hundred years before.

65 And probably I haven't got over those Poor Richard tags yet. I rankle still with them. They are thorns in young flesh.

66 Because, although I still believe that honesty is the best policy, I dislike policy altogether; though it is just as well not to count your chickens before they are hatched, it's still more hateful to count them with gloating when they *are* hatched. It has taken me many years and countless smarts to get out of that barbed wire moral enclosure that Poor Richard rigged up. Here am I now in tatters and scratched to ribbons, sitting in the middle of Benjamin's America looking at the barbed wire, and the fat sheep crawling under the fence to get fat outside, and the watchdogs yelling at the gate lest by chance anyone should get out by the proper exit. Oh America! Oh Benjamin! And I just utter a long loud curse against Benjamin and the American corral.

67 Moral America! Most moral Benjamin. Sound, satisfied Ben!

68 He had to go to the frontiers of his State to settle some disturbance among the Indians. On this occasion he writes:

> "We found that they had made a great bonfire in the middle of the square; they were all drunk, men and women quarrelling and fighting. Their dark-coloured bodies, half-naked, seen only by the gloomy light of the bonfire, running after and beating one another with fire-brands, accompanied by their horrid yellings, formed a scene the most resembling our ideas of hell that could well be imagined. There was no appeasing the tumult, and we retired to our lodging. At midnight a number of them came thundering at our door, demanding more rum, of which we took no notice.
>
> "The next day, sensible they had misbehaved in giving us that disturbance, they sent three of their counsellors to make their apology. The orator acknowledged the fault, but laid it upon the rum, and then endeavoured to excuse the rum by saying: 'The Great Spirit, who made all things, made everything for some use; and whatever he designed anything for, that use it should always be put to. Now, when he had made the rum, he said: "Let this be for the Indians to get drunk with." And it must be so.'
>
> "And, indeed, if it be the design of Providence to extirpate these savages in order

to make room for the cultivators of the earth, it seems not improbable that rum may be the appointed means. It has already annihilated all the tribes who formerly inhabited all the seacoast. . . ."

69 This, from the good doctor with such suave complacency, is a little disenchanting. Almost too good to be true.

70 But there you are! The barbed wire fence. "Extirpate these savages in order to make room for the cultivators of the earth." Oh, Benjamin Franklin! He even "used venery" as a cultivator of seed.

71 Cultivate the earth, ye gods! The Indians did that, as much as they needed. And they left off there. Who built Chicago? Who cultivated the earth until it spawned Pittsburgh, Pa?

72 The moral issue! Just look at it! Cultivation included. If it's a mere choice of Kultur or cultivation, I give it up.

73 Which brings us right back to our question, what's wrong with Benjamin, that we can't stand him? Or else, what's wrong with us, that we find fault with such a paragon?

74 Man is a moral animal. All right. I am a moral animal. And I'm going to remain such. I'm not going to be turned into a virtuous little automaton as Benjamin would have me. "This is good, that is bad. Turn the little handle and let the good tap flow," saith Benjamin, and all America with him. "But first of all extirpate those savages who are always turning on the bad tap."

75 I am a moral animal. But I am not a moral machine. I don't work with a little set of handles or levers. The Temperance - silence - order - resolution - frugality - industry - sincerity - justice - moderation - cleanliness - tranquillity - chastity - humility keyboard is not going to get me going. I'm really not just an automatic piano with a moral Benjamin getting tunes out of me.

76 Here's my creed, against Benjamin's. This is what I believe:

"That I am I."

"That my soul is a dark forest."

"That my known self will never be more than a little clearing in the forest."

"That gods, strange gods, come forth from the forest into the clearing of my known self, and then go back."

"That I must have the courage to let them come and go."

"That I will never let mankind put anything over me, but that I will try always to recognize and submit to the gods in me and the gods in other men and women."

77 There is my creed. He who runs may read. He who prefers to crawl, or to go by gasoline, can call it rot.

78 Then for a "list." It is rather fun to play at Benjamin.

1. TEMPERANCE

79 Eat and carouse with Bacchus, or munch dry bread with Jesus, but don't sit down without one of the gods.

2. SILENCE

80 Be still when you have nothing to say; when genuine passion moves you, say what you've got to say, and say it hot.

3. ORDER

81 Know that you are responsible to the gods inside you and to the men in whom the gods are manifest. Recognize your superiors and your inferiors, according to the gods. This is the root of all order.

4. RESOLUTION

82 Resolve to abide by your own deepest promptings, and to sacrifice the smaller thing to the greater. Kill when you must, and be killed the same: the *must* coming from the gods inside you, or from the men in whom you recognize the Holy Ghost.

5. FRUGALITY

83 Demand nothing; accept what you see fit. Don't waste your pride or squander your emotion.

6. INDUSTRY

84 Lose no time with ideals; serve the Holy Ghost; never serve mankind.

7. SINCERITY

85 To be sincere is to remember that I am I, and that the other man is not me.

8. JUSTICE

86 The only justice is to follow the sincere intuition of the soul, angry or gentle. Anger is just, and pity is just, but judgment is never just.

9. MODERATION

87 Beware of absolutes. There are many gods.

10. CLEANLINESS

88 Don't be too clean. It impoverishes the blood.

11. TRANQUILLITY

89 The soul has many motions, many gods come and go. Try and find your deepest issue, in every confusion, and abide by that. Obey the man in whom you recognize the Holy Ghost; command when your honour comes to command.

12. CHASTITY

90 Never "use" venery at all. Follow your passional impulse, if it be answered in the other being; but never have any motive in mind, neither offspring nor health nor even pleasure, nor even service. Only know that "venery" is of the great gods. An offering-up of yourself to the very great gods, the dark ones, and nothing else.

13. HUMILITY

91 See all men and women according to the Holy Ghost that is within them. Never yield before the barren.

92 There's my list. I have been trying dimly to realize it for a long time, and only America and old Benjamin have at last goaded me into trying to formulate it.

93 And now I, at least, know why I can't stand Benjamin. He tries to take away my wholeness and my dark forest, my freedom. For how can any man be free,

without an illimitable background? And Benjamin tries to shove me into a barbed wire paddock and make me grow potatoes or Chicagoes.

94 And how can I be free, without gods that come and go? But Benjamin won't let anything exist except my useful fellow men, and I'm sick of them; as for his Godhead, his Providence, He is Head of nothing except a vast heavenly store that keeps every imaginable line of goods, from victrolas to cat-o'-nine tails.

95 And how can any man be free without a soul of his own, that he believes in and won't sell at any price? But Benjamin doesn't let me have a soul of my own. He says I am nothing but a servant of mankind—galley-slave I call it—and if I don't get my wages here below—that is, if Mr. Pierpont Morgan or Mr. Nosey Hebrew or the grand United States Government, the great US, US or SOMEOFUS, manages to scoop in my bit, along with their lump—why, never mind, I shall get my wages HEREAFTER.

96 Oh Benjamin! Oh Binjum! You do NOT suck me in any longer.

97 And why, oh why should the snuff-coloured little trap have wanted to take us all in? Why did he do it?

98 Out of sheer human cussedness, in the first place. We do all like to get things inside a barbed wire corral. Especially our fellow men. We love to round them up inside the barbed wire enclosure of FREEDOM, and make 'em work. "*Work, you free jewel, WORK!*" shouts the liberator, cracking his whip. Benjamin, I will not work. I do not choose to be a free democrat. I am absolutely a servant of my own Holy Ghost.

99 Sheer cussedness! But there was as well the salt of a subtler purpose. Benjamin was just in his eyeholes—to use an English vulgarism, meaning he was just delighted—when he was at Paris judiciously milking money out of the French monarchy for the overthrow of all monarchy. If you want to ride your horse to somewhere you must put a bit in his mouth. And Benjamin wanted to ride his horse so that it would upset the whole apple-cart of the old masters. He wanted the whole European apple-cart upset. So he had to put a strong bit in the mouth of his ass.

100 "Henceforth be masterless."

101 That is, he had to break-in the human ass completely, so that much more might be broken, in the long run. For the moment it was the British Government that had to have a hole knocked in it. The first real hole it ever had: the breach of the American rebellion.

102 Benjamin, in his sagacity, knew that the breaking of the old world was a long process. In the depths of his own under-consciousness he hated England, he hated Europe, he hated the whole corpus of the European being. He wanted to be American. But you can't change your nature and mode of consciousness like changing your shoes. It is a gradual shedding. Years must go by, and centuries must elapse before you have finished. Like a son escaping from the domination of his parents. The escape is not just one rupture. It is a long and half-secret process.

103 So with the American. He was a European when he first went over the Atlantic. He is in the main a recreant European still. From Benjamin Franklin to Woodrow Wilson may be a long stride, but it is a stride along the same road. There

is no new road. The same old road, become dreary and futile. Theoretic and materialistic.

104 Why then did Benjamin set up this dummy of a perfect citizen as a pattern to America? Of course, he did it in perfect good faith, as far as he knew. He thought it simply was the true ideal. But what we *think* we do is not very important. We never really know what we are doing. Either we are materialistic instruments, like Benjamin, or we move in the gesture of creation, from our deepest self, usually unconscious. We are only the actors, we are never wholly the authors of our own deeds or works. IT is the author, the unknown inside us or outside us. The best we can do is to try to hold ourselves in unison with the deeps which are inside us. And the worst we can do is to try to have things our own way, when we run counter to IT, and in the long run get our knuckles rapped for our presumption.

105 So Benjamin contriving money out of the Court of France. He was contriving the first steps of the overthrow of all Europe, France included. You can never have a new thing without breaking an old. Europe happens to be the old thing. America, unless the people in America assert themselves too much in opposition to the inner gods, should be the new thing. The new thing is the death of the old. But you can't cut the throat of an epoch. You've got to steal the life from it through several centuries.

106 And Benjamin worked for this both directly and indirectly. Directly, at the Court of France, making a small but very dangerous hole in the side of England, through which hole Europe has by now almost bled to death. And indirectly in Philadelphia, setting up this unlovely, snuff-coloured little ideal, or automaton, of a pattern American. The pattern American, this dry, moral, utilitarian little democrat, has done more to ruin the old Europe than any Russian nihilist. He has done it by slow attrition, like a son who has stayed at home and obeyed his parents, all the while silently hating their authority, and silently, in his soul, destroying not only their authority but their whole existence. For the American spiritually stayed at home in Europe. The spiritual home of America was, and still is, Europe. This is the galling bondage, in spite of several billions of heaped-up gold. Your heaps of gold are only so many muck-heaps, America, and will remain so till you become a reality to yourselves.

107 All this Americanizing and mechanizing has been for the purpose of overthrowing the past. And now look at America, tangled in her own barbed wire, and mastered by her own machines. Absolutely got down by her own barbed wire of shalt-nots, and shut up fast in her own "productive" machines like millions of squirrels running in millions of cages. It is just a farce.

108 Now is your chance, Europe. Now let Hell loose and get your own back, and paddle your own canoe on a new sea, while clever America lies on her muck-heaps of gold, strangled in her own barbed wire of shalt-not ideals and shalt-not moralisms. While she goes out to work like millions of squirrels in millions of cages. Production!

109 Let Hell loose, and get your own back, Europe!

(1923)

QUESTIONS

Thought and Structure

1. What, specifically, does Lawrence object to about Franklin's ideas and values?
2. Is Lawrence fair to Franklin? Does he accurately represent what Franklin believes and thinks?
3. Lawrence answers Franklin's list of virtues with a list of his own. Whose list do you prefer—and why? Whose writing do you find more appealing? More convincing? Why?
4. Explain how Lawrence organized this essay. Divide it into sections and comment on the logic and effect of their arrangement.
5. Lawrence uses Franklin to press an attack on something else. What? Where does he launch this attack?

Style and Strategy

6. Perhaps the most striking thing about Lawrence's response to Franklin is its tone. How would you describe this tone?
7. One of the ways Lawrence achieves his peculiar tone is by employing sentence fragments and short sentences. Reread paragraphs 1–10 aloud to see and hear the effect of such sentences.
8. Also contributing to his special tone is Lawrence's heavy reliance on interrogative sentences. What effects do his questions have in paragraphs 1–6?
9. What is the effect of Lawrence's use of parenthetical sentences in paragraphs 12–23?
10. What words and phrases does Lawrence use when referring to Franklin himself? Why? What is their tone?

SUGGESTIONS FOR WRITING

A. Write your own plan for self-improvement, commenting on its salient points. You can take a serious or a comic approach.

B. Imitate Lawrence by writing an essay attacking something you've read, something you strongly disagree with. Try to catch Lawrence's tone. (See the questions above, especially 6–10.)

C. Write an essay defending Franklin against Lawrence's attack. If you like, imitate Franklin's style. (Perhaps you can imagine that you are Franklin himself rebutting Lawrence.)

The Horse Dealer's Daughter

1 "Well, Mabel, and what are you going to do with yourself?" asked Joe, with foolish flippancy. He felt quite safe himself. Without listening for an answer, he turned aside, worked a grain of tobacco to the tip of his tongue, and spat it out. He did not care about anything, since he felt safe himself.

2 The three brothers and the sister sat round the desolate breakfast table,

attempting some sort of desultory consultation. The morning's post had given the final tap to the family fortune, and all was over. The dreary dining-room itself, with its heavy mahogany furniture, looked as if it were waiting to be done away with.

3 But the consultation amounted to nothing. There was a strange air of ineffectuality about the three men, as they sprawled at table, smoking and reflecting vaguely on their own condition. The girl was alone, a rather short, sullen-looking young woman of twenty-seven. She did not share the same life as her brothers. She would have been good-looking, save for the impassive fixity of her face, "bull-dog," as her brothers called it.

4 There was a confused tramping of horses' feet outside. The three men all sprawled round in their chairs to watch. Beyond the dark hollybushes that separated the strip of lawn from the high-road, they could see a cavalcade of shire horses swinging out of their own yard, being taken for exercise. This was the last time. These were the last horses that would go through their hands. The young men watched with critical, callous look. They were all frightened at the collapse of their lives, and the sense of disaster in which they were involved left them no inner freedom.

5 Yet they were three fine, well-set fellows enough. Joe, the eldest, was a man of thirty-three, broad and handsome in a hot, flushed way. His face was red, he twisted his black moustache over a thick finger, his eyes were shallow and restless. He had a sensual way of uncovering his teeth when he laughed, and his bearing was stupid. Now he watched the horses with a glazed look of helplessness in his eyes, a certain stupor of downfall.

6 The great draught-horses swung past. They were tied head to tail, four of them, and they heaved along to where a lane branched off from the high-road, planting their great hoofs floutingly in the fine black mud, swinging their great rounded haunches sumptuously, and trotting a few sudden steps as they were led into the lane, round the corner. Every movement showed a massive, slumbrous strength, and a stupidity which held them in subjection. The groom at the head looked back, jerking the leading rope. And the cavalcade moved out of sight up the lane, the tail of the last horse bobbed up tight and stiff, held out taut from the swinging great haunches as they rocked behind the hedges in a motion like sleep.

7 Joe watched with glazed hopeless eyes. The horses were almost like his own body to him. He felt he was done for now. Luckily he was engaged to a woman as old as himself, and therefore her father, who was steward of a neighbouring estate, would provide him with a job. He would marry and go into harness. His life was over, he would be a subject animal now.

8 He turned uneasily aside, the retreating steps of the horses echoing in his ears. Then, with foolish restlessness, he reached for the scraps of bacon-rind from the plates, and making a faint whistling sound, flung them to the terrier that lay against the fender. He watched the dog swallow them, and waited till the creature looked into his eyes. Then a faint grin came on his face, and in a high, foolish voice he said:

9 "You won't get much more bacon, shall you, you little bitch?"

10 The dog faintly and dismally wagged its tail, then lowered its haunches, circled round, and lay down again.

11 There was another helpless silence at the table. Joe sprawled uneasily in his seat, not willing to go till the family conclave was dissolved. Fred Henry, the second brother, was erect, clean-limbed, alert. He had watched the passing of the horses with more sangfroid. If he was an animal, like Joe, he was an animal which controls, not one which is controlled. He was master of any horse, and he carried himself with a well-tempered air of mastery. But he was not master of the situations of life. He pushed his coarse brown moustache upwards, off his lip, and glanced irritably at his sister, who sat impassive and inscrutable.

12 "You'll go and stop with Lucy for a bit, shan't you?" he asked. The girl did not answer.

13 "I don't see what else you can do," persisted Fred Henry.

14 "Go as a skivvy," Joe interpolated laconically.

15 The girl did not move a muscle.

16 "If I was her, I should go in for training for a nurse," said Malcolm, the youngest of them all. He was the baby of the family, a young man of twenty-two, with a fresh, jaunty *museau.*

17 But Mabel did not take any notice of him. They had talked at her and round her for so many years, that she hardly heard them at all.

18 The marble clock on the mantelpiece softly chimed the half-hour, the dog rose uneasily from the hearthrug and looked at the party at the breakfast table. But still they sat on in ineffectual conclave.

19 "Oh, all right," said Joe suddenly, apropos of nothing. "I'll get a move on."

20 He pushed back his chair, straddled his knees with a downward jerk, to get them free, in horsey fashion, and went to the fire. Still he did not go out of the room; he was curious to know what the others would do or say. He began to charge his pipe, looking down at the dog and saying, in a high, affected voice:

21 "Going wi' me? Going wi' me are ter? Tha'rt goin' further than the counts on just now, dost hear?"

22 The dog faintly wagged its tail, the man stuck out his jaw and covered his pipe with his hands, and puffed intently, losing himself in the tobacco, looking down all the while at the dog with an absent brown eye. The dog looked up at him in mournful distrust. Joe stood with his knees stuck out, in real horsey fashion.

23 "Have you had a letter from Lucy?" Fred Henry asked of his sister.

24 "Last week," came the neutral reply.

25 "And what does she say?"

26 There was no answer.

27 "Does she *ask* you to go and stop there?" persisted Fred Henry.

28 "She says I can if I like."

29 "Well, then, you'd better. Tell her you'll come on Monday."

30 This was received in silence.

31 "That's what you'll do then, is it?" said Fred Henry, in some exasperation.

32 But she made no answer. There was a silence of futility and irritation in the room. Malcolm grinned fatuously.

33 "You'll have to make up your mind between now and next Wednesday," said Joe loudly, "or else find yourself lodgings on the kerbstone."

34 The face of the young woman darkened, but she sat on immutable.

35 "Here's Jack Fergusson!" exclaimed Malcolm, who was looking aimlessly out of the window.

36 "Where?" exclaimed Joe, loudly.

37 "Just gone past."

38 "Coming in?"

39 Malcolm craned his neck to see the gate.

40 "Yes," he said.

41 There was a silence. Mabel sat on like one condemned, at the head of the table. Then a whistle was heard from the kitchen. The dog got up and barked sharply. Joe opened the door and shouted:

42 "Come on."

43 After a moment a young man entered. He was muffled up in overcoat and a purple woollen scarf, and his tweed cap, which he did not remove, was pulled down on his head. He was of medium height, his face was rather long and pale, his eyes looked tired.

44 "Hello, Jack! Well, Jack!" exclaimed Malcolm and Joe. Fred Henry merely said, "Jack."

45 "What's doing?" asked the newcomer, evidently addressing Fred Henry.

46 "Same. We've got to be out by Wednesday. Got a cold?"

47 "I have—got it bad, too."

48 "Why don't you stop in?"

49 "*Me* stop in? When I can't stand on my legs, perhaps I shall have a chance." The young man spoke huskily. He had a slight Scotch accent.

50 "It's a knock-out, isn't it?" said Joe, boisterously, "if a doctor goes round croaking with a cold. Looks bad for the patients, doesn't it?"

51 The young doctor looked at him slowly.

52 "Anything the matter with *you,* then?" he asked sarcastically.

53 "Not as I know of. Damn your eyes, I hope not. Why?"

54 "I thought you were very concerned about the patients, wondered if you might be one yourself."

55 "Damn it, no, I've never been patient to no flaming doctor, and hope I never shall be," returned Joe.

56 At this point Mabel rose from the table, and they all seemed to become aware of her existence. She began putting the dishes together. The young doctor looked at her, but did not address her. He had not greeted her. She went out of the room with the tray, her face impassive and unchanged.

57 "When are you off then, all of you?" asked the doctor.

58 "I'm catching the eleven-forty," replied Malcolm. "Are you goin' down wi' th' trap, Joe?"

59 "Yes, I've told you I am going down wi' th' trap, haven't I?"

60 "We'd better be getting her in then. So long, Jack, if I don't see you before I go," said Malcolm, shaking hands.

61 He went out, followed by Joe, who seemed to have his tail between his legs.

62 "Well, this is the devil's own," exclaimed the doctor, when he was left alone with Fred Henry. "Going before Wednesday, are you."

63 "That's the orders," replied the other.

64 "Where, to Northampton?"

65 "That's it."

66 "The devil!" exclaimed Fergusson, with quiet chagrin.

67 And there was silence between the two.

68 "All settled up, are you?" asked Fergusson.

69 "About."

70 There was another pause.

71 "Well, I shall miss yer, Freddy, boy," said the young doctor.

72 "And I shall miss thee, Jack," returned the other.

73 "Miss you like hell," mused the doctor.

74 Fred Henry turned aside. There was nothing to say. Mabel came in again, to finish clearing the table.

75 "What are *you* going to do, then, Miss Pervin?" asked Fergusson. "Going to your sister's, are you?"

76 Mabel looked at him with her steady, dangerous eyes, that always made him uncomfortable, unsettling his superficial ease.

77 "No," she said.

78 "Well, what in the name of fortune are *you* going to do? Say what you mean to do," cried Fred Henry, with futile intensity.

79 But she only averted her head, and continued her work. She folded the white table-cloth, and put on the chenille cloth.

80 "The sulkiest bitch that ever trod!" muttered her brother.

81 But she finished her task with perfectly impassive face, the young doctor watching her interestedly all the while. Then she went out.

82 Fred Henry stared after her, clenching his lips, his blue eyes fixing in sharp antagonism, as he made a grimace of sour exasperation.

83 "You could bray her into bits, and that's all you'd get out of her," he said in a small, narrowed tone.

84 The doctor smiled faintly.

85 "What's she *going* to do, then?" he asked.

86 "Strike me if I know!" returned the other.

87 There was a pause. Then the doctor stirred.

88 "I'll be seeing you to-night, shall I?" he said to his friend.

89 "Ay—where's it to be? Are we going over to Jessdale?"

90 "I don't know. I've got such a cold on me. I'll come round to the Moon and Stars, anyway."

91 "Let Lizzie and May miss their night for once, eh?"

92 "That's it—if I feel as I do now."

93 "All's one—"

94 The two young men went through the passage and down to the back door together. The house was large, but it was servantless now, and desolate. At the back was a small bricked house-yard, and beyond that a big square, gravelled fine and red, and having stables on two sides. Sloping, dank, winter-dark fields stretched away on the open sides.

95 But the stables were empty. Joseph Pervin, the father of the family, had been a man of no education, who had become a fairly large horse dealer. The stables had

been full of horses, there was a great turmoil and come-and-go of horses and of dealers and grooms. Then the kitchen was full of servants. But of late things had declined. The old man had married a second time, to retrieve his fortunes. Now he was dead and everything was gone to the dogs, there was nothing but debt and threatening.

96 For months, Mabel had been servantless in the big house, keeping the home together in penury for her ineffectual brothers. She had kept house for ten years. But previously it was with unstinted means. Then, however brutal and coarse everything was, the sense of money had kept her proud, confident. The men might be foul-mouthed, the women in the kitchen might have bad reputations, her brothers might have illegitimate children. But so long as there was money, the girl felt herself established and brutally proud, reserved.

97 No company came to the house, save dealers and coarse men. Mabel had no associates of her own sex, after her sister went away. But she did not mind. She went regularly to church, she attended to her father. And she lived in the memory of her mother, who had died when she was fourteen, and whom she had loved. She had loved her father, too, in a different way, depending upon him, and feeling secure in him, until at the age of fifty-four he married again. And then she had set hard against him. Now he had died and left them all hopelessly in debt.

98 She had suffered badly during the period of poverty. Nothing, however, could shake the curious sullen, animal pride that dominated each member of the family. Now, for Mabel, the end had come. Still she would not cast about her. She would follow her own way just the same. She would always hold the keys of her own situation. Mindless and persistent, she endured from day to day. What should she think? Why should she answer anybody? It was enough that this was the end and there was no way out. She need not pass any more darkly along the main street of the small town, avoiding every eye. She need not demean herself any more, going into the shops and buying the cheapest food. This was at an end. She thought of nobody, not even of herself. Mindless and persistent, she seemed in a sort of ecstasy to be coming nearer to her fulfillment, her own glorification, approaching her dead mother, who was glorified.

99 In the afternoon she took a little bag, with shears and sponge and a small scrubbing brush, and went out. It was a grey, wintry day, with saddened, dark green fields and an atmosphere blackened by the smoke of foundries not far off. She went quickly, darkly along the causeway, heeding nobody, through the town to the churchyard.

100 There she always felt secure, as if no one could see her, although as a matter of fact she was exposed to the stare of every one who passed along under the churchyard wall. Nevertheless, once under the shadow of the great looming church, among the graves, she felt immune from the world, reserved within the thick churchyard wall as in another country.

101 Carefully she clipped the grass from the grave, and arranged the pinky white, small chrysanthemums in the tin cross. When this was done, she took an empty jar from a neighbouring grave, brought water, and carefully, most scrupulously sponged the marble head-stone and the coping-stone.

102 It gave her sincere satisfaction to do this. She felt in immediate contact with

the world of her mother. She took minute pains, went through the park in a state bordering on pure happiness, as if in performing this task she came into a subtle, intimate connection with her mother. For the life she followed here in the world was far less real than the world of death she inherited from her mother.

103 The doctor's house was just by the church. Fergusson, being a mere hired assistant, was slave to the country-side. As he hurried now to attend to the out-patients in the surgery, glancing across the graveyard with his quick eye, he saw the girl at her task at the grave. She seemed so intent and remote, it was like looking into another world. Some mystical element was touched in him. He slowed down as he walked, watching her as if spell-bound.

104 She lifted her eyes, feeling him looking. Their eyes met. And each looked away again at once, each feeling, in some way, found out by the other. He lifted his cap and passed on down the road. There remained distinct in his consciousness, like a vision, the memory of her face, lifted from the tombstone in the churchyard, and looking at him with slow, large, portentous eyes. It *was* portentous, her face. It seemed to mesmerize him. There was a heavy power in her eyes which laid hold of his whole being, as if he had drunk some powerful drug. He had been feeling weak and done before. Now the life came back into him, he felt delivered from his own fretted, daily self.

105 He finished his duties at the surgery as quickly as might be, hastily filling up the bottle of the waiting people with cheap drugs. Then, in perpetual haste, he set off again to visit several cases in another part of his round, before tea-time. At all times he preferred to walk if he could, but particularly when he was not well. He fancied the motion restored him.

106 The afternoon was falling. It was grey, deadened, and wintry, with a slow, moist, heavy coldness sinking in and deadening all the faculties. But why should he think or notice? He hastily climbed the hill and turned across the dark green fields, following the black cinder-track. In the distance, across a shallow dip in the country, the small town was clustered like smouldering ash, a tower, a spire, a heap of low, raw, extinct houses. And on the nearest fringe of the town, sloping into the dip, was Oldmeadow, the Pervins' house. He could see the stables and the outbuildings distinctly, as they lay towards him on the slope. Well, he would not go there many more times! Another resource would be lost to him, another place gone: the only company he cared for in the alien, ugly little town he was losing. Nothing but work, drudgery, constant hastening from dwelling to dwelling among the colliers and the ironworkers. It wore him out, but at the same time he had a craving for it. It was a stimulant to him to be in the homes of the working people, moving as it were through the innermost body of their life. His nerves were excited and gratified. He could come so near, into the very lives of the rough, inarticulate, powerfully emotional men and women. He grumbled, he said he hated the hellish hole. But as a matter of fact it excited him, the contact with the rough, strongly-feeling people was a stimulant applied direct to his nerves.

107 Below Oldmeadow, in the green, shallow, soddened hollow of fields lay a square, deep pond. Roving across the landscape, the doctor's quick eye detected a figure in black passing through the gate of the field, down towards the pond. He

looked again. It would be Mabel Pervin. His mind suddenly became alive and attentive.

108 Why was she going down there? He pulled up on the path on the slope above, and stood staring. He could just make sure of the small black figure moving in the hollow of the failing day. He seemed to see her in the midst of such obscurity, that he was like a clairvoyant, seeing rather with the mind's eye than with ordinary sight. Yet he could see her positively enough, whilst he kept his eye attentive. He felt, if he looked away from her, in the thick, ugly falling dusk, he would lose her altogether.

109 He followed her minutely as she moved, direct and intent, like something transmitted rather than stirring in voluntary activity, straight down the field towards the pond. There she stood on the bank for a moment. She never raised her head. Then she waded slowly into the water.

110 He stood motionless as the small black figure walked slowly and deliberately towards the centre of the pond, very slowly, gradually moving deeper into the motionless water, and still moving forward as the water got up to her breast. Then he could see her no more in the dusk of the dead afternoon.

111 "There!" he exclaimed. "Would you believe it?"

112 And he hastened straight down, running over the wet, soddened fields, pushing through the hedges, down into the depression of callous wintry obscurity. It took him several minutes to come to the pond. He stood on the bank, breathing heavily. He could see nothing. His eyes seemed to penetrate the dead water. Yes, perhaps that was the dark shadow of her black clothing beneath the surface of the water.

113 He slowly ventured into the pond. The bottom was deep, soft clay, he sank in, and the water clasped dead cold round his legs. As he stirred he could smell the cold, rotten clay that fouled up into the water. It was objectionable in his lungs. Still, repelled and yet not heeding, he moved deeper into the pond. The cold water rose over his thighs, over his loins, upon his abdomen. The lower part of his body was all sunk in the hideous cold element. And the bottom was so deeply soft and uncertain, he was afraid of pitching with his mouth underneath. He could not swim, and was afraid.

114 He crouched a little, spreading his hands under the water and moving them round, trying to feel for her. The dead cold pond swayed upon his chest. He moved again, a little deeper, and again, with his hands underneath, he felt all around the water. And he touched her clothing. But it evaded his fingers. He made a desperate effort to grasp it.

115 And so doing he lost his balance and went under, horribly, suffocating in the foul earthy water, struggling madly for a few moments. At last, after what seemed an eternity, he got his footing, rose again into the air and looked around. He gasped, and knew he was in the world. Then he looked at the water. She had risen near him. He grasped her clothing, and drawing her nearer, turned to take his way to land again.

116 He went very slowly, carefully, absorbed in the slow progress. He rose higher, climbing out of the pond. The water was now only about his legs; he was thankful, full of relief to be out of the clutches of the pond. He lifted her and staggered on to the bank, out of the horror of wet, grey clay.

117 He laid her down on the bank. She was quite unconscious and running with

water. He made the water come from her mouth, he worked to restore her. He did not have to work very long before he could feel the breathing begin again in her; she was breathing naturally. He worked a little longer. He could feel her live beneath his hands; she was coming back. He wiped her face, wrapped her in his overcoat, looked round into the dim, dark grey world, then lifted her and staggered down the bank and across the fields.

118 It seemed an unthinkably long way, and his burden so heavy he felt he would never get to the house. But at last he was in the stable-yard, and then in the house-yard. He opened the door and went into the house. In the kitchen he laid her down on the hearthrug, and called. The house was empty. But the fire was burning in the grate.

119 Then again he kneeled to attend to her. She was breathing regularly, her eyes were wide open and as if conscious, but there seemed something missing in her look. She was conscious in herself, but unconscious of her surroundings.

120 He ran upstairs, took blankets from a bed, and put them before the fire to warm. Then he removed her saturated, earthy-smelling clothing, rubbed her dry with a towel, and wrapped her naked in the blankets. Then he went into the dining-room, to look for spirits. There was a little whisky. He drank a gulp himself, and put some into her mouth.

121 The effect was instantaneous. She looked full into his face, as if she had been seeing him for some time, and yet had only just become conscious of him.

122 "Dr. Fergusson?" she said.

123 "What?" he answered.

124 He was divesting himself of his coat, intending to find some dry clothing upstairs. He could not bear the smell of the dead, clayey water, and he was mortally afraid for his own health.

125 "What did I do?" she asked.

126 "Walked into the pond," he replied. He had begun to shudder like one sick, and could hardly attend to her. Her eyes remained full-on him, he seemed to be going dark in his mind, looking back at her helplessly. The shuddering became quieter in him, his life came back in him, dark and unknowing, but strong again.

127 "Was I out of my mind?" she asked, while her eyes were fixed on him all the time.

128 "Maybe, for the moment," he replied. He felt quiet, because his strength had come back. The strange fretful strain had left him.

129 "Am I out of my mind now?" she asked.

130 "Are you?" he reflected a moment. "No," he answered truthfully. "I don't see that you are." He turned his face aside. He was afraid now, because he felt dazed, and felt dimly that her power was stronger than his, in this issue. And she continued to look at him fixedly all the time. "Can you tell me where I shall find some dry things to put on?" he asked.

131 "Did you dive into the pond for me?" she asked.

132 "No," he answered. "I walked in. But I went in overhead as well."

133 There was silence for a moment. He hesitated. He very much wanted to go upstairs to get into dry clothing. But there was another desire in him. And she seemed to hold him. His will seemed to have gone to sleep, and left him, standing

there slack before her. But he felt warm inside himself. He did not shudder at all, though his clothes were sodden on him.

134 "Why did you?" she asked.

135 "Because I didn't want you to do such a foolish thing," he said.

136 "It wasn't foolish," she said, still gazing at him as she lay on the floor, with a sofa cushion under her head. "It was the right thing to do. *I* knew best, then."

137 "I'll go and shift these wet things," he said. But still he had not the power to move out of her presence, until she sent him. It was as if she had the life of his body in her hands, and he could not extricate himself. Or perhaps he did not want to.

138 Suddenly she sat up. Then she became aware of her own immediate condition. She felt the blankets about her, she knew her own limbs. For a moment it seemed as if her reason were going. She looked round, with wild eye, as if seeking something. He stood still with fear. She saw her clothing lying scattered.

139 "Who undressed me?" she asked, her eyes resting full and inevitable on his face.

140 "I did," he replied, "to bring you round."

141 For some moments she sat and gazed at him awfully, her lips parted.

142 "Do you love me, then?" she asked.

143 He only stood and stared at her, fascinated. His soul seemed to melt.

144 She shuffled forward on her knees, and put her arms around him, round his legs, as he stood there, pressing her breasts against his knees and thighs, clutching him with strange, convulsive certainty, pressing his thighs against her, drawing him to her face, her throat, as she looked up at him with flaring, humble eyes of transfiguration, triumphant in first possession.

145 "You love me," she murmured, in strange transport, yearning and triumphant and confident. "You love me. I know you love me. I know."

146 And she was passionately kissing his knees, through the wet clothing, passionately and indiscriminately kissing his knees, his legs, as if unaware of everything.

147 He looked down at the tangled wet hair, the wild, bare, animal shoulders. He was amazed, bewildered, and afraid. He had never thought of loving her. He had never wanted to love her. When he rescued her and restored her, he was a doctor, and she was a patient. He had had no single personal thought of her. Nay, this introduction of the personal element was very distasteful to him, a violation of his professional honour. It was horrible to have her there embracing his knees. It was horrible. He revolted from it, violently. And yet—and yet—he had not the power to break away.

148 She looked at him again, with the same supplication of powerful love, and that same transcendent, frightening light of triumph. In view of the delicate flame which seemed to come from her face like a light, he was powerless. And yet he had never intended to love her. He had never intended. And something stubborn in him could not give way.

149 "You love me," she repeated, in a murmur of deep rhapsodic assurance. "You love me."

150 Her hands were drawing him, drawing him down to her. He was afraid, even a little horrified. For he had, really, no intention of loving her. Yet her hands were

drawing him towards her. He put out his hand quickly to steady himself, and grasped her bare shoulder. A flame seemed to burn the hand that grasped her soft shoulder. He had no intention of loving her: his whole will was against his yielding. It was horrible. And yet wonderful was the touch of her shoulders, beautiful the shining of her face. Was she perhaps mad? He had a horror of yielding to her. Yet something in him ached also.

151 He had been staring away at the door, away from her. But his hand remained on her shoulder. She had gone suddenly very still. He looked down at her. Her eyes were now wide with fear, with doubt, the light was dying from her face, a shadow of terrible greyness was returning. He could not bear the touch of her eyes' question upon him, and the look of death behind the question.

152 With an inward groan he gave way, and let his heart yield towards her. A sudden gentle smile came on his face. And her eyes, which never left his face, slowly, slowly filled with tears. He watched the strange water rise in her eyes, like some slow fountain coming up. And his heart seemed to burn and melt away in his breast.

153 He could not bear to look at her any more. He dropped on his knees and caught her head with his arms and pressed her face against his throat. She was very still. His heart, which seemed to have broken, was burning with a kind of agony in his breast. And he felt her slow, hot tears wetting his throat. But he could not move.

154 He felt the hot tears wet his neck and the hollows of his neck, and he remained motionless, suspended through one of man's eternities. Only now it had become indispensable to him to have her face pressed close to him; he could never let her go again. He could never let her head go away from the close clutch of his arm. He wanted to remain like that for ever, with his heart hurting him in a pain that was also life to him. Without knowing, he was looking down on her damp, soft brown hair.

155 Then, as it were suddenly, he smelt the horrid stagnant smell of that water. And at the same moment she drew away from him and looked at him. Her eyes were wistful and unfathomable. He was afraid of them, and he fell to kissing her, not knowing what he was doing. He wanted her eyes not to have that terrible, wistful, unfathomable look.

156 When she turned her face to him again, a faint delicate flush was glowing, and there was again dawning that terrible shining of joy in her eyes, which really terrified him, and yet which he now wanted to see, because he feared the look of doubt still more.

157 "You love me?" she said, rather faltering.

158 "Yes." The word cost him a painful effort. Not because it wasn't true. But because it was too newly true, the *saying* seemed to tear open again his newly-torn heart. And he hardly wanted it to be true, even now.

159 She lifted her face to him, and he bent forward and kissed her on the mouth, gently, with the one kiss that is an eternal pledge. And as he kissed her his heart strained again in his breast. He never intended to love her. But now it was over. He had crossed over the gulf to her, and all that he had left behind had shrivelled and become void.

160 After the kiss, her eyes again slowly filled with tears. She sat still, away from him, with her face drooped aside, and her hands folded in her lap. The tears fell

very slowly. There was complete silence. He too sat there motionless and silent on the hearthrug. The strange pain of his heart that was broken seemed to consume him. That he should love her? That this was love! That he should be ripped open in this way! Him, a doctor! How they would all jeer if they knew! It was agony to him to think they might know.

161 In the curious naked pain of the thought he looked again to her. She was sitting there drooped into a muse. He saw a tear fall, and his heart flared hot. He saw for the first time that one of her shoulders was quite uncovered, one arm bare, he could see one of her small breasts; dimly, because it had become almost dark in the room.

162 "Why are you crying?" he asked, in an altered voice.

163 She looked up at him, and behind her tears the consciousness of her situation for the first time brought a dark look of shame to her eyes.

164 "I'm not crying, really," she said, watching him half frightened.

165 He reached his hand, and softly closed it on her bare arm.

166 "I love you! I love you!" he said in a soft, low vibrating voice, unlike himself.

167 She shrank, and dropped her head. The soft, penetrating grip of his hand on her arm distressed her. She looked up at him.

168 "I want to go," she said. "I want to go and get you some dry things."

169 "Why?" he said. "I'm all right."

170 "But I want to go," she said. "And I want you to change your things."

171 He released her arm, and she wrapped herself in the blanket, looking at him rather frightened. And still she did not rise.

172 "Kiss me," she said wistfully.

173 He kissed her, but briefly, half in anger.

174 Then, after a second, she rose nervously, all mixed up in the blanket. He watched her in her confusion, as she tried to extricate herself and wrap herself up so that she could walk. He watched her relentlessly, as she knew. And as she went, the blanket trailing, and as he saw a glimpse of her feet and her white leg, he tried to remember her as she was when he had wrapped her in the blanket. But then he didn't want to remember, because she had been nothing to him then, and his nature revolted from remembering her as she was when she was nothing to him.

175 A tumbling, muffled noise from within the dark house startled him. Then he heard her voice:—"There are clothes." He rose and went to the foot of the stairs, and gathered up the garments she had thrown down. Then he came back to the fire, to rub himself down and dress. He grinned at his own appearance when he had finished.

176 The fire was sinking, so he put on coal. The house was now quite dark, save for the light of a street-lamp that shone in faintly from beyond the holly trees. He lit the gas with matches he found on the mantelpiece. Then he emptied the pockets of his own clothes, and threw all his wet things in a heap into the scullery. After which he gathered up her sodden clothes, gently, and put them in a separate heap on the copper-top in the scullery.

177 It was six o'clock on the clock. His own watch had stopped. He ought to go back to the surgery. He waited, and still she did not come down. So he went to the foot of the stairs and called:

178 "I shall have to go."

179 Almost immediately he heard her coming down. She had on her best dress of black voile, and her hair was tidy, but still damp. She looked at him—and in spite of herself, smiled.

180 "I don't like you in those clothes," she said.

181 "Do I look a sight?" he answered.

182 They were shy of one another.

183 "I'll make you some tea," she said.

184 "No, I must go."

185 "Must you?" And she looked at him again with the wide, strained, doubtful eyes. And again, from the pain of his breast, he knew how he loved her. He went and bent to kiss her, gently, passionately, with his heart's painful kiss.

186 "And my hair smells so horrible," she murmured in distraction. "And I'm so awful, I'm so awful! Oh, no, I'm too awful." And she broke into bitter, heartbroken sobbing. "You can't want to love me, I'm horrible."

187 "Don't be silly, don't be silly," he said, trying to comfort her, kissing her, holding her in his arms. "I want you, I want to marry you, we're going to be married, quickly, quickly—tomorrow if I can."

188 But she only sobbed terribly, and cried:

190 "I feel awful. I feel awful. I feel I'm horrible to you."

191 "No, I want you, I want you," was all he answered, blindly, with that terrible intonation which frightened her almost more than her horror lest he should *not* want her.

(1922)

QUESTIONS

1. What is the purpose of the opening paragraphs? Besides being apprised of the circumstances of the Pervin family, what else are we shown? Consider especially the description of the horses in paragraph 6.
2. From early in the story, Lawrence includes many references to eyes. Mabel's eyes, for example, are described as "steady, dangerous eyes, that always made him [Dr. Fergusson] uncomfortable, unsettling his superficial ease" (paragraph 76). Find three or four additional passages where eyes are mentioned, and explain their significance.
3. Read carefully the description of the pond as Dr. Fergusson wades in to rescue Mabel (paragraphs 113–115). What is revealed about the doctor in this passage? Consider the symbolic implications of the pond.
4. In the dialogue following the rescue, Mabel asks: "Did you dive into the pond for me?" (paragraph 131). Suppose Lawrence had written "walk" for "dive" and also had omitted "for me." How would those changes alter the implications of Mabel's question. What are the implications of Dr. Fergusson's answer: "No . . . I walked in. But I went in overhead as well" (paragraph 132)?
5. In the ensuing dialogue, Lawrence shows the doctor struggling to overcome both a fascination for, and a fear of, Mabel. He resists Mabel's assertion: "You love me . . . You love me. I know you love me, I know" (paragraph 145). Why does he resist? Are his fear

and resistance plausible? How would you describe his feelings during this scene? How do his feelings change? Why?

6. Eventually, unable to withstand Mabel's power and attraction, Fergusson yields. After carefully examining the language through which Lawrence conveys the feelings of both Fergusson and Mabel (paragraphs 146–174), explain what he seems to be trying to achieve. Why does he extend the scene so long? What would be gained or lost if it were cut in half with the repetitions and hesitations omitted?
7. How is "The Horse Dealer's Daughter" as much the doctor's story as Mabel's? What does Mabel do for Fergusson, and he for her?
8. Explain the significance of Dr. Fergusson's profession as it influences his attitude, behavior, and self-image. Explain why he is attracted to the miners and also what he derives from working with them.

SUGGESTIONS FOR WRITING

A. Discuss the transformation of Mabel and of Dr. Fergusson.

B. Discuss the role of the brothers in the story.

C. Discuss the symbolism of the story. Consider especially the horses, the grave, the pond.

D. Compare the treatment of sexual love here with its portrayal or its consideration in another of Lawrence's works, whether essay or short story.

FIVE

Katherine Anne Porter

(1890–1980)

Katherine Anne Porter's very first published book, *Flowering Judas and Other Stories* (1930), earned her the high critical praise her subsequent work continued to merit. Porter grew up in the home of her grandmother in Kyle, Texas; her own mother died when she was two. In her grandmother's house she was surrounded by volumes of Shakespeare, Dante, Homer, Montaigne, Jane Austen, Thomas Hardy, Charles Dickens, and Henry James. And although Porter felt a compulsion to write from an early age, she did not attempt to have her fiction published until many years after first writing her stories. (She needed, as she pointed out in an interview, to learn the craft of writing before she dared go public with her literary efforts.) Porter did, however, achieve publication of news stories while working as a newspaper reporter in Chicago, Denver, and Fort Worth.

Porter attended boarding schools, and for a while, an Ursuline convent. She was married at sixteen and divorced at twenty-one. Supporting herself as an actress and ballad singer as well as a journalist, she struggled financially until the 1930s when she published, in addition to her first collection of stories, *Noon Wine* (1937) and *Pale Horse, Pale Rider: Three Short Novels* (1939). Financial security came only with the publication of her sole full-length novel, the commercially successful *Ship of Fools* (1962), on which she'd worked off and on for twenty years.

Porter's short fiction is carefully crafted with great attention to her characters' consciousness. Her language is exact and her images powerfully suggestive. Most often her stories concern moments of revelation—acute understandings and glimpses of awareness shared by characters and readers. Perhaps her own critical evaluation of a writer who influenced her, Katherine Mansfield, best describes Porter's own achievement:

> With fine objectivity she bares a moment of experience, real experience, in the life of some one human being; she states no belief, gives no motive, airs no theories, but simply presents a situation, a place, and a character . . . and the emotional content is present as implicitly as the germ is in the grain of wheat.

About writing, Porter has noted that the vocation chose her; she didn't choose it. Compared to her work as a writer, a vocation for which she was "willing to live and die," as she put it, she considered "very few other things of the slightest importance." Writing was such an essential aspect of her life, that Porter has described it as the strongest bond she ever had—"stronger than any bond or any engagement with any human being or with any other work" she ever did. In fact even while doing the other work she often did to support herself, Porter was preparing herself, as she came to see later, to be an artist. She firmly believed that "all our lives we are preparing to be somebody or something, even if we don't do it consciously." For Porter this meant to become "a good writer, a good artist."

What does Porter mean by being a good writer and a good artist? Essentially this: to take the confusion of human experience, its disparateness and irreconcilable elements, and out of its fragments to "frame some kind of shape and meaning." For Porter, the art of writing consists in ordering language and experience, giving it form, and in doing so, creating, as she has noted, "the feeling of reconciliation . . . the purification of mind and imagination."

How does a writer accomplish these ambitious goals? By the hard work of learning the writer's craft and by telling the truth about experience as simply and directly as possible. Porter has put it bluntly: "There is a technique; there is a craft, and you have to learn it." Beyond that there is the desire to tell the stories (whether factual or imaginative) you feel compelled to tell, an experience Porter has described like this: "I have something to tell you that I, for some reason, think is worth telling, and so I want to tell it as clearly and purely and simply as I can."

Perhaps the most important single piece of advice Porter has given aspiring writers is to avoid using any sort of jargon or specialized language, primarily because jargon goes in and out of fashion. Instead of jargon, advises Porter, "strive for the basic pure human speech that exists in every language." Try to write, she urges, "in a language that a six-year-old child can understand; and yet have the meanings and the overtones of language, and the implications, that appeal to the highest intelligence."

A tall order, but one Porter herself consistently filled.

Virginia Woolf

1 Leonard Woolf, in selecting and publishing the shorter writings of his wife, Virginia Woolf, has taken occasion to emphasize, again and again, her long painstaking ways of working, her habit of many revisions and rewritings, and her refusal to publish anything until she had brought it to its final state. The four volumes to appear in the nine years since her death will probably be the lot, Mr. Woolf tells us. There seems to remain a certain amount of unfinished manuscripts—unfinished in the sense that she had intended still to reconsider them and would not herself have published them in their present versions. One cannot respect enough the devoted care and love and superb literary judgment of the executor of this precious estate.

2 "In the previous volumes," Mr. Woolf writes in his foreword to the latest collection, *The Captain's Death Bed,* "I made no attempt to select essays in accordance with what I thought to be their merit or importance; I aimed at including in each volume some of all the various kinds of essay."

3 It is easy to agree with him when he finds "The essays in this volume are

. . . no different in merit and achievement from those previously published." Indeed, I found old favorites and new wonders in each of the earlier collections, finding still others again in this: the celebrated "Mr. Bennett and Mrs. Brown"; "Memories of a Working Woman's Guild"; "The Novels of Turgenev"; "Oliver Goldsmith." She speaks a convincing good word for Ruskin, such was her independence of taste, for surely this word is the first Ruskin has received in many a long year. She does a really expert taxidermy job on Sir Walter Raleigh, poor man, though he certainly deserved it; does another on reviewing, so severe her husband feels he must modify it a little with a footnote.

4 *The Captain's Death Bed* contains in fact the same delicious things to read as always; apparently her second or third draft was as good as her ninth or fifteenth; her last would be a little different, but surely not much better writing, that is clear. Only she, the good artist, without self-indulgence, would have known how much nearer with each change she was getting to the heart of her thought. For an example of how near she could come to it, read the three and one-half pages called "Gas." It is about having a tooth out, in the same sense, as E. M. Forster once remarked, that *Moby Dick* is a novel about catching a whale.

5 Now it is to be supposed that with this final gathering up of her life's work the critics will begin their formal summings-up, analyses, exegeses; the various schools will attack or defend her; she will be "placed" here and there; Freud will be involved, if he has not been already; elegies will be written: Cyril Connolly has already shed a few morning tears, and advised us not to read her novels for at least another decade: she is too painfully near to our most disastrous memories.

6 It turns out merely that Mr. Connolly wishes us to neglect her because she reminds him of the thirties, which he, personally, cannot endure. A great many of us who have no grudges against either the twenties or the thirties will find this advice mystifying. And there is a whole generation springing up, ready to read what is offered, who know and care nothing for either of those decades. My advice must be exactly the opposite: read everything of Virginia Woolf's now, for she has something of enormous importance to say at this time, here, today; let her future take care of itself.

7 I cannot pretend to be coldly detached about her work, nor, even if I were able, would I be willing to write a purely literary criticism of it. It is thirty-five years since I read her first novel, *The Voyage Out.* She was one of the writers who touched the real life of my mind and feeling very deeply; I had from that book the same sense of some mysterious revelation of truth I had got in earliest youth from Laurence Sterne ("of all people!" jeers a Shandy-hating friend of mine), from Jane Austen, from Emily Brontë, from Henry James. I had grown up with these, and I went on growing with W. B. Yeats, the first short stories of James Joyce, the earliest novels of Virginia Woolf.

8 In the most personal way, all of these seemed and do seem to be my contemporaries; their various visions of reality, their worlds, merged for me into one vision, one world view that revealed to me little by little my familiar place. Living as I did in a world of readers devoted to solid, tried and true literature, in which unimpeachable moral grandeur and inarguable doctrine were set forth in balanced paragraphs,

these writers were my own private discoveries. Reading as I did almost no contemporary criticism, talking to no one, still it did not occur to me that these were not great artists, who if only people could be persuaded to read them (even if by the light of Dr. Johnson or Dean Swift) they would be accepted as simply and joyously as I accepted them.

9 In some instances I was to have rude surprises. I could never understand the "revival" of Henry James; I had not heard that he was dead. Rather suddenly Jane Austen came back into fashionable favor; I had not dreamed she had ever been out of it.

10 In much the same way I have been amazed at the career of Virginia Woolf among the critics. To begin with, there has been very little notice except of the weekly review variety. Compared to the libraries of criticism published about Joyce, Lawrence, Eliot and all her other fellow artists of comparable stature, she has had little consideration. In 1925 she puzzled E. M. Forster, whose fountain pen disappeared when he was all prepared in his mind to write about her early novels.

11 Almost everything has been said, over and over, about Virginia Woolf's dazzling style, her brilliant humor, her extraordinary sensibility. She has been called neurotic, and hypersensitive. Her style has been compared to cobwebs with dew drops, rainbows, landscapes seen by moonlight, and other unsubstantial but showy stuff. She has been called a Phoenix, Muse, a Sybil, a Prophetess, in praise, or a Feminist, in dispraise. Her beauty and remarkable personality, her short way with fools and that glance of hers, which chilled many a young literary man with its expression of seeing casually through a millstone—all of this got in the way. It disturbed the judgment and drew the attention from the true point of interest.

12 Virginia Woolf was a great artist, one of the glories of our time, and she never published a line that was not worth reading. The least of her novels would have made the reputation of a lesser writer, the least of her critical writings compare more than favorably with the best criticism of the past half-century. In a long, sad period of fear, a world broken by wars, in which the artists have in the most lamentable way been the children of their time, knees knocking, teeth chattering, looking for personal salvation in the midst of world calamity, there appeared this artist, Virginia Woolf.

13 She was full of secular intelligence primed with the profane virtues, with her love not only of the world of all the arts created by the human imagination, but a love of life itself and of daily living, a spirit at once gay and severe, exacting and generous, a born artist and a sober craftsman; and she had no plan whatever for her personal salvation; or the personal salvation even of someone else; brought no doctrine; no dogma. Life, the life of this world, here and now, was a great mystery, no one could fathom it; and death was the end. In short, she was what the true believers always have called a heretic.

14 What she did, then, in the way of breaking up one of the oldest beliefs of mankind, is more important than the changes she made in the form of the novel. She wasn't even a heretic—she simply lived outside of dogmatic belief. She lived in the naturalness of her vocation. The world of the arts was her native territory;

she ranged freely under her own sky, speaking her mother tongue fearlessly. She was at home in that place as much as anyone ever was.

(1950)

QUESTIONS

Thought and Structure

1. Porter's essay is a form of testimony and tribute. What impresses Porter most about Woolf's writing? What has been the central effect of Woolf's writing on Porter? How has Porter been influenced by Woolf?
2. E. M. Forster is mentioned directly in paragraph 10. More important, however, than this direct reference is the way Forster's essay, "What I Believe" touches on Porter's praise of Woolf in paragraphs 13–14. Look back at Forster's essay and comment on the relationship of his views to Porter's portrait of Woolf.
3. What impresses you about Porter's view of Woolf? Does her view coincide with your own on the basis of your reading of Woolf's work? Why or why not?
4. How would you characterize the organization of this essay? What does Porter begin with, how does she follow that up, and how does she conclude?

Style and Strategy

5. What do you think Porter means by saying Woolf does a "taxidermy" job on Sir Walter Raleigh (paragraph 3)? What does she mean by her remark that Woolf's essay "Gas" is as much about having a tooth extracted as *Moby Dick* is about a whale (paragraph 4)?
6. Notice the balanced syntax of the following sentences from paragraph 9. Comment on their function.
   a. I could never understand the "revival" of Henry James;
   I had not heard that he was dead.
   b. Rather suddenly Jane Austen came back into fashionable favor;
   I had not dreamed she had ever been out of it.
7. In paragraph 11 Porter speaks of Woolf's style. What images does she use to identify Woolf's style? Does Porter agree or disagree with the view of Woolf's writing implied by the images associated with her style?
8. Identify the images Porter employs in discussing Woolf's importance as a writer. See especially paragraphs 12–14.

SUGGESTIONS FOR WRITING

A. Write an essay discussing the image of the writer that emerges from Porter's portrait of Woolf. You may, if you like, develop your ideas by referring also to Woolf's essays.

B. Write your own tribute to a writer whose work you admire. Like Porter, try to identify the salient features of the written work.

C. Discuss in an essay what it means to live beyond the compass of dogmatic belief. Explain what you think Porter means by "living in the naturalness of a vocation."

St. Augustine and the Bullfight

1 Adventure. The word has become a little stale to me, because it has been applied too often to the dull physical exploits of professional "adventurers" who write books about it, if they know how to write; if not, they hire ghosts who quite often can't write either.

2 I don't read them, but rumors of them echo, and re-echo. The book business at least is full of heroes who spend their time, money and energy worrying other animals, manifestly their betters such as lions and tigers, to death in trackless jungles and deserts only to be crossed by the stoutest motorcar; or another feeds hooks to an inedible fish like the tarpon; another crosses the ocean on a raft, living on plankton and seaweed, why ever, I wonder? And always always, somebody is out climbing mountains, and writing books about it, which are read by quite millions of persons who feel, apparently, that the next best thing to going there yourself is to hear from somebody who went. And I have heard more than one young woman remark that, though she did not want to get married, still, she would like to have a baby, for the adventure: not lately though. That was a pose of the 1920s and very early '30s. Several of them did it, too, but I do not know of any who wrote a book about it—good for them.

3 W. B. Yeats remarked—I cannot find the passage now, so must say it in other words—that the unhappy man (unfortunate?) was one whose adventures outran his capacity for experience, capacity for experience being, I should say, roughly equal to the faculty for understanding what has happened to one. The difference then between mere adventure and a real experience might be this? That adventure is something you seek for pleasure, or even for profit, like a gold rush or invading a country; for the illusion of being more alive than ordinarily, the thing you will to occur; but experience is what really happens to you in the long run; the truth that finally overtakes you.

4 Adventure is sometimes fun, but not too often. Not if you can remember what really happened; all of it. It passes, seems to lead nowhere much, is something to tell friends to amuse them, maybe. "Once upon a time," I can hear myself saying, for I once said it, "I scaled a cliff in Boulder, Colorado, with my bare hands, and in Indian moccasins, bare-legged. And at nearly the top, after six hours of feeling for toe- and fingerholds, and the gayest feeling in the world that when I got to the top I should see something wonderful, something that sounded awfully like a bear growled out of a cave, and I scuttled down out of there in a hurry." This is a fact. I had never climbed a mountain in my life, never had the least wish to climb one. But there I was, for perfectly good reasons, in a hut on a mountainside in heavenly sunny though sometimes stormy weather, so I went out one morning and scaled a very minor cliff; alone, unsuitably clad, in the season when rattlesnakes are casting their skins; and if it was not a bear in that cave, it was some kind of unfriendly animal who growls at people; and this ridiculous escapade, which was nearly six hours of the hardest work I ever did in my life, toeholds and fingerholds on a cliff, put me to bed for just nine days with a complaint the local people called "muscle poisoning."

I don't know exactly what they meant, but I do remember clearly that I could not turn over in bed without help and in great agony. And did it teach me anything? I think not, for three years later I was climbing a volcano in Mexico, that celebrated unpronounceably named volcano, Popocatepetl which everybody who comes near it climbs sooner or later; but was that any reason for me to climb it? No. And I was knocked out for weeks, and that finally did teach me: I am not supposed to go climbing things. Why did I not know in the first place? For me, this sort of thing must come under the head of Adventure.

5 I think it is pastime of rather an inferior sort; yet I have heard men tell yarns like this only a very little better: their mountains were higher, or their sea was wider, or their bear was bigger and noisier, or their cliff was steeper and taller, yet there was no point whatever to any of it except that it had happened. This is not enough. May it not be, perhaps, that experience, that is, the thing that happens to a person living from day to day, is anything at all that sinks in? is, without making any claims, a part of your growing and changing life? what it is that happens in your mind, your heart?

6 Adventure hardly ever seems to be that at the time it is happening: not under that name, at least. Adventure may be an afterthought, something that happens in the memory with imaginative trimmings if not downright lying, so that one should suppress it entirely, or go the whole way and make honest fiction of it. My own habit of writing fiction has provided a wholesome exercise to my natural, incurable tendency to try to wangle the sprawling mess of our existence in this bloody world into some kind of shape: almost any shape will do, just so it is recognizably made with human hands, one small proof the more of the validity and reality of the human imagination. But even within the most limited frame what utter confusion shall prevail if you cannot take hold firmly, and draw the exact line between what really happened, and what you have since imagined about it. Perhaps my soul will be saved after all in spite of myself because now and then I take some unmanageable, indigestible fact and turn it into fiction; cause things to happen with some kind of logic—my own logic, of course—and everything ends as I think it should end and no back talk, or very little, from anybody about it. Otherwise, and except for this safety device, I should be the greatest liar unhung. (When was the last time anybody was hanged for lying?) What is Truth? I often ask myself. Who knows?

7 A publisher asked me a great while ago to write a kind of autobiography, and I was delighted to begin; it sounded very easy when he said, "Just start, and tell everything you remember until now!" I wrote about a hundred pages before I realized, or admitted, the hideous booby trap into which I had fallen. First place, I remember quite a lot of stupid and boring things: there were other times when my life seemed merely an endurance test, or a quite mysterious but not very interesting and often monotonous effort at survival on the most primitive terms. There are dozens of things that might be entertaining but I have no intention of telling them, because they are nobody's business; and endless little gossipy incidents that might entertain indulgent friends for a minute, but in print they look as silly as they really are. Then, there are the tremendous, unmistakable, life-and-death crises, the scalding, the bone-breaking events, the lightnings that shatter the landscape of the soul—who would write that by request? No, that is for a secretly written

manuscript to be left with your papers, and if your executor is a good friend, who has probably been brought up on St. Augustine's *Confessions,* he will read it with love and attention and gently burn it to ashes for your sake.

8 Yet I intend to write something about my life, here and now, and so far as I am able without one touch of fiction, and I hope to keep it as shapeless and unforeseen as the events of life itself from day to day. Yet, look! I have already betrayed my occupation, and dropped a clue in what would be the right place if this were fiction, by mentioning St. Augustine when I hadn't meant to until it came in its right place in life, not in art. Literary art, at least, is the business of setting human events to rights and giving them meanings that, in fact, they do not possess, or not obviously, or not the meanings the artist feels they should have—we do understand so little of what is really happening to us in any given moment. Only by remembering, comparing, waiting to know the consequences can we sometimes, in a flash of light, see what a certain event really meant, what it was trying to tell us. So this will be notes on a fateful thing that happened to me when I was young and did not know much about the world or about myself. I had been reading St. Augustine's *Confessions* since I was able to read at all, and I thought I had read every word, perhaps because I did know certain favorite passages by heart. But then, it was something like having read the Adventures of Gargantua by Rabelais when I was twelve and enjoying it; when I read it again at thirty-odd, I was astounded at how much I had overlooked in the earlier reading, and wondered what I thought I had seen there.

9 So it was with St. Augustine and my first bullfight. Looking back nearly thirty-five years on my earliest days in Mexico, it strikes me that, for a fairly serious young woman who was in the country for the express purpose of attending a Revolution, and studying Mayan people art, I fell in with a most lordly gang of fashionable international hoodlums. Of course I had Revolutionist friends and artist friends, and they were gay and easy and poor as I was. This other mob was different: they were French, Spanish, Italian, Polish, and they all had titles and good names: a duke, a count, a marquess, a baron, and they all were in some flashy money-getting enterprise like importing cognac wholesale, or selling sports cars to newly rich politicians; and they all drank like fish and played fast games like polo or tennis or jai alai; they haunted the wings of theaters, drove slick cars like maniacs, but expert maniacs, never missed a bullfight or a boxing match; all were reasonably young and they had ladies to match, mostly imported and all speaking French. These persons stalked pleasure as if it were big game—they took their fun exactly where they found it, and the way they liked it, and they worked themselves to exhaustion at it. A fast, tough, expensive, elegant, high low-life they led, for the ladies and gentlemen each in turn had other friends you would have had to see to believe; and from time to time, without being in any way involved or engaged, I ran with this crowd of shady characters and liked their company and ways very much. I don't like gloomy sinners, but the merry ones charm me. And one of them introduced me to Shelley. And Shelley, whom I knew in the most superficial way, who remained essentially a stranger to me to the very end, led me, without in the least ever knowing what he had done, into one of the most important and lasting experiences of my life.

10 He was British, a member of the poet's family; said to be an authentic great-great-nephew; he was rich and willful, and had come to Mexico young and

wild, and mad about horses, of course. Coldly mad—he bred them and raced them and sold them with the stony detachment and merciless appraisal of the true horse lover—they call it love, and it could be that: but he did not like them. "What is there to like about a horse but his good points? If he has a vice, shoot him or send him to the bullring; that is the only way to work a vice out of the breed!"

11 Once, during a riding trip while visiting a ranch, my host gave me a stallion to ride, who instantly took the bit in his teeth and bolted down a steep mountain trail. I managed to stick on, held an easy rein, and he finally ran himself to a standstill in an open field. My disgrace with Shelley was nearly complete. Why? Because the stallion was not a good horse. I should have refused to mount him. I said it was a question how to refuse the horse your host offered you—Shelley thought it no question at all. "A lady," he reminded me, "can always excuse herself gracefully from anything she doesn't wish to do." I said, "I wish that were really true," for the argument about the bullfight was already well started. But the peak of his disapproval of me, my motives, my temperament, my ideas, my ways, was reached when, to provide a diversion and end a dull discussion, I told him the truth: that I had liked being run away with, it had been fun and the kind of thing that had to happen unexpectedly, you couldn't arrange for it. I tried to convey to him my exhilaration, my pure joy when this half-broken, crazy beast took off down that trail with just a hoofhold between a cliff on one side and a thousand-foot drop on the other. He said merely that such utter frivolity surprised him in someone whom he had mistaken for a well-balanced, intelligent girl; and I remember thinking how revoltingly fatherly he sounded, exactly like my own father in his stuffier moments.

12 He was a stocky, red-faced, muscular man with broad shoulders, hard-jowled, with bright blue eyes glinting from puffy lids; his hair was a grizzled tan, and I guessed him about fifty years old, which seemed a great age to me then. But he mentioned that his Mexican wife had "died young" about three years before, and that his eldest son was only eleven years old. His whole appearance was so remarkably like the typical horsy, landed-gentry sort of Englishman one meets in books by Frenchmen or Americans, if this were fiction I should feel obliged to change his looks altogether, thus falling into one stereotype to avoid falling into another. However, so Shelley did look, and his clothes were magnificent and right beyond words, and never new-looking and never noticeable at all except one could not help observing sooner or later that he was beyond argument the best-dressed man in America, North or South; it was that kind of typical British inconspicuous good taste: he had it, superlatively. He was evidently leading a fairly rakish life, or trying to, but he was of a cast-iron conventionality even in that. We did not fall in love—far from it. We struck up a hands-off, quaint, farfetched, tetchy kind of friendship which consisted largely of good advice about worldly things from him, mingled with critical marginal notes on my character—a character of which I could not recognize a single trait; and if I said, helplessly, "But I am not in the least like that," he would answer, "Well, you should be!" or "Yes, you are, but you don't know it."

13 This man took me to my first bullfight. I'll tell you later how St. Augustine comes into it. It was the first bullfight of that season; Covadonga Day; April; clear, hot blue sky; and a long procession of women in flower-covered carriages; wearing their finest lace veils and highest combs and gauziest fans; but I shan't describe a

bullfight. By now surely there is no excuse for anyone who can read or even hear or see not to know pretty well what goes on in a bullring. I shall say only that Sánchez Mejías and Rudolfo Gaona each killed a bull that day; but before the Grand March of the toreros, Hattie Weston rode her thoroughbred High School gelding into the ring to thunders of shouts and brassy music.

14 She was Shelley's idol. "Look at that girl, for God's sake," and his voice thickened with feeling, "the finest rider in the world," he said in his dogmatic way, and it is true I have not seen better since.

15 She was a fine buxom figure of a woman, a highly colored blonde with a sweet, childish face; probably forty years old, and perfectly rounded in all directions; a big round bust, and that is the word, there was nothing plural about it, just a fine, warm-looking bolster straight across her front from armpit to armpit; fine firm round hips—again, why the plural? It was an ample seat born to a sidesaddle, as solid and undivided as the bust, only more of it. She was tightly laced and her waist was small. She wore a hard-brimmed dark gray Spanish sailor hat, sitting straight and shallow over her large golden knot of hair; a light gray bolero and a darker gray riding skirt—not a Spanish woman's riding dress, nor yet a man's, but something tight and fit and formal and appropriate. And there she went, the most elegant woman in the saddle I have ever seen, graceful and composed in her perfect style, with her wonderful, lightly dancing, learned horse, black and glossy as shoe polish, perfectly under control—no, not under control at all, you might have thought, but just dancing and showing off his paces by himself for his own pleasure.

16 "She makes the bullfight seem like an anticlimax," said Shelley, tenderly.

17 I had not wanted to come to this bullfight. I had never intended to see a bullfight at all. I do not like the slaughtering of animals as sport. I am carnivorous, I love all the red juicy meats and all the fishes. Seeing animals killed for food on the farm in summers shocked and grieved me sincerely, but it did not cure my taste for flesh. My family for as far back as I know anything about them, only about 450 years, were the huntin', shootin', fishin' sort: their houses were arsenals and their dominion over the animal kingdom was complete and unchallenged. When I was older, my father remarked on my tiresome timidity, or was I just pretending to finer feelings than those of the society around me? He hardly knew which was the more tiresome. But that was perhaps only a personal matter. Morally, if I wished to eat meat I should be able to kill the animal—otherwise it appeared that I was willing to nourish myself on other people's sins? For he supposed I considered it a sin. Otherwise why bother about it? Or was it just something unpleasant I wished to avoid? Maintaining my own purity—and a very doubtful kind of purity he found it, too—at the expense of the guilt of others? Altogether, my father managed to make a very sticky question of it, and for some years at intervals I made it a matter of conscience to kill an animal or bird, something I intended to eat. I gave myself and the beasts some horrible times, through fright and awkwardness, and to my shame, nothing cured me of my taste for flesh. All forms of cruelty offend me bitterly, and this repugnance is inborn, absolutely impervious to any arguments, or even insults, at which the red-blooded lovers of blood sports are very expert; they don't admire me at all, any more than I admire them. . . . Ah, me, the contradictions, the paradoxes! I was once perfectly capable of keeping a calf for a pet until he

outgrew the yard in the country and had to be sent to the pastures. His subsequent fate I leave you to guess. Yes, it is all revoltingly sentimental and, worse than that, confused. My defense is that no matter whatever else this world seemed to promise me, never once did it promise to be simple.

18 So, for a great tangle of emotional reasons I had no intention of going to a bullfight. But Shelley was so persistently unpleasant about my cowardice, as he called it flatly, I just wasn't able to take the thrashing any longer. Partly, too, it was his natural snobbery: smart people of the world did not have such feelings; it was to him a peculiarly provincial if not downright Quakerish attitude. "I have some Quaker ancestors," I told him. "How absurd of you!" he said, and really meant it.

19 The bullfight question kept popping up and had a way of spoiling other occasions that should have been delightful. Shelley was one of those men, of whose company I feel sometimes that I have had more than my fair share, who simply do not know how to drop a subject, or abandon a position once they have declared it. Constitutionally incapable of admitting defeat, or even its possibility, even when he had not the faintest shadow of right to expect a victory—for why should he make a contest of my refusal to go to a bullfight?—he would start an argument during the theater intermissions, at the fronton, at a street fair, on a stroll in the Alameda, at a good restaurant over coffee and brandy; there was no occasion so pleasant that he could not shatter it with his favorite gambit: "If you would only see one, you'd get over this nonsense."

20 So there I was, at the bullfight, with cold hands, trembling innerly, with painful tinglings in the wrists and collarbone: yet my excitement was not altogether painful; and in my happiness at Hattie Weston's performance I was calmed and off guard when the heavy barred gate to the corral burst open and the first bull charged through. The bulls were from the Duke of Veragua's* ranch, as enormous and brave and handsome as any I ever saw afterward. (This is not a short story, so I don't have to maintain any suspense.) This first bull was a beautiful monster of brute courage: his hide was a fine pattern of black and white, much enhanced by the goad with fluttering green ribbons stabbed into his shoulder as he entered the ring; this in turn furnished an interesting design in thin rivulets of blood, the enlivening touch of scarlet in his sober color scheme, with highly aesthetic effect.

21 He rushed at the waiting horse, blindfolded in one eye and standing at the proper angle for the convenience of his horns, the picador making only the smallest pretense of staving him off, and disemboweled the horse with one sweep of his head. The horse trod in his own guts. It happens at least once every bullfight. I could not pretend not to have expected it; but I had not been able to imagine it. I sat back and covered my eyes. Shelley, very deliberately and as inconspicuously as he could, took both my wrists and held my hands down on my knees. I shut my eyes and turned my face away, away from the arena, away from him, but not before I had seen in his eyes a look of real, acute concern and almost loving anxiety for me—he really believed that my feelings were the sign of a grave flaw of character, or at least an unbecoming, unworthy weakness that he was determined to overcome in me. He

---

*Lineal descendant of Christopher Columbus.

couldn't shoot me, alas, or turn me over to the bullring; he had to deal with me in human terms, and he did it according to his lights. His voice was hoarse and fierce: "Don't you dare come here and then do this! You must face it!"

22 Part of his fury was shame, no doubt, at being seen with a girl who would behave in such a pawky way. But at this point he was, of course, right. Only he had been wrong before to nag me into this, and I was altogether wrong to have let him persuade me. Or so I felt then. "You have got to face this!" By then he was right; and I did look and I did face it, though not for years and years.

23 During those years I saw perhaps a hundred bullfights, all in Mexico City, with the finest bulls from Spain and the greatest bullfighters—but not with Shelley—never again with Shelley, for we were not comfortable together after that day. Our odd, mismatched sort of friendship declined and neither made any effort to revive it. There was bloodguilt between us, we shared an evil secret, a hateful revelation. He hated what he had revealed in me to himself, and I hated what he had revealed to me about myself, and each of us for entirely opposite reasons; but there was nothing more to say or do, and we stopped seeing each other.

24 I took to the bullfights with my Mexican and Indian friends. I sat with them in the cafés where the bullfighters appeared; more than once went at two o'clock in the morning with a crowd to see the bulls brought into the city; I visited the corral back of the ring where they could be seen before the corrida. Always, of course, I was in the company of impassioned adorers of the sport, with their special vocabulary and mannerisms and contempt for all others who did not belong to their charmed and chosen cult. Quite literally there were those among them I never heard speak of anything else; and I heard then all that can be said—the topic is limited, after all, like any other—in love and praise of bullfighting. But it can be tiresome, too. And I did not really live in that world, so narrow and so trivial, so cruel and so unconscious; I was a mere visitor. There was something deeply, irreparably wrong with my being there at all, something against the grain of my life; except for this (and here was the falseness I had finally to uncover): I loved the spectacle of the bullfights, I was drunk on it, I was in a strange, wild dream from which I did not want to be awakened. I was now drawn irresistibly to the bullring as before I had been drawn to the race tracks and the polo fields at home. But this had death in it, and it was the death in it that I loved. . . . And I was bitterly ashamed of this evil in me, and believed it to be in me only—no one had fallen so far into cruelty as this! These bullfight buffs I truly believed did not know what they were doing—but I did, and I knew better because I had once known better; so that spiritual pride got in and did its deadly work, too. How could I face the cold fact that at heart I was just a killer, like any other, that some deep corner of my soul consented not just willingly but with rapture? I still clung obstinately to my flattering view of myself as a unique case, as a humane, blood-avoiding civilized being, somehow a fallen angel, perhaps? Just the same, what was I doing there? And why was I beginning secretly to abhor Shelley as if he had done me a great injury, when in fact he had done me the terrible and dangerous favor of helping me to find myself out?

25 In the meantime I was reading St. Augustine; and if Shelley had helped me find myself out, St. Augustine helped me find myself again. I read for the first time then his story of a friend of his, a young man from the provinces who came to Rome and was taken up by the gang of clever, wellborn young hoodlums Augustine then

ran with; and this young man, also wellborn but severely brought up, refused to go with the crowd to the gladiatorial combat; he was opposed to them on the simple grounds that they were cruel and criminal. His friends naturally ridiculed such dowdy sentiments; they nagged him slyly, bedeviled him openly, and, of course, finally some part of him consented—but only to a degree. He would go with them, he said, but he would not watch the games. And he did not, until the time for the first slaughter, when the howling of the crowd brought him to his feet, staring: and afterward he was more bloodthirsty than any.

26 Why, of course: oh, it might be a commonplace of human nature, it might be it could happen to anyone! I longed to be free of my uniqueness, to be a fellow-sinner at least with someone: I could not bear my guilt alone—and here was this student, this boy at Rome in the fourth century, somebody I felt I knew well on sight, who had been weak enough to be led into adventure but strong enough to turn it into experience. For no matter how we both attempted to deceive ourselves, our acts had all the earmarks of adventure: violence of motive, events taking place at top speed, at sustained intensity, under powerful stimulus and a willful seeking for pure sensation; willful, I say, because I was not kidnapped and forced, after all, nor was that young friend of St. Augustine's. We both proceeded under the power of our own weakness. When the time came to kill the splendid black and white bull, I who had pitied him when he first came into the ring stood straining on tiptoe to see everything, yet almost blinded with excitement, and crying out when the crowd roared, and kissing Shelley on the cheekbone when he shook my elbow and shouted in the voice of one justified: "Didn't I tell you? Didn't I?"

(1955)

QUESTIONS

Thought and Structure

1. What is Porter's attitude toward adventure and adventurers? Cite a few examples of typical adventures and comment on Porter's view of them.
2. What distinction does Porter make between adventure and experience? Do you think this is a valid and necessary distinction? Why or why not?
3. How has Porter's personal experience contributed to her ideas and feelings about "adventure"?
4. Explain how St. Augustine and his *Confessions* are important to Porter.
5. Sketch out the organization of the essay. Identify the major parts of the piece and explain their relationship.
6. Discuss why Porter stopped seeing Shelley. Consider especially her comments at the end of paragraphs 23 and 24.

Style and Strategy

7. A number of Porter's sentences take the form of questions. Consider, for example, those in paragraphs 3–6. Comment on their purpose and effect.
8. What impression of Shelley does Porter convey? How does she accomplish this?

9. Single out two sentences you find especially striking, and explain what you like about them.
10. Look up the meanings of the following words: escapade (4), rakish (12), impervious (17), and rapture (24).

SUGGESTIONS FOR WRITING

A. Discuss one or both of the following comments about literary art with reference to Porter's own writing or to that of any other writer in this book:
   a. Literary art . . . is the business of setting human events to rights and giving them meanings that, in fact, they do not possess (paragraph 8).
   b. My own habit of writing fiction has provided a wholesome exercise to my natural, incurable tendency to try to wangle the sprawling mess of our existence in this bloody world into some kind of shape . . . one small proof the more of the validity and reality of the human imagination (paragraph 6).
B. Discuss Porter's ideas about experience and adventure and comment on their significance for your own life.
C. Recount an "adventure" that for you has become "experience" in Porter's sense of the term. Explain how and why this has happened.

The Necessary Enemy

1 She is a frank, charming, fresh-hearted young woman who married for love. She and her husband are one of those gay, good-looking young pairs who ornament this modern scene rather more in profusion perhaps than ever before in our history. They are handsome, with a talent for finding their way in their world, they work at things that interest them, their tastes agree and their hopes. They intend in all good faith to spend their lives together, to have children and do well by them and each other—to be happy, in fact, which for them is the whole point of their marriage. And all in stride, keeping their wits about them. Nothing romantic, mind you; their feet are on the ground.

2 Unless they were this sort of person, there would be not much point to what I wish to say; for they would seem to be an example of the high-spirited, right-minded young whom the critics are always invoking to come forth and do their duty and practice all those sterling old-fashioned virtues which in every generation seem to be falling into disrepair. As for virtues, these young people are more or less on their own, like most of their kind; they get very little moral or other aid from their society; but after three years of marriage this very contemporary young woman finds herself facing the oldest and ugliest dilemma of marriage.

3 She is dismayed, horrified, full of guilt and forebodings because she is finding out little by little that she is capable of hating her husband, whom she loves faithfully. She can hate him at times as fiercely and mysteriously, indeed in terribly much the same way, as often she hated her parents, her brothers and sisters, whom

she loves, when she was a child. Even then it had seemed to her a kind of black treacherousness in her, her private wickedness that, just the same, gave her her only private life. That was one thing her parents never knew about her, never seemed to suspect. For it was never given a name. They did and said hateful things to her and to each other as if by right, as if in them it was a kind of virtue. But when they said to her, "Control your feelings," it was never when she was amiable and obedient, only in the black times of her hate. So it was her secret, a shameful one. When they punished her, sometimes for the strangest reasons, it was, they said, only because they loved her—it was for her good. She did not believe this, but she thought herself guilty of something worse than ever they had punished her for. None of this really frightened her: the real fright came when she discovered that at times her father and mother hated each other; this was like standing on the doorsill of a familiar room and seeing in a lightning flash that the floor was gone, you were on the edge of a bottomless pit. Sometimes she felt that both of them hated her, but that passed, it was simply not a thing to be thought of, much less believed. She thought she had outgrown all this, but here it was again, an element in her own nature she could not control, or feared she could not. She would have to hide from her husband, if she could, the same spot in her feelings she had hidden from her parents, and for the same no doubt disreputable, selfish reason: she wants to keep his love.

4 Above all, she wants him to be absolutely confident that she loves him, for that is the real truth, no matter how unreasonable it sounds, and no matter how her own feelings betray them both at times. She depends recklessly on his love; yet while she is hating him, he might very well be hating her as much or even more, and it would serve her right. But she does not want to be served right, she wants to be loved and forgiven—that is, to be sure he would forgive her anything, if he had any notion of what she had done. But best of all she would like not to have anything in her love that should ask forgiveness. She doesn't mean about their quarrels—they are not so bad. Her feelings are out of proportion, perhaps. She knows it is perfectly natural for people to disagree, have fits of temper, fight it out; they learn quite a lot about each other that way, and not all of it disappointing either. When it passes, her hatred seems quite unreal. It always did.

5 Love. We are early taught to say it. I love you. We are trained to the thought of it as if there were nothing else, or nothing else worth having without it, or nothing worth having which it could not bring with it. Love is taught, always by precept, sometimes by example. Then hate, which no one meant to teach us, comes of itself. It is true that if we say I love you, it may be received with doubt, for there are times when it is hard to believe. Say I hate you, and the one spoken to believes it instantly, once for all.

6 Say I love you a thousand times to that person afterward and mean it every time, and still it does not change the fact that once we said I hate you, and meant that too. It leaves a mark on that surface love had worn so smooth with its eternal caresses. Love must be learned, and learned again and again; there is no end to it. Hate needs no instruction, but waits only to be provoked . . . hate, the unspoken word, the unacknowledged presence in the house, that faint smell of brimstone

among the roses, that invisible tongue-tripper, that unkempt finger in every pie, that sudden oh-so-curiously *chilling* look—could it be boredom?—on your dear one's features, making them quite ugly. Be careful: love, perfect love, is in danger.

7 If it is not perfect, it is not love, and if it is not love, it is bound to be hate sooner or later. This is perhaps a not too exaggerated statement of the extreme position of Romantic Love, more especially in America, where we are all brought up on it, whether we know it or not. Romantic Love is changeless, faithful, passionate, and its sole end is to render the two lovers happy. It has no obstacles save those provided by the hazards of fate (that is to say, society), and such sufferings as the lovers may cause each other are only another word for delight: exciting jealousies, thrilling uncertainties, the ritual dance of courtship within the charmed closed circle of their secret alliance; all *real* troubles come from without, they face them unitedly in perfect confidence. Marriage is not the end but only the beginning of true happiness, cloudless, changeless to the end. That the candidates for this blissful condition have never seen an example of it, nor ever knew anyone who had, makes no difference. That is the ideal and they will achieve it.

8 How did Romantic Love manage to get into marriage at last, where it was most certainly never intended to be? At its highest it was tragic: the love of Héloïse and Abélard. At its most graceful, it was the homage of the trouvère for his lady. In its most popular form, the adulterous strayings of solidly married couples who meant to stray for their own good reasons, but at the same time do nothing to upset the property settlements or the line of legitimacy; at its most trivial, the pretty trifling of shepherd and shepherdess.

9 This was generally condemned by church and state and a word of fear to honest wives whose mortal enemy it was. Love within the sober, sacred realities of marriage was a matter of personal luck, but in any case, private feelings were strictly a private affair having, at least in theory, no bearing whatever on the fixed practice of the rules of an institution never intended as a recreation ground for either sex. If the couple discharged their religious and social obligations, furnished forth a copious progeny, kept their troubles to themselves, maintained public civility and died under the same roof, even if not always on speaking terms, it was rightly regarded as a successful marriage. Apparently this testing ground was too severe for all but the stoutest spirits; it too was based on an ideal, as impossible in its way as the ideal Romantic Love. One good thing to be said for it is that society took responsibility for the conditions of marriage, and the sufferers within its bonds could always blame the system, not themselves. But Romantic Love crept into the marriage bed, very stealthily, by centuries, bringing its absurd notions about love as eternal springtime and marriage as a personal adventure meant to provide personal happiness. To a Western romantic such as I, though my views have been much modified by painful experience, it still seems to me a charming work of the human imagination, and it is a pity its central notion has been taken too literally and has hardened into a convention as cramping and enslaving as the older one. The refusal to acknowledge the evils in ourselves which therefore are implicit in any human situation is as extreme and unworkable a proposition as the doctrine of total depravity; but somewhere between them, or maybe beyond them, there does exist a possibility for reconciliation between our desires for impossible satisfactions and the

simple unalterable fact that we also desire to be unhappy and that we create our own sufferings; and out of these sufferings we salvage our fragments of happiness.

10 Our young woman who has been taught that an important part of her human nature is not real because it makes trouble and interferes with her peace of mind and shakes her self-love, has been very badly taught; but she has arrived at a most important stage of her re-education. She is afraid her marriage is going to fail because she has not love enough to face its difficulties; and this because at times she feels a painful hostility toward her husband, and cannot admit its reality because such an admission would damage in her own eyes her view of what love should be, an absurd view, based on her vanity of power. Her hatred is real as her love is real, but her hatred has the advantage at present because it works on a blind instinctual level, it is lawless; and her love is subjected to a code of ideal conditions, impossible by their very nature of fulfillment, which prevents its free growth and deprives it of its right to recognize its human limitations and come to grips with them. Hatred is natural in a sense that love, as she conceives it, a young person brought up in the tradition of Romantic Love, is not natural at all. Yet it did not come by hazard, it is the very imperfect expression of the need of the human imagination to create beauty and harmony out of chaos, no matter how mistaken its notion of these things may be, nor how clumsy its methods. It has conjured love out of the air, and seeks to preserve it by incantations; when she spoke a vow to love and honor her husband until death, she did a very reckless thing, for it is not possible by an act of the will to fulfill such an engagement. But it was the necessary act of faith performed in defense of a mode of feeling, the statement of honorable intention to practice as well as she is able the noble, acquired faculty of love, that very mysterious overtone to sex which is the best thing in it. Her hatred is part of it, the necessary enemy and ally.

(1948)

QUESTIONS

Thought and Structure

1. What is the relationship between love and hatred as suggested in this essay? How do you see their relationship? Why?
2. Do the woman's feelings of hatred and her strategy for concealing it from her husband (and from parents and siblings as well) seem plausible? Why or why not?
3. Do you agree with what Porter says about love and hate in paragraph 5? Why or why not?
4. What characteristics of "Romantic love" does Porter identify and what is her attitude toward them?
5. Explain Porter's attitude toward the images of love she presents in paragraph 9. What do you think she means by the last sentence of that paragraph.
6. Porter's essay falls into three major sections. Provide a title for each, and explain how the three parts are related.

Style and Strategy

7. How would you characterize the tone of the opening paragraph? What seems to be Porter's attitude toward the young couple?
8. In paragraph 6 Porter presents a series of images: "the unspoken word, the unacknowledged presence . . . [the] *chilling* look . . ." What are their point and purpose?
9. Intermittently throughout the essay Porter addresses her readers directly. Sometimes she seems to warn us. Identify two or three places where she does this most emphatically and comment on their effectiveness.
10. Porter's control of syntax is remarkably assured. She is especially adept at using short sentences. Look, for example, at the end of paragraphs 1, 4, 6, 7, and 10—and all of paragraph 5. Select two examples of short sentences you find particularly effective and explain why.

SUGGESTIONS FOR WRITING

A. Read this essay in conjunction with Porter's short story "Rope." Write an essay analyzing the portrayal of marriage in the two works.

B. Write your own essay on love, on hate, or on the relationship between them. You can use Porter's essay to support your views, you can refute her, or you can ignore her.

C. Read the following selections—the opening paragraph of Richard Selzer's *Love Sick* and Robert Graves's poem "Symptoms of Love"—and discuss their vision of Romantic love in relation to Porter's.

LOVE SICK

Love is an illness, and has its own set of obsessive thoughts. Behold the poor wretch afflicted with love: one moment strewn upon a sofa, scarcely breathing save for an occasional sigh upsucked from the deep well of his despair; the next, pacing *agitato,* his cheek alternately pale and flushed. Is he pricked? What barb, what gnat stings him thus?

At noon he waves away his plate of food. Unloved, he loathes his own body, and refuses it the smallest nourishment. At half-past twelve, he receives a letter. She loves him! And soon he is snout-deep in his dish, voracious as any wolf at entrails. Greeted by a friend, a brother, he makes no discernible reply, but gazes to and fro, unable to recall who it is that salutes him. Distraught, he picks up a magazine, only to stand wondering what it is he is holding. Was he once clever at the guitar? He can no longer play at all. And so it goes.

SYMPTOMS OF LOVE

Love is a universal migraine,
A bright stain on the vision
Blotting out reason.

Symptoms of true love
Are leanness, jealousy,
Laggard dawns;

Are omens and nightmares—
Listening for a knock.
Waiting for a sign:

For a touch of her fingers
In a darkened room,
For a searching look.

Take courage, lover!
Could you endure such pain
At any hand but hers?

Rope

1 On the third day after they moved to the country he came walking back from the village carrying a basket of groceries and a twenty-four-yard coil of rope. She came out to meet him, wiping her hands on her green smock. Her hair was tumbled, her nose was scarlet with sunburn; he told her that already she looked like a born country woman. His gray flannel shirt stuck to him, his heavy shoes were dusty. She assured him he looked like a rural character in a play.

2 Had he brought the coffee? She had been waiting all day long for coffee. They had forgot it when they ordered at the store the first day.

3 Gosh, no, he hadn't. Lord, now he'd have to go back. Yes, he would if it killed him. He thought, though, he had everything else. She reminded him it was only because he didn't drink coffee himself. If he did he would remember it quick enough. Suppose they ran out of cigarettes? Then she saw the rope. What was that for? Well, he thought it might do to hang clothes on, or something. Naturally she asked him if he thought they were going to run a laundry? They already had a fifty-foot line hanging right before his eyes? Why, hadn't he noticed it, really? It was a blot on the landscape to her.

4 He thought there were a lot of things a rope might come in handy for. She wanted to know what, for instance. He thought a few seconds, but nothing occurred. They could wait and see, couldn't they? You need all sorts of strange odds and ends around a place in the country. She said, yes, that was so; but she thought just at that time when every penny counted, it seemed funny to buy more rope. That was all. She hadn't meant anything else. She hadn't just seen, not at first, why he felt it was necessary.

5 Well, thunder, he had bought it because he wanted to, and that was all there was to it. She thought that was reason enough, and couldn't understand why he hadn't said so, at first. Undoubtedly it would be useful, twenty-four yards of rope, there were hundreds of things, she couldn't think of any at the moment, but it would come in handy. Of course. As he had said, things always did in the country.

6 But she was a little disappointed about the coffee, and oh, look, look, look at the eggs! Oh, my, they're all running! What had he put on top of them? Hadn't he known eggs mustn't be squeezed? Squeezed, who had squeezed them, he wanted to know. What a silly thing to say. He had simply brought them along in the basket with the other things. If they got broke it was the grocer's fault. He should know better than to put heavy things on top of eggs.

7 She believed it was the rope. That was the heaviest thing in the pack, she saw him plainly when he came in from the road, the rope was a big package on top of everything. He desired the whole wide world to witness that this was not a fact. He had carried the rope in one hand and the basket in the other, and what was the use of her having eyes if that was the best they could do for her?

8 Well, anyhow, she could see one thing plain: no eggs for breakfast. They'd have to scramble them now, for supper. It was too damned bad. She had planned to have steak for supper. No ice, meat wouldn't keep. He wanted to know why she couldn't finish breaking the eggs in a bowl and set them in a cool place.

9 Cool place! if he could find one for her, she'd be glad to set them there. Well, then, it seemed to him they might very well cook the meat at the same time they cooked the eggs and then warm up the meat for tomorrow. The idea simply choked her. Warmed-over meat, when they might as well have had it fresh. Second best and scraps and makeshifts, even to the meat! He rubbed her shoulder a little. It doesn't really matter so much, does it, darling? Sometimes when they were playful, he would rub her shoulder and she would arch and purr. This time she hissed and almost clawed. He was getting ready to say that they could surely manage somehow when she turned on him and said, if he told her they could manage somehow she would certainly slap his face.

10 He swallowed the words red hot, his face burned. He picked up the rope and started to put it on the top shelf. She would not have it on the top shelf, the jars and tins belonged there; positively she would not have the top shelf cluttered up with a lot of rope. She had borne all the clutter she meant to bear in the flat in town, there was space here at least and she meant to keep things in order.

11 Well, in that case, he wanted to know what the hammer and nails were doing up there? And why had she put them there when she knew very well he needed that hammer and those nails upstairs to fix the window sashes? She simply slowed down everything and made double work on the place with her insane habit of changing things around and hiding them.

12 She was sure she begged his pardon, and if she had had any reason to believe he was going to fix the sashes this summer she would have left the hammer and nails right where he put them; in the middle of the bedroom floor where they could step on them in the dark. And now if he didn't clear the whole mess out of there she would throw them down the well.

13 Oh, all right, all right—could he put them in the closet? Naturally not, there were brooms and mops and dustpans in the closet, and why couldn't he find a place for his rope outside her kitchen? Had he stopped to consider there were seven God-forsaken rooms in the house, and only one kitchen?

14 He wanted to know what of it? And did she realize she was making a complete fool of herself? And what did she take him for, a three-year-old idiot? The whole trouble with her was she needed something weaker than she was to heckle and tyrannize over. He wished to God now they had a couple of children she could take it out on. Maybe he'd get some rest.

15 Her face changed at this, she reminded him he had forgot the coffee and had bought a worthless piece of rope. And when she thought of all the things they actually needed to make the place even decently fit to live in, well, she could cry, that was all. She looked so forlorn, so lost and despairing he couldn't believe it was only a piece of rope that was causing all the racket. What *was* the matter, for God's sake?

16 Oh, would he please hush and go away, and *stay* away, if he could, for five minutes? By all means, yes, he would. He'd stay away indefinitely if she wished. Lord,

yes, there was nothing he'd like better than to clear out and never come back. She couldn't for the life of her see what was holding him, then. It was a swell time. Here she was, stuck, miles from a railroad, with a half-empty house on her hands, and not a penny in her pocket, and everything on earth to do; it seemed the God-sent moment for him to get out from under. She was surprised he hadn't stayed in town as it was until she had come out and done the work and got things straightened out. It was his usual trick.

17 It appeared to him that this was going a little far. Just a touch out of bounds, if she didn't mind his saying so. Why the hell had he stayed in town the summer before? To do a half-dozen extra jobs to get the money he had sent her. That was it. She knew perfectly well they couldn't have done it otherwise. She had agreed with him at the time. And that was the only time so help him he had ever left her to do anything by herself.

18 Oh, he could tell that to his great-grandmother. She had her notion of what had kept him in town. Considerably more than a notion, if he wanted to know. So, she was going to bring all that up again, was she? Well, she could just think what she pleased. He was tired of explaining. It may have looked funny but he had simply got hooked in, and what could he do? It was impossible to believe that she was going to take it seriously. Yes, yes, she knew how it was with a man: if he was left by himself a minute, some woman was certain to kidnap him. And naturally he couldn't hurt her feelings by refusing!

19 Well, what was she raving about? Did she forget she had told him those two weeks alone in the country were the happiest she had known for four years? And how long had they been married when she said that? All right, shut up! If she thought that hadn't stuck in his craw.

20 She hadn't meant she was happy because she was away from him. She meant she was happy getting the devilish house nice and ready for him. That was what she had meant, and now look! Bringing up something she had said a year ago simply to justify himself for forgetting her coffee and breaking the eggs and buying a wretched piece of rope they couldn't afford. She really thought it was time to drop the subject, and now she wanted only two things in the world. She wanted him to get that rope from underfoot, and go back to the village and get her coffee, and if he could remember it, he might bring a metal mitt for the skillets, and two more curtain rods, and if there were any rubber gloves in the village, her hands were simply raw, and a bottle of milk of magnesia from the drugstore.

21 He looked out at the dark blue afternoon sweltering on the slopes, and mopped his forehead and sighed heavily and said, if only she could wait a minute for *anything*, he was going back. He had said so, hadn't he, the very instant they found he had overlooked it?

22 Oh, yes, well . . . run along. She was going to wash windows. The country was so beautiful! She doubted they'd have a moment to enjoy it. He meant to go, but he could not until he had said that if she wasn't such a hopeless melancholiac she might see that this was only for a few days. Couldn't she remember anything pleasant about the other summers? Hadn't they ever had any fun? She hadn't time to talk about it, and now would he please not leave that rope lying around for her

to trip on? He picked it up, somehow it had toppled off the table, and walked out with it under his arm.

23 Was he going this minute? He certainly was. She thought so. Sometimes it seemed to her he had second sight about the precisely perfect moment to leave her ditched. She had meant to put the mattresses out to sun, if they put them out this minute they would get at least three hours, he must have heard her say that morning she meant to put them out. So of course he would walk off and leave her to it. She supposed he thought the exercise would do her good.

24 Well, he was merely going to get her coffee. A four-mile walk for two pounds of coffee was ridiculous, but he was perfectly willing to do it. The habit was making a wreck of her, but if she wanted to wreck herself there was nothing he could do about it. If he thought it was coffee that was making a wreck of her, she congratulated him: he must have a damned easy conscience.

25 Conscience or no conscience, he didn't see why the mattresses couldn't very well wait until tomorrow. And anyhow, for God's sake, were they living *in* the house, or were they going to let the house ride them to death? She paled at this, her face grew livid about the mouth, she looked quite dangerous, and reminded him that housekeeping was no more her work than it was his: she had other work to do as well, and when did he think she was going to find time to do it at this rate?

26 Was she going to start on that again? She knew as well as he did that his work brought in the regular money, hers was only occasional, if they depended on what *she* made—and she might as well get straight on this question once for all!

27 That was positively not the point. The question was, when both of them were working on their own time, was there going to be a division of the housework, or wasn't there? She merely wanted to know, she had to make her plans. Why, he thought that was all arranged. It was understood that he was to help. Hadn't he always, in summers?

28 Hadn't he, though? Oh, just hadn't he? And when, and where, and doing what? Lord, what an uproarious joke!

29 It was such a very uproarious joke that her face turned slightly purple, and she screamed with laughter. She laughed so hard she had to sit down, and finally a rush of tears spurted from her eyes and poured down into the lifted corners of her mouth. He dashed towards her and dragged her up to her feet and tried to pour water on her head. The dipper hung by a string on a nail and he broke it loose. Then he tried to pump water with one hand while she struggled in the other. So he gave it up and shook her instead.

30 She wrenched away, crying out for him to take his rope and go to hell, she had simply given him up: and ran. He heard her high-heeled bedroom slippers clattering and stumbling on the stairs.

31 He went out around the house and into the lane; he suddenly realized he had a blister on his heel and his shirt felt as if it were on fire. Things broke so suddenly you didn't know where you were. She could work herself into a fury about simply nothing. She was terrible, damn it: not an ounce of reason. You might as well talk to a sieve as that woman when she got going. Damned if he'd spend his life humoring her! Well, what to do now? He would take back the rope and exchange it for something else. Things accumulated, things were mountainous, you couldn't

move them or sort them out or get rid of them. They just lay and rotted around. He'd take it back. Hell, why should he? He wanted it. What was it anyhow? A piece of rope. Imagine anybody caring more about a piece of rope than about a man's feelings. What earthly right had she to say a word about it? He remembered all the useless, meaningless things she bought for herself: Why? because I wanted it, that's why! He stopped and selected a large stone by the road. He would put the rope behind it. He would put it in the tool-box when he got back. He'd heard enough about it to last him a life-time.

32 When he came back she was leaning against the post box beside the road waiting. It was pretty late, the smell of broiled steak floated nose high in the cooling air. Her face was young and smooth and fresh-looking. Her unmanageable funny black hair was all on end. She waved to him from a distance, and he speeded up. She called out that supper was ready and waiting, was he starved?

33 You bet he was starved. Here was the coffee. He waved it at her. She looked at his other hand. What was that he had there?

34 Well, it was the rope again. He stopped short. He had meant to exchange it but forgot. She wanted to know why he should exchange it, if it was something he really wanted. Wasn't the air sweet now, and wasn't it fine to be here?

35 She walked beside him with one hand hooked into his leather belt. She pulled and jostled him a little as he walked, and leaned against him. He put his arm clear around her and patted her stomach. They exchanged wary smiles. Coffee, coffee for the Ootsum-Wootsums! He felt as if he were bringing her a beautiful present.

36 He was a love, she firmly believed, and if she had had her coffee in the morning, she wouldn't have behaved so funny . . . There was a whippoorwill still coming back, imagine, clear out of season, sitting in the crab-apple tree calling all by himself. Maybe his girl stood him up. Maybe she did. She hoped to hear him once more, she loved whippoorwills . . . He knew how she was, didn't he?

37 Sure, he knew how she was.

(1928)

QUESTIONS

1. Is the basic situation of this story believable? Why or why not?
2. What qualities of character distinguish the man and the woman? Why aren't the characters named?
3. What is the effect of not being given the direct speech of the husband and wife? We do know what they say to each other, but this knowledge is filtered through a narrator, who reports their conversation indirectly. What is different about this manner of presentation?
4. What is the author's attitude toward her characters? Does she seem to side with one or the other? Do you? Why or why not?
5. What do you make of the ending? Were you surprised at the couple's behavior? Why or why not?
6. What is the significance of the rope? What does it represent?

SUGGESTIONS FOR WRITING

A. Discuss the nature of the marital relationship portrayed here. Offer a prognosis for the couple's marital future.

B. Compare the portrayal of marriage in this story with that in Porter's essay "A Necessary Enemy."

The Grave

1 The grandfather, dead for more than thirty years, had been twice disturbed in his long repose by the constancy and possessiveness of his widow. She removed his bones first to Louisiana and then to Texas as if she had set out to find her own burial place, knowing well she would never return to the places she had left. In Texas she set up a small cemetery in a corner of her first farm, and as the family connection grew, and oddments of relations came over from Kentucky to settle, it contained at last about twenty graves. After the grandmother's death, part of her land was to be sold for the benefit of certain of her children, and the cemetery happened to lie in the part set aside for sale. It was necessary to take up the bodies and bury them again in the family plot in the big new public cemetery, where the grandmother had been buried. At last her husband was to lie beside her for eternity, as she had planned.

2 The family cemetery had been a pleasant small neglected garden of tangled rose bushes and ragged cedar trees and cypress, the simple flat stones rising out of uncropped sweet-smelling wild grass. The graves were lying open and empty one burning day when Miranda and her brother Paul, who often went together to hunt rabbits and doves, propped their twenty-two Winchester rifles carefully against the rail fence, climbed over and explored among the graves. She was nine years old and he was twelve.

3 They peered into the pits all shaped alike with such purposeful accuracy, and looking at each other with pleased adventurous eyes, they said in solemn tones: "These were graves!" trying by words to shape a special, suitable emotion in their minds, but they felt nothing except an agreeable thrill of wonder: they were seeing a new sight, doing something they had not done before. In them both there was also a small disappointment at the entire commonplaceness of the actual spectacle. Even if it had once contained a coffin for years upon years, when the coffin was gone a grave was just a hole in the ground. Miranda leaped into the pit that had held her grandfather's bones. Scratching around aimlessly and pleasurably as any young animal, she scooped up a lump of earth and weighed it in her palm. It had a pleasantly sweet, corrupt smell, being mixed with cedar needles and small leaves, and as the crumbs fell apart, she saw a silver dove no larger than a hazel nut, with spread wings and a neat fan-shaped tail. The breast had a deep round hollow in it. Turning it up to the fierce sunlight, she saw that the inside of the hollow was cut in little whorls. She scrambled out, over the pile of loose earth that had fallen back into one end of the grave, calling to Paul that she had found something, he must guess what

. . . His head appeared smiling over the rim of another grave. He waved a closed hand at her. "I've got something too!" They ran to compare treasures, making a game of it, so many guesses each, all wrong, and a final showdown with opened palms. Paul had found a thin wide gold ring carved with intricate flowers and leaves. Miranda was smitten at sight of the ring and wished to have it. Paul seemed more impressed by the dove. They made a trade, with some little bickering. After he had got the dove in his hand, Paul said, "Don't you know what this is? This is a screw head for a *coffin!* . . . I'll bet nobody else in the world has one like this!"

4 Miranda glanced at it without covetousness. She had the gold ring on her thumb; it fitted perfectly. "Maybe we ought to go now," she said, "maybe one of the niggers 'll see us and tell somebody." They knew the land had been sold, the cemetery was no longer theirs, and they felt like trespassers. They climbed back over the fence, slung their rifles loosely under their arms—they had been shooting at targets with various kinds of firearms since they were seven years old—and set out to look for the rabbits and doves or whatever small game might happen along. On these expeditions Miranda always followed at Paul's heels along the path, obeying instructions about handling her gun when going through fences; learning how to stand it up properly so it would not slip and fire unexpectedly; how to wait her time for a shot and not just bang away in the air without looking, spoiling shots for Paul, who really could hit things if given a chance. Now and then, in her excitement at seeing birds whizz up suddenly before her face, or a rabbit leap across her very toes, she lost her head, and almost without sighting she flung her rifle up and pulled the trigger. She hardly ever hit any sort of mark. She had no proper sense of hunting at all. Her brother would be often completely disgusted with her. "You don't care whether you get your bird or not," he said. "That's no way to hunt." Miranda could not understand his indignation. She had seen him smash his hat and yell with fury when he had missed his aim. "What I like about shooting," said Miranda, with exasperating inconsequence, "is pulling the trigger and hearing the noise."

5 "Then, by golly," said Paul, "whyn't you go back to the range and shoot at bulls-eyes?"

6 "I'd just as soon," said Miranda, "only like this, we walk around more."

7 "Well, you just stay behind and stop spoiling my shots," said Paul, who, when he made a kill, wanted to be certain he had made it. Miranda, who alone brought down a bird once in twenty rounds, always claimed as her own any game they got when they fired at the same moment. It was tiresome and unfair and her brother was sick of it.

8 "Now, the first dove we see, or the first rabbit, is mine," he told her. "And the next will be yours. Remember that and don't get smarty."

9 "What about snakes?" asked Miranda idly. "Can I have the first snake?"

10 Waving her thumb gently and watching her gold ring glitter, Miranda lost interest in shooting. She was wearing her summer roughing outfit: dark blue overalls, a light blue shirt, a hired-man's straw hat, and thick brown sandals. Her brother had the same outfit except his was a sober hickory-nut color. Ordinarily Miranda preferred her overalls to any other dress, though it was making rather a scandal in the countryside, for the year was 1903, and in the back country the law of female decorum had teeth in it. Her father had been criticized for letting his girls dress like

boys and go careering around astride barebacked horses. Big sister Maria, the really independent and fearless one, in spite of her rather affected ways, rode at a dead run with only a rope knotted around her horse's nose. It was said the motherless family was running down, with the Grandmother no longer there to hold it together. It was known that she had discriminated against her son Harry in her will, and that he was in straits about money. Some of his old neighbors reflected with vicious satisfaction that now he would probably not be so stiffnecked, nor have any more high-stepping horses either. Miranda knew this, though she could not say how. She had met along the road old women of the kind who smoked corn-cob pipes, who had treated her grandmother with most sincere respect. They slanted their gummy old eyes side-ways at the granddaughter and said, "Ain't you ashamed of yoself, Missy? It's aginst the Scriptures to dress like that. Whut yo Pappy thinkin about?" Miranda, with her powerful social sense, which was like a fine set of antennae radiating from every pore of her skin, would feel ashamed because she knew well it was rude and ill-bred to shock anybody, even bad-tempered old crones, though she had faith in her father's judgment and was perfectly comfortable in the clothes. Her father had said, "They're just what you need, and they'll save your dresses for school . . ." This sounded quite simple and natural to her. She had been brought up in rigorous economy. Wastefulness was vulgar. It was also a sin. These were truths; she had heard them repeated many times and never once disputed.

11 Now the ring, shining with the serene purity of fine gold on her rather grubby thumb, turned her feelings against her overalls and sockless feet, toes sticking through the thick brown leather straps. She wanted to go back to the farmhouse, take a good cold bath, dust herself with plenty of Maria's violet talcum powder—provided Maria was not present to object, of course—put on the thinnest, most becoming dress she owned, with a big sash, and sit in a wicker chair under the trees . . . These things were not all she wanted, of course; she had vague stirrings of desire for luxury and a grand way of living which could not take precise form in her imagination but were founded on family legend of past wealth and leisure. These immediate comforts were what she could have, and she wanted them at once. She lagged rather far behind Paul, and once she thought of just turning back without a word and going home. She stopped, thinking that Paul would never do that to her, and so she would have to tell him. When a rabbit leaped, she let Paul have it without dispute. He killed it with one shot.

12 When she came up with him, he was already kneeling, examining the wound, the rabbit trailing from his hands. "Right through the head," he said complacently, as if he had aimed for it. He took out his sharp, competent bowie knife and started to skin the body. He did it very cleanly and quickly. Uncle Jimbilly knew how to prepare the skins so that Miranda always had fur coats for her dolls, for though she never cared much for her dolls she liked seeing them in fur coats. The children knelt facing each other over the dead animal. Miranda watched admiringly while her brother stripped the skin away as if he were taking off a glove. The flayed flesh emerged dark scarlet, sleek, firm; Miranda with thumb and finger felt the long fine muscles with the silvery flat strips binding them to the joints. Brother lifted the oddly bloated belly. "Look," he said, in a low amazed voice. "It was going to have young ones."

13 Very carefully he slit the thin flesh from the center ribs to the flanks, and a scarlet bag appeared. He slit again and pulled the bag open, and there lay a bundle of tiny rabbits, each wrapped in a thin scarlet veil. The brother pulled these off and there they were, dark gray, their sleek wet down lying in minute even ripples, like a baby's head just washed, their unbelievably small delicate ears folded close, their little blind faces almost featureless.

14 Miranda said, "Oh, I want to *see,*" under her breath. She looked and looked—excited but not frightened, for she was accustomed to the sight of animals killed in hunting—filled with pity and astonishment and a kind of shocked delight in the wonderful little creatures for their own sakes, they were so pretty. She touched one of them ever so carefully, "Ah, there's blood running over them," she said and began to tremble without knowing why. Yet she wanted most deeply to see and to know. Having seen, she felt at once as if she had known all along. The very memory of her former ignorance faded, she had always known just this. No one had ever told her anything outright, she had been rather unobservant of the animal life around her because she was so accustomed to animals. They seemed simply disorderly and unaccountably rude in their habits, but altogether natural and not very interesting. Her brother had spoken as if he had known about everything all along. He may have seen all this before. He had never said a word to her, but she knew now a part at least of what he knew. She understood a little of the secret, formless intuitions in her own mind and body, which had been clearing up, taking form, so gradually and so steadily she had not realized that she was learning what she had to know. Paul said cautiously, as if he were talking about something forbidden: "They were just about ready to be born." His voice dropped on the last word. "I know," said Miranda, "like kittens. I know, like babies." She was quietly and terribly agitated, standing again with her rifle under her arm, looking down at the bloody heap. "I don't want the skin," she said, "I won't have it." Paul buried the young rabbits again in their mother's body, wrapped the skin around her, carried her to a clump of sage bushes, and hid her away. He came out again at once and said to Miranda, with an eager friendliness, a confidential tone quite unusual in him, as if he were taking her into an important secret on equal terms: "Listen now. Now you listen to me, and don't ever forget. Don't you ever tell a living soul that you saw this. Don't tell a soul. Don't tell Dad because I'll get into trouble. He'll say I'm leading you into things you ought not to do. He's always saying that. So now don't you go and forget and blab out sometime the way you're always doing . . . Now, that's a secret. Don't you tell."

15 Miranda never told, she did not even wish to tell anybody. She thought about the whole worrisome affair with confused unhappiness for a few days. Then it sank quietly into her mind and was heaped over by accumulated thousands of impressions, for nearly twenty years. One day she was picking her path among the puddles and crushed refuse of a market street in a strange city of a strange country, when without warning, plain and clear in its true colors as if she looked through a frame upon a scene that had not stirred nor changed since the moment it happened, the episode of that far-off day leaped from its burial place before her mind's eye. She was so reasonlessly horrified she halted suddenly staring, the scene before her eyes dimmed by the vision back of them. An Indian vendor had held up before her a tray of dyed

sugar sweets, in the shapes of all kinds of small creatures: birds, baby chicks, baby rabbits, lambs, baby pigs. They were in gay colors and smelled of vanilla, maybe. . . . It was a very hot day and the smell in the market, with its piles of raw flesh and wilting flowers, was like the mingled sweetness and corruption she had smelled that other day in the empty cemetery at home: the day she had remembered always until now vaguely as the time she and her brother had found treasure in the opened graves. Instantly upon this thought the dreadful vision faded, and she saw clearly her brother, whose childhood face she had forgotten, standing again in the blazing sunshine, again twelve years old, a pleased sober smile in his eyes, turning the silver dove over and over in his hands.

(1944)

QUESTIONS

1. What, for you, is the most dramatic moment in the story? Why?
2. What does Miranda learn from her experience?
3. What is the significance of the open grave? Of the dove and ring the children find there? Their swapping of the items?
4. What triggers Miranda's memory some twenty years later about the experience described when she was nine years old?
5. What attitude toward the natural world do the children exhibit? Why?
6. Discuss what happens to Miranda in terms of Porter's distinction between "adventure" and "experience" in her essay "St. Augustine and the Bullfight."

SUGGESTIONS FOR WRITING

A. Write an essay in which you describe an experience whose meaning was not clear to you until some time later. Illuminate the later meaning the experience came to have for you.

B. Compare and contrast the male and female attitudes toward birth and death exhibited in this story.

SIX

E. B. White

(1899–1985)

E. B. White is generally recognized as one of America's finest writers. Long associated with *The New Yorker,* for which he wrote stories, sketches, essays, and editorials, White has also contributed to another prominent magazine, *Harper's,* writing a monthly column, "One Man's Meat," from 1938 to 1943. These columns were collected and published with a few additional pieces from *The New Yorker* as *One Man's Meat* (1944). This book was followed by two other collections of miscellany, *The Second Tree from the Corner* (1954) and *The Points of My Compass* (1962). Besides these collections, White published, over a slightly longer span of years, three children's books: *Stuart Little* (1945), *Charlotte's Web* (1952), and *The Trumpet of the Swan* (1970). In 1976, White published a selection of his best essays, those, as he says, which had "an odor of durability clinging to them." *The Essays of E. B. White* were followed a year later by a selection of White's letters. *Poems and Sketches of E. B. White* appeared in 1981.

Though not a complete bibliography of White's published work, this list does suggest White's range and versatility, as well as the way writing was for him steady work over a long stretch of time. And the steadiest of White's work, in both senses of the word, has been his essays. In fact, it is as an essayist that White is best known and most highly acclaimed. And it is as an essayist that he identifies himself, defining essayist as "a self-liberated man sustained by the childish belief that everything he thinks about, everything that happens to him, is of general interest." And again, as one who is "content with living a free life and enjoying the satisfactions of a somewhat undisciplined existence."

Edward Hoagland, himself a respected essayist, considers White's name nearly synonymous with "essay." And for good reason, since it is a form congenial to White's temperament, one that allows him enough latitude in thought and structure to stamp the form indelibly with his own imprint. This imprint is reflected in White's scrupulous respect for his readers, his uncanny accuracy in the use of language, and his uncommon delight in everyday things. White sees the extraordinary in the ordinary, noticing and valuing what many of us either overlook or take for granted. From his repeated acts of attention flow reminiscences, speculations, explorations, and questions about our common humanity, our relationships with one another, our connections with the past, with nature, and with the world of technology.

White's insight derives directly from observation, from what he sees. Henry David Thoreau, one of White's favorite writers—and one with whom he has much in common—once remarked that "you can't say more than you can see." White's writing bears this out. The relationship between sight and insight, between observation and speculation, is evident in essays such as "The Ring of Time," which begins with a description of a circus act and ends with speculations about time and change; and in "Once More to The Lake," in which White reminisces about his boyhood summer holidays in Maine, describing the place with startling vividness and offering unsettling speculations about the meaning of his memories.

White's best writing, however, is more than a record of what he has seen and thought. It is also literary art. It is crafted with the same attention to details of structure, texture, image, and tone that poets and novelists, painters and sculptors, give their work. In "The Ring of Time" and "Once More to the Lake," details of time, place, and circumstance give way to larger concerns. The circus is more than a circus ring: it becomes a symbol of time; the lake is more than a summer vacation: it becomes an image of serenity and a reminder of mortality. The images of light and water, the symbolism of circus ring and lake, along with a concern for understanding the present in relation to the past and the future—these lift the essays beyond the merely personal and the ordinary into the extraordinary universality of art.

About writing itself White has a said a good deal, and said it well. In the chapter he contributed to the famous *Elements of Style,* White notes that when we speak of a writer's style we mean "the sound his words make on paper." The voice that we hear is what distinguishes one writer from another; and it is one good reason why, to acquire a good sense of a writer's style, we should read his or her work aloud. Beyond this concern for hearing what language can do, White notes that a writer's style "reveals something of his spirit, his habits, his capacities, his bias . . . it is the Self escaping into the open." And, as White suggests, this Self cannot be hidden, for a writer's style "reveals his identity as surely as would his fingerprints."

Recognizing that writing is hard work requiring endurance, thought, and revision ("revising is part of writing," White remarks) he advises beginning writers to develop an ear for language, to avoid all tricks and mannerisms, to see writing as "one way to go about thinking," and finally, to achieve style by affecting none and by believing "in the truth and worth" of their writing.

Throughout his years as a writer, White has often been asked for advice about writing. To one seeker he wrote: "Remember that writing is translation, and the opus to be translated is yourself." On another occasion he responded to a seventeen-year-old girl this way:

> You asked me about writing—how I did it. There is no trick to it. If you like to write and want to write, you write, no matter where you are or what else you are doing or whether anyone pays any heed . . . If you want to write about feelings, about the end of summer, about growing, write about it. A great deal of writing is not "plotted"—most of my essays have no plot structure; they are a ramble in the woods, or a ramble in the basement of my mind.

There is a naturalness, an ease about White's writing both in these offhand remarks from his letters and in his more elaborately developed essays. It is an ease that derives in part from a refusal to be either pompous or pedantic; it is an ease that derives also from a consistent attempt to be honest, to achieve the candor he admires in Montaigne. White's naturalness is reflected in his style, which mingles the high subject and the low, the big word and the small without flamboyance or ostentation. White's style, in short, is a badge of his character—intelligent, honest, witty, exact, and fundamentally endearing.

The Geese

1 To give a clear account of what took place in the barnyard early in the morning on that last Sunday in June, I will have to go back more than a year in time, but a year is nothing to me these days. Besides, I intend to be quick about it, and not dawdle.

2 I have had a pair of elderly gray geese—a goose and a gander—living on this place for a number of years, and they have been my friends. "Companions" would be a better word; geese are friends with no one, they badmouth everybody and everything. But they are companionable once you get used to their ingratitude and their false accusations. Early in the spring, a year ago, as soon as the ice went out of the pond, my goose started to lay. She laid three eggs in about a week's time and then died. I found her halfway down the lane that connects the barnyard with the pasture. There were no marks on her—she lay with wings partly outspread, and with her neck forward in the grass, pointing downhill. Geese are rarely sick, and I think this goose's time had come and she had simply died of old age. I had noticed that her step had slowed on her trips back from the pond to the barn where her nest was. I had never known her age, and so had nothing else to go on. We buried her in our private graveyard, and I felt sad at losing an acquaintance of such long standing—long standing and loud shouting.

3 Her legacy, of course, was the three eggs. I knew they were good eggs and did not like to pitch them out. It seemed to me that the least I could do for my departed companion was to see that the eggs she had left in my care were hatched. I checked my hen pen to find out whether we had a broody, but there was none. During the next few days, I scoured the neighborhood for a broody hen, with no success. Years ago, if you needed a broody hen, almost any barn or henhouse would yield one. But today broodiness is considered unacceptable in a hen; the modern hen is an egg-laying machine, and her natural tendency to sit on eggs in springtime has been bred out of her. Besides, not many people keep hens anymore—when they want a dozen eggs, they don't go to the barn, they go to the First National.

4 Days went by. My gander, the widower, lived a solitary life—nobody to swap gossip with, nobody to protect. He seemed dazed. The three eggs were not getting any younger, and I myself felt dazed—restless and unfulfilled. I had stored the eggs down cellar in the arch where it is cool, and every time I went down there for something they seemed silently to reproach me. My plight had become known around town, and one day a friend phoned and said he would lend me an incubator designed for hatching the eggs of waterfowl. I brought the thing home, cleaned it up, plugged it in, and sat down to read the directions. After studying them, I realized that if I were to tend eggs in that incubator, I would have to withdraw from the world for thirty days—give up everything, just as a broody goose does. Obsessed

though I was with the notion of bringing life into three eggs, I wasn't quite prepared to pay the price.

5 Instead, I abandoned the idea of incubation and decided to settle the matter by acquiring three ready-made goslings, as a memorial to the goose and a gift for the lonely gander. I drove up the road about five miles and dropped in on Irving Closson. I knew Irving had geese; he has everything—even a sawmill. I found him shoeing a very old horse in the doorway of his barn, and I stood and watched for a while. Hens and geese wandered about the yard, and a turkey tom circled me, wings adroop, strutting. The horse, with one forefoot between the man's knees, seemed to have difficulty balancing himself on three legs but was quiet and sober, almost asleep. When I asked Irving if he planned to put shoes on the horse's hind feet, too, he said, "No, it's hard work for me, and he doesn't use those hind legs much anyway." Then I brought up the question of goslings, and he took me into the barn and showed me a sitting goose. He said he thought she was covering more than twenty eggs and should bring off her goslings in a couple of weeks and I could buy a few if I wanted. I said I would like three.

6 I took to calling at Irving's every few days—it is about the pleasantest place to visit anywhere around. At last, I was rewarded: I pulled into the driveway one morning and saw a goose surrounded by green goslings. She had been staked out, like a cow. Irving had simply tied a piece of string to one leg and fastened the other end to a peg in the ground. She was a pretty goose—not as large as my old one had been, and with a more slender neck. She appeared to be a cross-bred bird, two-toned gray, with white markings—a sort of particolored goose. The goslings had the cheerful, bright, innocent look that all baby geese have. We scooped up three and tossed them into a box, and I paid Irving and carried them home.

7 My next concern was how to introduce these small creatures to their foster father, my old gander. I thought about this all the way home. I've had just enough experience with domesticated animals and birds to know that they are a bundle of eccentricities and crotchets, and I was not at all sure what sort of reception three strange youngsters would get from a gander who was full of sorrows and suspicions. (I once saw a gander, taken by surprise, seize a newly hatched gosling and hurl it the length of the barn floor.) I had an uneasy feeling that my three little charges might be dead within the hour, victims of a grief-crazed old fool. I decided to go slow. I fixed a makeshift pen for the goslings in the barn, arranged so that they would be separated from the gander but visible to him, and he would be visible to them. The old fellow, when he heard youthful voices, hustled right in to find out what was going on. He studied the scene in silence and with the greatest attention. I could not tell whether the look in his eye was one of malice or affection—a goose's eye is a small round enigma. After observing this introductory scene for a while, I left and went into the house.

8 Half an hour later, I heard a commotion in the barnyard: the gander was in full cry. I hustled out. The goslings, impatient with life indoors, had escaped from their hastily constructed enclosure in the barn and had joined their foster father in the barnyard. The cries I had heard were his screams of welcome—the old bird was delighted with the turn that events had taken. His period of mourning was over, he now had interesting and useful work to do, and he threw himself into the role of father with immense satisfaction and zeal, hissing at me with renewed malevolence, shep-

herding the three children here and there, and running interference against real and imaginary enemies. My fears were laid to rest. In the rush of emotion that seized him at finding himself the head of a family, his thoughts turned immediately to the pond, and I watched admiringly as he guided the goslings down the long, tortuous course through the weedy lane and on down across the rough pasture between blueberry knolls and granite boulders. It was a sight to see him hold the heifers at bay so the procession could pass safely. Summer was upon us, the pond was alive again. I brought the three eggs up from the cellar and dispatched them to the town dump.

9 At first, I did not know the sex of my three goslings. But nothing on two legs grows any faster than a young goose, and by early fall it was obvious that I had drawn one male and two females. You tell the sex of a goose by its demeanor and its stance—the way it holds itself, its general approach to life. A gander carries his head high and affects a threatening attitude. Females go about with necks in a graceful arch and are less aggressive. My two young females looked like their mother, particolored. The young male was quite different. He feathered out white all over except for his wings, which were a very light, pearly gray. Afloat on the pond, he looked almost like a swan, with his tall, thin white neck and his cocked-up white tail—a real dandy, full of pompous thoughts and surly gestures.

10 Winter is a time of waiting, for man and goose. Last winter was a long wait, the pasture deep in drifts, the lane barricaded, the pond inaccessible and frozen. Life centered in the barn and the barnyard. When the time for mating came, conditions were unfavorable, and this was upsetting to the old gander. Geese like a body of water for their coupling; it doesn't have to be a large body of water—just any wet place in which a goose can become partly submerged. My old gander, studying the calendar, inflamed by passion, unable to get to the pond, showed signs of desperation. On several occasions, he tried to manage with a ten-quart pail of water that stood in the barnyard. He would chivvy one of his young foster daughters over to the pail, seize her by the nape, and hold her head under water while he made his attempt. It was never a success and usually ended up looking more like a comedy tumbling act than like coitus. One got the feeling during the water-pail routine that the gander had been consulting one of the modern sex manuals describing peculiar positions. Anyway, I noticed two things: the old fellow confined his attentions to one of the two young geese and let the other alone, and he never allowed his foster son to approach either of the girls—he was very strict about that, and the handsome young male lived all spring in a state of ostracism.

11 Eventually, the pond opened up, the happy band wended its way down across the melting snows, and the breeding season was officially opened. My pond is visible from the house, but it is at quite a distance. I am not a voyeur and do not spend my time watching the sex antics of geese or anything else. But I try to keep reasonably well posted on all the creatures around the place, and it was apparent that the young gander was not allowed by his foster father to enjoy the privileges of the pond and that the old gander's attentions continued to be directed to just one of the young geese. I shall call her Liz to make this tale easier to tell.

12 Both geese were soon laying. Liz made her nest in the barn cellar; her sister, Apathy, made hers in the tie-ups on the main floor of the barn. It was the end of April or the beginning of May. Still awfully cold—a reluctant spring.

13 Apathy laid three eggs, then quit. I marked them with a pencil and left them

for the time being in the nest she had constructed. I made a mental note that they were infertile. Liz, unlike her sister, went right on laying, and became a laying fool. She dallied each morning at the pond with her foster father, and she laid and laid and laid, like a commercial hen. I dutifully marked the eggs as they arrived—1, 2, 3, and so on. When she had accumulated a clutch of fifteen, I decided she had all she could cover. From then on, I took to removing the oldest egg from the nest each time a new egg was deposited. I also removed Apathy's three eggs from *her* nest, discarded them, and began substituting the purloined eggs from the barn cellar—the ones that rightfully belonged to Liz. Thus I gradually contrived to assemble a nest of fertile eggs for each bird, all of them laid by the fanatical Liz.

14 During the last week in May, Apathy, having produced only three eggs of her own but having acquired ten through the kind offices of her sister and me, became broody and began to sit. Liz, with a tally of twenty-five eggs, ten of them stolen, showed not the slightest desire to sit. Laying was her thing. She laid and laid, while the other goose sat and sat. The old gander, marveling at what he had wrought, showed a great deal of interest in both nests. The young gander was impressed but subdued. I continued to remove the early eggs from Liz's nest, holding her to a clutch of fifteen and discarding the extras. In late June, having produced forty-one eggs, ten of which were under Apathy, she at last sat down.

15 I had marked Apathy's hatching date on my desk calendar. On the night before the goslings were due to arrive, when I made my rounds before going to bed, I looked in on her. She hissed, as usual, and ran her neck out. When I shone my light at her, two tiny green heads were visible, thrusting their way through her feathers. The goslings were here—a few hours ahead of schedule. My heart leapt up. Outside, in the barnyard, both ganders stood vigil. They knew very well what was up: ganders take an enormous interest in family affairs and are deeply impressed by the miracle of the egg-that-becomes-goose. I shut the door against them and went to bed.

16 Next morning, Sunday, I rose early and went straight to the barn to see what the night had brought. Apathy was sitting quietly while five goslings teetered about on the slopes of the nest. One of them, as I watched, strayed from the others, and, not being able to find his way back, began sending out cries for help. They were the kind of distress signal any anxious father would instantly respond to. Suddenly, I heard sounds of a rumble outside in the barnyard where the ganders were—loud sounds of scuffling. I ran out. A fierce fight was in progress—it was no mere skirmish, it was the real thing. The young gander had grabbed the old one by the stern, his white head buried in feathers right where it would hurt the most, and was running him around the yard, punishing him at every turn—thrusting him on ahead and beating him unmercifully with his wings. It was an awesome sight, these two great male birds locked in combat, slugging it out—not for the favors of a female but for the dubious privilege of assuming the responsibilities of parenthood. The young male had suffered all spring the indignities of a restricted life at the pond; now he had turned, at last, against the old one, as though to get even. Round and round over rocks and through weeds, they raced, struggling and tripping, the old one in full retreat and in apparent pain. It was a beautiful late—June morning, with fair-weather clouds and a light wind going, the grasses long in the orchard—the kind of morning that always carries for me overtones of summer sadness, I don't know

why. Overhead, three swallows circled at low altitude, pursuing one white feather, the coveted trophy of nesting time. They were like three tiny fighter planes giving air support to the battle that raged below. For a moment, I thought of climbing the fence and trying to separate the combatants, but instead I just watched. The engagement was soon over. Plunging desperately down the lane, the old gander sank to the ground. The young one let go, turned, and walked back, screaming in triumph, to the door behind which his newly won family were waiting: a strange family indeed—the sister who was not even the mother of the babies, and the babies who were not even his own get.

17 When I was sure the fight was over, I climbed the fence and closed the barnyard gate, effectively separating victor from vanquished. The old gander had risen to his feet. He was in almost the same spot in the lane where his first wife had died mysteriously more than a year ago. I watched as he threaded his way slowly down the narrow path between clumps of thistles and daisies. His head was barely visible above the grasses, but his broken spirit was plain to any eye. When he reached the pasture bars, he hesitated, then painfully squatted and eased himself under the bottom bar and into the pasture, where he sat down on the cropped sward in the bright sun. I felt very deeply his sorrow and his defeat. As things go in the animal kingdom, he is about my age, and when he lowered himself to creep under the bar, I could feel in my own bones his pain at bending down so far. Two hours later, he was still sitting there, the sun by this time quite hot. I had seen his likes often enough on the benches of the treeless main street of a Florida city—spent old males, motionless in the glare of the day.

18 Toward the end of the morning, he walked back up the lane as far as the gate, and there he stood all afternoon, his head and orange bill looking like the head of a great snake. The goose and her goslings had emerged into the barnyard. Through the space between the boards of the gate, the old fellow watched the enchanting scene: the goslings taking their frequent drinks of water, climbing in and out of the shallow pan for their first swim, closely guarded by the handsome young gander, shepherded by the pretty young goose.

19 After supper, I went into the tie-ups and pulled the five remaining, unhatched eggs from the nest and thought about the five lifeless chicks inside the eggs—the unlucky ones, the ones that lacked what it takes to break out of an egg into the light of a fine June morning. I put the eggs in a basket and set the basket with some other miscellany consigned to the dump. I don't know anything sadder than a summer's day.

(1971)

QUESTIONS

Thought and Structure

1. What is the point of this piece? How can it be related to the point of "The Ring of Time" or "Once More to the Lake"?
2. Why does White purchase three goslings? What does that reveal about him?

3. "The Geese" is organized chronologically. It recounts the events of a specific time in their order of occurrence. List in time order the significant events White describes.
4. Consider White's essay as a three-part structure. Identify the introduction, body, and conclusion. What do you notice about the relative space alotted each?

Style and Strategy

5. Identify the transitions White uses to move from one paragraph to another. (Read the opening words of each paragraph, noting what they have in common.)
6. Examine any one paragraph from the standpoint of sentence length. Observe how White varies the length of his sentences, mixing long and short.
7. Notice the frequent use of dashes in both single and double versions. Look back, for example, at paragraphs 2, 4, and 6. Explain the effect of these uses of the dash.
8. Identify words and phrases that although used to describe the geese, are more suggestive of human behavior, attitudes, and feelings. Why do you think White made those language choices? (Look, for example, at paragraph 8.)

SUGGESTIONS FOR WRITING

A. Condense White's essay into a fable of one page or less (250 words).
B. Write an essay about the behavior of an animal you've observed. Make some connection between your story about the animal and human experience.
C. Write imitations of any three "dash" and/or "colon" sentences from this essay.
D. Write an imitation of one paragraph, styling your sentences in the manner of White's. Pay particular attention to sentence length.

The Ring of Time

I

Fiddler Bayou, March 22, 1956

1 After the lions had returned to their cages, creeping angrily through the chutes, a little bunch of us drifted away and into an open doorway nearby, where we stood for a while in semidarkness, watching a big brown circus horse go harumphing around the practice ring. His trainer was a woman of about forty, and the two of them, horse and woman, seemed caught up in one of those desultory treadmills of afternoon from which there is no apparent escape. The day was hot, and we kibitzers were grateful to be briefly out of the sun's glare. The long rein, or tape, by which the woman guided her charge counterclockwise in his dull career formed the radius of their private circle, of which she was the revolving center; and she, too, stepped a tiny circumference of her own, in order to accommodate the horse and allow him his maximum scope. She had on a short-skirted costume and a conical straw hat. Her legs were bare and she wore high heels, which probed deep into the

loose tanbark and kept her ankles in a state of constant turmoil. The great size and meekness of the horse, the repetitious exercise, the heat of the afternoon, all exerted a hypnotic charm that invited boredom; we spectators were experiencing a languor—we neither expected relief nor felt entitled to any. We had paid a dollar to get into the grounds, to be sure, but we had got our dollar's worth a few minutes before, when the lion trainer's whiplash had got caught around a toe of one of the lions. What more did we want for a dollar?

2 Behind me I heard someone say, "Excuse me, please," in a low voice. She was halfway into the building when I turned and saw her—a girl of sixteen or seventeen, politely threading her way through us onlookers who blocked the entrance. As she emerged in front of us, I saw that she was barefoot, her dirty little feet fighting the uneven ground. In most respects she was like any of two or three dozen showgirls you encounter if you wander about the winter quarters of Mr. John Ringling North's circus, in Sarasota—cleverly proportioned, deeply browned by the sun, dusty, eager, and almost naked. But her grave face and the naturalness of her manner gave her a sort of quick distinction and brought a new note into the gloomy octagonal building where we had all cast our lot for a few moments. As soon as she had squeezed through the crowd, she spoke a word or two to the older woman, whom I took to be her mother, stepped to the ring, and waited while the horse coasted to a stop in front of her. She gave the animal a couple of affectionate swipes on his enormous neck and then swung herself aboard. The horse immediately resumed his rocking canter, the woman goading him on, chanting something that sounded like "Hop! Hop!"

3 In attempting to recapture this mild spectacle, I am merely acting as recording secretary for one of the oldest of societies—the society of those who, at one time or another, have surrendered, without even a show of resistance, to the bedazzlement of a circus rider. As a writing man, or secretary, I have always felt charged with the safekeeping of all unexpected items of worldly or unworldly enchantment, as though I might be held personally responsible if even a small one were to be lost. But it is not easy to communicate anything of this nature. The circus comes as close to being the world in microcosm as anything I know; in a way, it puts all the rest of show business in the shade. Its magic is universal and complex. Out of its wild disorder comes order; from its rank smell rises the good aroma of courage and daring; out of its preliminary shabbiness comes the final splendor. And buried in the familiar boasts of its advance agents lies the modesty of most of its people. For me the circus is at its best before it has been put together. It is at its best at certain moments when it comes to a point, as through a burning glass, in the activity and destiny of a single performer out of so many. One ring is always bigger than three. One rider, one aerialist, is always greater than six. In short, a man has to catch the circus unawares to experience its full impact and share its gaudy dream.

4 The ten-minute ride the girl took achieved—as far as I was concerned, who wasn't looking for it, and quite unbeknownst to her, who wasn't even striving for it—the thing that is sought by performers everywhere, on whatever stage, whether struggling in the tidal currents of Shakespeare or bucking the difficult motion of a horse. I somehow got the idea she was just cadging a ride, improving a shining ten minutes in the diligent way all serious artists seize free moments to hone the blade

of their talent and keep themselves in trim. Her brief tour included only elementary postures and tricks, perhaps because they were all she was capable of, perhaps because her warmup at this hour was unscheduled and the ring was not rigged for a real practice session. She swung herself off and on the horse several times, gripping his mane. She did a few knee-stands—or whatever they are called—dropping to her knees and quickly bouncing back up on her feet again. Most of the time she simply rode in a standing position, well aft on the beast, her hands hanging easily at her sides, her head erect, her straw-colored ponytail lightly brushing her shoulders, the blood of exertion showing faintly through the tan of her skin. Twice she managed a one-foot stance—a sort of ballet pose, with arms outstretched. At one point the neck strap of her bathing suit broke and she went twice around the ring in the classic attitude of a woman making minor repairs to a garment. The fact that she was standing on the back of a moving horse while doing this invested the matter with a clownish significance that perfectly fitted the spirit of the circus—jocund, yet charming. She just rolled the strap into a neat ball and stowed it inside her bodice while the horse rocked and rolled beneath her in dutiful innocence. The bathing suit proved as self-reliant as its owner and stood up well enough without benefit of strap.

5 The richness of the scene was in its plainness, its natural condition—of horse, of ring, of girl, even to the girl's bare feet that gripped the bare back of her proud and ridiculous mount. The enchantment grew not out of anything that happened or was performed but out of something that seemed to go round and around and around with the girl, attending her, a steady gleam in the shape of a circle—a ring of ambition, of happiness, of youth. (And the positive pleasures of equilibrium under difficulties.) In a week or two, all would be changed, all (or almost all) lost: the girl would wear makeup, the horse would wear gold, the ring would be painted, the bark would be clean for the feet of the horse, the girl's feet would be clean for the slippers that she'd wear. All, all would be lost.

6 As I watched with the others, our jaws adroop, our eyes alight, I became painfully conscious of the element of time. Everything in the hideous old building seemed to take the shape of a circle, conforming to the course of the horse. The rider's gaze, as she peered straight ahead, seemed to be circular, as though bent by force of circumstance; then time itself began running in circles, and so the beginning was where the end was, and the two were the same, and one thing ran into the next and time went round and around and got nowhere. The girl wasn't so young that she did not know the delicious satisfaction of having a perfectly behaved body and the fun of using it to do a trick most people can't do, but she was too young to know that time does not really move in a circle at all. I thought: "She will never be as beautiful as this again"—a thought that made me acutely unhappy—and in a flash my mind (which is too much of a busybody to suit me) had projected her twenty-five years ahead, and she was now in the center of the ring, on foot, wearing a conical hat and high-heeled shoes, the image of the older woman, holding the long rein, caught in the treadmill of an afternoon long in the future. "She is at that enviable moment in life [I thought] when she believes she can go once around the ring, make one complete circuit, and at the end be exactly the same age as at the start." Everything in her movements, her expression, told you that for her the ring of time

was perfectly formed, changeless, predictable, without beginning or end, like the ring in which she was traveling at this moment with the horse that wallowed under her. And then I slipped back into my trance, and time was circular again—time, pausing quietly with the rest of us, so as not to disturb the balance of a performer.

7 Her ride ended as casually as it had begun. The older woman stopped the horse, and the girl slid to the ground. As she walked toward us to leave, there was a quick, small burst of applause. She smiled broadly, in surprise and pleasure; then her face suddenly regained its gravity and she disappeared through the door.

8 It has been ambitious and plucky of me to attempt to describe what is indescribable, and I have failed, as I knew I would. But I have discharged my duty to my society; and besides, a writer, like an acrobat, must occasionally try a stunt that is too much for him. At any rate, it is worth reporting that long before the circus comes to town, its most notable performances have already been given. Under the bright lights of the finished show, a performer need only reflect the electric candle power that is directed upon him; but in the dark and dirty old training rings and in the makeshift cages, whatever light is generated, whatever excitement, whatever beauty, must come from original sources—from internal fires of professional hunger and delight, from the exuberance and gravity of youth. It is the difference between planetary light and the combustion of stars.

II

9 The South is the land of the sustained sibilant. Everywhere, for the appreciative visitor, the letter "s" insinuates itself in the scene: in the sound of sea and sand, in the singing shell, in the heat of sun and sky, in the sultriness of the gentle hours, in the siesta, in the stir of birds and insects. In contrast to the softness of its music, the South is also cruel and hard and prickly. A little striped lizard, flattened along the sharp green bayonet of a yucca, wears in its tiny face and watchful eye the pure look of death and violence. And all over the place, hidden at the bottom of their small sandy craters, the ant lions lie in wait for the ant that will stumble into their trap. (There are three kinds of lions in this region: the lions of the circus, the ant lions, and the Lions of the Tampa Lions Club, who roared their approval of segregation at a meeting the other day—all except one, a Lion named Monty Gurwit, who declined to roar and thereby got his picture in the paper.)

10 The day starts on a note of despair: the sorrowing dove, alone on its telephone wire, mourns the loss of night, weeps at the bright perils of the unfolding day. But soon the mocking bird wakes and begins an early rehearsal, setting the dove down by force of character, running through a few slick imitations, and trying a couple of original numbers into the bargain. The redbird takes it from there. Despair gives way to good humor. The Southern dawn is a pale affair, usually, quite different from our northern daybreak. It is a triumph of gradualism; night turns to day imperceptibly, softly, with no theatrics. It is subtle and undisturbing. As the first light seeps in through the blinds I lie in bed half awake, despairing with the dove, sounding the A for the brothers Alsop. All seems lost, all seems sorrowful. Then a mullet jumps in the bayou outside the bedroom window. It falls back into the water with a smart

smack. I have asked several people why the mullet incessantly jump and I have received a variety of answers. Some say the mullet jump to shake off a parasite that annoys them. Some say they jump for the love of jumping—as the girl on the horse seemed to ride for the love of riding (although she, too, like all artists, may have been shaking off some parasite that fastens itself to the creative spirit and can be got rid of only by fifty turns around a ring while standing on a horse).

11 In Florida at this time of year, the sun does not take command of the day until a couple of hours after it has appeared in the east. It seems to carry no authority at first. The sun and the lizard keep the same schedule; they bide their time until the morning has advanced a good long way before they come fully forth and strike. The cold lizard waits astride his warming leaf for the perfect moment; the cold sun waits in his nest of clouds for the crucial time.

12 On many days, the dampness of the air pervades all life, all living. Matches refuse to strike. The towel, hung to dry, grows wetter by the hour. The newspaper, with its headlines about integration, wilts in your hand and falls limply into the coffee and the egg. Envelopes seal themselves. Postage stamps mate with one another as shamelessly as grasshoppers. But most of the time the days are models of beauty and wonder and comfort, with the kind sea stroking the back of the warm sand. At evening there are great flights of birds over the sea, where the light lingers; the gulls, the pelicans, the terns, the herons stay aloft for half an hour after land birds have gone to roost. They hold their ancient formations, wheel and fish over the Pass, enjoying the last of day like children playing outdoors after suppertime.

13 To a beachcomber from the North, which is my present status, the race problem has no pertinence, no immediacy. Here in Florida I am a guest in two houses—the house of the sun, the house of the State of Florida. As a guest, I mind my manners and do not criticize the customs of my hosts. It gives me a queer feeling, though, to be at the center of the greatest social crisis of my time and see hardly a sign of it. Yet the very absence of signs seems to increase one's awareness. Colored people do not come to the public beach to bathe, because they would not be made welcome there; and they don't fritter away their time visiting the circus, because they have other things to do. A few of them turn up at the ballpark, where they occupy a separate but equal section of the left-field bleachers and watch Negro players on the visiting Braves team using the same bases as the white players, instead of separate (but equal) bases. I have had only two small encounters with "color." A colored woman named Viola, who had been a friend of my wife's sister years ago, showed up one day with some laundry of ours that she had consented to do for us, and with the bundle she brought a bunch of nasturtiums, as a sort of natural accompaniment to the delivery of clean clothes. The flowers seemed a very acceptable thing and I was touched by them. We asked Viola about her daughter, and she said she was at Kentucky State College, studying voice.

14 The other encounter was when I was explaining to our cook, who is from Finland, the mysteries of bus travel in the American Southland. I showed her the bus stop, armed her with a timetable, and then, as a matter of duty, mentioned the customs of the Romans. "When you get on the bus," I said, "I think you'd better sit in one of the front seats—the seats in back are for colored people." A look of great weariness came into her face, as it does when we use too many dishes, and she replied, "Oh, I know—isn't it silly!"

15 Her remark, coming as it did all the way from Finland and landing on this sandbar with a plunk, impressed me. The Supreme Court said nothing about silliness, but I suspect it may play more of a role than one might suppose. People are, if anything, more touchy about being thought silly than they are about being thought unjust. I note that one of the arguments in the recent manifesto of Southern Congressmen in support of the doctrine of "separate but equal" was that it had been founded on "common sense." The sense that is common to one generation is uncommon to the next. Probably the first slave ship, with Negroes lying in chains on its decks, seemed commonsensical to the owners who operated it and to the planters who patronized it. But such a vessel would not be in the realm of common sense today. The only sense that is common, in the long run, is the sense of change—and we all instinctively avoid it, and object to the passage of time, and would rather have none of it.

16 The Supreme Court decision is like the Southern sun, laggard in its early stages, biding its time. It has been the law in Florida for two years now, and the years have been like the hours of the morning before the sun has gathered its strength. I think the decision is as incontrovertible and warming as the sun, and, like the sun, will eventually take charge.

17 But there is certainly a great temptation in Florida to duck the passage of time. Lying in warm comfort by the sea, you receive gratefully the gift of the sun, the gift of the South. This is true seduction. The day is a circle—morning, afternoon, and night. After a few days I was clearly enjoying the same delusion as the girl on the horse—that I could ride clear around the ring of day, guarded by wind and sun and sea and sand, and be not a moment older.

18 P.S. (April 1962). When I first laid eyes on Fiddler Bayou, it was wild land, populated chiefly by the little crabs that gave it its name, visited by wading birds and by an occasional fisherman. Today, houses ring the bayou, and part of the mangrove shore has been bulkheaded with a concrete wall. Green lawns stretch from patio to water's edge, and sprinklers make rainbows in the light. But despite man's encroachment, Nature manages to hold her own and assert her authority: high tides and high winds in the gulf sometimes send the sea crashing across the sand barrier, depositing its wrack on lawns and ringing everyone's front door bell. The birds and the crabs accommodate themselves quite readily to the changes that have taken place; every day brings herons to hunt around among the roots of the mangroves, and I have discovered that I can approach to within about eight feet of a Little Blue Heron simply by entering the water and swimming slowly toward him. Apparently he has decided that when I'm in the water, I am without guile—possibly even desirable, like a fish.

19 The Ringling circus has quit Sarasota and gone elsewhere for its hibernation. A few circus families still own homes in the town, and every spring the students at the high school put on a circus, to let off steam, work off physical requirements, and provide a promotional spectacle for Sarasota. At the drugstore you can buy a postcard showing the bed John Ringling slept in. Time has not stood still for anybody but the dead, and even the dead must be able to hear the acceleration of little sports cars and know that things have changed.

20 From the all-wise *New York Times,* which has the animal kingdom ever in

mind, I have learned that one of the creatures most acutely aware of the passing of time is the fiddler crab himself. Tiny spots on his body enlarge during daytime hours, giving him the same color as the mudbank he explores and thus protecting him from his enemies. At night the spots shrink, his color fades, and he is almost invisible in the light of the moon. These changes are synchronized with the tides, so that each day they occur at a different hour. A scientist who experimented with the crabs to learn more about the phenomenon discovered that even when they are removed from their natural environment and held in confinement, the rhythm of their bodily change continues uninterrupted, and they mark the passage of time in their laboratory prison, faithful to the tides in their fashion.

(1956)

QUESTIONS

Thought and Structure

1. What connections can you find between parts I and II? What is the focus of each part? Consider especially paragraphs 9–10, 13, and 15. What is the purpose of the postscript? Would it be better incorporated as part of the essay proper?
2. What does White mean by his suggestion in paragraph 3 that the circus is a microcosm? In what sense is this an essay about the circus, about performance, about race, about time and change?
3. Twice in the essay White refers to his task and responsibility as a writer. What is his point? Has White failed to accomplish what he set out to do (paragraph 8)? What has he set out to do?
4. In the opening paragraph White locates and describes the scene. Later, he moves from that initial description to speculation about what he has seen. During the remainder of the essay, he alternates between description and speculation. Which paragraphs are primarily descriptive and which speculative? What would be gained or lost if the essay were to be reorganized with the paragraphs arranged in the following order: 1, 2, 4, 7, 3, 5, 6, 8, 9–conclusion?
5. What connections exist between the end of the first part of the essay and its beginning? Explain why paragraph 8 does or does not sound like a conclusion.

Style and Strategy

6. Read paragraph 5 aloud. Mark off the repeated sounds at the level of phrase, word, and syllable.
7. The following sentence appears in paragraph 3; its parts have been numbered here for ease of reference:

   (1) Out of its wild disorder comes order;
   (2) from its rank smell rises the good aroma of courage and daring;
   (3) out of its preliminary shabbiness comes the final splendor.

   Read the sentence aloud as it is written. Then read it aloud as you reorder its parts. Try these combinations: 2, 3, 1; 2, 1, 3; 1, 3, 2; 3, 2, 1; 3, 1, 2. Which version(s) do you prefer and why?

8. Reread the opening paragraphs and underline, circle, or list all the words suggesting circularity. Why does White include so many of them? Look through paragraph 6 for echoes and repetitions of the details of the opening paragraph. What is the effect of such repetitions? How are they related to what White suggests about the girl and about time?
9. Paragraph 3 introduces the language of light which burns so brilliantly in the essay's final sentences. List all the "light" words (and "dark" words) you can find in this paragraph. Explain what each of the images means, especially the last one: "out of its preliminary shabbiness comes the final splendor." Then reread the final paragraph and explain how White uses light-imagery to make his point.
10. In paragraph 9 White emphasizes the sound of the sibilant "s." Read the paragraph aloud noting how he does this, and to what effect.

SUGGESTIONS FOR WRITING

A. Recall an incident in your life which made you feel old, perhaps when something had passed you by, when someone else was moving into the place you once held. You might think, for example, of periods of transition or graduation—from elementary or high school, from Little League, Girl Scouts, or something similar. Recreate the scene from your past with concrete details. Weave into your description your insights and speculations.

B. Write an analysis of this essay. Explain what White is saying. Discuss his strategy of organization and his use of language.

C. Write an imitation of the sentence discussed in question 7.

D. Write an imitation of paragraph 5 or 8.

E. Compare the feeling in White's essay with the feeling of being present at the circus as it is reflected in the following vignette, "Up in the Gallery," by Franz Kafka (translated by Willa and Edwin Muir).

> If some frail, consumptive equestrienne in the circus were to be urged around and around on an undulating horse for months on end without respite by a ruthless, whip-flourishing ringmaster, before an insatiable public, whizzing along on her horse, throwing kisses, swaying from the waist, and if this performance were likely to continue in the infinite perspective of a drab future to the unceasing roar of the orchestra and hum of the ventilators, accompanied by ebbing and renewed swelling bursts of applause which are really steam hammers—then, perhaps, a young visitor to the gallery might race down the long stairs through all the circles, rush into the ring, and yell: Stop! against the fanfares of the orchestra still playing the appropriate music.
>
> But since that is not so; a lovely lady, pink and white, floats in between the curtains, which proud lackeys open before her; the ringmaster, deferentially catching her eye, comes toward her breathing animal devotion; tenderly lifts her up on the dapple-gray, as if she were his own most precious granddaughter about to start on a dangerous journey; cannot make up his mind to give the signal with his whip, finally masters himself enough to crack the whip loudly; runs along beside the horse, open-mouthed; follows with a sharp eye the leaps taken by its rider; finds her artistic skill almost beyond belief; calls to her with English shouts of warning; angrily exhorts the grooms who hold the hoops to be most closely attentive; before the great somersault lifts up his arms and implores the orchestra to be silent; finally lifts the little one down from her trembling horse, kisses her on both cheeks, and finds that all the ovation she gets from the audience is barely sufficient; while she herself, supported by him, right up on the tips of her toes, in a cloud of dust, with outstretched arms and small head

thrown back, invites the whole circus to share her triumph—since that is so, the visitor to the gallery lays his face on the rail before him and, sinking into the closing march as into a heavy dream, weeps without knowing it.

Once More to the Lake

August 1941

1 One summer, along about 1904, my father rented a camp on a lake in Maine and took us all there for the month of August. We all got ringworm from some kittens and had to rub Pond's Extract on our arms and legs night and morning, and my father rolled over in a canoe with all his clothes on; but outside of that the vacation was a success and from then on none of us ever thought there was any place in the world like that lake in Maine. We returned summer after summer—always on August 1 for one month. I have since become a salt-water man, but sometimes in summer there are days when the restlessness of the tides and the fearful cold of the sea water and the incessant wind that blows across the afternoon and into the evening make me wish for the placidity of a lake in the woods. A few weeks ago this feeling got so strong I bought myself a couple of bass hooks and a spinner and returned to the lake where we used to go, for a week's fishing and to revisit old haunts.

2 I took along my son, who had never had any fresh water up his nose and who had seen lily pads only from train windows. On the journey over to the lake I began to wonder what it would be like. I wondered how time would have marred this unique, this holy spot—the coves and streams, the hills that the sun set behind, the camps and the paths behind the camps. I was sure that the tarred road would have found it out and I wondered in what other ways it would be desolated. It is strange how much you can remember about places like that once you allow your mind to return into the grooves that lead back. You remember one thing, and that suddenly reminds you of another thing. I guess I remembered clearest of all the early mornings, when the lake was cool and motionless, remembered how the bedroom smelled of the lumber it was made of and of the wet woods whose scent entered through the screen. The partitions in the camp were thin and did not extend clear to the top of the rooms, and as I was always the first up I would dress softly so as not to wake the others, and sneak out into the sweet outdoors and start out in the canoe, keeping close along the shore in the long shadows of the pines. I remembered being very careful never to rub my paddle against the gunwale for fear of disturbing the stillness of the cathedral.

3 The lake had never been what you would call a wild lake. There were cottages sprinkled around the shores, and it was in farming country although the shores of the lake were quite heavily wooded. Some of the cottages were owned by nearby farmers, and you would live at the shore and eat your meals at the farmhouse. That's what our family did. But although it wasn't wild, it was a fairly large and undisturbed lake and there were places in it that, to a child at least, seemed infinitely remote and primeval.

4 I was right about the tar: it led to within half a mile of the shore. But when

I got back there, with my boy, and we settled into a camp near a farmhouse and into the kind of summertime I had known, I could tell that it was going to be pretty much the same as it had been before—I knew it, lying in bed the first morning, smelling the bedroom and hearing the boy sneak quietly out and go off along the shore in a boat. I began to sustain the illusion that he was I, and therefore, by simple transposition, that I was my father. This sensation persisted, kept cropping up all the time we were there. It was not an entirely new feeling, but in this setting it grew much stronger. I seemed to be living a dual existence. I would be in the middle of some simple act, I would be picking up a bait box or laying down a table fork, or I would be saying something, and suddenly it would be not I but my father who was saying the words or making the gesture. It gave me a creepy sensation.

5 We went fishing the first morning. I felt the same damp moss covering the worms in the bait can, and saw the dragonfly alight on the tip of my rod as it hovered a few inches from the surface of the water. It was the arrival of this fly that convinced me beyond any doubt that everything was as it always had been, that the years were a mirage and that there had been no years. The small waves were the same, chucking the rowboat under the chin as we fished at anchor, and the boat was the same boat, the same color green and the ribs broken in the same places, and under the floor-boards the same fresh-water leavings and débris—the dead helgramite, the wisps of moss, the rusty discarded fishhook, the dried blood from yesterday's catch. We stared silently at the tips of our rods, at the dragonflies that came and went. I lowered the tip of mine into the water, tentatively, pensively dislodging the fly, which darted two feet away, poised, darted two feet back, and came to rest again a little farther up the rod. There had been no years between the ducking of this dragonfly and the other one—the one that was part of memory. I looked at the boy, who was silently watching his fly, and it was my hands that held his rod, my eyes watching. I felt dizzy and didn't know which rod I was at the end of.

6 We caught two bass, hauling them in briskly as though they were mackerel, pulling them over the side of the boat in a businesslike manner without any landing net, and stunning them with a blow on the back of the head. When we got back for a swim before lunch, the lake was exactly where we had left it, the same number of inches from the dock, and there was only the merest suggestion of a breeze. This seemed an utterly enchanted sea, this lake you could leave to its own devices for a few hours and come back to, and find that it had not stirred, this constant and trustworthy body of water. In the shallows, the dark, water-soaked sticks and twigs, smooth and old, were undulating in clusters on the bottom against the clean ribbed sand, and the track of the mussel was plain. A school of minnows swam by, each minnow with its small individual shadow, doubling the attendance, so clear and sharp in the sunlight. Some of the other campers were in swimming, along the shore, one of them with a cake of soap, and the water felt thin and clear and unsubstantial. Over the years there had been this person with the cake of soap, this cultist, and here he was. There had been no years.

7 Up to the farmhouse to dinner through the teeming, dusty field, the road under our sneakers was only a two-track road. The middle track was missing, the one with the marks of the hooves and the splotches of dried, flaky manure. There had always been three tracks to choose from in choosing which track to walk in; now the choice was narrowed down to two. For a moment I missed terribly the middle

alternative. But the way led past the tennis court, and something about the way it lay there in the sun reassured me; the tape had loosened along the backline, the alleys were green with plantains and other weeds, and the net (installed in June and removed in September) sagged in the dry noon, and the whole place steamed with midday heat and hunger and emptiness. There was a choice of pie for dessert, and one was blueberry and one was apple, and the waitresses were the same country girls, there having been no passage of time, only the illusion of it as in a dropped curtain—the waitresses were still fifteen; their hair had been washed, that was the only difference—they had been to the movies and seen the pretty girls with the clean hair.

8 Summertime, oh, summertime, pattern of life indelible, the fade-proof lake, the woods unshatterable, the pasture with the sweetfern and the juniper forever and ever, summer without end; this was the background, and the life along the shore was the design, the cottagers with their innocent and tranquil design, their tiny docks with the flagpole and the American flag floating against the white clouds in the blue sky, the little paths over the roots of the trees leading from camp to camp and the paths leading back to the outhouses and the can of lime for sprinkling, and at the souvenir counters at the store the miniature birch-bark canoes and the postcards that showed things looking a little better than they looked. This was the American family at play, escaping the city heat, wondering whether the newcomers in the camp at the head of the cove were "common" or "nice," wondering whether it was true that the people who drove up for Sunday dinner at the farmhouse were turned away because there wasn't enough chicken.

9 It seemed to me, as I kept remembering all this, that those times and those summers had been infinitely precious and worth saving. There had been jollity and peace and goodness. The arriving (at the beginning of August) had been so big a business in itself, at the railway station the farm wagon drawn up, the first smell of the pine-laden air, the first glimpse of the smiling farmer, and the great importance of the trunks and your father's enormous authority in such matters, and the feel of the wagon under you for the long ten-mile haul, and at the top of the last long hill catching the first view of the lake after eleven months of not seeing this cherished body of water. The shouts and cries of the other campers when they saw you, and the trunks to be unpacked, to give up their rich burden. (Arriving was less exciting nowadays, when you sneaked up in your car and parked it under a tree near the camp and took out the bags and in five minutes it was all over, no fuss, no loud wonderful fuss about trunks.)

10 Peace and goodness and jollity. The only thing that was wrong now, really, was the sound of the place, an unfamiliar nervous sound of the outboard motors. This was the note that jarred, the one thing that would sometimes break the illusion and set the years moving. In those other summertimes all motors were inboard; and when they were at a little distance, the noise they made was a sedative, an ingredient of summer sleep. They were one-cylinder and two-cylinder engines, and some were make-and-break and some were jump-spark, but they all made a sleepy sound across the lake. The one-lungers throbbed and fluttered, and the twin-cylinder ones purred and purred, and that was a quiet sound, too. But now the campers all had outboards. In the daytime, in the hot mornings, these motors made a petulant, irritable sound;

at night, in the still evening when the afterglow lit the water, they whined about one's ears like mosquitoes. My boy loved our rented outboard, and his great desire was to achieve single-handed mastery over it, and authority, and he soon learned the trick of choking it a little (but not too much), and the adjustment of the needle valve. Watching him I would remember the things you could do with the old one-cylinder engine with the heavy flywheel, how you could have it eating out of your hand if you got really close to it spiritually. Motorboats in those days didn't have clutches, and you would make a landing by shutting off the motor at the proper time and coasting in with a dead rudder. But there was a way of reversing them, if you learned the trick, by cutting the switch and putting it on again exactly on the final dying revolution of the flywheel, so that it would kick back against compression and begin reversing. Approaching a dock in a strong following breeze, it was difficult to slow up sufficiently by the ordinary coasting method, and if a boy felt he had complete mastery over his motor, he was tempted to keep it running beyond its time and then reverse it a few feet from the dock. It took a cool nerve, because if you threw the switch a twentieth of a second too soon you would catch the flywheel when it still had speed enough to go up past center, and the boat would leap ahead, charging bull-fashion at the dock.

11 We had a good week at the camp. The bass were biting well and the sun shone endlessly, day after day. We would be tired at night and lie down in the accumulated heat of the little bedrooms after the long hot day and the breeze would stir almost imperceptibly outside and the smell of the swamp drift in through the rusty screens. Sleep would come easily and in the morning the red squirrel would be on the roof, tapping out his gay routine. I kept remembering everything, lying in bed in the mornings—the small steamboat that had a long rounded stern like the lip of a Ubangi, and how quietly she ran on the moonlight sails, when the older boys played their mandolins and the girls sang and we ate doughnuts dipped in sugar, and how sweet the music was on the water in the shining night, and what it had felt like to think about girls then. After breakfast we would go up to the store and the things were in the same place—the minnows in a bottle, the plugs and spinners disarranged and pawed over by the youngsters from the boys' camp, the Fig Newtons and the Beeman's gum. Outside, the road was tarred and cars stood in front of the store. Inside, all was just as it had always been, except there was more Coca-Cola and not so much Moxie and root beer and birch beer and sarsaparilla. We would walk out with the bottle of pop apiece and sometimes the pop would backfire up our noses and hurt. We explored the streams, quietly, where the turtles slid off the sunny logs and dug their way into the soft bottom; and we lay on the town wharf and fed worms to the tame bass. Everywhere we went I had trouble making out which was I, the one walking at my side, the one walking in my pants.

12 One afternoon while we were there at that lake a thunderstorm came up. It was like the revival of an old melodrama that I had seen long ago with childish awe. The second-act climax of the drama of the electrical disturbance over a lake in America had not changed in any important respect. This was the big scene, still the big scene. The whole thing was so familiar, the first feeling of oppression and heat and a general air around camp of not wanting to go very far away. In mid-afternoon (it was all the same) a curious darkening of the sky, and a lull in everything that had

made life tick; and then the way the boats suddenly swung the other way at their moorings with the coming of a breeze out of the new quarter, and the premonitory rumble. Then the kettle drum, then the snare, then the bass drum and cymbals, then crackling light against the dark, and the gods grinning and licking their chops in the hills. Afterward the calm, the rain steadily rustling in the calm lake, the return of light and hope and spirits, and the campers running out in joy and relief to go swimming in the rain, their bright cries perpetuating the deathless joke about how they were getting simply drenched, and the children screaming with delight at the new sensation of bathing in the rain, and the joke about getting drenched linking the generations in a strong indestructible chain. And the comedian who waded in carrying an umbrella.

13 When the others went swimming, my son said he was going in, too. He pulled his dripping trunks from the line where they had hung all through the shower and wrung them out. Languidly, and with no thought of going in, I watched him, his hard little body, skinny and bare, saw him wince slightly as he pulled up around his vitals the small, soggy, icy garment. As he buckled the swollen belt, suddenly my groin felt the chill of death.

(1941)

QUESTIONS

Thought and Structure

1. Like "The Ring of Time," "Once More to the Lake" is a lyrical and speculative essay. It is, of course, a reminiscence of a memorable summer. But it is something more: a meditation on time. What ideas about time does White suggest? Consider especially what he says in paragraphs 4, 5, and 6.
2. Explain what you think White means by the following statements:

   I seemed to be living a dual existence. (4)
   I felt dizzy and didn't know which rod I was at the end of. (5)
   I began to sustain the illusion that he was I, and therefore, by simple transposition, that I was my father. (4)

3. Besides time and change, what is this essay about?
4. Divide the essay into sections, and provide titles for each part. In deciding upon your sections and titles, consider which paragraphs are primarily descriptive and which speculative.
5. White gains emphasis by positioning key ideas at the ends of paragraphs. Reread paragraphs 4, 5, and 6, attending to the final sentence of each. Locate at least one additional example of a striking ending to a paragraph. Explain how it completes the paragraph and why it is noteworthy.
6. Examine paragraphs 9 and 10 for their use of comparison and contrast. Identify the important comparative and contrastive words and phrases, and comment on their significance.

Style and Strategy

7. A number of White's sentences reverberate with repeated words and phrases. Read the following sentence aloud, noting its repetitions:

 > The small waves were the same, chucking the rowboat under the chin as we fished at anchor, and the boat was the same boat, the same color green and the ribs broken in the same places, and under the floorboards the same fresh-water leavings and débris—the dead helgramite, the wisps of moss, the rusty discarded fishhook, the dried blood from yesterday's catch.

 What are the effects of these repetitions?

8. In the sentences that follow, White expands his thought and accumulates details toward the end—after a brief direct statement of idea. You might think of the sentence formed this way as a string or a stack of details laid out in a series of parallel clauses or phrases.

 > It was the arrival of this fly that convinced me beyond any doubt
 > that everything was as it always had been,
 > that the years were a mirage
 > and that there had been no years.

 > We caught two bass,
 > hauling them in briskly as though they were mackerel,
 > pulling them in over the side of the boat in a businesslike manner without any landing net,
 > and stunning them with a blow on the back of the head.

 Is this parallelism effective? Explain.

9. Compare the following sentence by White with the alternate for sound and rhythm.

 WHITE: I wondered how time would have marred this unique, this holy spot—the coves and streams, the hills that the sun set behind, the camps and the paths behind the camps.

 ALTERNATE: I wondered how time would have marred this unique, holy spot—the coves, streams, hills, camps, and paths.

10. What words in paragraphs 1 and 2 describe the lake? What connotations does each possess? What overall impression of the lake is created by the accumulation of these words? How do the final words of paragraph 3 reinforce this impression?

11. "Once More to the Lake" is rich in sensuous detail—in images of sight, sound, smell, taste, and touch. List the visual details of paragraph 7 and the sound and sense details of paragraphs 10, 11, and 12. What is the overall effect of each paragraph?

12. White's diction in this essay and in others combines the high and the low, the common and the unusual, the formally elegant and the colloquially casual. Compare the tone, sound, and rhythm of the following two voices: (a) "the restlessness of the tides"; "the incessant wind that blows across the afternoon"; "the placidity of a lake in the woods." (b) "A few weeks ago this feeling got so strong I bought myself a couple of bass hooks and a spinner and returned to the lake where we used to go, for a week's fishing and to revisit old haunts." What is different about the second voice?

SUGGESTIONS FOR WRITING

A. Write an essay about a place you have revisited after a long absence. Try to account for what the place meant to you after the first visit and after the later one. Provide some sense of what you expected and hoped for on the later visit. Comment on what changed and what remained the same.

B. Explain the sources of White's appeal as a writer. Does it have something to do with his subjects? His ideas? His attitude and tone? His style?

C. Write an essay explaining White's ideas in two of his essays. You might compare and contrast his treatment of a similar subject or discuss his use of a similar theme with two different subjects (e.g., *Time* in "Ring" and in "Lake").

D. Write imitations of the sentences discussed in questions 7, 8, and 9.

E. Compare the ideas about time in the following poem—"Men at Forty" by Donald Justice—with those about time in White's essay. (Consider especially the last stanza of the poem and the final paragraph of the essay.)

Men at forty
Learn to close softly
The doors to rooms they will not be
Coming back to.

At rest on a stair landing,
They feel it moving
Beneath them now like the deck of a ship,
Though the swell is gentle.

And deep in mirrors
They rediscover
The face of the boy as he practices tying
His father's tie there in secret

And the face of that father,
Still warm with the mystery of lather.
They are more fathers than sons themselves now.
Something is filling them, something

That is like the twilight sound
Of the crickets, immense,
Filling the woods at the foot of the slope
Behind their mortgaged houses.

The Door

1 Everything (he kept saying) is something it isn't. And everybody is always somewhere else. Maybe it was the city, being in the city, that made him feel how queer everything was and that it was something else. Maybe (he kept thinking) it was the names of the things. The names were tex and frequently koid. Or they were flex and oid or they were duroid (sani) or flexsan (duro), but everything was glass (but not quite glass) and the thing that you touched (the surface, washable, crease-resistant) was rubber, only it wasn't quite rubber and you didn't quite touch it but almost. The wall, which was glass but thrutex, turned out on being approached not to be a wall, it was something else, it was an opening or doorway—and the doorway (through which he saw himself approaching) turned out to be something else, it was a wall. And what he had eaten not having agreed with him.

2 He was in a washable house, but he wasn't sure. Now about those rats, he kept saying to himself. He meant the rats that the Professor had driven crazy by forcing them to deal with problems which were beyond the scope of rats, the insoluble problems. He meant the rats that had been trained to jump at the square card with the circle in the middle, and the card (because it was something it wasn't) would give way and let the rat into a place where the food was, but then one day it would be a trick played on the rat, and the card would be changed, and the rat would jump but the card wouldn't give way, and it was an impossible situation (for a rat) and the rat would go insane and into its eyes would come the unspeakably bright imploring look of the frustrated, and after the convulsions were over and the frantic racing around, then the passive stage would set in and the willingness to let anything be done to it, even if it was something else.

3 He didn't know which door (or wall) or opening in the house to jump at, to get through, because one was an opening that wasn't a door (it was a void, or koid) and the other was a wall that wasn't an opening, it was a sanitary cupboard of the same color. He caught a glimpse of his eyes staring into his eyes, in the thrutex, and in them was the expression he had seen in the picture of the rats—weary after convulsions and the frantic racing around, when they were willing and did not mind having anything done to them. More and more (he kept saying) I am confronted by a problem which is incapable of solution (for this time even if he chose the right door, there would be no food behind it) and that is what madness is, and things seeming different from what they are. He heard, in the house where he was, in the city to which he had gone (as toward a door which might, or might not, give way), a noise—not a loud noise but more of a low prefabricated humming. It came from a place in the base of the wall (or stat) where the flue carrying the filterable air was, and not far from the Minipiano, which was made of the same material nailbrushes are made of, and which was under the stairs. "This, too, has been tested," she said, pointing, but not at it, "and found viable." It wasn't a loud noise, he kept thinking, sorry that he had seen his eyes, even though it was through his own eyes that he had seen them.

4 First will come the convulsions (he said), then the exhaustion, then the willingness to let anything be done. "And you better believe it *will* be."

5 All his life he had been confronted by situations which were incapable of being solved, and there was a deliberateness behind all this, behind this changing of the card (or door), because they would always wait till you had learned to jump at the certain card (or door)—the one with the circle—and then they would change it on you. There have been so many doors changed on me, he said, in the last twenty years, but it is now becoming clear that it is an impossible situation, and the question is whether to jump again, even though they ruffle you in the rump with a blast of air—to make you jump. He wished he wasn't standing by the Minipiano. First they would teach you the prayers and the Psalms, and that would be the right door (the one with the circle), and the long sweet words with the holy sound, and that would be the one to jump at to get where the food was. Then one day you jumped and it didn't give way, so that all you got was the bump on the nose, and the first bewilderment, the first young bewilderment.

6 I don't know whether to tell her about the door they substituted or not, he

said, the one with the equation on it and the picture of the amoeba reproducing itself by division. Or the one with the photostatic copy of the check for thirty-two dollars and fifty cents. But the jumping was so long ago, although the bump is . . . how those old wounds hurt! Being crazy this way wouldn't be so bad if only, if only. If only when you put your foot forward to take a step, the ground wouldn't come up to meet your foot the way it does. And the same way in the street (only I may never get back to the street unless I jump at the right door), the curb coming up to meet your foot, anticipating ever so delicately the weight of the body, which is somewhere else. "We could take your name," she said, "and send it to you." And it wouldn't be so bad if only you could read a sentence all the way through without jumping (your eye) to something else on the same page; and then (he kept thinking) there was that man out in Jersey, the one who started to chop his trees down, one by one, the man who began talking about how he would take his house to pieces, brick by brick, because he faced a problem incapable of solution, probably, so he began to hack at the trees in the yard, began to pluck with trembling fingers at the bricks in the house. Even if a house is not washable, it is worth taking down. It is not till later that the exhaustion sets in.

7 But it is inevitable that they will keep changing the doors on you, he said, because that is what they are for; and the thing is to get used to it and not let it unsettle the mind. But that would mean not jumping, and you can't. Nobody can not jump. There will be no not-jumping. Among rats, perhaps, but among people never. Everybody has to keep jumping at a door (the one with the circle on it) because that is the way everybody is, specially some people. You wouldn't want me, standing here, to tell you, would you, about my friend the poet (deceased) who said, "My heart has followed all my days something I cannot name"? (It had the circle on it.) And like many poets, although few so beloved, he is gone. It killed him, the jumping. First, of course, there were the preliminary bouts, the convulsions, and the calm and the willingness.

8 I remember the door with the picture of the girl on it (only it was spring), her arms outstretched in loveliness, her dress (it was the one with the circle on it) uncaught, beginning the slow, clear, blinding cascade—and I guess we would all like to try that door again, for it seemed like the way and for a while it was the way, the door would open and you would go through winged and exalted (like any rat) and the food would be there, the way the Professor had it arranged, everything O.K., and you had chosen the right door for the world was young. The time they changed that door on me, my nose bled for a hundred hours—how do you like that, Madam? Or would you prefer to show me further through this so strange house, or you could take my name and send it to me, for although my heart has followed all my days something I cannot name, I am tired of the jumping and I do not know which way to go, Madam, and I am not even sure that I am not tried beyond the endurance of man (rat, if you will) and have taken leave of sanity. What are you following these days, old friend, after your recovery from the last bump? What is the name, or is it something you cannot name? The rats have a name for it by this time, perhaps, but I don't know what they call it. I call it plexikoid and it comes in sheets, something like insulating board, unattainable and ugli-proof.

9 And there was the man out in Jersey, because I keep thinking about his terrible

necessity and the passion and trouble he had gone to all those years in the indescribable abundance of a householder's detail, building the estate and the planting of the trees and in spring the lawn-dressing and in fall the bulbs for the spring burgeoning, and the watering of the grass on the long light evenings in summer and the gravel for the driveway (all had to be thought out, planned) and the decorative borders, probably, the perennials and the bug spray, and the building of the house from plans of the architect, first the sills, then the studs, then the full corn in the ear, the floors laid on the floor timbers, smoothed, and then the carpets upon the smooth floors and the curtains and the rods therefor. And then, almost without warning, he would be jumping at the same old door and it wouldn't give: they had changed it on him, making life no longer supportable under the elms in the elm shade, under the maples in the maple shade.

10 "Here you have the maximum of openness in a small room."

11 It was impossible to say (maybe it was the city) what made him feel the way he did, and I am not the only one either, he kept thinking—ask any doctor if I am. The doctors, they know how many there are, they even know where the trouble is only they don't like to tell you about the prefrontal lobe because that means making a hole in your skull and removing the work of centuries. It took so long coming, this lobe, so many, many years. (Is it something you read in the paper, perhaps?) And now, the strain being so great, the door having been changed by the Professor once too often . . . but it only means a whiff of ether, a few deft strokes, and the higher animal becomes a little easier in his mind and more like the lower one. From now on, you see, that's the way it will be, the ones with the small prefrontal lobes will win because the other ones are hurt too much by this incessant bumping. They can stand just so much, eh, Doctor? (And what is that, pray, that you have in your hand?) Still, you never can tell, eh, Madam?

12 He crossed (carefully) the room, the thick carpet under him softly, and went toward the door carefully, which was glass and he could see himself in it, and which, at his approach, opened to allow him to pass through; and beyond he half expected to find one of the old doors that he had known, perhaps the one with the circle, the one with the girl her arms outstretched in loveliness and beauty before him. But he saw instead a moving stairway, and descended in light (he kept thinking) to the street below and to the other people. As he stepped off, the ground came up slightly, to meet his foot.

(1954)

QUESTIONS

1. Where does the action of this story take place? Does the setting change?
2. What does the door represent?
3. Why are the rats included? What connection exists between the rats and the main character?
4. What is the importance of the *koid*'s, *oid*'s, *tex*'s, and *flex*'s: "duroid," "plexikoid," "thrutex," and "flexsan."

5. Explain the meaning of the first sentence. Explain what happens at the end of the story.
6. How would this work be different if it were written as an essay rather than as a short story?

SUGGESTIONS FOR WRITING

A. Recast the story as a 500–750 word essay.
B. Compare the style and tone of "The Door" with one of White's essays.
C. Compare the central character of the story with the central character in Richard Selzer's "Minor Surgery."

SEVEN

George Orwell

(1903–1950)

George Orwell was not always George Orwell. He was born Eric Blair to English parents in 1903 in Bengal, India. Blair became Orwell only with the publication of his first book, *Down and Out in Paris and London,* in 1933. Orwell was educated in England, at Crossgates School, and at Eton as a King's Scholar from 1917–1921. The next year he returned to British India, this time to Burma, where he served as a subdivisional officer in the Indian Imperial Police. His Burmese experience had a profound impact on his life, burdening him with an intolerable sense of guilt from which he seems never to have entirely escaped. This guilt resulted from the discrepancy Orwell discovered between the lives of the privileged class of rulers and the subjugated underprivileged native population. But his curse of guilt was also a blessing since Orwell spent the rest of his life thinking through its implications in one work after another. His Burmese experience transformed Orwell from an ordinary, educated middle-class man into an extraordinary and unconventional writer with an acute political consciousness.

Orwell is best known for his fictional allegories, *Animal Farm* and *1984.* He is less well known for his remarkable nonfiction, especially his essays, autobiography, and documentary reportage. And he is perhaps known least for his more-or-less satirical novels of manners. Of the novels, the one most closely related to his nonfiction is *Burmese Days* (1934), a book that reflects the anti-imperialism so vividly illustrated and so eloquently denounced in his essays "Shooting an Elephant" and "Marrakech." Like these works Orwell's documentary books are noteworthy for their powerful revelation of political and social conditions. *Homage to Catalonia* (1938) provides an eyewitness account of the Spanish Civil War, Orwell having served as a soldier on the Republican side. *The Road to Wigan Pier* (1937) provides an account of mining conditions in northern England, focusing on the lives and work of the miners while including statistical information Orwell used to argue for improved conditions. Both books illustrate Orwell's remarkable ability to transform personal experience into literary art.

The same can be said for his other documentary works, especially *Down and Out in Paris and London,* for which Orwell deliberately lived the life of a vagabond bereft of home and money. With this book, Orwell found his voice and subject as a writer. His subject would be his experience, which he would project outside of himself while describing it as spectator and witness. Through an act of deliberate self-distancing, Orwell became a participant observer of his own life. He learned to step back from his experience, to analyze and generalize from it as well as present it subjectively from the inside. This double perspective gives his best work both a concrete particularity and a universality. Orwell's experience becomes, vicariously, ours.

In the manner of his documentary books, Orwell's essays combine narrative and argument, story and point. In "A Hanging" Orwell presents both a description of an actual hanging and an implied argument against capital punishment. What is interesting about this early essay (1931) is not only the way Orwell interpolates his argument, but also the way he strengthens it. Of interest, too, is what Orwell omits about the victim. We know nothing of his crime, of his motives, of his previous life. We see him only as a man condemned to death, a restriction necessary for Orwell's literary and rhetorical purposes. Besides considering Orwell's rhetorical skill in this essay, we might also consider "A Hanging" as a work of fiction. More than one biographer has argued that Orwell never personally witnessed a hanging.

Like "A Hanging," "Shooting an Elephant" derives from Orwell's Burma experience. Although there is no evidence to suggest that he did not shoot an elephant, we might consider the effects of the work if it, too, were found to be fictional rather than factual. Perhaps Orwell's most famous and memorable essay, "Shooting an Elephant" should be read with an eye to its use of detail, its rendering of the narrator's feelings, its imagery of theater, and its clear exposition of an idea.

The same can be said for "Marrakech," an essay in which Orwell makes political writing into an art. As anti-imperialistic as "Shooting an Elephant," "Marrakech" is organized very differently. Instead of a sustained narrative with the advantages of continuity and suspense, "Marrakech" is a mosaic composed of vignettes or little scenes. The scenes together build up an impression of the place and its people. By considering what the scenes imply individually and what they suggest cumulatively, we can infer Orwell's point before he explicitly states it. And though his method is indirect, his prose and point are as clear as a windowpane.

Throughout his work Orwell has maintained a reputation for honesty, for telling the truth as he experienced it. Along with this has gone a concern for the way language is used to distort and conceal truth as well as to reveal it. In "Politics and the English Language" Orwell assumes the role of prophet, warning us of the decay of language and its pernicious effects on thought. His argument, essentially, is that language can corrupt thought, and thought can corrupt language. Language is not a neutral medium, and thought is not a neutral process. Both are weighted with values, especially political and ideological ones. Both are subject to abuse. For better or worse the two are indissolubly wedded. And when language and thought are allowed to decay, we have the inevitable result of a disintegrated society and a decayed humanity. Orwell presents both in the nightmarish vision of *1984*.

Orwell once described what he took to be the four major reasons why writers write. They are (1) sheer egoism; (2) esthetic enthusiasm; (3) historical impulse; (4) political purpose. The most important of these for Orwell was the last, political purpose. Whatever form his writing took, and whatever occasion precipitated it, its animating impulse was to make readers see injustice or dishonesty or cruelty and care enough to want to eradicate them. He cared about the kind of society he lived in; he cared enough to push the world in the direction he believed it should take. And he did this repeatedly in prose that is a model of clarity, honesty, and directness. It is these qualities in part that account for his preeminence as a modern essayist. Equally compelling, however, is the intensity of his moral and political convictions.

Inscribed in each of his works is a man with a conscience and a set of passionate convictions, determined to make us see and hear and feel. He fully deserves his reputation as "the conscience of his generation."

A Hanging

1 It was in Burma, a sodden morning of the rains. A sickly light, like yellow tinfoil, was slanting over the high walls into the jail yard. We were waiting outside the condemned cells, a row of sheds fronted with double bars, like small animal cages. Each cell measured about ten feet by ten and was quite bare within except for a plank bed and a pot for drinking water. In some of them brown silent men were squatting at the inner bars, with their blankets draped round them. These were the condemned men, due to be hanged within the next week or two.

2 One prisoner had been brought out of his cell. He was a Hindu, a puny wisp of a man, with a shaven head and vague liquid eyes. He had a thick, sprouting moustache, absurdly too big for his body, rather like the moustache of a comic man on the films. Six tall Indian warders were guarding him and getting him ready for the gallows. Two of them stood by with rifles and fixed bayonets, while the others handcuffed him, passed a chain through his handcuffs and fixed it to their belts, and lashed his arms tight to his sides. They crowded very close about him, with their hands always on him in a careful, caressing grip, as though all the while feeling him to make sure he was there. It was like men handling a fish which is still alive and may jump back into the water. But he stood quite unresisting, yielding his arms limply to the ropes, as though he hardly noticed what was happening.

3 Eight o'clock struck and a bugle call, desolately thin in the wet air, floated from the distant barracks. The superintendent of the jail, who was standing apart from the rest of us, moodily prodding the gravel with his stick, raised his head at the sound. He was an army doctor, with a gray toothbrush moustache and a gruff voice. "For God's sake hurry up, Francis," he said irritably. "The man ought to have been dead by this time. Aren't you ready yet?"

4 Francis, the head jailer, a fat Dravidian in a white drill suit and gold spectacles, waved his black hand. "Yes sir, yes sir," he bubbled. "All iss satisfactorily prepared. The hangman iss waiting. We shall proceed."

5 "Well, quick march, then. The prisoners can't get their breakfast till this job's over."

6 We set out for the gallows. Two warders marched on either side of the prisoner, with their rifles at the slope; two others marched close against him, gripping him by arm and shoulder, as though at once pushing and supporting him. The rest of us, magistrates and the like, followed behind. Suddenly, when we had gone ten yards, the procession stopped short without any order or warning. A dreadful thing had happened—a dog, come goodness knows whence, had appeared in the yard. It came bounding among us with a loud volley of barks, and leapt round us wagging

its whole body, wild with glee at finding so many human beings together. It was a large woolly dog, half Airedale, half pariah. For a moment it pranced round us, and then, before anyone could stop it, it had made a dash for the prisoner and, jumping up, tried to lick his face. Everyone stood aghast, too taken aback even to grab at the dog.

7 "Who let that bloody brute in here?" said the superintendent angrily. "Catch it, someone!"

8 A warder, detached from the escort, charged clumsily after the dog, but it danced and gamboled just out of his reach, taking everything as part of the game. A young Eurasian jailer picked up a handful of gravel and tried to stone the dog away, but it dodged the stones and came after us again. Its yaps echoed from the jail walls. The prisoner, in the grasp of the two warders, looked on incuriously, as though this was another formality of the hanging. It was several minutes before someone managed to catch the dog. Then we put my handkerchief through its collar and moved off once more, with the dog still straining and whimpering.

9 It was about forty yards to the gallows. I watched the bare brown back of the prisoner marching in front of me. He walked clumsily with his bound arms, but quite steadily, with that bobbing gait of the Indian who never straightens his knees. At each step his muscles slid neatly into place, the lock of hair on his scalp danced up and down, his feet printed themselves on the wet gravel. And once, in spite of the men who gripped him by each shoulder, he stepped slightly aside to avoid a puddle on the path.

10 It is curious, but till that moment I had never realized what it means to destroy a healthy, conscious man. When I saw the prisoner step aside to avoid the puddle I saw the mystery, the unspeakable wrongness, of cutting a life short when it is in full tide. This man was not dying, he was alive just as we are alive. All the organs of his body were working—bowels digesting food, skin renewing itself, nails growing, tissues forming—all toiling away in solemn foolery. His nails would still be growing when he stood on the drop, when he was falling through the air with a tenth of a second to live. His eyes saw the yellow gravel and the gray walls, and his brain still remembered, foresaw, reasoned—reasoned even about puddles. He and we were a party of men walking together, seeing, hearing, feeling, understanding the same world; and in two minutes, with a sudden snap, one of us would be gone—one mind less, one world less.

11 The gallows stood in a small yard, separate from the main grounds of the prison, and overgrown with tall prickly weeds. It was a brick erection like three sides of a shed, with planking on top, and above that two beams and a crossbar with the rope dangling. The hangman, a gray-haired convict in the white uniform of the prison, was waiting beside his machine. He greeted us with a servile crouch as we entered. At a word from Francis the two warders, gripping the prisoner more closely than ever, half led half pushed him to the gallows and helped him clumsily up the ladder. Then the hangman climbed up and fixed the rope round the prisoner's neck.

12 We stood waiting, five yards away. The warders had formed in a rough circle round the gallows. And then, when the noose was fixed, the prisoner began crying out to his god. It was a high, reiterated cry of "Ram! Ram! Ram! Ram!" not urgent

and fearful like a prayer or cry for help, but steady, rhythmical, almost like the tolling of a bell. The dog answered the sound with a whine. The hangman, still standing on the gallows, produced a small cotton bag like a flour bag and drew it down over the prisoner's face. But the sound, muffled by the cloth, still persisted, over and over again: "Ram! Ram! Ram! Ram! Ram!"

13 The hangman climbed down and stood ready, holding the lever. Minutes seemed to pass. The steady, muffled crying from the prisoner went on and on, "Ram! Ram! Ram!" never faltering for an instant. The superintendent, his head on his chest, was slowly poking the ground with his stick; perhaps he was counting the cries, allowing the prisoner a fixed number—fifty, perhaps, or a hundred. Everyone had changed color. The Indians had gone gray like bad coffee, and one or two of the bayonets were wavering. We looked at the lashed, hooded man on the drop, and listened to his cries—each cry another second of life; the same thought was in all our minds: oh, kill him quickly, get it over, stop that abominable noise!

14 Suddenly the superintendent made up his mind. Throwing up his head he made a swift motion with his stick. "Chalo!" he shouted almost fiercely.

15 There was a clanking noise, and then dead silence. The prisoner had vanished, and the rope was twisting on itself. I let go of the dog, and it galloped immediately to the back of the gallows; but when it got there it stopped short, barked, and then retreated into a corner of the yard, where it stood among the weeds, looking timorously out at us. We went round the gallows to inspect the prisoner's body. He was dangling with his toes pointed straight downward, very slowly revolving, as dead as a stone.

16 The superintendent reached out with his stick and poked the bare brown body; it oscillated slightly. "*He's* all right," said the superintendent. He backed out from under the gallows, and blew out a deep breath. The moody look had gone out of his face quite suddenly. He glanced at his wrist watch. "Eight minutes past eight. Well, that's all for this morning, thank God."

17 The warders unfixed bayonets and marched away. The dog, sobered and conscious of having misbehaved itself, slipped after them. We walked out of the gallows yard, past the condemned cells with their waiting prisoners, into the big central yard of the prison. The convicts, under the command of warders armed with lathis, were already receiving their breakfast. They squatted in long rows, each man holding a tin pannikin, while two warders with buckets marched round ladling out rice; it seemed quite a homely, jolly scene, after the hanging. An enormous relief had come upon us now that the job was done. One felt an impulse to sing, to break into a run, to snigger. All at once everyone began chattering gaily.

18 The Eurasian boy walking beside me nodded toward the way we had come, with a knowing smile: "Do you know, sir, our friend [he meant the dead man] when he heard his appeal had been dismissed, he pissed on the floor of his cell. From fright. Kindly take one of my cigarettes, sir. Do you not admire my new silver case, sir? From the boxwalah, two rupees eight annas. Classy European style."

19 Several people laughed—at what, nobody seemed certain.

20 Francis was walking by the superintendent, talking garrulously: "Well, sir, all hass passed off with the utmost satisfactoriness. It was all finished—flick! like that.

It iss not always so—oah, no! I have known cases where the doctor wass obliged to go beneath the gallows and pull the prissoner's legs to ensure decease. Most disagreeable!"

21 "Wriggling about, eh? That's bad," said the superintendent.

22 "Ach, sir, it iss worse when they become refractory! One man, I recall, clung to the bars of hiss cage when we went to take him out. You will scarcely credit, sir, that it took six warders to dislodge him, three pulling at each leg. We reasoned with him. 'My dear fellow,' we said, 'think of all the pain and trouble you are causing to us!' But no, he would not listen! Ach, he wass very troublesome!"

23 I found that I was laughing quite loudly. Everyone was laughing. Even the superintendent grinned in a tolerant way. "You'd better all come out and have a drink," he said quite genially. "I've got a bottle of whisky in the car. We could do with it."

24 We went through the big double gates of the prison into the road. "Pulling at his legs!" exclaimed a Burmese magistrate suddenly, and burst into a loud chuckling. We all began laughing again. At that moment Francis' anecdote seemed extraordinarily funny. We all had a drink together, native and European alike, quite amicably. The dead man was a hundred yards away.

(1931)

QUESTIONS

Thought and Structure

1. As a story, how interesting is "A Hanging"? As an argument against capital punishment, how persuasive is it?
2. If you discovered that Orwell never attended a hanging, would that affect your response to his essay? How, and why?
3. What is the point and purpose of paragraph 10? Why does Orwell emphasize physiological details? How and why does he bring us into the essay at this point? For what purpose? What does he mean by "one mind less, one world less"?
4. After rereading paragraph 10 carefully and responding to question 3, backtrack a bit and reread paragraph 9. What details there prepare for and set up the emphasis and point of paragraph 10?
5. What is the overall structure of "A Hanging"? How does it begin, where does it go, and how does it end? In the narrative, there are two interruptions of the walk to the gallows. What are they, and what effect do they have—on the narrator, the characters, and on the reader?
6. Where does Orwell make his point most explicitly? Does he explain his view in more than one place?

Style and Strategy

7. Orwell's language in "A Hanging" frequently stimulates the senses. Consider, for example, the following words and phrases: "slanting" light, "sodden morning," "yellow

gravel," the "caressing grip," the "loud volley of barks." What other words and phrases indicating sound, sense, taste, or touch can you find?

8. Comparisons are scattered throughout the essay. Consider the point and the effect of the following:

   It was like men handling a fish. (2)

   It was a high reiterated cry of "Ram! Ram! Ram! Ram!" not urgent and fearful like a prayer or cry for help, but steady, rhythmical, almost like the tolling of a bell. (12)

   The Indians had gone gray like bad coffee. (13)

   What other comparisons can you find, and how effective do you think they are? What would be lost if such comparisons were omitted?

9. A number of the people described in "A Hanging" are given direct speech—dialogue—in the manner of a story or a play. Is the dialogue necessary? What does it contribute?

10. The sentences in paragraph 10 contain a considerable amount of stacking—piling up two, three, or more parallel words, phrases, or clauses. Both the second and third sentences, for example, balance two statements—somewhat in the manner of a seesaw, with the comma as a fulcrum:

    I saw the mystery,
    the unspeakable wrongness . . .

    This man was not dying,
    he was alive
    just as we are alive.

    Other sentences in the same paragraph—and elsewhere in the essay—stack three and four elements with separating commas. What is the effect of this kind of accumulation?

11. The final sentence of paragraph 10 contains an appended detail after the dash. Try reading the sentence without the dash—simply omitting the words after "gone." Can the appended thought be included somehow in the sentence without using a dash, without, that is, setting it off the way Orwell does. What is the effect of having that final remark appear after a dash?

SUGGESTIONS FOR WRITING

A. Write an essay arguing for or against capital punishment. You might want to write a strictly argumentative essay, relying on logic, evidence, concession, qualification—applying primarily or even exclusively to reason. Or you might, as Orwell does here, use personal experience in the form of a story or brief anecdote to convey your view, in which case you would probably rely more on feeling to convey your point. Or you might combine the two kinds of persuasion.

B. Describe an event you witnessed. Include both what you saw—the details of fact and vision—and how it affected you. You might include, as Orwell does in "A Hanging," an idea that derives from the experience. You'll need to decide where you want to put this explanatory information, and how full you want it to be.

C. Explain what Orwell means when he writes that with the death of this man there was "one mind less, one world less." Consider as part of your thinking, the following poem, "People," by the contemporary Russian poet, Yevgeny Yevtushenko.

No people are uninteresting.
Their fate is like the chronicle of planets.

Nothing in them is not particular,
and planet is dissimilar from planet.

And if a man lived in obscurity
making his friends in that obscurity
obscurity is not uninteresting.

To each his world is private,
and in that world one excellent minute.

And in that world one tragic minute.
These are private.

In any man who dies there dies with him
his first snow and kiss and fight.
It goes with him.

They are left books and bridges
and painted canvas and machinery.

Whose fate is to survive.
But what has gone is also not nothing:

by the rule of the game something has gone.
Not people die but worlds die in them.

Whom we knew as faulty, the earth's creatures.
Of whom, essentially, what did we know?

Brother of a brother? Friend of friends?
Lover of lover?

We who knew our fathers
in everything, in nothing.

They perish. They cannot be brought back.
The secret worlds are not regenerated.

And every time again and again
I make my lament against destruction.

D. The following news report, which appeared in a British newspaper, is an eyewitness account of a hanging. It shares some common details with Orwell's essay. But it is also quite different. Make a list of similarities and differences between the two pieces. Consider the following: the purpose and point of each; the intended or implied audience of each; the number and kind of details included; the voice and tone of each; the style.

Michael Lake Describes What the Executioner Actually Faces,
Guardian 9 April, 1973

It is doubtful if those who seek the reintroduction of capital punishment have ever seen a hanging. It is a grim business, far removed from the hurly burly of Parliament, from the dusty gloom of the Old Bailey and a million light years away from the murder.

In New Zealand hangings were always in the evening. There were never any crowds, but three journalists were always summoned to witness the hanging. Their names were published later that night, along with those of the sheriff, the coroner and others, in the Official Gazette. I watched the last hanging in New Zealand.

Walter James Bolton was a farmer from the west coast of the North Island. He had poisoned his wife. He was 62, and the oldest and heaviest man ever hanged in New Zealand. They had to make sure they got the length of rope right so the drop wouldn't tear off his head.

I arrived at Mt Eden Gaol, Auckland, at 6 o'clock on a Monday evening. With the other witnesses I was led through the main administrative block, down some steps, and along a wing which, it turned out, was a sort of Death Row.

We were led to the foot of the scaffold in a yard immediately at the end of the wing. The sky was darkening and a canvas canopy over the yard flapped gently in the breeze.

After a long time, there was a murmuring. Into view came a strange procession; the deputy governor of the prison, leading four warders and among them, walked or rather shambled the hulking figure of Bolton. His arms were pinioned by ropes to his trunk.

Behind him walked a parson reading aloud. It was with disbelief and shock that I recognised the Burial Service from the Book of Common Prayer.

High upon the scaffold, 17 steps away, the executioner stood immobile. He wore a black broad-brimmed hat, a black trench coat, and heavy boots, and he was masked. Only the slit for his eyes and his white hands gleamed in the light.

Bolton was helped up the steps by the warders, who bound his ankles together. The sheriff then asked him if he had anything to say before sentence was carried out.

Bolton mumbled. After a few seconds mumbling the parson, apparently unaware that the prisoner was talking, interrupted with further readings from the Burial Service.

I checked my shorthand notes with the other reporters. One, an elderly man who had witnessed 19 hangings, had heard nothing. The other man's shorthand outlines matched my own. He had said: 'The only thing I want to say is. . . .'

The warders did all the work. They bound him and put a white canvas hood over his head as he stood there, swaying in their grasp. Then they dropped the loop over his head, with the traditional hangman's knot, tidied it up, and stepped back.

The sheriff lifted his hand and lowered it. The executioner moved for the first and only time. He pulled a lever, and stepped back. Bolton dropped behind a canvas screen. The rope ran fast through the pulley at the top, and then when the Turk's Head knotted in the end jammed in the pulley, the block clanged loudly up against the beam to which it was fixed. The rope quivered, and that was the end of Walter James Bolton.

A doctor repaired behind the screen which hid the body from us. A hanged man usually ejaculates and evacuates his bowels. In New Zealand, at any rate he also hanged for an hour. Bolton hung while we sat back in the deputy governor's office drinking the whisky traditionally provided by the Government for these occasions—'Who's for a long drop,' asked some macabre wit.

The city coroner, Mr Alf Addison, an old friend of mine, called us across to his office where we duly swore we had seen the sentence of the court carried out.

I went back to my newspaper office and wrote three paragraphs. No sensations, I told the night editor, the bloke hadn't made a fuss. Then I went home with a sense of loss and corruption I have never quite shed.

Politics and the English Language

1 Most people who bother with the matter at all would admit that the English language is in a bad way, but it is generally assumed that we cannot by conscious action do anything about it. Our civilization is decadent and our lan-

guage—so the argument runs—must inevitably share in the general collapse. It follows that any struggle against the abuse of language is a sentimental archaism, like preferring candles to electric light or hansom cabs to aeroplanes. Underneath this lies the half-conscious belief that language is a natural growth and not an instrument which we shape for our own purposes.

2 Now, it is clear that the decline of a language must ultimately have political and economic causes: it is not due simply to the bad influence of this or that individual writer. But an effect can become a cause, reinforcing the original cause and producing the same effect in an intensified form, and so on indefinitely. A man may take to drink because he feels himself to be a failure, and then fail all the more completely because he drinks. It is rather the same thing that is happening to the English language. It becomes ugly and inaccurate because our thoughts are foolish, but the slovenliness of our language makes it easier for us to have foolish thoughts. The point is that the process is reversible. Modern English, especially written English, is full of bad habits which spread by imitation and which can be avoided if one is willing to take the necessary trouble. If one gets rid of these habits one can think more clearly, and to think clearly is a necessary first step toward political regeneration: so that the fight against bad English is not frivolous and is not the exclusive concern of professional writers. I will come back to this presently, and I hope that by that time the meaning of what I have said here will have become clearer. Meanwhile, here are five specimens of the English language as it is now habitually written.

3 These five passages have not been picked out because they are especially bad—I could have quoted far worse if I had chosen—but because they illustrate various of the mental vices from which we now suffer. They are a little below the average, but are fairly representative samples. I number them so that I can refer back to them when necessary:

> (1) I am not, indeed, sure whether it is not true to say that the Milton who once seemed not unlike a seventeenth-century Shelley had not become, out of an experience ever more bitter in each year, more alien [*sic*] to the founder of that Jesuit sect which nothing could induce him to tolerate.
>
> Professor Harold Laski (Essay in *Freedom of Expression*)

> (2) Above all, we cannot play ducks and drakes with a native battery of idioms which prescribes such egregious collocations of vocables as the Basic *put up with* for *tolerate* or *put at a loss* for *bewilder.*
>
> Professor Lancelot Hogben *(Interglossa)*

> (3) On the one side we have the free personality: by definition it is not neurotic, for it has neither conflict nor dream. Its desires, such as they are, are transparent, for they are just what institutional approval keeps in the forefront of consciousness; another institutional pattern would alter their number and intensity; there is little in them that is natural, irreducible, or culturally dangerous. But *on the other side,* the social bond itself is nothing but the mutual reflection of these self-secure integrities. Recall the definition of love. Is not this the very picture of a small academic? Where is there a place in this hall of mirrors for either personality or fraternity?
>
> Essay on psychology in *Politics* (New York)

> (4) All the "best people" from the gentlemen's clubs, and all the frantic fascist captains,

united in common hatred of Socialism and bestial horror of the rising tide of the mass revolutionary movement, have turned to acts of provocation, to foul incendiarism, to medieval legends of poisoned wells, to legalize their own destruction of proletarian organizations, and rouse the agitated petty-bourgeoisie to chauvinistic fervor on behalf of the fight against the revolutionary way out of the crisis.

Communist pamphlet

(5) If a new spirit *is* to be infused into this old country, there is one thorny and contentious reform which must be tackled, and that is the humanization and galvanization of the B.B.C. Timidity here will bespeak canker and atrophy of the soul. The heart of Britain may be sound and of strong beat, for instance, but the British lion's roar at present is like that of Bottom in Shakespeare's *Midsummer Night's Dream*—as gentle as any sucking dove. A virile new Britain cannot continue indefinitely to be traduced in the eyes or rather ears, of the world by the effete languors of Langham Place, brazenly masquerading as "standard English." When the Voice of Britain is heard at nine o'clock, better far and infinitely less ludicrous to hear aitches honestly dropped than the present priggish, inflated, inhibited, school-ma'amish arch braying of blameless bashful mewing maidens!

Letter in *Tribune*

4 Each of these passages has faults of its own, but, quite apart from avoidable ugliness, two qualities are common to all of them. The first is staleness of imagery; the other is lack of precision. The writer either has a meaning and cannot express it, or he inadvertently says something else, or he is almost indifferent as to whether his words mean anything or not. This mixture of vagueness and sheer incompetence is the most marked characteristic of modern English prose, and especially of any kind of political writing. As soon as certain topics are raised, the concrete melts into the abstract and no one seems able to think of turns of speech that are not hackneyed: prose consists less and less of *words* chosen for the sake of their meaning, and more and more of *phrases* tacked together like the sections of a prefabricated henhouse. I list below, with notes and examples, various of the tricks by means of which the work of prose-construction is habitually dodged:

5 *Dying metaphors.* A newly invented metaphor assists thought by evoking a visual image, while on the other hand a metaphor which is technically "dead" (e.g. *iron resolution*) has in effect reverted to being an ordinary word and can generally be used without loss of vividness. But in between these two classes there is a huge dump of worn-out metaphors which have lost all evocative power and are merely used because they save people the trouble of inventing phrases for themselves. Examples are: *Ring the changes on, take up the cudgels for, toe the line, ride roughshod over, stand shoulder to shoulder with, play into the hands of, no axe to grind, grist to the mill, fishing in troubled waters, on the order of the day, Achilles' heel, swan song, hotbed.* Many of these are used without knowledge of their meaning (what is a "rift," for instance?), and incompatible metaphors are frequently mixed, a sure sign that the writer is not interested in what he is saying. Some metaphors now current have been twisted out of their original meaning without those who use them even being aware of the fact. For example, *toe the line* is sometimes written *tow the line.* Another example is *the hammer and the anvil,* now always used with the implication that the anvil gets the worst of it. In real life it is always the anvil that breaks the hammer, never the other

way about: a writer who stopped to think what he was saying would be aware of this, and would avoid perverting the original phrase.

6 *Operators* or *verbal false limbs.* These save the trouble of picking out appropriate verbs and nouns, and at the same time pad each sentence with extra syllables which give it an appearance of symmetry. Characteristic phrases are *render inoperative, militate against, make contact with, be subjected to, give rise to, give grounds for, have the effect of, play a leading part (role) in, make itself felt, take effect, exhibit a tendency to, serve the purpose of, etc., etc.* The keynote is the elimination of simple verbs. Instead of being a single word, such as *break, stop, spoil, mend, kill,* a verb becomes a *phrase,* made up of a noun or adjective tacked on to some general-purpose verb such as *prove, serve, form, play, render.* In addition, the passive voice is wherever possible used in preference to the active, and noun constructions are used instead of gerunds *(by examination of* instead of *by examining).* The range of verbs is further cut down by means of the *-ize* and *de-* formations, and the banal statements are given an appearance of profundity by means of the *not un-* formation. Simple conjunctions and prepositions are replaced by such phrases as *with respect to, having regard to, the fact that, by dint of, in view of, in the interests of, on the hypothesis that;* and the ends of sentences are saved by anticlimax by such resounding commonplaces as *greatly to be desired, cannot be left out of account, a development to be expected in the near future, deserving of serious consideration, brought to a satisfactory conclusion,* and so on and so forth.

7 *Pretentious diction.* Words like *phenomenon, element, individual* (as noun), *objective, categorical, effective, virtual, basic, primary, promote, constitute, exhibit, exploit, utilize, eliminate, liquidate,* are used to dress up simple statements and give an air of scientific impartiality to biased judgments. Adjectives like *epoch-making, epic, historic, unforgettable, triumphant, age-old, inevitable, inexorable, veritable,* are used to dignify the sordid processes of international politics, while writing that aims at glorifying war usually takes on an archaic color, its characteristic words being: *realm, throne, chariot, mailed fist, trident, sword, shield, buckler, banner, jackboot, clarion.* Foreign words and expressions such as *cul de sac, ancien régime, deus ex machina, mutatis mutandis, status quo, gleichschaltung, weltanschauung,* are used to give an air of culture and elegance. Except for the useful abbreviations *i.e., e.g.,* and *etc.,* there is no real need for any of the hundreds of foreign phrases now current in English. Bad writers, and especially scientific, political, and sociological writers, are nearly always haunted by the notion that Latin or Greek words are grander than Saxon ones, and unnecessary words like *expedite, ameliorate, predict, extraneous, deracinated, clandestine, subaqueous,* and hundreds of others constantly gain ground from their Anglo-Saxon opposite numbers.* The jargon peculiar to Marxist writing

*An interesting illustration of this is the way in which the English flower names which were in use till very recently are being ousted by Greek ones, *snapdragon* becoming *antirrhinum, forget-me-not* becoming *myosotis,* etc. It is hard to see any practical reason for this change of fashion: it is probably due to an instinctive turning away from the more homely word and a vague feeling that the Greek word is scientific.

(*hyena, hangman, cannibal, petty bourgeois, these gentry, lackey, flunkey, mad dog, White Guard,* etc.) consists largely of words and phrases translated from Russian, German, or French; but the normal way of coining a new word is to use a Latin or Greek root with the appropriate affix and, where necessary, the size formation. It is often easier to make up words of this kind (*deregionalize, impermissible, extramarital, nonfragmentary* and so forth) than to think up the English words that will cover one's meaning. The result, in general, is an increase in slovenliness and vagueness.

8 *Meaningless words.* In certain kinds of writing, particularly in art criticism and literary criticism, it is normal to come across long passages which are almost completely lacking in meaning.† Words like *romantic, plastic, values, human, dead, sentimental, natural, vitality,* as used in art criticism, are strictly meaningless, in the sense that they not only do not point to any discoverable object, but are hardly ever expected to do so by the reader. When one critic writes, "The outstanding feature of Mr. X's work is its living quality," while another writes, "The immediately striking thing about Mr. X's work is its peculiar deadness," the reader accepts this as a simple difference of opinion. If words like *black* and *white* were involved, instead of the jargon words *dead* and *living,* he would see at once that language was being used in an improper way. Many political words are similarly abused. The word *Fascism* has now no meaning except in so far as it signifies "something not desirable." The words *democracy, socialism, freedom, patriotic, realistic, justice,* have each of them several different meanings which cannot be reconciled with one another. In the case of a word like *democracy,* not only is there no agreed definition, but the attempt to make one is resisted from all sides. It is almost universally felt that when we call a country democratic we are praising it: consequently the defenders of every kind of régime claim that it is a democracy, and fear that they might have to stop using the word if it were tied down to any one meaning. Words of this kind are often used in a consciously dishonest way. That is, the person who uses them has his own private definition, but allows his hearer to think he means something quite different. Statements like *Marshal Pétain was a true patriot, The Soviet press is the freest in the world, The Catholic Church is opposed to persecution,* are almost always made with intent to deceive. Other words used in variable meanings, in most cases more or less dishonestly, are: *class, totalitarian, science, progressive, reactionary, bourgeois, equality.*

9 Now that I have made this catalogue of swindles and perversions, let me give another example of the kind of writing that they lead to. This time it must of its nature be an imaginary one. I am going to translate a passage of good English into modern English of the worst sort. Here is a well-known verse from *Ecclesiastes:*

---

†Example: "Comfort's catholicity of perception and image, strangely Whitmanesque in range, almost the exact opposite in aesthetic compulsion, continues to evoke that trembling atmospheric accumulative hinting at a cruel, an inexorably serene timelessness. . . . Wrey Gardiner scores by aiming at simple bull's-eyes with precision. Only they are not so simple, and through this contented sadness runs more than the surface bittersweet of resignation." *(Poetry Quarterly.)*

> I returned and saw under the sun, that the race is not to the swift, nor the battle to the strong, neither yet bread to the wise, nor yet riches to men of understanding, nor yet favour to men of skill; but time and chance happeneth to them all.

Here it is in modern English:

> Objective considerations of contemporary phenomena compels the conclusion that success or failure in competitive activities exhibits no tendency to be commensurate with innate capacity, but that a considerable element of the unpredictable must invariably be taken into account.

10 This is a parody, but not a very gross one. Exhibit (3), above, for instance, contains several patches of the same kind of English. It will be seen that I have not made a full translation. The beginning and ending of the sentence follow the original meaning fairly closely, but in the middle the concrete illustrations—race, battle, bread—dissolve into the vague phrase "success or failure in competitive activities." This had to be so, because no modern writer of the kind I am discussing—no one capable of using phrases like "objective consideration of contemporary phenomena"—would ever tabulate his thoughts in that precise and detailed way. The whole tendency of modern prose is away from concreteness. Now analyze these two sentences a little more closely. The first contains forty-nine words but only sixty syllables, and all its words are those of everyday life. The second contains thirty-eight words of ninety syllables: eighteen of its words are from Latin roots, and one from Greek. The first sentence contains six vivid images, and only one phrase ("time and chance") that could be called vague. The second contains not a single fresh, arresting phrase, and in spite of its ninety syllables it gives only a shortened version of the meaning contained in the first. Yet without a doubt it is the second kind of sentence that is gaining ground in modern English. I do not want to exaggerate. This kind of writing is not yet universal, and outcrops of simplicity will occur here and there in the worst-written page. Still, if you or I were told to write a few lines on the uncertainty of human fortunes, we should probably come much nearer to my imaginary sentence than to the one from *Ecclesiastes.*

11 As I have tried to show, modern writing at its worst does not consist in picking out words for the sake of their meaning and inventing images in order to make the meaning clearer. It consists in gumming together long strips of words which have already been set in order by someone else, and making the results presentable by sheer humbug. The attraction of this way of writing is that it is easy. It is easier—even quicker, once you have the habit—to say *In my opinion it is not an unjustifiable assumption that* than to say *I think.* If you use ready-made phrases, you not only don't have to hunt about for words; you also don't have to bother with the rhythms of your sentences, since these phrases are generally so arranged as to be more or less euphonious. When you are composing in a hurry—when you are dictating to a stenographer, for instance, or making a public speech—it is natural to fall into a pretentious, Latinized style. Tags like *a consideration which we should do well to bear in mind* or *a conclusion to which all of us would readily assent* will save many a sentence from coming down with a bump. By using stale metaphors, similes, and

idioms, you save much mental effort, at the cost of leaving your meaning vague, not only for your reader but for yourself. This is the significance of mixed metaphors. The sole aim of a metaphor is to call up a visual image. When these images clash—as in *The Fascist octopus has sung its swan song, the jackboot is thrown into the melting pot*—it can be taken as certain that the writer is not seeing a mental image of the objects he is naming; in other words he is not really thinking. Look again at the examples I gave at the beginning of this essay. Professor Laski (1) uses five negatives in fifty-three words. One of these is superfluous, making nonsense of the whole passage, and in addition there is the slip—*alien* for akin—making further nonsense, and several avoidable pieces of clumsiness which increase the general vagueness. Professor Hogben (2) plays ducks and drakes with a battery which is able to write prescriptions, and, while disapproving of the everyday phrase *put up with,* is unwilling to look *egregious* up in the dictionary and see what it means; (3), if one takes an uncharitable attitude towards it, is simply meaningless: probably one could work out its intended meaning by reading the whole of the article in which it occurs. In (4), the writer knows more or less what he wants to say, but an accumulation of stale phrases chokes him like tea leaves blocking a sink. In (5), words and meaning have almost parted company. People who write in this manner usually have a general emotional meaning—they dislike one thing and want to express solidarity with another—but they are not interested in the detail of what they are saying. A scrupulous writer, in every sentence that he writes, will ask himself at least four questions, thus: What am I trying to say? What words will express it? What image or idiom will make it clearer? Is this image fresh enough to have an effect? And he will probably ask himself two more: Could I put it more shortly? Have I said anything that is avoidably ugly? But you are not obliged to go to all this trouble. You can shirk it by simply throwing your mind open and letting the ready-made phrases come crowding in. They will construct your sentences for you—even think your thoughts for you, to a certain extent—and at need they will perform the important service of partially concealing your meaning even from yourself. It is at this point that the special connection between politics and the debasement of language becomes clear.

12 In our time it is broadly true that political writing is bad writing. Where it is not true, it will generally be found that the writer is some kind of rebel, expressing his private opinions and not a "party line." Orthodoxy, of whatever color, seems to demand a lifeless, imitative style. The political dialects to be found in pamphlets, leading articles, manifestoes, White Papers and the speeches of undersecretaries do, of course, vary from party to party, but they are all alike in that one almost never finds in them a fresh, vivid, homemade turn of speech. When one watches some tired hack on the platform mechanically repeating the familiar phrases—*bestial atrocities, iron heel, bloodstained tyranny, free peoples of the world, stand shoulder to shoulder*—one often has a curious feeling that one is not watching a live human being but some kind of dummy: a feeling which suddenly becomes stronger at moments when the light catches the speaker's spectacles and turns them into blank discs which seem to have no eyes behind them. And this is not altogether fanciful. A speaker who uses that kind of phraseology has gone some distance toward turning himself into a machine. The appropriate noises are coming out of his larynx, but

his brain is not involved as it would be if he were choosing his words for himself. If the speech he is making is one that he is accustomed to make over and over again, he may be almost unconscious of what he is saying, as one is when one utters the responses in church. And this reduced state of consciousness, if not indispensable, is at any rate favorable to political conformity.

13 In our time, political speech and writing are largely the defense of the indefensible. Things like the continuance of British rule in India, the Russian purges and deportations, the dropping of the atom bombs on Japan, can indeed be defended, but only by arguments which are too brutal for most people to face, and which do not square with the professed aims of political parties. Thus political language has to consist largely of euphemisms, question-begging and sheer cloudy vagueness. Defenseless villages are bombarded from the air, the inhabitants driven out into the countryside, the cattle machine-gunned, the huts set on fire with incendiary bullets: this is called *pacification.* Millions of peasants are robbed of their farms and sent trudging along the roads with no more than they can carry: this is called *transfer of population* or *rectification of frontiers.* People are imprisoned for years without trial, or shot in the back of the neck or sent to die of scurvy in Arctic lumber camps: this is called *elimination of unreliable elements.* Such phraseology is needed if one wants to name things without calling up mental pictures of them. Consider for instance some comfortable English professor defending Russian totalitarianism. He cannot say outright, "I believe in killing off your opponents when you can get good results by doing so." Probably, therefore, he will say something like this:

14 "While freely conceding that the Soviet régime exhibits certain features which the humanitarian may be inclined to deplore, we must, I think, agree that a certain curtailment of the right to political opposition is an unavoidable concomitant of transitional periods, and that the rigors which the Russian people have been called upon to undergo have been amply justified in the sphere of concrete achievement."

15 The inflated style is itself a kind of euphemism. A mass of Latin words falls upon the facts like soft snow, blurring the outlines and covering up all the details. The great enemy of clear language is insincerity. When there is a gap between one's real and one's declared aims, one turns as it were instinctively to long words and exhausted idioms, like a cuttlefish squirting out ink. In our age there is no such thing as "keeping out of politics." All issues are political issues, and politics itself is a mass of lies, evasions, folly, hatred, and schizophrenia. When the general atmosphere is bad, language must suffer. I should expect to find—this is a guess which I have not sufficient knowledge to verify—that the German, Russian and Italian languages have all deteriorated in the last ten or fifteen years, as a result of dictatorship.

16 But if thought corrupts language, language can also corrupt thought. A bad usage can spread by tradition and imitation, even among people who should and do know better. The debased language that I have been discussing is in some ways very convenient. Phrases like *a not unjustifiable assumption, leaves much to be desired, would serve no good purpose, a consideration which we should do well to bear in mind,* are a continuous temptation, a packet of aspirins always at one's elbow. Look back through this essay, and for certain you will find that I have again and again committed the very faults I am protesting against. By this morning's

post I have received a pamphlet dealing with conditions in Germany. The author tells me that he "felt impelled" to write it. I open it at random, and here is almost the first sentence that I see: "[The Allies] have an opportunity not only of achieving a radical transformation of Germany's social and political structure in such a way as to avoid a nationalistic reaction in Germany itself, but at the same time of laying the foundations of a co-operative and unified Europe." You see, he "feels impelled" to write—feels, presumably, that he has something new to say—and yet his words, like cavalry horses answering the bugle, group themselves automatically into the familiar dreary pattern. This invasion of one's mind by ready-made phrases *(lay the foundations, achieve a radical transformation)* can only be prevented if one is constantly on guard against them, and every such phrase anesthetizes a portion of one's brain.

17 I said earlier that the decadence of our language is probably curable. Those who deny this would argue, if they produced an argument at all, that language merely reflects existing social conditions, and that we cannot influence its development by any direct tinkering with words and constructions. So far as the general tone or spirit of a language goes, this may be true, but it is not true in detail. Silly words and expressions have often disappeared, not through any evolutionary process but owing to the conscious action of a minority. Two recent examples were *explore every avenue* and *leave no stone unturned,* which were killed by the jeers of a few journalists. There is a long list of flyblown metaphors which could similarly be got rid of if enough people would interest themselves in the job; and it should also be possible to laugh the *not un-* formation out of existence,* to reduce the amount of Latin and Greek in the average sentence, to drive out foreign phrases and strayed scientific words, and, in general, to make pretentiousness unfashionable. But all these are minor points. The defense of the English language implies more than this, and perhaps it is best to start by saying what it does *not* imply.

18 To begin with it has nothing to do with archaism, with the salvaging of obsolete words and turns of speech, or with the setting up of a "standard English" which must never be departed from. On the contrary, it is especially concerned with the scrapping of every word or idiom which has outworn its usefulness. It has nothing to do with correct grammar and syntax, which are of no importance so long as one makes one's meaning clear, or with the avoidance of Americanisms, or with having what is called a "good prose style." On the other hand it is not concerned with fake simplicity and the attempt to make written English colloquial. Nor does it even imply in every case preferring the Saxon word to the Latin one, though it does imply using the fewest and shortest words that will cover one's meaning. What is above all needed is to let the meaning choose the word, and not the other way about. In prose, the worst thing one can do with words is to surrender to them. When you think of a concrete object, you think wordlessly, and then, if you want to describe the thing you have been visualizing you probably hunt about till you find the exact words that seem to fit it. When you think of something abstract you are

*One can cure oneself of the *not un-* formation by memorizing this sentence: *A not unblack dog was chasing a not unsmall rabbit across a not ungreen field.*

more inclined to use words from the start, and unless you make a conscious effort to prevent it, the existing dialect will come rushing in and do the job for you, at the expense of blurring or even changing your meaning. Probably it is better to put off using words as long as possible and get one's meaning as clear as one can through pictures or sensations. Afterward one can choose—not simply *accept*—the phrases that will best cover the meaning, and then switch round and decide what impression one's words are likely to make on another person. This last effort of the mind cuts out all stale or mixed images, all prefabricated phrases, needless repetitions, and humbug and vagueness generally. But one can often be in doubt about the effect of a word or a phrase, and one needs rules that one can rely on when instinct fails. I think the following rules will cover most cases:

(i) Never use a metaphor, simile, or other figure of speech which you are used to seeing in print.
(ii) Never use a long word where a short one will do.
(iii) If it is possible to cut a word out, always cut it out.
(iv) Never use the passive where you can use the active.
(v) Never use a foreign phrase, a scientific word, or a jargon word if you can think of an everyday English equivalent.
(vi) Break any of these rules sooner than say anything outright barbarous.

These rules sound elementary, and so they are, but they demand a deep change of attitude in anyone who has grown used to writing in the style now fashionable. One could keep all of them and still write bad English, but one could not write the kind of stuff that I quoted in those five specimens at the beginning of this article.

19 I have not here been considering the literary use of language, but merely language as an instrument for expressing and not for concealing or preventing thought. Stuart Chase and others have come near to claiming that all abstract words are meaningless, and have used this as a pretext for advocating a kind of political quietism. Since you don't know what Fascism is, how can you struggle against Fascism? One need not swallow such absurdities as this, but one ought to recognize that the present political chaos is connected with the decay of language, and that one can probably bring about some improvement by starting at the verbal end. If you simplify your English, you are freed from the worst follies of orthodoxy. You cannot speak any of the necessary dialects, and when you make a stupid remark its stupidity will be obvious, even to yourself. Political language—and with variations this is true of all political parties, from Conservatives to Anarchists—is designed to make lies sound truthful and murder respectable, and to give an appearance of solidity to pure wind. One cannot change this all in a moment, but one can at least change one's own habits, and from time to time one can even, if one jeers loudly enough, send some worn-out and useless phrase—some *jackboot, Achilles' heel, hotbed, melting pot, acid test, veritable inferno,* or other lump of verbal refuse—into the dustbin where it belongs.

(1946)

QUESTIONS

1. Who is Orwell addressing and why? What is his general point and how does the example of the man who drinks (paragraph 2) help clarify and illustrate it? What connection between thought and language does Orwell postulate? Compare what he says in paragraph 2 with his remarks in paragraph 12.
2. What common problems do the five passages exemplifying bad writing share? What is wrong with the writing in each?
3. What point does Orwell make in his translation of the passage from Ecclesiastes? Why is the original biblical passage in the King James Version an example of good writing?
4. What does Orwell have against clichés? What examples has he included? Provide an update with some clichés you have heard or seen in print.
5. In paragraph 11 Orwell lists a series of questions writers ought constantly to ask themselves as they write and revise. What are they, and how might they be helpful to any writer? What common bad writing habits are they meant to overcome?
6. In paragraph 18 Orwell presents guidelines for good writing. Examine one of your essays to see how you measure up against these standards. Analyze one of Orwell's essays to see if he follows his own advice.

SUGGESTIONS FOR WRITING

A. In a 500–1000 word essay, agree or disagree with Orwell's assertion that "thought corrupts language, [and] language can also corrupt thought."

B. Revise one of your papers or a few pages from one of your textbooks to bring it into line with Orwell's standards for good writing.

C. Keep a journal for a week or two of violations of Orwell's standards made by politicians in their public statements.

Shooting an Elephant

1 In Moulmein, in lower Burma, I was hated by large numbers of people—the only time in my life that I have been important enough for this to happen to me. I was sub-divisional police officer of the town, and in an aimless, petty kind of way anti-European feeling was very bitter. No one had the guts to raise a riot, but if a European woman went through the bazaars alone somebody would probably spit betel juice over her dress. As a police officer I was an obvious target and was baited whenever it seemed safe to do so. When a nimble Burman tripped me up on the football field and the referee (another Burman) looked the other way, the crowd yelled with hideous laughter. This happened more than once. In the end the sneering yellow faces of young men that met me everywhere, the insults hooted after me when I was at a safe distance, got badly on my nerves. The young Buddhist priests were the worst of all. There were several thousands of them in the town and none of them seemed to have anything to do except stand on street corners and jeer at Europeans.

2 All this was perplexing and upsetting. For at that time I had already made up my mind that imperialism was an evil thing and the sooner I chucked up my job and got out of it the better. Theoretically—and secretly, of course—I was all for the Burmese and all against their oppressors, the British. As for the job I was doing, I hated it more bitterly than I can perhaps make clear. In a job like that you see the dirty work of Empire at close quarters. The wretched prisoners huddling in the stinking cages of the lock-ups, the gray, cowed faces of the long-term convicts, the scarred buttocks of the men who had been flogged with bamboos—all these oppressed me with an intolerable sense of guilt. But I could get nothing into perspective. I was young and ill educated and I had had to think out my problems in the utter silence that is imposed on every Englishman in the East. I did not even know that the British Empire is dying, still less did I know that it is a great deal better than the younger empires that are going to supplant it. All I knew was that I was stuck between my hatred of the empire I served and my rage against the evil-spirited little beasts who tried to make my job impossible. With one part of my mind I thought of the British Raj as an unbreakable tyranny, as something clamped down, in *saecula saeculorum,* upon the will of prostrate peoples; with another part I thought that the greatest joy in the world would be to drive a bayonet into a Buddhist priest's guts. Feelings like these are the normal by-products of imperialism; ask any Anglo-Indian official, if you can catch him off duty.

3 One day something happened which in a roundabout way was enlightening. It was a tiny incident in itself, but it gave me a better glimpse than I had had before of the real nature of imperialism—the real motives for which despotic governments act. Early one morning the sub-inspector at a police station the other end of the town rang me up on the 'phone and said that an elephant was ravaging the bazaar. Would I please come and do something about it? I did not know what I could do, but I wanted to see what was happening and I got on to a pony and started out. I took my rifle, an old .44 Winchester and much too small to kill an elephant, but I thought the noise might be useful *in terrorem.* Various Burmans stopped me on the way and told me about the elephant's doings. It was not, of course, a wild elephant, but a tame one which had gone "must." It had been chained up, as tame elephants always are when their attack of "must" is due, but on the previous night it had broken its chain and escaped. Its mahout, the only person who could manage it when it was in that state, had set out in pursuit, but had taken the wrong direction and was now twelve hours' journey away, and in the morning the elephant had suddenly reappeared in the town. The Burmese population had no weapons and were quite helpless against it. It had already destroyed somebody's bamboo hut, killed a cow and raided some fruit-stalls and devoured the stock; also it had met the municipal rubbish van and, when the driver jumped out and took to his heels, had turned the van over and inflicted violences upon it.

4 The Burmese sub-inspector and some Indian constables were waiting for me in the quarter where the elephant had been seen. It was a very poor quarter, a labyrinth of squalid bamboo huts, thatched with palm-leaf, winding all over a steep hillside. I remember that it was a cloudy, stuffy morning at the beginning of the rains. We began questioning the people as to where the elephant had gone and, as usual, failed to get any definite information. That is invariably the case in the East;

a story always sounds clear enough at a distance, but the nearer you get to the scene of events the vaguer it becomes. Some of the people said that the elephant had gone in one direction, some said that he had gone in another, some professed not even to have heard of any elephant. I had almost made up my mind that the whole story was a pack of lies, when we heard yells a little distance away. There was a loud, scandalized cry of "Go away, child! Go away this instant!" and an old woman with a switch in her hand came round the corner of a hut, violently shooing away a crowd of naked children. Some more women followed, clicking their tongues and exclaiming; evidently there was something that the children ought not to have seen. I rounded the hut and saw a man's dead body sprawling in the mud. He was an Indian, a black Dravidian coolie, almost naked, and he could not have been dead many minutes. The people said that the elephant had come suddenly upon him round the corner of the hut, caught him with its trunk, put its foot on his back and ground him into the earth. This was the rainy season and the ground was soft, and his face had scored a trench a foot deep and a couple of yards long. He was lying on his belly with arms crucified and head sharply twisted to one side. His face was coated with mud, the eyes wide open, the teeth bared and grinning with an expression of unendurable agony. (Never tell me, by the way, that the dead look peaceful. Most of the corpses I have seen looked devilish.) The friction of the great beast's foot had stripped the skin from his back as neatly as one skins a rabbit. As soon as I saw the dead man I sent an orderly to a friend's house nearby to borrow an elephant rifle. I had already sent back the pony, not wanting it to go mad with fright and throw me if it smelt the elephant.

5 The orderly came back in a few minutes with a rifle and five cartridges, and meanwhile some Burmans had arrived and told us that the elephant was in the paddy fields below, only a few hundred yards away. As I started forward practically the whole population of the quarter flocked out of the houses and followed me. They had seen the rifle and were all shouting excitedly that I was going to shoot the elephant. They had not shown much interest in the elephant when he was merely ravaging their homes, but it was different now that he was going to be shot. It was a bit of fun to them, as it would be to an English crowd; besides they wanted the meat. It made me vaguely uneasy. I had no intention of shooting the elephant—I had merely sent for the rifle to defend myself if necessary—and it is always unnerving to have a crowd following you. I marched down the hill, looking and feeling a fool, with the rifle over my shoulder and an ever-growing army of people jostling at my heels. At the bottom, when you got away from the huts, there was a metalled road and beyond that a miry waste of paddy fields a thousand yards across, not yet ploughed but soggy from the first rains and dotted with coarse grass. The elephant was standing eight yards from the road, his left side toward us. He took not the slightest notice of the crowd's approach. He was tearing up bunches of grass, beating them against his knees to clean them, and stuffing them into his mouth.

6 I had halted on the road. As soon as I saw the elephant I knew with perfect certainty that I ought not to shoot him. It is a serious matter to shoot a working elephant—it is comparable to destroying a huge and costly piece of machinery—and obviously one ought not to do it if it can possibly be avoided. And at that distance, peacefully eating, the elephant looked no more dangerous than a cow. I thought then

and I think now that his attack of "must" was already passing off; in which case he would merely wander harmlessly about until the mahout came back and caught him. Moreover, I did not in the least want to shoot him. I decided that I would watch him for a little while to make sure that he did not turn savage again, and then go home.

7 But at that moment I glanced round at the crowd that had followed me. It was an immense crowd, two thousand at the least and growing every minute. It blocked the road for a long distance on either side. I looked at the sea of yellow faces above the garish clothes—faces all happy and excited over this bit of fun, all certain that the elephant was going to be shot. They were watching me as they would watch a conjurer about to perform a trick. They did not like me, but with the magical rifle in my hands I was momentarily worth watching. And suddenly I realized that I should have to shoot the elephant after all. The people expected it of me and I had got to do it; I could feel their two thousand wills pressing me forward, irresistibly. And it was at this moment, as I stood there with the rifle in my hands, that I first grasped the hollowness, the futility of the white man's dominion in the East. Here was I, the white man with his gun, standing in front of the unarmed native crowd—seemingly the leading actor of the piece; but in reality I was only an absurd puppet pushed to and fro by the will of those yellow faces behind. I perceived in this moment that when the white man turns tyrant it is his own freedom that he destroys. He becomes a sort of hollow, posing dummy, the conventionalized figure of a sahib. For it is the condition of his rule that he shall spend his life in trying to impress the "natives," and so in every crisis he has got to do what the "natives" expect of him. He wears a mask, and his face grows to fit it. I had got to shoot the elephant. I had committed myself to doing it when I sent for the rifle. A sahib has got to act like a sahib; he has got to appear resolute, to know his own mind and do definite things. To come all that way, rifle in hand, with two thousand people marching at my heels, and then to trail feebly away, having done nothing—no, that was impossible. The crowd would laugh at me. And my whole life, every white man's life in the East, was one long struggle not to be laughed at.

8 But I did not want to shoot the elephant. I watched him beating his bunch of grass against his knees with that preoccupied grandmotherly air that elephants have. It seemed to me that it would be murder to shoot him. At that age I was not squeamish about killing animals, but I had never shot an elephant and never wanted to. (Somehow it always seems worse to kill a *large* animal.) Besides, there was the beast's owner to be considered. Alive, the elephant was worth at least a hundred pounds; dead, he would only be worth the value of his tusks, five pounds, possibly. But I had got to act quickly. I turned to some experienced-looking Burmans who had been there when we arrived, and asked them how the elephant had been behaving. They all said the same thing: he took no notice of you if you left him alone, but he might charge if you went too close to him.

9 It was perfectly clear to me what I ought to do. I ought to walk up to within, say, twenty-five yards of the elephant and test his behavior. If he charged, I could shoot; if he took no notice of me, it would be safe to leave him until the mahout came back. But also I knew that I was going to do no such thing. I was a poor shot with a rifle and the ground was soft mud into which one would sink at every step.

If the elephant charged and I missed him, I should have about as much chance as a toad under a steam-roller. But even then I was not thinking particularly of my own skin, only of the watchful yellow faces behind. For at that moment, with the crowd watching me, I was not afraid in the ordinary sense, as I would have been if I had been alone. A white man mustn't be frightened in front of "natives"; and so, in general, he isn't frightened. The sole thought in my mind was that if anything went wrong those two thousand Burmans would see me pursued, caught, trampled on, and reduced to a grinning corpse like that Indian up the hill. And if that happened it was quite probable that some of them would laugh. That would never do. There was only one alternative. I shoved the cartridges into the magazine and lay down on the road to get a better aim.

10 The crowd grew very still, and a deep, low, happy sigh, as of people who see the theater curtain go up at last, breathed from innumerable throats. They were going to have their bit of fun after all. The rifle was a beautiful German thing with cross-hair sights. I did not then know that in shooting an elephant one would shoot to cut an imaginary bar running from ear-hole to ear-hole. I ought, therefore, as the elephant was sideways on, to have aimed straight at his ear-hole; actually I aimed several inches in front of this, thinking the brain would be further forward.

11 When I pulled the trigger I did not hear the bang or feel the kick—one never does when a shot goes home—but I heard the devilish roar of glee that went up from the crowd. In that instant, in too short a time, one would have thought, even for the bullet to get there, a mysterious, terrible change had come over the elephant. He neither stirred nor fell, but every line of his body had altered. He looked suddenly stricken, shrunken, immensely old, as though the frightful impact of the bullet had paralyzed him without knocking him down. At last, after what seemed a long time—it might have been five seconds, I dare say—he sagged flabbily to his knees. His mouth slobbered. An enormous senility seemed to have settled upon him. One could have imagined him thousands of years old. I fired again into the same spot. At the second shot he did not collapse but climbed with desperate slowness to his feet and stood weakly upright, with legs sagging and head drooping. I fired a third time. That was the shot that did for him. You could see the agony of it jolt his whole body and knock the last remnant of strength from his legs. But in falling he seemed for a moment to rise, for as his hind legs collapsed beneath him he seemed to tower upward like a huge rock toppling, his trunk reaching skyward like a tree. He trumpeted, for the first and only time. And then down he came, his belly toward me, with a crash that seemed to shake the ground even where I lay.

12 I got up. The Burmans were already racing past me across the mud. It was obvious that the elephant would never rise again, but he was not dead. He was breathing very rhythmically with long rattling gasps, his great mound of a side painfully rising and falling. His mouth was wide open—I could see far down into caverns of pale pink throat. I waited a long time for him to die, but his breathing did not weaken. Finally I fired my two remaining shots into the spot where I thought his heart must be. The thick blood welled out of him like red velvet, but still he did not die. His body did not even jerk when the shots hit him, the tortured breathing continued without a pause. He was dying, very slowly and in great agony, but in some world remote from me where not even a bullet could damage him

further. I felt that I had got to put an end to that dreadful noise. It seemed dreadful to see the great beast lying there, powerless to move and yet powerless to die, and not even to be able to finish him. I sent back for my small rifle and poured shot after shot into his heart and down his throat. They seemed to make no impression. The tortured gasps continued as steadily as the ticking of a clock.

13 In the end I could not stand it any longer and went away. I heard later that it took him half an hour to die. Burmans were bringing dahs and baskets even before I left, and I was told they had stripped his body almost to the bones by the afternoon.

14 Afterward, of course, there were endless discussions about the shooting of the elephant. The owner was furious, but he was only an Indian and could do nothing. Besides, legally I had done the right thing, for a mad elephant has to be killed, like a mad dog, if its owner fails to control it. Among the Europeans opinion was divided. The older men said I was right, the younger men said it was a damn shame to shoot an elephant for killing a coolie, because an elephant was worth more than any damn Coringhee coolie. And afterward I was very glad that the coolie had been killed; it put me legally in the right and it gave me a sufficient pretext for shooting the elephant. I often wondered whether any of the others grasped that I had done it solely to avoid looking a fool.

(1936)

QUESTIONS

Thought and Structure

1. Where does the action of "Shooting an Elephant" begin? Could the essay begin without the preliminary introductory section? Why is that section included and how does it both prepare for and lead into the incident concerning the elephant?
2. Where does Orwell interrupt the action to explain a point? What is this point? How does the final paragraph reinforce it?
3. Would the essay be more effective if the discussion of the main idea were left until the end? Why or why not? What advantages do you see in the essay's current structure?
4. Is the elephant symbolic? If so, of what? If not, why not?

Style and Strategy

5. Reread the first two paragraphs, paying attention to verbs and adjectives. Note especially words such as "hooted" and "jeer." What do these and the other descriptive details suggest about the attitude of the Burmans toward the British?
6. Throughout the essay Orwell makes extensive use of comparisons. How does the imagery of acting and theater reinforce Orwell's point in paragraph 7? How does Orwell use comparisons there to describe his position?
7. In paragraphs 11 and 12 Orwell has managed a triumph of style, a tour de force of controlled language. What impression of the elephant comes through, and what words

convey it? Why does Orwell divide this description into two paragraphs rather than treat the whole episode as a single unit?

8. Besides imagery, Orwell exploits the sounds of words and the rhythms of phrase and sentence. Again, look at paragraphs 11 and 12, noting how Orwell expands his sentences, opening them up, letting them breathe. And notice how he tempers long sentences with short ones. Read the paragraphs aloud.

9. One of the ways Orwell controls the rhythms of his sentences is with balanced phrases and clauses. Another is with carefully placed interrupting words and phrases. Examine the balanced phrases of the following sentence:

   The wretched prisoners huddling in the stinking cages of the lock-ups,
   the gray, cowed faces of the long-term convicts,
   the scarred buttocks of the men who had been flogged with bamboos—
   all these oppressed me with an intolerable sense of guilt.

   And notice how the dash is used to introduce an umbrella statement that covers the stack of parallel details with which the sentence begins. Listen to the interruptions of the following sentences:

   It is a serious matter to shoot a working elephant—it is comparable to destroying a huge and costly piece of machinery—and obviously one ought not to do it if it can possibly be avoided. (6)

   When I pulled the trigger I did not hear the bang or feel the kick—one never does when a shot goes home—but I heard the devilish roar of glee that went up from the crowd. (11)

   Consider also the interpolated, interrupting words in the following sentences. After reading them aloud, try rereading them without the embedded information and comment. What do you notice?

   In that instant, in too short a time, one would have thought, even for the bullet to get there, a mysterious, terrible change had come over the elephant. (11)

   And my whole life, every white man's life in the East, was one long struggle not to be laughed at. (7)

10. Orwell occasionally begins sentences with coordinating conjunctions: *and, but, or, nor, for*. Although some handbooks advise against this practice it is perfectly acceptable. Reread paragraphs 7, 8, and 9 to see how Orwell does this, and to see how effective these opening conjunctions can be. Imagine one of these paragraphs revised so that no sentence begins with a coordinating conjunction. What is gained or lost? Which version do you prefer, and why?

SUGGESTIONS FOR WRITING

A. Write an essay in which you describe a time when you were pressured into doing something you didn't want to do. Explain the circumstances, how and why you did what you did, and how you felt about it then and perhaps how you feel now. Discuss also the consequences and implications of what happened.

B. Analyze Orwell's essay by concentrating on key passages, which you will explicate. Attend especially to Orwell's choice of words and images.

Marrakech

I

1 As the corpse went past the flies left the restaurant table in a cloud and rushed after it, but they came back a few minutes later.

2 The little crowd of mourners—all men and boys, no women—threaded their way across the market-place between the piles of pomegranates and the taxis and the camels, wailing a short chant over and over again. What really appeals to the flies is that the corpses here are never put into coffins, they are merely wrapped in a piece of rag and carried on a rough wooden bier on the shoulders of four friends. When the friends get to the burying-ground they hack an oblong hole a foot or two deep, dump the body in it and fling over it a little of the dried-up, lumpy earth, which is like broken brick. No gravestone, no name, no identifying mark of any kind. The burying-ground is merely a huge waste of hummocky earth, like a derelict building-lot. After a month or two no one can even be certain where his own relatives are buried.

II

3 When you walk through a town like this—two hundred thousand inhabitants, of whom at least twenty thousand own literally nothing except the rags they stand up in—when you see how the people live, and still more how easily they die, it is always difficult to believe that you are walking among human beings. All colonial empires are in reality founded upon that fact. The people have brown faces—besides, there are so many of them! Are they really the same flesh as yourself? Do they even have names? Or are they merely a kind of undifferentiated brown stuff, about as individual as bees or coral insects? They rise out of the earth, they sweat and starve for a few years, and then they sink back into the nameless mounds of the graveyard and nobody notices that they are gone. And even the graves themselves soon fade back into the soil. Sometimes, out for a walk, as you break your way through the prickly pear, you notice that it is rather bumpy underfoot, and only a certain regularity in the bumps tells you that you are walking over skeletons.

4 I was feeding one of the gazelles in the public gardens.

5 Gazelles are almost the only animals that look good to eat when they are still alive, in fact, one can hardly look at their hindquarters without thinking of mint sauce. The gazelle I was feeding seemed to know that this thought was in my mind, for though it took the piece of bread I was holding out it obviously did not like me. It nibbled rapidly at the bread, then lowered its head and tried to butt me, then took another nibble and then butted again. Probably its idea was that if it could drive me away the bread would somehow remain hanging in mid-air.

6 An Arab navvy working on the path nearby lowered his heavy hoe and sidled slowly towards us. He looked from the gazelle to the bread and from the bread to

the gazelle, with a sort of quiet amazement, as though he had never seen anything quite like this before. Finally he said shyly in French:

7 "*I* could eat some of that bread."

8 I tore off a piece and he stowed it gratefully in some secret place under his rags. This man is an employee of the Municipality.

III

9 When you go through the Jewish quarters you gather some idea of what the medieval ghettoes were probably like. Under their Moorish rulers the Jews were only allowed to own land in certain restricted areas, and after centuries of this kind of treatment they have ceased to bother about overcrowding. Many of the streets are a good deal less than six feet wide, the houses are completely windowless, and sore-eyed children cluster everywhere in unbelievable numbers, like clouds of flies. Down the centre of the street there is generally running a little river of urine.

10 In the bazaar huge families of Jews, all dressed in the long black robe and little black skull-cap, are working in dark fly-infested booths that look like caves. A carpenter sits cross-legged at a prehistoric lathe, turning chair-legs at lightning speed. He works the lathe with a bow in his right hand and guides the chisel with his left foot, and thanks to a lifetime of sitting in this position his left leg is warped out of shape. At his side his grandson, aged six, is already starting on the simpler parts of the job.

11 I was just passing the coppersmiths' booths when somebody noticed that I was lighting a cigarette. Instantly, from the dark holes all round, there was a frenzied rush of Jews, many of them old grandfathers with flowing grey beards, all clamoring for a cigarette. Even a blind man somewhere at the back of one of the booths heard a rumour of cigarettes and came crawling out, groping in the air with his hand. In about a minute I had used up the whole packet. None of these people, I suppose, works less than twelve hours a day, and every one of them looks on a cigarette as a more or less impossible luxury.

12 As the Jews live in self-contained communities they follow the same trades as the Arabs, except for agriculture. Fruit-sellers, potters, silversmiths, blacksmiths, butchers, leather-workers, tailors, water-carriers, beggars, porters—whichever way you look you see nothing but Jews. As a matter of fact there are thirteen thousand of them, all living in the space of a few acres. A good job Hitler wasn't here. Perhaps he was on his way, however. You hear the usual dark rumours about the Jews, not only from the Arabs but from the poorer Europeans.

13 "Yes, mon vieux, they took my job away from me and gave it to a Jew. The Jews! They're the real rulers of this country, you know. They've got all the money. They control the banks, finance—everything."

14 "But," I said, "isn't it a fact that the average Jew is a labourer working for about a penny an hour?"

15 "Ah, that's only for show! They're all moneylenders really. They're cunning, the Jews."

16 In just the same way, a couple of hundred years ago, poor old women used

to be burned for witchcraft when they could not even work enough magic to get themselves a square meal.

IV

17 All people who work with their hands are partly invisible, and the more important the work they do, the less visible they are. Still, a white skin is always fairly conspicuous. In northern Europe, when you see a labourer ploughing a field, you probably give him a second glance. In a hot country, anywhere south of Gibraltar or east of Suez, the chances are that you don't even see him. I have noticed this again and again. In a tropical landscape one's eye takes in everything except the human beings. It takes in the dried-up soil, the prickly pear, the palm tree and the distant mountain, but it always misses the peasant hoeing at his patch. He is the same colour as the earth, and a great deal less interesting to look at.

18 It is only because of this that the starved countries of Asia and Africa are accepted as tourist resorts. No one would think of running cheap trips to the Distressed Areas. But where the human beings have brown skins their poverty is simply not noticed. What does Morocco mean to a Frenchman? An orange-grove or a job in Government service. Or to an Englishman? Camels, castles, palm trees, Foreign Legionnaires, brass trays, and bandits. One could probably live there for years without noticing that for nine-tenths of the people the reality of life is an endless, back-breaking struggle to wring a little food out of an eroded soil.

19 Most of Morocco is so desolate that no wild animal bigger than a hare can live on it. Huge areas which were once covered with forest have turned into a treeless waste where the soil is exactly like broken-up brick. Nevertheless a good deal of it is cultivated, with frightful labour. Everything is done by hand. Long lines of women, bent double like inverted capital L's, work their way slowly across the fields, tearing up the prickly weeds with their hands, and the peasant gathering lucerne for fodder pulls it up stalk by stalk instead of reaping it, thus saving an inch or two on each stalk. The plough is a wretched wooden thing, so frail that one can easily carry it on one's shoulder, and fitted underneath with a rough iron spike which stirs the soil to a depth of about four inches. This is as much as the strength of the animals is equal to. It is usual to plough with a cow and a donkey yoked together. Two donkeys would not be quite strong enough, but on the other hand two cows would cost a little more to feed. The peasants possess no harrows, they merely plough the soil several times over in different directions, finally leaving it in rough furrows, after which the whole field has to be shaped with hoes into small oblong patches to conserve water. Except for a day or two after the rare rainstorms there is never enough water. Along the edges of the fields channels are hacked out to a depth of thirty or forty feet to get at the tiny trickles which run through the subsoil.

20 Every afternoon a file of very old women passes down the road outside my house, each carrying a load of firewood. All of them are mummified with age and the sun, and all of them are tiny. It seems to be generally the case in primitive communities that the women, when they get beyond a certain age, shrink to the size of children. One day a poor old creature who could not have been more than

four feet tall crept past me under a vast load of wood. I stopped her and put a five-sou piece (a little more than a farthing) into her hand. She answered with a shrill wail, almost a scream, which was partly gratitude but mainly surprise. I suppose that from her point of view, by taking any notice of her, I seemed almost to be violating a law of nature. She accepted her status as an old woman, that is to say as a beast of burden. When a family is travelling it is quite usual to see a father and a grown-up son riding ahead on donkeys, and an old woman following on foot, carrying the baggage.

21 But what is strange about these people is their invisibility. For several weeks, always at about the same time of day, the file of old women had hobbled past the house with their firewood, and though they had registered themselves on my eyeballs I cannot truly say that I had seen them. Firewood was passing—that was how I saw it. It was only that one day I happened to be walking behind them, and the curious up-and-down motion of a load of wood drew my attention to the human being beneath it. Then for the first time I noticed the poor old earth-coloured bodies, bodies reduced to bones and leathery skin, bent double under the crushing weight. Yet I suppose I had not been five minutes on Moroccan soil before I noticed the overloading of the donkeys and was infuriated by it. There is no question that the donkeys are damnably treated. The Moroccan donkey is hardly bigger than a St. Bernard dog, it carries a load which in the British Army would be considered too much for a fifteen-hands mule, and very often its pack-saddle is not taken off its back for weeks together. But what is peculiarly pitiful is that it is the most willing creature on earth, it follows its master like a dog and does not need either bridle or halter. After a dozen years of devoted work it suddenly drops dead, whereupon its master tips it into the ditch and the village dogs have torn its guts out before it is cold.

22 This kind of thing makes one's blood boil, whereas—on the whole—the plight of the human beings does not. I am not commenting, merely pointing to a fact. People with brown skins are next door to invisible. Anyone can be sorry for the donkey with its galled back, but it is generally owing to some kind of accident if one even notices the old woman under her load of sticks.

V

23 As the storks flew northward the Negroes were marching southward—a long, dusty column, infantry, screw-gun batteries, and then more infantry, four or five thousand men in all, winding up the road with a clumping of boots and a clatter of iron wheels.

24 They were Senegalese, the blackest Negroes in Africa, so black that sometimes it is difficult to see whereabouts on their necks the hair begins. Their splendid bodies were hidden in reach-me-down khaki uniforms, their feet squashed into boots that looked like blocks of wood, and every tin hat seemed to be a couple of sizes too small. It was very hot and the men had marched a long way. They slumped under the weight of their packs and the curiously sensitive black faces were glistening with sweat.

25 As they went past a tall, very young Negro turned and caught my eye. But the look he gave me was not in the least the kind of look you might expect. Not

hostile, not contemptuous, not sullen, not even inquisitive. It was the shy, wide-eyed Negro look, which actually is a look of profound respect. I saw how it was. This wretched boy, who is a French citizen and has therefore been dragged from the forest to scrub floors and catch syphilis in garrison towns, actually has feelings of reverence before a white skin. He has been taught that the white race are his masters, and he still believes it.

26 But there is one thought which every white man (and in this connection it doesn't matter twopence if he calls himself a socialist) thinks when he sees a black army marching past. "How much longer can we go on kidding these people? How long before they turn their guns in the other direction?"

27 It was curious, really. Every white man there had this thought stowed somewhere or other in his mind. I had it, so had the other onlookers, so had the officers on their sweating chargers and the white N.C.O.'s marching in the ranks. It was a kind of secret which we all knew and were too clever to tell; only the Negroes didn't know it. And really it was like watching a flock of cattle to see the long column, a mile or two miles of armed men, flowing peacefully up the road, while the great white birds drifted over them in the opposite direction, glittering like scraps of paper.

(1939)

QUESTIONS

Thought and Structure

1. This essay says something about Marrakech the place and about its people, especially their poverty and their powerlessness. What political point links these aspects of the essay?
2. In the essay overall, Orwell presents a series of scenes—the burial ground, the zoo, the ghetto, the women carrying firewood, the Senegalese troops—all to create his view of Marrakech. What does each scene imply, and how are the scenes related?
3. To make his point, Orwell relies on incident, illustration, and analogy. In section II, for example (the gazelle episode), a brief scenario is described and a bit of conversation included. What is implied by the man's remark, "I could eat some of that bread" (paragraph 7)? What is implied by his action of putting the bread in his clothes (paragraph 8)?
4. You might think of section III as a miniature version of the essay as a whole. This section contains a series of vignettes, each of which describes a scene and suggests, by implication, an idea. Identify the vignettes and explain what they have in common.
5. Consider the way the essay begins: "As the corpse went past the flies left the restaurant table in a cloud and rushed after it, but they came back a few minutes later." What is implied here? Compare the effectiveness of this opening sentence with the following opening sentences from some of Orwell's other essays:

   Saints should always be judged guilty until they are proved innocent . . .

   "Reflections on Gandhi"

   Dickens is one of those writers who are well worth stealing.

   "Charles Dickens"

As I write, highly civilized human beings are flying overhead, trying to kill me.
"England, Your England"

Style and Strategy

6. One of Orwell's strengths as a writer is his use of vivid and precise verbs. The following passage from paragraph 2 has been stripped of its verbs. Before looking back to see what verbs Orwell used, fill in the blanks with your own choices.

   When the friends get to the burying-ground they ____________ an oblong hole a foot or two deep, ____________ the body in it and ____________ over it a little of the dried-up, lumpy earth, which is like broken brick.

   How is the paragraph affected by different sets of verbs?
7. How do the comparisons in paragraph 2 reinforce the point carried by its verbs?
8. In section IV Orwell writes, "Firewood was passing." He could have written instead: "Women with firewood were passing." What is the difference?
9. At two different points in the essay Orwell shifts from making statements to asking questions. In fact, on both occasions, he strings questions together. What is the effect of the accumulated questions, and what are the implied answers? (See paragraphs 3 and 26.)
10. Twice Orwell uses fragments:

    No gravestone, no name, no identifying mark of any kind.
    Not hostile, not contemptuous, not sullen, not even inquisitive.

    What do you gain and lose if you rewrite these fragments as grammatically complete sentences?
11. Orwell also includes an occasional inverted sentence like this one from paragraph 9:

    Down the centre of the street there is generally running a little river of urine.

    If you think of this as a three-part sentence, you can separate it like this:

    (1) Down the centre of the street
    (2) there is generally running
    (3) a little river of urine.

    Move the parts around like this: 3, 2, 1; 1, 3, 2. Which version do you prefer and why?
12. Examine the sentences of the fourth paragraph of section IV (paragraph 20) and the fourth paragraph of section V (paragraph 26), particularly those that include parentheses. What is the tone of those sentences? Could the parentheses be removed or the words within the parentheses deleted? If you replaced the parentheses with commas or with dashes how would the tone of the sentences differ?

SUGGESTIONS FOR WRITING

A. Write an advertisement or travel poster inviting Americans to vacation in Marrakech, either Orwell's Marrakech or the Marrakech of today. You might think of yourself as a representative for public relations for the Morrocan government. Or you might write as a member of a United Nations committee on world brotherhood. Or . . .

B. Write an imitation of paragraph 3.

C. Visit an area of your city, your neighborhood, or your campus. If you were to concentrate on your campus, for example, you could go to the library, the cafeteria, student center, gymnasium, and classroom buildings. Describe each mini-locale without directly explaining the idea behind the description. In doing so try to suggest rather than explicitly state the impression of the place you wish to convey. Choose your mini-locales and select your details so they reinforce one another, so that together they suggest a unified impression of the place overall.

1984 (Chapter One)

1 It was a bright cold day in April, and the clocks were striking thirteen. Winston Smith, his chin nuzzled into his breast in an effort to escape the vile wind, slipped quickly through the glass doors of Victory Mansions, though not quickly enough to prevent a swirl of gritty dust from entering along with him.

2 The hallway smelt of boiled cabbage and old rag mats. At one end of it a colored poster, too large for indoor display, had been tacked to the wall. It depicted simply an enormous face, more than a meter wide: the face of a man of about forty-five, with a heavy black mustache and ruggedly handsome features. Winston made for the stairs. It was no use trying the lift. Even at the best of times it was seldom working, and at present the electric current was cut off during daylight hours. It was part of the economy drive in preparation for Hate Week. The flat was seven flights up, and Winston, who was thirty-nine and had a varicose ulcer above his right ankle, went slowly, resting several times on the way. On each landing, opposite the lift shaft, the poster with the enormous face gazed from the wall. It was one of those pictures which are so contrived that the eyes follow you about when you move. Big Brother Is Watching You, the caption beneath it ran.

3 Inside the flat a fruity voice was reading out a list of figures which had something to do with the production of pig iron. The voice came from an oblong metal plaque like a dulled mirror which formed part of the surface of the right-hand wall. Winston turned a switch and the voice sank somewhat, though the words were still distinguishable. The instrument (the telescreen, it was called) could be dimmed, but there was no way of shutting it off completely. He moved over to the window: a smallish, frail figure, the meagerness of his body merely emphasized by the blue overalls which were the uniform of the Party. His hair was very fair, his face naturally sanguine, his skin roughened by coarse soap and blunt razor blades and the cold of the winter that had just ended.

4 Outside, even through the shut window pane, the world looked cold. Down in the street little eddies of wind were whirling dust and torn paper into spirals, and though the sun was shining and the sky a harsh blue, there seemed to be no color in anything except the posters that were plastered everywhere. The black-mustachio'd face gazed down from every commanding corner. There was one on the house front immediately opposite. Big Brother Is Watching You, the caption said, while the dark eyes looked deep into Winston's own. Down at street level another poster, torn at one corner, flapped fitfully in the wind, alternately covering and

uncovering the single word INGSOC. In the far distance a helicopter skimmed down between the roofs, hovered for an instant like a bluebottle, and darted away again with a curving flight. It was the Police Patrol, snooping into people's windows. The patrols did not matter, however. Only the Thought Police mattered.

5 Behind Winston's back the voice from the telescreen was still babbling away about pig iron and the overfulfillment of the Ninth Three-Year Plan. The telescreen received and transmitted simultaneously. Any sound that Winston made, above the level of a very low whisper, would be picked up by it; moreover, so long as he remained within the field of vision which the metal plaque commanded, he could be seen as well as heard. There was of course no way of knowing whether you were being watched at any given moment. How often, or on what system, the Thought Police plugged in on any individual wire was guesswork. It was even conceivable that they watched everybody all the time. But at any rate they could plug in your wire whenever they wanted to. You had to live—did live, from habit that became instinct—in the assumption that every sound you made was overheard, and, except in darkness, every movement scrutinized

6 Winston kept his back turned to the telescreen. It was safer; though, as he well knew, even a back can be revealing. A kilometer away the Ministry of Truth, his place of work, towered vast and white above the grimy landscape. This, he thought with a sort of vague distaste—this was London, chief city of Airstrip One, itself the third most populous of the provinces of Oceania. He tried to squeeze out some childhood memory that should tell him whether London had always been quite like this. Were there always these vistas of rotting nineteenth-century houses, their sides shored up with balks of timber, their windows patched with cardboard and their roofs with corrugated iron, their crazy garden walls sagging in all directions? And the bombed sites where the plaster dust swirled in the air and the willow herb straggled over the heaps of rubble; and the places where the bombs had cleared a larger patch and there had sprung up sordid colonies of wooden dwellings like chicken houses? But it was no use, he could not remember: nothing remained of his childhood except a series of bright-lit tableaux, occurring against no background and mostly unintelligible.

7 The Ministry of Truth—Minitrue, in Newspeak—was startlingly different from any other object in sight. It was an enormous pyramidal structure of glittering white concrete, soaring up, terrace after terrace, three hundred meters into the air. From where Winston stood it was just possible to read, picked out on its white face in elegant lettering the three slogans of the Party:

WAR IS PEACE

FREEDOM IS SLAVERY

IGNORANCE IS STRENGTH.

The Ministry of Truth contained, it was said, three thousand rooms above ground level, and corresponding ramifications below. Scattered about London there were just three other buildings of similar appearance and size. So completely did they dwarf the surrounding architecture that from the roof of Victory Mansions you could see all four of them simultaneously. They were the homes of the four Ministries between which the entire apparatus of government was divided: the Ministry of Truth, which concerned itself with news, entertainment, education, and the fine arts; the Ministry of Peace, which concerned itself with war; the Ministry of Love, which maintained law and order; and the Ministry of Plenty, which was responsible for economic affairs. Their names, in Newspeak: Minitrue, Minipax, Miniluv, and Miniplenty.

8 The Ministry of Love was the really frightening one. There were no windows in it at all. Winston had never been inside the Ministry of Love, nor within half a kilometer of it. It was a place impossible to enter except on official business, and then only by penetrating through a maze of barbed-wire entanglements, steel doors, and hidden machine-gun nests. Even the streets leading up to its outer barriers were roamed by gorilla-faced guards in black uniforms, armed with jointed truncheons.

9 Winston turned round abruptly. He had set his features into the expression of quiet optimism which it was advisable to wear when facing the telescreen. He crossed the room into the tiny kitchen. By leaving the Ministry at this time of day he had sacrificed his lunch in the canteen, and he was aware that there was no food in the kitchen except a hunk of dark-colored bread which had got to be saved for tomorrow's breakfast. He took down from the shelf a bottle of colorless liquid with a plain white label marked VICTORY GIN. It gave off a sickly, oily smell, as of Chinese rice-spirit. Winston poured out nearly a teacupful, nerved himself for a shock, and gulped it down like a dose of medicine.

10 Instantly his face turned scarlet and the water ran out of his eyes. The stuff was like nitric acid, and moreover, in swallowing it one had the sensation of being hit on the back of the head with a rubber club. The next moment, however, the burning in his belly died down and the world began to look more cheerful. He took a cigarette from a crumpled packet marked VICTORY CIGARETTES and incautiously held it upright, whereupon the tobacco fell out onto the floor. With the next he was more successful. He went back to the living room and sat down at a small table that stood to the left of the telescreen. From the table drawer he took out a penholder, a bottle of ink, and a thick, quarto-sized blank book with a red back and a marbled cover.

11 For some reason the telescreen in the living room was in an unusual position. Instead of being placed, as was normal, in the end wall, where it could command the whole room, it was in the longer wall, opposite the window. To one side of it there was a shallow alcove in which Winston was now sitting, and which, when the flats were built, had probably been intended to hold bookshelves. By sitting in the alcove, and keeping well back, Winston was able to remain outside the range of the telescreen, so far as sight went. He could be heard, of course, but so long as he stayed in his present position he could not be seen. It was partly the unusual geography of the room that had suggested to him the thing that he was now about to do.

12 But it had also been suggested by the book that he had just taken out of the drawer. It was a peculiarly beautiful book. Its smooth creamy paper, a little yellowed by age, was of a kind that had not been manufactured for at least forty years past. He could guess, however, that the book was much older than that. He had seen it lying in the window of a frowsy little junk shop in a slummy quarter of the town (just what quarter he did not now remember) and had been stricken immediately

by an overwhelming desire to possess it. Party members were supposed not to go into ordinary shops ("dealing on the free market," it was called), but the rule was not strictly kept, because there were various things such as shoelaces and razor blades which it was impossible to get hold of in any other way. He had given a quick glance up and down the street and then had slipped inside and bought the book for two dollars fifty. At the time he was not conscious of wanting it for any particular purpose. He had carried it guiltily home in his brief case. Even with nothing written in it, it was a compromising possession.

13 The thing that he was about to do was to open a diary. This was not illegal (nothing was illegal, since there were no longer any laws), but if detected it was reasonably certain that it would be punished by death, or at least by twenty-five years in a forced-labor camp. Winston fitted a nib into the penholder and sucked it to get the grease off. The pen was an archaic instrument, seldom used even for signatures, and he had procured one, furtively and with some difficulty, simply because of a feeling that the beautiful creamy paper deserved to be written on with a real nib instead of being scratched with an ink pencil. Actually he was not used to writing by hand. Apart from very short notes, it was usual to dictate everything into the speak-write, which was of course impossible for his present purpose. He dipped the pen into the ink and then faltered for just a second. A tremor had gone through his bowels. To mark the paper was the decisive act. In small clumsy letters he wrote:

April 4th, 1984.

14 He sat back. A sense of complete helplessness had descended upon him. To begin with, he did not know with any certainty that this *was* 1984. It must be round about that date, since he was fairly sure that his age was thirty-nine, and he believed that he had been born in 1944 or 1945; but it was never possible nowadays to pin down any date within a year or two.

15 For whom, it suddenly occurred to him to wonder, was he writing this diary? For the future, for the unborn. His mind hovered for a moment round the doubtful date on the page, and then fetched up with a bump against the Newspeak word *doublethink.* For the first time the magnitude of what he had undertaken came home to him. How could you communicate with the future? It was of its nature impossible. Either the future would resemble the present, in which case it would not listen to him, or it would be different from it, and his predicament would be meaningless.

16 For some time he sat gazing stupidly at the paper. The telescreen had changed over to strident military music. It was curious that he seemed not merely to have lost the power of expressing himself, but even to have forgotten what it was that he had originally intended to say. For weeks past he had been making ready for this moment, and it had never crossed his mind that anything would be needed except courage. The actual writing would be easy. All he had to do was to transfer to paper the interminable restless monologue that had been running inside his head, literally for years. At this moment, however, even the monologue had dried up. Moreover, his varicose ulcer had begun itching unbearably. He dared not scratch it, because if he did so it always became inflamed. The seconds were ticking by. He was

conscious of nothing except the blankness of the page in front of him, the itching of the skin above his ankle, the blaring of the music, and a slight booziness caused by the gin.

17 Suddenly he began writing in sheer panic, only imperfectly aware of what he was setting down. His small but childish handwriting straggled up and down the page, shedding first its capital letters and finally even its full stops:

April 4th, 1984. Last night to the flicks. All war films. One very good one of a ship full of refugees being bombed somewhere in the Mediterranean. Audience much amused by shots of a great huge fat man trying to swim away with a helicopter after him, first you saw him wallowing along in the water like a porpoise, then you saw him through the helicopters gunsights, then he was full of holes and the sea round him turned pink and he sank as suddenly as though the holes had let in the water. audience shouting with laughter when he sank. then you saw a lifeboat full of children with a helicopter hovering over it. there was a middleaged woman might have been a jewess sitting up in the bow with a little boy about three years old in her arms. little boy screaming with fright and hiding his head between her breasts as if he was trying to burrow right into her and the woman putting her arms round him and comforting him although she was blue with fright herself. all the time covering him up as much as possible as if she thought her arms could keep the bullets off him. then the helicopter planted a 20 kilo bomb in among them terrific flash and the boat went all to matchwood. then there was a wonderful shot of a childs arm going up up up right up into the air a helicopter with a camera in its nose must have followed it up and there was a lot of applause from the party seats but a woman down in the prole part of the house suddenly started kicking up a fuss and shouting they didnt oughter of showed it not in front of kids they didnt it aint right not in front of kids it aint until the police turned her out i dont suppose anything happened to her nobody cares what the proles say typical prole reaction they never—

18 Winston stopped writing, partly because he was suffering from cramp. He did not know what had made him pour out this stream of rubbish. But the curious thing was that while he was doing so a totally different memory had clarified itself in his mind, to the point where he almost felt equal to writing it down. It was, he now realized, because of this other incident that he had suddenly decided to come home and begin the diary today.

19 It had happened that morning at the Ministry, if anything so nebulous could be said to happen.

20 It was nearly eleven hundred, and in the Records Department, where Winston worked, they were dragging the chairs out of the cubicles and grouping them in the center of the hall, opposite the big telescreen, in preparation for the Two Minutes Hate. Winston was just taking his place in one of the middle rows when two people whom he knew by sight, but had never spoken to, came unexpectedly into the room. One of them was a girl whom he often passed in the corridors. He did not know her name, but he knew that she worked in the Fiction Department. Presumably—since he had sometimes seen her with oily hands and carrying a spanner—she had some mechanical job on one of the novel-writing machines. She was a bold-looking girl of about twenty-seven, with thick dark hair, a freckled face, and swift, athletic

movements. A narrow scarlet sash, emblem of the Junior Anti-Sex League, was wound several times round the waist of her overalls, just tightly enough to bring out the shapeliness of her hips. Winston had disliked her from the very first moment of seeing her. He knew the reason. It was because of the atmosphere of hockey fields and cold baths and community hikes and general clean-mindedness which she managed to carry about with her. He disliked nearly all women, and especially the young and pretty ones. It was always the women, and above all the young ones, who were the most bigoted adherents of the Party, the swallowers of slogans, the amateur spies and nosers-out of unorthodoxy. But this particular girl gave him the impression of being more dangerous than most. Once when they passed in the corridor she had given him a quick sidelong glance which seemed to pierce right into him and for a moment had filled him with black terror. The idea had even crossed his mind that she might be an agent of the Thought Police. That, it was true, was very unlikely. Still, he continued to feel a peculiar uneasiness, which had fear mixed up in it as well as hostility, whenever she was anywhere near him.

21 The other person was a man named O'Brien, a member of the Inner Party and holder of some post so important and remote that Winston had only a dim idea of its nature. A momentary hush passed over the group of people round the chairs as they saw the black overalls of an Inner Party member approaching. O'Brien was a large, burly man with a thick neck and a coarse, humorous, brutal face. In spite of his formidable appearance he had a certain charm of manner. He had a trick of resettling his spectacles on his nose which was curiously disarming—in some indefinable way, curiously civilized. It was a gesture which, if anyone had still thought in such terms, might have recalled an eighteenth-century nobleman offering his snuff-box. Winston had seen O'Brien perhaps a dozen times in almost as many years. He felt deeply drawn to him, and not solely because he was intrigued by the contrast between O'Brien's urbane manner and his prizefighter's physique. Much more it was because of a secretly held belief—or perhaps not even a belief, merely a hope—that O'Brien's political orthodoxy was not perfect. Something in his face suggested it irresistibly. And again, perhaps it was not even unorthodoxy that was written in his face, but simply intelligence. But at any rate he had the appearance of being a person that you could talk to, if somehow you could cheat the telescreen and get him alone. Winston had never made the smallest effort to verify this guess; indeed, there was no way of doing so. At this moment O'Brien glanced at his wristwatch, saw that it was nearly eleven hundred, and evidently decided to stay in the Records Department until the Two Minutes Hate was over. He took a chair in the same row as Winston, a couple of places away. A small, sandy-haired woman who worked in the next cubicle to Winston was between them. The girl with dark hair was sitting immediately behind.

22 The next moment a hideous, grinding screech, as of some monstrous machine running without oil, burst from the big telescreen at the end of the room. It was a noise that set one's teeth on edge and bristled the hair at the back of one's neck. The Hate had started.

23 As usual, the face of Emmanuel Goldstein, the Enemy of the People, had flashed onto the screen. There were hisses here and there among the audience. The little sandy-haired woman gave a squeak of mingled fear and disgust. Goldstein was the renegade and backslider who once, long ago (how long ago, nobody quite

remembered), had been one of the leading figures of the Party, almost on a level with Big Brother himself, and then had engaged in counterrevolutionary activities, had been condemned to death, and had mysteriously escaped and disappeared. The program of the Two Minutes Hate varied from day to day, but there was none in which Goldstein was not the principal figure. He was the primal traitor, the earliest defiler of the Party's purity. All subsequent crimes against the Party, all treacheries, acts of sabotage, heresies, deviations, sprang directly out of his teaching. Somewhere or other he was still alive and hatching his conspiracies: perhaps somewhere beyond the sea, under the protection of his foreign paymasters; perhaps even—so it was occasionally rumored—in some hiding place in Oceania itself.

24 Winston's diaphragm was constricted. He could never see the face of Goldstein without a painful mixture of emotions. It was a lean Jewish face, with a great fuzzy aureole of white hair and a small goatee beard—a clever face, and yet somehow inherently despicable, with a kind of senile silliness in the long thin nose near the end of which a pair of spectacles was perched. It resembled the face of a sheep, and the voice, too, had a sheeplike quality. Goldstein was delivering his usual venomous attack upon the doctrines of the Party—an attack so exaggerated and perverse that a child should have been able to see through it, and yet just plausible enough to fill one with an alarmed feeling that other people, less level-headed than oneself, might be taken in by it. He was abusing Big Brother, he was denouncing the dictatorship of the Party, he was demanding the immediate conclusion of peace with Eurasia, he was advocating freedom of speech, freedom of the press, freedom of assembly, freedom of thought, he was crying hysterically that the revolution had been betrayed—and all this in rapid polysyllabic speech which was a sort of parody of the habitual style of the orators of the Party, and even contained Newspeak words: more Newspeak words, indeed, than any Party member would normally use in real life. And all the while, lest one should be in any doubt as to the reality which Goldstein's specious claptrap covered, behind his head on the telescreen there marched the endless columns of the Eurasian army—row after row of solid-looking men with expressionless Asiatic faces, who swam up to the surface of the screen and vanished, to be replaced by others exactly similar. The dull, rhythmic tramp of the soldiers' boots formed the background to Goldstein's bleating voice.

25 Before the Hate had proceeded for thirty seconds, uncontrollable exclamations of rage were breaking out from half the people in the room. The self-satisfied sheeplike face on the screen, and the terrifying power of the Eurasian army behind it, were too much to be borne; besides, the sight or even the thought of Goldstein produced fear and anger automatically. He was an object of hatred more constant than either Eurasia or Eastasia, since when Oceania was at war with one of these powers it was generally at peace with the other. But what was strange was that although Goldstein was hated and despised by everybody, although every day, and a thousand times a day, on platforms, on the telescreen, in newspapers, in books, his theories were refuted, smashed, ridiculed, held up to the general gaze for the pitiful rubbish that they were—in spite of all this, his influence never seemed to grow less. Always there were fresh dupes waiting to be seduced by him. A day never passed when spies and saboteurs acting under his directions were not unmasked by the Thought Police. He was the commander of a vast shadowy army, an underground

network of conspirators dedicated to the overthrow of the State. The Brotherhood, its name was supposed to be. There were also whispered stories of a terrible book, a compendium of all the heresies, of which Goldstein was the author and which circulated clandestinely here and there. It was a book without a title. People referred to it, if at all, simply as *the book.* But one knew of such things only through vague rumors. Neither the Brotherhood nor *the book* was a subject that any ordinary Party member would mention if there was a way of avoiding it.

26 In its second minute the Hate rose to a frenzy. People were leaping up and down in their places and shouting at the tops of their voices in an effort to drown the maddening bleating voice that came from the screen. The little sandy-haired woman had turned bright pink, and her mouth was opening and shutting like that of a landed fish. Even O'Brien's heavy face was flushed. He was sitting very straight in his chair, his powerful chest swelling and quivering as though he were standing up to the assault of a wave. The dark-haired girl behind Winston had begun crying out "Swine! Swine! Swine!" and suddenly she picked up a heavy Newspeak dictionary and flung it at the screen. It struck Goldstein's nose and bounced off; the voice continued inexorably. In a lucid moment Winston found that he was shouting with the others and kicking his heel violently against the rung of his chair. The horrible thing about the Two Minutes Hate was not that one was obliged to act a part, but that it was impossible to avoid joining in. Within thirty seconds any pretense was always unnecessary. A hideous ecstasy of fear and vindictiveness, a desire to kill, to torture, to smash faces in with a sledge hammer, seemed to flow through the whole group of people like an electric current, turning one even against one's will into a grimacing, screaming lunatic. And yet the rage that one felt was an abstract, undirected emotion which could be switched from one object to another like the flame of a blowlamp. Thus, at one moment Winston's hatred was not turned against Goldstein at all, but, on the contrary, against Big Brother, the Party, and the Thought Police; and at such moments his heart went out to the lonely, derided heretic on the screen, sole guardian of truth and sanity in a world of lies. And yet the very next instant he was at one with the people about him, and all that was said of Goldstein seemed to him to be true. At those moments his secret loathing of Big Brother changed into adoration, and Big Brother seemed to tower up, an invincible, fearless protector, standing like a rock against the hordes of Asia, and Goldstein, in spite of his isolation, his helplessness, and the doubt that hung about his very existence, seemed like some sinister enchanter, capable by the mere power of his voice of wrecking the structure of civilization.

27 It was even possible, at moments, to switch one's hatred this way or that by a voluntary act. Suddenly, by the sort of violent effort with which one wrenches one's head away from the pillow in a nightmare, Winston succeeded in transferring his hatred from the face on the screen to the dark-haired girl behind him. Vivid, beautiful hallucinations flashed through his mind. He would flog her to death with a rubber truncheon. He would tie her naked to a stake and shoot her full of arrows like Saint Sebastian. He would ravish her and cut her throat at the moment of climax. Better than before, moreover, he realized *why* it was that he hated her. He hated her because she was young and pretty and sexless, because he wanted to go to bed with her and would never do so, because round her sweet supple waist, which

seemed to ask you to encircle it with your arm, there was only the odious scarlet sash, aggressive symbol of chastity.

28 The Hate rose to its climax. The voice of Goldstein had become an actual sheep's bleat, and for an instant the face changed into that of a sheep. Then the sheep-face melted into the figure of a Eurasian soldier who seemed to be advancing, huge and terrible, his submachine gun roaring, and seeming to spring out of the surface of the screen, so that some of the people in the front row actually flinched backward in their seats. But in the same moment, drawing a deep sigh of relief from everybody, the hostile figure melted into the face of Big Brother, black-haired, black mustachio'd, full of power and mysterious calm, and so vast that it almost filled up the screen. Nobody heard what Big Brother was saying. It was merely a few words of encouragement, the sort of words that are uttered in the din of battle, not distinguishable individually but restoring confidence by the fact of being spoken. Then the face of Big Brother faded away again, and instead the three slogans of the Party stood out in bold capitals:

WAR IS PEACE

FREEDOM IS SLAVERY

IGNORANCE IS STRENGTH.

29 But the face of Big Brother seemed to persist for several seconds on the screen, as though the impact that it had made on everyone's eyeballs were too vivid to wear off immediately. The little sandy-haired woman had flung herself forward over the back of the chair in front of her. With a tremulous murmur that sounded like "My Savior!" she extended her arms toward the screen. Then she buried her face in her hands. It was apparent that she was uttering a prayer.

30 At this moment the entire group of people broke into a deep, slow, rhythmical chant of "B-B! . . . B-B! . . . B-B!" over and over again, very slowly, with a long pause between the first "B" and the second—a heavy, murmurous sound, somehow curiously savage, in the background of which one seemed to hear the stamp of naked feet and the throbbing of tom-toms. For perhaps as much as thirty seconds they kept it up. It was a refrain that was often heard in moments of overwhelming emotion. Partly it was a sort of hymn to the wisdom and majesty of Big Brother, but still more it was an act of self-hypnosis, a deliberate drowning of consciousness by means of rhythmic noise. Winston's entrails seemed to grow cold. In the Two Minutes Hate he could not help sharing in the general delirium, but this subhuman chanting of "B-B! . . . B-B!" always filled him with horror. Of course he chanted with the rest: it was impossible to do otherwise. To dissemble your feelings, to control your face, to do what everyone else was doing, was an instinctive reaction. But there was a space of a couple of seconds during which the expression in his eyes might conceivably have betrayed him. And it was exactly at this moment that the significant thing happened—if, indeed, it did happen.

31 Momentarily he caught O'Brien's eye. O'Brien had stood up. He had taken off his spectacles and was in the act of resettling them on his nose with his character-

istic gesture. But there was a fraction of a second when their eyes met, and for as long as it took to happen Winston knew—yes, he *knew!*—that O'Brien was thinking the same thing as himself. An unmistakable message had passed. It was as though their two minds had opened and the thoughts were flowing from one into the other through their eyes. "I am with you," O'Brien seemed to be saying to him. "I know precisely what you are feeling. I know all about your contempt, your hatred, your disgust. But don't worry, I am on your side!" And then the flash of intelligence was gone, and O'Brien's face was as inscrutable as everybody else's.

32 That was all, and he was already uncertain whether it had happened. Such incidents never had any sequel. All that they did was to keep alive in him the belief, or hope, that others besides himself were the enemies of the Party. Perhaps the rumors of vast underground conspiracies were true after all—perhaps the Brotherhood really existed! It was impossible, in spite of the endless arrests and confessions and executions, to be sure that the Brotherhood was not simply a myth. Some days he believed in it, some days not. There was no evidence, only fleeting glimpses that might mean anything or nothing: snatches of overheard conversation, faint scribbles on lavatory walls—once, even, when two strangers met, a small movement of the hands which had looked as though it might be a signal of recognition. It was all guesswork: very likely he had imagined everything. He had gone back to his cubicle without looking at O'Brien again. The idea of following up their momentary contact hardly crossed his mind. It would have been inconceivably dangerous even if he had known how to set about doing it. For a second, two seconds, they had exchanged an equivocal glance, and that was the end of the story. But even that was a memorable event, in the locked loneliness in which one had to live.

33 Winston roused himself and sat up straighter. He let out a belch. The gin was rising from his stomach.

34 His eyes refocused on the page. He discovered that while he sat helplessly musing he had also been writing, as though by automatic action. And it was no longer the same cramped awkward handwriting as before. His pen had slid voluptuously over the smooth paper, printing in large neat capitals—

DOWN WITH BIG BROTHER

DOWN WITH BIG BROTHER

DOWN WITH BIG BROTHER

DOWN WITH BIG BROTHER

DOWN WITH BIG BROTHER

over and over again, filling half a page.

35 He could not help feeling a twinge of panic. It was absurd, since the writing of those particular words was not more dangerous than the initial act of opening the diary; but for a moment he was tempted to tear out the spoiled pages and abandon the enterprise altogether.

36 He did not do so, however, because he knew that it was useless. Whether he wrote DOWN WITH BIG BROTHER, or whether he refrained from writing it,

made no difference. Whether he went on with the diary, or whether he did not go on with it, made no difference. The Thought Police would get him just the same. He had committed—would still have committed, even if he had never set pen to paper—the essential crime that contained all others in itself. Thoughtcrime, they called it. Thoughtcrime was not a thing that could be concealed forever. You might dodge successfully for a while, even for years, but sooner or later they were bound to get you.

37 It was always at night—the arrests invariably happened at night. The sudden jerk out of sleep, the rough hand shaking your shoulder, the lights glaring in your eyes, the ring of hard faces round the bed. In the vast majority of cases there was no trial, no report of the arrest. People simply disappeared, always during the night. Your name was removed from the registers, every record of everything you had ever done was wiped out, your one-time existence was denied and then forgotten. You were abolished, annihilated: *vaporized* was the usual word.

38 For a moment he was seized by a kind of hysteria. He began writing in a hurried untidy scrawl:

theyll shoot me i dont care theyll shoot me in the back of the neck i dont care down with big brother they always shoot you in the back of the neck i dont care down with big brother—

39 He sat back in his chair, slightly ashamed of himself, and laid down the pen. The next moment he started violently. There was a knocking at the door.

40 Already! He sat as still as a mouse, in the futile hope that whoever it was might go away after a single attempt. But no, the knocking was repeated. The worst thing of all would be to delay. His heart was thumping like a drum, but his face, from long habit, was probably expressionless. He got up and moved heavily toward the door.

(1949)

QUESTIONS

1. What impression of Oceania is created in this opening chapter? What incongruous details are mentioned in the first paragraph? To what effect?
2. How is Winston Smith characterized? Why does he begin writing a diary?
3. Comment on Orwell's presentation of group psychology in his rendition of the "Two Minutes Hate." Consider the details Orwell includes and also their order of appearance.
4. What impression are we given of the girl from the Junior Anti-Sex League? of O'Brien? How sure can we be about Winston's response to them?
5. What impression do we have of the citizenry of Oceania? What details convey this impression?
6. If Winston is our angle of perception in this opening scene, Big Brother is its dominating force. What characteristics are associated with him?
7. If you have never read *1984,* will you be inclined to continue? Why or why not? If you have read it, do you think it is worth an additional reading?

SUGGESTIONS FOR WRITING

A. Discuss the three slogans from chapter one. Explain how they make sense, if you think they do. Explain how you think they function in the society. Draw a parallel with our society by identifying two or three contemporary slogans and analyzing their function.

B. Compare Orwell's opening of *1984* with Didion's first chapter of *Democracy.* Consider how each writer establishes the book's atmosphere, indicates a tone and point of view, and creates suspense.

EIGHT

Loren Eiseley

(1907–1977)

Loren Eiseley is perhaps the most difficult to classify of all the writers in this anthology and that difficulty provides a clue to his fascination. Although he was an anthropologist by profession—a professor and once the Provost of the University of Pennsylvania—Eiseley considered himself a writer. Other labels, some self-generated (social philosopher, scientist, naturalist, fugitive, drifter), satisfied him less. And what he wrote most and liked best, were the pieces he called "concealed" essays, essays in which "personal anecdote [is] allowed gently to bring under observation thoughts of a more purely scientific nature." Those essays, he tells us, found their evolutionary origins scattered from Montaigne to Emerson. And Leslie E. Gerber and Margaret McFadden, in the first book written about Eiseley, claim that for him as for Montaigne, the essay "serves as a vehicle for exploration rather than demonstration; it precedes a final argument, not the argument itself." They claim too that Eiseley's essays are part of a subgenre of the familiar essay: "a many-sided American natural-history essay . . . [a]t times sentimental, excessively aesthetic, and mawkishly spiritual." And they point out quite correctly that "the narrowly argumentative, positivistic, unadventurous modern temper" was *alien* to him (*Loren Eiseley,* pp. 21–23).

But those observations merely serve to place Eiseley within a tradition. The essays themselves give us a much clearer sense of Eiseley's writing habits and his thoughts about the writing process itself. Some might prefer to call some of the selections in this anthology metawriting, writing about writing. Although their range clearly exceeds such a classification, we can nevertheless learn a great deal about writing from an essay like "Willy"—a chapter from Eiseley's autobiography, *All the Strange Hours: The Excavation of a Life,* where he accounts for his storehouse of images. In that essay Eiseley calls those images out of his "artist's loft" and uses them in unusual and fascinating ways. Even on a subject as personal as private images, Eiseley pushes us beyond the boundaries of purely rational thought as he asks us to believe that he merely calls on the images so that he can tell the story "that already lies there" in those pictures of ordinary life. In that sense, he sees himself as different from a fiction writer like Robert Louis Stevenson who would say that the pictures, the images themselves, "demanded a story, a human story of equal proportions." Embedded in that distinction is the notion that one kind of mind apprehends and records, the other imposes. Eiseley's mind, the apprehending one, probes behind the appearance of things, searching for the message that is already there.

Eiseley is obsessed with the past, an obsession born of a deep concern for the present. So when he probes behind the ordinary and the apparently obvious, reaching back always to discover the hidden meaning behind some primal urge contained in the image in his mind, he does so in the interest of preserving life in the present. He does so for an audience that has become, in his mind, too narrowly rational, too scientific—an audience that has lost its fascination with "the kingdome of fairies in the dark." Nowhere is he more clear about these matters than in "The Illusion of Two Cultures" where he argues against an unnatural division between science and literature, between scientific thinking and literary thinking.

"The Dance of the Frogs" lies somewhere on the boundary zone between science and literature; it also lies somewhere on the boundary zone between the essay and fiction. For several years we have taught the piece as an essay; now in light of Gerber and McFadden's classification, we are also considering it as an example of the tall tale, a fictional work in the tradition of Twain, Bierce, and Poe. Such is the power and direction of Eiseley's mind. He pushes us into new considerations, begs that we not get hemmed in by our own ways of seeing, making here a strong case for archetypes and "shaking tent" rites while mocking the limitations of a young, narrow scientist—but doing it in a form that generally mocks its contents, the story itself. Nevertheless, within the form, and despite it, Eiseley makes another compelling case for the unbelievable, for the show that is going on behind the scenes.

Eiseley has enormous faith in the power of the human mind, and in stating what is only too obvious to all of us—that the mind distinguishes us from all other species—he goes on to point out what we too easily forget: it is the mind that has the potential to save us. It and it alone can apprehend our place at the center of the universe's web; it and it alone can fashion a way to change the shape of our future. He expresses his concern about our failure to imagine greater possibilities in "The Hidden Teacher," where he also offers a compelling account of a Teacher at the back of things showing us the way, if only we can see. And that essay, like many of the others, points to the mysteries, accessible but not obvious to the modern temper. What Eiseley tries to do is transport us beyond the boundaries, giving us a sense of what enormous potential we have, while reminding us how little we make of it. He is of this world, but sceptical of our direction, a lonely drifter writing for our salvation and for his own. His is a verbal fire that burns even after the heat from his brain has cooled in the grave.

All the Strange Hours: Willy

1 Nowadays, when I pass along the walk where the tenements were leveled, I persist in seeing, not the massive architecture of the new building, but the dust and the stones where, in my mind, the dogs still lie in the October wind. Man is a strange creature. I look upon this great building with its inner fountains and amenities, and though it is well over ten years since it was constructed, I see right through it to the bare field left by the demolition of the slum. Something has seized and held me there, created what is even more real than what currently exists. Perhaps it is my mother's unrestrained clairvoyant eye. I cannot control it.

2 My sight comes and goes of its own volition. Just today, for example, I turned a corner and passed a girl whose name I almost spoke. She had a certain cast of

cheekbone and a merry eye. Then, with a wrench, I realized I was seeing someone in youth who—if she still lives—is in her sixties. But here was the face, and I had immediately reached backward into time beyond the elapsed years. I had to restrain myself from speaking. We go away and the other person stays eternally young, to be seen at rare and sudden intervals on a far street corner, or down a pathway in the park. Time never touches such people. It is we who, in the very moment of speaking, draw back in embarrassment. We are never recognized; we have grown old.

3 In all the questioning about what makes a writer, and especially perhaps the personal essayist, I have seen little reference to this fact; namely, that the brain has become a kind of unseen artist's loft. There are pictures that hang askew, pictures with outlines barely chalked in, pictures torn, pictures the artist has striven unsuccessfully to erase, pictures that only emerge and glow in a certain light. They have all been teleported, stolen, as it were, out of time. They represent no longer the sequential flow of ordinary memory. They can be pulled about on easels, examined within the mind itself. The act is not one of total recall like that of the professional mnemonist. Rather it is the use of things extracted from their context in such a way that they have become the unique possession of a single life. The writer sees back to these transports alone, bare, perhaps few in number, but endowed with a symbolic life. He cannot obliterate them. He can only drag them about, magnify or reduce them as his artistic sense dictates, or juxtapose them in order to enhance a pattern. One thing he cannot do. He cannot destroy what will not be destroyed; he cannot determine in advance what will enter his mind.

4 By way of example, I cannot explain why, out of many forgotten childhood episodes, my mind should retain as bright as yesterday the peculiar actions of a redheaded woodpecker. I must have been about six years old, and in the alley behind our house I had found the bird lying beneath a telephone pole. Looking back, I can only assume that he had received in some manner a stunning but not fatal shock of electricity. Coming upon him, seemingly dead but uninjured, I had carried him back to our porch and stretched him out to admire his color.

5 In a few moments, much to my surprise, he twitched and jerked upright. Then in a series of quick hops he reached the corner of the house and began to ascend in true woodpecker fashion—a hitch of the grasping feet, the bracing of the tail, and then, wonder of wonders, the knock, knock, knock, of the questing beak against our house. He was taking up life where it had momentarily left him, somewhere on the telephone pole. When he reached the top of the porch he flew away.

6 So there the picture lies. Even the coarse-grained wood of the porch comes back to me. If anyone were to ask me what else happened in that spring of 1913 I would stare blindly and be unable to answer with surety. But, as I have remarked, somewhere amidst the obscure lumber loft of my head that persistent hammering still recurs. Did it stay because it was my first glimpse of unconsciousness, resurrection, and time lapse presented in bright color? I do not know. I have never chanced to meet another adult who has a childhood woodpecker almost audibly rapping in his skull.

7 Robert Louis Stevenson, who had an eye for such matters, maintained that there are landscapes that cry out for a story and I suspect that his tale of *The Merry*

Men, along a tide-ripped coast, revolves about some personal vision of his own. Similarly Dickens once spoke of the "cold wet shelterless streets of London," something I myself can attest to from memories of one foggy night in those same streets.

8 Amongst this odd collection of pictures I must confess that much of historical importance has passed me by. I do not travel to political rallies and it has not been my fortune to be present at the scene of great events. On the whole, as I pause to examine this lost studio in my head, the animals outnumber by far the famous people I have met. If I sense a dearth of presidents, I have still encountered, though he looked right through me, one magnificent snow leopard, and I have also danced with an African crane. The crane, which is nearly as tall as a man, has an intricate mating dance. I was once strolling in the Philadelphia zoo when I came upon one of these birds solitary in a barely retaining enclosure.

9 In the animal world lines of definition are not as severely drawn as in the civilized one that we inhabit. This bird, acting under the impulse of spring, made some intricate little steps in my direction and extended its wings. Now I too believe in friendliness and spring festivities. I realized that the bird saw me as a vertical creature of the proper appearance to be a potential mate. To simplify things for her unlettered offspring, nature imparts, as in this case, a recognition of the vertical. After all, what is a face to a creature with a large bill? But then, unfortunately, in order to prevent, in her wisdom, unwise mixtures such as I and this crane potentially represented, nature insists upon an extremely complicated recognition dance. If one fails the steps and gestures, nothing is going to happen.

10 I fitted the vertical line pattern all right and I tried to be a good sport about the rest. I extended my arms, fluttered and flapped them. After looking carefully up and down the walk to verify that we were alone, I executed what I hoped was the proper enticing shuffle and jigged about in a circle. So did my partner. We did this a couple of times with mounting enthusiasm when I happened to see a park policeman sauntering in our direction. I dropped my arms and came to a direct, meditative halt.

11 The bird, too, paused uncertainly. There were now two attractive vertical figures, but they really did not seem to know the approved steps. Furthermore, not having read up on African cranes, I was a bit uncertain about the sex role I was playing. Male, female? I looked at the policeman. He looked at me. Suddenly I felt it best to leave the vicinity. Three is a crowd at moments like this. I walked away with careful unconcern in the direction of the small mammal house.

12 But why should my dance with a crane supersede in vividness years of graduate study? One can see a certain lack of disciplined control in a mind of this sort. Either that or the artist eye of my deprived mother lingered in me so that I was too much taken with color and form. I remember the vast wastes of the Mohave but, much more than that, I recall a baby ground squirrel that I came suddenly upon sunning himself in some fresh-turned earth beside the family burrow. His mother must have been careless, for here was her little waif blissfully lying on his back and patting his stomach. He looked up at me without a trace of fear as I stood over him. There the image stays, yet close to fifty years have passed: one ground squirrel patting his paunch.

13 I think, you know, it is the innocence. A violent dog-eat-dog world, a murder-

ous world, but one in which the very young are truly innocent. I am always amazed at this aspect of creation, the small Eden that does not last, but recurs with the young of every generation. I can remember when I was just as innocent as that baby ground squirrel and expected good from everyone, as a puppy might. We lose our innocence inevitably, but isn't there some kind of message in this innocence, some hint of a world beyond this fallen one, some place where everything was otherwise? Why else do infants peer up with humorous, arch visages, as when I briefly scratched the ground squirrel's belly and saw him wriggle?

14 These are the pictures that haunt my mind so that I stare through brick or stone as if it were not quite there. I know that I have written of harsh events and of those memories I wish that some might be effaced, scratched over with great black erasure marks, but this is not the way the essayist writes. He sees as his own eye dictates. Once, far north in Canada, I came upon a tremendous pile of boulders tossed about like houses in a hurricane. I was dwarfed beside them. They were remnants dropped from the retreating Labradorean ice cap. The huge stones were spilled as carelessly as a child's playthings upon a sidewalk. They could be picked up again as readily, the timeless eye looking through the boulders predicted, just as the little blue lakes between the stones could once more be frozen permanently and rise to obliterate the present countryside. There is a place like this as far south as Nebraska, where in the evening light everything shifts and changes and the transported granite takes on the shapes of marching mammoth.

15 These pictures reduce us to miniscule proportions, but I have so long wandered among eroded pinnacles and teetering tablestones that I have felt as lost as an insect drifting into a colossal ruin, not alone of earth, but of ages. I suppose if these stones had been glimpsed by Stevenson he would have said that they demanded a story, a human story of equal proportions. Being of a different vision, I can only say the story already lies there.

16 Nothing human will compass it save this: we, mankind, arose amidst the wandering of the ice and marched with it. We are in some sense shaped by it, as it has shaped the stones. Perhaps our very fondness for the building of stone alignments, dolmens, and pyramids reveals unconsciously an ancient heritage from the ice itself, the earth shaper. Like the ice, we have been cruel to the face of the planet and the life upon it. A chill wind lingers about us. With a few slight exceptions we are merciless. We have invented giant, earth-scavenging machinery to do what the ice once did. Does this explain the nature of the man whose mind is lost among ancient pictures? No, not entirely. For again from that dim mental studio, he peers out upon modern pictures and transposes them as in some totemic ceremony.

17 I once visited a distinguished artist whose primary interest is landscape and buildings, not animals. He was giving me a little preview of his latest work. I glanced at a deserted farmyard containing a few abandoned wheels and a broken pump. "I see you have a fox's face hidden by the well curb," I said.

18 My friend jumped up and peered at his canvas. "No, no," he protested. "That is not a fox. I had no such intention."

19 "It's surprising," I said in turn. "I can still see it. Look," I tried to point. "See it now, the eyes, the ears? There, just over the wellhead, watching."

20 "It can't be there," cried the artist, starting to pace restlessly before his

picture. "Damn it, man, that's just a rusty pump, boards, and old wire. I didn't put a fox there. I didn't."

21 "It's there just the same, Dan," I said. "It's the perspective. You got him in somehow. Or he sneaked in. Stand over here and look."

22 Dan peered at me strangely. "I'm not going to look," he countered sullenly. "If I look, I'll begin to see him myself. I almost do now. I won't look. You're spoiling my picture. I won't show any more." He began to stack his pictures face to the wall.

23 "Dan," I said, "I'm sorry. I just thought I saw—maybe it's my eyes." I removed my glasses and waved them. "I thought you had actually intended—"

24 "Just forget it," he sulked. I knew he would never give me a private showing again. There are pictures that come to affect me like Rorschach tests, where the psychologists try to peer into your head by way of your interpretation of an ink blot. I begin to look and the blots turn out always to be animals. A picture of a tropical swamp painted by a friend now deceased once hung on my wall. The scene was admittedly weird, but finally I began to see so many little faces in the twisted stumps that the thing got on my nerves. I gave it away. Probably, however, all of the creatures merely retreated to my private storeroom to await the time they might emerge again.

25 This is the way of it, I think. One has just so many pictures in one's head which, after one has stared at them long enough, make a story or an essay. Beyond that one is helpless. Naturally, if one is sufficiently distracted, or has dreams, as I often do, one tries to jot something down as at least a brief reminder. This can be a very efficient device in the hands of a man like Thoreau. I practice it in these late years, but unless one records detail it can be folly. Leafing through the old notebooks of my busiest, most diversified years, I have recently come upon two mysterious notations as frustrating to me as the unexpected fox in my painter friend's farmyard. The lines run as follows and are obviously unrelated:

Story of the Three Bloodhounds
The power of the mice

26 Now the three bloodhounds, in spite of suggesting something out of Sherlock Holmes, must have been intended as a tag for some curious dog story I had heard. The quick note implied haste. Years had passed before I was able to read that line again. If the story lies lost in the room of memories, I have been unable to recover it. As for the power of the mice, whatever their power was, it has totally vanished. If I had my choice as to which notation I would rather be informed upon, it would be the latter. In each case I would venture that these lost phrases hinted at nothing so visual as a redheaded woodpecker or the eyes of a snow leopard. They are consciously literary and therefore they faded from my mind.

27 On the other hand, there is the case of Willy, whose life was so tangential to my own that he would never have drawn a line in a notebook. Nevertheless, Willy lives on because of a certain grandeur and pathos in his end. I never learned Willy's full name. He was a black who had the night shift in the garage of our apartment house.

28 I used to come home and see Willy leaning upon the little fence by the door

of the garage. Across that fence was a pharmacy and a brightly lighted shopping center. I would speak to Willy and wonder what so fascinated him across the fence by which he lingered. Only after Willy's death did I begin to understand his final days.

29 Willy must have known he was dying, but, like most of us in humble circumstances, he went on tending to the dark subterranean garage until his final days. By carefully leaning upon the fence, he could see across into the domain of life. It was a small break for him in the brightly lit evening. The fence, and it was a rickety affair, had begun for Willy to mark the boundary between life and death. He knew he was on the wrong side of the barrier, but there was nothing he could do about it. In his final days he had come unconsciously to yearn toward the lights and movement across the way. There were telephone booths there in which boys called girls, or girls called boys. It was all exceedingly attractive to a dying man.

30 I doubt if anyone else remembers Willy now, but I do. I can look at the fence where the roses grow each spring and see him standing there, a worn black shadow. I am Willy's last recorder. Have I made sufficiently clear the burdens that a writer carries? I sometimes think that men and their thoughts are like jack-o'-lanterns upheld on poles at Halloween. They float and grin awhile before some dark unanswering window, and then, like hollow pumpkins, they are taken down, dismantled, and cast out. Poor old heads, there was only a small light in them and a rotund expansiveness that soon withered. Our own case is no better. But Willy still stands immovably by the fence. I can just make him out. It is a matter of seeing, like the fox in the painting. The rotten fence pickets have become a vast menacing landscape, but Willy refuses to depart. He exists in me, he watches.

(1975)

QUESTIONS

Thought and Structure

1. Paragraph 3 of this essay is very important because it looks back to the first two paragraphs and sets forth the controlling image for the remainder of the essay. How does that pivotal paragraph help us understand the general idea in paragraph 1? What can we learn about Eiseley's inheritance from his mother (the "unrestrained clairvoyant eye") from reading paragraphs 1, 3, and 12 together? Do we get a clearer sense of Eiseley's fascination with things visual by considering what he attributes to his mother?
2. Paragraph 8 focuses on one of Eiseley's preoccupations. What is that preoccupation? Does it establish his kinship with other writers in this anthology? How about Dillard? Are there others?
3. Look at paragraphs 9–11 dealing with the crane dance. Think about that dance and what it tells us about Eiseley. See if you can list three ideas that Eiseley advances by telling that story. What do those ideas have to do with the essay in general?
4. Think about the transition Eiseley makes in paragraph 12. He turns momentarily from the task of describing the pictures in his mind to an analysis of the pictures he has just told us about. As we try to come to terms with what Eiseley is telling us, does it help

to know that he was an anthropologist? Does such knowledge become even more important as we consider the four paragraphs (13–16) that follow? What do we learn about the way Eiseley's mind works by looking at these five paragraphs (12–16) as a rhetorical unit?

5. In this essay about writing and about the writer's imagination, what can you learn that will help you write your own essays? Consider especially paragraphs 25 and 26. Try to pinpoint the quality of those images that stick in Eiseley's memory. How do you suppose they differ from those that fade, from those that are "consciously literary."
6. In paragraph 15, Eiseley suggests that his way of dealing with "pictures" is different from the way Robert Louis Stevenson might deal with them. See if you can come to terms with that difference. It might help to go back to paragraph 7 where Eiseley first mentions Stevenson and to consider paragraphs 7–15 as a unit of discourse, or a section of the argument. As you study that section, try to account for this, the last sentence of paragraph 15: "Being of a different vision, I can only say the story already lies there." Does Willy's story already lie there, or is Eiseley imposing a story on an image? Who is in charge, the image or the writer's transforming imagination?

Style and Strategy

7. Why do you suppose that in an essay titled "Willy," there is no mention of Willy until the last four paragraphs of the essay?
8. Let's go back to paragraph 3 again, looking this time at the way Eiseley develops his controlling metaphor: "the brain has become a kind of unseen artist's loft." The next sentence begins to develop and to account for that metaphor by accumulating meaning through a series of phrases that build on and modify one another:

   There are pictures that hang askew,
   pictures with outlines barely chalked in,
   pictures torn,
   pictures the artist has striven unsuccessfully to erase,
   pictures that only emerge and glow in a certain light.

   Clearly we have moved from the "artist's loft" itself, to the contents of the loft, to the pictures there. Is the term pictures a metaphor? In other words, is Eiseley reaching for something that he cannot define precisely and does that reaching beyond what he can actually account for have something to do with the shape of his sentence? Keep in mind the three sentences that follow the one we've just considered:

   They have all been teleported, stolen, as it were, out of time.
   They represent no longer the sequential flow of ordinary memory.
   They can be pulled about on easels, examined within the mind itself.

   How do these three sentences extend the range of Eiseley's inquiry about the nature of those pictures in the "artist's loft"? How does he make use of "They" to glue his thoughts together?
9. Keeping paragraph 3 in mind, what is Eiseley's writing strategy in paragraphs 4–5 and in paragraph 6? Can you distinguish between the two writing tasks that he sets for himself in those two sections?
10. What is Eiseley's strategy in paragraph 14? Why does he make us go back to reconsider the essay's first paragraph with these words: "so that I stare through brick or stone as if it were not quite there"?

11. Why does Eiseley include the story about his friend Dan (paragraphs 17–23)? What is the point of that section of the essay? Is it critical to Eiseley's argument or could he leave it out?
12. Is this just an essay about Eiseley's writing, or might it also be about our own? How can you tell?

SUGGESTIONS FOR WRITING

A. Write a short essay about how the "Eiseley" of this essay differs from the "Eiseley" in "The Dance of the Frogs." Take your clue from the crane dance. Think too about Dreyer. Which "Eiseley" is more like Dreyer?

B. Write two to four paragraphs comparing and contrasting Eiseley's dance with the crane with Annie Dillard's encounter with the weasel ("Living Like a Weasel," editors' introduction).

C. Write a short letter to your friend who is in the hospital and cannot attend class. Tell your friend how Forster's essay "English Prose Between 1918 and 1939" might give her a clue that will help her understand "Willy." Focus initially on the idea of relativity set forth in "Prose," paragraph 5. Forster is thinking more about the relativity of good and evil; Eiseley seems to have in mind the relativity of time as it exists inside the memory and out of it. Consider especially what Eiseley says through example in paragraph 2 and then builds on throughout the essay.

D. Try to recall one of those lingering and haunting memories from your "artist's loft" and write an interesting essay about either that memory or about an idea that you can use the memory to illuminate. In your prewriting, you might try it both ways. Start first with the memory; write about it and see if an idea develops. Or if an idea immediately pops into your mind, set out to develop the idea and see how the memory will work its way into your draft.

The Hidden Teacher

Sometimes the best teacher teaches only once to a single child or to a grownup past hope.

—*ANONYMOUS*

I

1 The putting of formidable riddles did not arise with today's philosophers. In fact, there is a sense in which the experimental method of science might be said merely to have widened the area of man's homelessness. Over two thousand years ago, a man named Job, crouching in the Judean desert, was moved to challenge what he felt to be the injustice of his God. The voice in the whirlwind, in turn, volleyed pitiless questions upon the supplicant—questions that have, in truth, precisely the ring of modern science. For the Lord asked of Job by whose wisdom the hawk soars, and who had fathered the rain, or entered the storehouses of the snow.

2 A youth standing by, one Elihu, also played a role in this drama, for he ventured diffidently to his protesting elder that it was not true that God failed to manifest Himself. He may speak in one way or another, though men do not perceive it. In consequence of this remark perhaps it would be well, whatever our individual beliefs, to consider what may be called the hidden teacher, lest we become too much concerned with the formalities of only one aspect of the education by which we learn.

3 We think we learn from teachers, and we sometimes do. But the teachers are not always to be found in school or in great laboratories. Sometimes what we learn depends upon our own powers of insight. Moreover, our teachers may be hidden, even the greatest teacher. And it was the young man Elihu who observed that if the old are not always wise, neither can the teacher's way be ordered by the young whom he would teach.

4 For example, I once received an unexpected lesson from a spider.

5 It happened far away on a rainy morning in the West. I had come up a long gulch looking for fossils, and there, just at eye level, lurked a huge yellow-and-black orb spider, whose web was moored to the tall spears of buffalo grass at the edge of the arroyo. It was her universe, and her senses did not extend beyond the lines and spokes of the great wheel she inhabited. Her extended claws could feel every vibration throughout that delicate structure. She knew the tug of wind, the fall of a raindrop, the flutter of a trapped moth's wing. Down one spoke of the web ran a stout ribbon of gossamer on which she could hurry out to investigate her prey.

6 Curious, I took a pencil from my pocket and touched a strand of the web. Immediately there was a response. The web, plucked by its menacing occupant, began to vibrate until it was a blur. Anything that had brushed claw or wing against that amazing snare would be thoroughly entrapped. As the vibrations slowed, I could see the owner fingering her guidelines for signs of struggle. A pencil point was an intrusion into this universe for which no precedent existed. Spider was circumscribed by spider ideas; its universe was spider universe. All outside was irrational, extraneous, at best raw material for spider. As I proceeded on my way along the gully, like a vast impossible shadow, I realized that in the world of spider I did not exist.

7 Moreover, I considered, as I tramped along, that to the phagocytes, the white blood cells, clambering even now with some kind of elementary intelligence amid the thin pipes and tubing of my body—creatures without whose ministrations I could not exist—the conscious "I" of which I was aware had no significance to these amoeboid beings. I was, instead, a kind of chemical web that brought meaningful messages to them, a natural environment seemingly immortal if they could have thought about it, since generations of them had lived and perished, and would continue to so live and die, in that odd fabric which contained my intelligence—a misty light that was beginning to seem floating and tenuous even to me.

8 I began to see that, among the many universes in which the world of living creatures existed, some were large, some small, but that all, including man's, were in some way limited or finite. We were creatures of many different dimensions passing through each other's lives like ghosts through doors.

9 In the years since, my mind has many times returned to that far moment of my encounter with the orb spider. A message has arisen only now from the misty shreds of that webbed universe. What was it that had so troubled me about the incident? Was it that spidery indifference to the human triumph?

10 If so, that triumph was very real and could not be denied. I saw, had many times seen, both mentally and in the seams of exposed strata, the long backward stretch of time whose recovery is one of the great feats of modern science. I saw the drifting cells of the early seas from which all life, including our own, has arisen. The salt of those ancient seas is in our blood, its lime is in our bones. Every time we walk along a beach some ancient urge disturbs us so that we find ourselves shedding shoes and garments or scavenging among seaweed and whitened timbers like the homesick refugees of a long war.

11 And war it has been indeed—the long war of life against its inhospitable environment, a war that has lasted for perhaps three billion years. It began with strange chemicals seething under a sky lacking in oxygen; it was waged through long ages until the first green plants learned to harness the light of the nearest star, our sun. The human brain, so frail, so perishable, so full of inexhaustible dreams and hungers, burns by the power of the leaf.

12 The hurrying blood cells charged with oxygen carry more of that element to the human brain than to any other part of the body. A few moments' loss of vital air and the phenomenon we know as consciousness goes down into the black night of inorganic things. The human body is a magical vessel, but its life is linked with an element it cannot produce. Only the green plant knows the secret of transforming the light that comes to us across the far reaches of space. There is no better illustration of the intricacy of man's relationship with other living things.

13 The student of fossil life would be forced to tell us that if we take the past into consideration the vast majority of earth's creatures—perhaps over 90 percent—have vanished. Forms that flourished for a far longer time than man has existed upon earth have become either extinct or so transformed that their descendants are scarcely recognizable. The specialized perish with the environment that created them, the tooth of the tiger fails at last, the lances of men strike down the last mammoth.

14 In three billion years of slow change and groping effort only one living creature has succeeded in escaping the trap of specialization that has led in time to so much death and wasted endeavor. It is man, but the word should be uttered softly, for his story is not yet done.

15 With the rise of the human brain, with the appearance of a creature whose upright body enabled two limbs to be freed for the exploration and manipulation of his environment, there had at last emerged a creature with a specialization—the brain—that, paradoxically, offered escape from specialization. Many animals driven into the nooks and crannies of nature have achieved momentary survival only at the cost of later extinction.

16 Was it this that troubled me and brought my mind back to a tiny universe among the grass blades, a spider's universe concerned with spider thought?

17 Perhaps.

18 The mind that once visualized animals on a cave wall is now engaged in a vast ramification of itself through time and space. Man has broken through the boundaries that control all other life. I saw, at last, the reason for my recollection of that great spider on the arroyo's rim, fingering its universe against the sky.

19 The spider was a symbol of man in miniature. The wheel of the web brought the analogy home clearly. Man, too, lies at the heart of a web, a web extending through the starry reaches of sidereal space, as well as backward into the dark realm of prehistory. His great eye upon Mount Palomar looks into a distance of millions of light-years, his radio ear hears the whisper of even more remote galaxies, he peers through the electron microscope upon the minute particles of his own being. It is a web no creature of earth has ever spun before. Like the orb spider, man lies at the heart of it, listening. Knowledge has given him the memory of earth's history beyond the time of his emergence. Like the spider's claw, a part of him touches a world he will never enter in the flesh. Even now, one can see him reaching forward into time with new machines, computing, analyzing, until elements of the shadowy future will also compose part of the invisible web he fingers.

20 Yet still my spider lingers in memory against the sunset sky. Spider thoughts in a spider universe—sensitive to raindrop and moth flutter, nothing beyond, nothing allowed for the unexpected, the inserted pencil from the world outside.

21 Is man at heart any different from the spider, I wonder: man thoughts, as limited as spider thoughts, contemplating now the nearest star with the threat of bringing with him the fungus rot from earth, wars, violence, the burden of a population he refuses to control, cherishing again his dream of the Adamic Eden he had pursued and lost in the green forests of America. Now it beckons again like a mirage from beyond the moon. Let man spin his web, I thought further; it is his nature. But I considered also the work of the phagocytes swarming in the rivers of my body, the unresting cells in their mortal universe. What is it we are a part of that we do not see, as the spider was not gifted to discern my face, or my little probe into her world?

22 We are too content with our sensory extensions, with the fulfillment of that Ice Age mind that began its journey amidst the cold of vast tundras and that pauses only briefly before its leap into space. It is no longer enough to see as a man sees—even to the ends of the universe. It is not enough to hold nuclear energy in one's hand like a spear, as a man would hold it, or to see the lightning, or times past, or time to come, as a man would see it. If we continue to do this, the great brain—the human brain—will be only a new version of the old trap, and nature is full of traps for the beast that cannot learn.

23 It is not sufficient any longer to listen at the end of a wire to the rustling of galaxies; it is not enough even to examine the great coil of DNA in which is coded the very alphabet of life. These are our extended perceptions. But beyond lies the great darkness of the ultimate Dreamer, who dreamed the light and the galaxies. Before act was, or substance existed, imagination grew in the dark. Man partakes of that ultimate wonder and creativeness. As we turn from the galaxies to the swarming cells of our own being, which toil for something, some entity beyond their grasp, let us remember man, the self-fabricator who came across an ice age to look into the mirrors and the magic of science. Surely he did not come to see himself

or his wild visage only. He came because he is at heart a listener and a searcher for some transcendent realm beyond himself. This he has worshiped by many names, even in the dismal caves of his beginning. Man, the self-fabricator, is so by reason of gifts he had no part in devising—and so he searches as the single living cell in the beginning must have sought the ghostly creature it was to serve.

II

24 The young man Elihu, Job's counselor and critic, spoke simply of the "Teacher," and it is of this teacher I speak when I refer to gifts man had no part in devising. Perhaps—though it is purely a matter of emotional reactions to words—it is easier for us today to speak of this teacher as "nature," that omnipresent all which contained both the spider and my invisible intrusion into her carefully planned universe. But nature does not simply represent reality. In the shapes of life, it prepares the future; it offers alternatives. Nature teaches, though what it teaches is often hidden and obscure, just as the voice from the spinning dust cloud belittled Job's thought but gave back no answers to its own formidable interrogation.

25 A few months ago I encountered an amazing little creature on a windy corner of my local shopping center. It seemed, at first glance, some long-limbed, feathery spider teetering rapidly down the edge of a store front. Then it swung into the air and, as hesitantly as a spider on a thread, blew away into the parking lot. It returned in a moment on a gust of wind and ran toward me once more on its spindly legs with amazing rapidity.

26 With great difficulty I discovered the creature was actually a filamentous seed, seeking a hiding place and scurrying about with the uncanny surety of a conscious animal. In fact, it *did* escape me before I could secure it. Its flexible limbs were stiffer than milkweed down, and, propelled by the wind, it ran rapidly and evasively over the pavement. It was like a gnome scampering somewhere with a hidden packet—for all that I could tell, a totally new one: one of the jumbled alphabets of life.

27 A new one? So stable seem the years and all green leaves, a botanist might smile at my imaginings. Yet bear with me a moment. I would like to tell a tale, a genuine tale of childhood. Moreover, I was just old enough to know the average of my kind and to marvel at what I saw. And what I saw was straight from the hidden Teacher, whatever be his name.

28 It is told in the Orient of the Hindu god Krishna that his mother, wiping his mouth when he was a child, inadvertently peered in and beheld the universe, though the sight was mercifully and immediately veiled from her. In a sense, this is what happened to me. One day there arrived at our school a newcomer, who entered the grade above me. After some days this lad, whose look of sleepy-eyed arrogance is still before me as I write, was led into my mathematics classroom by the principal. Our class was informed severely that we should learn to work harder.

29 With this preliminary exhortation, great rows of figures were chalked upon the blackboard, such difficult mathematical problems as could be devised by adults. The class watched in helpless wonder. When the preparations had been completed, the young pupil sauntered forward and, with a glance of infinite boredom that swept

from us to his fawning teachers, wrote the answers, as instantaneously as a modern computer, in their proper place upon the board. Then he strolled out with a carelessly exaggerated yawn.

30 Like some heavy-browed child at the wood's edge, clutching the last stone hand ax, I was witnessing the birth of a new type of humanity—one so beyond its teachers that it was being used for mean purposes while the intangible web of the universe in all its shimmering mathematical perfection glistened untaught in the mind of a chance little boy. The boy, by then grown self-centered and contemptuous, was being dragged from room to room to encourage us, the paleanthropes, to duplicate what, in reality, our teachers could not duplicate. He was too precious an object to be released upon the playground among us, and with reason. In a few months his parents took him away.

31 Long after, looking back from maturity, I realized that I had been exposed on that occasion, not to human teaching, but to the Teacher, toying with some sixteen billion nerve cells interlocked in ways past understanding. Or, if we do not like the anthropomorphism implied in the word teacher, then nature, the old voice from the whirlwind fumbling for the light. At all events, I had been the fortunate witness to life's unbounded creativity—a creativity seemingly still as unbalanced and chance-filled as in that far era when a black-scaled creature had broken from an egg and the age of the giant reptiles, the creatures of the prime, had tentatively begun.

32 Because form cannot be long sustained in the living, we collapse inward with age. We die. Our bodies, which were the product of a kind of hidden teaching by an alphabet we are only beginning dimly to discern, are dismissed into their elements. What is carried onward, assuming we have descendants, is the little capsule of instructions such as I encountered hastening by me in the shape of a running seed. We have learned the first biological lesson: that in each generation life passes through the eye of a needle. It exists for a time molecularly and in no recognizable semblance to its adult condition. It *instructs* its way again into man or reptile. As the ages pass, so do variants of the code. Occasionally, a species vanishes on a wind as unreturning as that which took the pterodactyls.

33 Or the code changes by subtle degrees through the statistical altering of individuals; until I, as the fading Neanderthals must once have done, have looked with still-living eyes upon the creature whose genotype was quite possibly to replace me. The genetic alphabets, like genuine languages, ramify and evolve along unreturning pathways.

34 If nature's instructions are carried through the eye of a needle, through the molecular darkness of a minute world below the field of human vision and of time's decay, the same, it might be said, is true of those monumental structures known as civilizations. They are transmitted from one generation to another in invisible puffs of air known as words—words that can also be symbolically incised on clay. As the delicate printing on the mud at the water's edge retraces a visit of autumn birds long since departed, so the little scrabbled tablets in perished cities carry the seeds of human thought across the deserts of millennia. In this instance the teacher is the social brain, but it, too, must be compressed into minute hieroglyphs, and the minds that wrought the miracle efface themselves amidst the jostling torrent of messages, which, like the genetic code, are shuffled and reshuffled as they hurry through

eternity. Like a mutation, an idea may be recorded in the wrong time, to lie latent like a recessive gene and spring once more to life in an auspicious era.

35 Occasionally, in the moments when an archaeologist lifts the slab over a tomb that houses a great secret, a few men gain a unique glimpse through that dark portal out of which all men living have emerged, and through which messages again must pass. Here the Mexican archaeologist Ruz Lhuillier speaks of his first penetration of the great tomb hidden beneath dripping stalactites at the pyramid of Palenque: "Out of the dark shadows, rose a fairy-tale vision, a weird ethereal spectacle from another world. It was like a magician's cave carved out of ice, with walls glittering and sparkling like snow crystals." After shining his torch over hieroglyphs and sculptured figures, the explorer remarked wonderingly: "We were the first people for more than a thousand years to look at it."

36 Or again, one may read the tale of an unknown pharaoh who had secretly arranged that a beloved woman of his household should be buried in the tomb of the god-king—an act of compassion carrying a personal message across the millennia in defiance of all precedent.

37 Up to this point we have been talking of the single hidden teacher, the taunting voice out of that old Biblical whirlwind which symbolizes nature. We have seen incredible organic remembrance passed through the needle's eye of a microcosmic world hidden completely beneath the observational powers of creatures preoccupied and ensorcelled by dissolution and decay. We have seen the human mind unconsciously seize upon the principles of that very code to pass its own societal memory forward into time. The individual, the momentary living cell of the society, vanishes, but the institutional structures stand, or if they change, do so in an invisible flux not too dissimilar from that persisting in the stream of genetic continuity.

38 Upon this world, life is still young, not truly old as stars are measured. Therefore it comes about that we minimize the role of the synapsid reptiles, our remote forerunners, and correspondingly exalt our own intellectual achievements. We refuse to consider that in the old eye of the hurricane we may be, and doubtless are, in aggregate, a slightly more diffuse and dangerous dragon of the primal morning that still enfolds us.

39 Note that I say "in aggregate." For it is just here, among men, that the role of messages, and, therefore, the role of the individual teacher—or, I should say now, the hidden teachers—begin to be more plainly apparent and their instructions become more diverse. The dead pharaoh, though unintentionally, by a revealing act, had succeeded in conveying an impression of human tenderness that has outlasted the trappings of a vanished religion.

40 Like most modern educators I have listened to student demands to grade their teachers. I have heard the words repeated until they have become a slogan, that no man over thirty can teach the young of this generation. How would one grade a dead pharaoh, millennia gone, I wonder, one who did not intend to teach, but who, to a few perceptive minds, succeeded by the simple nobility of an act.

41 Many years ago, a student who was destined to become an internationally known anthropologist sat in a course in linguistics and heard his instructor, a man of no inconsiderable wisdom, describe some linguistic peculiarities of Hebrew words. At the time, the young student, at the urging of his family, was contemplating a

career in theology. As the teacher warmed to his subject, the student, in the back row, ventured excitedly, "I believe I can understand that, sir. It is very similar to what exists in Mohegan."

42 The linguist paused and adjusted his glasses. "Young man," he said, "Mohegan is a dead language. Nothing has been recorded of it since the eighteenth century. Don't bluff."

43 "But sir," the young student countered hopefully, "It can't be dead so long as an old woman I know still speaks it. She is Pequot-Mohegan. I learned a bit of vocabulary from her and could speak with her myself. She took care of me when I was a child."

44 "Young man," said the austere, old-fashioned scholar, "be at my house for dinner at six this evening. You and I are going to look into this matter."

45 A few months later, under careful guidance, the young student published a paper upon Mohegan linguistics, the first of a long series of studies upon the forgotten languages and ethnology of the Indians of the northeastern forests. He had changed his vocation and turned to anthropology because of the attraction of a hidden teacher. But just who was the teacher? The young man himself, his instructor, or that solitary speaker of a dying tongue who had so yearned to hear her people's voice that she had softly babbled it to a child?

46 Later, this man was to become one of my professors. I absorbed much from him, though I hasten to make the reluctant confession that he was considerably beyond thirty. Most of what I learned was gathered over cups of coffee in a dingy campus restaurant. What we talked about were things some centuries older than either of us. Our common interest lay in snakes, scapulimancy, and other forgotten rites of benighted forest hunters.

47 I have always regarded this man as an extraordinary individual, in fact, a hidden teacher. But alas, it is all now so old-fashioned. We never protested the impracticality of his quaint subjects. We were all too ready to participate in them. He was an excellent canoeman, but he took me to places where I fully expected to drown before securing my degree. To this day, fragments of his unused wisdom remain stuffed in some back attic of my mind. Much of it I have never found the opportunity to employ, yet it has somehow colored my whole adult existence. I belong to that elderly professor in somewhat the same way that he, in turn, had become the wood child of a hidden forest mother.

48 There are, however, other teachers. For example, among the hunting peoples there were the animal counselors who appeared in prophetic dreams. Or, among the Greeks, the daemonic supernaturals who stood at the headboard while a man lay stark and listened—sometimes to dreadful things. "You are asleep," the messengers proclaimed over and over again, as though the man lay in a spell to hear his doom pronounced. "You, Achilles, you, son of Atreus. You are asleep, asleep," the hidden ones pronounced and vanished.

49 We of this modern time know other things of dreams, but we know also that they can be interior teachers and healers as well as the anticipators of disaster. It has been said that great art is the night thought of man. It may emerge without warning from the soundless depths of the unconscious, just as supernovas may blaze up suddenly in the farther reaches of void space. The critics, like astronomers, can afterward triangulate such worlds but not account for them.

50 A writer friend of mine with bitter memories of his youth, and estranged from his family, who, in the interim, had died, gave me this account of the matter in his middle years. He had been working, with an unusual degree of reluctance, upon a novel that contained certain autobiographical episodes. One night he dreamed; it was a very vivid and stunning dream in its detailed reality.

51 He found himself hurrying over creaking snow through the blackness of a winter night. He was ascending a familiar path through a long-vanished orchard. The path led to his childhood home. The house, as he drew near, appeared dark and uninhabited, but, impelled by the power of the dream, he stepped upon the porch and tried to peer through a dark window into his own old room.

52 "Suddenly," he told me, "I was drawn by a strange mixture of repulsion and desire to press my face against the glass. I knew intuitively they were all there waiting for me within, if I could but see them. My mother and my father. Those I had loved and those I hated. But the window was black to my gaze. I hesitated a moment and struck a match. For an instant in that freezing silence I saw my father's face glimmer wan and remote behind the glass. My mother's face was there, with the hard, distorted lines that marked her later years.

53 "A surge of fury overcame my cowardice. I cupped the match before me and stepped closer, closer toward that dreadful confrontation. As the match guttered down, my face was pressed almost to the glass. In some quick transformation, such as only a dream can effect, I saw that it was my own face into which I stared, just as it was reflected in the black glass. My father's haunted face was but my own. The hard lines upon my mother's aging countenance were slowly reshaping themselves upon my living face. The light burned out. I awoke sweating from the terrible psychological tension of that nightmare. I was in a far port in a distant land. It was dawn. I could hear the waves breaking on the reef."

54 "And how do you interpret the dream?" I asked, concealing a sympathetic shudder and sinking deeper into my chair.

55 "It taught me something," he said slowly, and with equal slowness a kind of beautiful transfiguration passed over his features. All the tired lines I had known so well seemed faintly to be subsiding.

56 "Did you ever dream it again?" I asked out of a comparable experience of my own.

57 "No, never," he said, and hesitated. "You see, I had learned it was just I, but more, much more, I had learned that I was they. It makes a difference. And at the last, late—much too late—it was all right. I understood. My line was dying, but I understood. I hope they understood, too." His voice trailed into silence.

58 "It is a thing to learn," I said. "You were seeking something and it came." He nodded, wordless. "Out of a tomb," he added after a silent moment, "my kind of tomb—the mind."

59 On the dark street, walking homeward, I considered my friend's experience. Man, I concluded, may have come to the end of that wild being who had mastered the fire and the lightning. He can create the web but not hold it together, not save himself except by transcending his own image. For at last, before the ultimate mystery, it is himself he shapes. Perhaps it is for this that the listening web lies open: that by knowledge we may grow beyond our past, our follies, and ever closer to what the Dreamer in the dark intended before the dust arose and walked. In the pages

of an old book it has been written that we are in the hands of a Teacher, nor does it yet appear what man shall be.

(1964)

QUESTIONS

Thought and Structure

1. After Eiseley completes his account of the spider in paragraphs 5 and 6, he begins to think in terms we might consider scientific; he thinks about white blood cells and elementary intelligence, but he quickly extends his considerations to matters that scientists might shun. What are those other matters, and why are they so hard to deal with scientifically? Consider paragraphs 7–23 as a cerebration, a kind of interior monologue in which Eiseley thinks about why his mind keeps going back to the spider. What are the reasons he considers and then rejects? What is the primary reason? Could we consider Part I of the essay a warning and a challenge? Explain.
2. To what extent do you agree with Eiseley that man "is at heart a listener and a searcher for some transcendent realm beyond himself"?
3. In paragraphs 27–30, Eiseley tells the story of a little boy who was brought into the classroom to perform feats of intelligence other children could not perform. What is the point that Eiseley wants us to glean from this story? Look to paragraphs 31–33 for part of the answer, but also look back to paragraphs 25 and 26, to the story of the "filamentous seed." Try to come to terms with what Eiseley means by "code" and by "genetic alphabets."
4. In paragraph 34, what does Eiseley mean when he says that an idea might be like "a mutation" or "like a recessive gene"?
5. From paragraph 35 to the end of the essay, Eiseley goes beyond his notion of Teacher ("a single hidden teacher") to a consideration of teachers. Which of his several examples of teachers do you think is most effectively presented? Why?

Style and Strategy

6. At the end of paragraph 6 Eiseley has three curious sentences in which articles are omitted:

   > Spider was circumscribed by spider ideas; its universe was spider universe. All outside was irrational, extraneous, at best raw material for spider. As I proceeded on my way along the gully, like a vast impossible shadow, I realized that in the world of spider I did not exist.

   What is the effect of these omissions?
7. Read aloud paragraphs 22 and 23. Pay particular attention to the repetition of word patterns: "It is no longer enough"; "It is not enough"; "It is not sufficient any longer." There are other repetitions within the sentences. What is the effect of those repetitions as you read the paragraph? Does the rhythm that builds as you read work on you in an interesting way? Do you think Eiseley might be trying to pull you into the argument in some subconscious way? In answering that last question, consider the function, the rhetorical purpose, of these last two paragraphs of part I.

8. In paragraphs 25 and 26 why does Eiseley personify the "filamentous seed" that is "scurrying about with the uncanny surety of a conscious animal"?
9. Compare the final paragraph of the essay with paragraphs 22 and 23. Which of those conclusions do you find more appealing? Why? Does paragraph 59 untangle the web of the essay for you, or does it complicate things?

SUGGESTIONS FOR WRITING

A. Write your own essay about learning and about teachers, but before you begin writing, consider what Eiseley says in this essay and others. How would Eiseley say that we do most of our learning? What does that learning depend on most, the teacher or "our own powers of insight"? Cite evidence from Eiseley's essays and from your own experience to support *your* ideas.

B. Richard Wilbur's poem "Mind" bears a strong kinship with this essay. In a journal entry in your notebook try to account for the relationship between poem and essay. How do the two comment on one another? Look for complementing ideas. Try particularly to account for this line from the poem: "A graceful error may correct the cave."

> Mind in its purest play is like some bat
> That beats about in caverns all alone,
> Contriving by a kind of senseless wit
> Not to conclude against a wall of stone.
>
> It has no need to falter or explore;
> Darkly it knows what obstacles are there,
> And so may weave and flitter, dip and soar
> In perfect courses through the blackest air.
>
> And has this simile a like perfection?
> The mind is like a bat. Precisely. Save
> That in the very happiest intellection
> A graceful error may correct the cave.

C. Write two or three paragraphs in your journal about what you think Eiseley means by Teacher.

The Illusion of the Two Cultures

1 Not long ago an English scientist, Sir Eric Ashby, remarked that "to train young people in the dialectic between orthodoxy and dissent is the unique contribution which universities make to society." I am sure that Sir Eric meant by this remark that nowhere but in universities are the young given the opportunity to absorb past tradition and at the same time to experience the impact of new ideas—in the sense of a constant dialogue between past and present—lived in every hour of the student's existence. This dialogue, ideally, should lead to a great winnowing and sifting of experience and to a heightened consciousness of self which, in turn, should lead on to greater sensitivity and perception on the part of the individual.

2 Our lives are the creation of memory and the accompanying power to extend ourselves outward into ideas and relive them. The finest intellect is that which employs an invisible web of gossamer running into the past as well as across the minds of living men and which constantly responds to the vibrations transmitted through these tenuous lines of sympathy. It would be contrary to fact, however, to assume that our universities always perform this unique function of which Sir Eric speaks, with either grace or perfection; in fact our investment in man, it has been justly remarked, is deteriorating even as the financial investment in science grows.

3 More than thirty years ago, George Santayana had already sensed this trend. He commented, in a now-forgotten essay, that one of the strangest consequences of modern science was that as the visible wealth of nature was more and more transferred and abstracted, the mind seemed to lose courage and to become ashamed of its own fertility. "The hard-pressed natural man will not indulge his imagination," continued Santayana, "unless it poses for truth; and being half-aware of this imposition, he is more troubled at the thought of being deceived than at the fact of being mechanized or being bored; and he would wish to escape imagination altogether."

4 "Man would wish to escape imagination altogether." I repeat that last phrase, for it defines a peculiar aberration of the human mind found on both sides of that bipolar division between the humanities and the sciences, which C. P. Snow has popularized under the title of *The Two Cultures.* The idea is not solely a product of this age. It was already emerging with the science of the seventeenth century; one finds it in Bacon. One finds the fear of it faintly foreshadowed in Thoreau. Thomas Huxley lent it weight when he referred contemptuously to the "caterwauling of poets."

5 Ironically, professional scientists berated the early evolutionists such as Lamarck and Chambers for overindulgence in the imagination. Almost eighty years ago John Burroughs observed that some of the animus once directed by science toward dogmatic theology seemed in his day increasingly to be vented upon the literary naturalist. In the early 1900s a quarrel over "nature faking" raised a confused din in America and aroused W. H. Hudson to some dry and pungent comment upon the failure to distinguish the purposes of science from those of literature. I know of at least one scholar who, venturing to develop some personal ideas in an essay for the layman, was characterized by a reviewer in a leading professional journal as a worthless writer, although, as it chanced, the work under discussion had received several awards in literature, one of them international in scope. More recently, some scholars not indifferent to humanistic values have exhorted poets to leave their personal songs in order to portray the beauty and symmetry of molecular structures.

6 Now some very fine verse has been written on scientific subjects, but, I fear, very little under the dictate of scientists as such. Rather there is evident here precisely that restriction of imagination against which Santayana inveighed; namely, an attempt to constrain literature itself to the delineation of objective or empiric truth, and to dismiss the whole domain of value, which after all constitutes the very nature of man, as without significance and beneath contempt.

7 Unconsciously, the human realm is denied in favor of the world of pure technics. Man, the tool user, grows convinced that he is himself only useful as a tool, that fertility except in the use of the scientific imagination is wasteful and without

purpose, even, in some indefinable way, sinful. I was reading J. R. R. Tolkien's great symbolic trilogy, *The Fellowship of the Ring,* a few months ago, when a young scientist of my acquaintance paused and looked over my shoulder. After a little casual interchange the man departed leaving an accusing remark hovering in the air between us. "I wouldn't waste my time with a man who writes fairy stories." He might as well have added, "or with a man who reads them."

8 As I went back to my book I wondered vaguely in what leafless landscape one grew up without Hans Christian Andersen, or Dunsany, or even Jules Verne. There lingered about the young man's words a puritanism which seemed the more remarkable because, as nearly as I could discover, it was unmotivated by any sectarian religiosity unless a total dedication to science brings to some minds a similar authoritarian desire to shackle the human imagination. After all, it is this impossible, fertile world of our imagination which gave birth to liberty in the midst of oppression, and which persists in seeking until what is sought is seen. Against such invisible and fearful powers, there can be found in all ages and in all institutions—even the institutions of professional learning—the humorless man with the sneer, or if the sneer does not suffice, then the torch, for the bright unperishing letters of the human dream.

9 One can contrast this recalcitrant attitude with an 1890 reminiscence from that great Egyptologist Sir Flinders Petrie, which steals over into the realm of pure literature. It was written, in unconscious symbolism, from a tomb:

10 "I here live, and do not scramble to fit myself to the requirements of others. In a narrow tomb, with the figure of Néfermaat standing on each side of me—as he has stood through all that we know as human history—I have just room for my bed, and a row of good reading in which I can take pleasure after dinner. Behind me is that Great Peace, the Desert. It is an entity—a power—just as much as the sea is. No wonder men fled to it from the turmoil of the ancient world."

11 It may now reasonably be asked why one who has similarly, if less dramatically, spent his life among the stones and broken shards of the remote past should be writing here about matters involving literature and science. While I was considering this with humility and trepidation, my eye fell upon a stone in my office. I am sure that professional journalists must recall times when an approaching deadline has keyed all their senses and led them to glance wildly around in the hope that something might leap out at them from the most prosaic surroundings. At all events my eyes fell upon this stone.

12 Now the stone antedated anything that the historians would call art; it had been shaped many hundreds of thousands of years ago by men whose faces would frighten us if they sat among us today. Out of old habit, since I like the feel of worked flint, I picked it up and hefted it as I groped for words over this difficult matter of the growing rift between science and art. Certainly the stone was of no help to me; it was a utilitarian thing which had cracked marrow bones, if not heads, in the remote dim morning of the human species. It was nothing if not practical. It was, in fact, an extremely early example of the empirical tradition which has led on to modern science.

13 The mind which had shaped this artifact knew its precise purpose. It had found out by experimental observation that the stone was tougher, sharper, more

enduring than the hand which wielded it. The creature's mind had solved the question of the best form of the implement and how it could be manipulated most effectively. In its day and time this hand ax was as grand an intellectual achievement as a rocket.

14 As a scientist my admiration went out to that unidentified workman. How he must have labored to understand the forces involved in the fracturing of flint, and all that involved practical survival in his world. My uncalloused twentieth-century hand caressed the yellow stone lovingly. It was then that I made a remarkable discovery.

15 In the mind of this gross-featured early exponent of the practical approach to nature—the technician, the no-nonsense practitioner of survival—two forces had met and merged. There had not been room in his short and desperate life for the delicate and supercilious separation of the arts from the sciences. There did not exist then the refined distinctions set up between the scholarly percipience of reality and what has sometimes been called the vaporings of the artistic imagination.

16 As I clasped and unclasped the stone, running my fingers down its edges, I began to perceive the ghostly emanations from a long-vanished mind, the kind of mind which, once having shaped an object of any sort, leaves an individual trace behind it which speaks to others across the barriers of time and language. It was not the practical experimental aspect of this mind that startled me, but rather that the fellow had wasted time.

17 In an incalculably brutish and dangerous world he had both shaped an instrument of practical application and then, with a virtuoso's elegance, proceeded to embellish his product. He had not been content to produce a plain, utilitarian implement. In some wistful, inarticulate way, in the grip of the dim aesthetic feelings which are one of the marks of man—or perhaps I should say, some men—this archaic creature had lingered over his handiwork.

18 One could still feel him crouching among the stones on a long-vanished river bar, turning the thing over in his hands, feeling its polished surface, striking, here and there, just one more blow that no longer had usefulness as its criterion. He had, like myself, enjoyed the texture of the stone. With skills lost to me, he had gone on flaking the implement with an eye to beauty until it had become a kind of rough jewel, equivalent in its day to the carved and gold-inlaid pommel of the iron dagger placed in Tutankhamen's tomb.

19 All the later history of man contains these impractical exertions expended upon a great diversity of objects, and, with literacy, breaking even into printed dreams. Today's secular disruption between the creative aspect of art and that of science is a barbarism that would have brought lifted eyebrows in a Cro-Magnon cave. It is a product of high technical specialization, the deliberate blunting of wonder, and the equally deliberate suppression of a phase of our humanity in the name of an authoritarian institution, science, which has taken on, in our time, curious puritanical overtones. Many scientists seem unaware of the historical reasons for this development or the fact that the creative aspect of art is not so remote from that of science as may seem, at first glance, to be the case.

20 I am not so foolish as to categorize individual scholars or scientists. I am, however, about to remark on the nature of science as an institution. Like all such

structures it is apt to reveal certain behavioral rigidities and conformities which increase with age. It is no longer the domain of the amateur, though some of its greatest discoverers could be so defined. It is now a professional body, and with professionalism there tends to emerge a greater emphasis upon a coherent system of regulations. The deviant is more sharply treated, and the young tend to imitate their successful elders. In short, an "Establishment"—a trade union—has appeared.

21 Similar tendencies can be observed among those of the humanities concerned with the professional analysis and interpretation of the works of the creative artist. Here too, a similar rigidity and exclusiveness make their appearance. It is not that in the case of both the sciences and the humanities standards are out of place. What I am briefly cautioning against is that too frequently they afford an excuse for stifling original thought or constricting much latent creativity within traditional molds.

22 Such molds are always useful to the mediocre conformist who instinctively castigates and rejects what he cannot imitate. Tradition, the continuity of learning, are, it is true, enormously important to the learned disciplines. What we must realize as scientists is that the particular institution we inhabit has its own irrational accretions and authoritarian dogmas which can be as unpleasant as some of those encountered in sectarian circles—particularly so since they are frequently unconsciously held and surrounded by an impenetrable wall of self-righteousness brought about because science is regarded as totally empiric and open-minded by tradition.

23 This type of professionalism, as I shall label it in order to distinguish it from what is best in both the sciences and humanities, is characterized by two assumptions: that the accretions of fact are cumulative and lead to progress, whereas the insights of art are, at best, singular, and lead nowhere, or, when introduced into the realm of science, produce obscurity and confusion. The convenient label "mystic" is, in our day, readily applied to men who pause for simple wonder, or who encounter along the borders of the known that "awful power" which Wordsworth characterized as the human imagination. It can, he says, rise suddenly from the mind's abyss and enwrap the solitary traveler like a mist.

24 We do not like mists in this era, and the word imagination is less and less used. We like, instead, a clear road, and we abhor solitary traveling. Indeed one of our great scientific historians remarked not long ago that the literary naturalist was obsolescent if not completely outmoded. I suppose he meant that with our penetration into the biophysical realm, life, like matter, would become increasingly represented by abstract symbols. To many it must appear that the more we can dissect life into its elements, the closer we are getting to its ultimate resolution. While I have some reservations on this score, they are not important. Rather, I should like to look at the symbols which in the one case denote science and in the other constitute those vaporings and cloud wraiths that are the abomination, so it is said, of the true scientist but are the delight of the poet and literary artist.

25 Creation in science demands a high level of imaginative insight and intuitive perception. I believe no one would deny this, even though it exists in varying degrees, just as it does, similarly, among writers, musicians, or artists. The scientist's achievement, however, is quantitatively transmissible. From a single point his discovery is verifiable by other men who may then, on the basis of corresponding data, accept

the innovation and elaborate upon it in the cumulative fashion which is one of the great triumphs of science.

26 Artistic creation, on the other hand, is unique. It cannot be twice discovered, as, say, natural selection was discovered. It may be imitated stylistically, in a genre, a school, but, save for a few items of technique, it is not cumulative. A successful work of art may set up reverberations and is, in this, just as transmissible as science, but there is a qualitative character about it. Each reverberation in another mind is unique. As the French novelist François Mauriac has remarked, each great novel is a separate and distinct world operating under its own laws with a flora and fauna totally its own. There is communication, or the work is a failure, but the communication releases our own visions, touches some highly personal chord in our own experience.

27 The symbols used by the great artist are a key releasing our humanity from the solitary tower of the self. "Man," says Lewis Mumford, "is first and foremost the self-fabricating animal." I shall merely add that the artist plays an enormous role in this act of self-creation. It is he who touches the hidden strings of pity, who searches our hearts, who makes us sensitive to beauty, who asks questions about fate and destiny. Such questions, though they lurk always around the corners of the external universe which is the peculiar province of science, the rigors of the scientific method do not enable us to pursue directly.

28 And yet I wonder.

29 It is surely possible to observe that it is the successful analogy or symbol which frequently allows the scientist to leap from a generalization in one field of thought to a triumphant achievement in another. For example, Progressionism in a spiritual sense later became the model contributing to the discovery of organic evolution. Such analogies genuinely resemble the figures and enchantments of great literature, whose meanings similarly can never be totally grasped because of their endless power to ramify in the individual mind.

30 John Donne gave powerful expression to a feeling applicable as much to science as to literature when he said devoutly of certain Biblical passages: "The literall sense is alwayes to be preserved; but the literall sense is not alwayes to be discerned; for the literall sense is not alwayes that which the very letter and grammar of the place presents." A figurative sense, he argues cogently, can sometimes be the most "literall intention of the Holy Ghost."

31 It is here that the scientist and artist sometimes meet in uneasy opposition, or at least along lines of tension. The scientist's attitude is sometimes, I suspect, that embodied in Samuel Johnson's remark that, wherever there is mystery, roguery is not far off.

32 Yet surely it was not roguery when Sir Charles Lyell glimpsed in a few fossil prints of raindrops the persistence of the world's natural forces through the incredible, mysterious aeons of geologic time. The fossils were a symbol of a vast hitherto unglimpsed order. They are, in Donne's sense, both literal and symbolic. As fossils they merely denote evidence of rain in a past era. Figuratively they are more. To the perceptive intelligence they afford the hint of lengthened natural order, just as the eyes of ancient trilobites tell us similarly of the unchanging laws of light. Equally, the educated mind may discern in a scratched pebble the retreating shadow of vast

ages of ice and gloom. In Donne's archaic phraseology these objects would bespeak the principal intention of the Divine Being—that is, of order beyond our power to grasp.

33 Such images drawn from the world of science are every bit as powerful as great literary symbolism and equally demanding upon the individual imagination of the scientist who would fully grasp the extension of meaning which is involved. It is, in fact, one and the same creative act in both domains.

34 Indeed evolution itself has become such a figurative symbol, as has also the hypothesis of the expanding universe. The laboratory worker may think of these concepts in a totally empirical fashion as subject to proof or disproof by the experimental method. Like Freud's doctrine of the subconscious, however, such ideas frequently escape from the professional scientist into the public domain. There they may undergo further individual transformation and embellishment. Whether the scholar approves or not, such hypotheses are now as free to evolve in the mind of the individual as are the creations of art. All the resulting enrichment and confusion will bear about it something suggestive of the world of artistic endeavor.

35 As figurative insights into the nature of things, such embracing conceptions may become grotesquely distorted or glow with added philosophical wisdom. As in the case of the trilobite eye or the fossil raindrop, there lurks behind the visible evidence vast shadows no longer quite of that world which we term natural. Like the words in Donne's Bible, enormous implications have transcended the literal expression of the thought. Reality itself has been superseded by a greater reality. As Donne himself asserted, "The substance of the truth is in the great images which lie behind."

36 It is because these two types of creation—the artistic and the scientific—have sprung from the same being and have their points of contact even in division that I have the temerity to assert that, in a sense, the "two cultures" are an illusion, that they are a product of unreasoning fear, professionalism, and misunderstanding. Because of the emphasis upon science in our society, much has been said about the necessity of educating the layman and even the professional student of the humanities upon the ways and the achievements of science. I admit that a barrier exists, but I am also concerned to express the view that there persists in the domain of science itself an occasional marked intolerance of those of its own membership who venture to pursue the way of letters. As I have remarked, this intolerance can the more successfully clothe itself in seeming objectivity because of the supposed open nature of the scientific society. It is not remarkable that this trait is sometimes more manifest in the younger and less secure disciplines.

37 There was a time, not too many centuries ago, when to be active in scientific investigation was to invite suspicion. Thus it may be that there now lingers among us, even in the triumph of the experimental method, a kind of vague fear of that other artistic world of deep emotion, of strange symbols, lest it seize upon us or distort the hard-won objectivity of our thinking—lest it corrupt, in other words, that crystalline and icy objectivity which, in our scientific guise, we erect as a model of conduct. This model, incidentally, if pursued to its absurd conclusion, would lead to a world in which the computer would determine all aspects of our existence; one in which the bomb would be as welcome as the discoveries of the physician.

38 Happily, the very great in science, or even those unique scientist-artists such as Leonardo, who foreran the emergence of science as an institution, have been singularly free from this folly. Darwin decried it even as he recognized that he had paid a certain price in concentrated specialization for his achievement. Einstein, it is well known, retained a simple sense of wonder; Newton felt like a child playing with pretty shells on a beach. All show a deep humility and an emotional hunger which is the prerogative of the artist. It is with the lesser men, with the institutionalization of method, with the appearance of dogma and mapped-out territories, that an unpleasant suggestion of fenced preserves begins to dominate the university atmosphere.

39 As a scientist, I can say that I have observed it in my own and others' specialties. I have had occasion, also, to observe its effects in the humanities. It is not science *per se;* it is, instead, in both regions of thought, the narrow professionalism which is also plainly evident in the trade union. There can be small men in science just as there are small men in government or business. In fact it is one of the disadvantages of big science, just as it is of big government, that the availability of huge sums attracts a swarm of elbowing and contentious men to whom great dreams are less than protected hunting preserves.

40 The sociology of science deserves at least equal consideration with the biographies of the great scientists, for powerful and changing forces are at work upon science, the institution, as contrasted with science as a dream and an ideal of the individual. Like other aspects of society, it is a construct of men and is subject, like other social structures, to human pressures and inescapable distortions.

41 Let me give an illustration. Even in learned journals, clashes occasionally occur between those who would regard biology as a separate and distinct domain of inquiry and the reductionists who, by contrast, perceive in the living organism only a vaster and more random chemistry. Understandably, the concern of the reductionists is with the immediate. Thomas Hobbes was expressing a similar point of view when he castigated poets as "working on mean minds with words and distinctions that of themselves signifie nothing, but betray (by their obscurity) that there walketh . . . another kingdome, as it were a kingdome of fayries in the dark." I myself have been similarly criticized for speaking of a nature "beyond the nature that we know."

42 Yet consider for a moment this dark, impossible realm of "fayrie." Man is not totally compounded of the nature we profess to understand. He contains, instead, a lurking unknown future, just as the man-apes of the Pliocene contained in embryo the future that surrounds us now. The world of human culture itself was an unpredictable fairy world until, in some pre-ice-age meadow, the first meaningful sounds in all the world broke through the jungle babble of the past, the nature, until that moment, "known."

43 It is fascinating to observe that, in the very dawn of science, Francis Bacon, the spokesman for the empirical approach to nature, shared with Shakespeare, the poet, a recognition of the creativeness which adds to nature, and which emerges from nature as "an art which nature makes." Neither the great scholar nor the great poet had renounced this "kingdome of fayries." Both had realized what Henri Bergson was later to express so effectively, that life inserts a vast "indetermination into matter." It is, in a sense, an intrusion from a realm which can never be completely subject to prophetic analysis by science. The novelties of evolution

emerge; they cannot be predicted. They haunt, until their arrival, a world of unimaginable possibilities behind the living screen of events, as these last exist to the observer confined to a single point on the time scale.

44 Oddly enough, much of the confusion that surrounded my phrase, "a nature beyond the nature that we know," resolves itself into pure semantics. I might have pointed out what must be obvious even to the most dedicated scientific mind—that the nature which we know has been many times reinterpreted in human thinking, and that the hard, substantial matter of the nineteenth century has already vanished into a dark, bodiless void, a web of "events" in space-time. This is a realm, I venture to assert, as weird as any we have tried, in the past, to exorcise by the brave use of seeming solid words. Yet some minds exhibit an almost instinctive hostility toward the mere attempt to wonder or to ask what lies below that microcosmic world out of which emerge the particles which compose our bodies and which now take on this wraithlike quality.

45 Is there something here we fear to face, except when clothed in safely sterilized professional speech? Have we grown reluctant in this age of power to admit mystery and beauty into our thoughts, or to learn where power ceases? I referred earlier to one of our own forebears on a gravel bar, thumbing a pebble. If, after the ages of building and destroying, if after the measuring of light-years and the powers probed at the atom's heart, if after the last iron is rust-eaten and the last glass lies shattered in the streets, a man, some savage, some remnant of what once we were, pauses on his way to the tribal drinking place and feels rising from within his soul the inexplicable mist of terror and beauty that is evoked from old ruins—even the ruins of the greatest city in the world—then, I say, all will still be well with man.

46 And if that savage can pluck a stone from the gravel because it shone like crystal when the water rushed over it, and hold it against the sunset, he will be as we were in the beginning, whole—as we were when we were children, before we began to split the knowledge from the dream. All talk of the two cultures is an illusion; it is the pebble which tells man's story. Upon it is written man's two faces, the artistic and the practical. They are expressed upon one stone over which a hand once closed, no less firm because the mind behind it was submerged in light and shadow and deep wonder.

47 Today we hold a stone, the heavy stone of power. We must perceive beyond it, however, by the aid of the artistic imagination, those humane insights and understandings which alone can lighten our burden and enable us to shape ourselves, rather than the stone, into the forms which great art has anticipated.

(1964)

QUESTIONS

Thought and Structure

1. Is there something in these sentences from paragraph 2 that makes you think of "The Hidden Teacher": "Our lives are the creation of memory and the accompanying power to extend ourselves outward into ideas and relive them. The finest intellect is that which

employs an invisible web of gossamer running into the past as well as across the minds of living men and which constantly responds to the vibrations transmitted through these tenuous lines of sympathy"? Compare the metaphor here with the one in paragraph 19 in "Teacher." Does Eiseley modify his metaphor in any way? If so, how does the modification alter the meaning?

2. In paragraphs 11–18 Eiseley attempts to illustrate the point of his essay by examining a stone that he finds in his office. Is his illustration effective? What point (or points) emerge from the illustration?
3. What does Eiseley mean by "Establishment" in paragraph 20? What are the larger implications of the term as it applies to the scientific community?
4. In paragraph 28, we see Eiseley change his mind in the midst of his argument. What is the point of the argument he advances in paragraphs 29–33? What is the meaning of "figurative" in the paragraphs that follow?
5. In your final analysis of this essay, do you consider it a criticism of the scientific community or a defense of the imagination?

Style and Strategy

6. Eiseley takes what many would consider an inordinate amount of space to get to his point. Look at the first ten paragraphs of the essay to see what he accomplishes before he considers his purpose in writing this essay (paragraph 11). Would the essay be better if he eliminated those early paragraphs? What purposes do they serve?
7. What is the effect of this embedded expression in paragraph 17: "or perhaps I should say, some men"? In the next paragraph, what does Eiseley mean by "one more blow that no longer had usefulness as its criterion"? How does he further his argument by these expressions?
8. Look at paragraphs 20 and 21. What is their relationship to one another? Is Eiseley trying to balance his attack? Or is he simply trying momentarily to soften his criticism of science? Eiseley goes to another pair of paragraphs (25 and 26) to compare scientific creation and artistic creation. How does he distinguish the two? Does the pairing in this second instance have a rhetorical purpose different from the first pairing?
9. What does Eiseley gain by his "clear road" metaphor in paragraph 24?
10. How effectively does Eiseley evoke Leonardo, Darwin, and Einstein in paragraph 38? Is he persuasive? Have you seen any evidence of "fenced preserves" in your classes?

SUGGESTIONS FOR WRITING

A. Write an epistolary essay in the form of a personal letter to Dr. Eiseley; discuss with him a matter of substance raised by his essay. Whatever your point happens to be, support it with evidence from your personal experience and from your reading.

B. Read all of the essays by Eiseley in this anthology and then write a character sketch of Eiseley. Do no outside research and do not extract any of your evidence from the headnote. Look within the essays to identify what you think are Eiseley's preoccupations. Think about what those preoccupations tell you about him. Consider his images too, his method of developing his essays, and the facts of his life as he outlines them. Take all of this information into account and use your "figurative" imagination to come to terms with your subject.

The Dance of the Frogs

I

1 He was a member of the Explorers Club, and he had never been outside the state of Pennsylvania. Some of us who were world travelers used to smile a little about that, even though we knew his scientific reputation had been, at one time, great. It is always the way of youth to smile. I used to think of myself as something of an adventurer, but the time came when I realized that old Albert Dreyer, huddling with his drink in the shadows close to the fire, had journeyed farther into the Country of Terror than any of us would ever go, God willing, and emerge alive.

2 He was a morose and aging man, without family and without intimates. His membership in the club dated back into the decades when he was a zoologist famous for his remarkable experiments upon amphibians—he had recovered and actually produced the adult stage of the Mexican axolotl, as well as achieving remarkable tissue transplants in salamanders. The club had been flattered to have him then, travel or no travel, but the end was not fortunate. The brilliant scientist had become the misanthrope; the achievement lay all in the past, and Albert Dreyer kept to his solitary room, his solitary drink, and his accustomed spot by the fire.

3 The reason I came to hear his story was an odd one. I had been north that year, and the club had asked me to give a little talk on the religious beliefs of the Indians of the northern forest, the Naskapi of Labrador. I had long been a student of the strange mélange of superstition and woodland wisdom that makes up the religious life of the nature peoples. Moreover, I had come to know something of the strange similarities of the "shaking tent rite" to the phenomena of the modern medium's cabinet.

4 "The special tent with its entranced occupant is no different from the cabinet," I contended. "The only difference is the type of voices that emerge. Many of the physical phenomena are identical—the movement of powerful forces shaking the conical hut, objects thrown, all this is familiar to Western psychical science. What is different are the voices projected. Here they are the cries of animals, the voices from the swamp and the mountain—the solitary elementals before whom the primitive man stands in awe, and from whom he begs sustenance. Here the game lords reign supreme; man himself is voiceless."

5 A low, halting query reached me from the back of the room. I was startled, even in the midst of my discussion, to note that it was Dreyer.

6 "And the game lords, what are they?"

7 "Each species of animal is supposed to have gigantic leaders of more than normal size," I explained. "These beings are the immaterial controllers of that particular type of animal. Legend about them is confused. Sometimes they partake of human qualities, will and intelligence, but they are of animal shape. They control the movements of game, and thus their favor may mean life or death to man."

8 "Are they visible?" Again Dreyer's low, troubled voice came from the back of the room.

9 "Native belief has it that they can be seen on rare occasions," I answered. "In a sense they remind one of the concept of the archetypes, the originals behind the petty show of our small, transitory existence. They are the immortal renewers of substance—the force behind and above animate nature."

10 "Do they dance?" persisted Dreyer.

11 At this I grew nettled. Old Dreyer in a heckling mood was something new. "I cannot answer that question," I said acidly. "My informants failed to elaborate upon it. But they believe implicitly in these monstrous beings, talk to and propitiate them. It is their voices that emerge from the shaking tent."

12 "The Indians believe it," pursued old Dreyer relentlessly, "but do *you* believe it?"

13 "My dear fellow"—I shrugged and glanced at the smiling audience—"I have seen many strange things, many puzzling things, but I am a scientist." Dreyer made a contemptuous sound in his throat and went back to the shadow out of which he had crept in his interest. The talk was over. I headed for the bar.

II

14 The evening passed. Men drifted homeward or went to their rooms. I had been a year in the woods and hungered for voices and companionship. Finally, however, I sat alone with my glass, a little mellow, perhaps, enjoying the warmth of the fire and remembering the blue snowfields of the North as they should be remembered—in the comfort of warm rooms.

15 I think an hour must have passed. The club was silent except for the ticking of an antiquated clock on the mantel and small night noises from the street. I must have drowsed. At all events it was some time before I grew aware that a chair had been drawn up opposite me. I started.

16 "A damp night," I said.

17 "Foggy," said the man in the shadow musingly. "But not too foggy. They like it that way."

18 "Eh?" I said. I knew immediately it was Dreyer speaking. Maybe I had missed something; on second thought, maybe not.

19 "And spring," he said. "Spring. That's part of it. God knows why, of course, but we feel it, why shouldn't they? And more intensely."

20 "Look—" I said. "I guess—" The old man was more human than I thought. He reached out and touched my knee with the hand that he always kept a glove over—burn, we used to speculate—and smiled softly.

21 "You don't know what I'm talking about," he finished for me. "And, besides, I ruffled your feelings earlier in the evening. You must forgive me. You touched on an interest of mine, and I was perhaps overeager. I did not intend to give the appearance of heckling. It was only that . . ."

22 "Of course," I said. "Of course." Such a confession from Dreyer was astounding. The man might be ill. I rang for a drink and decided to shift the conversation to a safer topic, more appropriate to a scholar.

23 "Frogs," I said desperately, like any young ass in a china shop. "Always admired your experiments. Frogs. Yes."

24 I give the old man credit. He took the drink and held it up and looked at me across the rim. There was a faint stir of sardonic humor in his eyes.

25 "Frogs, no," he said, "or maybe yes. I've never been quite sure. Maybe yes. But there was no time to decide properly." The humor faded out of his eyes. "Maybe I should have let go," he said. "It was what they wanted. There's no doubting that at all, but it came too quick for me. What would you have done?"

26 "I don't know," I said honestly enough and pinched myself.

27 "You had better know," said Albert Dreyer severely, "if you're planning to become an investigator of primitive religions. Or even not. I wasn't, you know, and the things came to me just when I least suspected—But I forget, you don't believe in them."

28 He shrugged and half rose, and for the first time, really, I saw the black-gloved hand and the haunted face of Albert Dreyer and knew in my heart the things he had stood for in science. I got up then, as a young man in the presence of his betters should get up, and I said, and I meant it, every word: "Please, Dr. Dreyer, sit down and tell me. I'm too young to be saying what I believe or don't believe in at all. I'd be obliged if you'd tell me."

29 Just at that moment a strange, wonderful dignity shone out of the countenance of Albert Dreyer, and I knew the man he was. He bowed and sat down, and there were no longer the barriers of age and youthful ego between us. There were just two men under a lamp, and around them a great waiting silence. Out to the ends of the universe, I thought fleetingly, that's the way with man and his lamps. One has to huddle in, there's so little light and so much space. One——

III

30 "It could happen to anyone," said Albert Dreyer. "And especially in the spring. Remember that. And all I did was to skip. Just a few feet, mark you, but I skipped. Remember that, too.

31 "You wouldn't remember the place at all. At least not as it was then." He paused and shook the ice in his glass and spoke more easily.

32 "It was a road that came out finally in a marsh along the Schuykill River. Probably all industrial now. But I had a little house out there with a laboratory thrown in. It was convenient to the marsh, and that helped me with my studies of amphibia. Moreover, it was a wild, lonely road, and I wanted solitude. It is always the demand of the naturalist. You understand that?"

33 "Of course," I said. I knew he had gone there, after the death of his young wife, in grief and loneliness and despair. He was not a man to mention such things. "It is best for the naturalist," I agreed.

34 "Exactly. My best work was done there." He held up his black-gloved hand and glanced at it meditatively. "The work on the axolotl, newt neoteny. I worked hard. I had—" he hesitated—"things to forget. There were times when I worked

all night. Or diverted myself, while waiting the result of an experiment, by midnight walks. It was a strange road. Wild all right, but paved and close enough to the city that there were occasional street lamps. All uphill and downhill, with bits of forest leaning in over it, till you walked in a tunnel of trees. Then suddenly you were in the marsh, and the road ended at an old, unused wharf.

35 "A place to be alone. A place to walk and think. A place for shadows to stretch ahead of you from one dim lamp to another and spring back as you reached the next. I have seen them get tall, tall, but never like that night. It was like a road into space."

36 "Cold?" I asked.

37 "No. I shouldn't have said 'space.' It gives the wrong effect. Not cold. Spring. Frog time. The first warmth, and the leaves coming. A little fog in the hollows. The way they like it then in the wet leaves and bogs. No moon, though; secretive and dark, with just those street lamps wandered out from the town. I often wondered what graft had brought them there. They shone on nothing—except my walks at midnight and the journeys of toads, but still . . ."

38 "Yes?" I prompted, as he paused.

39 "I was just thinking. The web of things. A politician in town gets a rake-off for selling useless lights on a useless road. If it hadn't been for that, I might not have seen them. I might not even have skipped. Or, if I had, the effect—How can you tell about such things afterwards? Was the effect heightened? Did it magnify their power? Who is to say?"

40 "The skip?" I said, trying to keep things casual. "I don't understand. You mean, just skipping? Jumping?"

41 Something like a twinkle came into his eyes for a moment. "Just that," he said. "No more. You are a young man. Impulsive? You should understand."

42 "I'm afraid—" I began to counter.

43 "But of course," he cried pleasantly. "I forget. You were not there. So how could I expect you to feel or know about this skipping. Look, look at me now. A sober man, eh?"

44 I nodded. "Dignified," I said cautiously.

45 "Very well. But, young man, there is a time to skip. On country roads in the spring. It is not necessary that there be girls. You will skip without them. You will skip because something within you knows the time—frog time. Then you will skip."

46 "Then I will skip," I repeated, hypnotized. Mad or not, there was a force in Albert Dreyer. Even there under the club lights, the night damp of an unused road began to gather.

IV

47 "It was a late spring," he said. "Fog and mist in those hollows in a way I had never seen before. And frogs, of course. Thousands of them, and twenty species, trilling, gurgling, and grunting in as many keys. The beautiful keen silver piping of spring peepers arousing as the last ice leaves the ponds—if you have heard that after a long winter alone, you will never forget it." He paused and leaned forward,

listening with such an intent inner ear that one could almost hear that far-off silver piping from the wet meadows of the man's forgotten years.

48 I rattled my glass uneasily, and his eyes came back to me.

49 "They come out then," he said more calmly. "All amphibia have to return to the water for mating and egg laying. Even toads will hop miles across country to streams and waterways. You don't see them unless you go out at night in the right places as I did, but that night—

50 "Well, it was unusual, put it that way, as an understatement. It was late, and the creatures seemed to know it. You could feel the forces of mighty and archaic life welling up from the very ground. The water was pulling them—not water as we know it, but the mother, the ancient life force, the thing that made us in the days of creation, and that lurks around us still, unnoticed in our sterile cities.

51 "I was no different from any other young fool coming home on a spring night, except that as a student of life, and of amphibia in particular, I was, shall we say, more aware of the creatures. I had performed experiments"—the black glove gestured before my eyes. "I was, as it proved, susceptible.

52 "It began on that lost stretch of roadway leading to the river, and it began simply enough. All around, under the street lamps, I saw little frogs and big frogs hopping steadily toward the river. They were going in my direction.

53 "At that time I had my whimsies, and I was spry enough to feel the tug of that great movement. I joined them. There was no mystery about it. I simply began to skip, to skip gaily, and enjoy the great bobbing shadow I created as I passed onward with that leaping host all headed for the river.

54 "Now skipping along a wet pavement in spring is infectious, particularly going downhill, as we were. The impulse to take mightier leaps, to soar farther, increases progressively. The madness worked into me. I bounded till my lungs labored, and my shadow, at first my own shadow, bounded and labored with me.

55 "It was only midway in my flight that I began to grow conscious that I was not alone. The feeling was not strong at first. Normally a sober pedestrian, I was ecstatically preoccupied with the discovery of latent stores of energy and agility which I had not suspected in my subdued existence.

56 "It was only as we passed under a street lamp that I noticed, beside my own bobbing shadow, another great, leaping grotesquerie that had an uncanny suggestion of the frog world about it. The shocking aspect of the thing lay in its size, and the fact that, judging from the shadow, it was soaring higher and more gaily than myself.

57 " 'Very well,' you will say"—and here Dreyer paused and looked at me tolerantly—" 'Why didn't you turn around? That would be the scientific thing to do.'

58 "It would be the scientific thing to do, young man, but let me tell you it is not done—not on an empty road at midnight—not when the shadow is already beside your shadow and is joined by another, and then another.

59 "No, you do not pause. You look neither to left nor right, for fear of what you might see there. Instead, you dance on madly, hopelessly. Plunging higher, higher, in the hope the shadows will be left behind, or prove to be only leaves dancing, when you reach the next street light. Or that whatever had joined you in this midnight bacchanal will take some other pathway and depart.

60 "You do not look—you cannot look—because to do so is to destroy the

universe in which we move and exist and have our transient being. You dare not look, because, beside the shadows, there now comes to your ears the loose-limbed slap of giant batrachian feet, not loud, not loud at all, but there, definitely there, behind you at your shoulder, plunging with the utter madness of spring, their rhythm entering your bones until you too are hurtling upward in some gigantic ecstasy that it is not given to mere flesh and blood to long endure.

61 "I was part of it, part of some mad dance of the elementals behind the show of things. Perhaps in that night of archaic and elemental passion, that festival of the wetlands, my careless hopping passage under the street lights had called them, attracted their attention, brought them leaping down some fourth-dimensional roadway into the world of time.

62 "Do not suppose for a single moment I thought so coherently then. My lungs were bursting, my physical self exhausted, but I sprang, I hurtled, I flung myself onward in a company I could not see, that never outpaced me, but that swept me with the mighty ecstasies of a thousand springs, and that bore me onward exultantly past my own doorstep, toward the river, toward some pathway long forgotten, toward some unforgettable destination in the wetlands and the spring.

63 "Even as I leaped, I was changing. It was this, I think, that stirred the last remnants of human fear and human caution that I still possessed. My will was in abeyance; I could not stop. Furthermore, certain sensations, hypnotic or otherwise, suggested to me that my own physical shape was modifying, or about to change. I was leaping with a growing ease. I was—

64 "It was just then that the wharf lights began to show. We were approaching the end of the road, and the road, as I have said, ended in the river. It was this, I suppose, that startled me back into some semblance of human terror. Man is a land animal. He does not willingly plunge off wharfs at midnight in the monstrous company of amphibious shadows.

65 "Nevertheless their power held me. We pounded madly toward the wharf, and under the light that hung above it, and the beam that made a cross. Part of me struggled to stop, and part of me hurtled on. But in that final frenzy of terror before the water below engulfed me I shrieked, *'Help! In the name of God, help me! In the name of Jesus, stop!'* "

66 Dreyer paused and drew in his chair a little closer under the light. Then he went on steadily.

67 "I was not, I suppose, a particularly religious man, and the cries merely revealed the extremity of my terror. Nevertheless this is a strange thing, and whether it involves the crossed beam, or the appeal to a Christian deity, I will not attempt to answer.

68 "In one electric instant, however, I was free. It was like the release from demoniac possession. One moment I was leaping in an inhuman company of elder things, and the next moment I was a badly shaken human being on a wharf. Strangest of all, perhaps, was the sudden silence of that midnight hour. I looked down in the circle of the arc light, and there by my feet hopped feebly some tiny froglets of the great migration. There was nothing impressive about them, but you will understand that I drew back in revulsion. I have never been able to handle them for research since. My work is in the past."

69 He paused and drank, and then, seeing perhaps some lingering doubt and

confusion in my eyes, held up his black-gloved hand and deliberately pinched off the glove.

70 A man should not do that to another man without warning, but I suppose he felt I demanded some proof. I turned my eyes away. One does not like a webbed batrachian hand on a human being.

71 As I rose embarrassedly, his voice came up to me from the depths of the chair.

72 "It is not the hand," Dreyer said. "It is the question of choice. Perhaps I was a coward, and ill prepared. Perhaps"—his voice searched uneasily among his memories—"perhaps I should have taken them and that springtime without question. Perhaps I should have trusted them and hopped onward. Who knows? They were gay enough, at least."

73 He sighed and set down his glass and stared so intently into empty space that, seeing I was forgotten, I tiptoed quietly away.

(1928)

QUESTIONS

Thought and Structure

1. In part I, we get a sense in the first paragraph that there may actually be two "Eiseleys" in this essay, one young and one older, one who had an encounter with Dreyer and one who looks back on that encounter as he tries to relate it to us. Does it help us understand the essay if we keep these two different Eiseleys in mind? Explain.
2. What does this sentence from paragraph 13 tell us about the younger Eiseley: "I have seen many strange things, many puzzling things, but I am a scientist"?
3. In part III, paragraphs 34, 37, and 39, we learn about the street lamps on that lonely road near Dreyer's little house. What do those street lamps have to do with the "web of things"? How important does that phrase become as we try to come to terms with the essay? Is Eiseley suggesting something about Fate? Why does Dreyer mention "girls" in paragraph 45? What is he suggesting about the nature of skipping?
4. In part IV, Dreyer tries to account for the force that moved him so close to the water. How effectively does his language account for that force? Consider these terms that he uses: "the mother, the ancient life force, the thing that made us in the days of creation"; "The madness worked into me"; "the utter madness of spring"; "hurtling upward in some gigantic ecstasy"; "part of some mad dance of the elementals behind the show of things." Do you get as much insight from those terms as you do from the rhythm of the last sentence in paragraph 62?
5. In paragraph 68, Dreyer claims that he was "free," released from "demoniac possession." Was he, or was he more free when he skipped with the frogs? Why does Dreyer wonder, as he concludes his account, whether he was a coward? Consider carefully what he says in paragraph 72. Why does Eiseley tiptoe quietly away?

Style and Strategy

6. What happens in terms of development in part I, paragraph 4, when Eiseley shifts to dialogue? What happens to time? How does Eiseley alter our sense of the relationship between himself and Dreyer? (See question 1 above: do we get a clearer sense of the two

"Eiseleys" if we consider paragraphs 1–3 as one unit of discourse and paragraphs 4–13 as another unit?)

7. In part II, we get an even clearer sense of the two "Eiseleys" in the essay, but with that clarification, other ambiguities are introduced: "the frogs," "the black-gloved hand," and the idea of "so little light" in the world. What is the author's strategy here? Why is he deliberately keeping us off guard? What do you make of Dreyer's warning in paragraph 27?
8. Part III begins with the indefinite pronoun "It" and then we learn about "skipping," but we have no sense of what either "It" or "skipping" means in the context of the essay. Before this section ends, the young "Eiseley" is "hypnotized." Does our own disorientation have anything to do with our understanding the experience Eiseley is trying to relate to us? Is he conjuring us as Dreyer conjured him that evening in the Explorers Club? If so, how effective is the method?
9. By the beginning of part IV, Dreyer seems to be in charge. Young "Eiseley" is hypnotized, ready to listen. The scientist seems to be losing control to the "misanthrope." Why then do you think Dreyer turns to a consideration of "the scientific thing to do" in paragraph 58? What effect does that consideration have on you as a reader? Is that consideration related in any way to the proof Dreyer provides at the end of his account—the webbed hand beneath the glove?

SUGGESTIONS FOR WRITING

A. In the questions above, we have treated "Frogs" as an essay. Gerber and McFadden, in their fine introductory book *Loren Eiseley,* classify "Frogs" as a "first-person tall tale, owing much to the legacy of Twain, Bierce, and Poe." Select a tall tale by one of these writers and compare and contrast that tale with "Frogs." Decide whether you think "Frogs" is a tale or an essay and make that decision the point of an essay you will write about this classification problem. Support your conclusion by citing evidence from the two specimen pieces and from any other general sources about the two forms of literature, the tale and the essay. You might also consider the characteristics of other Eiseley essays in this collection. How do those essays differ from this piece? How are they the same?

B. Write a short essay about how Eiseley uses light and shadows to convey meaning.

C. Write a short account of how our knowledge of the "Eiseley" in "Willy" (the one who dances with the crane) gives us a better sense of the two "Eiseleys" in "Frogs."

D. Do a bit of research in the library on archetypes. Write a short report for the other students in your class outlining your findings; include a final paragraph about whether you find Dreyer's story more or less believable as a result of your research and explain why.

NINE

James Baldwin

(1924–1987)

James Baldwin was born in Harlem, the son of fundamentalist religious parents. Baldwin followed his father's vocation and became, at fourteen, a preacher. At seventeen he abandoned the ministry and devoted himself to the craft of writing. He had been writing all along, from early childhood, but his writing had been discouraged by his family in favor of the religion that overshadowed it.

Baldwin received institutional support in the form of fellowships to help sustain him while he wrote and published his first two novels: *Go Tell It on the Mountain* (1953) and *Giovanni's Room* (1956), both of which were written abroad. Sandwiched between these works was a collection of essays, *Notes of a Native Son* (1955), which many readers consider his finest work. More fiction and essays followed: *Nobody Knows My Name* (essays, 1961), *Another Country* (novel, 1962), *The Fire Next Time* (essay, 1963), *Going to Meet the Man* (stories, 1965)—and much more.

In his early essays, for which he has received considerable praise, Baldwin struggled to define himself—as an American, as a writer, and as a Black. (And for Baldwin the three are inextricably intertwined.) In coming to terms with what was, for him, the most difficult thing in his life—the fact that he was born a Negro, "and was forced, therefore, to effect some kind of truce with this reality"—Baldwin revealed himself to be a passionate and eloquent writer. His most frequent subject has been the relations between the races, about which he has noted sardonically, "the color of my skin makes me, automatically, an expert."

Baldwin has written of pain, of rage and bitterness, of persecution and paranoia, of identity and responsibility, of the relations between fathers and sons, and of the search for equanimity, understanding, and love. Regardless of title, occasion, and place of composition, his essays revolve around these subjects, often stressing the importance of accepting and understanding one another, whatever our differences of race, sex, culture, religion, or intellectual disposition.

"Stranger in the Village" emphasizes Baldwin's sense of alienation from the culture and history of white Europeans and Americans. The essay records his struggle to come to terms with his sense of exclusion, with his foreignness less as an American in Europe than as a Black in a white world. The subject of alienation is given a different twist in Baldwin's short story, "Sonny's Blues." There the estrangement felt by the narrator is an alienation from his family, his social class, and his past. The story records the narrator's struggle to reestablish a relationship with his brother, whose values and life-style differ from his own.

In addition to alienation, Baldwin's writing frequently explores racial issues. "Fifth Avenue Uptown: A Letter From Harlem" and "Notes of a Native Son" are devoted to the problem of race relations in America. In "Fifth Avenue" Baldwin works largely by description and comparison, providing incisive commentary after he takes us on a "tour" of Harlem. His purpose is to help us understand the despair and hopelessness of the black ghetto. In "Notes," more strictly autobiographical than any of his other essays, Baldwin combines a reminiscence of his father with an account of his funeral. He also narrates an incident that brought home to him a painful racial fact and an important personal revelation about his feelings toward white people. As one of Baldwin's most impressive attempts to explore problematic social issues through personal experience, "Notes of a Native Son" fulfills the writer's most important obligation: "to examine attitudes, to go beneath the surface, to tap the source."

In the prefatory essay to the collection *Notes of a Native Son,* Baldwin stressed the absolute priority of his personal experience for his writing. He put it this way: "One writes out of one thing only—one's own experience. . . . Everything depends on how relentlessly one forces from this experience the last drop, sweet or bitter, it can possibly give." That Baldwin's experience was bitter helped his writing as much as it may have hindered it. For he himself noted that "any writer . . . finds that the things which hurt him and the things which helped him cannot be divorced from each other." Baldwin's anguished experience was essential for his acute understanding of the hatred and bitterness in his own heart and of the bitter hatred at the heart of the racial antagonisms felt by many Americans.

Although Baldwin may have resigned from his religious ministry at seventeen, his writing, nonetheless, is strongly influenced by the style of pulpit oratory. It possesses the same strong emotional cast, a similar quality of exhortation, and a common vision of apocalypse. In its rhythm, in its imagery, and in its ethical imperatives, Baldwin's style reveals the influence of both the King James Bible and the storefront church—the two influences he has specifically mentioned as formative.

Preacher, polemicist, social critic, autobiographer, essayist—Baldwin brought together repeatedly, in deeply affecting ways, public issues and private agonies with relentless candor and inexorable logic. On the success of his best essays rests his fame and fate as a writer, on what he himself claimed is the only real concern of the artist: "to recreate out of the disorder of life that order which is art."

Stranger in the Village

1 From all available evidence no black man had ever set foot in this tiny Swiss village before I came. I was told before arriving that I would probably be a "sight" for the village; I took this to mean that people of my complexion were rarely seen in Switzerland, and also that city people are always something of a "sight" outside of the city. It did not occur to me—possibly because I am an American—that there could be people anywhere who had never seen a Negro.

2 It is a fact that cannot be explained on the basis of the inaccessibility of the village. The village is very high, but it is only four hours from Milan and three hours

from Lausanne. It is true that it is virtually unknown. Few people making plans for a holiday would elect to come here. On the other hand, the villagers are able, presumably, to come and go as they please—which they do: to another town at the foot of the mountain, with a population of approximately five thousand, the nearest place to see a movie or go to the bank. In the village there is no movie house, no bank, no library, no theater; very few radios, one jeep, one station wagon; and, at the moment, one typewriter, mine, an invention which the woman next door to me here had never seen. There are about six hundred people living here, all Catholic—I conclude this from the fact that the Catholic church is open all year round, whereas the Protestant chapel, set off on a hill a little removed from the village, is open only in the summertime when the tourists arrive. There are four or five hotels, all closed now, and four or five *bistros,* of which, however, only two do any business during the winter. These two do not do a great deal, for life in the village seems to end around nine or ten o'clock. There are a few stores, butcher, baker, *épicerie,* a hardware store, and a money-changer—who cannot change travelers' checks, but must send them down to the bank, an operation which takes two or three days. There is something called the *Ballet Haus,* closed in the winter and used for God knows what, certainly not ballet, during the summer. There seems to be only one schoolhouse in the village, and this for the quite young children; I suppose this to mean that their older brothers and sisters at some point descend from these mountains in order to complete their education—possibly, again, to the town just below. The landscape is absolutely forbidding, mountains towering on all four sides, ice and snow as far as the eye can reach. In this white wilderness, men and women and children move all day, carrying washing, wood, buckets of milk or water, sometimes skiing on Sunday afternoons. All week long boys and young men are to be seen shoveling snow off the rooftops, or dragging wood down from the forest in sleds.

3 The village's only real attraction, which explains the tourist season, is the hot spring water. A disquietingly high proportion of these tourists are cripples, or semicripples, who come year after year—from other parts of Switzerland, usually—to take the waters. This lends the village, at the height of the season, a rather terrifying air of sanctity, as though it were a lesser Lourdes. There is often something beautiful, there is always something awful, in the spectacle of a person who has lost one of his faculties, a faculty he never questioned until it was gone, and who struggles to recover it. Yet people remain people, on crutches or indeed on deathbeds; and wherever I passed, the first summer I was here, among the native villagers or among the lame, a wind passed with me—of astonishment, curiosity, amusement, and outrage. That first summer I stayed two weeks and never intended to return. But I did return in the winter, to work; the village offers, obviously, no distractions whatever and has the further advantage of being extremely cheap. Now it is winter again, a year later, and I am here again. Everyone in the village knows my name, though they scarcely ever use it, knows that I come from America—though, this, apparently, they will never really believe: black men come from Africa—and everyone knows that I am the friend of the son of a woman who was born here, and that I am staying in their chalet. But I remain as much a stranger today as I was the first day I arrived, and the children shout *Neger! Neger!* as I walk along the streets.

4 It must be admitted that in the beginning I was far too shocked to have any

real reaction. In so far as I reacted at all, I reacted by trying to be pleasant—it being a great part of the American Negro's education (long before he goes to school) that he must make people "like" him. This smile-and-the-world-smiles-with-you routine worked about as well in this situation as it had in the situation for which it was designed, which is to say that it did not work at all. No one, after all, can be liked whose human weight and complexity cannot be, or has not been, admitted. My smile was simply another unheard-of phenomenon which allowed them to see my teeth—they did not, really, see my smile and I began to think that, should I take to snarling, no one would notice any difference. All of the physical characteristics of the Negro which had caused me, in America, a very different and almost forgotten pain were nothing less than miraculous—or infernal—in the eyes of the village people. Some thought my hair was the color of tar, that it had the texture of wire, or the texture of cotton. It was jocularly suggested that I might let it all grow long and make myself a winter coat. If I sat in the sun for more than five minutes some daring creature was certain to come along and gingerly put his fingers on my hair, as though he were afraid of an electric shock, or put his hand on my hand, astonished that the color did not rub off. In all of this, in which it must be conceded there was the charm of genuine wonder and in which there was certainly no element of intentional unkindness, there was yet no suggestion that I was human: I was simply a living wonder.

5 I knew that they did not mean to be unkind, and I know it now; it is necessary, nevertheless, for me to repeat this to myself each time that I walk out of the chalet. The children who shout *Neger!* have no way of knowing the echoes this sound raises in me. They are brimming with good humor and the more daring swell with pride when I stop to speak with them. Just the same, there are days when I cannot pause and smile, when I have no heart to play with them; when, indeed, I mutter sourly to myself, exactly as I muttered on the streets of a city these children have never seen, when I was no bigger than these children are now: *Your* mother *was a nigger.* Joyce is right about history being a nightmare—but it may be the nightmare from which no one *can* awaken. People are trapped in history and history is trapped in them.

6 There is a custom in the village—I am told it is repeated in many villages—of "buying" African natives for the purpose of converting them to Christianity. There stands in the church all year round a small box with a slot for money, decorated with a black figurine, and into this box the villagers drop their francs. During the *carnaval* which precedes Lent, two village children have their faces blackened—out of which bloodless darkness their blue eyes shine like ice—and fantastic horsehair wigs are placed on their blond heads; thus disguised, they solicit among the villagers for money for the missionaries in Africa. Between the box in the church and the blackened children, the village "bought" last year six or eight African natives. This was reported to me with pride by the wife of one of the *bistro* owners and I was careful to express astonishment and pleasure at the solicitude shown by the village for the souls of black folk. The *bistro* owner's wife beamed with a pleasure far more genuine than my own and seemed to feel that I might now breathe more easily concerning the souls of at least six of my kinsmen.

7 I tried not to think of these so lately baptized kinsmen, of the price paid for

them, or the peculiar price they themselves would pay, and said nothing about my father, who having taken his own conversion too literally never, at bottom, forgave the white world (which he described as heathen) for having saddled him with a Christ in whom, to judge at least from their treatment of him, they themselves no longer believed. I thought of white men arriving for the first time in an African village, strangers there, as I am a stranger here, and tried to imagine the astounded populace touching their hair and marveling at the color of their skin. But there is a great difference between being the first white man to be seen by Africans and being the first black man to be seen by whites. The white man takes the astonishment as tribute, for he arrives to conquer and to convert the natives, whose inferiority in relation to himself is not even to be questioned; whereas I, without a thought of conquest, find myself among a people whose culture controls me, has even, in a sense, created me, people who have cost me more in anguish and rage than they will ever know, who yet do not even know of my existence. The astonishment with which I might have greeted them, should they have stumbled into my African village a few hundred years ago, might have rejoiced their hearts. But the astonishment with which they greet me today can only poison mine.

8 And this is so despite everything I may do to feel differently, despite my friendly conversations with the *bistro* owner's wife, despite their three-year-old son who has at last become my friend, despite the *saluts* and *bonsoirs* which I exchange with people as I walk, despite the fact that I know that no individual can be taken to task for what history is doing, or has done. I say that the culture of these people controls me—but they can scarcely be held responsible for European culture. America comes out of Europe, but these people have never seen America, nor have most of them seen more of Europe than the hamlet at the foot of their mountain. Yet they move with an authority which I shall never have; and they regard me, quite rightly, not only as a stranger in their village but as a suspect latecomer, bearing no credentials, to everything they have—however unconsciously—inherited.

9 For this village, even were it incomparably more remote and incredibly more primitive, is the West, the West onto which I have been so strangely grafted. These people cannot be, from the point of view of power, strangers anywhere in the world; they have made the modern world, in effect, even if they do not know it. The most illiterate among them is related, in a way that I am not, to Dante, Shakespeare, Michelangelo, Aeschylus, Da Vinci, Rembrandt, and Racine; the cathedral at Chartres says something to them which it cannot say to me, as indeed would New York's Empire State Building, should anyone here ever see it. Out of their hymns and dances come Beethoven and Bach. Go back a few centuries and they are in their full glory—but I am in Africa, watching the conquerors arrive.

10 The rage of the disesteemed is personally fruitless, but it is also absolutely inevitable; this rage, so generally discounted, so little understood even among the people whose daily bread it is, is one of the things that makes history. Rage can only with difficulty, and never entirely, be brought under the domination of the intelligence and is therefore not susceptible to any arguments whatever. This is a fact which ordinary representatives of the *Herrenvolk,* having never felt this rage and being unable to imagine it, quite fail to understand. Also, rage cannot be hidden, it can only be dissembled. This dissembling deludes the thoughtless, and strengthens

rage and adds, to rage, contempt. There are, no doubt, as many ways of coping with the resulting complex of tensions as there are black men in the world, but no black man can hope ever to be entirely liberated from this internal warfare—rage, dissembling, and contempt having inevitably accompanied his first realization of the power of white men. What is crucial here is that, since white men represent in the black man's world so heavy a weight, white men have for black men a reality which is far from being reciprocal; and hence all black men have toward all white men an attitude which is designed, really, either to rob the white man of the jewel of his naïveté, or else to make it cost him dear.

11 The black man insists, by whatever means he finds at his disposal, that the white man cease to regard him as an exotic rarity and recognize him as a human being. This is a very charged and difficult moment, for there is a great deal of will power involved in the white man's naïveté. Most people are not naturally reflective any more than they are naturally malicious, and the white man prefers to keep the black man at a certain human remove because it is easier for him thus to preserve his simplicity and avoid being called to account for crimes committed by his forefathers, or his neighbors. He is inescapably aware, nevertheless, that he is in a better position in the world than black men are, nor can he quite put to death the suspicion that he is hated by black men therefore. He does not wish to be hated, neither does he wish to change places, and at this point in his uneasiness he can scarcely avoid having recourse to those legends which white men have created about black men, the most usual effect of which is that the white man finds himself enmeshed, so to speak, in his own language which describes hell, as well as the attributes which lead one to hell, as being as black as night.

12 Every legend, moreover, contains its residuum of truth, and the root function of language is to control the universe by describing it. It is of quite considerable significance that black men remain, in the imagination, and in overwhelming numbers in fact, beyond the disciplines of salvation; and this despite the fact that the West has been "buying" African natives for centuries. There is, I should hazard, an instantaneous necessity to be divorced from this so visibly unsaved stranger, in whose heart, moreover, one cannot guess what dreams of vengeance are being nourished; and, at the same time, there are few things on earth more attractive than the idea of the unspeakable liberty which is allowed the unredeemed. When, beneath the black mask, a human being begins to make himself felt one cannot escape a certain awful wonder as to what kind of human being it is. What one's imagination makes of other people is dictated, of course, by the laws of one's own personality and it is one of the ironies of black-white relations that, by means of what the white man imagines the black man to be, the black man is enabled to know who the white man is.

13 I have said, for example, that I am as much a stranger in this village today as I was the first summer I arrived, but this is not quite true. The villagers wonder less about the texture of my hair than they did then, and wonder rather more about me. And the fact that their wonder now exists on another level is reflected in their attitudes and in their eyes. There are the children who make those delightful, hilarious, sometimes astonishingly grave overtures of friendship in the unpredictable fashion of children; other children, having been taught that the devil is a black man,

scream in genuine anguish as I approach. Some of the older women never pass without a friendly greeting, never pass, indeed, if it seems that they will be able to engage me in conversation; other women look down or look away or rather contemptuously smirk. Some of the men drink with me and suggest that I learn how to ski—partly, I gather, because they cannot imagine what I would look like on skis—and want to know if I am married, and ask questions about my *métier.* But some of the men have accused *le sale nègre*—behind my back—of stealing wood and there is already in the eyes of some of them that peculiar, intent, paranoiac malevolence which one sometimes surprises in the eyes of American white men when, out walking with their Sunday girl, they see a Negro male approach.

14 There is a dreadful abyss between the streets of this village and the streets of the city in which I was born, between the children who shout *Neger!* today and those who shouted *Nigger!* yesterday—the abyss is experience, the American experience. The syllable hurled behind me today expresses, above all, wonder: I am a stranger here. But I am not a stranger in America and the same syllable riding on the American air expresses the war my presence has occasioned in the American soul.

15 For this village brings home to me this fact: that there was a day, and not really a very distant day, when Americans were scarcely Americans at all but discontented Europeans, facing a great unconquered continent and strolling, say, into a marketplace and seeing black men for the first time. The shock this spectacle afforded is suggested, surely, by the promptness with which they decided that these black men were not really men but cattle. It is true that the necessity on the part of the settlers of the New World of reconciling their moral assumptions with the fact—and the necessity—of slavery enhanced immensely the charm of this idea, and it is also true that this idea expresses, with a truly American bluntness, the attitude which to varying extents all masters have had toward all slaves.

16 But between all former slaves and slave-owners and the drama which begins for Americans over three hundred years ago at Jamestown, there are at least two differences to be observed. The American Negro slave could not suppose, for one thing, as slaves in past epochs had supposed and often done, that he would ever be able to wrest the power from his master's hands. This was a supposition which the modern era, which was to bring about such vast changes in the aims and dimensions of power, put to death; it only begins, in unprecedented fashion, and with dreadful implications, to be resurrected today. But even had this supposition persisted with undiminished force, the American Negro slave could not have used it to lend his condition dignity, for the reason that this supposition rests on another: that the slave in exile yet remains related to his past, has some means—if only in memory—of revering and sustaining the forms of his former life, is able, in short, to maintain his identity.

17 This was not the case with the American Negro slave. He is unique among the black men of the world in that his past was taken from him, almost literally, at one blow. One wonders what on earth the first slave found to say to the first dark child he bore. I am told that there are Haitians able to trace their ancestry back to African kings, but any American Negro wishing to go back so far will find his journey through time abruptly arrested by the signature on the bill of sale which served as the entrance paper for his ancestor. At the time—to say nothing of the circumstances—of the

enslavement of the captive black man who was to become the American Negro, there was not the remotest possibility that he would ever take power from his master's hands. There was no reason to suppose that his situation would ever change, nor was there, shortly, anything to indicate that his situation had ever been different. It was his necessity, in the words of E. Franklin Frazier, to find a "motive for living under American culture or die." The identity of the American Negro comes out of this extreme situation, and the evolution of this identity was a source of the most intolerable anxiety in the minds and the lives of his masters.

18 For the history of the American Negro is unique also in this: that the question of his humanity, and of his rights therefore as a human being, became a burning one for several generations of Americans, so burning a question that it ultimately became one of those used to divide the nation. It is out of this argument that the venom of the epithet *Nigger!* is derived. It is an argument which Europe has never had, and hence Europe quite sincerely fails to understand how or why the argument arose in the first place, why its effects are so frequently disastrous and always so unpredictable, why it refuses until today to be entirely settled. Europe's black possessions remained—and do remain—in Europe's colonies, at which remove they represented no threat whatever to European identity. If they posed any problem at all for the European conscience, it was a problem which remained comfortingly abstract: in effect, the black man, *as a man,* did not exist for Europe. But in America, even as a slave, he was an inescapable part of the general social fabric and no American could escape having an attitude toward him. Americans attempt until today to make an abstraction of the Negro, but the very nature of these abstractions reveals the tremendous effects the presence of the Negro has had on the American character.

19 When one considers the history of the Negro in America it is of the greatest importance to recognize that the moral beliefs of a person, or a people, are never really as tenuous as life—which is not moral—very often causes them to appear; these create for them a frame of reference and a necessary hope, the hope being that when life has done its worst they will be enabled to rise above themselves and to triumph over life. Life would scarcely be bearable if this hope did not exist. Again, even when the worst has been said, to betray a belief is not by any means to have put oneself beyond its power; the betrayal of a belief is not the same thing as ceasing to believe. If this were not so there would be no moral standards in the world at all. Yet one must also recognize that morality is based on ideas and that all ideas are dangerous—dangerous because ideas can only lead to action and where the action leads no man can say. And dangerous in this respect: that confronted with the impossibility of remaining faithful to one's beliefs, and the equal impossibility of becoming free of them, one can be driven to the most inhuman excesses. The ideas on which American beliefs are based are not, though Americans often seem to think so, ideas which originated in America. They came out of Europe. And the establishment of democracy on the American continent was scarcely as radical a break with the past as was the necessity, which Americans faced, of broadening this concept to include black men.

20 This was, literally, a hard necessity. It was impossible, for one thing, for Americans to abandon their beliefs, not only because these beliefs alone seemed able to justify the sacrifices they had endured and the blood that they had spilled, but

also because these beliefs afforded them their only bulwark against a moral chaos as absolute as the physical chaos of the continent it was their destiny to conquer. But in the situation in which Americans found themselves, these beliefs threatened an idea which, whether or not one likes to think so, is the very warp and woof of the heritage of the West, the idea of white supremacy.

21 Americans have made themselves notorious by the shrillness and the brutality with which they have insisted on this idea, but they did not invent it; and it has escaped the world's notice that those very excesses of which Americans have been guilty imply a certain, unprecedented uneasiness over the idea's life and power, if not, indeed, the idea's validity. The idea of white supremacy rests simply on the fact that white men are the creators of civilization (the present civilization, which is the only one that matters; all previous civilizations are simply "contributions" to our own) and are therefore civilization's guardians and defenders. Thus it was impossible for Americans to accept the black man as one of themselves, for to do so was to jeopardize their status as white men. But not so to accept him was to deny his human reality, his human weight and complexity, and the strain of denying the overwhelmingly undeniable forced Americans into rationalizations so fantastic that they approached the pathological.

22 At the root of the American Negro problem is the necessity of the American white man to find a way of living with the Negro in order to be able to live with himself. And the history of this problem can be reduced to the means used by Americans—lynch law and law, segregation and legal acceptance, terrorization and concession—either to come to terms with this necessity, or to find a way around it, or (most usually) to find a way of doing both these things at once. The resulting spectacle, at once foolish and dreadful, led someone to make the quite accurate observation that "the negro-in-America is a form of insanity which overtakes white men."

23 In this long battle, a battle by no means finished, the unforeseeable effects of which will be felt by many future generations, the white man's motive was the protection of his identity; the black man was motivated by the need to establish an identity. And despite the terrorization which the Negro in America endured and endures sporadically until today, despite the cruel and totally inescapable ambivalence of his status in his country, the battle for his identity has long ago been won. He is not a visitor to the West, but a citizen there, an American; as American as the Americans who despise him, the Americans who fear him, the Americans who love him—the Americans who became less than themselves, or rose to be greater than themselves by virtue of the fact that the challenge he represented was inescapable. He is perhaps the only black man in the world whose relationship to white men is more terrible, more subtle, and more meaningful than the relationship of bitter possessed to uncertain possessor. His survival depended, and his development depends, on his ability to turn his peculiar status in the Western world to his own advantage and, it may be, to the very great advantage of that world. It remains for him to fashion out of his experience that which will give him sustenance, and a voice.

24 The cathedral at Chartres, I have said, says something to the people of this village which it cannot say to me; but it is important to understand that this cathedral says something to me which it cannot say to them. Perhaps they are struck by the power of the spires, the glory of the windows; but they have known God,

after all, longer than I have known him, and in a different way, and I am terrified by the slippery bottomless well to be found in the crypt, down which heretics were hurled to death, and by the obscene, inescapable gargoyles jutting out of the stone and seeming to say that God and the devil can never be divorced. I doubt that the villagers think of the devil when they face a cathedral because they have never been identified with the devil. But I must accept the status which myth, if nothing else, gives me in the West before I can hope to change the myth.

25 Yet, if the American Negro has arrived at his identity by virtue of the absoluteness of his estrangement from his past, American white men still nourish the illusion that there is some means of recovering the European innocence, of returning to a state in which black men do not exist. This is one of the greatest errors Americans can make. The identity they fought so hard to protect has, by virtue of that battle, undergone a change: Americans are as unlike any other white people in the world as it is possible to be. I do not think, for example, that it is too much to suggest that the American vision of the world—which allows so little reality, generally speaking, for any of the darker forces in human life, which tends until today to paint moral issues in glaring black and white—owes a great deal to the battle waged by Americans to maintain between themselves and black men a human separation which could not be bridged. It is only now beginning to be borne in on us—very faintly, it must be admitted, very slowly, and very much against our will—that this vision of the world is dangerously inaccurate, and perfectly useless. For it protects our moral high-mindedness at the terrible expense of weakening our grasp of reality. People who shut their eyes to reality simply invite their own destruction, and anyone who insists on remaining in a state of innocence long after that innocence is dead turns himself into a monster.

26 The time has come to realize that the interracial drama acted out on the American continent has not only created a new black man, it has created a new white man, too. No road whatever will lead Americans back to the simplicity of this European village where white men still have the luxury of looking on me as a stranger. I am not, really, a stranger any longer for any American alive. One of the things that distinguishes Americans from other people is that no other people has ever been so deeply involved in the lives of black men, and vice versa. This fact faced, with all its implications, it can be seen that the history of the American Negro problem is not merely shameful, it is also something of an achievement. For even when the worst has been said, it must also be added that the perpetual challenge posed by this problem was always, somehow, perpetually met. It is precisely this black-white experience which may prove of indispensable value to us in the world we face today. This world is white no longer, and it will never be white again.

(1953)

QUESTIONS

Thought and Structure

1. What do you think Baldwin means when he writes that no one can be appreciated or liked "whose human weight and complexity cannot be . . . admitted"?

2. What impression of the Swiss villagers does Baldwin convey?
3. Explain what Baldwin felt about his experience as a stranger in the village. In what ways, specifically, was he a "stranger"?
4. What significant contrasts does Baldwin develop between the villagers and himself?
5. What point does Baldwin make about race relations in America? What does his experience in Europe contribute to this point?

Style and Strategy

6. Why does Baldwin open the essay with an inventory of details about the Swiss village?
7. Notice the use of repetition in the opening sentence of paragraph 8. Why do you think Baldwin wrote this long sentence with its repeating "despite"?
8. Baldwin includes a number of historical details. What purpose do they serve and how necessary are they?
9. Consider the way Baldwin blends long and short sentences in paragraph 19. Notice his alternation of long and short; notice too the way he varies his sentence openings. Consider, finally, the way Baldwin's sentence openings create continuity within the paragraph.
10. What words recur repeatedly in paragraph 19? Why? To what effect?

SUGGESTIONS FOR WRITING

A. In an argumentative essay agree or disagree with this statement of Baldwin's:

> People who shut their eyes to reality simply invite their own destruction, and anyone who insists on remaining in a state of innocence long after that innocence is dead turns himself into a monster.

B. Write an imitation of the sentence discussed in question 7.

C. Write an imitation of paragraph 19, staying as close as possible to the varied lengths, forms, and openings of Baldwin's sentences. Choose your own topic.

Fifth Avenue, Uptown: A Letter from Harlem

1 There is a housing project standing now where the house in which we grew up once stood, and one of those stunted city trees is snarling where our doorway used to be. This is on the rehabilitated side of the avenue. The other side of the avenue—for progress takes time—has not been rehabilitated yet and it looks exactly as it looked in the days when we sat with our noses pressed against the windowpane, longing to be allowed to go "across the street." The grocery store which gave us credit is still there, and there can be no doubt that it is still giving credit. The people in the project certainly need it—far more, indeed, than they ever needed the project. The last time I passed by, the Jewish proprietor was still standing among his shelves, looking sadder and heavier but scarcely any older. Farther down the block stands

the shoe-repair store in which our shoes were repaired until reparation became impossible and in which, then, we bought all our "new" ones. The Negro proprietor is still in the window, head down, working at the leather.

2 These two, I imagine, could tell a long tale if they would (perhaps they would be glad to if they could), having watched so many, for so long, struggling in the fishhooks, the barbed wire, of this avenue.

3 The avenue is elsewhere the renowned and elegant Fifth. The area I am describing, which, in today's gang parlance, would be called "the turf," is bounded by Lenox Avenue on the west, the Harlem River on the east, 135th Street on the north, and 130th Street on the south. We never lived beyond these boundaries; this is where we grew up. Walking along 145th Street—for example—familiar as it is, and similar, does not have the same impact because I do not know any of the people on the block. But when I turn east on 131st Street and Lenox Avenue, there is first a soda-pop joint, then a shoeshine "parlor," then a grocery store, then a dry cleaners', then the houses. All along the street there are people who watched me grow up, people who grew up with me, people I watched grow up along with my brothers and sisters; and, sometimes in my arms, sometimes underfoot, sometimes at my shoulder—or on it—their children, a riot, a forest of children, who include my nieces and nephews.

4 When we reach the end of this long block, we find ourselves on wide, filthy, hostile Fifth Avenue, facing that project which hangs over the avenue like a monument to the folly, and the cowardice, of good intentions. All along the block, for anyone who knows it, are immense human gaps, like craters. These gaps are not created merely by those who have moved away, inevitably into some other ghetto; or by those who have risen, almost always into a greater capacity for self-loathing and self-delusion; or yet by those who, by whatever means—War II, the Korean war, a policeman's gun or billy, a gang war, a brawl, madness, an overdose of heroin, or, simply, unnatural exhaustion—are dead. I am talking about those who are left, and I am talking principally about the young. What are they doing? Well, some, a minority, are fanatical churchgoers, members of the more extreme of the Holy Roller sects. Many, many more are "moslems," by affiliation or sympathy, that is to say that they are united by nothing more—and nothing less—than a hatred of the white world and all its works. They are present, for example, at every Buy Black street-corner meeting—meetings in which the speaker urges his hearers to cease trading with white men and establish a separate economy. Neither the speaker nor his hearers can possibly do this, of course, since Negroes do not own General Motors or RCA or the A & P, nor, indeed, do they own more than a wholly insufficient fraction of anything else in Harlem (those who *do* own anything are more interested in their profits than in their fellows). But these meetings nevertheless keep alive in the participators a certain pride of bitterness without which, however futile this bitterness may be, they could scarcely remain alive at all. Many have given up. They stay home and watch the TV screen, living on the earnings of their parents, cousins, brothers, or uncles, and only leave the house to go to the movies or to the nearest bar. "How're you making it?" one may ask, running into them along the block, or in the bar. "Oh, I'm TV-ing it"; with the saddest, sweetest, most shamefaced of smiles, and from a great distance. This distance one is compelled to respect; anyone

who has traveled so far will not easily be dragged again into the world. There are further retreats, of course, than the TV screen or the bar. There are those who are simply sitting on their stoops, "stoned," animated for a moment only, and hideously, by the approach of someone who may lend them the money for a "fix." Or by the approach of someone from whom they can purchase it, one of the shrewd ones, on the way to prison or just coming out.

5 And the others, who have avoided all of these deaths, get up in the morning and go downtown to meet "the man." They work in the white man's world all day and come home in the evening to this fetid block. They struggle to instill in their children some private sense of honor or dignity which will help the child to survive. This means, of course, that they must struggle, stolidly, incessantly, to keep this sense alive in themselves, in spite of the insults, the indifference, and the cruelty they are certain to encounter in their working day. They patiently browbeat the landlord into fixing the heat, the plaster, the plumbing; this demands prodigious patience; nor is patience usually enough. In trying to make their hovels habitable, they are perpetually throwing good money after bad. Such frustration, so long endured, is driving many strong, admirable men and women whose only crime is color to the very gates of paranoia.

6 One remembers them from another time—playing handball in the playground, going to church, wondering if they were going to be promoted at school. One remembers their return. Perhaps one remembers their wedding day. And one sees where the girl is now—vainly looking for salvation from some other embittered, trussed, and struggling boy—and sees the all-but-abandoned children in the streets.

7 Now I am perfectly aware that there are other slums in which white men are fighting for their lives, and mainly losing. I know that blood is also flowing through those streets and that the human damage there is incalculable. People are continually pointing out to me the wretchedness of white people in order to console me for the wretchedness of blacks. But an itemized account of the American failure does not console me and it should not console anyone else. That hundreds of thousands of white people are living, in effect, no better than the "niggers" is not a fact to be regarded with complacency. The social and moral bankruptcy suggested by this fact is of the bitterest, most terrifying kind.

8 The people, however, who believe that this democratic anguish has some consoling value are always pointing out that So-and-So, white, and So-and-So, black, rose from the slums into the big time. The existence—the public existence—of, say, Frank Sinatra and Sammy Davis, Jr. proves to them that America is still the land of opportunity and that inequalities vanish before the determined will. It proves nothing of the sort. The determined will is rare—at the moment, in this country, it is unspeakably rare—and the inequalities suffered by the many are in no way justified by the rise of a few. A few have always risen—in every country, every era, and in the teeth of regimes which can by no stretch of the imagination be thought of as free. Not all of these people, it is worth remembering, left the world better than they found it. The determined will is rare, but it is not invariably benevolent. Furthermore, the American equation of success with the big times reveals an awful disrespect for human life and human achievement. This equation has placed our cities among the most dangerous in the world and has placed our youth among the most empty and most

bewildered. The situation of our youth is not mysterious. Children have never been very good at listening to their elders, but they have never failed to imitate them. They must, they have no other models. That is exactly what our children are doing. They are imitating our immorality, our disrespect for the pain of others.

9 All other slum dwellers, when the bank account permits it, can move out of the slum and vanish altogether from the eye of persecution. No Negro in this country has ever made that much money and it will be a long time before any Negro does. The Negroes in Harlem, who have no money, spend what they have on such gimcracks as they are sold. These include "wider" TV screens, more "faithful" hi-fi sets, more "powerful" cars, all of which, of course, are obsolete long before they are paid for. Anyone who has ever struggled with poverty knows how extremely expensive it is to be poor; and if one is a member of a captive population, economically speaking, one's feet have simply been placed on the treadmill forever. One is victimized, economically, in a thousand ways—rent, for example, or car insurance. Go shopping one day in Harlem—for anything—and compare Harlem prices and quality with those downtown.

10 The people who have managed to get off this block have only got as far as a more respectable ghetto. This respectable ghetto does not even have the advantages of the disreputable one—friends, neighbors, a familiar church, and friendly tradesmen; and it is not, moreover, in the nature of any ghetto to remain respectable long. Every Sunday, people who have left the block take the lonely ride back, dragging their increasingly discontented children with them. They spend the day talking, not always with words, about the trouble they've seen and the trouble—one must watch their eyes as they watch their children—they are only too likely to see. For children do not like ghettos. It takes them nearly no time to discover exactly why they are there.

11 The projects in Harlem are hated. They are hated almost as much as policemen, and this is saying a great deal. And they are hated for the same reason: both reveal, unbearably, the real attitude of the white world, no matter how many liberal speeches are made, no matter how many lofty editorials are written, no matter how many civil-rights commissions are set up.

12 The projects are hideous, of course, there being a law, apparently respected throughout the world, that popular housing shall be as cheerless as a prison. They are lumped all over Harlem, colorless, bleak, high, and revolting. The wide windows look out on Harlem's invincible and indescribable squalor: the Park Avenue railroad tracks, around which, about forty years ago, the present dark community began; the unrehabilitated houses, bowed down, it would seem, under the great weight of frustration and bitterness they contain; the dark, the ominous schoolhouses from which the child may emerge maimed, blinded, hooked, or enraged for life; and the churches, churches, block upon block of churches, niched in the walls like cannon in the walls of a fortress. Even if the administration of the projects were not so insanely humiliating (for example: one must report raises in salary to the management, which will then eat up the profit by raising one's rent; the management has the right to know who is staying in your apartment; the management can ask you to leave, at their discretion), the projects would still be hated because they are an insult to the meanest intelligence.

13 Harlem got its first private project, Riverton*—which is now, naturally, a slum—about twelve years ago because at that time Negroes were not allowed to live in Stuyvesant Town. Harlem watched Riverton go up, therefore, in the most violent bitterness of spirit, and hated it long before the builders arrived. They began hating it at about the time people began moving out of their condemned houses to make room for this additional proof of how thoroughly the white world despised them. And they had scarcely moved in, naturally, before they began smashing windows, defacing walls, urinating in the elevators, and fornicating in the playgrounds. Liberals, both white and black, were appalled at the spectacle. I was appalled by the liberal innocence—or cynicism, which comes out in practice as much the same thing. Other people were delighted to be able to point to proof positive that nothing could be done to better the lot of the colored people. They were, and are, right in one respect: that nothing can be done as long as they are treated like colored people. The people in Harlem know they are living there because white people do not think they are good enough to live anywhere else. No amount of "improvement" can sweeten this fact. Whatever money is now being earmarked to improve this, or any other ghetto, might as well be burnt. A ghetto can be improved in one way only: out of existence.

14 Similarly, the only way to police a ghetto is to be oppressive. None of the Police Commissioner's men, even with the best will in the world, have any way of understanding the lives led by the people they swagger about in twos and threes controlling. Their very presence is an insult, and it would be, even if they spent their entire day feeding gumdrops to children. They represent the force of the white world, and that world's real intentions are, simply, for that world's criminal profit and ease, to keep the black man corraled up here, in his place. The badge, the gun in the holster, and the swinging club make vivid what will happen should his rebellion become overt. Rare, indeed, is the Harlem citizen, from the most circumspect church member to the most shiftless adolescent, who does not have a long tale to tell of police incompetence, injustice, or brutality. I myself have witnessed and endured it more than once. The businessmen and racketeers also have a story. And so do the prostitutes. (And this is not, perhaps, the place to discuss Harlem's very complex attitude toward black policemen, nor the reasons, according to Harlem, that they are nearly all downtown.)

15 It is hard, on the other hand, to blame the policeman, blank, good-natured, thoughtless, and insuperably innocent, for being such a perfect representative of the people he serves. He, too, believes in good intentions and is astounded and offended when they are not taken for the deed. He has never, himself, done anything for which to be hated—which of us has?—and yet he is facing, daily and nightly, people

---

*The inhabitants of Riverton were much embittered by this description; they have, apparently, forgotten how their project came into being; and have repeatedly informed me that I cannot possibly be referring to Riverton, but to another housing project which is directly across the street. It is quite clear, I think, that I have no interest in accusing any individuals or families of the depredations herein described: but neither can I deny the evidence of my own eyes. Nor do I blame anyone in Harlem for making the best of a dreadful bargain. But anyone who lives in Harlem and imagines that he has *not* struck this bargain, or that what he takes to be his status (in whose eyes?) protects him against the common pain, demoralization, and danger, is simply self deluded.

who would gladly see him dead, and he knows it. There is no way for him not to know it: there are few things under heaven more unnerving than the silent, accumulating contempt and hatred of a people. He moves through Harlem, therefore, like an occupying soldier in a bitterly hostile country; which is precisely what, and where, he is, and is the reason he walks in twos and threes. And he is not the only one who knows why he is always in company: the people who are watching him know why, too. Any street meeting, sacred or secular, which he and his colleagues uneasily cover has as its explicit or implicit burden the cruelty and injustice of the white domination. And these days, of course, in terms increasingly vivid and jubilant, it speaks of the end of that domination. The white policeman standing on a Harlem street corner finds himself at the very center of the revolution now occurring in the world. He is not prepared for it—naturally, nobody is—and, what is possibly much more to the point, he is exposed, as few white people are, to the anguish of the black people around him. Even if he is gifted with the merest mustard grain of imagination, something must seep in. He cannot avoid observing that some of the children, in spite of their color, remind him of children he has known and loved, perhaps even of his own children. He knows that he certainly does not want *his* children living this way. He can retreat from his uneasiness in only one direction: into a callousness which very shortly becomes second nature. He becomes more callous, the population becomes more hostile, the situation grows more tense, and the police force is increased. One day, to everyone's astonishment, someone drops a match in the powder keg and everything blows up. Before the dust has settled or the blood congealed, editorials, speeches, and civil-rights commissions are loud in the land, demanding to know what happened. What happened is that Negroes want to be treated like men.

16 *Negroes want to be treated like men:* a perfectly straightforward statement, containing only seven words. People who have mastered Kant, Hegel, Shakespeare, Marx, Freud, and the Bible find this statement utterly impenetrable. The idea seems to threaten profound, barely conscious assumptions. A kind of panic paralyzes their features, as though they found themselves trapped on the edge of a steep place. I once tried to describe to a very well-known American intellectual the conditions among Negroes in the South. My recital disturbed him and made him indignant; and he asked me in perfect innocence, "Why don't all the Negroes in the South move North?" I tried to explain what *has* happened, unfailingly, whenever a significant body of Negroes move North. They do not escape Jim Crow: they merely encounter another, not-less-deadly variety. They do not move to Chicago, they move to the South Side; they do not move to New York, they move to Harlem. The pressure within the ghetto causes the ghetto walls to expand, and this expansion is always violent. White people hold the line as long as they can, and in as many ways as they can, from verbal intimidation to physical violence. But inevitably the border which has divided the ghetto from the rest of the world falls into the hands of the ghetto. The white people fall back bitterly before the black horde; the landlords make a tidy profit by raising the rent, chopping up the rooms, and all but dispensing with the upkeep; and what has once been a neighborhood turns into a "turf." This is precisely what happened when the Puerto Ricans arrived in their thousands—and the bitterness thus caused is, as I write, being fought out all up and down those streets.

17 Northerners indulge in an extremely dangerous luxury. They seem to feel that because they fought on the right side during the Civil War, and won, they have earned the right merely to deplore what is going on in the South, without taking any responsibility for it; and that they can ignore what is happening in Northern cities because what is happening in Little Rock or Birmingham is worse. Well, in the first place, it is not possible for anyone who has not endured both to know which is "worse." I know Negroes who prefer the South and white Southerners, because "At least there, you haven't got to play any guessing games!" The guessing games referred to have driven more than one Negro into the narcotics ward, the madhouse, or the river. I know another Negro, a man very dear to me, who says, with conviction and with truth, "The spirit of the South is the spirit of America." He was born in the North and did his military training in the South. He did not, as far as I can gather, find the South "worse"; he found it, if anything, all too familiar. In the second place, though, even if Birmingham *is* worse, no doubt Johannesburg, South Africa, beats it by several miles, and Buchenwald was one of the worst things that ever happened in the entire history of the world. The world has never lacked for horrifying examples; but I do not believe that these examples are meant to be used as justification for our own crimes. This perpetual justification empties the heart of all human feeling. The emptier our hearts become, the greater will be our crimes. Thirdly, the South is not merely an embarrassingly backward region, but a part of this country, and what happens there concerns every one of us.

18 As far as the color problem is concerned, there is but one great difference between the Southern white and the Northerner: the Southerner remembers, historically and in his own psyche, a kind of Eden in which he loved black people and they loved him. Historically, the flaming sword laid across this Eden is the Civil War. Personally, it is the Southerner's sexual coming of age, when, without any warning, unbreakable taboos are set up between himself and his past. Everything, thereafter, is permitted him except the love he remembers and has never ceased to need. The resulting, indescribable torment affects every Southern mind and is the basis of the Southern hysteria.

19 None of this is true for the Northerner. Negroes represent nothing to him personally, except, perhaps, the dangers of carnality. He never sees Negroes. Southerners see them all the time. Northerners never think about them whereas Southerners are never really thinking of anything else. Negroes are, therefore, ignored in the North and are under surveillance in the South, and suffer hideously in both places. Neither the Southerner nor the Northerner is able to look on the Negro simply as a man. It seems to be indispensable to the national self-esteem that the Negro be considered either as a kind of ward (in which case we are told how many Negroes, comparatively, bought Cadillacs last year and how few, comparatively, were lynched), or as a victim (in which case we are promised that he will never vote in our assemblies or go to school with our kids). They are two sides of the same coin and the South will not change—*cannot* change—until the North changes. The country will not change until it re-examines itself and discovers what it really means by freedom. In the meantime, generations keep being born, bitterness is increased by incompetence, pride, and folly, and the world shrinks around us.

20 It is a terrible, an inexorable, law that one cannot deny the humanity of

another without diminishing one's own: in the face of one's victim, one sees oneself. Walk through the streets of Harlem and see what we, this nation, have become.

(1954)

QUESTIONS

Thought and Structure

1. What is Baldwin's purpose, who is his implied audience, and what is his major point?
2. Baldwin suggests that the housing project is "a monument to the folly, and the cowardice, of good intentions." What does he mean? And to whom is he referring?
3. In describing Harlem, Baldwin contrasts what he remembers from his childhood with what he later sees as an adult. What does he remember, what does he see, and what is the significance of the difference?
4. Twice Baldwin considers counterarguments (paragraphs 8 and 13). What are Baldwin's views about the problem of the ghetto and what are the counterviews? Which do you find more persuasive and why?
5. Children are mentioned five times (paragraphs 3, 5, 6, 10, and 15). What do these references have in common? Why are they important?
6. How does Baldwin characterize the relationship between the police and the people of Harlem? Reread paragraph 15 and outline the pattern of cause and effect Baldwin adduces for the inciting of riots.
7. Why does Baldwin bring South Africa and Buchenwald into his argument? Why does he discuss the South?
8. In the final paragraph Baldwin makes an important point: that in diminishing other people we diminish ourselves. Explain how and why this diminishment occurs.
9. One way of looking at the structure of this essay is to see it as composed of two major parts: paragraphs 1–10 and paragraphs 11–20. Provide a title for each, and explain how the two parts are related. Another way to see the essay's organization is as an oscillation between description and argumentation. How are the descriptive sections related to the polemical ones?
10. Baldwin structures part of the essay as a walk through Harlem. Where does the tour begin and end? How does Baldwin lead into and slide out of this section?

Style and Strategy

11. Paragraph 2 is only a single sentence. Why? Would this sentence be better attached to paragraph 1 or 3? Explain.
12. The last sentence of paragraph 5 packs in many details. Why does Baldwin cram them into one sentence? Would these details be more effectively presented in a series of short sentences? Why or why not?
12. The end of paragraph 15 and the beginning of paragraph 16 contain the same sentence—or part of the same sentence. What does Baldwin gain by repeating it?
13. What do you notice about how Baldwin concludes his paragraphs? Consider especially paragraphs 7–13, 15, 19–20.

14. Paragraphs 4–6 contain highly charged emotional language. Which words carry especially strong connotations? Of these, which have positive and which negative connotations? What is Baldwin's point here?
15. Throughout the essay, Baldwin places many words in quotation marks. Explain the tone of each, especially the following: "the turf" (3), "moslems" (4), "the man" (5), "powerful" (9), and "improvement" (13). Also explain the tone and point of the sentences quoted in paragraphs 4, 16, and 17.

SUGGESTIONS FOR WRITING

A. Write a polemical essay about a social problem, using a place as your central focus. Try to mix description of the problem with an analysis of how it got that way. Decide whether you want primarily to persuade readers to do something about the problem or whether you want them simply to better understand it. Decide on the relative proportions of description, explanation, and analysis—but only after you write a rough draft or two.

B. Argue with or support Baldwin. Choose one of the following statements from the essay and write an essay confirming or refuting Baldwin's idea.

> Negroes want to be treated like men. (15, 16)
>
> It is a terrible, an inexorable, law that one cannot deny the humanity of another without diminishing one's own: in the face of one's victim, one sees oneself. (20)
>
> Children have never been very good at listening to their elders, but they have never failed to imitate them. (8)

C. Go to the library and read Martin Luther King's "Letter from Birmingham Jail." Compare and contrast Baldwin's and King's "letters."

D. Write your own letter to a public of your own choosing. Choose as your topic a social grievance. Expose that grievance and offer suggestions for redressing it.

Notes of a Native Son

I

1 On the 29th of July, in 1943, my father died. On the same day, a few hours later, his last child was born. Over a month before this, while all our energies were concentrated in waiting for these events, there had been, in Detroit, one of the bloodiest race riots of the century. A few hours after my father's funeral, while he lay in state in the undertaker's chapel, a race riot broke out in Harlem. On the morning of the 3rd of August, we drove my father to the graveyard through a wilderness of smashed plate glass.

2 The day of my father's funeral had also been my nineteenth birthday. As we drove him to the graveyard, the spoils of injustice, anarchy, discontent, and hatred were all around us. It seemed to me that God himself had devised, to mark my father's end, the most sustained and brutally dissonant of codas. And it seemed to me, too, that the violence which rose all about us as my father left the world had

been devised as a corrective for the pride of his eldest son. I had declined to believe in that apocalypse which had been central to my father's vision; very well, life seemed to be saying, here is something that will certainly pass for an apocalypse until the real thing comes along. I had inclined to be contemptuous of my father for the conditions of his life, for the conditions of our lives. When his life had ended I began to wonder about that life and also, in a new way, to be apprehensive about my own.

3 I had not known my father very well. We had got on badly, partly because we shared, in our different fashions, the vice of stubborn pride. When he was dead I realized that I had hardly ever spoken to him. When he had been dead a long time I began to wish I had. It seems to be typical of life in America, where opportunities, real and fancied, are thicker than anywhere else on the globe, that the second generation has no time to talk to the first. No one, including my father, seems to have known exactly how old he was, but his mother had been born during slavery. He was of the first generation of free men. He, along with thousands of other Negroes, came North after 1919 and I was part of that generation which had never seen the landscape of what Negroes sometimes call the Old Country.

4 He had been born in New Orleans and had been a quite young man there during the time that Louis Armstrong, a boy, was running errands for the dives and honky-tonks of what was always presented to me as one of the most wicked of cities—to this day, whenever I think of New Orleans, I also helplessly think of Sodom and Gomorrah. My father never mentioned Louis Armstrong, except to forbid us to play his records; but there was a picture of him on our wall for a long time. One of my father's strong-willed female relatives had placed it there and forbade my father to take it down. He never did, but he eventually maneuvered her out of the house and when, some years later, she was in trouble and near death, he refused to do anything to help her.

5 He was, I think, very handsome. I gather this from photographs and from my own memories of him, dressed in his Sunday best and on his way to preach a sermon somewhere, when I was little. Handsome, proud, and ingrown, "like a toe-nail," somebody said. But he looked to me, as I grew older, like pictures I had seen of African tribal chieftains: he really should have been naked, with war-paint on and barbaric mementos, standing among spears. He could be chilling in the pulpit and indescribably cruel in his personal life and he was certainly the most bitter man I have ever met; yet it must be said that there was something else in him, buried in him, which lent him his tremendous power and, even, a rather crushing charm. It had something to do with his blackness, I think—he was very black—with his blackness and his beauty, and with the fact that he knew that he was black but did not know that he was beautiful. He claimed to be proud of his blackness but it had also been the cause of much humiliation and it had fixed bleak boundaries to his life. He was not a young man when we were growing up and he had already suffered many kinds of ruin; in his outrageously demanding and protective way he loved his children, who were black like him and menaced, like him; and all these things sometimes showed in his face when he tried, never to my knowledge with any success, to establish contact with any of us. When he took one of his children on his knee to play, the child always became fretful and began to cry; when he tried to help one of us with our homework the absolutely unabating tension which

emanated from him caused our minds and our tongues to become paralyzed, so that he, scarcely knowing why, flew into a rage and the child, not knowing why, was punished. If it ever entered his head to bring a surprise home for his children, it was, almost unfailingly, the wrong surprise and even the big watermelons he often brought home on his back in the summertime led to the most appalling scenes. I do not remember, in all those years, that one of his children was ever glad to see him come home. From what I was able to gather of his early life, it seemed that this inability to establish contact with other people had always marked him and had been one of the things which had driven him out of New Orleans. There was something in him, therefore, groping and tentative, which was never expressed and which was buried with him. One saw it most clearly when he was facing new people and hoping to impress them. But he never did, not for long. We went from church to smaller and more improbable church, he found himself in less and less demand as a minister, and by the time he died none of his friends had come to see him for a long time. He had lived and died in an intolerable bitterness of spirit and it frightened me, as we drove him to the graveyard through those unquiet, ruined streets, to see how powerful and overflowing this bitterness could be and to realize that this bitterness now was mine.

6 When he died I had been away from home for a little over a year. In that year I had had time to become aware of the meaning of all my father's bitter warnings, had discovered the secret of his proudly pursed lips and rigid carriage: I had discovered the weight of white people in the world. I saw that this had been for my ancestors and now would be for me an awful thing to live with and that the bitterness which had helped to kill my father could also kill me.

7 He had been ill a long time—in the mind, as we now realized, reliving instances of his fantastic intransigence in the new light of his affliction and endeavoring to feel a sorrow for him which never, quite, came true. We had not known that he was being eaten up by paranoia, and the discovery that his cruelty, to our bodies and our minds, had been one of the symptoms of his illness was not, then, enough to enable us to forgive him. The younger children felt, quite simply, relief that he would not be coming home anymore. My mother's observation that it was he, after all, who had kept them alive all these years meant nothing because the problems of keeping children alive are not real for children. The older children felt, with my father gone, that they could invite their friends to the house without fear that their friends would be insulted or, as had sometimes happened with me, being told that their friends were in league with the devil and intended to rob our family of everything we owned. (I didn't fail to wonder, and it made me hate him, what on earth we owned that anybody else would want.)

8 His illness was beyond all hope of healing before anyone realized that he was ill. He had always been so strange and had lived, like a prophet, in such unimaginably close communion with the Lord that his long silences which were punctuated by moans and hallelujahs and snatches of old songs while he sat at the living-room window never seemed odd to us. It was not until he refused to eat because, he said, his family was trying to poison him that my mother was forced to accept as a fact what had, until then, been only an unwilling suspicion. When he was committed, it was discovered that he had tuberculosis and, as it turned out, the disease of his

mind allowed the disease of his body to destroy him. For the doctors could not force him to eat, either, and, though he was fed intravenously, it was clear from the beginning that there was no hope for him.

9 In my mind's eye I could see him, sitting at the window, locked up in his terrors; hating and fearing every living soul including his children who had betrayed him, too, by reaching towards the world which had despised him. There were nine of us. I began to wonder what it could have felt like for such a man to have had nine children whom he could barely feed. He used to make little jokes about our poverty, which never, of course, seemed very funny to us; they could not have seemed very funny to him, either, or else our all too feeble response to them would never have caused such rages. He spent great energy and achieved, to our chagrin, no small amount of success in keeping us away from the people who surrounded us, people who had all-night rent parties to which we listened when we should have been sleeping, people who cursed and drank and flashed razor blades on Lenox Avenue. He could not understand why, if they had so much energy to spare, they could not use it to make their lives better. He treated almost everybody on our block with a most uncharitable asperity and neither they, nor, of course, their children were slow to reciprocate.

10 The only white people who came to our house were welfare workers and bill collectors. It was almost always my mother who dealt with them, for my father's temper, which was at the mercy of his pride, was never to be trusted. It was clear that he felt their very presence in his home to be a violation: this was conveyed by his carriage, almost ludicrously stiff, and by his voice, harsh and vindictively polite. When I was around nine or ten I wrote a play which was directed by a young, white schoolteacher, a woman, who then took an interest in me, and gave me books to read and, in order to corroborate my theatrical bent, decided to take me to see what she somewhat tactlessly referred to as "real" plays. Theatergoing was forbidden in our house, but, with the really cruel intuitiveness of a child, I suspected that the color of this woman's skin would carry the day for me. When, at school, she suggested taking me to the theater, I did not, as I might have done if she had been a Negro, find a way of discouraging her, but agreed that she should pick me up at my house one evening. I then, very cleverly, left all the rest to my mother, who suggested to my father, as I knew she would, that it would not be very nice to let such a kind woman make the trip for nothing. Also, since it was a schoolteacher, I imagine that my mother countered the idea of sin with the idea of "education," which word, even with my father, carried a kind of bitter weight.

11 Before the teacher came my father took me aside to ask *why* she was coming, what *interest* she could possibly have in our house, in a boy like me. I said I didn't know but I, too, suggested that it had something to do with education. And I understood that my father was waiting for me to say something—I didn't quite know what; perhaps that I wanted his protection against this teacher and her "education." I said none of these things and the teacher came and we went out. It was clear, during the brief interview in our living room, that my father was agreeing very much against his will and that he would have refused permission if he had dared. The fact that he did not dare caused me to despise him: I had no way of knowing that he was facing in that living room a wholly unprecedented and frightening situation.

12 Later, when my father had been laid off from his job, this woman became very important to us. She was really a very sweet and generous woman and went to a great deal of trouble to be of help to us, particularly during one awful winter. My mother called her by the highest name she knew; she said she was a "christian." My father could scarcely disagree but during the four or five years of our relatively close association he never trusted her and was always trying to surprise in her open, Midwestern face the genuine, cunningly hidden, and hideous motivation. In later years, particularly when it began to be clear that this "education" of mine was going to lead me to perdition, he became more explicit and warned me that my white friends in high school were not really my friends and that I would see, when I was older, how white people would do anything to keep a Negro down. Some of them could be nice, he admitted, but none of them were to be trusted and most of them were not even nice. The best thing was to have as little to do with them as possible. I did not feel this way and I was certain, in my innocence, that I never would.

13 But the year which preceded my father's death had made a great change in my life. I had been living in New Jersey, working in defense plants, working and living among southerners, white and black. I knew about the south, of course, and about how southerners treated Negroes and how they expected them to behave, but it had never entered my mind that anyone would look at me and expect *me* to behave that way. I learned in New Jersey that to be a Negro meant, precisely, that one was never looked at but was simply at the mercy of the reflexes the color of one's skin caused in other people. I acted in New Jersey as I had always acted, that is as though I thought a great deal of myself—I had to *act* that way—with results that were, simply, unbelievable. I had scarcely arrived before I had earned the enmity, which was extraordinarily ingenious, of all my superiors and nearly all my co-workers. In the beginning, to make matters worse, I simply did not know what was happening. I did not know what I had done, and I shortly began to wonder what *anyone* could possibly do, to bring about such unanimous, active, and unbearably vocal hostility. I knew about jim-crow but I had never experienced it. I went to the same self-service restaurant three times and stood with all the Princeton boys before the counter, waiting for a hamburger and coffee; it was always an extraordinarily long time before anything was set before me; but it was not until the fourth visit that I learned that, in fact, nothing had ever been set before me: I had simply picked something up. Negroes were not served there, I was told, and they had been waiting for me to realize that I was always the only Negro present. Once I was told this, I determined to go there all the time. But now they were ready for me and, though some dreadful scenes were subsequently enacted in that restaurant, I never ate there again.

14 It was the same story all over New Jersey, in bars, bowling alleys, diners, places to live. I was always being forced to leave, silently, or with mutual imprecations. I very shortly became notorious and children giggled behind me when I passed and their elders whispered or shouted—they really believed that I was mad. And it did begin to work on my mind, of course; I began to be afraid to go anywhere and to compensate for this I went places to which I really should not have gone and where, God knows, I had no desire to be. My reputation in town naturally enhanced my reputation at work and my working day became one long series of acrobatics de-

signed to keep me out of trouble. I cannot say that these acrobatics succeeded. It began to seem that the machinery of the organization I worked for was turning over, day and night, with but one aim: to eject me. I was fired once, and contrived, with the aid of a friend from New York, to get back on the payroll; was fired again, and bounced back again. It took a while to fire me for the third time, but the third time took. There were no loopholes anywhere. There was not even any way of getting back inside the gates.

15 That year in New Jersey lives in my mind as though it were the year during which, having an unsuspected predilection for it, I first contracted some dread, chronic disease, the unfailing symptom of which is a kind of blind fever, a pounding in the skull and fire in the bowels. Once this disease is contracted, one can never be really carefree again, for the fever, without an instant's warning, can recur at any moment. It can wreck more important things than race relations. There is not a Negro alive who does not have this rage in his blood—one has the choice, merely, of living with it consciously or surrendering to it. As for me, this fever has recurred in me, and does, and will until the day I die.

16 My last night in New Jersey, a white friend from New York took me to the nearest big town, Trenton, to go to the movies and have a few drinks. As it turned out, he also saved me from, at the very least, a violent whipping. Almost every detail of that night stands out very clearly in my memory. I even remember the name of the movie we saw because its title impressed me as being so patly ironical. It was a movie about the German occupation of France, starring Maureen O'Hara and Charles Laughton and called *This Land Is Mine.* I remember the name of the diner we walked into when the movie ended: it was the "American Diner." When we walked in the counterman asked what we wanted and I remember answering with the casual sharpness which had become my habit: "We want a hamburger and a cup of coffee, what do you think we want?" I do not know why, after a year of such rebuffs, I so completely failed to anticipate his answer, which was, of course, "We don't serve Negroes here." This reply failed to discompose me, at least for the moment. I made some sardonic comment about the name of the diner and we walked out into the streets.

17 This was the time of what was called the "brown-out," when the lights in all American cities were very dim. When we re-entered the streets something happened to me which had the force of an optical illusion, or a nightmare. The streets were very crowded and I was facing north. People were moving in every direction but it seemed to me, in that instant, that all of the people I could see, and many more than that, were moving toward me, against me, and that everyone was white. I remember how their faces gleamed. And I felt, like a physical sensation, a *click* at the nape of my neck as though some interior string connecting my head to my body had been cut. I began to walk. I heard my friend call after me, but I ignored him. Heaven only knows what was going on in his mind, but he had the good sense not to touch me—I don't know what would have happened if he had—and to keep me in sight. I don't know what was going on in my mind, either; I certainly had no conscious plan. I wanted to do something to crush these white faces, which were crushing me. I walked for perhaps a block or two until I came to an enormous, glittering, and fashionable restaurant in which I knew not even the intercession of

the Virgin would cause me to be served. I pushed through the doors and took the first vacant seat I saw, at a table for two, and waited.

18 I do not know how long I waited and I rather wonder, until today, what I could possibly have looked like. Whatever I looked like, I frightened the waitress who shortly appeared, and the moment she appeared all of my fury flowed towards her. I hated her for her white face, and for her great, astounded, frightened eyes. I felt that if she found a black man so frightening I would make her fright worth-while.

19 She did not ask me what I wanted, but repeated, as though she had learned it somewhere, "We don't serve Negroes here." She did not say it with the blunt, derisive hostility to which I had grown so accustomed, but, rather, with a note of apology in her voice, and fear. This made me colder and more murderous than ever. I felt I had to do something with my hands. I wanted her to come close enough for me to get her neck between my hands.

20 So I pretended not to have understood her, hoping to draw her closer. And she did step a very short step closer, with her pencil poised incongruously over her pad, and repeated the formula: ". . . don't serve Negroes here."

21 Somehow, with the repetition of that phrase, which was already ringing in my head like a thousand bells of a nightmare, I realized that she would never come any closer and that I would have to strike from a distance. There was nothing on the table but an ordinary water-mug half full of water, and I picked this up and hurled it with all my strength at her. She ducked and it missed her and shattered against the mirror behind the bar. And, with that sound, my frozen blood abruptly thawed, I returned from wherever I had been, I *saw,* for the first time, the restaurant, the people with their mouths open, already, as it seemed to me, rising as one man, and I realized what I had done, and where I was, and I was frightened. I rose and began running for the door. A round, potbellied man grabbed me by the nape of the neck just as I reached the doors and began to beat me about the face. I kicked him and got loose and ran into the streets. My friend whispered, *"Run!"* and I ran.

22 My friend stayed outside the restaurant long enough to misdirect my pursuers and the police, who arrived, he told me, at once. I do not know what I said to him when he came to my room that night. I could not have said much. I felt, in the oddest, most awful way, that I had somehow betrayed him. I lived it over and over and over again, the way one relives an automobile accident after it has happened and one finds oneself alone and safe. I could not get over two facts, both equally difficult for the imagination to grasp, and one was that I could have been murdered. But the other was that I had been ready to commit murder. I saw nothing very clearly but I did see this: that my life, my *real* life, was in danger, and not from anything other people might do but from the hatred I carried in my own heart.

II

23 I had returned home around the second week in June—in great haste because it seemed that my father's death and my mother's confinement were both but a matter of hours. In the case of my mother, it soon became clear that she had simply made a miscalculation. This had always been her tendency and I don't believe that

a single one of us arrived in the world, or has since arrived anywhere else, on time. But none of us dawdled so intolerably about the business of being born as did my baby sister. We sometimes amused ourselves, during those endless, stifling weeks, by picturing the baby sitting within in the safe, warm dark, bitterly regretting the necessity of becoming a part of our chaos and stubbornly putting it off as long as possible. I understood her perfectly and congratulated her on showing such good sense so soon. Death, however, sat as purposefully at my father's bedside as life stirred within my mother's womb and it was harder to understand why he so lingered in that long shadow. It seemed that he had bent, and for a long time, too, all of his energies towards dying. Now death was ready for him but my father held back.

24 All of Harlem, indeed, seemed to be infected by waiting. I had never before known it to be so violently still. Racial tensions throughout this country were exacerbated during the early years of the war, partly because the labor market brought together hundreds of thousands of ill-prepared people and partly because Negro soldiers, regardless of where they were born, received their military training in the south. What happened in defense plants and army camps had repercussions, naturally, in every Negro ghetto. The situation in Harlem had grown bad enough for clergymen, policemen, educators, politicians, and social workers to assert in one breath that there was no "crime wave" and to offer, in the very next breath, suggestions as to how to combat it. These suggestions always seemed to involve playgrounds, despite the fact that racial skirmishes were occurring in the playgrounds, too. Playground or not, crime wave or not, the Harlem police force had been augmented in March, and the unrest grew—perhaps, in fact, partly as a result of the ghetto's instinctive hatred of policemen. Perhaps the most revealing news item, out of the steady parade of reports of muggings, stabbings, shootings, assaults, gang wars, and accusations of police brutality is the item concerning six Negro girls who set upon a white girl in the subway because, as they all too accurately put it, she was stepping on their ties. Indeed she was, all over the nation.

25 I had never before been so aware of policemen, on foot, on horseback, on corners, everywhere, always two by two. Nor had I ever been so aware of small knots of people. They were on stoops and on corners and in doorways, and what was striking about them, I think, was that they did not seem to be talking. Never, when I passed these groups, did the usual sound of a curse or a laugh ring out and neither did there seem to be any hum of gossip. There was certainly, on the other hand, occurring between them communication extraordinarily intense. Another thing that was striking was the unexpected diversity of the people who made up these groups. Usually, for example, one would see a group of sharpies standing on the street corner, jiving the passing chicks; or a group of older men, usually, for some reason, in the vicinity of a barber shop, discussing baseball scores, or the numbers or making rather chilling observations about women they had known. Women, in a general way, tended to be seen less often together—unless they were church women, or very young girls, or prostitutes met together for an unprofessional instant. But that summer I saw the strangest combinations: large, respectable, churchly matrons standing on the stoops or the corners with their hair tied up, together with a girl in sleazy satin whose face bore the marks of gin and the razor, or heavyset, abrupt, no-nonsense older men, in company with the most disreputable and fanatical "race"

men or these same "race" men with the sharpies, or these sharpies with the churchly women. Seventh Day Adventists and Methodists and Spiritualists seemed to be hobnobbing with Holyrollers and they were all, alike, entangled with the most flagrant disbelievers; something heavy in their stance seemed to indicate that they had all, incredibly, seen a common vision, and on each face there seemed to be the same strange, bitter shadow.

26 The churchly women and the matter-of-fact, no-nonsense men had children in the Army. The sleazy girls they talked to had lovers there, the sharpies and the "race" men had friends and brothers there. It would have demanded an unquestioning patriotism, happily as uncommon in this country as it is undesirable, for these people not to have been disturbed by the bitter letters they received, by the newspaper stories they read, not to have been enraged by the posters, then to be found all over New York, which described the Japanese as "yellow-bellied Japs." It was only the "race" men, to be sure, who spoke ceaselessly of being revenged—how this vengeance was to be exacted was not clear—for the indignities and dangers suffered by Negro boys in uniform; but everybody felt a directionless, hopeless bitterness, as well as that panic which can scarcely be suppressed when one knows that a human being one loves is beyond one's reach, and in danger. This helplessness and this gnawing uneasiness does something, at length, to even the toughest mind. Perhaps the best way to sum all this up is to say that the people I knew felt, mainly, a peculiar kind of relief when they knew that their boys were being shipped out of the south, to do battle overseas. It was, perhaps, like feeling that the most dangerous part of a dangerous journey had been passed and that now, even if death should come, it would come with honor and without the complicity of their countrymen. Such a death would be, in short, a fact with which one could hope to live.

27 It was on the 28th of July, which I believe was a Wednesday, that I visited my father for the first time during his illness and for the last time in his life. The moment I saw him I knew why I had put off this visit so long. I had told my mother that I did not want to see him because I hated him. But this was not true. It was only that I *had* hated him and I wanted to hold on to this hatred. I did not want to look on him as a ruin: it was not a ruin I had hated. I imagine that one of the reasons people cling to their hates so stubbornly is because they sense, once hate is gone, that they will be forced to deal with pain.

28 We traveled out to him, his older sister and myself, to what seemed to be the very end of a very Long Island. It was hot and dusty and we wrangled, my aunt and I, all the way out, over the fact that I had recently begun to smoke and, as she said, to give myself airs. But I knew that she wrangled with me because she could not bear to face the fact of her brother's dying. Neither could I endure the reality of her despair, her unstated bafflement as to what had happened to her brother's life, and her own. So we wrangled and I smoked and from time to time she fell into a heavy reverie. Covertly, I watched her face, which was the face of an old woman; it had fallen in, the eyes were sunken and lightless; soon she would be dying, too.

29 In my childhood—it had not been so long ago—I had thought her beautiful. She had been quick-witted and quick-moving and very generous with all the children and each of her visits had been an event. At one time one of my brothers and myself had thought of running away to live with her. Now she could no longer produce out

of her handbag some unexpected and yet familiar delight. She made me feel pity and revulsion and fear. It was awful to realize that she no longer caused me to feel affection. The closer we came to the hospital the more querulous she became and at the same time, naturally, grew more dependent on me. Between pity and guilt and fear I began to feel that there was another me trapped in my skull like a jack-in-the-box who might escape my control at any moment and fill the air with screaming.

30 She began to cry the moment we entered the room and she saw him lying there, all shriveled and still, like a little black monkey. The great, gleaming apparatus which fed him and would have compelled him to be still even if he had been able to move brought to mind, not beneficence, but torture; the tubes entering his arm made me think of pictures I had seen when a child, of Gulliver, tied down by the pygmies on that island. My aunt wept and wept, there was a whistling sound in my father's throat; nothing was said; he could not speak. I wanted to take his hand, to say something. But I do not know what I could have said, even if he could have heard me. He was not really in that room with us, he had at last really embarked on his journey; and though my aunt told me that he said he was going to meet Jesus, I did not hear anything except that whistling in his throat. The doctor came back and we left, into that unbearable train again, and home. In the morning came the telegram saying that he was dead. Then the house was suddenly full of relatives, friends, hysteria, and confusion and I quickly left my mother and the children to the care of those impressive women, who, in Negro communities at least, automatically appear at times of bereavement armed with lotions, proverbs, and patience, and an ability to cook. I went downtown. By the time I returned, later the same day, my mother had been carried to the hospital and the baby had been born.

III

31 For my father's funeral I had nothing black to wear and this posed a nagging problem all day long. It was one of those problems, simple, or impossible of solution, to which the mind insanely clings in order to avoid the mind's real trouble. I spent most of that day at the downtown apartment of a girl I knew, celebrating my birthday with whiskey and wondering what to wear that night. When planning a birthday celebration one naturally does not expect that it will be up against competition from a funeral and this girl had anticipated taking me out that night, for a big dinner and a night club afterwards. Sometime during the course of that long day we decided that we would go out anyway, when my father's funeral service was over. I imagine I decided it, since, as the funeral hour approached, it became clearer and clearer to me that I would not know what to do with myself when it was over. The girl, stifling her very lively concern as to the possible effects of the whiskey on one of my father's chief mourners, concentrated on being conciliatory and practically helpful. She found a black shirt for me somewhere and ironed it and, dressed in the darkest pants and jacket I owned, and slightly drunk, I made my way to my father's funeral.

32 The chapel was full, but not packed, and very quiet. There were, mainly, my

father's relatives, and his children, and here and there I saw faces I had not seen since childhood, the faces of my father's one-time friends. They were very dark and solemn now, seeming somehow to suggest that they had known all along that something like this would happen. Chief among the mourners was my aunt, who had quarreled with my father all his life; by which I do not mean to suggest that her mourning was insincere or that she had not loved him. I suppose that she was one of the few people in the world who had, and their incessant quarreling proved precisely the strength of the tie that bound them. The only other person in the world, as far as I knew, whose relationship to my father rivaled my aunt's in depth was my mother, who was not there.

33 It seemed to me, of course, that it was a very long funeral. But it was, if anything, a rather shorter funeral than most, nor, since there were no overwhelming, uncontrollable expressions of grief, could it be called—if I dare to use the word—successful. The minister who preached my father's funeral sermon was one of the few my father had still been seeing as he neared his end. He presented to us in his sermon a man whom none of us had ever seen—a man thoughtful, patient, and forbearing, a Christian inspiration to all who knew him, and a model for his children. And no doubt the children, in their disturbed and guilty state, were almost ready to believe this; he had been remote enough to be anything and, anyway, the shock of the incontrovertible, that it was really our father lying up there in that casket, prepared the mind for anything. His sister moaned and this grief-stricken moaning was taken as corroboration. The other faces held a dark, non-committal thoughtfulness. This was not the man they had known, but they had scarcely expected to be confronted with *him;* this was, in a sense deeper than questions of fact, the man they had not known, and the man they had not known may have been the real one. The real man, whoever he had been, had suffered and now he was dead: this was all that was sure and all that mattered now. Every man in the chapel hoped that when his hour came he, too, would be eulogized, which is to say forgiven, and that all of his lapses, greeds, errors, and strayings from the truth would be invested with coherence and looked upon with charity. This was perhaps the last thing human beings could give each other and it was what they demanded, after all, of the Lord. Only the Lord saw the midnight tears, only He was present when one of His children, moaning and wringing hands, paced up and down the room. When one slapped one's child in anger the recoil in the heart reverberated through heaven and became part of the pain of the universe. And when the children were hungry and sullen and distrustful and one watched them, daily, growing wilder, and further away, and running headlong into danger, it was the Lord who knew what the charged heart endured as the strap was laid to the backside; the Lord alone who knew what one *would* have said if one had had, like the Lord, the gift of the living word. It was the Lord who knew of the impossibility every parent in that room faced: how to prepare the child for the day when the child would be despised and how to *create* in the child—by what means?—a stronger antidote to this poison than one had found for oneself. The avenues, side streets, bars, billiard halls, hospitals, police stations, and even the playgrounds of Harlem—not to mention the houses of correction, the jails, and the morgue—testified to the potency of the poison while remaining silent as to the efficacy of whatever antidote, irresistibly raising the question of

whether or not such an antidote existed; raising, which was worse, the question of whether or not an antidote was desirable; perhaps poison should be fought with poison. With these several schisms in the mind and with more terrors in the heart than could be named, it was better not to judge the man who had gone down under an impossible burden. It was better to remember: *Thou knowest this man's fall; but thou knowest not his wrassling.*

34 While the preacher talked and I watched the children—years of changing their diapers, scrubbing them, slapping them, taking them to school, and scolding them had had the perhaps inevitable result of making me love them, though I am not sure I knew this then—my mind was busily breaking out with a rash of disconnected impressions. Snatches of popular songs, indecent jokes, bits of books I had read, movie sequences, faces, voices, political issues—I thought I was going mad; all these impressions suspended, as it were, in the solution of the faint nausea produced in me by the heat and liquor. For a moment I had the impression that my alcoholic breath, inefficiently disguised with chewing gum, filled the entire chapel. Then someone began singing one of my father's favorite songs and, abruptly, I was with him, sitting on his knee, in the hot, enormous, crowded church which was the first church we attended. It was the Abyssinia Baptist Church on 138th Street. We had not gone there long. With this image, a host of others came. I had forgotten, in the rage of my growing up, how proud my father had been of me when I was little. Apparently, I had had a voice and my father had liked to show me off before the members of the church. I had forgotten what he had looked like when he was pleased but now I remembered that he had always been grinning with pleasure when my solos ended. I even remembered certain expressions on his face when he teased my mother—had he loved her? I would never know. And when had it all begun to change? For now it seemed that he had not always been cruel. I remembered being taken for a haircut and scraping my knee on the footrest of the barber's chair and I remembered my father's face as he soothed my crying and applied the stinging iodine. Then I remembered our fights, fights which had been of the worst possible kind because my technique had been silence.

35 I remembered the one time in all our life together when we had really spoken to each other.

36 It was on a Sunday and it must have been shortly before I left home. We were walking, just the two of us, in our usual silence, to or from church. I was in high school and had been doing a lot of writing and I was, at about this time, the editor of the high school magazine. But I had also been a Young Minister and had been preaching from the pulpit. Lately, I had been taking fewer engagements and preached as rarely as possible. It was said in the church, quite truthfully, that I was "cooling off."

37 My father asked me abruptly, "You'd rather write than preach, wouldn't you?"

38 I was astonished at his question—because it was a real question. I answered, "Yes."

39 That was all we said. It was awful to remember that that was all we had *ever* said.

40 The casket now was opened and the mourners were being led up the aisle to look for the last time on the deceased. The assumption was that the family was too

overcome with grief to be allowed to make this journey alone and I watched while my aunt was led to the casket and, muffled in black, and shaking, led back to her seat. I disapproved of forcing the children to look on their dead father, considering that the shock of his death, or, more truthfully, the shock of death as a reality, was already a little more than a child could bear, but my judgment in this matter had been overruled and there they were, bewildered and frightened and very small, being led, one by one, to the casket. But there is also something very gallant about children at such moments. It has something to do with their silence and gravity and with the fact that one cannot help them. Their legs, somehow, seem *exposed,* so that it is at once incredible and terribly clear that their legs are all they have to hold them up.

41 I had not wanted to go to the casket myself and I certainly had not wished to be led there, but there was no way of avoiding either of these forms. One of the deacons led me up and I looked on my father's face. I cannot say that it looked like him at all. His blackness had been equivocated by powder and there was no suggestion in that casket of what his power had or could have been. He was simply an old man dead, and it was hard to believe that he had ever given anyone either joy or pain. Yet, his life filled that room. Further up the avenue his wife was holding his newborn child. Life and death so close together, and love and hatred, and right and wrong, said something to me which I did not want to hear concerning man, concerning the life of man.

42 After the funeral, while I was downtown desperately celebrating my birthday, a Negro soldier, in the lobby of the Hotel Braddock, got into a fight with a white policeman over a Negro girl. Negro girls, white policemen, in or out of uniform, and Negro males—in or out of uniform—were part of the furniture of the lobby of the Hotel Braddock and this was certainly not the first time such an incident had occurred. It was destined, however, to receive an unprecedented publicity, for the fight between the policeman and the soldier ended with the shooting of the soldier. Rumor, flowing immediately to the streets outside, stated that the soldier had been shot in the back, an instantaneous and revealing invention, and that the soldier had died protecting a Negro woman. The facts were somewhat different—for example, the soldier had not been shot in the back, and was not dead, and the girl seems to have been as dubious a symbol of womanhood as her white counterpart in Georgia usually is, but no one was interested in the facts. They preferred the invention because this invention expressed and corroborated their hates and fears so perfectly. It is just as well to remember that people are always doing this. Perhaps many of those legends, including Christianity, to which the world clings began their conquest of the world with just some such concerted surrender to distortion. The effect, in Harlem, of this particular legend was like the effect of a lit match in a tin of gasoline. The mob gathered before the doors of the Hotel Braddock simply began to swell and to spread in every direction, and Harlem exploded.

43 The mob did not cross the ghetto lines. It would have been easy, for example, to have gone over Morningside Park on the west side or to have crossed the Grand Central railroad tracks at 125th Street on the east side, to wreak havoc in white neighborhoods. The mob seems to have been mainly interested in something more potent and real than the white face, that is, in white power, and the principal

damage done during the riot of the summer of 1943 was to white business establishments in Harlem. It might have been a far bloodier story, of course, if, at the hour the riot began, these establishments had still been open. From the Hotel Braddock the mob fanned out, east and west along 125th Street, and for the entire length of Lenox, Seventh, and Eighth avenues. Along each of these avenues, and along each major side street—116th, 125th, 135th, and so on—bars, stores, pawnshops, restaurants, even little luncheonettes had been smashed open and entered and looted—looted, it might be added, with more haste than efficiency. The shelves really looked as though a bomb had struck them. Cans of beans and soup and dog food, along with toilet paper, corn flakes, sardines and milk tumbled every which way, and abandoned cash registers and cases of beer leaned crazily out of the splintered windows and were strewn along the avenues. Sheets, blankets, and clothing of every description formed a kind of path, as though people had dropped them while running. I truly had not realized that Harlem *had* so many stores until I saw them all smashed open; the first time the word *wealth* ever entered my mind in relation to Harlem was when I saw it scattered in the streets. But one's first, incongruous impression of plenty was countered immediately by an impression of waste. None of this was doing anybody any good. It would have been better to have left the plate glass as it had been and the goods lying in the stores.

44 It would have been better, but it would also have been intolerable, for Harlem had needed something to smash. To smash something is the ghetto's chronic need. Most of the time it is the members of the ghetto who smash each other, and themselves. But as long as the ghetto walls are standing there will always come a moment when these outlets do not work. That summer, for example, it was not enough to get into a fight on Lenox Avenue, or curse out one's cronies in the barber shops. If ever, indeed, the violence which fills Harlem's churches, pool halls, and bars erupts outward in a more direct fashion, Harlem and its citizens are likely to vanish in an apocalyptic flood. That this is not likely to happen is due to a great many reasons, most hidden and powerful among them the Negro's real relation to the white American. This relation prohibits, simply, anything as uncomplicated and satisfactory as pure hatred. In order really to hate white people, one has to blot so much out of the mind—and the heart—that this hatred itself becomes an exhausting and self-destructive pose. But this does not mean, on the other hand, that love comes easily: the white world is too powerful, too complacent, too ready with gratuitous humiliation, and, above all, too ignorant and too innocent for that. One is absolutely forced to make perpetual qualifications and one's own reactions are always canceling each other out. It is this, really, which has driven so many people mad, both white and black. One is always in the position of having to decide between amputation and gangrene. Amputation is swift but time may prove that the amputation was not necessary—or one may delay the amputation too long. Gangrene is slow, but it is impossible to be sure that one is reading one's symptoms right. The idea of going through life as a cripple is more than one can bear, and equally unbearable is the risk of swelling up slowly, in agony, with poison. And the trouble, finally, is that the risks are real even if the choices do not exist.

45 "But as for me and my house," my father had said, "we will serve the Lord." I wondered, as we drove him to his resting place, what this line had meant for him.

I had heard him preach it many times. I had preached it once myself, proudly giving it an interpretation different from my father's. Now the whole thing came back to me, as though my father and I were on our way to Sunday school and I were memorizing the golden text: *And if it seem evil unto you to serve the Lord, choose you this day whom you will serve; whether the gods which your fathers served that were on the other side of the flood, or the gods of the Amorites, in whose land ye dwell: but as for me and my house, we will serve the Lord.* I suspected in these familiar lines a meaning which had never been there for me before. All of my father's texts and songs, which I had decided were meaningless, were arranged before me at his death like empty bottles, waiting to hold the meaning which life would give them for me. This was his legacy: nothing is ever escaped. That bleakly memorable morning I hated the unbelievable streets and the Negroes and whites who had, equally, made them that way. But I knew that it was folly, as my father would have said, this bitterness was folly. It was necessary to hold on to the things that mattered. The dead man mattered, the new life mattered; blackness and whiteness did not matter; to believe that they did was to acquiesce in one's own destruction. Hatred, which could destroy so much, never failed to destroy the man who hated and this was an immutable law.

46 It began to seem that one would have to hold in the mind forever two ideas which seemed to be in opposition. The first idea was acceptance, the acceptance, totally without rancor, of life as it is, and men as they are: in the light of this idea, it goes without saying that injustice is a commonplace. But this did not mean that one could be complacent, for the second idea was of equal power: that one must never, in one's own life, accept these injustices as commonplace but must fight them with all one's strength. This fight begins, however, in the heart and it now had been laid to my charge to keep my own heart free of hatred and despair. This intimation made my heart heavy and, now that my father was irrecoverable, I wished that he had been beside me so that I could have searched his face for the answers which only the future would give me now.

(1954)

QUESTIONS

Thought and Structure

1. In part I Baldwin describes his father, characterizing him. How does this characterization compare with what Baldwin says about him in part III? In these descriptions of his father, Baldwin reveals things about himself. What does he reveal and why is it important?
2. Throughout the essay Baldwin uses description and narration in the service of argumentation. What point does Baldwin make via the restaurant incident at the end of part I? What point does he make by his description of riding through Harlem on the day of his father's funeral?
3. What ironies of circumstance does Baldwin indicate in the first paragraph of part III? What other ironies do you detect in the essay? What is the point, for example, of

mentioning who attended the funeral? What does Baldwin mean when he suggests that his aunt was one of the few people in the world who had loved his father, and yet "their incessant quarreling proved precisely the strength of the tie that bound them"?

4. In paragraph 45 Baldwin brings together the personal and the social, the private and public, his father and Harlem. What conclusion does he draw about his relation to his father? About the hatred and rage and bitterness that sparked the riots? Explain the final sentence of the paragraph: "Hatred, which could destroy so much, never failed to destroy the man who hated and this was an immutable law." The essay ends with a pair of contradictory impulses, with two irreconcilable ideas. What are they, and how does Baldwin both emphasize them and tie them in with what has gone before—especially with what he suggests at the end of part I?
5. "Notes of a Native Son" is divided into three major sections. Provide a title for each part, explain the main point of each, and comment on the relationship among them. Take any one of the three parts and examine its structure. Explain how it begins, where it goes, and how it ends. Explain how each of its parts fits into the whole section and into the essay overall.
6. Baldwin ends part I with a narrative account of an episode at a New Jersey restaurant. He begins this account with an idea and he ends with one. Discuss each of these ideas and the connections between them.

Style and Strategy

7. How do the rhythm and word order of sentences 3–4 in the opening paragraph continue the structure and rhythm of the first and second sentences? What is the effect of this patterning?
8. In paragraph 2 Baldwin again uses parallel sentences. Look especially at sentences 3–4 and 5–7. Read the sentences aloud, noting pacing and pauses. Reread one of Baldwin's paragraphs, mentally deleting all material between commas. What happens to the sound and the weight of the sentences? Why?
9. In the narrative portions of the essay, especially in paragraphs 17, 21, and 22, Baldwin employs comparisons. What is the point of each? Explain how comparisons and other forms of imagery are used in paragraphs 28, 29, 30, and 43–45.
10. There are two vocabularies in "Notes of a Native Son": simple, common words; more formal, longer words, usually of Latin derivation. Read paragraphs 2 and 3, marking off words of each type. What is the effect of such a mixture?
11. In paragraph 43 Baldwin describes the effects of the looting. What comparisons does he use and how effective are they? In paragraph 44 he uses the language of disease to express the consequences for blacks of race relations in the U.S. What psychological difference is Baldwin suggesting by means of his description of the physical differences between gangrene and amputation?
12. The final paragraph of the essay achieves coherence, continuity, and emphasis by careful repetition of words and phrases. Circle or underline the words and phrases that establish this coherence and emphasis.

SUGGESTIONS FOR WRITING

A. Write an essay in which you describe something that happened to you that made you aware of yourself or made you aware of a social, political, religious, or racial problem. Begin and end your account with an idea.

B. Write your own "Notes of a Native Son or Daughter." Try to come to terms with your ethnic or racial heritage and with your place in relation to the society of which you are a part.

C. Examine your relationship with your mother or father in an extended essay.

D. Write imitations of the sentences discussed in questions 7 and 8.

E. Discuss the following poem—"A Man Feared" by Stephen Crane—in relation to what Baldwin says about himself in the final paragraph of part I.

> A man feared that he might find an assassin;
> Another that he might find a victim.
> One was more wise than the other.

(Who was the wiser, and why?)

Sonny's Blues

1 I read about it in the paper, in the subway, on my way to work. I read it, and I couldn't believe it, and I read it again. Then perhaps I just stared at it, at the newsprint spelling out his name, spelling out the story. I stared at it in the swinging lights of the subway car, and in the faces and bodies of the people, and in my own face, trapped in the darkness which roared outside.

2 It was not to be believed and I kept telling myself that, as I walked from the subway station to the high school. And at the same time I couldn't doubt it. I was scared, scared for Sonny. He became real to me again. A great block of ice got settled in my belly and kept melting there slowly all day long, while I taught my classes algebra. It was a special kind of ice. It kept melting, sending trickles of ice water all up and down my veins, but it never got less. Sometimes it hardened and seemed to expand until I felt my guts were going to come spilling out or that I was going to choke or scream. This would always be at a moment when I was remembering some specific thing Sonny had once said or done.

3 When he was about as old as the boys in my classes his face had been bright and open, there was a lot of copper in it; and he'd had wonderfully direct brown eyes, and great gentleness and privacy. I wondered what he looked like now. He had been picked up, the evening before, in a raid on an apartment downtown, for peddling and using heroin.

4 I couldn't believe it: but what I mean by that is that I couldn't find any room for it anywhere inside me. I had kept it outside me for a long time. I hadn't wanted to know. I had had suspicions, but I didn't name them, I kept putting them away. I told myself that Sonny was wild, but he wasn't crazy. And he'd always been a good boy, he hadn't ever turned hard or evil or disrespectful, the way kids can, so quick, so quick, especially in Harlem. I didn't want to believe that I'd ever see my brother going down, coming to nothing, all that light in his face gone out, in the condition I'd already seen so many others. Yet it had happened and here I was, talking about algebra to a lot of boys who might, every one of them for all I knew, be popping off needles every time they went to the head. Maybe it did more for them than algebra could.

5 I was sure that the first time Sonny had ever had horse, he couldn't have been much older than these boys were now. These boys, now, were living as we'd been living then, they were growing up with a rush and their heads bumped abruptly against the low ceiling of their actual possibilities. They were filled with rage. All they really knew were two darknesses, the darkness of their lives, which was now closing in on them, and the darkness of the movies, which had blinded them to that other darkness, and in which they now, vindictively, dreamed, at once more together than they were at any other time, and more alone.

6 When the last bell rang, the last class ended, I let out my breath. It seemed I'd been holding it for all that time. My clothes were wet—I may have looked as though I'd been sitting in a steam bath, all dressed up, all afternoon. I sat alone in the classroom a long time. I listened to the boys outside, downstairs, shouting and cursing and laughing. Their laughter struck me for perhaps the first time. It was not the joyous laughter which—God knows why—one associates with children. It was mocking and insular, its intent was to denigrate. It was disenchanted, and in this, also, lay the authority of their curses. Perhaps I was listening to them because I was thinking about my brother and in them I heard my brother. And myself.

7 One boy was whistling a tune, at once very complicated and very simple, it seemed to be pouring out of him as though he were a bird, and it sounded very cool and moving through all that harsh, bright air, only just holding its own through all those other sounds.

8 I stood up and walked over to the window and looked down into the courtyard. It was the beginning of the spring and the sap was rising in the boys. A teacher passed through them every now and again, quickly, as though he or she couldn't wait to get out of that courtyard, to get those boys out of their sight and off their minds. I started collecting my stuff. I thought I'd better get home and talk to Isabel.

9 The courtyard was almost deserted by the time I got downstairs. I saw this boy standing in the shadow of a doorway, looking just like Sonny. I almost called his name. Then I saw that it wasn't Sonny, but somebody we used to know, a boy from around our block. He'd been Sonny's friend. He'd never been mine, having been too young for me, and, anyway, I'd never liked him. And now, even though he was a grown-up man, he still hung around that block, still spent hours on the street corners, was always high and raggy. I used to run into him from time to time and he'd often work around to asking me for a quarter or fifty cents. He always had some real good excuse, too, and I always gave it to him, I don't know why.

10 But now, abruptly, I hated him. I couldn't stand the way he looked at me, partly like a dog, partly like a cunning child. I wanted to ask him what the hell he was doing in the school courtyard.

11 He sort of shuffled over to me, and he said, "I see you got the papers. So you already know about it."

12 "You mean about Sonny? Yes, I already know about it. How come they didn't get you?"

13 He grinned. It made him repulsive and it also brought to mind what he'd looked like as a kid. "I wasn't there. I stay away from them people."

14 "Good for you." I offered him a cigarette and I watched him through the smoke. "You come all the way down here just to tell me about Sonny?"

15 "That's right." He was sort of shaking his head and his eyes looked strange, as though they were about to cross. The bright sun deadened his damp dark brown skin and it made his eyes look yellow and showed up the dirt in his kinked hair. He smelled funky. I moved a little away from him and I said, "Well, thanks. But I already know about it and I got to get home."

16 "I'll walk you a little ways," he said. We started walking. There were a couple of kids still loitering in the courtyard and one of them said goodnight to me and looked strangely at the boy beside me.

17 "What're you going to do?" he asked me. "I mean, about Sonny?"

18 "Look. I haven't seen Sonny for over a year, I'm not sure I'm going to do anything. Anyway, what the hell *can* I do?"

19 "That's right," he said quickly, "ain't nothing you can do. Can't much help old Sonny no more, I guess."

20 It was what I was thinking and so it seemed to me he had no right to say it.

21 "I'm surprised at Sonny, though," he went on—he had a funny way of talking, he looked straight ahead as though he were talking to himself—"I thought Sonny was a smart boy, I thought he was too smart to get hung."

22 "I guess he thought so too," I said sharply, "and that's how he got hung. And how about you? You're pretty goddamn smart, I bet."

23 Then he looked directly at me, just for a minute. "I ain't smart," he said. "If I was smart, I'd have reached for a pistol a long time ago."

24 "Look. Don't tell *me* your sad story, if it was up to me, I'd give you one." Then I felt guilty—guilty, probably, for never having supposed that the poor bastard *had* a story of his own, much less a sad one, and I asked, quickly, "What's going to happen to him now?"

25 He didn't answer this. He was off by himself some place. "Funny thing," he said, and from his tone we might have been discussing the quickest way to get to Brooklyn, "when I saw the papers this morning, the first thing I asked myself was if I had anything to do with it. I felt sort of responsible."

26 I began to listen more carefully. The subway station was on the corner, just before us, and I stopped. He stopped, too. We were in front of a bar and he ducked slightly, peering in, but whoever he was looking for didn't seem to be there. The juke box was blasting away with something black and bouncy and I half watched the barmaid as she danced her way from the juke box to her place behind the bar. And I watched her face as she laughingly responded to something someone said to her, still keeping time to the music. When she smiled one saw the little girl, one sensed the doomed, still-struggling woman beneath the battered face of the semi-whore.

27 "I never *give* Sonny nothing," the boy said finally, "but a long time ago I come to school high and Sonny asked me how it felt." He paused, I couldn't bear to watch him, I watched the barmaid, and I listened to the music which seemed to be causing the pavement to shake. "I told him it felt great." The music stopped, the barmaid paused and watched the juke box until the music began again. "It did."

28 All this was carrying me some place I didn't want to go. I certainly didn't want to know how it felt. It filled everything, the people, the houses, the music, the dark, quicksilver barmaid, with menace; and this menace was their reality.

29 "What's going to happen to him now?" I asked again.

30 "They'll send him away some place and they'll try to cure him." He shook his head. "Maybe he'll even think he's kicked the habit. Then they'll let him loose"—he gestured, throwing his cigarette into the gutter. "That's all."

31 "What do you mean, that's *all?*"

32 But I knew what he meant.

33 "I *mean,* that's *all.*" He turned his head and looked at me, pulling down the corners of his mouth. "Don't you know what I mean?" he asked, softly.

34 "How the hell *would* I know what you mean?" I almost whispered it, I don't know why.

35 "That's right," he said to the air, "how would *he* know what I mean?" He turned toward me again, patient and calm, and yet I somehow felt him shaking, shaking as though he were going to fall apart. I felt that ice in my guts again, the dread I'd felt all afternoon; and again I watched the barmaid, moving about the bar, washing glasses, and singing. "Listen. They'll let him out and then it'll just start all over again. That's what I mean."

36 "You mean—they'll let him out. And then he'll just start working his way back in again. You mean he'll never kick the habit. Is that what you mean?"

37 "That's right," he said, cheerfully. "*You* see what I mean."

38 "Tell me," I said at last, "why does he want to die? He must want to die, he's killing himself, why does he want to die?"

39 He looked at me in surprise. He licked his lips. "He don't want to die. He wants to live. Don't nobody want to die, ever."

40 Then I wanted to ask him—too many things. He could not have answered, or if he had, I could not have borne the answers. I started walking. "Well, I guess it's none of my business."

41 "It's going to be rough on old Sonny," he said. We reached the subway station. "This is your station?" he asked. I nodded. I took one step down. "Damn!" he said, suddenly. I looked up at him. He grinned again. "Damn it if I didn't leave all my money home. You ain't got a dollar on you, have you? Just for a couple of days, is all."

42 All at once something inside gave and threatened to come pouring out of me. I didn't hate him any more. I felt that in another moment I'd start crying like a child.

43 "Sure," I said. "Don't swear." I looked in my wallet and didn't have a dollar, I only had a five. "Here," I said. "That hold you?"

44 He didn't look at it—he didn't want to look at it. A terrible, closed look came over his face, as though he were keeping the number on the bill a secret from him and me. "Thanks," he said, and now he was dying to see me go. "Don't worry about Sonny. Maybe I'll write him or something."

45 "Sure," I said. "You do that. So long."

46 "Be seeing you," he said. I went down the steps.

47 And I didn't write Sonny or send him anything for a long time. When I finally did, it was just after my little girl died, he wrote me back a letter which made me feel like a bastard.

48 Here's what he said:

Dear Brother,

You don't know how much I needed to hear from you. I wanted to write you many a time but I dug how much I must have hurt you and so I didn't write. But now I feel like a man who's been trying to climb up out of some deep, real deep and funky hole and just saw the sun up there, outside. I got to get outside.

I can't tell you much about how I got here. I mean I don't know how to tell you. I guess I was afraid of something or I was trying to escape from something and you know I have never been very strong in the head (smile). I'm glad Mama and Daddy are dead and can't see what's happened to their son and I swear if I'd known what I was doing I would never have hurt you so, you and a lot of other fine people who were nice to me and who believed in me.

I don't want you to think it had anything to do with me being a musician. It's more than that. Or maybe less than that. I can't get anything straight in my head down here and I try not to think about what's going to happen to me when I get outside again. Sometime I think I'm going to flip and *never* get outside and sometime I think I'll come straight back. I tell you one thing, though, I'd rather blow my brains out than go through this again. But that's what they all say, so they tell me. If I tell you when I'm coming to New York and if you could meet me, I sure would appreciate it. Give my love to Isabel and the kids and I was sure sorry to hear about little Gracie. I wish I could be like Mama and say the Lord's will be done, but I don't know it seems to me that trouble is the one thing that never does get stopped and I don't know what good it does to blame it on the Lord. But maybe it does some good if you believe it.

Your brother,
Sonny

49 Then I kept in constant touch with him and I sent him whatever I could and I went to meet him when he came back to New York. When I saw him many things I thought I had forgotten came flooding back to me. This was because I had begun, finally, to wonder about Sonny, about the life that Sonny lived inside. This life, whatever it was, had made him older and thinner and it had deepened the distant stillness in which he had always moved. He looked very unlike my baby brother. Yet, when he smiled, when we shook hands, the baby brother I'd never known looked out from the depths of his private life, like an animal waiting to be coaxed into the light.

50 "How you been keeping?" he asked me.

51 "All right. And you?"

52 "Just fine." He was smiling all over his face. "It's good to see you again."

53 "It's good to see you."

54 The seven years' difference in our ages lay between us like a chasm: I wondered if these years would ever operate between us as a bridge. I was remembering, and it made it hard to catch my breath, that I had been there when he was born; and I had heard the first words he had ever spoken. When he started to walk, he walked from our mother straight to me. I caught him just before he fell when he took the first steps he ever took in this world.

55 "How's Isabel?"

56 "Just fine. She's dying to see you."

57 "And the boys?"

58 "They're fine, too. They're anxious to see their uncle."

59 "Oh, come on. You know they don't remember me."

60 "Are you kidding? Of course they remember you."

61 He grinned again. We got into a taxi. We had a lot to say to each other, far too much to know how to begin.

62 As the taxi began to move, I asked, "You still want to go to India?"

63 He laughed. "You still remember that. Hell, no. This place is Indian enough for me."

64 "It used to belong to them," I said.

65 And he laughed again. "They damn sure knew what they were doing when they got rid of it."

66 Years ago, when he was around fourteen, he'd been all hipped on the idea of going to India. He read books about people sitting on rocks, naked, in all kinds of weather, but mostly bad, naturally, and walking barefoot through hot coals and arriving at wisdom. I used to say that it sounded to me as though they were getting away from wisdom as fast as they could. I think he sort of looked down on me for that.

67 "Do you mind," he asked, "if we have the driver drive alongside the park? On the west side—I haven't seen the city in so long."

68 "Of course not," I said. I was afraid that I might sound as though I were humoring him, but I hoped he wouldn't take it that way.

69 So we drove along, between the green of the park and the stony, lifeless elegance of hotels and apartment buildings, toward the vivid, killing streets of our childhood. These streets hadn't changed, though housing projects jutted up out of them now like rocks in the middle of a boiling sea. Most of the houses in which we had grown up had vanished, as had the stores from which we had stolen, the basements in which we had first tried sex, the rooftops from which we had hurled tin cans and bricks. But houses exactly like the houses of our past yet dominated the landscape, boys exactly like the boys we once had been found themselves smothering in these houses, came down into the streets for light and air and found themselves encircled by disaster. Some escaped the trap, most didn't. Those who got out always left something of themselves behind, as some animals amputate a leg and leave it in the trap. It might be said, perhaps, that I had escaped, after all, I was a school teacher; or that Sonny had, he hadn't lived in Harlem for years. Yet, as the cab moved uptown through streets which seemed, with a rush, to darken with dark people, and as I covertly studied Sonny's face, it came to me that what we both were seeking through our separate cab windows was that part of ourselves which had been left behind. It's always at the hour of trouble and confrontation that the missing member aches.

70 We hit 110th Street and started rolling up Lenox Avenue. And I'd known this avenue all my life, but it seemed to me again, as it had seemed on the day I'd first heard about Sonny's trouble, filled with a hidden menace which was its very breath of life.

71 "We almost there," said Sonny.

72 "Almost." We were both too nervous to say anything more.

73 We lived in a housing project. It hasn't been up long. A few days after it was up it seemed uninhabitably new, now, of course, it's already rundown. It looks like a parody of the good, clean, faceless life—God knows the people who live in it do their best to make it a parody. The beat-looking grass lying around isn't enough to make their lives green, the hedges will never hold out the streets, and they know it. The big windows fool no one, they aren't big enough to make space out of no space. They don't bother with the windows, they watch the TV screen instead. The playground is most popular with the children who don't play at jacks, or skip rope, or roller skate, or swing, and they can be found in it after dark. We moved in partly because it's not too far from where I teach, and partly for the kids; but it's really just like the houses in which Sonny and I grew up. The same things happen, they'll have the same things to remember. The moment Sonny and I started into the house I had the feeling that I was simply bringing him back into the danger he had almost died trying to escape.

74 Sonny has never been talkative. So I don't know why I was sure he'd be dying to talk to me when supper was over the first night. Everything went fine, the oldest boy remembered him, and the youngest boy liked him, and Sonny had remembered to bring something for each of them; and Isabel, who is really much nicer than I am, more open and giving, had gone to a lot of trouble about dinner and was genuinely glad to see him. And she's always been able to tease Sonny in a way that I haven't. It was nice to see her face so vivid again and to hear her laugh and watch her make Sonny laugh. She wasn't, or, anyway, she didn't seem to be, at all uneasy or embarrassed. She chatted as though there were no subject which had to be avoided and she got Sonny past his first, faint stiffness. And thank God she was there, for I was filled with that icy dread again. Everything I did seemed awkward to me, and everything I said sounded freighted with hidden meaning. I was trying to remember everything I'd heard about dope addiction and I couldn't help watching Sonny for signs. I wasn't doing it out of malice. I was trying to find out something about my brother. I was dying to hear him tell me he was safe.

75 "Safe!" my father grunted, whenever Mama suggested trying to move to a neighborhood which might be safer for children. "Safe, hell! Ain't no place safe for kids, nor nobody."

76 He always went on like this, but he wasn't, ever, really as bad as he sounded, not even on weekends, when he got drunk. As a matter of fact, he was always on the lookout for "something a little better," but he died before he found it. He died suddenly, during a drunken weekend in the middle of the war, when Sonny was fifteen. He and Sonny hadn't ever got on too well. And this was partly because Sonny was the apple of his father's eye. It was because he loved Sonny so much and was frightened for him, that he was always fighting with him. It doesn't do any good to fight with Sonny. Sonny just moves back, inside himself, where he can't be reached. But the principal reason that they never hit it off is that they were so much alike. Daddy was big and rough and loud-talking, just the opposite of Sonny, but they both had—that same privacy.

77 Mama tried to tell me something about this, just after Daddy died. I was home on leave from the army.

78 This was the last time I ever saw my mother alive. Just the same, this picture gets all mixed up in my mind with pictures I had of her when she was younger. The way I always see her is the way she used to be on a Sunday afternoon, say, when the old folks were talking after the big Sunday dinner. I always see her wearing pale blue. She'd be sitting on the sofa. And my father would be sitting in the easy chair, not far from her. And the living room would be full of church folks and relatives. There they sit, in chairs all around the living room, and the night is creeping up outside, but nobody knows it yet. You can see the darkness growing against the windowpanes and you hear the street noises every now and again, or maybe the jangling beat of a tambourine from one of the churches close by, but it's real quiet in the room. For a moment nobody's talking, but every face looks darkening, like the sky outside. And my mother rocks a little from the waist, and my father's eyes are closed. Everyone is looking at something a child can't see. For a minute they've forgotten the children. Maybe a kid is lying on the rug, half asleep. Maybe somebody's got a kid in his lap and is absent-mindedly stroking the kid's head. Maybe there's a kid, quiet and big-eyed, curled up in a big chair in the corner. The silence, the darkness coming, and the darkness in the faces frightens the child obscurely. He hopes that the hand which strokes his forehead will never stop—will never die. He hopes that there will never come a time when the old folks won't be sitting around the living room, talking about where they've come from, and what they've seen, and what's happened to them and their kinfolk.

79 But something deep and watchful in the child knows that this is bound to end, is already ending. In a moment someone will get up and turn on the light. Then the old folks will remember the children and they won't talk any more that day. And when light fills the room, the child is filled with darkness. He knows that every time this happens he's moved just a little closer to that darkness outside. The darkness outside is what the old folks have been talking about. It's what they've come from. It's what they endure. The child knows that they won't talk any more because if he knows too much about what's happened to *them,* he'll know too much too soon, about what's going to happen to *him.*

80 The last time I talked to my mother, I remember I was restless. I wanted to get out and see Isabel. We weren't married then and we had a lot to straighten out between us.

81 There Mama sat, in black, by the window. She was humming an old church song, *Lord, you brought me from a long ways off.* Sonny was out somewhere. Mama kept watching the streets.

82 "I don't know," she said, "if I'll ever see you again, after you go off from here. But I hope you'll remember the things I tried to teach you."

83 "Don't talk like that," I said, and smiled. "You'll be here a long time yet."

84 She smiled, too, but she said nothing. She was quiet for a long time. And I said, "Mama, don't you worry about nothing. I'll be writing all the time, and you be getting the checks. . . ."

85 "I want to talk to you about your brother," she said, suddenly. "If anything happens to me he ain't going to have nobody to look out for him."

86 "Mama," I said, "ain't nothing going to happen to you *or* Sonny. Sonny's all right. He's a good boy and he's got good sense."

87 "It ain't a question of his being a good boy," Mama said, "nor of his having good sense. It ain't only the bad ones, nor yet the dumb ones that gets sucked under." She stopped, looking at me. "Your Daddy once had a brother," she said, and she smiled in a way that made me feel she was in pain. "You didn't never know that, did you?"

88 "No," I said, "I never knew that," and I watched her face.

89 "Oh, yes," she said, "your Daddy had a brother." She looked out of the window again. "I know you never saw your Daddy cry. But *I* did—many a time, through all these years."

90 I asked her. "What happened to his brother? How come nobody's ever talked about him?"

91 This was the first time I ever saw my mother look old.

92 "His brother got killed," she said, "when he was just a little younger than you are now. I knew him. He was a fine boy. He was maybe a little full of the devil, but he didn't mean nobody no harm."

93 Then she stopped and the room was silent, exactly as it had sometimes been on those Sunday afternoons. Mama kept looking out into the streets.

94 "He used to have a job in the mill," she said, "and, like all young folks, he just liked to perform on Saturday nights. Saturday nights, him and your father would drift around to different places, go to dances and things like that, or just sit around with people they knew, and your father's brother would sing, he had a fine voice, and play along with himself on his guitar. Well, this particular Saturday night, him and your father was coming home from some place, and they were both a little drunk and there was a moon that night, it was bright like day. Your father's brother was feeling kind of good, and he was whistling to himself, and he had his guitar slung over his shoulder. They was coming down a hill and beneath them was a road that turned off from the highway. Well, your father's brother, being always kind of frisky, decided to run down this hill, and he did, with that guitar banging and clanging behind him, and he ran across the road, and he was making water behind a tree. And your father was sort of amused at him and he was still coming down the hill, kind of slow. Then he heard a car motor and that same minute his brother stepped from behind the tree, into the road, in the moonlight. And he started to cross the road. And your father started to run down the hill, he says he don't know why. This car was full of white men. They was all drunk, and when they seen your father's brother they let out a great whoop and holler and they aimed the car straight at him. They was having fun, they just wanted to scare him, the way they do sometimes, you know. But they was drunk. And I guess the boy, being drunk, too, and scared, kind of lost his head. By the time he jumped it was too late. Your father says he heard his brother scream when the car rolled over him, and he heard the wood of that guitar when it give, and he heard them strings go flying, and he heard them white men shouting, and the car kept on a-going and it ain't stopped till this day. And, time your father got down the hill, his brother weren't nothing but blood and pulp."

95 Tears were gleaming on my mother's face. There wasn't anything I could say.

96 "He never mentioned it," she said, "because I never let him mention it before you children. Your Daddy was like a crazy man that night and for many a night thereafter. He says he never in his life seen anything as dark as that road after the lights of that car had gone away. Weren't nothing; weren't nobody on that road, just your Daddy and his brother and that busted guitar. Oh, yes. Your Daddy never did really get right again. Till the day he died he weren't sure but that every white man he saw was the man that killed his brother."

97 She stopped and took out her handkerchief and dried her eyes and looked at me.

98 "I ain't telling you all this," she said, "to make you scared or bitter or to make you hate nobody. I'm telling you this because you got a brother. And the world ain't changed."

99 I guess I didn't want to believe this. I guess she saw this in my face. She turned away from me, toward the window again, searching those streets.

100 "But I praise my Redeemer," she said at last, "that He called your Daddy home before me. I ain't saying it to throw no flowers at myself, but, I declare, it keeps me from feeling too cast down to know I helped your father get safely through this world. Your father always acted like he was the roughest, strongest man on earth. And everybody took him to be like that. But if he hadn't had *me* there—to see his tears!"

101 She was crying again. Still, I couldn't move. I said, "Lord, Lord, Mama, I didn't know it was like that."

102 "Oh, honey," she said, "There's a lot that you don't know. But you are going to find it out." She stood up from the window and came over to me. "You got to hold on to your brother," she said, "and don't let him fall, no matter what it looks like is happening to him and no matter how evil you gets with him. You going to be evil with him many a time. But don't you forget what I told you, you hear?"

103 "I won't forget," I said. "Don't you worry, I won't forget. I won't let nothing happen to Sonny."

104 My mother smiled as though she were amused at something she saw in my face. Then, "You may not be able to stop nothing from happening. But you got to let him know you's *there.*"

105 Two days later I was married, and then I was gone. And I had a lot of things on my mind and I pretty well forgot my promise to Mama until I got shipped home on a special furlough for her funeral.

106 And, after the funeral, with just Sonny and me alone in the empty kitchen, I tried to find out something about him.

107 "What do you want to do?" I asked him.

108 "I'm going to be a musician," he said.

109 For he had graduated, in the time I had been away, from dancing to the juke box to finding out who was playing what, and what they were doing with it, and he had bought himself a set of drums.

110 "You mean, you want to be a drummer?" I somehow had the feeling that being a drummer might be all right for other people but not for my brother Sonny.

111 "I don't think," he said, looking at me very gravely, "that I'll ever be a good drummer. But I think I can play a piano."

112 I frowned. I'd never played the role of the older brother quite so seriously before, had scarcely ever, in fact, *asked* Sonny a damn thing. I sensed myself in the presence of something I didn't really know how to handle, didn't understand. So I made my frown a little deeper as I asked: "What kind of musician do you want to be?"

113 He grinned. "How many kinds do you think there are?"

114 "Be *serious,*" I said.

115 He laughed, throwing his head back, and then looked at me. "I *am* serious."

116 "Well, then, for Christ's sake, stop kidding around and answer a serious question. I mean, do you want to be a concert pianist, you want to play classical music and all that, or—or what?" Long before I finished he was laughing again. "For Christ's *sake,* Sonny!"

117 He sobered, but with difficulty. "I'm sorry. But you sound so—*scared!*" and he was off again.

118 "Well, you may think it's funny now, baby, but it's not going to be so funny when you have to make your living at it, let me tell you *that.*" I was furious because I knew he was laughing at me and I didn't know why.

119 "No," he said, very sober now, and afraid, perhaps, that he'd hurt me, "I don't want to be a classical pianist. That isn't what interests me. I mean"—he paused, looking hard at me, as though his eyes would help me to understand, and then gestured helplessly, as though perhaps his hand would help—"I mean, I'll have a lot of studying to do, and I'll have to study *everything,* but, I mean, I want to play *with*—jazz musicians." He stopped. "I want to play jazz," he said.

120 Well, the word had never before sounded as heavy, as real, as it sounded that afternoon in Sonny's mouth. I just looked at him and I was probably frowning a real frown by this time. I simply couldn't see why on earth he'd want to spend his time hanging around nightclubs, clowning around on bandstands, while people pushed each other around a dance floor. It seemed—beneath him, somehow. I had never thought about it before, had never been forced to, but I suppose I had always put jazz musicians in a class with what Daddy called "goodtime people."

121 "Are you *serious?*"

122 "Hell, *yes,* I'm serious."

123 He looked more helpless than ever, and annoyed, and deeply hurt.

124 I suggested, helpfully: "You mean—like Louis Armstrong?"

125 His face closed as though I'd struck him. "No. I'm not talking about none of that old-time, down home crap."

126 "Well, look, Sonny, I'm sorry, don't get mad. I just don't altogether get it, that's all. Name somebody—you know, a jazz musician you admire."

127 "Bird."

128 "Who?"

129 "Bird! Charlie Parker! Don't they teach you nothing in the goddamn army?"

130 I lit a cigarette. I was surprised and then a little amused to discover that I was trembling. "I've been out of touch," I said. "You'll have to be patient with me. Now. Who's this Parker character?"

131 "He's just one of the greatest jazz musicians alive," said Sonny, sullenly, his hands in his pockets, his back to me. "Maybe *the* greatest," he added, bitterly, "that's probably why *you* never heard of him."

132 "All right," I said, "I'm ignorant. I'm sorry. I'll go out and buy all the cat's records right away, all right?"

133 "It don't," said Sonny, with dignity, "make any difference to me. I don't care what you listen to. Don't do me no favors."

134 I was beginning to realize that I'd never seen him so upset before. With another part of my mind I was thinking that this would probably turn out to be one of those things kids go through and that I shouldn't make it seem important by pushing it too hard. Still, I didn't think it would do any harm to ask: "Doesn't all this take a lot of time? Can you make a living at it?"

135 He turned back to me and half leaned, half sat, on the kitchen table. "Everything takes time," he said, "and—well, yes, sure, I can make a living at it. But what I don't seem to be able to make you understand is that it's the only thing I want to do."

136 "Well, Sonny," I said, gently, "you know people can't always do exactly what they *want* to do—"

137 "*No,* I don't know that," said Sonny, surprising me. "I think people *ought* to do what they want to do, what else are they alive for?"

138 "You getting to be a big boy," I said desperately, "it's time you started thinking about your future."

139 "I'm thinking about my future," said Sonny, grimly. "I think about it all the time."

140 I gave up. I decided, if he didn't change his mind, that we could always talk about it later. "In the meantime," I said, "you got to finish school." We had already decided that he'd have to move in with Isabel and her folks. I knew this wasn't the ideal arrangement because Isabel's folks are inclined to be dicty and they hadn't especially wanted Isabel to marry me. But I didn't know what else to do. "And we have to get you fixed up at Isabel's."

141 There was a long silence. He moved from the kitchen table to the window. "That's a terrible idea. You know it yourself."

142 "Do you have a *better* idea?"

143 He just walked up and down the kitchen for a minute. He was as tall as I was. He had started to shave. I suddenly had the feeling that I didn't know him at all.

144 He stopped at the kitchen table and picked up my cigarettes. Looking at me with a kind of mocking, amused defiance, he put one between his lips. "You mind?"

145 "You smoking already?"

146 He lit the cigarette and nodded, watching me through the smoke. "I just wanted to see if I'd have the courage to smoke in front of you." He grinned and blew a great cloud of smoke to the ceiling. "It was easy." He looked at my face. "Come on, now. I bet you was smoking at my age, tell the truth."

147 I didn't say anything but the truth was on my face, and he laughed. But now there was something very strained in his laugh. "Sure. And I bet that ain't all you was doing."

148 He was frightening me a little. "Cut the crap," I said. "We already decided that you was going to go and live at Isabel's. Now what's got into you all of a sudden?"

149 "*You* decided it," he pointed out. "*I* didn't decide nothing." He stopped in

front of me, leaning against the stove, arms loosely folded. "Look, brother. I don't want to stay in Harlem no more, I really don't." He was very earnest. He looked at me, then over toward the kitchen window. There was something in his eyes I'd never seen before, some thoughtfulness, some worry all his own. He rubbed the muscle of one arm. "It's time I was getting out of here."

150 "Where do you want to *go,* Sonny?"

151 "I want to join the army. Or the navy, I don't care. If I say I'm old enough, they'll believe me."

152 Then I got mad. It was because I was so scared. "You must be crazy. You goddamn fool, what the hell do you want to go and join the *army* for?"

153 "I just told you. To get out of Harlem."

154 "Sonny, you haven't even finished *school.* And if you really want to be a musician, how do you expect to study if you're in the *army?"*

155 He looked at me, trapped and in anguish. "There's ways. I might be able to work out some kind of deal. Anyway, I'll have the G.I. Bill when I come out."

156 *"If* you come out." We stared at each other. "Sonny, please. Be reasonable. I know the setup is far from perfect. But we got to do the best we can."

157 "I ain't learning nothing in school," he said. "Even when I go." He turned away from me and opened the window and threw his cigarette out into the narrow alley. I watched his back. "At least, I ain't learning nothing you'd want me to learn." He slammed the window so hard I thought the glass would fly out, and turned back to me. "And I'm sick of the stink of these garbage cans!"

158 "Sonny," I said, "I know how you feel. But if you don't finish school now, you're going to be sorry later that you didn't." I grabbed him by the shoulders. "And you only got another year. It ain't so bad. And I'll come back and I swear I'll help you do *whatever* you want to do. Just try to put up with it till I come back. Will you please do that? For me?"

159 He didn't answer and he wouldn't look at me.

160 "Sonny. You hear me?"

161 He pulled away. "I hear you. But you never hear anything *I* say."

162 I didn't know what to say to that. He looked out of the window and then back at me. "OK," he said, and sighed. "I'll try."

163 Then I said, trying to cheer him up a little, "They got a piano at Isabel's. You can practice on it."

164 And as a matter of fact, it did cheer him up for a minute. "That's right," he said to himself. "I forgot that." His face relaxed a little. But the worry, the thoughtfulness, played on it still, the way shadows play on a face which is staring into the fire.

165 But I thought I'd never hear the end of that piano. At first, Isabel would write me, saying how nice it was that Sonny was so serious about his music and how, as soon as he came in from school, or wherever he had been when he was supposed to be at school, he went straight to that piano and stayed there until suppertime. And, after supper, he went back to that piano and stayed there until everybody went to bed. He was at the piano all day Saturday and all day Sunday. Then he bought a record player and started playing records. He'd play one record over and over again,

all day long sometimes, and he'd improvise along with it on the piano. Or he'd play one section of the record, one chord, one change, one progression, then he'd do it on the piano. Then back to the record. Then back to the piano.

166 Well, I really don't know how they stood it. Isabel finally confessed that it wasn't like living with a person at all, it was like living with sound. And the sound didn't make any sense to her, didn't make any sense to any of them—naturally. They began, in a way, to be afflicted by this presence that was living in their home. It was as though Sonny were some sort of god, or monster. He moved in an atmosphere which wasn't like theirs at all. They fed him and he ate, he washed himself, he walked in and out of their door; he certainly wasn't nasty or unpleasant or rude, Sonny isn't any of those things; but it was as though he were all wrapped up in some cloud, some fire, some vision all his own; and there wasn't any way to reach him.

167 At the same time, he wasn't really a man yet, he was still a child, and they had to watch out for him in all kinds of ways. They certainly couldn't throw him out. Neither did they dare to make a great scene about that piano because even they dimly sensed, as I sensed, from so many thousands of miles away, that Sonny was at that piano playing for his life.

168 But he hadn't been going to school. One day a letter came from the school board and Isabel's mother got it—there had, apparently, been other letters but Sonny had torn them up. This day, when Sonny came in, Isabel's mother showed him the letter and asked where he'd been spending his time. And she finally got it out of him that he'd been down in Greenwich Village, with musicians and other characters, in a white girl's apartment. And this scared her and she started to scream at him and what came up, once she began—though she denies it to this day—was what sacrifices they were making to give Sonny a decent home and how little he appreciated it.

169 Sonny didn't play the piano that day. By evening, Isabel's mother had calmed down but then there was the old man to deal with, and Isabel herself. Isabel says she did her best to be calm but she broke down and started crying. She says she just watched Sonny's face. She could tell, by watching him, what was happening with him. And what was happening was that they penetrated his cloud, they had reached him. Even if their fingers had been a thousand times more gentle than human fingers ever are, he could hardly help feeling that they had stripped him naked and were spitting on that nakedness. For he also had to see that his presence, that music, which was life or death to him, had been torture for them and that they had endured it, not at all for his sake, but only for mine. And Sonny couldn't take that. He can take it a little better today than he could then but he's still not very good at it and, frankly, I don't know anybody who is.

170 The silence of the next few days must have been louder than the sound of all the music ever played since time began. One morning, before she went to work, Isabel was in his room for something and she suddenly realized that all of his records were gone. And she knew for certain that he was gone. And he was. He went as far as the navy would carry him. He finally sent me a postcard from some place in Greece and that was the first I knew that Sonny was still alive. I didn't see him any more until we were both back in New York and the war had long been over.

171 He was a man by then, of course, but I wasn't willing to see it. He came by

the house from time to time, but we fought almost every time we met. I didn't like the way he carried himself, loose and dreamlike all the time, and I didn't like his friends, and his music seemed to be merely an excuse for the life he led. It sounded just that weird and disordered.

172 Then we had a fight, a pretty awful fight, and I didn't see him for months. By and by I looked him up, where he was living, in a furnished room in the Village, and I tried to make it up. But there were lots of other people in the room and Sonny just lay on his bed, and he wouldn't come downstairs with me, and he treated these other people as though they were his family and I weren't. So I got mad and then he got mad, and then I told him that he might just as well be dead as live the way he was living. Then he stood up and he told me not to worry about him any more in life, that he *was* dead as far as I was concerned. Then he pushed me to the door and the other people looked on as though nothing were happening, and he slammed the door behind me. I stood in the hallway, staring at the door. I heard somebody laugh in the room and then the tears came to my eyes. I started down the steps, whistling to keep from crying, I kept whistling to myself, *You going to need me, baby, one of these cold, rainy days.*

173 I read about Sonny's trouble in the spring. Little Grace died in the fall. She was a beautiful little girl. But she only lived a little over two years. She died of polio and she suffered. She had a slight fever for a couple of days, but it didn't seem like anything and we just kept her in bed. And we would certainly have called the doctor, but the fever dropped, she seemed to be all right. So we thought it had just been a cold. Then, one day, she was up, playing, Isabel was in the kitchen fixing lunch for the two boys when they'd come in from school, and she heard Grace fall down in the living room. When you have a lot of children you don't always start running when one of them falls, unless they start screaming or something. And, this time, Grace was quiet. Yet, Isabel says that when she heard that *thump* and then that silence, something happened in her to make her afraid. And she ran to the living room and there was little Grace on the floor, all twisted up, and the reason she hadn't screamed was that she couldn't get her breath. And when she did scream, it was the worst sound, Isabel says, that she'd ever heard in all her life, and she still hears it sometimes in her dreams. Isabel will sometimes wake me up with a low, moaning, strangled sound and I have to be quick to awaken her and hold her to me and where Isabel is weeping against me seems a mortal wound.

174 I think I may have written Sonny the very day that little Grace was buried. I was sitting in the living room in the dark, by myself, and I suddenly thought of Sonny. My trouble made his real.

175 One Saturday afternoon, when Sonny had been living with us, or, anyway, been in our house, for nearly two weeks, I found myself wandering aimlessly about the living room, drinking from a can of beer, and trying to work up the courage to search Sonny's room. He was out, he was usually out whenever I was home, and Isabel had taken the children to see their grandparents. Suddenly I was standing still in front of the living room window, watching Seventh Avenue. The idea of searching Sonny's room made me still. I scarcely dared to admit to myself what I'd be searching for. I didn't know what I'd do if I found it. Or if I didn't.

176 On the sidewalk across from me, near the entrance to a barbecue joint, some people were holding an old-fashioned revival meeting. The barbecue cook, wearing a dirty white apron, his conked hair reddish and metallic in the pale sun, and a cigarette between his lips, stood in the doorway, watching them. Kids and older people paused in their errands and stood there, along with some older men and a couple of very tough-looking women who watched everything that happened on the avenue, as though they owned it, or were maybe owned by it. Well, they were watching this, too. The revival was being carried on by three sisters in black, and a brother. All they had were their voices and their Bibles and a tambourine. The brother was testifying and while he testified two of the sisters stood together, seeming to say, amen, and the third sister walked around with the tambourine outstretched and a couple of people dropped coins into it. Then the brother's testimony ended and the sister who had been taking up the collection dumped the coins into her palm and transferred them to the pocket of her long black robe. Then she raised both hands, striking the tambourine against the air, and then against one hand, and she started to sing. And the two other sisters and the brother joined in.

177 It was strange, suddenly, to watch, though I had been seeing these street meetings all my life. So, of course, had everybody else down there. Yet, they paused and watched and listened and I stood still at the window. *"'Tis the old ship of Zion,"* they sang, and the sister with the tambourine kept a steady, jangling beat, *"it has rescued many a thousand!"* Not a soul under the sound of their voices was hearing this song for the first time, not one of them had been rescued. Nor had they seen much in the way of rescue work being done around them. Neither did they especially believe in the holiness of the three sisters and the brother, they knew too much about them, knew where they lived, and how. The woman with the tambourine, whose voice dominated the air, whose face was bright with joy, was divided by very little from the woman who stood watching her, a cigarette between her heavy, chapped lips, her hair a cuckoo's nest, her face scarred and swollen from many beatings, and her black eyes glittering like coal. Perhaps they both knew this, which was why, when, as rarely, they addressed each other, they addressed each other as Sister. As the singing filled the air the watching, listening faces underwent a change, the eyes focusing on something within; the music seemed to soothe a poison out of them; and time seemed, nearly, to fall away from the sullen, belligerent, battered faces, as though they were fleeing back to their first condition, while dreaming of their last. The barbecue cook half shook his head and smiled, and dropped his cigarette and disappeared into his joint. A man fumbled in his pockets for change and stood holding it in his hand impatiently, as though he had just remembered a pressing appointment further up the avenue. He looked furious. Then I saw Sonny, standing on the edge of the crowd. He was carrying a wide, flat notebook with a green cover, and it made him look, from where I was standing, almost like a schoolboy. The coppery sun brought out the copper in his skin, he was very faintly smiling, standing very still. Then the singing stopped, the tambourine turned into a collection plate again. The furious man dropped in his coins and vanished, so did a couple of the women, and Sonny dropped some change in the plate, looking directly at the woman with a little smile. He started across the avenue, toward the house. He has a slow, loping walk, something like the way Harlem hipsters walk, only he's imposed on this his own half-beat. I had never really noticed it before.

178 I stayed at the window, both relieved and apprehensive. As Sonny disappeared from my sight, they began singing again. And they were still singing when his key turned in the lock.

179 "Hey," he said.

180 "Hey, yourself. You want some beer?"

181 "No. Well, maybe." But he came up to the window and stood beside me, looking out. "What a warm voice," he said.

182 They were singing *If I could only hear my mother pray again!*

183 "Yes," I said, "and she can sure beat that tambourine."

184 "But what a terrible song," he said, and laughed. He dropped his notebook on the sofa and disappeared into the kitchen. "Where's Isabel and the kids?"

185 "I think they went to see their grandparents. You hungry?"

186 "No." He came back into the living room with his can of beer. "You want to come some place with me tonight?"

187 I sensed, I don't know how, that I couldn't possibly say no. "Sure. Where?"

188 He sat down on the sofa and picked up his notebook and started leafing through it. "I'm going to sit in with some fellows in a joint in the Village."

189 "You mean, you're going to play, tonight?"

190 "That's right." He took a swallow of his beer and moved back to the window. He gave me a sidelong look. "If you can stand it."

191 "I'll try," I said.

192 He smiled to himself and we both watched as the meeting across the way broke up. The three sisters and the brother, heads bowed, were singing *God be with you till we meet again.* The faces around them were very quiet. Then the song ended. The small crowd dispersed. We watched the three women and the lone man walk slowly up the avenue.

193 "When she was singing before," said Sonny, abruptly, "her voice reminded me for a minute of what heroin feels like sometimes—when it's in your veins. It makes you feel sort of warm and cool at the same time. And distant. And—and sure." He sipped his beer, very deliberately not looking at me. I watched his face. "It makes you feel—in control. Sometimes you've got to have that feeling."

194 "Do you?" I sat down slowly in the easy chair.

195 "Sometimes." He went to the sofa and picked up his notebook again. "Some people do."

196 "In order," I asked, "to play?" And my voice was very ugly, full of contempt and anger.

197 "Well"—he looked at me with great, troubled eyes, as though, in fact, he hoped his eyes would tell me things he could never otherwise say—"they *think* so. And *if* they think so—!"

198 "And what do *you* think?" I asked.

199 He sat on the sofa and put his can of beer on the floor. "I don't know," he said, and I couldn't be sure if he were answering my question or pursuing his thoughts. His face didn't tell me. "It's not so much to *play.* It's to *stand* it, to be able to make it at all. On any level." He frowned and smiled: "In order to keep from shaking to pieces."

200 "But these friends of yours," I said, "they seem to shake themselves to pieces pretty goddamn fast."

201 "Maybe." He played with the notebook. And something told me that I should curb my tongue, that Sonny was doing his best to talk, that I should listen. "But of course you only know the ones that've gone to pieces. Some don't—or at least they haven't *yet* and that's just about all *any* of us can say." He paused. "And then there are some who just live, really, in hell, and they know it and they see what's happening and they go right on. I don't know." He sighed, dropped the notebook, folded his arms. "Some guys, you can tell from the way they play, they on something *all* the time. And you can see that, well, it makes something real for them. But of course," he picked up his beer from the floor and sipped it and put the can down again, "they *want* to, too, you've got to see that. Even some of them that say they don't—*some,* not all."

202 "And what about you?" I asked—I couldn't help it. "What about you? Do *you* want to?"

203 He stood up and walked to the window and remained silent for a long time. Then he sighed. "Me," he said. Then: "While I was downstairs before, on my way here, listening to that woman sing, it struck me all of a sudden how much suffering she must have had to go through—to sing like that. It's *repulsive* to think you have to suffer that much."

204 I said: "But there's no way not to suffer—is there, Sonny?"

205 "I believe not," he said and smiled, "but that's never stopped anyone from trying." He looked at me. "Has it?" I realized, with this mocking look, that there stood between us, forever, beyond the power of time or forgiveness, the fact that I had held silence—so long!—when he had needed human speech to help him. He turned back to the window. "No, there's no way not to suffer. But you try all kinds of ways to keep from drowning in it, to keep on top of it, and to make it seem—well, like *you.* Like you did something, all right, and now you're suffering for it. You know?" I said nothing. "Well you know," he said, impatiently, "Why *do* people suffer? Maybe it's better to do something to give it a reason, *any* reason."

206 "But we just agreed," I said, "that there's no way not to suffer. Isn't it better, then, just to—take it?"

207 "But nobody just takes it," Sonny cried, "that's what I'm telling you! *Everybody* tries not to. You're just hung up on the *way* some people try—it's not *your* way!"

208 The hair on my face began to itch, my face felt wet. "That's not true," I said, "that's not true. I don't give a damn what other people do, I don't even care how they suffer. I just care how *you* suffer." And he looked at me. "Please believe me," I said, "I don't want to see you—die—trying not to suffer."

209 "I won't," he said, flatly, "die trying not to suffer. At least, not any faster than anybody else."

210 "But there's no need," I said, trying to laugh, "is there? in killing yourself."

211 I wanted to say more, but I couldn't. I wanted to talk about will power and how life could be—well, beautiful. I wanted to say that it was all within; but was it? or, rather, wasn't that exactly the trouble? And I wanted to promise that I would never fail him again. But it would all have sounded—empty words and lies.

212 So I made the promise to myself and prayed that I would keep it.

213 "It's terrible sometimes, inside," he said, "that's what's the trouble. You walk these streets, black and funky and cold, and there's not really a living ass to talk to,

and there's nothing shaking, and there's no way of getting it out—that storm inside. You can't talk it and you can't make love with it, and when you finally try to get with it and play it, you realize *nobody's* listening. So *you've* got to listen. You got to find a way to listen."

214 And then he walked away from the window and sat on the sofa again, as though all the wind had suddenly been knocked out of him. "Sometimes you'll do *anything* to play, even cut your mother's throat." He laughed and looked at me. "Or your brother's." Then he sobered. "Or your own." Then: "Don't worry. I'm all right now and I think I'll *be* all right. But I can't forget—where I've been. I don't mean just the physical place I've been, I mean where I've *been.* And *what* I've been."

215 "What have you been, Sonny?" I asked.

216 He smiled—but sat sideways on the sofa, his elbow resting on the back, his fingers playing with his mouth and chin, not looking at me. "I've been something I didn't recognize, didn't know I could be. Didn't know anybody could be." He stopped, looking inward, looking helplessly young, looking old. "I'm not talking about it now because I feel *guilty* or anything like that—maybe it would be better if I did, I don't know. Anyway, I can't really talk about it. Not to you, not to anybody," and now he turned and faced me. "Sometimes, you know, and it was actually when I was most *out* of the world, I felt that I was in it, that I was *with* it, really, and I could play or I didn't really have to *play,* it just came out of me, it was there. And I don't know how I played, thinking about it now, but I know I did awful things, those times, sometimes, to people. Or it wasn't that I *did* anything to them—it was that they weren't real." He picked up the beer can; it was empty; he rolled it between his palms: "And other times—well, I needed a fix, I needed to find a place to lean, I needed to clear a space to *listen*—and I couldn't find it, and I—went crazy, I did terrible things to *me,* I was terrible *for* me." He began pressing the beer can between his hands, I watched the metal begin to give. It glittered, as he played with it, like a knife, and I was afraid he would cut himself, but I said nothing. "Oh well. I can never tell you. I was all by myself at the bottom of something, stinking and sweating and crying and shaking, and I smelled it, you know? *my* stink, and I thought I'd die if I couldn't get away from it and yet, all the same, I knew that everything I was doing was just locking me in with it. And I didn't know," he paused, still flattening the beer can, "I didn't know, I still *don't* know, something kept telling me that maybe it was good to smell your own stink, but I didn't think that *that* was what I'd been trying to do—and—who can stand it?" and he abruptly dropped the ruined beer can, looking at me with a small, still smile, and then rose, walking to the window as though it were the lodestone rock. I watched his face, he watched the avenue. "I couldn't tell you when Mama died—but the reason I wanted to leave Harlem so bad was to get away from drugs. And then, when I ran away, that's what I was running from—really. When I came back, nothing had changed, *I* hadn't changed, I was just—older." And he stopped, drumming with his fingers on the windowpane. The sun had vanished, soon darkness would fall. I watched his face. "It can come again," he said, almost as though speaking to himself. Then he turned to me. "It can come again," he repeated. "I just want you to know that."

217 "All right," I said, at last. "So it can come again, All right."

218 He smiled, but the smile was sorrowful. "I had to try to tell you," he said.

219 "Yes," I said. "I understand that."

220 "You're my brother," he said, looking straight at me, and not smiling at all.

221 "Yes," I repeated, "yes. I understand that."

222 He turned back to the window, looking out. "All that hatred down there," he said, "all that hatred and misery and love. It's a wonder it doesn't blow the avenue apart."

223 We went to the only nightclub on a short, dark street, downtown. We squeezed through the narrow, chattering, jam-packed bar to the entrance of the big room, where the bandstand was. And we stood there for a moment, for the lights were very dim in this room and we couldn't see. Then, "Hello, boy," said a voice and an enormous black man, much older than Sonny or myself, erupted out of all that atmospheric lighting and put an arm around Sonny's shoulder. "I been sitting right here," he said, "waiting for you."

224 He had a big voice, too, and heads in the darkness turned toward us.

225 Sonny grinned and pulled a little away, and said, "Creole, this is my brother. I told you about him."

226 Creole shook my hand. "I'm glad to meet you, son," he said, and it was clear that he was glad to meet me *there* for Sonny's sake. And he smiled, "You got a real musician in *your* family," and he took his arm from Sonny's shoulder and slapped him, lightly, affectionately, with the back of his hand.

227 "Well. Now I've heard it all," said a voice behind us. This was another musician, and a friend of Sonny's, a coal-black, cheerful-looking man, built close to the ground. He immediately began confiding to me, at the top of his lungs, the most terrible things about Sonny, his teeth gleaming like a lighthouse and his laugh coming up out of him like the beginning of an earthquake. And it turned out that everyone at the bar knew Sonny, or almost everyone; some were musicians, working there, or nearby, or not working, some were simply hangers-on, and some were there to hear Sonny play. I was introduced to all of them and they were all very polite to me. Yet, it was clear that, for them, I was only Sonny's brother. Here, I was in Sonny's world. Or, rather: his kingdom. Here, it was not even a question that his veins bore royal blood.

228 They were going to play soon and Creole installed me, by myself, at a table in a dark corner. Then I watched them, Creole, and the little black man, and Sonny, and the others, while they horsed around, standing just below the bandstand. The light from the bandstand spilled just a little short of them and, watching them laughing and gesturing and moving about, I had the feeling that they, nevertheless, were being most careful not to step into that circle of light too suddenly: that if they moved into the light too suddenly, without thinking, they would perish in flame. Then, while I watched, one of them, the small, black man, moved into the light and crossed the bandstand and started fooling around with his drums. Then—being funny and being, also, extremely ceremonious—Creole took Sonny by the arm and led him to the piano. A woman's voice called Sonny's name and a few hands started clapping. And Sonny, also being funny and being ceremonious, and so touched, I think, that he could have cried, but neither hiding it nor showing it, riding it like a man, grinned, and put both hands to his heart and bowed from the waist.

229 Creole then went to the bass fiddle and a lean, very bright-skinned brown man jumped up on the bandstand and picked up his horn. So there they were, and the atmosphere on the bandstand and in the room began to change and tighten. Someone stepped up to the microphone and announced them. Then there were all kinds of murmurs. Some people at the bar shushed others. The waitress ran around, frantically getting in the last orders, guys and chicks got closer to each other, and the lights on the bandstand, on the quartet, turned to a kind of indigo. Then they all looked different there. Creole looked about him for the last time, as though he were making certain that all his chickens were in the coop, and then he—jumped and struck the fiddle. And there they were.

230 All I know about music is that not many people ever really hear it. And even then, on the rare occasions when something opens within, and the music enters, what we mainly hear, or hear corroborated, are personal, private, vanishing evocations. But the man who creates the music is hearing something else, is dealing with the roar rising from the void and imposing order on it as it hits the air. What is evoked in him, then, is of another order, more terrible because it has no words, and triumphant, too, for that same reason. And his triumph, when he triumphs, is ours. I just watched Sonny's face. His face was troubled, he was working hard, but he wasn't with it. And I had the feeling that, in a way, everyone on the bandstand was waiting for him, both waiting for him and pushing him along. But as I began to watch Creole, I realized that it was Creole who held them all back. He had them on a short rein. Up there, keeping the beat with his whole body, wailing on the fiddle, with his eyes half closed, he was listening to everything, but he was listening to Sonny. He was having a dialogue with Sonny. He wanted Sonny to leave the shoreline and strike out for the deep water. He was Sonny's witness that deep water and drowning were not the same thing—he had been there, and he knew. And he wanted Sonny to know. He was waiting for Sonny to do the things on the keys which would let Creole know that Sonny was in the water.

231 And, while Creole listened, Sonny moved, deep within, exactly like someone in torment. I had never before thought of how awful the relationship must be between the musician and his instrument. He has to fill it, this instrument, with the breath of life, his own. He has to make it do what he wants it to do. And a piano is just a piano. It's made out of so much wood and wires and little hammers and big ones, and ivory. While there's only so much you can do with it, the only way to find this out is to try; to try and make it do everything.

232 And Sonny hadn't been near a piano for over a year. And he wasn't on much better terms with his life, not the life that stretched before him now. He and the piano stammered, started one way, got scared, stopped; started another way, panicked, marked time, started again; then seemed to have found a direction, panicked again, got stuck. And the face I saw on Sonny I'd never seen before. Everything had been burned out of it, and, at the same time, things usually hidden were being burned in, by the fire and fury of the battle which was occurring in him up there.

233 Yet, watching Creole's face as they neared the end of the first set, I had the feeling that something had happened, something I hadn't heard. Then they finished, there was scattered applause, and then, without an instant's warning, Creole started into something else, it was almost sardonic, it was *Am I Blue*. And,

as though he commanded, Sonny began to play. Something began to happen. And Creole let out the reins. The dry, low, black man said something awful on the drums, Creole answered, and the drums talked back. Then the horn insisted, sweet and high, slightly detached perhaps, and Creole listened, commenting now and then, dry, and driving, beautiful and calm and old. Then they all came together again, and Sonny was part of the family again. I could tell this from his face. He seemed to have found, right there beneath his fingers, a damn brand-new piano. It seemed that he couldn't get over it. Then, for a while, just being happy with Sonny, they seemed to be agreeing with him that brand-new pianos certainly were a gas.

234 Then Creole stepped forward to remind them that what they were playing was the blues. He hit something in all of them, he hit something in me, myself, and the music tightened and deepened, apprehension began to beat the air. Creole began to tell us what the blues were all about. They were not about anything very new. He and his boys up there were keeping it new, at the risk of ruin, destruction, madness, and death, in order to find new ways to make us listen. For, while the tale of how we suffer, and how we are delighted, and how we may triumph is never new, it always must be heard. There isn't any other tale to tell, it's the only light we've got in all this darkness.

235 And this tale, according to that face, that body, those strong hands on those strings, has another aspect in every country, and a new depth in every generation. Listen, Creole seemed to be saying, listen. Now these are Sonny's blues. He made the little black man on the drums know it, and the bright, brown man on the horn. Creole wasn't trying any longer to get Sonny in the water. He was wishing him Godspeed. Then he stepped back, very slowly, filling the air with the immense suggestion that Sonny speak for himself.

236 Then they all gathered around Sonny and Sonny played. Every now and again one of them seemed to say, amen. Sonny's fingers filled the air with life, his life. But that life contained so many others. And Sonny went all the way back, he really began with the spare, flat statement of the opening phrase of the song. Then he began to make it his. It was very beautiful because it wasn't hurried and it was no longer a lament. I seemed to hear with what burning he had made it his, with what burning we had yet to make it ours, how we could cease lamenting. Freedom lurked around us and I understood, at last, that he could help us to be free if we would listen, that he would never be free until we did. Yet, there was no battle in his face now. I heard what he had gone through, and would continue to go through until he came to rest in earth. He had made it his: that long line, of which we knew only Mama and Daddy. And he was giving it back, as everything must be given back, so that, passing through death, it can live forever. I saw my mother's face again, and felt, for the first time, how the stones of the road she had walked on must have bruised her feet. I saw the moonlit road where my father's brother died. And it brought something else back to me, and carried me past it, I saw my little girl again and felt Isabel's tears again, and I felt my own tears begin to rise. And I was yet aware that this was only a moment, that the world waited outside, as hungry as a tiger, and that trouble stretched above us, longer than the sky.

237 Then it was over. Creole and Sonny let out their breath, both soaking wet, and grinning. There was a lot of applause and some of it was real. In the dark, the girl came by and I asked her to take drinks to the bandstand. There was a long pause,

while they talked up there in the indigo light and after awhile I saw the girl put a Scotch and milk on top of the piano for Sonny. He didn't seem to notice it, but just before they started playing again, he sipped from it and looked toward me, and nodded. Then he put it back on top of the piano. For me, then, as they began to play again, it glowed and shook above my brother's head like the very cup of trembling.

(1965)

QUESTIONS

1. What are Sonny's "blues"? Consider both the musical and the nonmusical meanings.
2. Compare the values of the narrator with those of his brother. What do you find admirable about the values of either or both?
3. What kind of relationship do the brothers have? How does the narrator feel about Sonny? Account for his sense of responsibility for his younger brother.
4. Why does Baldwin include a return visit to their old neighborhood? What do we learn about their past? What more general point is implied?
5. What is the significance of the story about Sonny's uncle—his father's brother? What would be gained or lost if it were omitted?
6. How does Baldwin structure the story? Outline its organization of time and incident.
7. What precipitates the narrator's change of heart about his brother? What does the older brother learn from his experience of loss?
8. What connections does the story suggest among religion, music, drugs, and work.
9. Find a few passages that employ the imagery of darkness and images of entrapment. Comment on their significance.
10. What is the significance of the narrator's attendance at Sonny's performance? Of his buying a drink for Sonny?
11. Read the extended passage near the end of the story where Baldwin describes the musical performance of Creole, Sonny, and the others (paragraphs 230–236). Explain what is happening literally and symbolically. What does the music do for Sonny? For his brother?
12. What are we left with at the end? How promising is Sonny's future? What do you envision for the future of the brothers' relationship? Why?

SUGGESTIONS FOR WRITING

A. Compare the narrator of Baldwin's story with Wangero in Alice Walker's "Everyday Use."

B. Compare "Sonny's Blues" with one of Baldwin's essays. Consider their ideas, selection of detail, style, and tone.

C. Write an essay about your own relationship with a brother or sister. Trace the development of your relationship over time, highlighting significant incidents that contributed to it. Use dialogue and description along with explanation and analysis.

TEN

Richard Selzer

(1928–)

Richard Selzer is both a doctor and a writer. Like the American poet and pediatrician William Carlos Williams, Selzer combines practicing medicine with writing about it. His books include one collection of stories, *Rituals of Surgery* (1974) and four collections of essays—*Mortal Lessons* (1977), *Confessions of a Knife* (1979), *Letters to a Young Doctor* (1982), *Taking the World in for Repairs* (1986). Throughout his work, Selzer explores the role and image of the physician, the relations between doctor and patient, and the workings of the diseased and healthy body in all its splendor.

Born in Troy, New York, in 1928, Selzer was educated at Union College, Albany Medical College, and Yale University. Since 1960 he has lived in New Haven, where he writes, teaches at the Yale Medical School, and conducts a private practice in surgery, his father's medical specialty.

Selzer did not begin his writing career until he was nearly forty, when he experienced a restless urgency to do something besides practice medicine. When he realized that he possessed the talent and the desire to be a writer, Selzer dedicated himself to learning the craft of writing as he had earlier devoted himself to the art of surgery. He began, as he put it, "suturing words together," a suturing he had to teach himself. His major preparation for this writerly work was reading. Among the writers Selzer cites as formative influences were the English essayists, particularly G. K. Chesterton, Charles Lamb, and William Hazlitt. Important also were the fiction writers, Edgar Allan Poe and Patrick White, and the Catholic mystics, especially St. Catherine of Siena and St. John of the Cross. To these prose writers Selzer adds the French symbolist poets Arthur Rimbaud, Paul Verlaine, Charles Baudelaire and Stephan Mallarmé. From these diverse writers Selzer derived a sense of linguistic precision and artistic passion. His own writing combines these elements in striking ways.

In "The Masked Marvel's Last Toehold" Selzer describes his encounter as a surgeon with a retired wrestler whose professional name had been "The Masked Marvel." When Selzer realizes the identity of his patient, he recalls a boyhood experience when he had seen the wrestler perform. The essay records Selzer's response as doctor in light of his memory of the earlier experience. Especially exciting is the way Selzer dovetails and telescopes the two experiences.

"Four Appointments with the Discus Thrower" also describes an encounter with a patient. But Selzer is unable to help the discus thrower the way he did the wrestler. Surgery can not adequately address this patient's problem. Selzer's attitude toward the discus thrower, moreover, differs from his response to the retired wrestler. Interestingly enough, however, the language and structure of the two essays offer striking parallels. Selzer's handling of time in both selections and his inclusion of vivid pictorial detail through vivid verbs and striking figures of comparison are worthy of careful attention.

"Minor Surgery" differs from the other selections. As a short piece of narrative fiction, it offers an imaginative inside view of the central character's experience with the surgical removal of a birthmark. The story shifts the focus from doctor to patient, describing his feelings about the birthmark and the consequences of its removal. Like much good fiction, it invites us into its imaginative world without telling us exactly what to think about what we discover there.

The longest and most complex of Selzer's essays included here is "Imelda," which concerns one of his medical school experiences. It describes how Selzer learned some memorable lessons from an older surgeon and teacher, Dr. Franciscus, who performed intricate facial surgery on a young South American girl, Imelda. The essay explores the impact Imelda and Dr. Franciscus have on one another and on the medical students who learn of his experiences. Like Selzer's other essays, "Imelda" reveals his profoundly personal response to his professional experience. For Selzer the two are inseparable and reciprocal.

We are fortunate in having Selzer's comments about his experience as a writer. In an interview with Charles Schuster, Selzer described writing as a solitary experience. He writes in longhand, which he says possesses "a special kind of magic" in which "the manual work of fashioning the words . . . flows out of your hand as though it were a secretion from your own body." The energy of writing carries Selzer along as he goes on line-by-line "to get it down as the burst comes." Following this "initial fever" of writing comes what Selzer describes as the work of the "sly fox" who calculates and manipulates the draft, tinkering with it, reconstructing and polishing it. And Selzer enjoys both these stages—the impetuous commitment of words to paper and the discipline of revising and editing.

Selzer has calculated that he writes sixty to seventy polished, publishable pages a year—and hundreds more from which he distills those. In his published prose he aims to accomplish a number of things: to evoke experience, to amuse, to inform. Amid his lyric outpourings of language, his sometimes sensational subjects and details, Selzer aims to establish, as he points out, "a kinship with the reader," as if to say, "we're both in this together." (And by "this" Selzer means both this life about which the writing centers and also the writing itself.)

Beneath these purposes lie two others: to come to terms with his vocation and identity as doctor and writer; to make out of his experience as surgeon works of literary art. Selzer himself has put it clearly and forcefully: "I am writing," he says, "to make art. That's the whole thing. To write the best I can." And when he is writing to this high standard, Selzer's words perform a double function: they teach and they heal. They heal the writer, who makes himself whole in finding language to express his sense of self and world; and they heal the reader, who experiences the power and pleasure of art. In the act of writing, Richard Selzer the surgeon of the body, becomes a doctor of the soul.

 The Masked Marvel's Last Toehold

MORNING ROUNDS.

1 On the fifth floor of the hospital, in the west wing, I know that a man is sitting up in his bed, waiting for me. Elihu Koontz is seventy-five, and he is diabetic. It is two weeks since I amputated his left leg just below the knee. I walk down the corridor, but I do not go straight into his room. Instead, I pause in the doorway. He is not yet aware of my presence, but gazes down at the place in the bed where his leg used to be, and where now there is the collapsed leg of his pajamas. He is totally absorbed, like an athlete appraising the details of his body. What is he thinking, I wonder. Is he dreaming the outline of his toes. Does he see there his foot's incandescent ghost? Could he be angry? Feel that I have taken from him something for which he yearns now with all his heart? Has he forgotten so soon the pain? It was a pain so great as to set him apart from all other men, in a red-hot place where he had no kith or kin. What of those black gorilla toes and the soupy mess that was his heel? I watch him from the doorway. It is a kind of spying, I know.

2 Save for a white fringe open at the front, Elihu Koontz is bald. The hair has grown too long and is wilted. He wears it as one would wear a day-old laurel wreath. He is naked to the waist, so that I can see his breasts. They are the breasts of Buddha, inverted triangles from which the nipples swing, dark as garnets.

3 I have seen enough. I step into the room, and he sees that I am there.

4 "How did the night go, Elihu?"

5 He looks at me for a long moment. "Shut the door," he says.

6 I do, and move to the side of the bed. He takes my left hand in both of his, gazes at it, turns it over, then back, fondling, at last holding it up to his cheek. I do not withdraw from this loving. After a while he relinquishes my hand, and looks up at me.

7 "How is the pain?" I ask.

8 He does not answer, but continues to look at me in silence. I know at once that he has made a decision.

9 "Ever hear of The Masked Marvel?" He says this in a low voice, almost a whisper.

10 "What?"

11 "The Masked Marvel," he says. "You never heard of him?"

12 "No."

13 He clucks his tongue. He is exasperated.

14 All at once there is a recollection. It is dim, distant, but coming near.

15 "Do you mean the wrestler?"

16 Eagerly, he nods, and the breasts bob. How gnomish he looks, oval as the huge helpless egg of some outlandish lizard. He has very long arms, which, now and then, he unfurls to reach for things—a carafe of water, a get-well card. He gazes up at me, urging. He *wants* me to remember.

17 "Well . . . yes," I say. I am straining backward in time. "I saw him wrestle in Toronto long ago."

18 "Ha!" He smiles. "You saw *me.* And his index finger, held rigid and upright, bounces in the air.

19 The man has said something shocking, unacceptable. It must be challenged.

20 "You?" I am trying to smile.

21 Again that jab of the finger. "You saw *me.*"

22 "No," I say. But even then, something about Elihu Koontz, those prolonged arms, the shape of his head, the sudden agility with which he leans from his bed to get a large brown envelope from his nightstand, something is forcing me toward a memory. He rummages through his papers, old newspaper clippings, photographs, and I remember . . .

23 It is almost forty years ago. I am ten years old. I have been sent to Toronto to spend the summer with relatives. Uncle Max has bought two tickets to the wrestling match. He is taking me that night.

24 "He isn't allowed," says Aunt Sarah to me. Uncle Max has angina.

25 "He gets too excited," she says.

26 "I wish you wouldn't go, Max," she says.

27 "You mind your own business," he says.

28 And we go. Out into the warm Canadian evening. I am not only abroad, I am abroad in the *evening!* I have never been taken out in the evening. I am terribly excited. The trolleys, the lights, the horns. It is a bazaar. At the Maple Leaf Gardens, we sit high and near the center. The vast arena is dark except for the brilliance of the ring at the bottom.

29 It begins.

30 The wrestlers circle. They grapple. They are all haunch and paunch. I am shocked by their ugliness, but I do not show it. Uncle Max is exhilarated. He leans forward, his eyes unblinking, on his face a look of enormous happiness. One after the other, a pair of wrestlers enter the ring. The two men join, twist, jerk, tug, bend, yank, and throw. Then they leave and are replaced by another pair. At last it is the main event. "The Angel vs. The Masked Marvel."

31 On the cover of the program notes, there is a picture of The Angel hanging from the limb of a tree, a noose of thick rope around his neck. The Angel hangs just so for an hour every day, it is explained, to strengthen his neck. The Masked Marvel's trademark is a black stocking cap with holes for the eyes and mouth. He is never seen without it, states the program. No one knows who The Masked Marvel really is!

32 "Good," says Uncle Max. "Now you'll see something." He is fidgeting, waiting for them to appear. They come down separate aisles, climb into the ring from opposite sides. I have never seen anything like them. It is The Angel's neck that first captures the eye. The shaved nape rises in twin columns to puff into the white hood of a sloped and bosselated skull that is too small. As though, strangled by the sinews of that neck, the skull had long since withered and shrunk. The thing about The Angel is the absence of any mystery in his body. It is simply *there.* A monosyllabic announcement. A grunt. One looks and knows everything at once, the fat

thighs, the gigantic buttocks, the great spine from which hang knotted ropes and pale aprons of beef. And that prehistoric head. He is all of a single hideous piece, The Angel is. No detachables.

33 The Masked Marvel seems dwarfish. His fingers dangle kneeward. His short legs are slightly bowed as if under the weight of the cask they are forced to heft about. He has breasts that swing when he moves! I have never seen such breasts on a man before.

34 There is a sudden ungraceful movement, and they close upon one another. The Angel stoops and hugs The Marvel about the waist, locking his hands behind The Marvel's back. Now he straightens and lifts The Marvel as though he were uprooting a tree. Thus he holds him, then stoops again, thrusts one hand through The Marvel's crotch, and with the other grabs him by the neck. He rears and . . . The Marvel is aloft! For a long moment, The Angel stands as though deciding where to make the toss. Then throws. Was that board or bone that splintered there? Again and again, The Angel hurls himself upon the body of The Masked Marvel.

35 Now The Angel rises over the fallen Marvel, picks up one foot in both of his hands, and twists the toes downward. It is far beyond the tensile strength of mere ligament, mere cartilage. The Masked Marvel does not hide his agony, but pounds and slaps the floor with his hand, now and then reaching up toward The Angel in an attitude of supplication. I have never seen such suffering. And all the while his black mask rolls from side to side, the mouth pulled to a tight slit through which issues an endless hiss that I can hear from where I sit. All at once, I hear a shouting close by.

36 "Break it off! Tear off a leg and throw it up here!"

37 It is Uncle Max. Even in the darkness I can see that he is gray. A band of sweat stands upon his upper lip. He is on his feet now, panting, one fist pressed at his chest, the other raised warlike toward the ring. For the first time I begin to think that something terrible might happen here. Aunt Sarah was right.

38 "Sit down, Uncle Max," I say. "Take a pill, please."

39 He reaches for the pillbox, gropes, and swallows without taking his gaze from the wrestlers. I wait for him to sit down.

40 "That's not fair," I say, "twisting his toes like that."

41 "It's the toehold," he explains.

42 "But it's not *fair,*" I say again. The whole of the evil is laid open for me to perceive. I am trembling.

43 And now The Angel does something unspeakable. Holding the foot of The Marvel at full twist with one hand, he bends and grasps the mask where it clings to the back of The Marvel's head. And he pulls. He is going to strip it off! Lay bare an ultimate carnal mystery! Suddenly it is beyond mere physical violence. Now I am on my feet, shouting into the Maple Leaf Gardens.

44 "Watch out," I scream. "Stop him. Please, somebody, stop him."

45 Next to me, Uncle Max is chuckling.

46 Yet The Masked Marvel hears me, I know it. And rallies from his bed of pain. Thrusting with his free heel, he strikes The Angel at the back of the knee. The Angel falls. The Masked Marvel is on top of him, pinning his shoulders to the mat. One!

Two! Three! And it is over. Uncle Max is strangely still. I am gasping for breath. All this I remember as I stand at the bedside of Elihu Koontz.

47 Once again, I am in the operating room. It is two years since I amputated the left leg of Elihu Koontz. Now it is his right leg which is gangrenous. I have already scrubbed. I stand to one side wearing my gown and gloves. And . . . *I am masked.* Upon the table lies Elihu Koontz, pinned in a fierce white light. Spinal anesthesia has been administered. One of his arms is taped to a board placed at a right angle to his body. Into this arm, a needle has been placed. Fluid drips here from a bottle overhead. With his other hand, Elihu Koontz beats feebly at the side of the operating table. His head rolls from side to side. His mouth is pulled into weeping. It seems to me that I have never seen such misery.

48 An orderly stands at the foot of the table, holding Elihu Koontz's leg aloft by the toes so that the intern can scrub the limb with antiseptic solutions. The intern paints the foot, ankle, leg, and thigh, both front and back, three times. From a corner of the room where I wait, I look down as from an amphitheater. Then I think of Uncle Max yelling, "Tear off a leg. Throw it up here." And I think that forty years later I am making the catch.

49 "It's not fair," I say aloud. But no one hears me. I step forward to break The Masked Marvel's last toehold.

(1979)

QUESTIONS

Thought and Structure

1. What are the point and purpose of this essay. What do you think Selzer tries to accomplish in it? Does the essay have a single main point or thesis? If so, what do think it is?
2. In what way(s) does the surgeon break the Masked Marvel's toehold? Consider the various meanings of "break."
3. Compare the reactions of the boy and his uncle as they watch the wrestling match. How do you respond and evaluate the reactions of each? Why?
4. Selzer arranges his essay in three parts. Explain the relationship among the three sections. Consider how time is shaped—how chronology is broken—and with what effects.
5. What details from the second section parallel those of the first? What parallels exist between parts two and three? (Consider especially the opening paragraph of part three.)

Style and Strategy

6. What are the purpose and effect of the interrogative sentences in the opening paragraph? How would the tone of the paragraph change if these questions were converted to declarative sentences?
7. On occasion Selzer employs sentence fragments, especially in paragraphs 21, 32, and 46. Identify the fragments and consider whether they would be more or less effective if revised into complete sentences.

8. Identify and consider the effectiveness of the similes and metaphors in paragraphs 1 and 32. Explain the purposes and bases of each of the comparisons.
9. Note the profusion and precision of verbs at specific points in the essay—in paragraphs 30 and 34, for example. Account for the accuracy of each verb in these paragraphs. Substitute alternatives and consider their effectiveness.

SUGGESTIONS FOR WRITING

A. Using the questions above, write an analysis of "The Masked Marvel's Last Toehold." Interpret the essay, considering not only what Selzer says, but *how* he says it as well.

B. Describe a climactic moment of an athletic event—or of any kind of performance or contest. Try to recapture your experience of the event and provide the reader with a sense of being there.

C. Write an essay comparing or classifying different kinds of sports fans. You might compare two kinds of wrestling or baseball fans. Or you might identify characteristics that distinguish baseball fans from football fans. As another possibility, consider defining the word *fan* in an essay that highlights and explains the qualities that make a fan what he or she is.

Four Appointments with the Discus Thrower

One

1 I spy on my patients. Ought not a doctor to observe his patients by any means and from any stance, that he might the more fully assemble the evidence? So I stand in the doorways of hospital rooms and gaze. Oh, it is not all that furtive an act. Those in bed need only look up in order to discover me. But they never do.

2 From the doorway of Room 542, the man in the bed seems deeply tanned. Blue eyes and close-cropped white hair give him the appearance of vigor and good health. But I know that his skin is not brown from the sun. It is rusted, rather, in the last stage of containing the vile repose within. And the blue eyes are frosted, looking inward like the windows of a snowbound cottage. This man is blind. This man is also legless—the right leg missing from midthigh down, the left from just below the knee. It gives him the look of an ornamental tree, roots and branches pruned to the purpose that the thing should suggest a great tree but be the dwarfed facsimile thereof.

3 Propped on pillows, he cups his right thigh in both hands. Now and then, he shakes his head as though acknowledging the intensity of his suffering. In all of this, he makes no sound. Is he mute as well as blind?

4 If he is in pain, why do I not see it in his face? Why is the mouth not opened for shrieking? The eyes not spun skyward? Where are tears? He appears to be waiting for something, something that a blind man cannot watch for, but for which he is no less alert. He is listening.

5 The room in which he dwells is empty of all possessions—the get-well cards, the small private caches of food, the day-old flowers, the slippers—all the usual kickshaws of the sickroom. There is only a bed, a chair, a nightstand, and a tray on wheels that can be swung across his lap for meals. It is a wild island upon which he has been cast. It is Room 542.

Two

6 "What time is it?" he asks.

7 "Three o'clock."

8 "Morning or afternoon?"

9 "Afternoon."

10 He is silent. There is nothing else he wants to know. Only that another block of time has passed.

11 "How are you?" I say.

12 "Who is it?" he asks.

13 "It's the doctor. How do you feel?"

14 He does not answer right away.

15 "Feel?" he says.

16 "I hope you feel better," I say.

17 I press the button at the side of the bed.

18 "Down you go," I say.

19 "Yes, down," he says.

20 He falls back upon the bed awkwardly. His stumps, unweighted by legs and feet, rise in the air, presenting themselves. I unwrap the bandages from the stumps, and begin to cut away the black scabs and the dead glazed fat with scissors and forceps. A shard of white bone comes loose. I pick it away. I wash the wounds with disinfectant and redress the stumps. All this while, he does not speak. What is he thinking behind those lids that do not blink? Is he remembering the burry prickle of love? A time when he was whole? Does he dream of feet? Of when his body was not a rotting log?

21 He lies solid and inert. In spite of everything, he remains beautiful, as though he were a sailor standing athwart a slanting deck.

22 "Anything more I can do for you?" I ask.

23 For a long moment he is silent.

24 "Yes," he says at last and without the least irony, "you can bring me a pair of shoes."

25 In the corridor, the head nurse is waiting for me.

26 "We have to do something about him," she says. "Every morning he orders scrambled eggs for breakfast, and instead of eating them, he picks up the plate and throws it against the wall."

27 "Throws his plate?"

28 "Nasty. That's what he is. No wonder his family doesn't come to visit. They probably can't stand him any more than we can."

29 She is waiting for me to do something.

30 "Well?"

31 "We'll see," I say.

Three

32 The next morning, I am waiting in the corridor when the kitchen delivers his breakfast. I watch the aide place the tray on the stand and swing it across his lap. She presses the button to raise the head of the bed. Then she leaves.

33 In this time, which he has somehow identified as morning, the man reaches to find the rim of the tray, then on to find the dome of the covered dish. He lifts off the cover and places it on the stand. He fingers across the plate until he probes the eggs. He lifts the plate in both of his hands, sets it on the palm of his right hand, centers it, balances it. He hefts it up and down slightly, getting the feel of it. Abruptly, he draws back his right arm as far as he can.

34 There is the crack of the plate breaking against the wall at the foot of his bed and the small wet sound of the scrambled eggs dropping to the floor. Just so does this man break his fast.

35 And then he laughs. It is a sound you have never heard. It is something new under the sun.

36 Out in the corridor the eyes of the head nurse narrow.

37 "Laughed, did he?"

38 She writes something down on her clipboard.

39 A second aide arrives, brings a second breakfast tray, puts it on the nightstand out of his reach. She looks over at me, shaking her head and making her mouth go. I see that we are to be accomplices.

40 "I've got to feed you," she says to the man.

41 "Oh, no you don't," the man says.

42 "Oh, yes I do," the aide says, "after what you just did. Nurse says so."

43 "Get me my shoes," the man says.

44 "Here's oatmeal," the aide says. "Open." And she touches the spoon to his lower lip.

45 "I ordered scrambled eggs," says the man.

46 "That's right," the aide says.

47 I step forward.

48 "Is there anything I can do?" I say.

49 "Who are you?" the man asks.

Four

50 In the evening, I go once more to that ward to make my rounds. The head nurse reports to me that Room 542 is deceased. She has discovered this quite by accident, she says. No, there had been no sound. Nothing. It's a blessing, she says.

51 I go into his room, a spy looking for secrets. He is still there in his bed. His face is relaxed, grave, dignified, as the faces of the newly dead are. After a while,

I turn to leave. My gaze sweeps the wall at the foot of the bed, and I see the place where it has been repeatedly washed, where the wall looks very clean and very white in contrast to the rest, which is dirty and gray.

(1979)

QUESTIONS

Thought and Structure

1. Is this an essay or a story? Does it read like fact or fiction? Why?
2. How do you answer the question posed in part one about the doctor's right and responsibility to observe his patients. How far does this privilege extend?
3. Why is the essay arranged in four parts? Provide a title for each, explain the point of each, and identify the relationship among the four sections.
4. Why does the patient hurl his scrambled-egg discus? What are the connotations of "discus thrower"?
5. What do you make of the ending? How does it clarify the essay's meaning?

Style and Strategy

6. How many words for seeing can you identify in the piece? What are their denotations and connotations?
7. Identify three similes or metaphors, and explain their significance.
8. Identify two striking or unusual details, explain your reaction to them, and comment on their significance.
9. Selzer employs numerous questions in this selection. Why? Discuss their effectiveness.
10. Look at Selzer's use of verbs in part three. Comment on their appropriateness and their effects.

SUGGESTIONS FOR WRITING

A. Write an essay describing an unusual relationship you have been involved in or an experience you've had. Employ simile, metaphor, and imagery to convey your attitude toward the subject. Divide the essay into three or more sections or scenes.

B. Write an essay comparing the image and role of the doctor in this essay with those in "The Masked Marvel's Last Toehold" or "Imelda"—or both.

Imelda

I

1 I heard the other day that Hugh Franciscus had died. I knew him once. He was the Chief of Plastic Surgery when I was a medical student at Albany Medical

College. Dr. Franciscus was the archetype of the professor of surgery—tall, vigorous, muscular, as precise in his technique as he was impeccable in his dress. Each day a clean lab coat monkishly starched, that sort of thing. I doubt that he ever read books. One book only, that of the human body, took the place of all others. He never raised his eyes from it. He read it like a printed page as though he knew that in the calligraphy there just beneath the skin were all the secrets of the world. Long before it became visible to anyone else, he could detect the first sign of granulation at the base of a wound, the first blue line of new epithelium at the periphery that would tell him that a wound would heal, or the barest hint of necrosis that presaged failure. This gave him the appearance of a prophet. "This skin graft will take," he would say, and you must believe beyond all cyanosis, exudation and inflammation that it would.

2 He had enemies, of course, who said he was arrogant, that he exalted activity for its own sake. Perhaps. But perhaps it was no more than the honesty of one who knows his own worth. Just look at a scalpel, after all. What a feeling of sovereignty, megalomania even, when you know that it is you and you alone who will make certain use of it. It was said, too, that he was a ladies' man. I don't know about that. It was all rumor. Besides, I think he had other things in mind than mere living. Hugh Franciscus was a zealous hunter. Every fall during the season he drove upstate to hunt deer. There was a glass-front case in his office where he showed his guns. How could he shoot a deer? we asked. But he knew better. To us medical students he was someone heroic, someone made up of several gods, beheld at a distance, and always from a lesser height. If he had grown accustomed to his miracles, we had not. He had no close friends on the staff. There was something a little sad in that. As though once long ago he had been flayed by friendship and now the slightest breeze would hurt. Confidences resulted in dishonor. Perhaps the person in whom one confided would scorn him, betray. Even though he spent his days among those less fortunate, weaker than he—the sick, after all—Franciscus seemed aware of an air of personal harshness in his environment to which he reacted by keeping his own counsel, by a certain remoteness. It was what gave him the appearance of being haughty. With the patients he was forthright. All the facts laid out, every question anticipated and answered with specific information. He delivered good news and bad with the same dispassion.

3 I was a third-year student, just turned onto the wards for the first time, and clerking on Surgery. Everything—the operating room, the morgue, the emergency room, the patients, professors, even the nurses—was terrifying. One picked one's way among the mines and booby traps of the hospital, hoping only to avoid the hemorrhage and perforation of disgrace. The opportunity for humiliation was everywhere.

4 It all began on Ward Rounds. Dr. Franciscus was demonstrating a cross-leg flap graft he had constructed to cover a large fleshy defect in the leg of a merchant seaman who had injured himself in a fall. The man was from Spain and spoke no English. There had been a comminuted fracture of the femur, much soft tissue damage, necrosis. After weeks of débridement and dressings, the wound had been made ready for grafting. Now the patient was in his fifth postoperative day. What we saw was a thick web of pale blue flesh arising from the man's left thigh, and which had been sutured to the open wound on the right thigh. When the surgeon pressed

the pedicle with his finger, it blanched; when he let up, there was a slow return of the violaceous color.

5 "The circulation is good," Franciscus announced. "It will get better." In several weeks, we were told, he would divide the tube of flesh at its site of origin, and tailor it to fit the defect to which, by then, it would have grown more solidly. All at once, the webbed man in the bed reached out, and gripping Franciscus by the arm, began to speak rapidly, pointing to his groin and hip. Franciscus stepped back at once to disengage his arm from the patient's grasp.

6 "Anyone here know Spanish? I didn't get a word of that."

7 "The cast is digging into him up above," I said. "The edges of the plaster are rough. When he moves, they hurt."

8 Without acknowledging my assistance, Dr. Franciscus took a plaster shears from the dressing cart and with several large snips cut away the rough edges of the cast.

9 *"Gracias, gracias."* The man in the bed smiled. But Franciscus had already moved on to the next bed. He seemed to me a man of immense strength and ability, yet without affection for the patients. He did not want to be touched by them. It was less kindness that he showed them than a reassurance that he would never give up, that he would bend every effort. If anyone could, he would solve the problems of their flesh.

10 Ward Rounds had disbanded and I was halfway down the corridor when I heard Dr. Franciscus' voice behind me.

11 "You speak Spanish." It seemed a command.

12 "I lived in Spain for two years," I told him.

13 "I'm taking a surgical team to Honduras next week to operate on the natives down there. I do it every year for three weeks, somewhere. This year, Honduras. I can arrange the time away from your duties here if you'd like to come along. You will act as interpreter. I'll show you how to use the clinical camera. What you'd see would make it worthwhile."

14 So it was that, a week later, the envy of my classmates, I joined the mobile surgical unit—surgeons, anesthetists, nurses and equipment—aboard a Military Air Transport plane to spend three weeks performing plastic surgery on people who had been previously selected by an advance team. Honduras. I don't suppose I shall ever see it again. Nor do I especially want to. From the plane it seemed a country made of clay—burnt umber, raw sienna, dry. It had a deadweight quality, as though the ground had no buoyancy, no air sacs through which a breeze might wander. Our destination was Comayagua, a town in the Central Highlands. The town itself was situated on the edge of one of the flatlands that were linked in a network between the granite mountains. Above, all was brown, with only an occasional Spanish cedar tree; below, patches of luxuriant tropical growth. It was a day's bus ride from the airport. For hours, the town kept appearing and disappearing with the convolutions of the road. At last, there it lay before us, panting and exhausted at the bottom of the mountain.

15 That was all I was to see of the countryside. From then on, there was only the derelict hospital of Comayagua, with the smell of spoiling bananas and the accumulated odors of everyone who had been sick there for the last hundred years.

Of the two, I much preferred the frank smell of the sick. The heat of the place was incendiary. So hot that, as we stepped from the bus, our own words did not carry through the air, but hung limply at our lips and chins. Just in front of the hospital was a thirsty courtyard where mobs of waiting people squatted or lay in the meager shade, and where, on dry days, a fine dust rose through which untethered goats shouldered. Against the walls of this courtyard, gaunt, dejected men stood, their faces, like their country, preternaturally solemn, leaden. Here no one looked up at the sky. Every head was bent beneath a wide-brimmed straw hat. In the days that followed, from the doorway of the dispensary, I would watch the brown mountains sliding about, drinking the hospital into their shadow as the afternoon grew later and later, flattening us by their very altitude.

16 The people were mestizos, of mixed Spanish and Indian blood. They had flat, broad, dumb museum feet. At first they seemed to me indistinguishable the one from the other, without animation. All the vitality, the hidden sexuality, was in their black hair. Soon I was to know them by the fissures with which each face was graven. But, even so, compared to us, they were masked, shut away. My job was to follow Dr. Franciscus around, photograph the patients before and after surgery, interpret and generally act as aide-de-camp. It was exhilarating. Within days I had decided that I was not just useful, but essential. Despite that we spent all day in each other's company, there were no overtures of friendship from Dr. Franciscus. He knew my place, and I knew it, too. In the afternoon he examined the patients scheduled for the next day's surgery. I would call out a name from the doorway to the examining room. In the courtyard someone would rise. I would usher the patient in, and nudge him to the examining table where Franciscus stood, always, I thought, on the verge of irritability. I would read aloud the case history, then wait while he carried out his examination. While I took the "before" photographs, Dr. Franciscus would dictate into a tape recorder:

17 "Ulcerating basal cell carcinoma of the right orbit—six by eight centimeters—involving the right eye and extending into the floor of the orbit. Operative plan: wide excision with enucleation of the eye. Later, bone and skin grafting." The next morning we would be in the operating room where the procedure would be carried out.

18 We were more than two weeks into our tour of duty—a few days to go—when it happened. Earlier in the day I had caught sight of her through the window of the dispensary. A thin, dark Indian girl about fourteen years old. A figurine, orange-brown, terra-cotta, and still attached to the unshaped clay from which she had been carved. An older, sun-weathered woman stood behind and somewhat to the left of the girl. The mother was short and dumpy. She wore a broad-brimmed hat with a high crown, and a shapeless dress like a cassock. The girl had long, loose black hair. There were tiny gold hoops in her ears. The dress she wore could have been her mother's. Far too big, it hung from her thin shoulders at some risk of slipping down her arms. Even with her in it, the dress was empty, something hanging on the back of a door. Her breasts made only the smallest imprint in the cloth, her hips none at all. All the while, she pressed to her mouth a filthy, pink, balled-up rag as though to stanch a flow or buttress against pain. I knew that what she had come to show us, what we were there to see, was hidden beneath that pink cloth. As I watched,

the woman handed down to her a gourd from which the girl drank, lapping like a dog. She was the last patient of the day. They had been waiting in the courtyard for hours.

19 "Imelda Valdez," I called out. Slowly she rose to her feet, the cloth never leaving her mouth, and followed her mother to the examining-room door. I shooed them in.

20 "You sit up there on the table," I told her. "Mother, you stand over there, please." I read from the chart:

21 "This is a fourteen-year-old girl with a complete, unilateral, left-sided cleft lip and cleft palate. No other diseases or congenital defects. Laboratory tests, chest X ray—negative."

22 "Tell her to take the rag away," said Dr. Franciscus. I did, and the girl shrank back, pressing the cloth all the more firmly.

23 "Listen, this is silly," said Franciscus. "Tell her I've got to see it. Either she behaves, or send her away."

24 "Please give me the cloth," I said to the girl as gently as possible. She did not. She could not. Just then, Franciscus reached up and, taking the hand that held the rag, pulled it away with a hard jerk. For an instant the girl's head followed the cloth as it left her face, one arm still upflung against showing. Against all hope, she would hide herself. A moment later, she relaxed and sat still. She seemed to me then like an animal that looks outward at the infinite, at death, without fear, with recognition only.

25 Set as it was in the center of the girl's face, the defect was utterly hideous—a nude rubbery insect that had fastened there. The upper lip was widely split all the way to the nose. One white tooth perched upon the protruding upper jaw projected through the hole. Some of the bone seemed to have been gnawed away as well. Above the thing, clear almond eyes and long black hair reflected the light. Below, a slender neck where the pulse trilled visibly. Under our gaze the girl's eyes fell to her lap where her hands lay palms upward, half open. She was a beautiful bird with a crushed beak. And tense with the expectation of more shame.

26 "Open your mouth," said the surgeon. I translated. She did so, and the surgeon tipped back her head to see inside.

27 "The palate, too. Complete," he said. There was a long silence. At last he spoke.

28 "What is your name?" The margins of the wound melted until she herself was being sucked into it.

29 "Imelda." The syllables leaked through the hole with a slosh and a whistle.

30 "Tomorrow," said the surgeon, "I will fix your lip. *Mañana.*"

31 It seemed to me that Hugh Franciscus, in spite of his years of experience, in spite of all the dreadful things he had seen, must have been awed by the sight of this girl. I could see it flit across his face for an instant. Perhaps it was her small act of concealment, that he had had to demand that she show him the lip, that he had had to force her to show it to him. Perhaps it was her resistance that intensified the disfigurement. Had she brought her mouth to him willingly, without shame, she would have been for him neither more nor less than any other patient.

32 He measured the defect with calipers, studied it from different angles, turning her head with a finger at her chin.

33 "How can it ever be put back together?" I asked.

34 "Take her picture," he said. And to her, "Look straight ahead." Through the eye of the camera she seemed more pitiful than ever, her humiliation more complete.

35 "Wait!" The surgeon stopped me. I lowered the camera. A strand of her hair had fallen across her face and found its way to her mouth, becoming stuck there by saliva. He removed the hair and secured it behind her ear.

36 "Go ahead," he ordered. There was the click of the camera. The girl winced.

37 "Take three more, just in case."

38 When the girl and her mother had left, he took paper and pen and with a few lines drew a remarkable likeness of the girl's face.

39 "Look," he said. "If this dot is *A*, and this one *B*, this, *C* and this, *D*, the incisions are made *A* to *B*, then *C* to *D*. *CD* must equal *AB*. It is all equilateral triangles." All well and good, but then came *X* and *Y* and rotation flaps and the rest.

40 "Do you see?" he asked.

41 "It is confusing," I told him.

42 "It is simply a matter of dropping the upper lip into a normal position, then crossing the gap with two triangular flaps. It is geometry," he said.

43 "Yes," I said. "Geometry." And relinquished all hope of becoming a plastic surgeon.

II

44 In the operating room the next morning the anesthesia had already been administered when we arrived from Ward Rounds. The tube emerging from the girl's mouth was pressed against her lower lip to be kept out of the field of surgery. Already, a nurse was scrubbing the face which swam in a reddish-brown lather. The tiny gold earrings were included in the scrub. Now and then, one of them gave a brave flash. The face was washed for the last time, and dried. Green towels were placed over the face to hide everything but the mouth and nose. The drapes were applied.

45 "Calipers!" The surgeon measured, locating the peak of the distorted Cupid's bow.

46 "Marking pen!" He placed the first blue dot at the apex of the bow. The nasal sills were dotted; next, the inferior philtral dimple, the vermilion line. The *A* flap and the *B* flap were outlined. On he worked, peppering the lip and nose, making sense out of chaos, realizing the lip that lay waiting in that deep essential pink, that only he could see. The last dot and line were placed. He was ready.

47 "Scalpel!" He held the knife above the girl's mouth.

48 "O.K. to go ahead?" he asked the anesthetist.

49 "Yes."

50 He lowered the knife.

51 "No! Wait!" The anesthetist's voice was tense, staccato. "Hold it!"

52 The surgeon's hand was motionless.

53 "What's the matter?"

54 "Something's wrong. I'm not sure. God, she's hot as a pistol. Blood pressure is way up. Pulse one eighty. Get a rectal temperature." A nurse fumbled beneath the drapes. We waited. The nurse retrieved the thermometer.

55 "One hundred seven . . . no . . . eight." There was disbelief in her voice.

56 "Malignant hyperthermia," said the anesthetist. "Ice! Ice! Get lots of ice!" I raced out the door, accosted the first nurse I saw.

57 "Ice!" I shouted. *"Hielo!* Quickly! *Hielo!"* The woman's expression was blank. I ran to another. *"Hielo! Hielo!* For the love of God, ice."

58 *"Hielo?"* She shrugged. *"Nada."* I ran back to the operating room.

59 "There isn't any ice," I reported. Dr. Franciscus had ripped off his rubber gloves and was feeling the skin of the girl's abdomen. Above the mask his eyes were the eyes of a horse in battle.

60 "The EKG is wild . . ."

61 "I can't get a pulse . . ."

62 "What the hell . . ."

63 The surgeon reached for the girl's groin. No femoral pulse.

64 "EKG flat. My God! She's dead!"

65 "She can't be."

66 "She is."

67 The surgeon's fingers pressed the groin where there was no pulse to be felt, only his own pulse hammering at the girl's flesh to be let in.

III

68 It was noon, four hours later, when we left the operating room. It was a day so hot and humid I felt steamed open like an envelope. The woman was sitting on a bench in the courtyard in her dress like a cassock. In one hand she held the piece of cloth the girl had used to conceal her mouth. As we watched, she folded it once neatly, and then again, smoothing it, cleaning the cloth which might have been the head of the girl in her lap that she stroked and consoled.

69 "I'll do the talking here," he said. He would tell her himself, in whatever Spanish he could find. Only if she did not understand was I to speak for him. I watched him brace himself, set his shoulders. How could he tell her? I wondered. What? But I knew he would tell her everything, exactly as it had happened. As much for himself as for her, he needed to explain. But suppose she screamed, fell to the ground, attacked him, even? All that hope of love . . . gone. Even in his discomfort I knew that he was teaching me. The way to do it was professionally. Now he was standing above her. When the woman saw that he did not speak, she lifted her eyes and saw what he held crammed in his mouth to tell her. She knew, and rose to her feet.

70 *"Señora,"* he began, "I am sorry." All at once he seemed to me shorter than he was, scarcely taller than she. There was a place at the crown of his head where the hair had grown thin. His lips were stones. He could hardly move them. The voice dry, dusty.

71 "No one could have known. Some bad reaction to the medicine for sleeping. It poisoned her. High fever. She did not wake up." The last, a whisper. The woman studied his lips as though she were deaf. He tried, but could not control a twitching at the corner of his mouth. He raised a thumb and forefinger to press something back into his eyes.

72 "*Muerte,*" the woman announced to herself. Her eyes were human, deadly.

73 "*Sí, muerte.*" At that moment he was like someone cast, still alive, as an effigy for his own tomb. He closed his eyes. Nor did he open them until he felt the touch of the woman's hand on his arm, a touch from which he did not withdraw. Then he looked and saw the grief corroding her face, breaking it down, melting the features so that eyes, nose, mouth ran together in a distortion, like the girl's. For a long time they stood in silence. It seemed to me that minutes passed. At last her face cleared, the features rearranged themselves. She spoke, the words coming slowly to make certain that he understood her. She would go home now. The next day her sons would come for the girl, to take her home for burial. The doctor must not be sad. God has decided. And she was happy now that the harelip had been fixed so that her daughter might go to Heaven without it. Her bare feet retreating were the felted pads of a great bereft animal.

IV

74 The next morning I did not go to the wards, but stood at the gate leading from the courtyard to the road outside. Two young men in striped ponchos lifted the girl's body wrapped in a straw mat onto the back of a wooden cart. A donkey waited. I had been drawn to this place as one is drawn, inexplicably, to certain scenes of desolation—executions, battlefields. All at once, the woman looked up and saw me. She had taken off her hat. The heavy-hanging coil of her hair made her head seem larger, darker, noble. I pressed some money into her hand.

75 "For flowers," I said. "A priest." Her cheeks shook as though minutes ago a stone had been dropped into her navel and the ripples were just now reaching her head. I regretted having come to that place.

76 "*Sí, sí,*" the woman said. Her own face was stitched with flies. "The doctor is one of the angels. He has finished the work of God. My daughter is beautiful."

77 What could she mean! The lip had not been fixed. The girl had died before he would have done it.

78 "Only a fine line that God will erase in time," she said.

79 I reached into the cart and lifted a corner of the mat in which the girl had been rolled. Where the cleft had been there was now a fresh line of tiny sutures. The Cupid's bow was delicately shaped, the vermilion border aligned. The flattened nostril had now the same rounded shape as the other one. I let the mat fall over the face of the dead girl, but not before I had seen the touching place where the finest black hairs sprang from the temple.

80 "*Adiós, adiós . . .*" And the cart creaked away to the sound of hooves, a tinkling bell.

V

81 There are events in a doctor's life that seem to mark the boundary between youth and age, seeing and perceiving. Like certain dreams, they illuminate a whole lifetime of past behavior. After such an event, a doctor is not the same as he was before. It had seemed to me then to have been the act of someone demented, or at least insanely arrogant. An attempt to reorder events. Her death had come to him out of order. It should have come after the lip had been repaired, not before. He could have told the mother that, no, the lip had not been fixed. But he did not. He said nothing. It had been an act of omission, one of those strange lapses to which all of us are subject and which we live to regret. It must have been then, at that moment, that the knowledge of what he would do appeared to him. The words of the mother had not consoled him; they had hunted him down. He had not done it for her. The dire necessity was his. He would not accept that Imelda had died before he could repair her lip. People who do such things break free from society. They follow their own lonely path. They have a secret which they can never reveal. I must never let on that I knew.

VI

82 How often I have imagined it. Ten o'clock at night. The hospital of Comayagua is all but dark. Here and there lanterns tilt and skitter up and down the corridors. One of these lamps breaks free from the others and descends the stone steps to the underground room that is the morgue of the hospital. This room wears the expression as if it had waited all night for someone to come. No silence so deep as this place with its cargo of newly dead. Only the slow drip of water over stone. The door closes gassily and clicks shut. The lock is turned. There are four tables, each with a body encased in a paper shroud. There is no mistaking her. She is the smallest. The surgeon takes a knife from his pocket and slits open the paper shroud, that part in which the girl's head is enclosed. The wound seems to be living on long after she has died. Waves of heat emanate from it, blurring his vision. All at once, he turns to peer over his shoulder. He sees nothing, only a wooden crucifix on the wall.

83 He removes a package of instruments from a satchel and arranges them on a tray. Scalpel, scissors, forceps, needle holder. Sutures and gauze sponges are produced. Stealthy, hunched, engaged, he begins. The dots of blue dye are still there upon her mouth. He raises the scalpel, pauses. A second glance into the darkness. From the wall a small lizard watches and accepts. The first cut is made. A sluggish flow of dark blood appears. He wipes it away with a sponge. No new blood comes to take its place. Again and again he cuts, connecting each of the blue dots until the whole of the zigzag slice is made, first on one side of the cleft, then on the other. Now the edges of the cleft are lined with fresh tissue. He sets down the scalpel and takes up scissors and forceps, undermining the little flaps until each triangle is attached only at one side. He rotates each flap into its new position. He must be certain that they can be swung without tension. They can. He is ready to suture.

He fits the tiny curved needle into the jaws of the needle holder. Each suture is placed precisely the same number of millimeters from the cut edge, and the same distance apart. He ties each knot down until the edges are apposed. Not too tightly. These are the most meticulous sutures of his life. He cuts each thread close to the knot. It goes well. The vermilion border with its white skin roll is exactly aligned. One more stitch and the Cupid's bow appears as if by magic. The man's face shines with moisture. Now the nostril is incised around the margin, released, and sutured into a round shape to match its mate. He wipes the blood from the face of the girl with gauze that he has dipped in water. Crumbs of light are scattered on the girl's face. The shroud is folded once more about her. The instruments are handed into the satchel. In a moment the morgue is dark and a lone lantern ascends the stairs and is extinguished.

VII

84 Six weeks later I was in the darkened amphitheater of the Medical School. Tiers of seats rose in a semicircle above the small stage where Hugh Franciscus stood presenting the case material he had encountered in Honduras. It was the highlight of the year. The hall was filled. The night before he had arranged the slides in the order in which they were to be shown. I was at the controls of the slide projector.

85 "Next slide!" he would order from time to time in that military voice which had called forth blind obedience from generations of medical students, interns, residents and patients.

86 "This is a fifty-seven-year-old man with a severe burn contracture of the neck. You will notice the rigid webbing that has fused the chin to the presternal tissues. No motion of the head on the torso is possible. . . . Next slide!"

87 "Click," went the projector.

88 "Here he is after the excision of the scar tissue and with the head in full extension for the first time. The defect was then covered. . . . Next slide!"

89 "Click."

90 ". . . with full-thickness drums of skin taken from the abdomen with the Padgett dermatome. Next slide!"

91 "Click."

92 And suddenly there she was, extracted from the shadows, suspended above and beyond all of us like a resurrection. There was the oval face, the long black hair unbraided, the tiny gold hoops in her ears. And that luminous gnawed mouth. The whole of her life seemed to have been summed up in this photograph. A long silence followed that was the surgeon's alone to break. Almost at once, like the anesthetist in the operating room in Comayagua, I knew that something was wrong. It was not that the man would not speak as that he could not. The audience of doctors, nurses and students seemed to have been infected by the black, limitless silence. My own pulse doubled. It was hard to breathe. Why did he not call out for the next slide? Why did he not save himself? Why had he not removed this slide from the ones to be shown? All at once I knew that he had used his camera on her again. I could see the long black shadows of her hair flowing into the darker shadows of the morgue.

The sudden blinding flash . . . The next slide would be the one taken in the morgue. He would be exposed.

93 In the dim light reflected from the slide, I saw him gazing up at her, seeing not the colored photograph, I thought, but the negative of it where the ghost of the girl was. For me, the amphitheater had become Honduras. I saw again that courtyard littered with patients. I could see the dust in the beam of light from the projector. It was then that I knew that she was his measure of perfection and pain—the one lost, the other gained. He, too, had heard the click of the camera, had seen her wince and felt his mercy enlarge. At last he spoke.

94 "Imelda." It was the one word he had heard her say. At the sound of his voice I removed the next slide from the projector. "Click" . . . and she was gone. "Click" again, and in her place the man with the orbital cancer. For a long moment Franciscus looked up in my direction, on his face an expression that I have given up trying to interpret. Gratitude? Sorrow? It made me think of the gaze of the girl when at last she understood that she must hand over to him the evidence of her body.

95 "This is a sixty-two-year-old man with a basal cell carcinoma of the temple eroding into the bony orbit . . ." he began as though nothing had happened.

96 At the end of the hour, even before the lights went on, there was loud applause. I hurried to find him among the departing crowd. I could not. Some weeks went by before I caught sight of him. He seemed vaguely convalescent, as though a fever had taken its toll before burning out.

97 Hugh Franciscus continued to teach for fifteen years, although he operated a good deal less, then gave it up entirely. It was as though he had grown tired of blood, of always having to be involved with blood, of having to draw it, spill it, wipe it away, stanch it. He was a quieter, softer man, I heard, the ferocity diminished. There were no more expeditions to Honduras or anywhere else.

98 I, too, have not been entirely free of her. Now and then, in the years that have passed, I see that donkey-cart cortège, or his face bent over hers in the morgue. I would like to have told him what I now know, that his unrealistic act was one of goodness, one of those small, persevering acts done, perhaps, to ward off madness. Like lighting a lamp, boiling water for tea, washing a shirt. But, of course, it's too late now.

(1982)

QUESTIONS

Thought and Structure

1. Identify three ideas that emerge in the essay. Comment briefly on each.
2. Explain the purpose of the essay. How do you think Selzer wants us to respond to Imelda, to Dr. Franciscus, and to himself as a medical student?
3. "Imelda" is arranged in seven sections. Provide a title and explain the purpose of each.

4. Provide another way of thinking about the organization of the essay, one that comprises fewer than the seven sections Selzer has established. Can any of the short sections be grouped? On what basis?

Style and Strategy

5. Notice the way each of the following sentences employs units of three:

   There was the oval face, the long black hair unbraided, the tiny gold hoops in her ears. (92)

   Like lighting a lamp, boiling water for tea, washing a shirt. (98)

   It was as though he had grown tired of blood, of always having to be involved with blood, of having to draw it, spill it, wipe it away, stanch it. (97)

   The heavy-hanging coil of her hair made her head seem larger, darker, noble. (74)

   Then he looked and saw the grief corroding her face, breaking it down, melting the features so that eyes, nose, mouth ran together in a distortion, like the girl's. (73)

   Stealthy, hunched, engaged, he begins. (83)

   What is the effect of these rhetorical groupings?

6. Notice how in the following sentences Selzer preserves a balance of word against word, phrase against phrase, clause against clause.

   There are events in a doctor's life that seem to mark the boundary between youth and age, seeing and perceiving. (81)

   It had seemed to me then to have been the act of someone demented, or at least insanely arrogant. (81)

   The words of the mother had not consoled him; they had hunted him down. (81)

   The door closes gassily and clicks shut. (82)

   It was then that I knew that she was his measure of perfection and pain—the one lost, the other gained. (93)

   What does Selzer gain from such balancing?

7. Consider carefully the diction (word choices) and comparisons in section III. Comment on their tone, their effect, their descriptive power, their precision, and their emotional weight.

8. What is the effect of using Spanish words throughout the essay rather than English equivalents? Substitute English for the Spanish and consider the differences.

SUGGESTIONS FOR WRITING

A. Write an essay in which you describe your feelings as you were reading "Imelda." Try to account for your state of mind and heart as you read. Include also your responses upon finishing the piece and then again after having had some time to think about it.

B. Discuss what you take to be an important idea that emerges in the essay: perhaps something Selzer states in one of the more reflective moments in the piece; perhaps something you discover in its dialogue or action.

C. Write imitations of the sentences referred to in questions 5 and 6.

Minor Surgery

1 What am I doing here? he thought. This is crazy. I don't want to do it. I should get up and leave—now, while there's still time. Why did I listen to her?

2 But Nathan stayed.

3 "This will be just a little pinprick and a slight burning for a minute. You won't feel anything after that. Ready? Here goes."

4 Nathan felt the sting of the needle, a moment of heat, then nothing.

5 "Good boy," said the voice behind the mask. The eyes looked approvingly at him.

6 Get up, get up, run, quick, he thought. But Nathan stayed. He looked downward as far as he could, so as to watch the operation. He could see only the brown rubber-gloved hand, the handles of the clamps and scalpel. He lay still, stopped trying to see, and closed his eyes.

7 It was just a month ago that he lay on his back, playing who would blink first with the moon. The lecherous tide fingered and licked his heels in a kind of foreplay of the swim he was intending to take. From the periphery of his stare he could see a disembodied hand moving confidently up his arm, stuffing itself greedily with the muscles of his chest, playing with the nipple, then moving across his center. Suddenly it stopped and flung itself away as though scalded.

8 "Why don't you get rid of it, Nathan?"

9 With effort, he remained motionless, fighting off the urgent need to blink, then abruptly surrendered to the moon and closed his eyes.

10 "What?" He rolled onto his stomach.

11 "Have it removed. It's not as though it would take a big operation. I'm sure it wouldn't be very painful, and then only for a short time."

12 "Do you know the definition of a 'minor operation,' Sheila? It's one that's done on somebody else."

13 "For me, Nathan?" The voice was soft, persuasive.

14 "Why?"

15 "I hate it. It's so ugly, I don't want to touch it. And any time I try to avoid it, there it is, the furry soft disgusting thing."

16 He had risen to a kneeling position and pulled his shirt on over his head.

17 "There. That better?"

18 "No. It's there and I know it. I can almost see it through your shirt. It's—it's pink and buttery and squat."

19 "You really couldn't be worrying too much about it, Sheila."

20 "Don't get sensitive, please, Nat. It isn't that. It's repulsive to me. Can't you do it for me? To satisfy me? I love you."

21 "All right," he whispered at last. He rose as he said it and turned to step into the water.

22 "All right?" she asked quickly. "Did you say 'all right'? You will? Oh, Nathan, thank you, my darling. When, when?" She knelt in front of him, her face buried in his abdomen, her arms encircling his waist. With a steady, meaningful pull she

drew him to his knees and down on all fours. In a sudden movement, she slithered beneath him and wrapped her arms about his neck. Her legs encircled his body as she pulled herself up to him from the sand, clinging like a suckling pig, all but their chests touching.

23 His mother had called it his strawberry. It was about that size, pink in color, although deepening to a red when he laughed or cried. The surface was smooth, with a little lawn of short pale velvety hair. She hadn't minded looking at it, would even formally examine it from time to time, remarking:

24 "Well, now, Nathan, I do believe your strawberry is shrinking. It certainly looks paler to me today."

25 It never did shrink, and in fact grew as he grew, so that it always occupied the same percentage of his body surface. After a while his mother stopped examining it and giving her homely progress reports. Once he had asked her, "Why do I have this, Mother?"

26 "Your strawberry, Nat? That's because you're special. It means you're going to be somebody, yes you are."

27 He remembered (or did someone tell him?) how, when he was two years old, he had stood, delighted, before the mirror, having found the birthmark with a finger, looking from flesh to glass, then back again. He was fascinated by it. He would find his hand wandering to that spot on his chest, burrowing beneath his shirt. At night in his bed, it was soothing to touch it; there was a reassurance in it, as though, by virtue of its being extra, added on, he could focus on it, as a boat upon its anchor, a kite upon its string. So long as he knew it was there he was all right, moored. Even today, he would fall asleep touching it, as though it were a button which, pressed, sent beams of sleep penetrating his body.

28 At sixteen, he dreamed of a voluptuous woman who, among other things, would lick the mole and bite it softly with her small even teeth, picking at the small folds and letting them drop back from her lips. She would have to be a prostitute. No nice girl would do it. He would pay her a fortune, but it would be worth it, and each time she did it, he would go mad for days at a time, during which he would experience oracular visions of stunning importance.

29 Sheila had come with him to the doctor's office and was waiting in the outer room to take him home. "I know you're doing it just for me. I'm so terribly grateful. As soon as you're through I'll drive you home and we'll rest there together, play some records. You can take a nap."

30 "All right, Sheila, it's coming off. Let's not talk about it anymore."

31 "You won't hate me afterwards, will you? Please don't resent me. It's because I love you so, I want you to be perfect, and now you will be."

32 He rose at the nurse's call. There was a firm squeeze of his hand from Sheila. "Be brave, darling."

33 "There, it's done," said the muffled mouth. "It wasn't so bad, was it?"

34 Nathan knew that he was fundamentally altered. It was as though he had become an adjunct to the birthmark, and now that it lay some distance from him, he was bereft in some elemental way. He raised his head to see it lying on a square of white gauze, stained with a corona of blood. It glowed like a jewel.

35 Oh, God, he thought. At that moment, he wanted only one thing: He wanted

it back. He felt that his head had also been injected with Novocaine. He tried to think of something, anything, but like a numb lip his brain refused to move. He lay there stiff and lumpy, knowing that when he did start to think, it would come out like a lopsided smile. He watched the doctor grasp it with a forceps, hold it briefly to the light, then shake it into a small bottle of formaldehyde. The birthmark resisted stickily, and in the end the doctor pushed it from the end of his forceps with a rubber-gloved finger. It swam jerkily around in the jar, as though measuring its tiny grave, and sank joylessly to the bottom and lay still.

36 "Here. Inhale this." The doctor broke a pellet in his fingers and held it under Nathan's nose. "Take deep breaths and it will pass soon. Don't worry about it."

37 Acrid fumes bit him sharply. He coughed and turned away, then sat up and swung his legs over the side.

38 "Are you all right? You're still pale. Better stay a while longer."

39 The nurse was mechanically concerned. He walked from the operating room and into the crowded waiting room. Sheila stood as soon as he appeared and linked her arm in his. "It wasn't too bad, was it, darling?"

40 Nathan looked at her as though for the first time. His arm freed itself from her grasp, rose, and swung dryly with a crackling sound and great force across the side of her head. The smile broke off her face and crashed to the floor. Its splinters flew among the startled patients.

(1974)

QUESTIONS

1. Why is Nat reluctant to get rid of his "strawberry"? Why does he finally agree to have it removed? Comment on his reaction after the surgery.
2. Why does Sheila want it removed? How does she react afterward? Why?
3. How is the story organized? Identify its major scenes, and explain its handling of time.
4. Identify three comparisons, and comment on their point and purpose.
5. How much justification do we have to take the birthmark symbolically? What might Nat's birthmark represent?

SUGGESTIONS FOR WRITING

A. Describe a physical imperfection or difference you possess. Explain how you feel about it, how others respond to it, and what you have done to come to terms with it.

B. Compare Nat's reaction to his physical imperfection with Alice Walker's to hers as described in "Beauty: When the Other Dancer Is the Self."

C. Read Nathaniel Hawthorne's short story, "The Birthmark," and compare it to "Minor Surgery."

ELEVEN

Larry L. King
(1929–)

Larry L. King was born and raised in Texas. He has worked as a farmhand, oil-field worker, journalist, and politician. Although skeptical of academics, King has received and accepted some academic distinctions, including a Neiman Fellowship at Harvard University, and a Fellowship in Communications at Duke University. He has also been a professor of journalism and political science at Princeton University.

Mostly, however, Larry L. King has been a writer, and most persistently a political journalist. He has served as writer-in-residence for the *Washington Star,* and has been a contributing editor for *Harper's, The Texas Monthly, The Texas Observer,* and *New Times.* He has also written for many other periodicals including *Esquire, Sport, Playboy,* and *American Heritage.* King has published a novel, *The One-Eyed Man* (1966), and five books of nonfiction: *Wheeling and Dealing* (1978), *The Old Man and Other Lesser Mortals* (1974), *. . . And Other Dirty Stories* (1968), *Confessions of a White Racist,* (1971) and what is perhaps his best known and most consistently successful book: *Of Outlaws, Con Men, Whores, Politicians, and Other Artists* (1980). He has also coauthored two plays, one of which, *The Best Little Whorehouse in Texas* (1978), was a Broadway hit. His most recent book, *None But a Blockhead* (1985) reviews his life and experience as a writer.

Much of King's work is autobiographical, especially his best work. King has himself recognized the importance of his personal experience for his writing. In the Preface to *Of Outlaws, Con Men, Whores, Politicians, and Other Artists* he put it like this:

> Let an editor assign almost any subject, and I'll find a way to mine my past so that conclusions are drawn from it and comparisons are made against it. Sometimes I fret that this may be a weakness. And yet I believe that my better stuff is derived from my roots: from where I've been and what I saw or heard or felt there.

King sees himself as a teller of stories, one who is personally involved in them. His persistent subject is human behavior, particularly its less glorious aspects. He is drawn to various kinds of rascals because they provide, as he has noted, entertaining shows. He captures their language and their manner. Politeness, elegance, decorum, pretension—all go by the board in King's prose, as he strives to entertain as well as argue a position or explain a point. His is a popular style, serious without being solemn, informal, easy on eye and ear, his voice a pleasure to listen to.

In "Remembering the Hard Times," King recalls his boyhood, growing up during the depression of the 1930s. With vivid detail he recreates his own experience of the time, and in the process conveys what it was like for many families like his own. "Playing Cowboy" and "Shoot-out with Amarillo Slim" are more humorous pieces. "Shoot-out" tells of King's duel of dominoes, not pistols, with a skilled gambler and cagey con artist. "Playing Cowboy" is more ambitious. Drawing on his life as Texan and New Yorker, King explores his double identity, raising important questions about the power of place to affect identity. He also demolishes some of the more common myths easterners and southwesterners harbor about one another.

King makes still another and different use of personal experience in "The American Redneck." Like "Cowboy," this piece explores King's past, his roots, and his identity. Unlike that essay, however, "Redneck" is developed partly as factual autobiographical essay, partly as fictional short story. The combination of fact and fiction allows King to accomplish things impossible with either fact or fiction alone.

As a writer from the southwest King can be fruitfully compared with Alice Walker, though Walker is more strictly a southerner, whose work derives from a powerful autobiographical impulse. But he can also be aligned in this respect with George Orwell and James Baldwin. Like Baldwin, King exhibits a strong interest in social issues and personal identity. And like Orwell political concerns mingle with personal experience to animate much of what he writes. As a social analyst with a penchant for humor, King shares an affinity with Tom Wolfe.

King is honest enough to admit that writing is hard work. He quotes Samuel Johnson approvingly, agreeing that "no man but a blockhead ever wrote except for money."

King describes writing as "serious combat," as a "battle" with a typewriter that doesn't speak unless spoken to. And although "writing," says King, "looks easier than trapeze work," it really isn't. It involves for most writers, the painful admission that they will not become the next Shakespeare, Twain, or Faulkner. It involves the corollary recognition that all that is realistically available is to do decent work. For King, that seems to be enough. If and when other rewards come—fame, money, prestige—they are accepted and enjoyed. But what lasts, and what matters most is the work of writing itself.

Playing Cowboy

1 When I was young, I didn't know that when you leave a place, it may not be forever. The past, I thought, had served its full uses and could bury its own dead; bridges were for burning; "good-bye" meant exactly what it said. One never looked back except to judge how far one had come.

2 Texas was the place I left behind. And not reluctantly. The leave-taking was so random I trusted the United States Army to relocate me satisfactorily. It did, in 1946, choosing to establish in Queens (then but a five-cent subway ride from the clamorous glamour of Manhattan) a seventeen-year-old former farm boy and small-town sapling green enough to challenge chlorophyll. The assignment would shape

my life far more than I then suspected; over the years it would teach me to "play cowboy"—to become, strangely, more "Texas" than I had been.

3 New York offered everything to make an ambitious kid dizzy; I moved through its canyons in a hot walking dream. Looking back, I see myself starring in a bad movie I then accepted as high drama: the Kid, a.k.a. the Bumptious Innocent, discovering the theater, books, a bewildering variety of nightclubs and bars; subways and skyscrapers and respectable wines. There were glancing encounters with Famous Faces: Walter Winchell, the actor Paul Kelly, the ex-heavyweight champion Max Baer, bandleader Stan Kenton. It was easy; spotting them, I simply rushed up, stuck out my hand, sang out my name, and began asking personal questions.

4 Among my discoveries was that I dreaded returning to Texas; where were its excitements, celebrities, promises? As corny as it sounds, one remembers the final scene of that bad movie. Crossing the George Washington Bridge in a Greyhound bus in July 1949—Army discharge papers in my duffel bag—I looked back at Manhattan's spires and actually thought, *I'll be back, New York.* I did not know that scene had been played thousands of times by young men or young women from the provinces, nor did I know that New York cared not a whit whether we might honor the pledge. In time, I got back. On my recent forty-sixth birthday, it dawned that I had spent more than half my life—or twenty-four years—on the eastern seaboard. I guess there's no getting around the fact that this makes me an expatriate Texan.

5 "Expatriate" remains an exotic word. I think of it as linked to Paris or other European stations in the 1920s: of Sylvia Beach and her famous bookstore; of Hemingway, Fitzgerald, Dos Passos, Ezra Pound, and Gertrude Stein Stein Stein. There is wine in the Paris air, wine and cheese and sunshine, except on rainy days when starving young men in their attics write or paint in contempt of their gut rumbles. Spain. The brave bulls. Dublin's damp fog. Movable feasts. *That's* what "expatriate" means, so how can it apply to one middle-aged grandfather dodging Manhattan's muggers and dogshit pyramids while grunting a son through boarding school and knocking on the doors of magazine editors? True expatriates, I am certain, do not wait in dental offices, the Port Authority Bus Terminal, or limbo. Neither do they haunt their original root sources three or four times each year, while dreaming of accumulating enough money to return home in style as a gentlemanly rustic combining the best parts of J. Frank Dobie, Lyndon Johnson, Stanley Walker, and the Old Man of the Mountain. Yet that is my story, and that is my plan.

6 I miss the damned place. Texas is my mind's country, that place I most want to understand and record and preserve. Four generations of my people sleep in its soil; I have children there, and a grandson; the dead past and the living future tie me to it. Not that I always approve it or love it. It vexes and outrages and disappoints me—especially when I am there. It is now the third most urbanized state, behind New York and California, with all the tangles, stench, random violence, architectural rape, historical pillage, neon blight, pollution, and ecological imbalance the term implies. Money and mindless growth remain high on the list of official priorities, breeding a crass boosterism not entirely papered over by an infectious energy. The state legislature—though improving as slowly as an old man's mending bones—still harbors excessive, coon-ass, rural Tory Democrats who fail to understand that 79.7 percent of Texans have flocked to urban areas and may need fewer farm-to-

market roads, hide-and-tick inspectors, or outraged orations almost comically declaiming against welfare loafers, creeping socialism, the meddling ol' feds, and sin in the aggregate.

7 Too much, now, the Texas landscape sings no native notes. The impersonal, standardized superhighways—bending around or by most small towns, and then blatting straightaway toward the urban sprawls—offer homogenized service stations, fast-food-chain outlets, and cluttered shopping centers one might find duplicated in Ohio, Maryland, Illinois, or Anywhere, U.S.A. Yes, there is much to make me protest, as did Mr. Faulkner's Quentin Compson, of the South—"I *don't* hate it. I don't hate it, I *don't*. . . ." For all its shrinkages of those country pleasures I once eschewed, and now covet and vainly wish might return, Texas remains in my mind's eye that place to which I shall eventually return to rake the dust for my formative tracks; that place where one hopes to grow introspective and wise as well as old. It is a romantic foolishness, of course; the opiate dream of a nostalgia junkie. When I go back to stay—and I fancy that I will—there doubtless will be opportunities to wonder at my plan's imperfections.

8 For already I have created in my mind, you see, an improbable corner of paradise: the rustic, rambling ranch house with the clear-singing creek nearby, the clumps of shade trees (under which, possibly, the Sons of the Pioneers will play perpetual string-band concerts), the big cozy library where I will work and read and cogitate between issuing to the Dallas *Times-Herald* or the Houston *Post* those public pronouncements befitting an Elder Statesman of Life and Letters. I will become a late-blooming naturalist and outdoorsman: hiking and camping, and piddling in cattle; never mind that to date I have preferred the sidewalks of New York, and my beef not on the hoof but tricked up with mushroom sauces.

9 All this will occur about one easy hour out of Austin—my favorite Texas city—and exactly six miles from a tiny, unnamed town looking remarkably like what Walt Disney would have built for a cheery, heart-tugging Texas-based story happening about 1940. The nearest neighbor will live 3.7 miles away, have absolutely no children or dogs, but will have one beautiful young wife, who adores me; it is she who will permit me, by her periodic attentions, otherwise to live the hermit's uncluttered life. Politicians will come to my door hats in hand, and fledgling Poets and young Philosophers. Basically, they will want to know exactly what is Life's Purpose. Looking out across the gently blowing grasslands, past the grazing blooded cattle, toward a perfect sunset, with even the wind in my favor, and being the physical reincarnation of Hemingway with a dash of Twain in my mood, I shall—of course—be happy to tell them.

10 Well, we all know that vast gap between fantasy and reality when True Life begins playing the scenario. Likely I will pay twice to thrice the value for a run-down old "farmhouse" where the plumbing hasn't worked since Coolidge, and shall die of a heart attack while digging a cesspool. The nearest neighbor will live directly across the road; he will own seven rambunctious children, five mad dogs, and an ugly harridan with sharp elbows, a shrill voice, and a perverse hatred for dirty old writing men. The nearest town—less than a half mile away and growing by leaps, separated from my digs only by a subdivision of mock Bavarian castles and the new smeltering

plant—will be made of plastics, paved parking lots, and puppy-dog tails. The trip to Austin will require three hours if one avoids rush-hour crushes; when I arrive—to preen in Scholz Garten or The Raw Deal or other watering holes where artists congregate—people will say, "Who's that old fart?" Unfortunately I may try to tell them. My books will long have been out of print; probably my secret yearning will be to write a column for the local weekly newspaper. Surrounded by strangers, memories, and galloping growth, I shall sit on my porch—rocking and cackling and talking gibberish to the wind—while watching them build yet another Kwik Stop Kwality Barbecue Pit on the west edge of my crowded acreage. Occasionally I will walk the two dozen yards to the interstate highway to throw stones at passing trucks; my ammunition will peter out long before traffic does. But when I die digging that cesspool, by God, I'll have died at home. That knowledge makes me realize where my heart is.

11 But the truth, dammit, is that I feel much more the Texan when in the East. New Yorkers, especially, encourage and expect one to perform a social drill I think of as "playing cowboy." Even as a young soldier I discovered a presumption among a high percentage of New Yorkers that my family owned shares in the King Ranch and that my natural equestrian talents were unlimited; all one needed to affirm such groundless suspicions were a drawl and a grin. To this day you may spot me in Manhattan wearing boots and denim jeans with a matching vest and western-cut hat—topped by a furry cattleman's coat straight out of Marlboro Country; if you've seen Dennis Weaver play McCloud, then you've seen me, without my beard.

12 Never mind that I *like* such garb, grew up wearing it, or that I find it natural, practical, and inexpensive; no, to a shameful degree, I dress for my role. When I learned that Princeton University would pay good money to a working writer for teaching his craft—putting insulated students in touch with the workaday salts and sours of the literary world—do you think I went down there wrapped in an ascot and puffing a briar pipe from Dunhill's? No, good neighbors, I donned my Cowboy Outfit to greet the selection committee and aw-shucksed and consarned 'em half to death; easterners just can't resist a John Wayne quoting Shakespeare; I've got to admit there's satisfaction in it for every good ol' boy who country-slicks the city dudes.

13 New Yorkers tend to think of Mississippians or Georgians or Virginians under the catchall category of "southerners," of Californians as foreigners, and of Texans as the legendary Texan. We are the only outlanders, I think, that they define within a specific state border and assign the burden of an obligatory—i.e., "cowboy"—culture. Perhaps we court such treatment; let it be admitted that Texans are a clannish people. We tend to think of ourselves as Texans no matter how long ago we strayed or how tenuous our home connections. When I enter a New York store and some clerk—alerted by my nasal twang—asks where I am from, I do not answer "East Thirty-second Street," but "Texas," yet my last permanent address there was surrendered when Eisenhower was freshly President and old George Blanda was little more than a rookie quarterback.

14 More than half my close friends—and maybe 20 percent of my overall eastern seaboard acquaintances—are expatriate Texans: writers, musicians, composers, editors, lawyers, athletes, showfolk, a few businessmen, and such would-be politicians

or former politicians as Bill Moyers and Ramsey Clark. Don Meredith, Liz Smith, Judy Buie, Dan Jenkins, you name 'em, and to one degree or another we play cowboy together. Many of us gather for chili suppers, tell stories with origins in Fort Worth or Odessa or Abilene; sometimes we even play dominoes or listen to country-western records.

15 There is, God help us, an organization called The New York Texans, and about 2,000 of us actually belong to it. We meet each March 2—Texas Independence Day—to drink beer, hoo-haw at each other in the accents of home, and honor some myth that we can, at best, only ill define. We even have our own newspaper, published quarterly by a lady formerly of Spur, Texas, which largely specializes in stories bragging on how well we've done in the world of the Big Apple. Since people back home are too busy to remind us of our good luck and talents, we remind ourselves.

16 No matter where you go, other Texans discover you. Sometimes they are themselves expatriates, sometimes tourists, sometimes business-bent travelers. In any case, we whoop a mutual recognition, even though we're strangers or would be unlikely to attract each other if meeting within our native borders. Indeed, one of the puzzling curiosities is why the Dallas banker, or the George Wallace fanatic who owns the little drygoods store in Beeville, and I may drop all prior plans in order to spend an evening together in Monterrey or Oshkosh when—back home—we would consider each other social lepers. Many times I have found myself buddy-buddying with people not all that likable or interesting, sharing Aggie jokes or straight tequila shots or other peculiarities of home.

17 If you think that sounds pretty dreadful, it often is. Though I am outraged when called a "professional Texan," or when I meet one, certainly I am not always purely innocent. Much of it is a big put-on, of course. We enjoy sharing put-ons against those who expect all Texans to eat with the wrong fork, offer coarse rebel yells, and get all vomity-drunk at the nearest football game. There is this regional defensiveness—LBJ would have known what I mean—leading us to order "a glass of clabber and a mess of chitlins" when faced by the haughty ministrations of the finest French restaurants. (My group does, anyway, though I don't know about the stripe of Texan epitomized, say, by Rex Reed; that bunch has got so smooth you can't see behind the sheen). I hear my Texas friends, expatriates and otherwise, as their accents thicken and their drawls slow down on approaching representatives of other cultures. I observe them as they attempt to come on more lordly and sophisticated than Dean Acheson or more country than Ma and Pa Kettle, depending on what they feel a need to prove.

18 That they (or I) need to prove anything is weird in itself. It tells you what they—yes, the omnipotent They—put in our young Texas heads. The state's history is required teaching in the public schools, and no student by law may escape the course. They teach Texas history very much fumigated—the Alamo's martyrs, the Indian-killing frontiersmen, the heroic Early Day Pioneers, the Rugged Plainsmen, the Builders and Doers; these had hearts pure where others were soiled—and they teach it and teach it and teach it. I came out of the public schools of Texas knowing naught of Disraeli, Darwin, or Darrow—though well versed in the lore of Sam Houston, Stephen F. Austin, Jim Bowie, the King Ranch, the Goodnight-Loving

Trail over which thundered the last of the big herds. No school day was complete but that we sang "The Eyes of Texas," "Texas Our Texas," "Beautiful Texas." I mean, try substituting "Rhode Island" or "North Dakota," and it sounds about half-silly even to a Texan. We were taught again and again that Texas was the biggest state, one of the richest, possibly the toughest, surely the most envied. Most Americans, I guess, grow up convinced that their little corners of the universe are special; Texas, however, takes care to institutionalize the preachment.

19 To discover a wider world, then, where others fail to hold those views—to learn that Texans are thought ignorant or rich or quite often both, though to the last in number capable of sitting a mean steed—is to begin at once a new education and feel sneaky compulsions toward promoting useless old legends. Long after I knew that the Texas of my youth dealt more with myth than reality, and long past that time when I knew that the vast majority of Texans lived in cities, I continued to play cowboy. This was a social and perhaps a professional advantage in the East; it marked one as unique, permitted one to pose as a son of yesterday, furnished a handy identity among the faceless millions. In time one has a way of becoming in one's head something of the role one has assumed. Often I have actually felt myself the reincarnation or the extension of the old range lords or bedroll cowpokes or buffalo hunters. Such playacting is harmless so long as one confines it to wearing costumes or to speech patterns—"I'm a-hankerin' for a beefsteak, y'all, and thank I'll mosey on over to P. J. Clarke's"—but becomes counterproductive unless regulated. Nobody has been able to coax me atop a horse since that day a dozen years ago when I proved to be the most comic equestrian ever to visit a given riding stable on Staten Island. Misled by my range garb, accent, and sunlamp tan, the stable manager assigned what surely must have been his most spirited steed. Unhorsed after much graceless grabbing and grappling, I heard my ride described by a laughing fellow with Brooklyn in his voice: "Cheez, at foist we thought youse was a trick rider. But just before youse fell, we seen youse wasn't nothing but a shoemaker."

20 Though I wear my Texas garb in Texas, I am more the New Yorker there; not so much in my own mind, perhaps, as in the minds of others. People hold me to account for criticisms I've written of Texas or accuse me of having gone "New York" in my thinking or attitudes. "Nobody's more parochial than a goddamn New Yorker," some of my friends snort—and often they are right. I, too, feel outraged at Manhattan cocktail parties when some clinch-jawed easterner makes it clear he thinks that everything on the wrong side of the George Washington Bridge is quaint, hasn't sense enough to come in from the rain, and maybe lacks toilet training. Yet my Texas friends have their own misconceptions of my adopted home and cause me to defend it. They warn of its violent crime, even though Houston annually vies with Detroit for the title of "Murder Capital of the World." They deride New York's slums and corruptions, even though in South El Paso (and many another Texas city) may be found shameful dirt poverty and felonious social neglect, and Texas erupts in its own political Watergates—banking, insurance, real estate scandals—at least once each decade. So I find myself in the peculiar defense of New York, waving my arms, and my voice growing hotter, saying things like "You

goddamn Texans gotta learn that you're not so damned special. . . ." *You* goddamn Texans, now.

21 My friends charge that despite my frequent visits home and my summering on Texas beaches, my view of the place is hopelessly outdated. Fletcher Boone, an Austin artist and entrepreneur—now owner of The Raw Deal—was the latest to straighten out my thinking. "All you goddamn expatriates act like time froze somewhere in the nineteen-fifties or earlier," he said. "You'd think we hadn't discovered television down here, or skin flicks, or dope. Hell, we grew us a *President* down here. We've got tall buildings and long hairs and some of us know how to ski!" Mr. Boone had recently visited New York and now held me to account for its sins: "It's mental masturbation. You go to a party up there, and instead of people making real conversation, they stop the proceedings so somebody can sing opera or play the piano or do a tap dance. It's show biz, man—buncha egomaniacal people using a captive audience to stroke themselves. Whatta they talk about? 'I, I, I. Me, me, me. Mine, mine, mine.' " Well, no, I rebut; they also talk about books, politics, and even *ideas;* only the middle of these, I say, is likely to be remarked in Texas. Boone is offended; he counterattacks that easterners do not live life so much as they attempt to dissect it or, worse, dictate how others should live it by the manipulations of fashion, art, the media. We shout gross generalities, overstatements, "facts" without support. I become the Visiting Smart-ass New Yorker, losing a bit of my drawl.

22 Well, bless him, there may be something to Fletcher Boone's charge, I found recently when I returned as a quasi sociologist. It was my plan to discover some young, green blue-collar or white-collar, recently removed to the wicked city from upright rural upbringings, and record that unfortunate hick's slippages or shocks. Then I would return to the hick's small place of origin, comparing what he or she had traded for a mess of modern city pottage; family graybeards left behind would be probed for their surrogate shocks and would reveal their fears for their urbanized young. It would be a whiz of a story, having generational gaps and cultural shocks and more disappointments or depletions than the Nixon White House. It would be at once nostalgic, pitiful, and brave; one last angry shout against modernity before Houston sinks beneath the waves, Lubbock dries up and blows away for lack of drinking water, and Dallas-Fort Worth grows together as firmly as Siamese twins. Yes, it would have everything but three tits and, perhaps, originality.

23 Telephone calls to old friends produced no such convenient study. Those recommended turned out to have traveled abroad, attended college in distant places, or otherwise been educated by an urban, mobile society. A young airline hostess in Houston talked mainly of San Francisco or Hawaii; a bank clerk in Dallas sniggered that even in high school days he had spent most of his weekends away from his native village—in city revelry—and thought my idea of "cultural shock" quaint; a petrochemical plant worker failed to qualify when he said, "Shit, life's not all that much different. I live here in Pasadena"—an industrial morass with all the charms and odors of Gary, Indiana—"and I go to my job, watch TV, get drunk with my buddies. Hail, it's not no different from what it was back there in Monahans. Just more traffic and more people and a little less sand." I drove around the state for days, depressed by the urbanization of my former old outback even as I marveled at its energy, before returning to New York, where I might feel, once more, like a Texan: where I might play cowboy; dream again the ancient dreams.

24 It is somehow easier to conjure up the Texas I once knew from Manhattan. What an expatriate most remembers are not the hardscrabble times of the 1930s, or the narrow attitudes of a people not then a part of the American mainstream, but a way of life that was passing without one's then realizing it. Quite without knowing it, I witnessed the last of the region's horse culture. Schoolboys tied their mounts to mesquite trees west of the Putnam school and at noon fed them bundled roughage; the pickup truck and the tractor had not yet clearly won out over the horse, though within the decade they would. While the last of the great cattle herds had long ago disappeared up the Chisholm or the Goodnight-Loving Trail, I would see small herds rounded up on my Uncle Raymond's Bar-T-Bar Ranch and loaded from railside corrals for shipment to the stockyards of Fort Worth—or "Cowtown," as it was then called without provoking smiles. (The rough-planked saloons of the brawling North Side of "Cowtown," near the old stockyards, are gone now save for a small stretch lacquered and refurbished in a way so as to make tourists feel they've been where they ain't.) In Abilene, only thirty-two miles to the west, I would hear the chants of cattle auctioneers while smelling feedlot dung, tobacco, saddle leather, and the sweat of men living the outdoor life. Under the watchful eye of my father, I sometimes rode a gentle horse through the shinnery and scrub oaks of the old family farm, helping him bring in the five dehorned milk cows while pretending to be a bad-assed gunslinger herding longhorns on a rank and dangerous trail drive.

25 But it was all maya, illusion. Even a dreaming little tad knew the buffalo hunters were gone, along with the old frontier forts, the Butterfield stage, the first sodbusters whose barbed wire fenced in the open range and touched off wars continuing to serve Clint Eastwood or James Arness. This was painful knowledge for one succored on myths and legends, on real-life tales of his father's boyhood peregrinations in a covered wagon. Nothing of my original time and place, I felt, would be worth living through or writing about. What I did not then realize (and continue having trouble remembering) is that the past never was as good as it looks from a distance.

26 The expatriate, returning, thus places an unfair burden upon his native habitat: He demands it to have impossibly marked time, to have marched in place, during the decades he has absented himself. He expects it to have preserved itself as his mind recalls it; to furnish evidence that he did not memorize in vain its legends, folk and folklore, mountains and streams and villages. Never mind that he may have removed himself to other places because they offered rapid growth, new excitements, and cultural revolutions not then available at home.

27 We expatriate sons may sometimes be unfair: too critical; fail to give due credit; employ the double standard. Especially do those of us who write flay Texas in the name of our disappointments and melted snows. Perhaps it's good that we do this, the native press being so boosterish and critically timid; but there are times, I suspect, when our critical duty becomes something close to a perverse pleasure. Easterners I have known, visiting my homeplace, come away impressed by its dynamic qualities; they see a New Frontier growing in my native bogs, a continuing spirit of adventure, a bit of trombone and swashbuckle, something fresh and good. Ah, but they did not know Texas when she was young.

28 There is a poignant tale told by the writer John Graves of the last, tamed remnants of a formerly free and proud Indian tribe in Texas: how a small band of

them approached an old rancher, begged a scrawny buffalo bull from him, and—spurring their thin ponies—clattered and whooped after it, running it ahead of them, and killed it in the old way—with lances and arrows. They were foolish, I guess, in trying to hold history still for one more hour; probably I'm foolish in the same sentimental way when I sneak off the freeways to snake across the Texas back roads in search of my own past. But there are a couple of familiar stretches making the ride worth it; I most remember one out in the lonely windblown ranch country, between San Angelo and Water Valley, with small rock-dotted hills ahead at the end of a long, flat stretch of road bordered by grasslands, random clumps of trees, wild flowers, grazing cattle, a single distant ranch house whence—one fancies—issues the perfume of baking bread, simmering beans, beef over the flames. There are no billboards, no traffic cloverleafs, no neon, no telephone poles, no Jiffy Tacos or Stuckey's stands, no oil wells, no Big Rich Bastards, no ship channels threatening to ignite because of chemical pollutions, no Howard Johnson flavors. Though old Charley Goodnight lives, Lee Harvey Oswald and Charles Whitman remain unborn.

29 Never have I rounded the turn leading into that peaceful valley, with the spiny ridge of hills beyond it, that I failed to feel new surges and exhilarations and hope. For a precious few moments I exist in a time warp: I'm back in Old Texas, under a high sky, where all things are again possible and the wind blows free. Invariably, I put the heavy spurs to my trusty Hertz or Avis steed: go flying lickety-split down that lonesome road, whooping a crazy yell and taking deep joyous breaths, sloshing Lone Star beer on my neglected dangling safety belt, and scattering roadside gravel like bursts of buckshot. Ride 'im, cowboy! *Ride* 'im. . . .

(1980)

QUESTIONS

Thought and Structure

1. In what sense is the title a clue to King's idea and attitude? What does King mean by "playing cowboy"?
2. "Playing Cowboy" is divided into four sections. Provide a title for each, and explain how the parts are related.
3. What is King's attitude toward Texas? What does it mean to him? How has it influenced who and what he is?
4. What image of Texans does King present? What image of New Yorkers does he offer? What attitude does each seem to harbor about the other? To what extent are these attitudes accurate?
5. What does King mean when he says that "one has a way of becoming in one's head something of the role one has assumed"? You might like to compare Orwell's comment about masks in "Shooting an Elephant," paragraph 7.
6. Is it true as King notes in paragraph 25 that "the past never [is] as good as it looks from a distance"? What does he mean?

Style and Strategy

7. Notice the pile-up of short sentences and clauses in the first three paragraphs. Comment on their effect. Find another place where King relies heavily on short sentences. Comment on their effectiveness.
8. What image of himself does King present in the beginning of the essay? Later? How consistent are they?
9. How does King's language reveal him "playing cowboy" in this essay? Where does he do this most insistently? For what purpose? To what effect?
10. King quotes a number of people. What purposes do these direct quotations serve? Could they be dispensed with? Why or why not? (See especially paragraphs 19–23.)
11. Look at the string of negatives in the next-to-last sentence of paragraph 28. What is the effect of repeating "no" nine times?
12. What is the governing principle behind King's selection of detail in the final paragraph?

SUGGESTIONS FOR WRITING

A. Discuss your experience in returning to a place after having moved away, perhaps attempting to escape it. Discuss its hold on you, particularly how you may have tried to neutralize its influence and effects—and whether or not you succeeded—and why.

B. Compare King's discussion of Texas with Gretel Ehrlich's discussion of Wyoming.

C. Compare King's discussion of New York with Didion's in "Goodbye to All That." Or compare her experience of returning to California with King's return to Texas.

Shoot-out with Amarillo Slim

1 The grapevine had it that thirty-four men, putting up $10,000 each, would convene in Benny Binion's Horseshoe Casino in Las Vegas to settle the world poker championship and thereby make the winner temporarily rich.

2 Among the high rollers would be Amarillo Slim Preston, who had the reputation of beating people at their own game. My game was dominoes. I began to fantasize about giving Amarillo Slim a chance to beat me. Never mind that he once had defeated a Ping-Pong ace while playing him with a Coke bottle or that he'd trimmed Minnesota Fats at pool while employing a broomstick as a cue. I could think of no such flashy tricks available to him in a domino game, unless he wished to play me blindfolded. In which case I would merrily tattoo him and take his money.

3 I first played dominoes on the kitchen table in my father's Texas farmhouse before reaching school age. By age nine or ten I could beat or hold my own against most adults and had graduated to contests staged in feedstores, icehouses, cotton gins, and crossroads domino parlors. My father delighted in introducing me to unsuspecting farmers, ranchers, or rural merchants and then observing their embarrassment as they got whipped by a fuzzless kid.

4 As a teenager I hustled domino games in pool halls and beer joints, rarely

failing to relieve oil-field workers of their hard-earned cash. In the Army, while others sought their victims in crap games or at the poker table, I prospered from those who fancied themselves good domino players. In later life I had written articles on the art of dominoes and, indeed, had been asked to write a book about it. I recite all this so you will know that Amarillo Slim would not be getting his hooks into any innocent rookie should he accept my challenge.

5 A few words here about the game itself. It is played with twenty-eight rectangular blocks known as dominoes, or rocks. The face of each is divided in two, each half containing markings similar to a pair of dice—except that some are blank. The twenty-eight dominoes represent all possible combinations from double blank to double six.

6 In two-handed dominoes, the players draw for the right to start the game, known as the down. After the dominoes are reshuffled, each player draws seven; the remaining fourteen rocks go into the boneyard to await the unwary, unlucky, or inattentive player.

7 Any domino may be played on the down, but subsequent play is restricted: Players must follow suit by matching the pips, or spots, on the exposed ends of the dominoes. Rocks are placed end to end, except for doubles, which are set down at right angles to the main line of dominoes. The first double played becomes the spinner and may be developed in all four directions.

8 Players may score in three ways: (1) After each play, the number of spots on all open ends is added; if the sum is divisible by five, the player last playing scores the total; (2) when a player puts down his last rock with a triumphant "Domino!" he scores the value of the spots in his opponent's hand; (3) should the game be "blocked"—that is, if neither opponent can play—the one caught with the fewer points adds to his score the points his opponent has been stuck with, to the nearest complement of five.

9 The basic strategy is simple: Score, keep your opponent from scoring, block his plays and make him draw from the boneyard, and then domino on him. The first player to score 250 points is the winner.

10 Dominoes is an easy game to learn and a difficult one to master. Any kid can grasp its fundamentals. After that, progress is largely determined by the player's ability to recall what has been played and what is out, by his understanding of the mathematical probabilities, and by his being able to read what his opponent is trying to do. The luck of the draw plays a part in any given game, sure. But over the long haul, what might be called personality skills are more important than luck. These cannot be taught, but develop out of each player's inner core and chemistry. Either you got 'em or you ain't. My successful record as a domino player satisfied me that I had 'em, and I wondered if Amarillo Slim did. So I tracked the fabled gamesman down in Las Vegas to find out and to see if I could compete with the legendary gambler. In short, I wanted to know if I could play with the Big Boys.

11 "How many spots in a deck of dominoes?" Amarillo Slim asked.

12 "Er-rah," I said. "You mean total spots? In the whole deck?" Amarillo Slim pushed his considerable cowboy hat to the back of his head, further elongating his weathered and bony face, and nodded.

13 I took a swig of beer to cover my frantic mental arithmetic. It was a question that never had occurred to me.* Slim patiently waited while dozens of big-time gamblers, participants in or witnesses to the World Series of Poker, milled about in the flashy Horseshoe Casino. "Well," I ultimately said with great certainty, "I'm not exactly sure."

14 Amarillo Slim Preston shook his head, as if somebody had told him his favorite dog had died, and the sorrow was just too much to bear. His eyes said, *What is this poor fool doing challenging me to play dominoes for money when he don't know his elbow from Pike's Peak?*

15 Slim said, "I'm tied up in this big poker game right now, pal; but I ain't catchin' the cards, and my stake's so small it looks like a elephant stepped on it. Soon as I'm out of it, I'll be happy to accommodate you."

16 After he'd been eliminated from the high-stakes world championship tournament (which, on another occasion, he had won), we agreed to meet the following morning at eleven. We would play three games for $50 each, though Slim made it clear he probably would show more profit pitching pennies than in playing dominoes for such a paltry sum. "I'm a fair country domino player," he admitted, "but I'm not any world's expert. You wouldn't be hustlin' ol' Slim, would you?" I think I thought I told the truth when I denied it.

17 I had a few drinks to celebrate my opportunity and mentally calculated that a twenty-eight-piece set of dominoes contained exactly 172 spots. When I recalculated to corroborate this scientific fact, I got exactly 169. And then 166. Using pencil and paper and rechecking four times, I became convinced the correct answer was 165. Exactly. Yes. *Seven-and-eight are fifteen, carry the one. . . .*

18 Then I realized what I had been doing and said to myself: *Don't let Amarillo Slim psych you out. Why, he's trying to play the Coke-bottle-and-broomstick trick on you! It doesn't matter how many spots are in the deck. He's trying to get you to occupy your mind with extraneous matters. Forget it.* One hour after I'd completely and totally forgotten it, I thought: *Hell, he probably doesn't know the answer. He didn't give it, did he?* Then I calculated the spots three more times: 165, yep. But it didn't make any difference. Couldn't possibly have any bearing on the game. . . .

19 I was in the Horseshoe Casino at the appointed hour. Amarillo Slim was not. I searched the poker pits, the blackjack tables, the roulette-wheel crowds; among the rows of clickety-clacking slot machines; in the bars and restaurants. No Slim. I inquired of his whereabouts among gamblers, dealers, security guards, and perplexed tourists. I telephoned Slim's room three times and had him paged twice in two other casinos. No Slim.

20 Sitting at the bar nearest the poker pits and reminding myself not to drink excessively, I pep-talked my soul: *You're good. You haven't been beaten in years. Remember to play your hand and not to worry about his. Don't listen to his jabber, because you know he's a talker. Concentrate.*

---

*It should have. It would be vital to rapid calculation if one wondered whether to "block" the game. Since the odds rarely would be that close, I'd never bothered.

21 In the midst of my tenth or eleventh drink I spotted the big cowboy hat. Under it stood Amarillo Slim, more than six feet tall and exactly two hours late. *Shoot-out time!* "Slim!" I cheerfully cried. He gave me a vague wave and a who-are-you look and continued to talk with one of his cronies. Could he have *forgotten* so important a match?

22 "Oh, yeah, pal," he said when reminded. "You got a deck of dominoes with you?" When I said I did not, Slim looked incredulous. "You *don't!*" he exclaimed. You never would have suspected that the night before, he had assured me the house would provide a deck.

23 "Well, pal," Slim said a trifle sadly. "No matter how good you are, I kinda doubt you can beat me without a deck."

24 "I'll go get one," I volunteered, eagerly plunging out of the casino onto the sunny and garish sidewalks of Las Vegas, dodging among crowds of people who looked as if maybe God had run out of good clay when it came their turn and had made them from Silly Putty. As I visited my fourth novelty shop ("Naw, sir, we don't get many calls for dominoes no more"), it suddenly occurred to me that Amarillo Slim had his opponent running errands for him. Here I was rushing around, getting all sweaty and hot, while spending $10 besides, in order that Slim Preston might have an opportunity to take fifteen times that amount from me. *No, forget that! It's defeatist thinking! Keep your cool!*

25 When I returned to the Horseshoe, Slim was playing in a pickup poker game. I caught his eye and held up the domino deck. Amarillo Slim looked at me—no, *through* me—as if he'd never seen such a sight in his life and then raked in a pot of chips big enough to choke a longhorn steer. After I'd waved the dominoes four or five times, faint recognition dawned in his eyes. "Oh, yeah, pal," he called. "Just wait there for me."

26 I waited. And waited. And waited some more. By now I was doing a slow burn. *Okay for you, Slim, you shitass. When I finally corner your stalling ass, it belongs to the gypsies, pal!* A lot of Walter Mitty stuff began roistering in my head. I would so crush Amarillo Slim that he would retire from gaming for all time, publicly apologizing for his ineptitude. Meanwhile, however, I had time to eat a bowl of chili, whomp up on a friend in a practice game—250 to 95—and count the number of spots in the deck again. No doubt about it: 165.

27 Fully four hours after the appointed time, Amarillo Slim approached his challenger. He was tucking away a large role of bills newly accepted from two amateur poker players, who, now wiser and lighter, began to sneak away as if guilty of large crimes. *Play him tough,* I instructed myself. *Don't give him anything. He's just another ol' Texas boy, like you. He's just a little skinnier, that's all.*

28 "You bring your photographer?" Slim asked.

29 "Uh, beg pardon?"

30 "I thought you said this was gonna be in *Sport* magazine," he said. "You mean you didn't bring a photographer?"

31 "I forgot," I said, before realizing I'd made absolutely no promise of a photographer.

32 Slim grunted and sat down at the table. So as to reestablish authority, I said, "Here are the ground rules. Fifty bucks per game. Two hundred fifty points wins

a game. You play the seven dominoes you draw, no matter how many doubles." Slim gave me a who-don't-know-that look.

33 I poured the new deck onto the table. Slim bent over the dominoes and said, "Whut the *hail?*"

34 "Beg pardon?"

35 "Is this here a *deuce?*" he demanded of a rock he held before his eyes. Squinting like Mr. Magoo.

36 "Yeah. Sure."

37 "Damnedest-lookin' deuce *I* ever saw," Slim proclaimed. "All the deuces look like that, pal?" I decided not to answer. Though the deuces in this particular deck were a shade peculiar in appearance, they were not enough different from the norm to make a federal case. Which Amarillo Slim now was doing. "Pal," he said, "I'm in a whole heap of trouble. I can't tell these funny-lookin' deuces from the aces. Why, you can wet in this hat if I can tell 'em apart."

38 Slim's lament began to attract a sizable crowd of professional gamblers and the merely curious. Among those pressing close to the table was a huge, grinning fat man called Texas Dolly, Doyle Brunson, who had reason enough to grin, having the previous evening won $340,000 playing poker. *The winnah and new world champ-een!* I suddenly was very aware of where I was, and who Amarillo Slim was, and that he'd been winning big stakes around the globe while I had been taking lunch money away from oil-field grunts and Pfcs. *If you're not nervous,* whispered a small inner voice, *then why are your hands shaking?* It was something like being the rookie deep back waiting to receive the opening kickoff in the Super Bowl, I imagine. And Vince Lombardi was coaching the other side.

39 I had decided on a conservative strategy for the first few hands, much as a football team might carefully probe the opposition's defense with basic fundamentals rather than quickly go for the long bomb. I would take any count available to me, no matter how small, rather than scheme to send Slim to the boneyard. If you send a skilled opponent to the boneyard too early, and he gets enough dominoes, he has more options and more scoring rocks available. So I would wait until the major scoring rocks had been played before going for the jugular; would settle for the field goal on my first possession. Grunt gains.

40 I won the down—coin toss?—and played the double five, at once scoring 10 and establishing the spinner. Fine; I'd run the kickoff back to my own 47; I held three other fives and figured to prosper from that spinner. Sure enough, I scored 25 points before Slim got on the board. Slim countered with combinations of sixes and fours, all the time mumbling how he couldn't tell aces from deuces "and here we are playin' for the whole kit and kaboodle." *Don't listen to him. Play your hand.* Every time I played a deuce—and often when I didn't—Slim said, "Is that thang a deuce, pal?" At the end of the first hand I led him, 40–25. I'd kicked my field goal.

41 In the second go-round I again was blessed with fives. Slim, however, was equally blessed with blanks. We traded large counts; I was reminded of a baseball game in which neither side could get anybody out. I'd make 10 and Slim would make 15; then he would make 15 and I would make 20. We each scored 65 points, so that after two hands I was up 105 to 90; Slim, of course, chattered incessantly about the funny-lookin' deuces I'd rung in on him.

42 The third hand was tense and low-scoring, each of us waiting for the other fellow to make a major mistake. Nobody did. We only made 15 points each; the game now stood 120 to 105; I silently congratulated myself on having not yet fallen behind for a single moment.

43 After the fourth hand I was certain that I had him. He pulled within 5 points early; but then I turned treys on him, and he had none. He went to the boneyard twice and got nothing that helped him. I dominoed on him for 30 points and now led, 195 to 155. *Duck soup. I got him. How's it feel, pal?*

44 Now Slim was rattling and jabbering like monkeys climbing chains. I resolved to shut him out. *Keep track of what's played and what's out. You're playing good dominoes. But you'll blow it if you permit him to break your concentration.*

45 Having discovered that I preferred to play rapid-fire dominoes, Amarillo Slim now began to slow the pace. Though surely he had not read it, he was utilizing a technique I had recommended: "Should your opponent prefer to play quickly, slow the game. Conversely, should *he* slow it, then you should give a wham-bam-thankee-ma'am response. Once you rob your opponent of his preferred pace, you control the tempo—and he who controls the tempo usually will control the game."

46 Slim edged up on me, nickeling and diming me to death; I began to feel like a team that had tried to freeze the ball too early and had lost its momentum, its . . . yes . . . *tempo!* My lead had dwindled to 15 points when it suddenly became clear why he'd made such a fuss about the funny-lookin' deuces. I'd turned it all fours on him, and he had none. He was drawing from the boneyard, hunting for a four, when he suddenly exposed a domino in his hand and, peering at it as if he might qualify for aid to the blind, innocently asked, "Is that thang a deuce, pal?" I was astonished; clearly, it was not. Nor were the next three or four dominoes he deliberately exposed to my view.

47 By now the gamblers were hoo-hawing and laughing. The cardinal rule of dominoes, the very *first* rule—its being a game dependent on the calculating of odds and based upon the memory of what's been played and what has not—is that you never, but *never,* reveal anything of your hand to your opponent. Amarillo Slim was, in effect, playing me with an open hand! It was an insult of the magnitude a street fighter offers when he slaps another rather than hits him with a clenched fist. Such gestures say, *I can take you whenever I want you. You probably got to squat to pee.*

48 With the gamblers' laughter crashing about my reddening ears, I offered a good-sport grin as false and empty as an old maid's dream. There was a reason my face felt frozen somewhere between a grimace and a death mask: I now hated the bastard.

49 "Hey, pal," Slim said, "I'll make you a side bet of five hundred dollars that I can name the three rocks remainin' in the boneyard."

50 "No side bets," I said. "Play the game."

51 "Give you two to one," he offered.

52 "No, no. Dammit, play dominoes!"

53 By now it was all the old gamblers could do not to dance, so they settled for snickering, tee-heeing, and nudging each other with happy elbows. Without having any idea, then or now, of how it happened, I suddenly was behind by 20 points. You might say Slim had broken my concentration.

54 Slim then played a deuce, did an exaggerated double take, and said, "Whoee, kiss me sweet, damn if that wasn't a *deuce* and I didn't know I had any! Hell, pal, you'd of won that five hundred dollar side bet 'cause I was *sure* there was a deuce in that boneyard. And here I was lookin' at it all the time!" The gamblers enjoyed new spasms of mirth while I wondered if Nevada imposed the death penalty for mass murder.

55 Going into what proved to be the first game's final hand, I led by 10 points—245 to 235. How, I don't know.

56 "All you need's a nickel," Slim said. "I'll give you two to one and bet on you to win."

57 "No," I said, "No, no. . . ."

58 I searched my hand and the board but could find no combination that would make the decisive 5 points. It just wasn't there. *Play it close to the vest. You don't have any fives and only one blank and, therefore, no repeater rocks should he make a nickel or a dime. Play small dominoes. Nothing that'll let him get 15. Try for a combination of twos and threes so you can make that goddamn 5 playing defense. Since you don't have any counting rocks, he must have a pisspot full. Stop the long bomb! Intercept!*

59 I played the six-three, the three-outward; there was a blank at the other end of the board.

60 Slim said, "Uh-oh. What you thought was cookin' ain't on the fire. Now, pal, I'll bet you three to two that *I* win."

61 "No," I said. "No, no. . . ."

62 While I tried to calculate what obvious blunder I'd made that so dramatically had changed the odds, Amarillo Slim played the blank six. Now there was a six at one end and a three at the other and—*oh, outhouse mouse! I didn't have another six!* So I couldn't cut the six off. I didn't have a four, so I couldn't play on the spinner, which was the double four. The only three I had was the double three. And if I played it—and I had no choice, the rules said I *had* to play it; it was the only play I had—there would be 12 points on the board. And should Slim have the four-three and play it on the spinner, he'd make 15 and win. I cursed the gods for having given me a handful of sorry aces and funny-lookin' deuces and little else, in a hand where I would have been the prohibitive favorite given even minimal fives or blanks.

63 I put down the double trey, as the rules required. Sure enough, Slim played his four-three on the spinner and made the 15 points that did me in. I sat there feeling like the guy who'd had a three-lap lead in the Indianapolis 500 and then, fifty yards from the finish line, burned out his motor and died. *Five lousy points!*

64 "Hail, I just got lucky," Slim said. "You know, pal, if you'd taken that two to one bet on yourself, I'd owe you money. And that game could have went either way. . . ."

65 Round two. One of Slim's big-time gambler buddies stepped close to him and said, "Okay, you've had your fun, but you cut it a little close. Now settle down and play dominoes." Slim winked at him.

66 Amarillo Slim played no more open hands, though he resorted to physical

tricks: holding a half dozen rocks easily in his big left hand (*you* try it); shuffling his own dominoes while I tried to concentrate on my next play; dropping a domino and permitting it to bounce a shade too long before snatching it back to say, "You didn't see that one, did you, pal?" *Now why,* I wondered, *did he want me to see that one?*

67 While the second game was still nip-and-tuck, tied at 130, Slim so loudly and frequently dreaded my "slappin' me with that ace-five" that I feared a trap. Did he truly fear the ace-five or . . . *no!* He wanted me to play it! Sure! He was using double-think on me! I paused so long, looking for the trap, that Slim said, "Ain't it your play, pal?" I ignored him, continuing to look for the trap. *Just because you don't see it doesn't mean it isn't there.*

68 So, naturally, I did not play the ace-five. I would not have played it with a gun at my head. Instead, I played the ace-four. And no sooner had done so than I realized, sickeningly, that I'd made my biggest goof since agreeing to the match. Now I was left with the ace-five as the lone rock in my hand, while neither aces nor fives were available to be played on. I would be forced to visit the boneyard. Even worse, there *was* a four available on the board; had I played my ace-five and held onto my four—*the last available in the suit, which meant that Slim could not possibly have cut it off*—then I would have guaranteed myself a cinch "Domino" and would have caught Slim with about 50 points in his hand. *Oh, you jackass!* My perceptions were arriving a flash late; it was like a victim flying through the air while realizing that if he'd taken one half step to the right, the truck wouldn't have hit him.

69 I had flat let Slim talk me out of playing that goddamned ace-five, had been conned and flummoxed and sent off on a wild-goose chase looking for a trap that didn't exist. This had blinded me to what *was* there. I had reacted as a rank amateur, making the kind of blunder I had always relied on my kitchen-table opponents to make.

70 Amarillo Slim flashed a private grin that said, *We know who's gonna win now, don't we, pal? You dropped more than you can pick up, and it's all over.* It very shortly was. Slim dominoed on me for a crushing 55-point profit, making my blunder one of more than 100 points, considering what I properly should have extracted from him, and handily accounting for more than the margin by which he ultimately won: 250 to 165.

71 By now my game was in shambles. I worried not about winning that third game, or even hanging tough, for my pride and poise had deserted me and sneaked off to hide. I was concerned, instead, with not additionally making an ass of myself through the use of more sophomoric blunders. I imagined that the onlooking gamblers were rolling their eyes and giggling and perhaps whispering that I should take up paper dolls. Consequently, I played the last game as if blind, airless, and in a hurry to catch a bus. Slim won, 250 to 190, to complete his sweep. Don't ask me how, if you're talking about the play by play.

72 I counted out seven $20 bills and a lone ten-spot to Amarillo Slim, who scooped them off the table with a practiced hand while offering the other in tardy fellowship. "Pal," he said, "I really and truly enjoyed it."

73 I showed him the teeth through which I was lying and said, "Me, too, pal."

Then I leaned in and said softly, only for his ears, "Slim, there are a hundred sixty-five spots in a deck of dominoes." Slim grinned and winked.

74 As a friend and I tried to leave the gambling arena by an invisible path, one of the chuckling leather-lunged old gamblers called out, "What did you boys beat ol' Slim out of?"

75 "About thirty minutes," I said.

(1980)

QUESTIONS

Thought and Structure

1. What is King's purpose in this essay? Does he ever directly state his thesis or main point? How did you respond to the essay?
2. "Shoot-out" divides into four parts. Title each and explain how the parts are related.
3. Are the first two paragraphs necessary? Why or why not? How about paragraphs 5–9?
4. How does King characterize Amarillo Slim? How does he characterize himself? Why?
5. How much of the essay would you consider its conclusion? Why?

Style and Strategy

6. What is the importance of the question Slim asks King about the number of spots on a domino? Why does King open part two with it?
7. What is the significance of the italicized sentences in the essay? Can you think of another way to accomplish the same thing?
8. How does King prepare us for the big match? How does he build suspense? Are his methods effective?
9. Look at the dialogue. Compare Slim's comments with King's. What do you notice?
10. What is the function of the onlookers? Why does King include them? Could they be eliminated? Why or why not?

SUGGESTIONS FOR WRITING

A. Describe a contest or a game you've watched. Try to recreate the game's strategy and its tension.

B. Describe a game or contest or conversation you have participated in. Include not only the external action, but your internal monologue of thought as you played and/or spoke. In doing so you will offer a double perspective on the action or conversation: what goes on externally and what you think about it.

C. Compare King's comic techniques and effects in this selection with his comic techniques in another essay. Or compare King's humor with Tom Wolfe's as displayed in one or more of his essays.

Remembering the Hard Times

1 I don't know your reaction to all this woolly Depression talk—though I might if I knew your age—but here's one ol' boy it scares. Not mildly worries, mind you, or causes an occasional fretful tic, but simply disorders his brain and his innards. There are millions of us, in our mid-forties or over, who vividly recall the economic bust of Hoover's time. And a high percentage of us fear another depression more than we worry about heart attacks, cancer, hardened arteries, or like awards planned for us by the actuarial charts. Short of nature's most perverse inversion, that of burying one of my own children, I can't think of a more frightening nightmare.

2 Mounting Depression talk lately has influenced my daily conduct. I work more, feverishly hoping to gain a nest egg against whatever dread awaits, and have begun dogged small economies: turning off surplus lights; considering the cheaper cuts of meat; spending less on my twin indulgences—good books and good scotch—and I'm thinking of writing a letter of apology to an old friend, John Henry Faulk, who was a big-time network-radio star until blacklisted during the Joe McCarthy madness. I snickered on first hearing that John Henry had quit the city for a small Texas farm supplied with chickens and milk cows as a survival hedge against expected new privations. It doesn't seem so laughable anymore.

3 I am kicking myself, too, for having been such a spendthrift over the past ten years. Oh, yes, I have been a real butter-and-egg man, hitting all the whiskey and trombone towns, buying drinks for the crowd, and urging the good times to roll from New Orleans to Nantucket; it is a disease afflicting a certain stripe of man who once didn't have a pit to poss in, a reckless dispensation of resources almost as if one feared that the banks might fail again. In a manic spree about two years ago, I divested myself within three months of more than $12,000 on purely hedonistic pursuits—money above my true requirements or real obligations; funny money just burned and whoopeed away—and now, monitoring the gloomy economic forecasts, I think of how many chickens and moo cows it might have bought.

4 But where John Henry Faulk had the foresight to retreat to the earth's basic places and shelters, I did not. While deep in the Watergate dumps, I promised myself to move from Washington—that dreary ruin of marble monuments, rhinestone dreams, and brassy interlopers, where for years I had felt much the transient and grew no roots—to more commodious Manhattan quarters. Despite gathering misgivings and a plunging stock market heralding future economic turndowns, I accomplished the deed—just in time to witness the collapse of the Franklin National Bank, a branch of which reposed around the corner from my new digs. Although the Franklin's fall was played down in the press, publishers being businessmen first and sponsors of artists and prophets later, it represented the largest single bank failure in American history. Not the best possible welcome to the neighborhood.

5 I love it here—the apartment with its airy open view and light, the new gear and accouterments, those surging excitements of the Big Apple so long merely sampled by a visiting country boy hoping to throw his money away—but I am newly terrified at assuming the permanent cost of the place. My rent has doubled, and the

taxicabs are metered. One encounters formerly prosperous ex-stockbrokers in the bars, searching the want ads and nursing their midday drinks. Construction men can't find work, in a city perpetually building and in constant need of rebuilding, and sit over their beers with haunted eyes and many damnations of their former hard-hat hero, Dick Nixon, on their lips. I think more on the $8,000 required to keep a teenaged son in boarding school, of older family members infirm or otherwise disadvantaged who increasingly require helpful attentions, of skyrocketing taxes (sales; property; city, state, and federal income taxes) and business expenses; and of my own loose excesses.

6 Most of all, I think of how unfriendly were the nation's Gothams to their hopeless millions in that earlier dark penniless time. I conjure up visions from old books and ancient newsreels of the special miseries of the cities: their breadlines, soup kitchens, corner apple salesmen, park-bench sleepers; grim gray men in endless ranks profitlessly seeking work, and their dismal Hooverville settlements of cardboard, fruit crates, tin, and rags. These had it rougher, I know, than those of us relatively fortunate enough to hunker down in the hinterlands, where we might grow a few vegetables and produce our own eggs, with a little creek fishing on the side; there are damn few squirrels or rabbits to be bagged for the family stew pot on the sidewalks of New York. So I sit here within spitting range of Park Avenue, luxury-spoiled and more prosperous than yesteryear might have believed, wondering what in God's good name I am doing taking for neighbors those Wall Street bastards my father railed and warned against in the long ago.

7 There are brave words from President Ford and his White House advisers that no new depression will be tolerated; apparently, Mr. Hard Times is to be run out of town like a ragged hobo and by a prosperous mob wearing WIN buttons. These jawbonings afford small comfort to one who remembers the optimistic rhetoric and arrogant explanations of the Great Depression. President Hoover: "Prosperity is just around the corner. . . . The worst will be over in sixty days. . . . Many people left their jobs for the more profitable one of selling apples [!!!]. . . ." Calvin Coolidge: "When more and more people are thrown out of work, unemployment results. . . ." J. P. Morgan: "The stock market will fluctuate." Jackson Reynolds, president of the First National Bank of New York: "Ninety-nine out of a hundred persons haven't good sense." John D. Rockefeller: "Believing that fundamental conditions are sound, my son and I have for some days been purchasing sound common stocks." Thomas W. Lamont of J. P. Morgan and Company: "It is the consensus of financiers that many of the quotations on the stock exchange do not fairly represent the situation."

8 Well, thanks a heap, old fellows; and thanks, too, to all publications from *Fortune* to *Reader's Digest* for their cheery reports of 1929–32 even as our belt buckles grew closer to our backbones and grass grew in the streets. And a special thanks to all you determined jawboners of the present moment who have succeeded to the pep squad. But, damn it, I *still* think I ought to be back home, trading cows with John Henry Faulk, and canning prickly pear preserves.

9 When I am required to write an autobiographical sketch, it invariably begins: "I was born on the first day of the first year of the Great Depression—1929." My

subconscious imagines the Fates, wearing black capes and hideous grins, as they danced jigs and gleefully slapped their withered thighs in celebration of the tough surprises they had prepared for Baby King. My father then was a prospering blacksmith and had just built one of the finer houses in Putnam, Texas. I would mewl and gurgle in it little more than a year before the local oil boom would go bust and fly-by-night operators would escape, owing the village blacksmith more than 10,000 hard-money dollars. The Great Depression soon would show itself. My father lost everything; though he would live another forty years, he never recovered. The King family, like Steinbeck's wretched Joads, took to the road in search of that elusive prosperity President Hoover insisted was just around the corner.

10 My first memories are of living in a farmer's converted garage while my parents and older siblings went off to pick cotton each day. Sometimes they found somebody to stay with me, and sometimes they stationed me under a tree with an old collie dog to stand guard. The new Model T from Mr. Ford's new assembly lines, which my father had paid cash for just before the crash, was pulled by mules from cotton field to cotton field; gasoline was purchased only when it became necessary to find new work in distant places. We ultimately retreated to my father's old homeplace, where he had settled with his farming family in 1894; its fields had long lain fallow, so that older members of the family had to grub stumps and battle Johnson grass before being able to plant. There was a baking drought and a grasshopper plague. I don't know if you've ever seen thousands or millions of grasshoppers assault a cornfield, a grainfield, or a vegetable garden. First they chew down the main plants, not only stripping the blades or leaves but eating the stalk and then burrowing into the ground after the roots; when they're gone, it looks as if the field had been bombed or burned. Even when one had a bountiful harvest, prices were so depressed that little or no profit resulted.

11 By the time I was seven I, too, pulled a cotton sack or performed other agrarian tortures when not struggling with the mysteries of the rural Texas school. I cannot claim to have excessively enjoyed it. Indeed, my earliest private vow was to escape that farm and all the unrewarding toil it provided. I dreamed of running away from home but deduced that the road might not be a terribly profitable place after seeing streams of hobos hop off freight trains on the Texas & Pacific Railroad to fan out in our rural community and beg back-door food handouts. My mother was terrified of them, especially when my father might be working in some distant field or pasture; he established an old iron bell on the veranda, and she was under instructions to ring it in times of peril. I recall my father's being ashamed to turn away hungry men, but my mother's fear overcame his humanitarian instincts. It was, simply, a time of fear.

12 I have since heard, or read, the Depression memories of others of my generation; almost uniformly, they claim not to have especially noticed their poverty because everyone was in the same boat. That knowledge did not comfort me: I knew we were dirt poor, knew it every waking hour, and I resented it and hated it as some deep personal affront. When my parents reminisced of the good times—in an effort, I suppose, to bolster themselves—I stewed and grew angry because I could not remember having shared them. When school adjourned each fall for crop gathering, I loathed being part of itinerant cotton-picking crews; we crowded like cattle into a series of failed old trucks, clattering from one cotton patch to another among

exhausted parents and their crying kids; the hours were from daylight until dark, from "can to can't."

13 I hated going door to door with my mother in Cisco on Saturdays, trying to sell eggs or vegetables to people I imagined to be rich. I envied their radios, cars, telephones, and other superiorities. Bile sloshed in my innards when the high school football team played on Friday afternoons and found me short of the ten-cent admission price, and those of us without the where-withal were herded into the tiny school library for guarding while our luckier companions skipped gaily off to the big game. " 'Pride goeth before a mighty fall,' " my mother quoted in an effort to make me accept the realities. But I became a quarrelsome kid, full of hates and aggressions, one likely to explode into fistfights or pointless rages. I could not have defined either a communist, socialist, revolutionary, or capitalist; my instincts and sympathies certainly were with all of those, save the capitalist, however. Alternately I despised what he represented and wanted to be cut in on what he had.

14 That we ate well, by raising our own hogs and chickens and cows and vegetables, did not satisfy the urge for coins to click. There simply was *no* money. I heard my worried parents talk at night, when they thought young ears were deaf in sleep, about the impossibility of new shoes or new clothes or a new plow. I eavesdropped while my father and his angry contemporaries in their faded blue-ducking overalls cursed the banks and threatened violence should mortgages be foreclosed or seed-crop loans be denied. Sometimes I would find my father standing on the porch or in the yard staring blankly into space, and the expression on his face frightened me. There were stretches when he might be gone for days, riding horseback through the countryside in search of stumps to grub or horses to shoe or any odd jobs that might contribute a dollar. As often as not, he returned with nothing to show; I began to dread his returns for the fresh despair they produced.

15 After such disappointments, my mother privately lectured me to make something of myself: to seek an education and some vague main chance; to get up and get out as soon as nature and circumstance permitted; to find some yellow-brick road. I had the notion that she somehow blamed my father, though I didn't think it quite fair. My father preached harsh sermons against the Goddamn Republicans; I learned, early on, that they were rich to the very last in number and didn't give a shit for the little man. To this day I feel obscurely guilty about once having voted for one.

16 I was too young to know of Franklin D. Roosevelt's election in 1932; four years later, however, I knew that everyone save the Goddamn Republicans and inmates of insane asylums strongly backed him over Alf Landon. FDR had made it possible for my brother to obtain work in the Civilian Conservation Corps (he got bed, board, and $1 per day, $5 of which he kept at the end of the month, while a vital $25 came home to the family) and for my father to find occasional paydays improving country roads or bridges or building outdoor privies under the sponsorship of the Works Progress Administration. Obviously, FDR wanted us to have work and money; just as obviously, his opponents did not. *That* certain knowledge, combined with once seeing a weeping farm family's goods publicly sold at a sheriff's sale to satisfy creditors, would early make me a "yellow dog" Democrat—one who would vote for a "yellow dog" before crossing party lines to assist any living Republican.

17 Intellectually, I cannot now quarrel with contentions that for all of FDR's

pump priming, America did not truly recover from its Great Depression blues until that full-employment boom provided by World War II. There was, yes, some economic marching up and down again. But you cannot convince me that all the midnight schemes of the brain trusters went for naught or that the paper shufflings of the New Deal's alphabet-soup agencies failed to make important improvements or contributions. In addition to the tangibles—jobs, new schools and other useful edifices, emergency food and clothing; even a slight relaxation in the skinflint loan policies of formerly heartless bankers—the New Deal brought hope where no hope had lived. And it brought the faint promise, at least, of a better tomorrow. When hope was all you had, it was worth much more than the dry and distant recapitulations of historians can make later generations understand.

18 When I learned at school that FDR would be making yet another of his fireside chats, it was my bounden duty to take the word home. After a hurried early supper, we walked a mile to a neighboring farm, there to listen with other families who had assembled for the latest radio word from the new messiah. Those were vital gatherings, the adults listening so intently that even the most high-spirited child knew not to require shushing. I clung to every word the man said; though I didn't understand much of it, I was comforted by the sound and roll.

19 Afterward—when Roosevelt's confident voice had wished us good night—while popcorn and parched peanuts were passed around, the old snuff-dipping farmers would wave their arms and say, "By gum, now, Clyde, that feller Rusavelt; he's got some good i-deers; why, I wouldn't be a-tall surprised if cotton went up! Yessir!" Then they would make their bitter jokes about Hoover steak (rabbits or squirrels) or Hoover cars (mule-drawn wagons) or Hoover cake (cornbread), and surely some old nester—his eyes glowing mischief—would say something like "I tole my ol' woman t'other day that I figger the Depression's purt near over cause I seen a jackrabbit runnin' down the road and they wasn't no more than three fellers chasin' it." They would explode in rough laughter, then, the sharper edges momentarily knocked off their fear. Uncle Tal Horn and Old Man Luther Parks might commence sawing on their fiddles—playing "Cotton-Eyed Joe" or "Buffalo Gals" or "Old Joe Clark"—while feet tapped, children squealed, and for a little while you could forget those new burdens soon to come up with the sun.

20 Remembering all that, I have aggressively caused severe social embarrassments over the years should some academic dandy or cretin ideologue look too smug and too well fed in contending that FDR was the opiate of the masses and delivered the masses not; some things, goddammit, you just can't put a price tag on, though the high-domed thinkers can't seem to get that through their noggins. I particularly recall going all spluttery and inarticulate in the home of John Kenneth Galbraith, Warburg Professor of Economics at Harvard, when some dinner guest said over the fine wine and cigars—in response to my Depression memories, issued while I was voluntarily straightening out everybody's economic misconceptions—"But why didn't your family move elsewhere, where opportunities might have been greater?" The sumbitch actually *said* that. He was a young professor, and so I suppose allowances perhaps should be made; but from that moment forward I have pretty well despaired of the Ivy League.

21 A woman named Caroline Bird wrote a fine book about the Depression and

perfectly titled it *The Invisible Scar;* her theory ran that many of us shall go to our graves deeply wounded in our psyches by those have-not years. She's right as rain. My mother is in her late eighties now, living in that misty netherworld where yesteryear is more real than this living moment; I recently saw her cry anew in relating her deep hurt when my older brother went off to a CCC camp being established in distant Arizona: "We had two dollars and a dime. I tried to give Weldon a dollar, but he wouldn't take it. He struck off across the pasture, walkin' eight miles to Cisco to catch a government train, and it nearly killed me to see that boy go without a nickel in his pocket. I cried a long time after he was out of sight."

22 That brother is my senior by about fifteen years; though I worshiped him as a kid brother will, I grew extremely tired of hearing from others how he had dropped out of high school to wash dishes in a café so that I might be bought an infant's survival milk. No doubt it has colored our relationship through life; I was much older than I should have been before I could fully appreciate his sacrifice, simply because the guilt was too much. Indeed, I hardly had come of legal age when I provoked a fight with him in order to declare my independence. Not until I was nearing thirty did I forgive him for all he'd done for me.

23 As a young man in his earliest low-paying jobs I was torn between a natural instinct to instruct unreasonable, nit-picking bosses to go screw themselves and a deep, unspoken fear that should I lose *that* job, I might not find another. It was a thing I noted among many of my generation. They suffered dull mulework, performed overtime without compensation, and paled in the company of irascible supervisors; no matter that they then functioned in the post-World War II boom and had the added sweetener of a record local oil-based prosperity. Several old companions, I am certain, limited their career opportunities out of fear that should they fail in new adventures, they might find themselves on the streets. Sometimes, now, when they and the moon are high, they grouse in their cups of having been born in the wrong time. One old friend actually gave a party celebrating the tardy death of Herbert Hoover, who long had been past hurting him—if, indeed, he ever had—and though mildly appalled, I might have attended had I been in town.

24 It is good, I suppose, that each succeeding generation has difficulty transmitting its darker experiences to the next. Thus, fresh hope is not stillborn, people dare to dream, and the young are free to take those foolish risks and experimentations necessary to the full life. But whether attempting to replant their fears in a new generation or honestly hoping to help the young avoid their own mistakes, parents have a way of harping or preaching on their own private dreads; as these dreads are the product of their own histories, their children—of another time and place—cannot identify with them. It was maddening, when I chastised my own children for wasting food or time or opportunity, to comprehend ultimately that my Great Depression sermons were accepted as nothing more than the private preoccupations of an old fossil. They humored me along, sometimes exchanging quick, secret smiles, but I knew they could no more envision breadlines or failed banks or one-third of a nation ill-fed, ill-housed, and ill-clothed than I might understand the gibberings of some little green Martian. They are products of the affluent society and can imagine no other.

25 For all my occasional uses of the Depression in making the obligatory parental

preachments, I did not truly think—for years—that it would be possible to have another. Indeed, as a young man working on Capitol Hill, I had the personal assurances of the late Speaker Sam Rayburn. One postwork afternoon in the late fifties, over whiskey in his hideaway office in the Capitol building, where the fortunate might be invited to attend what he called meetings of "the board of education," the old man said of bankers and businessmen who had the temerity to vote Republican, "Why, Roosevelt saved the bastards; he fixed it so things can't *ever* go bust again. He put in laws propping up the economy, and he saved those bastards, and now they don't appreciate it." I believed him, for had not Rayburn personally sponsored dozens of FDR's bills in Congress? Was not America booming again? It was a time when few Americans questioned the authority of Authority; a time when myths were for promoting and old bad dreams were for forgetting. Yes, we had coins to rattle and folding stuff in our pokes, and you could count on the future unless the Russians blew up Wall Street with the Bomb.

26 We were almost a decade away from the time when we might begin to suspect that many of our problems might be beyond quick solutions, that the answer did not always handily repose in the back of the book, that we paid for our factories and highways and shiny shopping centers in the coin of polluted streams, disfigured countrysides, new slums, and urban tangles. In Sam Rayburn's time, we could not have imagined that day when the oil-producing nations not only would cease snatching off their hats in Uncle Sam's presence—mighty, unconquerable Uncle Sam, who always won his wars and ruled supreme as the quintessential industrial and technological state—but would actually back him against the wall and then shake a finger in his face. The time had not yet come when Europe would suspect the dollar and puzzled American tourists would find themselves stranded in foreign ports because suddenly their money wasn't preferred. We gave little or no thought to the increasing problem of constant balance-of-trade deficits, and we really couldn't imagine that Americans in significant numbers would take to those cheap imitations of radios, cameras, and such that the Japanese shipped here in such astounding quantities.

27 For some time now we've lived with the uneasy notion that certain external events may be beyond the economic control of Washington or Wall Street; the cat's long been out of the bag where official infallibility is concerned. We don't like to ponder it, but maybe we've got to be willing to risk an uncontrollable and unconscionable war if we're to get all the oil or other scarce resources we require. Nobody's saying "war" out loud from public podiums in Washington, but there are mutterings; those who understand that wars are fought more for material gain than for those more ethereal reasons found in wartime rhetoric or brushed-up history books must have had the dark, unthinkable thought even before Washington began "warning" the oil-producing nations of the dangers inherent in their escalating profits; not for nothing, I suspect, does the Pentagon have a paper plan for seizing certain Mideastern oil fields should things become intolerable. These, of course, are just "war games" the Pentagon says, and they are plotted to cover any eventuality, however remote; so don't worry about it.

28 We are, face it, no longer a country or a society of unlimited resources. We never were, of course; but it *seemed* that we were, and we acted accordingly. The

economic and political realities of the world are such that my older nightmares have come back into fashion. I fear that it *can* happen here again, and probably will. One of these days this nation of pyramiding credit, inflationary spirals, impossible taxes, suspect dollars, gross waste, bloated bureaucracies, union demands, cheating business ethics, and conflicting international complications may go down in such a heap that the dust and roar may not subside until we've scrapped the old ways and the old system. Morose thoughts, indeed, for one who knows that midtown Manhattan doesn't look like a good place to stake a cow and who knows, too, that fireside chats are unlikely to comfort as they did in that earlier time.

(1980)

QUESTIONS

Thought and Structure

1. King begins this essay with something of a prologue. What is the point of these opening paragraphs (1–8)? Would King have been better off beginning at paragraph 9? Why or why not?
2. What is King's attitude toward capitalist enterprise? Why?
3. What image of the Great Depression has King created? What does he do to enable those of us who did not experience it directly to understand it? Is intellectual comprehension King's aim? Something else?
4. King is able to present history from a personal vantage point. He not only gives us a feeling for what the depression was like for him, but he also is able to suggest a larger historical perspective. What, essentially, is his point about Hoover? About Roosevelt? About the consequences of the depression for the common man?
5. If paragraphs 1–8 form a prologue, which paragraphs constitute the conclusion? How are they related to the prologue? Once you have identified the concluding paragraphs, you are left with the body or heart of the essay. How is that central section organized?

Style and Strategy

6. King's writing is consistently concrete and specific. Instead of saying, for example, that although he had enough food, he lacked money, he writes that "raising our own hogs and chickens and cows and vegetables, did not satisfy the urge for coins to click." Find two additional examples of concrete language effectively used and account for their effectiveness.
7. Read the last sentence of paragraphs 1, 2, 4, 11, 13–15, 17, 20–22, and 24. What do they have in common? How effectively do they close their respective paragraphs?
8. What is the effect of the double dash interpolations King includes in his sentences in paragraphs 1–5? In paragraphs 17, 19, 20, 23–26? Would commas do as well as the double dashes? Why or why not?
9. Where is King's language most colloquial and informal—most consistently conversationally idiomatic? Where is it most formal and bookish? Are both voices necessary? What does each contribute?
10. In paragraph 20 King engages in some name-calling. He uses terms like "academic

dandy," "cretin ideologue," and "high-domed thinkers." Why does he employ this sort of language? How effective and convincing is it?

SUGGESTIONS FOR WRITING

A. Write an essay about a part of your life that profoundly affected you. Describe your circumstances in sufficient detail for readers to see what you went through. Explain its effects on your personality, character, behavior, thinking.

B. Read a chapter from an historical record of the depression. Write an essay comparing King's version with the historical account. Consider style, tone, purpose, details, point.

C. Compare this essay's tone and texture with that of Didion's "Goodbye to All That." How do the two writers recreate a remembered past? How different are those two remembrances?

The American Redneck

I

1 The maddest I remember being at my late wife (a Yankee lady, of Greek extraction and mercurial moods) was when she shouted, during a quarrel the origins of which are long lost, that I was "a dumb Redneck." My heart dangerously palpitated; my eyes bugged; I ran in tight circles and howled inarticulate general profanities until, yes . . . my neck turned red. Literally. I felt the betraying hot flush as real as a cornfield tan. My wife collapsed in a mirthful heap, little knowing how truly close I felt to righteous killing.

2 Being called dumb wasn't what had excited me. No, for I judged myself ignorant only to the extent that mankind is and knew I was no special klutz. But being called a Redneck, now, especially when you know in your genes and in the dirty back roads of your mind that you *are* one—despite having spent years trying not to be—well, when that happens, all fair has gone out of the fight. I do not cherish Rednecks, which means I dislike certain persistent old parts of myself.

3 Of late the Redneck has been wildly romanticized; somehow he threatens to become a cultural hero. Perhaps this is because heroes are in short supply—we seem to burn them up faster nowadays—or maybe it's a manifestation of our urge to return to simpler times: to be free of computers, pollution, the urban tangle, shortages of energy or materials or elbowroom. Even George Wallace is "respectable" now, having been semimartyred by gunfire and defanged by defeat. Since 'Necks have long been identified with overt racism, we may be embracing them because we long ago tired of bad niggers who spooked and threatened us; perhaps the revival is a backlash against hairy hippies, peaceniks, weirdos of all stripes. Or the recent worship of Redneckism may be no more than the clever manipulations of music and movie czars, ever on the lookout for profitable new crazes. Anyway,

a lot of foolishness disguised as noble folklore is going down as the 'Neck is praised in song and story.

4 There are "good" people, yes, who might properly answer to the appellation "Redneck": people who operate mom-and-pop stores or their lathes, dutifully pay their taxes, lend a helping hand to neighbors, love their country and their God and their dogs. But even among a high percentage of these salts-of-the-earth lives a terrible reluctance toward even modest passes at social justice, a suspicious regard of the mind as an instrument of worth, a view of the world extending little farther than the ends of their noses, and only vague notions that they are small quills writing a large, if indifferent, history.

5 Not that these are always mindless. Some value "common sense" or "horse sense" and in the basics may be less foolish than certain determined rote sophisticates and any number of pompous academicians. Some few may read Plato or Camus or otherwise astonish; it does not necessarily follow that he who is poor knows nothing or cares little. On the other hand, you can make boatloads of money and still be a Redneck in your bones, values, and attitudes. But largely, I think—even at the risk of being accused of elitism or class prejudice—the worse components of 'Neckery are found among the unlettered poor.

6 Attempts to deify the Redneck, to represent his life-style as close to that of the noble savage are, at best, unreal and naïve. For all their native wit—and sometimes they have keen senses of the absurd as applied to their daily lives—Rednecks generally comprise a sad lot. They flounder in perilous financial waters and are mired in the sociopolitical shallows. Their lives are hard: long on work and short on money; full of vile bossmen, hounding creditors, debilitating quarrels, routine disappointments, confrontations, ignorance, a treadmill hopelessness. It may sound good on a country-western record when Tom T. Hall and Waylon Jennings lift their voices, baby, but it neither sounds nor feels good when life is real and the alarm clock's jarring jangle soon must be followed by the time clock's tuneless bells.

7 Now, the Rednecks I'm talking about are not those counterfeit numbers who hang around Austin digging the Cosmic Cowboy scene, sucking up to Jerry Jeff Walker and Willie Nelson, wearing bleached color-patched overalls, and rolling their own dope, saying how they hanker to go live off the land and then winging off to stay six weeks in a Taos commune before flying back on daddy's credit card. May such toy Rednecks choke on their own romantic pretensions.

8 No, and I'm not talking about Good Ol' Boys. Do not, please, confuse the two; so many have. A Good Ol' Boy is a Redneck who has acquired a smidgen or much more of polish; I could call him a "former Redneck" except that there ain't no such when you bore bone-deep. One born a 'Neck of the true plastic-Jesus-on-the-dashboard and pink-rubber-haircurlers-in-the-supermarket variety can no more shuck his condition than may the Baptist who, once saved, becomes doctrinarily incapable of talking his way into hell.

9 The Good Ol' Boy may or may not have been refurbished by college. But bet your ass he's a climber, an achiever, a con man looking for the edge and the hedge. He'll lay a lot of semi-smarmy charm on you, and bullshit grading from middling to high. He acts dumber than he is when he knows something and smarter than he

is when he doesn't. He would be dangerous game to hunt. Such parts of his Redneck heritage as may be judged eccentric or humorous enough to be useful will be retained in his mildly self-deprecating stories and may come in handy while he's working up to relieving you of your billfold or your panties. Such Redneck parts as no longer serve him, he attempts to bury in the mute and dead past. And he becomes maniacal when, say, a domestic quarrel causes him to blow his cool enough that those old red bones briefly rise from their interment so that others may glimpse them.

10 A Good Ol' Boy turns his radio down at red lights so that other drivers won't observe him enjoying Kitty Wells singing through her nose. He carefully says "Negro," though it slips to "Nigra" with a shade much scotch, or even—under stress, or for purposes of humor among close associates—slides all the way down to "nigger." He does not dip snuff or chaw tobacco, preferring cigarettes or cigars or perhaps an occasional sly hip toke of pot. He has forgotten, or tells himself he has forgotten, the daily fear of being truly ragged and dirt poor—and, perhaps, how to ride a horse, or the cruel tug of the cotton sack, or the strength of the laborer's sun. He may belong to a civic club, play golf, travel, own his own shop, or run somebody else's. For a long time he's been running uphill; sometimes he doesn't know when he's reached level ground and keeps on struggling. Having fought and sweated for his toehold, he'll likely be quick to kick those who attempt to climb along behind him.

11 While all Good Ol' Boys have been at least fringe Rednecks, not nearly all Rednecks rise to be Good Ol' Boys. No. Their gizzards don't harbor enough of something—grit, ambition, good fortune, con, education, flint, self-propellants, saddle burrs, chickenshit, opportunity, whatever—and so they continue to breed and largely perpetuate themselves in place, defanged Snopeses never to attain, accumulate, bite the propertied gentry, or smite their tormentors. These are no radicals; though the resentful juices of revolution may ache their bloodstreams, they remain—with rare, crazed exceptions—amazingly docile. They simply can't find the handles of things and drop more than they can pick up.

12 Though broad generalities deserve their dangerous reputation, one hazards the judgment that always such unreconstructed Rednecks shall vote to the last in number for the George Wallaces or Lester Maddoxes or other dark ogres of their time; will fear God at least in the abstract and Authority and Change even more; will become shade-tree mechanics, factory robots, salesmen of small parts, peacetime soldiers or sailors; random serfs. (Yes, good neighbors, do you know what it is to envy the man who no longer carries the dinner bucket, and hope someday you'll reach his plateau: maybe shill for Allstate?) The women of such men are beauticians and waitresses and laundry workers and notions-counter clerks and generally pregnant. Their children may be hauled in joustabout pickup trucks or an old Ford dangling baby booties, giant furry dice, toy lions, nodding doggies and plastered with down-home bumper stickers: "Honk If You Love Jesus," maybe, or "Goat Ropers Need Love Too." Almost certainly it's got a steady mortgage against it, and at least one impatient lien.

13 We are talking, good buddies, about America's white niggers: the left behind, the luckless, the doomed. It is these we explore: my clay, native roots, mutha culture. . . .

14 I didn't know I was a Redneck as a kid. The Housenwrights were Rednecks, I knew—even though I was ignorant of the term; couldn't have defined it had I heard it—and so were the Spagles and certain branches of the Halls, the Peoples, the Conines, the many broods of Hawks. These were the raggedest of the ragged in a time when even FDR judged one-third of a nation to be out-at-elbows. There was a hopelessness about them, a feckless wildness possible only in the truly surrendered, a community sense that their daddies didn't try as hard as some or, simply, had been born to such ill luck, silly judgments, whiskey thirsts, or general rowdiness as to preclude twitches of upward mobility. Such families were less likely than others to seek church; their breadwinners idled more; their children came barefoot to the rural school even in winter. They were more likely to produce domestic violence, blood feuds, boys who fought their teachers. They no longer cared and, not caring, might cheerfully flatten you or stab you in a playground fight or at one of the Saturday-night country dances held in rude plank homes along the creek banks. Shiftless badasses. Poor tacky peckerwoods who did us the favor of providing somebody to look down on. For this service we children of the "better" homes rewarded them with rock fights or other torments: "Dessie Hall, Dessie Hall/Haw Haw Haw/Your Daddy Never Bathes/But He's Cleaner Than Your Maw."

15 Ours was a reluctant civilization. Eastland County, Texas, had its share of certified illiterates in the 1930s and later, people who could no more read a Clabber Girl Baking Powder billboard than they could translate from the French. I recall witnessing old nesters who made their laborious "marks" should documents require signatures. A neighboring farmer in middle age boasted that his sons had taught him simple long division; on Saturdays he presided from the wooden veranda of Morgan Brothers General Store in Scranton, demonstrating on a brown paper sack exactly how many times 13 went into 39, while whiskered old farmers gathered for their small commerce looked on as if he might be revealing the internal rules of heaven.

16 We lived in one of the more remote nooks of Eastland County, in cotton and goober and scrub-oak country. There were no paved roads and precious few tractors among that settlement of marginal farms populated by snuff dippers, their sunbonneted women, and broods of jittery shy kids who might regard unexpected visitors from concealment. We were broken-plow farmers, holding it all together with baling wire, habit, curses, and prayers. Most families were on FDR's relief agency rolls; county agriculture agents taught our parents to card their cotton by hand so they might stuff homemade mattresses. They had less success in teaching crop rotation, farmers feeling that the plot where daddy and granddaddy had grown cotton remained a logical place for cotton still. There were many who literally believed in a flat earth and the haunting presence of ghosts; if the community contained any individual who failed to believe that eternal damnation was a fair reward for the sinner, he never came forward to declare it.

17 Churches grew in wild profusion. Proud backwoodsmen, their best doctrines disputed by fellow parishioners, were quick to establish their rival rump churches under brush arbors or tabernacles or in plank cracker boxes. One need have no formal training to preach; the Call was enough, a personal conviction that God had beckoned one from a hot cornfield or cattle pen to spread the Word; this was easy enough for God to do, He being everywhere and so little inclined toward snobbery

that He frequently visited the lowliest Eastland County dirt farmer for consultations. Converts were baptized in muddy creeks or stock tanks, some flocks—in the words of the late Governor Earl Long of Louisiana—"chunking snakes and catching fevers."

18 It was not uncommon, when my father was a young man, for righteous vigilantes to pay nocturnal calls on erring wife beaters or general ne'er-do-wells, flogging them with whips and Scriptures while demanding their immediate improvement. Such godly posses did not seek to punish those who lived outside the law, however, should commerce be involved; when times were hard, so were the people. Bootleggers flourished in those woods in my youth, and it was not our responsibility to reveal them. Even cattle thieves were ignored so long as they traveled safe distances to improve their small herds.

19 My father's house was poor but proud: law-abiding, church-ridden, hardworking, pin-neat; innocent, it seems in retrospect, of conscious evil, and innocent, even, of the modern world. Certainly we had good opinions of ourselves and a worthy community standing. And yet even in that "good" family of work-worn, self-starting, self-designated country aristocrats there were tragedies and explosions as raw as the land we inhabited: My paternal grandfather was shot to death by a neighbor; an uncle went to the pen for carnal knowledge of an underaged girl; my father's fists variously laid out a farmer who had the temerity to cut in front of his wagon in the cotton-gin line, a ranch hand who'd reneged on a promise to pay out of his next wages for having his horse shod, a kinsman who threatened to embarrass the clan by running unsuccessfully for county commissioner a ninth straight time. My father was the family enforcer, handing out summary judgments and corporal punishments to any in the bloodline whose follies he judged trashy or a source of community scorn or ridicule. It was most tribal: Walking Bear has disgraced the Sioux; very well, off with Walking Bear's head.

20 So while we may have had no more money than others, no more of education or raw opportunity, I came to believe that the Kings were somehow special and that my mother's people, the proud and clannish Clarks, were more special still. A certain deference was paid my parents in their rural domain; they gave advice, helped shape community affairs, were arbiters and unofficial judges. I became a "leader" at the country school and in Bethel Methodist Church, where we took pride in worships free of snake handling or foot washings—although it was proper to occasionally talk in tongues or grovel at the mourners' bench.

21 I strutted when my older brother, Weldon, returned in his secondhand Model A Ford to visit from Midland, a huge metropolis of 9,000 noblemen in oil, cowboy, and rattlesnake country more than 200 miles to the west. I imagined him a leading citizen there; he had found Success as manager of the lunch counter and fountain at Piggly Wiggly's and announced cowpoke melodies part time over the facilities of radio station KCRS. More, he was a hot-fielding second baseman with the semiprofessional Midland Cowboys baseball team. Any day I expected the New York Yankees to call him up and wondered when they did not.

22 Weldon epitomized sophistication in my young mind; he wore smart two-toned shoes with air holes allowing his feet to breathe, oceans of Red Rose hair oil, and a thin go-to-hell mustache. In the jargon of the time and the place he was "a

jellybean." Where rustics rolled their own from nickel bags of Duke's Mixture or Country Gentlemen, my brother puffed luxurious "ready rolls." When he walked among local stay-at-homes on his rare visits, he turned the heads of milkmaids and drew the dark envied stares of male contemporaries who labored on their fathers' farms or, if especially enterprising, had found jobs at the broom factory in Cisco. He was walking proof of the family's industry and ambition, and he reinforced my own dreams of escape to bigger things.

23 Imagine my shocked surprise, then, when—in my early teens—I accompanied my family in its move to Midland City, there to discover that *I* was the Redneck: the bumpkin, the new boy with feedlot dung on his shoes and the funny homemade haircuts. Nobody in Midland had heard of the Kings or even of the Clarks; nobody rushed to embrace us. Where in the rural consolidated school I had boasted a grade average in the high nineties, in Midland the mysteries of algebra, geometry, and biology kept me clinging by my nails to scholastic survival. Where I had captained teams, I now stood uninvited on the fringes of playground games. My clothes, as good as most and better than some in Eastland County, now betrayed me as a poor clod.

24 I withdrew to the company of other misfits who lived in clapboard shacks or tents on the jerry-built South Side, wore tattered time-faded jeans and stained teeth, cursed, fought, swigged beer, and skipped school to hang around South Main Street pool halls or domino parlors. These were East Texans, Okies, and Arkies whose parents—like mine—had starved off their native acres and had followed the war boom west. Our drawls and twangs and marginal grammar had more of the dirt farmer or drifting fruit picker in them than of the cattleman or small merchant; our homes utilized large lard buckets as stools or chairs and such paltry art as adorned the wall likely showed Jesus on the cross suffering pain and a Woolworth's framing job; at least one member of almost every family boasted its musician: guitar or banjo or mandolin pickers who cried the old songs while their instruments whined or wailed of griefs and losses in places dimly remembered.

25 We hated the Townies who catcalled us as shitkickers . . . plowboys . . . Luke Plukes. We were a sneering lot, victims of cultural shock, defensive and dangerous as only the cornered can be. If you were a Townie, you very much wished not to encounter us unless you had the strength of numbers; we would whip your ass and take your money, pledging worse punishments should the authorities be notified. We hated niggers and meskins almost as much as we hated the white Townies, though it would be years before I knew how desperately we hated ourselves.

26 In time, deposits of ambition, snobbery, and pride caused me to work exceedingly hard at rising above common Redneckery. Not being able to beat the Townies, I opted to join them through pathways opened by athletics, debating, drama productions. It was simply better to be in than out, even if one must desert his own kind. I had discovered, simply, that nothing much on the bottom was worth having.

27 I began avoiding my Redneck companions at school and dodging their invitations to hillbilly jam sessions, pool hall recreations, forays into the scabbier honkytonks. The truth is, the Rednecks had come to depress me. Knowing they were losers, they acted as such. No matter their tough exteriors when tormenting Townies, they privately whined and sniveled and raged. The deeper their alienations, the

smaller they seemed to become physically; excepting an occasional natural jug-butted Ol' Boy, Rednecks appeared somehow to be stringier, knottier, more shriveled than others. They hacked the coughs of old men and moved about in old men's motions somehow furtive and fugitive. I did not want to be like them.

28 Nor did I want to imitate their older brothers or fathers, with whom I worked in the oil fields during summers and on weekends. They lived nomadic lives, following booms and rumors and their restless, unguided hearts. It puzzled me that they failed to seek better and more far-flung adventures, break with the old ways and start anew; I was very young then and understood less than all the realities. Their abodes were tin-topped old hotels in McCamey, gasping-hot tents perched on the desert floor near Crane, a crummy tourist court outside Sundown, any number of peeled fading houses decorating Wink, Odessa, Monahans. Such places smelled of sweat, fried foods, dirty socks, the bottoms of the barrel, too much sorry history.

29 By day we dug sump pits, pissanted heavy lengths of pipe, mixed cement and pushed it in iron wheelbarrows ("wheelbars"), chemically blistered our skins while hot-doping new pipeline, swabbed oil storage tanks, grubbed mesquite or other prickly desert growths to make way for new pump stations. We worked ten hours; the pay ranged from seventy to ninety-four cents for each of them, and we strangely disbelieved in labor unions.

30 There was a certain camaraderie, yes, a brotherhood of the lower rungs; kidding could be rough, raw, personal. Often, however, the day's sun combined with the evening's beer or liquor to produce a special craziness. Then fights erupted, on the job or in beer joints or among roommates in their quarters. Few rules burdened such fights, and the gentle or unwary could suffer real damage. Such people frightened me. They frighten me now, when I encounter them on visits to West Texas beer joints or lolling about a truckstop café. If you permit them to know it, however, your life will become a special long-running hell: *Grady, let's me and you whup that booger's ass for him agin.* Often, in the oil patch, one had to act much tougher than the stuff he knew to be in his bones. It helped to pick a fight occasionally and to put the boots to your adversary once you got him down. Fear and rage being first cousins, you could do it if you had to.

31 But I can't tell you what it's really like, day to day, being a Redneck: not in the cool language of one whom time has refurbished a bit or by analytical uses of whatever sensibilities may have been superimposed through the years. That approach can hint at it in a general way, knock the rough edges off. But it isn't raw enough to put you down in the pit: let you smell the blood, know the bone dread, the debts, the random confrontations, the pointless migrations, or purposeless days. I must speak to you from an earlier time, bring it up from the gut. Somehow fiction is more suited to that.

32 You may consider this next section, then, to be a fictional interlude . . . or near-fiction, maybe . . . voices from the past . . . essence of Redneck. Whatever. Anyway, it's something of what life was like for many West Texas people in the late 1940s or early 1950s; I suspect that even today it remains relatively true there and in other sparse grazing places of America's unhorsed riders: those who fight our dirtier wars, make us rich by the schlock and dreck they buy and the usurious interest rates they pay, those who suffer the invisible rule of deaf masters and stew in their

own poor juices. Those white niggers who live on the fringes out near the very edge and hope, mostly, to accumulate enough survival techniques to skate by. What follows is, at once, a story that didn't really happen and one that has happened again and again.

II

33 Me and Bobby Jack and Red Turpin was feeling real good that day. We'd told this old fat fart bossing the gang to shove his pipeline up his ass sideways, and then we'd hitched a ride to Odessa and drawed our time. He was a sorry old bastard, that gang boss. He'd been laying around in such shade as he could find, hollering at us for about six weeks when we didn't pissant pipe fast enough to suit him. Hisself, he looked like he hadn't carried nothing heavier than a lunch bucket in twenty years.

34 What happened had happened in the morning, just before we would of broke for dinner. Red Turpin was down in the dumps because the finance company had found him and drove his old Chevy away. We tried to tell him not to sweat it, that it wasn't worth near half of what he owed on it, but that never wiped out the fact that he was left afoot.

35 The gang boss had been bitching and moaning more than usual that day. All at once Red spun around to him and said, "I'm gona git me a piece of yore ass, Mr. Poot, if you don't git offa mine." Well, the gang boss waved his arms and hollered that ol' Red was sacked, and Red said, "Fuck you, Mr. Poot. I was a-huntin' a job when I found this 'un."

36 Me and Bobby Jack was standing there with our mouths dropped open when the gang boss started yelling at us to git back to work and to show him nothing but assholes and elbows. He was jumping around all red in the face, acting like a stroke was on him. Bobby Jack said, "Shit on such shit as this. Lincoln's done freed the slaves," and about that time he dropped his end of that length of pipe and told that gang boss to shove it.

37 "Sideways, Mr. Poot," I hollered. And then I dropped *my* end in the dirt.

38 Mr. Poot squealed like a girl rabbit and grabbed a monkey wrench off the crew truck and warned us not to come no closer. Which would of been hard to do, fast as he was backing up. So we cussed him for seventeen kinds of a fool and pissed on the pipe we'd dropped and then left, feeling free as the blowing wind. I never been in jail long enough to have give thought to busting out, but I bet there'd be some of the same feeling in it.

39 Out on the Crane Highway we laughed and hooted about calling that old gang boss "Mr. Poot" to his face, which is what we'd been calling him behind his back on account of he just laid around in the shade by the water cans and farted all day. But finally, after four or five cars and several oil trucks passed us up, we kinda sagged. You could see down that flat old highway for about three days, and all there was was hot empty. Red got down in the mouth about his old lady raising hell soon as she learned how he'd cussed his way off the job. Bobby Jack said hell, just tell 'er he got laid off. "Shit," Red said. "She don't care if it's fared or laid off or carried off on a silk pillar. All she knows is, it ain't no paycheck next week."

40 By the time we'd grunted answers to questions and signed papers and drawed our time at the Morrison Brothers Construction Company there in Odessa, and got a few cool 'uns down in a East Eighth Street beer joint, we was back on top. I swear, a certain amount of beer can make a man feel like he could beat cancer. We played the jukebox—Hank Williams, he'd just come out with one that reached out and grabbed you; seems to me like it was "Lovesick Blues," and there was plenty of Tubbs and Tillman and Frizzell—and shot a few games of shuffleboard at two bits a go. It was more fun than a regular day off because we was supposed to be working. I recollect Bobby Jack wallowing a swig of beer around in his mouth and saying, "You know what we doin'? We stealin' time." He looked real pleased.

41 Bobby Jack danced twice with a heavyset woman in red slacks from Conroe, who'd come out to Odessa on the Greyhound to find her twin sister that had been run off from by a driller. But all she'd found was a mad landlord that said the woman's sister had skipped out on a week's rent and had stole two venetian blinds besides. "I called that landlord a damn liar," the Conroe woman said. "My twin sister don't steal, and she wadn't raised to stealin'. We come from good stock and got a uncle that's been a deputy sheriff in Bossier City, Louisiana, for nearly twenty years."

42 Bobby Jack had enough nookie on the brain to buy her four or five beers, but all she done was flash a little brassiere strap and give him two different names and tell him about being a fan dancer at the Texas Centennial in 19-and-36. She babbled on about what all she'd been—a blues singer, a automobile dealer's wife, a registered nurse; everything but a lion tamer it seemed like—until Bobby Jack said, "Lissen, hon, I don't care what all you been. All I care about's what you are now and what *I* am. And I'm horny as a range bull with equipment hard as Christmas candy. How 'bout you?" She got in a mother huff and claimed it was the worst she'd ever been insulted. When Bobby Jack reached over and taken back the last beer he'd bought her, she moved over to a table by herself. I didn't care; she'd struck me as a high hat anyway.

43 A fleshy ol' boy wearing a Mead's Fine Bread uniform straddled a stool by us and said, "Man, I taken a leak that was better'n young love. I still say if they'd *give* the beer away and charge a dollar to piss, they'd make more money." We talked about how once you'd went to take a beer piss, you had to go ever five minutes, where you could hold a good gallon up until you'd went the first time.

44 Red Turpin got real quiet like he does when he's bothered bad. I whispered to Bobby Jack to keep an eye on the sumbitch because when Red quits being quiet, he usually gets real loud and rambunctious in a hurry. Then, along between sundown and dark, Bobby Jack got real blue. He went to mumbling about owing on his new bedroom set and how much money his wife spent on home permanents and started cussing the government for different things. Bobby Jack had always hated Harry Truman for some reason and blamed him ever time a barmaid drawed a hot beer or he dropped a dime in a crack. Now it seemed like he was working up to blaming Truman for losing him his job. I didn't much care about Harry Truman either way, but I'd liked President Roosevelt for ending hard times even though ol' Eleanor traipsed all over the world and run with too many niggers. My daddy's people come

from Georgia before they settled over around Clarksville, and hadn't none of us ever been able to stomach niggers.

45 Bobby Jack kept getting bluer and bluer, and I commenced worrying about what he might do. He may be little; but he's wound tight, and I've seen him explode. Finally a flyboy from the Midland Air Base tapped his shoulder and asked if he had a match. Bobby Jack grinned that grin that don't have no fun in it and said, "Sure, airplane jockey. My ass and your face." The flyboy grinned kinda sickly. Before he could back off, Bobby Jack said, "Hey, Yankee boy, what you think about that shitass Harry Truman?" The flyboy mumbled about not being able to discuss his Commander in Chief on account of certain regulations. "I got your Commander in Chief swangin'," Bobby Jack said, cupping his privates in one hand. "Come 'ere and salute 'im." The flyboy set his beer down and took off like a nigger aviator, lurching this way and that.

46 Bobby Jack felt better for a little bit; I even got him and Red Turpin to grinning a little by imitating Mr. Poot when we'd cussed him. But it's hard to keep married men perked up very long. I married a girl in beautician's college in Abilene in '46, but we didn't live together but five months. She was a Hardshell Baptist and talked to God while she ironed and pestered me to get a job in a office and finish high school at night. She had a plan for me to go on to junior college and then make a tent preacher.

47 Red Turpin went to the pay phone back by the men's pisser to tell his wife to borrow her daddy's pickup and come get him. He had to wait a long spell for her to come to the neighbor's phone, because Red's had been cut off again, and I could tell right off she wasn't doing a great deal of rejoicing.

48 "Goddammit, Emma," Red said. "We'll thresh all that shit out later. Come git me and chew my ass out in person. It's cheaper than doin' it long distance." Red and Emma lived in Midland behind the Culligan Bottled Water place. "Lissen," Red said, "I can't do nothin' about it right now. I'll whup his ass when I can find him, but all I'm tryin' to do right now is git a ride home. . . . What? . . . Well, all right, goddammit *I* don't like hearing the little farknocker cry neither. Promise 'im we'll buy 'im another 'un." He listened for a minute, got real red in the face, and yelled, "Lissen, Emma, *just fuck you!* How many meals you missed since we been married? *Just fuck you!*" From the way he banged the phone down I couldn't tell for sure which one of 'em had hung up first. Red looked right through me, and his eyes was hard and glittery. "Some cocksucker stole my kid's trike," he said, and stumbled on back toward the bar.

49 Two old range cowboys come in about then, their faces like leather that had been left out in the sun, and the potbellied one was right tipsy. He was hollering *"Ahha, Santa Flush!"* and singing about how he was a plumb fool about "Ida Red," which was a song that had been made popular by Bob Wills and the Texas Playboys. He slammed me on the back in a good-natured way and said, "Howdy, stud. Gettin' any strange?"

He grinned when I said, "It's all strange to me," and went on in the pisser real happy. When Red followed the old cowhand in, I just naturally figured he'd went to take a leak. I moseyed over to the jukebox and played "Slippin' Around" by Floyd Tillman, which, when I seen him play the Midland VFW Hall, he said he had wrote on a napkin late one night at a café in Dumas when all between him and starvation was forty-some cents and a bottle of Thunderbird wine.

50 In a little bit Red Turpin slid back on his stool and started drinking Pearl again, big as you please. About a half a beer later the second cowboy went to the pisser and come out like a cannon had shot him, yelling for a doctor and the po-leece. "They done killed ol' Dinger," he hollered. "I seen that big 'un go in right behind him. They's enough blood in there to float a log."

51 Four or five people run back toward the pisser; a general commotion started, and I said real quick, "Come on. Let's shuck outta here." But Bobby Jack was hopping around cussin' Red Turpin, asking what the hell he'd did. Red had a peculiar glaze in his eye; he just kept growling and slapping out at Bobby Jack like a bear swatting with his paw at a troublesome bee.

52 The barkeep run up and said, "You boys hold what you got." He yanked a sawed-off shotgun from under the bar and throwed down on us. "Skeeter," he hollered, "call the po-leece. And don't you damn bohunks move a hair." I wouldn't a-moved for big money.

53 The old cowboy had been helped out of the pisser and was sitting all addled at a back table, getting the blood wiped off his face. He groaned too loud to be good dead and kept asking, "What happened?" which was the same thing everybody was asking him. He seemed to think maybe a bronc had unhorsed him, and somebody laughed.

54 The barkeep relaxed his shotgun a smidgen. But when I leaned across the bar and offered him $12 to let us go on our way, he just shook his head and said, "It's gonna cost you a heap more'n that if I hafta blow you a twin asshole."

55 Two city cops come in, one fatter than the other; hog fat and jowly. They jangled with cuffs, sappers, and all kinds of hardwear; them sumbitches got more gear than Sears and Roebuck. The biggest cop huffed and puffed like he'd run a hill and said, "What kinda new shit we got stirred up here, Frankie?"

56 The barkeep poked a thumb in our direction and said, "That big ol' red-haired booger yonder beat up a Scharbauer Ranch cowboy." I didn't like the sound of that, on account of the Scharbauers owned everything that didn't belong to God and had the rest of it under lease.

57 "What about it, big 'un?" the fattest cop asked Red.

58 "I never hit *him,*" Red said.

59 "Oh, I see," the big cop said. "That feller just musta had bad luck and slipped and fell on his ass in somebody else's blood." You could tell he was enjoying hisself, that he would of po-leeced for free.

60 "I never hit *him,*" Red said again. He commenced to cry, which I found disgusting. From the way Bobby Jack looked at me and shook his head I could tell it pissed him off, too.

61 "Yeah, he did," the barkeep said. "Near as I unnerstan' it, the boomer hit the cowboy without a word passin'. Far as the cowboy knows he might been knocked flat by a runaway dump truck."

62 "On your feet." The big cop jerked Red off of the barstool. He tightened his

grip and lowered his voice and said, "You twitch just one of them fat ol' shitty muscles, big 'un, and I'll sap you a new hat size. And if 'at ain't enough, my partner'll shoot you where you real tender." Red kept on blubbering, whining something about somebody stealing his kid's trike, while the short cop fumbled the cuffs on him; me and Bobby Jack looked away and was careful not to say nothing. One time up in Snyder, I ask this constable what a buddy's fine would be when he was being hauled off for common public drunk, and the sumbitch taken me in, too. Next morning in court I found out the fine for common public drunk: $22 and costs.

63 The big cop went back and talked to the hurt cowboy awhile and wrote down in a notebook. Now that his health was better the hurt cowboy wanted more beer. The barkeep give him one and said, "On the house, Hoss. Sorry about the trouble."

64 Then the big cop come walking back to me and Bobby Jack, giving us the hard-eyed. He said, "You two peckerwoods holdin' cards in this game?" We naw-sirred him. The barkeep nodded, which I thought it was nice of him not to have told I'd offered a $12 bribe. The big cop looked us over: "Where you boys work at?" We told him Morrison Brothers Construction. "Him, too?" He nodded toward Red, who was standing with his head down and studying his cuffed wrists.

65 "Well," I said, "I heard he quit lately."

66 The cop grunted and tapped Bobby Jack on the ass with his billy club and said, "Keep it down to a dull roar, little 'un. I'm tard, and done had six Maggie-and-Jiggs calls. Old ladies throwin' knives and pots at their husbands, or their husbands kickin' the crap out of 'em. I don't wanta come back in this sumbitch till my shift's over and I'm scenting beer."

67 They taken the old cowboy to the county hospital for stitches. When he passed by, being about half helt up, I seen his face had been laid open like a busted watermelon. I guess maybe Red's ring that he got in a gyp joint in that spick town acrost from Del Rio done it. Just seeing it made my belly swim and pitch. One time at Jal, New Mexico, I seen a driller gouge out a roughneck's eye with a corkscrew when they fell out over wages, and I got the same feeling then, only more so.

68 The Conroe woman in red slacks was sashaying around, telling everybody with a set of ears how we'd broke a record insulting her just before Red beat up the old cowboy, and you could tell she'd be good at stirring up a lynch mob and would of enjoyed the work. Everybody kept looking at us like they was trying to make up their minds about something. After we'd drank another beer and belched loud to show they wasn't spooking us, and dropped a quarter in the jukebox like nothing had happened, we eased on out the door.

69 I wanted to hit Danceland on East Second because a lot of loose hair pie hung out there. Or the Ace of Clubs, where they had a French Quarter stripper who could twirl her titty tassels two different directions at once and pick half dollars up off the bar top with her snatch. But Bobby Jack said naw, hell, he reckoned he'd go on home and face the music. I sure was glad I didn't have no wife waiting to chew on my ass and remind me that I owed too much money or had too many kids to go around acting free. I walked with Bobby Jack up to where he turned down the alley running between the Phillips 66 Station and Furr's Cafeteria, which was close to the trailer park where he lived. "Well," Bobby Jack said, "at least ol' Red won't have to worry

'bout gettin' a ride to Midland. He's got him a free bed in the crossbar hotel." We talked a little about checking on how much Red's bail had been set at, but didn't much come of it. To tell the truth, what he had did didn't make much sense and ruined the best part of the night. Without saying so, we kinda agreed he'd brought it on hisself.

70 I went over to the Club Café and ate me a chicken-fried steak with a bowl of chili beans on the side and listened to some ol' humpbacked waitresses talk about how much trouble their kids was. Next day I caught on with a drilling crew up in Gaines County, and it wasn't but about six weeks more that I joined the Army just in time to see sunny Korea, so I never did learn what all Red got charged with or how he come out.

(1980)

QUESTIONS

Thought and Structure

1. King opens the essay with a specific and detailed example. His wife calls him "a dumb Redneck" and he responds physically. What would be gained or lost if King had begun with paragraph 3 or 4?
2. This selection is divided into two major sections. Identify the principle difference between them and explain how the two parts are related.
3. What is King's purpose in this piece? Who is his intended audience? And what is his main point?
4. What distinctions among rednecks does King draw in part I? Why?
5. What is King's attitude toward rednecks? Toward himself as redneck? In what ways has he escaped redneckism? In what ways retained it?
6. What does King mean when he says that the story he tells in part II "didn't really happen" and yet "happened again and again"?

Style and Strategy

7. Listen to the rhythm of the following sentence. Where does it pick up speed? "Their lives are hard: long on work and short on money; full of vile bossmen, hounding creditors, debilitating quarrels, routine disappointments, confrontations, ignorance, a treadmill hopelessness." The sentence is essentially a list—a brief catalog. Why do you think King strung it together in this way? Find another similar example and comment on its effectiveness.
8. King's language descends to such phrases as "shiftless badasses," "poor tacky peckerwoods," "pisser," "shitass," "shitkickers," and "sumbitch." Is such language necessary in the essay? Why or why not?
9. Select two details—concrete specific details—that you find especially striking, illuminating, or otherwise noteworthy. Explain why.
10. Comment on the language of the opening paragraph of part II. Characterize its tone.
11. Identify three uses of comparison, and comment on their point and effect. (There are quite a few in part II.)

12. Examine two passages of dialogue and comment on your impression of the character speaking in both.

SUGGESTIONS FOR WRITING

A. Imitate King by describing some ethnic, social, racial, religious, or other subgroup to which you belong. Use fact, fiction, or a combination of the two to describe and explain what it means to be a member of that group. (You might also read some of James Baldwin's essays before you attempt this assignment.)

B. Write an essay in which you explain how part II of "The American Redneck" illustrates the observations King makes about rednecks in part I.

C. Compare King's description of rednecks with Gretel Ehrlich's description of cowboys in one or more of her essays. Pay particular attention to the way both writers represent speech.

TWELVE

Tom Wolfe

(1931–)

Tom Wolfe is one of the most famous of the New Journalists, a group of writers who imported the techniques of fiction into journalism. Wolfe's account of how he wrote his essay on custom cars, "The Kandy-Kolored Tangerine-Flake Streamline Baby," provides an insight into both his working habits and the new style he was unwittingly developing.

With an abundance of material about his subject and with too little time to organize, write, revise, and edit in the conventional manner, Wolfe began typing his notes in a letter to his editor at *Esquire,* where the piece was to be published. His letter took the form of a long memorandum, Wolfe supposing that somebody at the magazine would be responsible for shaping his rambling notes and writing the story. Wolfe describes the experience of writing the piece this way: "I just recorded it all, and inside a couple of hours, typing along like a madman, I could tell that something was beginning to happen. By midnight this memorandum was . . . twenty pages long and I was still typing like a maniac. . . . about 6:15 A.M. . . . it was 49 pages long." *Esquire* published it as written, inaugurating thereby an alternate writing style that was later named the "New Journalism."

In an introduction to an anthology of new-journalistic essays entitled, appropriately enough, *The New Journalism,* Wolfe singles out four techniques as being especially important for this new style. The basic device, he notes, is "scene-by-scene construction, telling the story by moving from scene to scene and resorting as little as possible to sheer historical narrative." Another technique is to rely heavily on dialogue since, as Wolfe has pointed out, "realistic dialogue involves the reader more completely than any other single device. It also establishes and defines character more quickly than any other single device." The third device involves manipulating the point of view, the angle of vision, the perspective from which a scene is presented. New Journalists will interview someone at the center of a scene, then import into their write-ups the thoughts and emotions of those interviewed. The purpose of this strategy, as Wolfe notes, is to "give the reader the feeling of being inside the character's mind and experiencing the emotional reality of the scene as he experiences it." The fourth technique concerns what Wolfe describes as "the recording of everyday gestures, habits, manners, customs . . . looks, glances, poses, styles of walking and other symbolic details. . . ."

To these can be added what Winston Weathers in his fine book *An Alternate Style* calls the *crot*—an obsolete word meaning "bit" or "fragment": "an autonomous unit, characterized by the absence of any transitional devices . . . in its most intense form . . . by a certain abruptness in its termination." Crots are something like snapshots, something like vignettes. Putting them together without transitions can make for effects of montage, collage, surprise—and sometimes confusion. They challenge readers and involve them by inviting them to figure out how the fragments are related to one another. Besides the crot, about which Wolfe has said, "it will have you making crazy leaps of logic, leaps you never dreamed of before," Weathers singles out other devices frequently used by Wolfe and his new-journalistic colleagues: the labyrinthine sentence, the fragment, and the use of repetitions, lists, and refrains.

Wolfe began his career as an academic, earning a doctorate in American Studies at Yale. But his inclination was more journalistic than academic, and he worked for the *Washington Post* as a reporter and then as a magazine writer for the *New York Herald-Tribune.* Since 1968 he has been a contributing editor to *New York* magazine. He has written articles on trends in American popular culture, primarily essays that have been published first in magazines and later in books. Following his first collection, *The Kandy-Kolored Tangerine-Flake Streamline Baby* (1965), came a series of books with such zany titles as *The Electric Kool-Aid Acid Test* (1968)—on pot; *The Pump House Gang* (1968)—on California surfers (among other things); *Radical Chic and Mau-Mauing the Flak Catchers* (1970)—on rich New Yorkers vis-à-vis the Black Panthers; *Mauve Gloves and Madmen, Clutter and Vine* (1976)—on miscellaneous subjects; *The Right Stuff* (1979)—on the astronauts; *In Our Time* (1980), a collection of satirical pictorial sketches with brief notes and comments; *From Bauhaus to Our House* (1981), a critique of modern architecture; and more.

Wolfe takes great risks in his writing: his style is daring, flamboyant, energetic, humorous, and satirical. Reading him is like listening to a talented raconteur who reenacts the scenes and situations he describes, who comments on them in a free-wheeling style filled with digressions and associative ramblings, with less concern to instruct and moralize than to entertain and delight. His essays tend to be long and steeped in detail. He seems to need room to present the various facets of his subjects, time to amass details, and space to allow his characters to reveal, even display themselves. The masses of detail, the loose structure, the transcriptions of dialogue, the crots, lists, repetitions, and refrains cumulatively create a sense of immediacy and authenticity which suggests the reality of "This is how it is; this is what it's like."

The Right Stuff, Wolfe's longest and most ambitious work, has drawn wide critical acclaim, as well as becoming a best seller. Early in the book Wolfe describes just what the right stuff is that men need to become successful test pilots and astronauts. His comments relate as much to his own style and performance as a writer as they do to the astronauts. The right stuff, Wolfe explains, is "an amalgam of stamina, guts, fast neural synapses and old-fashioned hell raising." These elements, along with nerve, exhilaration, and a satirically edged humor, suggest something of Wolfe's tone and voice.

The five selections here show us Wolfe working in several mediums: a nonfiction short story ("The Angels") from *The Right Stuff;* an essay within that same novel ("The Right Stuff"); two essays about social status and culture ("Funky Chic" and "Honks and Wonks") from *Mauve Gloves and Madmen, Clutter and Vine;* and an excerpt from his new novel *The Bonfire of the Vanities.* In each of these selections we get glimpses of Wolfe using the techniques we have already discussed. But we also find Wolfe skating circles around his favorite subject, what he calls the lodestone of his writing: class. He is not so much interested in class as a divisive force as he is in the way people group themselves together, working in closed units, creating their own special language, developing their own life-styles and aspirations. He is especially curious about the way different classes of people interact, how they come into conflict with one another, how they merge, split off, assimilate. In his own special way, Wolfe is writing the history of our culture; he does so by focusing on the stuff of everyday: demolition derbies, art movements, cults, youth gangs, government welfare programs, fashions, fraternities, political groups, celebrities. He is doing for our culture what the realistic novelists did for earlier cultures; he is writing an illuminating history of our time.

Wolfe has been interviewed frequently and has commented extensively on writing. On one occasion he noted that "writing, unlike painting or drawing, is a process in which you *can't* tell right away whether it's successful or not. Some nights you go to bed thinking you've written some brilliant stuff, and you wake up the next morning and you realize it *is* just pure bullshit." His own regimen includes writing nine pages a day. Writing is so painful he limits the pages to limit the pain. In response to a question about why he writes, Wolfe noted that he doesn't have a ready answer, but that if pressed he thinks that he writes out of a concern for his own glory, with more concern for how he handles the materials of his craft than for the issues he writes about. The challenge in writing, for Wolfe, seems to reside in the compositional problem that he faces each day. Aesthetic and linguistic challenges excite him as much as the subjects he writes about. But this subjective priority of form over content hasn't kept Wolfe from offering dazzling and intelligent analyses of our contemporary life.

The Angels

1 Within five minutes, or ten minutes, no more than that, three of the others had called her on the telephone to ask her if she had heard that something had happened out there.

2 "Jane, this is Alice. Listen, I just got a call from Betty, and she said she heard something's happened out there. Have you heard anything?" That was the way they phrased it, call after call. She picked up the telephone and began relaying this same message to some of the others.

3 "Connie, this is Jane Conrad. Alice just called me, and she says something's happened . . ."

4 *Something* was part of the official Wife Lingo for tiptoeing blindfolded around the subject. Being barely twenty-one years old and new around here, Jane Conrad knew very little about this particular subject, since nobody ever talked about it. But the day was young! And what a setting she had for her imminent enlightenment! And what a picture she herself presented! Jane was tall and slender and had rich brown hair and high cheekbones and wide brown eyes. She looked a little like the actress Jean Simmons. Her father was a rancher in southwestern Texas. She had gone East to college, to Bryn Mawr, and had met her husband, Pete, at a debutante's party at the Gulph Mills Club in Philadelphia, when he was a senior at Princeton.

Pete was a short, wiry, blond boy who joked around a lot. At any moment his face was likely to break into a wild grin revealing the gap between his front teeth. The Hickory Kid sort, he was; a Hickory Kid on the deb circuit, however. He had an air of energy, self-confidence, ambition, *joi de vivre.* Jane and Pete were married two days after he graduated from Princeton. Last year Jane gave birth to their first child, Peter. And today, here in Florida, in Jacksonville, in the peaceful year 1955, the sun shines through the pines outside, and the very air takes on the sparkle of the ocean. The ocean and a great mica-white beach are less than a mile away. Anyone driving by will see Jane's little house gleaming like a dream house in the pines. It is a brick house, but Jane and Pete painted the bricks white, so that it gleams in the sun against a great green screen of pine trees with a thousand little places where the sun peeks through. They painted the shutters black, which makes the white walls look even more brilliant. The house has only eleven hundred square feet of floor space, but Jane and Pete designed it themselves and that more than makes up for the size. A friend of theirs was the builder and gave them every possible break, so that it cost only eleven thousand dollars. Outside, the sun shines, and inside, the fever rises by the minute as five, ten, fifteen, and, finally, nearly all twenty of the wives join the circuit, trying to find out what has happened, which, in fact, means: to whose husband.

5 After thirty minutes on such a circuit—this is not an unusual morning around here—a wife begins to feel that the telephone is no longer located on a table or on the kitchen wall. It is exploding in her solar plexus. Yet it would be far worse right now to hear the front doorbell. The protocol is strict on that point, although written down nowhere. No woman is supposed to deliver the final news, and certainly not on the telephone. The matter mustn't be bungled!—that's the idea. No, a man should bring the news when the time comes, a man with some official or moral authority, a clergyman or a comrade of the newly deceased. Furthermore, he should bring the bad news in person. He should turn up at the front door and ring the bell and be standing there like a pillar of coolness and competence, bearing the bad news on ice, like a fish. Therefore, all the telephone calls from the wives were the frantic and portentous beating of the wings of the death angels, as it were. When the final news came, there would be a ring at the front door—a wife in this situation finds herself staring at the front door as if she no longer owns it or controls it—and outside the door would be a man . . . come to inform her that unfortunately something has happened out there, and her husband's body now lies incinerated in the swamps or the pines or the palmetto grass, "burned beyond recognition," which anyone who had been around an air base for very long (fortunately Jane had not) realized was quite an artful euphemism to describe a human body that now looked like an enormous fowl that has burned up in a stove, burned a blackish brown all over, greasy and blistered, fried, in a word, with not only the entire face and all the hair and the ears burned off, not to mention all the clothing, but also the *hands* and *feet,* with what remains of the arms and legs bent at the knees and elbows and burned into absolutely rigid angles, burned a greasy blackish brown like the bursting body itself, so that this husband, father, officer, gentleman, this *ornamentum* of some mother's eye, His Majesty the Baby of just twenty-odd years back, has been reduced to a charred hulk with wings and shanks sticking out of it.

6 *My own husband*—how could this be what they were talking about? Jane had heard the young men, Pete among them, talk about other young men who had "bought it" or "augered in" or "crunched," but it had never been anyone they knew, no one in the squadron. And in any event, the way they talked about it, with such breezy, slangy terminology, was the same way they talked about sports. It was as if they were saying, "He was thrown out stealing second base." And that was all! Not one word, not in print, not in conversation—not in this amputated language!—about an incinerated corpse from which a young man's spirit has vanished in an instant, from which all smiles, gestures, moods, worries, laughter, wiles, shrugs, tenderness, and loving looks—*you, my love!*—have disappeared like a sigh, while the terror consumes a cottage in the woods, and a young woman, sizzling with the fever, awaits her confirmation as the new widow of the day.

7 The next series of calls greatly increased the possibility that it was Pete to whom something had happened. There were only twenty men in the squadron, and soon nine or ten had been accounted for . . . by the fluttering reports of the death angels. Knowing that the word was out that an accident had occurred, husbands who could get to a telephone were calling home to say *it didn't happen to me.* This news, of course, was immediately fed to the fever. Jane's telephone would ring once more, and one of the wives would be saying:

8 "Nancy just got a call from Jack. He's at the squadron and he says something's happened, but he doesn't know what. He said he saw Frank D——take off about ten minutes ago with Greg in back, so they're all right. What have you heard?"

9 But Jane has heard nothing except that other husbands, and not hers, are safe and accounted for. And thus, on a sunny day in Florida, outside of the Jacksonville Naval Air Station, in a little white cottage, a veritable dream house, another beautiful young woman was about to be apprised of the *quid pro quo* of her husband's line of work, of the trade-off, as one might say, the subparagraphs of a contract written in no visible form. Just as surely as if she had the entire roster in front of her, Jane now realized that only two men in the squadron were unaccounted for. One was a pilot named Bud Jennings; the other was Pete. She picked up the telephone and did something that was much frowned on in a time of emergency. She called the squadron office. The duty officer answered.

10 "I want to speak to Lieutenant Conrad," said Jane. "This is Mrs. Conrad."

11 "I'm sorry," the duty officer said—and then his voice cracked. "I'm sorry . . . I . . ." He couldn't find the words! He was about to cry! "I'm—that's—I mean . . . he can't come to the phone!"

12 *He can't come to the phone!*

13 "It's very important!" said Jane.

14 "I'm sorry—it's impossible—" The duty officer could hardly get the words out because he was so busy gulping back sobs. *Sobs!* "He can't come to the phone."

15 "Why not? Where is he?"

16 "I'm sorry—" More sighs, wheezes, snuffling gasps. "I can't tell you that. I—I have to hang up now!"

17 And the duty officer's voice disappeared in a great surf of emotion and he hung up.

18 The duty officer! *The very sound of her voice was more than he could take!*

19 The world froze, congealed, in that moment. Jane could no longer calculate the interval before the front doorbell would ring and some competent long-faced figure would appear, some Friend of Widows and Orphans, who would inform her, officially, that Pete was dead.

20 Even out in the middle of the swamp, in this rot-bog of pine trunks, scum slicks, dead dodder vines, and mosquito eggs, even out in this great overripe sump, the smell of "burned beyond recognition" obliterated everything else. When airplane fuel exploded, it created a heat so intense that everything but the hardest metals not only *burned*—everything of rubber, plastic, celluloid, wood, leather, cloth, flesh, gristle, calcium, horn, hair, blood, and protoplasm—it not only burned, it gave up the ghost in the form of every stricken putrid gas known to chemistry. One could smell the horror. It came in through the nostrils and burned the rhinal cavities raw and penetrated the liver and permeated the bowels like a black gas until there was nothing in the universe, inside or out, except the stench of the char. As the helicopter came down between the pine trees and settled onto the bogs, the smell hit Pete Conrad even before the hatch was completely open, and they were not even close enough to see the wreckage yet. The rest of the way Conrad and the crewmen had to travel on foot. After a few steps the water was up to their knees, and then it was up to their armpits, and they kept wading through the water and the scum and the vines and the pine trunks, but it was nothing compared to the smell. Conrad, a twenty-five-year-old lieutenant junior grade, happened to be on duty as squadron safety officer that day and was supposed to make the on-site investigation of the crash. The fact was, however, that this squadron was the first duty assignment of his career, and he had never been at a crash site before and had never smelled any such revolting stench or seen anything like what awaited him.

21 When Conrad finally reached the plane, which was an SNJ, he found the fuselage burned and blistered and dug into the swamp with one wing sheared off and the cockpit canopy smashed. In the front seat was all that was left of his friend Bud Jennings. Bud Jennings, an amiable fellow, a promising young fighter pilot, was now a horrible roasted hulk—with no head. His head was completely gone, apparently torn off the spinal column like a pineapple off a stalk, except that it was nowhere to be found.

22 Conrad stood there soaking wet in the swamp bog, wondering what the hell to do. It was a struggle to move twenty feet in this freaking muck. Every time he looked up, he was looking into a delirium of limbs, vines, dappled shadows, and a chopped-up white light that came through the tree-tops—the ubiquitous screen of trees with a thousand little places where the sun peeked through. Nevertheless, he started wading back out into the muck and the scum, and the others followed. He kept looking up. Gradually he could make it out. Up in the treetops there was a pattern of broken limbs where the SNJ had come crashing through. It was like a tunnel through the treetops. Conrad and the others began splashing through the swamp, following the strange path ninety or a hundred feet above them. It took a sharp turn. That must have been where the wing broke off. The trail veered to one side and started downward. They kept looking up and wading through the muck. Then they stopped. There was a great green sap wound up there in the middle of

a tree trunk. It was odd. Near the huge gash was . . . tree disease . . . some sort of brownish lumpy sac up in the branches, such as you see in trees infested by bagworms, and there were yellowish curds on the branches around it, as if the disease had caused the sap to ooze out and fester and congeal—except that it couldn't be sap because it was streaked with blood. In the next instant—Conrad didn't have to say a word. Each man could see it all. The lumpy sac was the cloth liner of a flight helmet, with the earphones attached to it. The curds were Bud Jennings's brains. The tree trunk had smashed through the cockpit canopy of the SNJ and knocked Bud Jennings's head to pieces like a melon.

23 In keeping with the protocol, the squadron commander was not going to release Bud Jennings's name until his widow, Loretta, had been located and a competent male death messenger had been dispatched to tell her. But Loretta Jennings was not at home and could not be found. Hence, a delay—and more than enough time for the other wives, the death angels, to burn with panic over the telephone lines. All the pilots were accounted for except the two who were in the woods, Bud Jennings and Pete Conrad. One chance in two, acey-deucey, one finger-two finger, and this was not an unusual day around here.

24 Loretta Jennings had been out at a shopping center. When she returned home, a certain figure was waiting outside, a man, a solemn Friend of Widows and Orphans, and it was Loretta Jennings who lost the game of odd and even, acey-deucey, and it was Loretta whose child (she was pregnant with a second) would have no father. It was this young woman who went through all the final horrors that Jane Conrad had imagined—*assumed!*—would be hers to endure forever. Yet this grim stroke of fortune brought Jane little relief.

25 On the day of Bud Jennings's funeral, Pete went into the back of the closet and brought out his bridge coat, per regulations. This was the most stylish item in the Navy officer's wardrobe. Pete had never had occasion to wear his before. It was a double-breasted coat made of navy-blue melton cloth and came down almost to the ankles. It must have weighed ten pounds. It had a double row of gold buttons down the front and loops for shoulder boards, big beautiful belly-cut collar and lapels, deep turnbacks on the sleeves, a tailored waist, and a center vent in back that ran from the waistline to the bottom of the coat. Never would Pete, or for that matter many other American males in the mid-twentieth century, have an article of clothing quite so impressive and aristocratic as that bridge coat. At the funeral the nineteen little Indians who were left—Navy boys!—lined up manfully in their bridge coats. They looked so young. Their pink, lineless faces with their absolutely clear, lean jawlines popped up bravely, correctly, out of the enormous belly-cut collars of the bridge coats. They sang an old Navy hymn, which slipped into a strange and lugubrious minor key here and there, and included a stanza added especially for aviators. It ended with: "Oh hear us when we lift our prayer for those in peril in the air."

26 Three months later another member of the squadron crashed and was burned beyond recognition and Pete hauled out the bridge coat again and Jane saw eighteen little Indians bravely going through the motions at the funeral. Not long after that,

Pete was transferred from Jacksonville to the Patuxent River Naval Air Station in Maryland. Pete and Jane had barely settled in there when they got word that another member of the Jacksonville squadron, a close friend of theirs, someone they had had over to dinner many times, had died trying to take off from the deck of a carrier in a routine practice session a few miles out in the Atlantic. The catapult that propelled aircraft off the deck lost pressure, and his ship just dribbled off the end of the deck, with its engine roaring vainly, and fell sixty feet into the ocean and sank like a brick, and he vanished, *just like that.*

27 Pete had been transferred to Patuxent River, which was known in Navy vernacular as Pax River, to enter the Navy's new test-pilot school. This was considered a major step up in the career of a young Navy aviator. Now that the Korean War was over and there was no combat flying, all the hot young pilots aimed for flight test. In the military they always said "flight test" and not "test flying." Jet aircraft had been in use for barely ten years at the time, and the Navy was testing new jet fighters continually. Pax River was the Navy's prime test center.

28 Jane liked the house they bought at Pax River. She didn't like it as much as the little house in Jacksonville, but then she and Pete hadn't designed this one. They lived in a community called North Town Creek, six miles from the base. North Town Creek, like the base, was on a scrub-pine peninsula that stuck out into Chesapeake Bay. They were tucked in amid the pine trees. (Once more!) All around were rhododendron bushes. Pete's classwork and his flying duties were very demanding. Everyone in his flight test class, Group 20, talked about how difficult it was—and obviously loved it, because in Navy flying this was the big league. The young men in Group 20 and their wives were Pete's and Jane's entire social world. They associated with no one else. They constantly invited each other to dinner during the week; there was a Group party at someone's house practically every weekend; and they would go off on outings to fish or waterski in Chesapeake Bay. In a way they could not have associated with anyone else, at least not easily, because the boys could talk only about one thing: their flying. One of the phrases that kept running through the conversation was "pushing the outside of the envelope." The "envelope" was a flight-test term referring to the limits of a particular aircraft's performance, how tight a turn it could make at such-and-such a speed, and so on. "Pushing the outside," probing the outer limits, of the envelope seemed to be the great challenge and satisfaction of flight test. At first "pushing the outside of the envelope" was not a particularly terrifying phrase to hear. It sounded once more as if the boys were just talking about sports.

29 Then one sunny day a member of the Group, one of the happy lads they always had dinner with and drank with and went waterskiing with, was coming in for a landing at the base in an A3J attack plane. He let his airspeed fall too low before he extended his flaps, and the ship stalled out, and he crashed and was burned beyond recognition. And they brought out the bridge coats and sang about those in peril in the air and put the bridge coats away, and the Indians who were left talked about the accident after dinner one night. They shook their heads and said it was a damned shame, but he should have known better than to wait so long before lowering the flaps.

30 Barely a week had gone by before another member of the Group was coming

in for a landing in the same type of aircraft, the A3J, making a ninety-degree turn to his final approach, and something went wrong with the controls, and he ended up with one rear stabilizer wing up and the other one down, and his ship rolled in like a corkscrew from 800 feet up and crashed, and he was burned beyond recognition. And the bridge coats came out and they sang about those in peril in the air and then they put the bridge coats away and after dinner one night they mentioned that the departed had been a good man but was inexperienced, and when the malfunction in the controls put him in that bad corner, he didn't know how to get out of it.

31 Every wife wanted to cry out: "Well, my God! The *machine* broke! What makes *any* of you think you would have come out of it any better!" Yet intuitively Jane and the rest of them knew it wasn't right even to suggest that. Pete never indicated for a moment that he thought any such thing could possibly happen to him. It seemed not only wrong but dangerous to challenge a young pilot's confidence by posing the question. And that, too, was part of the unofficial protocol for the Officer's Wife. From now on every time Pete was late coming in from the flight line, she would worry. She began to wonder if—no! *assume!*— he had found his way into one of those corners they all talked about so spiritedly, one of those little dead ends that so enlivened conversation around here.

32 Not long after that, another good friend of theirs went up in an F-4, the Navy's newest and hottest fighter plane, known as the Phantom. He reached twenty thousand feet and then nosed over and dove straight into Chesapeake Bay. It turned out that a hose connection was missing in his oxygen system and he had suffered hypoxia and passed out at the high altitude. And the bridge coats came out and they lifted a prayer about those in peril in the air and the bridge coats were put away and the little Indians were incredulous. How could anybody fail to check his hose connections? And how could anybody be in such poor condition as to pass out *that quickly* from hypoxia?

33 A couple of days later Jane was standing at the window of her house in North Town Creek. She saw some smoke rise above the pines from over in the direction of the flight line. Just that, a column of smoke; no explosion or sirens or any other sound. She went to another room, so as not to have to think about it but there was no explanation for the smoke. She went back to the window. In the yard of a house across the street she saw a group of people . . . standing there and looking at her house, as if trying to decide what to do. Jane looked away—but she couldn't keep from looking out again. She caught a glimpse of *a certain figure* coming up the walkway toward her front door. She knew exactly who it was. She had had nightmares like this. And yet this was no dream. She was wide awake and alert. Never more alert in her entire life! Frozen, completely defeated by the sight, she simply waited for the bell to ring. She waited, but there was not a sound. Finally she could stand it no more. In real life, unlike her dream life, Jane was both too self-possessed and too polite to scream through the door: "Go away!" So she opened it. There was no one there, no one at all. There was no group of people on the lawn across the way and no one to be seen for a hundred yards in any direction along the lawns and leafy rhododendron roads of North Town Creek.

34 Then began a cycle in which she had both the nightmares and the hallucina-

tions, continually. Anything could touch off an hallucination: a ball of smoke, a telephone ring that stopped before she could answer it, the sound of a siren, even the sound of trucks starting up (crash trucks!). Then she would glance out the window, and a certain figure would be coming up the walk, and she would wait for the bell. The only difference between the dreams and the hallucinations was that the scene of the dreams was always the little white house in Jacksonville. In both cases, the feeling that *this time it has happened* was quite real.

35 The star pilot in the class behind Pete's, a young man who was the main rival of their good friend Al Bean, went up in a fighter to do some power-dive tests. One of the most demanding disciplines in flight test was to accustom yourself to making precise readings from the control panel in the same moment that you were pushing the outside of the envelope. This young man put his ship into the test dive and was still reading out the figures, with diligence and precision and great discipline, when he augered straight into the oyster flats and was burned beyond recognition. And the bridge coats came out and they sang about those in peril in the air and the bridge coats were put away, and the little Indians remarked that the departed was a swell guy and a brilliant student of flying; a little too *much* of a student, in fact; he hadn't bothered to look out the window at the real world soon enough. Beano—Al Bean—wasn't quite so brilliant; on the other hand, he was still here.

36 Like many other wives in Group 20 Jane wanted to talk about the whole situation, the incredible series of fatal accidents, with her husband and the other members of the Group, to find out how they were taking it. But somehow the unwritten protocol forbade discussions of this subject, which was the fear of death. Nor could Jane or any of the rest of them talk, really *have a talk,* with anyone around the base. You could talk to another wife about being worried. But what good did it do? Who *wasn't* worried? You were likely to get a look that said: "*Why dwell on it?*" Jane might have gotten away with divulging the matter of the nightmares. But *hallucinations?* There was no room in Navy life for any such anomalous tendency as that.

37 By now the bad string had reached ten in all, and almost all of the dead had been close friends of Pete and Jane, young men who had been in their house many times, young men who had sat across from Jane and chattered like the rest of them about the grand adventure of military flying. And the survivors still sat around *as before*—with the same inexplicable exhilaration! Jane kept watching Pete for some sign that his spirit was cracking, but she saw none. He talked a mile a minute, kidded and joked, laughed with his Hickory Kid cackle. He always had. He still enjoyed the company of members of the group like Wally Schirra and Jim Lovell. Many young pilots were taciturn and cut loose with the strange fervor of this business only in the air. But Pete and Wally and Jim were not reticent; not in any situation. They loved to kid around. Pete called Jim Lovell "Shaky," because it was the last thing a pilot would want to be called. Wally Schirra was outgoing to the point of hearty; he loved practical jokes and dreadful puns, and so on. The three of them—*even in the midst of this bad string!*—would love to get on a subject such as accident-prone Mitch Johnson. Accident-prone Mitch Johnson, it seemed, was a Navy pilot whose life was in the hands of two angels, one of them bad and the other one good. The bad angel would put him into accidents that would have annihilated any ordinary pilot, and

the good angel would bring him out of them without a scratch. Just the other day—this was the sort of story Jane would hear them tell—Mitch Johnson was coming in to land on a carrier. But he came in short, missed the flight deck, and crashed into the fantail, below the deck. There was a tremendous explosion, and the rear half of the plane fell into the water in flames. Everyone on the flight deck said, "Poor Johnson. The good angel was off duty." They were still debating how to remove the debris and his mortal remains when a phone rang on the bridge. A somewhat dopey voice said, "This is Johnson. Say, listen, I'm down here in the supply hold and the hatch is locked and I can't find the lights and I can't see a goddamned thing and I tripped over a cable and I think I hurt my leg." The officer on the bridge slammed the phone down, then vowed to find out what morbid sonofabitch could pull a phone prank at a time like this. Then the phone rang again, and the man with the dopey voice managed to establish the fact that he was, indeed, Mitch Johnson. The good angel had not left his side. When he smashed into the fantail, he hit some empty ammunition drums, and they cushioned the impact, leaving him groggy but not seriously hurt. The fuselage had blown to pieces; so he just stepped out onto the fantail and opened a hatch that led into the supply hold. It was pitch black in there, and there were cables all across the floor, holding down spare aircraft engines. Accident-prone Mitch Johnson kept tripping over these cables until he found a telephone. Sure enough, the one injury he had was a bruised shin from tripping over a cable. The man was accident-prone! Pete and Wally and Jim absolutely cracked up over stories like this. It was amazing. Great sports yarns! Nothing more than that.

38 A few days later Jane was out shopping at the Pax River commissary on Saunders Road, near the main gate to the base. She heard the sirens go off at the field, and then she heard the engines of the crash trucks start up. This time Jane was determined to keep calm. Every instinct made her want to rush home, but she forced herself to stay in the commissary and continue shopping. For thirty minutes she went through the motions of completing her shopping list. Then she drove home to North Town Creek. As she reached the house, she saw a figure going up the sidewalk. It was a man. Even from the back there was no question as to who he was. He had on a black suit, and there was a white band around his neck. It was her minister, from the Episcopal Church. She stared, and this vision did not come and go. The figure kept on walking up the front walk. She was not asleep now, and she was not inside her house glancing out the front window. She was outside in her car in front of her house. She was not dreaming, and she was not hallucinating, and the figure kept walking up toward her front door.

39 The commotion at the field was over one of the most extraordinary things that even veteran pilots had ever seen at Pax River. And they had all seen it, because practically the entire flight line had gathered out on the field for it, as if it had been an air show.

40 Conrad's friend Ted Whelan had taken a fighter up, and on takeoff there had been a structural failure that caused a hydraulic leak. A red warning light showed up on Whelan's panel, and he had a talk with the ground. It was obvious that the leak would cripple the controls before he could get the ship back down to the field

for a landing. He would have to bail out; the only question was where and when, and so they had a talk about that. They decided that he should jump at 8,100 feet at such-and-such a speed, directly over the field. The plane would crash into the Chesapeake Bay, and he would float down to the field. Just as coolly as anyone could have asked for it, Ted Whelan lined the ship up to come across the field at 8,100 feet precisely and he punched out, ejected.

41 Down on the field they all had their faces turned up to the sky. They saw Whelan pop out of the cockpit. With his Martin-Baker seat-parachute rig strapped on, he looked like a little black geometric lump a mile and a half up in the blue. They watched him as he started dropping. Everyone waited for the parachute to open. They waited a few more seconds, and then they waited some more. The little shape was getting bigger and bigger and picking up tremendous speed. Then there came an unspeakable instant at which everyone on the field who knew anything about parachute jumps knew what was going to happen. Yet even for them it was an unearthly feeling, for no one had ever seen any such thing happen so close up, from start to finish, from what amounted to a grandstand seat. Now the shape was going so fast and coming so close it began to play tricks on the eyes. It seemed to stretch out. It became much bigger and hurtled toward them at a terrific speed, until they couldn't make out its actual outlines at all. Finally there was just a streaking black blur before their eyes, followed by what seemed like an explosion. Except that it was not an explosion; it was the tremendous *crack* of Ted Whelan, his helmet, his pressure suit, and his seat-parachute rig smashing into the center of the runway, precisely on target, right in front of the crowd; an absolute bull's-eye. Ted Whelan had no doubt been alive until the instant of impact. He had had about thirty seconds to watch the Pax River base and the peninsula and Baltimore County and continental America and the entire comprehensible world rise up to smash him. When they lifted his body up off the concrete, it was like a sack of fertilizer.

42 Pete took out the bridge coat again and he and Jane and all the little Indians went to the funeral for Ted Whelan. That it hadn't been Pete was not solace enough for Jane. That the preacher had not, in fact, come to her front door as the Solemn Friend of Widows and Orphans, but merely for a church call . . . had not brought peace and relief. That Pete still didn't show the slightest indication of thinking that any unkind fate awaited him no longer lent her even a moment's courage. The next dream and the next hallucination, and the next and the next, merely seemed more real. For she now *knew.* She now knew the subject and the essence of this enterprise, even though not a word of it had passed anybody's lips. She even knew why Pete—the Princeton boy she met at a deb party at the Gulph Mills Club!—would never quit, never withdraw from this grim business, unless in a coffin. And God knew, and she knew, there was a coffin waiting for each little Indian.

43 Seven years later, when a reporter and a photographer from *Life* magazine actually stood near her in her living room and watched her face, while outside, on the lawn, a crowd of television crewmen and newspaper reporters waited for a word, an indication, anything—perhaps a glimpse through a part in a curtain!—waited for some sign of what she felt—when one and all asked with their ravenous eyes and, occasionally, in so many words: "How do you feel?" and "Are you scared?"—America wants to know!—it made Jane want to laugh, but in fact she couldn't even manage a smile.

44 "Why ask *now?*" she wanted to say. But they wouldn't have had the faintest notion of what she was talking about.

(1979)

QUESTIONS

Thought and Structure

1. Wolfe has called this chapter from *The Right Stuff* a nonfiction short story. What distinguishes this nonfiction story from an essay?
2. In the beginning of this story, Wolfe keeps us in suspense for four paragraphs, leading us into the trap he springs in paragraph 5. Why does he create suspense about a series of phone calls among a group of unidentified wives? Does he assume that we will know their husbands' occupation, or does he want to keep us in the dark for some particular reason?
3. Why do we have the long interlude about Pete and Jane's background in paragraph 4? What is Wolfe's attitude about this young couple? Can you pinpoint his tone?
4. Wolfe doesn't actually reveal Jane Conrad's predicament until paragraph 9. At that point, we know only that she doesn't know whether her husband is dead or alive. After her conversation with the duty officer (paragraphs 10–19), Wolfe makes us think that Conrad is dead. In paragraph 20, he tells us again, but in much more gruesome terms, what "burned beyond recognition" means. Finally, we learn that Conrad is alive and that he is investigating the death of one of his squadron officers. We never find out how Jane Conrad learned that her husband was alive. Why do you think Wolfe creates this suspense?
5. Paragraph 26 accounts for two additional deaths. Paragraphs 29 and 30 account for still two more deaths. Paragraph 32 records yet another death. Finally in paragraph 33, we find that Jane Conrad is beginning to confuse reality and dream. She imagines the *man* is coming to tell her about her husband's death; she thinks that she sees the messenger walking up her sidewalk. But no one is there. What does Wolfe expect us to think about her hallucinations? Is he more concerned about Jane than he is about the "little Indians"? What does he think about the pilots?
6. What is the purpose of the story about the test pilot in paragraph 35? Every time Wolfe records one of these deaths, he tells us what the other pilots' collective reaction is to the death. What does Wolfe gain finally from this repetition? He sums up those reactions in paragraph 37 with the words "inexplicable exhilaration!" What is Wolfe suggesting about the pilots?
7. Why does Wolfe tell the stories of Mitch Johnson (paragraph 37) and Ted Whelan (paragraphs 40–42)? Why does he reintroduce the sports metaphor in paragraph 37?
8. If this is indeed a nonfiction short story and not an essay, does Wolfe nevertheless have a point to make in this piece? Can we tell where his sentiments lie?

Style and Strategy

9. In paragraphs 5 and 6 Wolfe tries to reveal the meaning of several official military phrases: "burned beyond recognition," "bought it," "augered in," or "crunched." Find

the two long sentences that account for the reality of those terms. What is the cumulative effect of those sentences?

10. Look at the last sentence in paragraphs 21 and 22. What rhetorical advantage does Wolfe gain by placing those two sentences last?
11. In paragraph 25 Wolfe introduces the "bridge coat" and the "little Indians." He repeats those terms throughout the rest of the essay. Why? What is the effect of those repetitions? Why in paragraph 25 does Wolfe give us so much detail about the "impressive and aristocratic" nature of the bridge coat?
12. Who believes in the "good angel" and who believes in the "bad angel" in this story about real people? How do you know?

SUGGESTIONS FOR WRITING

A. Wolfe was once upon a time a fledgling newspaper reporter. Then he became a New Journalist. Then he became a novelist. Along the way, he kept bringing more and more literary techniques into his reports and into his essays. Take several steps backward and think of yourself as a new reporter without Wolfe's experience. Rewrite this nonfiction short story as a single column for your local newspaper. Focus on the death of Ted Whelan, but try to give your readers a sense of the entire story.

B. Imagine that you are Jane Conrad. Write a letter to your husband's commanding officer asking him to revise the procedures for notifying wives about accidents on the flight line. Remember that you must be persuasive without being overbearing.

C. In a short paragraph try to explain why Wolfe would begin a book about the astronauts with "The Angels." What does he gain by starting with this story instead of a story about the successful launching of a space shuttle?

The Right Stuff

1 What an extraordinary grim stretch that had been . . . and yet thereafter Pete and Jane would keep running into pilots from other Navy bases, from the Air Force, from the Marines, who had been through their own extraordinary grim stretches. There was an Air Force pilot named Mike Collins, a nephew of former Army Chief of Staff J. Lawton Collins. Mike Collins had undergone eleven weeks of combat training at Nellis Air Force Base, near Las Vegas, and in that eleven weeks twenty-two of his fellow trainees had died in accidents, which was an extraordinary rate of two per week. Then there was a test pilot, Bill Bridgeman. In 1952, when Bridgeman was flying at Edwards Air Force Base, sixty-two Air Force pilots died in the course of thirty-six weeks of training, an extraordinary rate of 1.7 per week. Those figures were for fighter-pilot trainees only; they did not include the test pilots, Bridgeman's own confreres, who were dying quite regularly enough.

2 Extraordinary, to be sure; except that every veteran of flying small high-performance jets seemed to have experienced these bad strings.

3 In time, the Navy would compile statistics showing that for a career Navy pilot, i.e., one who intended to keep flying for twenty years as Conrad did, there

was a 23 percent probability that he would die in an aircraft accident. This did not even include combat deaths, since the military did not classify death in combat as accidental. Furthermore, there was a better than even chance, a 56 percent probability, to be exact, that at some point a career Navy pilot would have to eject from his aircraft and attempt to come down by parachute. In the era of jet fighters, ejection meant being exploded out of the cockpit by a nitroglycerine charge, like a human cannonball. The ejection itself was so hazardous—men lost knees, arms, and their lives on the rim of the cockpit or had the skin torn off their faces when they hit the "wall" of air outside—that many pilots chose to wrestle their aircraft to the ground rather than try it . . . and died that way instead.

4 The statistics were not secret, but neither were they widely known, having been eased into print rather obliquely in a medical journal. No pilot, and certainly no pilot's wife, had any need of the statistics in order to know the truth, however. The funerals took care of that in the most dramatic way possible. Sometimes, when the young wife of a fighter pilot would have a little reunion with the girls she went to school with, an odd fact would dawn on her: *they* have not been going to funerals. And then Jane Conrad would look at Pete . . . Princeton, Class of 1953 . . . Pete had already worn his great dark sepulchral bridge coat more than most boys of the Class of '53 had worn their tuxedos. How many of those happy young men had buried more than a dozen friends, comrades, and co-workers? (Lost through violent death in the execution of everyday duties.) At the time, the 1950's, students from Princeton took great pride in going into what they considered highly competitive, aggressive pursuits, jobs on Wall Street, on Madison Avenue, and at magazines such as *Time* and *Newsweek.* There was much fashionably brutish talk of what "dog-eat-dog" and "cutthroat" competition they found there; but in the rare instances when one of these young men died on the job, it was likely to be from choking on a chunk of Chateaubriand, while otherwise blissfully boiled, in an expense-account restaurant in Manhattan. How many would have gone to work, or stayed at work, on cutthroat Madison Avenue if there had been a 23 percent chance, nearly one chance in four, of dying from it? Gentlemen, we're having this little problem with chronic violent death . . .

5 And yet was there any basic way in which Pete (or Wally Schirra or Jim Lovell or any of the rest of them) was different from other college boys his age? There didn't seem to be, other than his love of flying. Pete's father was a Philadelphia stockbroker who in Pete's earliest years had a house in the Main Line suburbs, a limousine, and a chauffeur. The Depression eliminated the terrific brokerage business, the house, the car, and the servants; and by and by his parents were divorced and his father moved to Florida. Perhaps because his father had been an observation balloonist in the First World War—an adventurous business, since the balloons were prized targets of enemy aircraft—Pete was fascinated by flying. He went to Princeton on the Holloway Plan, a scholarship program left over from the Second World War in which a student trained with midshipmen from the Naval Academy during the summers and graduated with a commission in the Regular Navy. So Pete graduated, received his commission, married Jane, and headed off to Pensacola, Florida, for flight training.

6 Then came the difference, looking back on it.

7 A young man might go into military flight training believing that he was entering some sort of technical school in which he was simply going to acquire a certain set of skills. Instead, he found himself all at once enclosed in a fraternity. And in this fraternity, even though it was military, men were not rated by their outward rank as ensigns, lieutenants, commanders, or whatever. No, herein the world was divided into those who had it and those who did not. This quality, this *it,* was never named, however, nor was it talked about in any way.

8 As to just what this ineffable quality was . . . well, it obviously involved bravery. But it was not bravery in the simple sense of being willing to risk your life. The idea seemed to be that any fool could do that, if that was all that was required, just as any fool could throw away his life in the process. No, the idea here (in the all-enclosing fraternity) seemed to be that a man should have the ability to go up in a hurtling piece of machinery and put his hide on the line and then have the moxie, the reflexes, the experience, the coolness, to pull it back in the last yawning moment—and then to go up again *the next day,* and the next day, and every next day, even if the series should prove infinite—and, ultimately, in its best expression, do so in a cause that means something to thousands, to a people, a nation, to humanity, to God. Nor was there *a test* to show whether or not a pilot had this righteous quality. There was, instead, a seemingly infinite series of tests. A career in flying was like climbing one of those ancient Babylonian pyramids made up of a dizzy progression of steps and ledges, a ziggurat, a pyramid extraordinarily high and steep; and the idea was to prove at every foot of the way up that pyramid that you were one of the elected and anointed ones who had *the right stuff* and could move higher and higher and even—ultimately, God willing, one day—that you might be able to join that special few at the very top, that elite who had the capacity to bring tears to men's eyes, the very Brotherhood of the Right Stuff itself.

9 None of this was to be mentioned, and yet it was acted out in a way that a young man could not fail to understand. When a new flight (i.e., a class) of trainees arrived at Pensacola, they were brought into an auditorium for a little lecture. An officer would tell them: "Take a look at the man on either side of you." Quite a few actually swiveled their heads this way and that, in the interest of appearing diligent. Then the officer would say: "One of the three of you is not going to make it!"—meaning, not get his wings. That was the opening theme, the *motif* of primary training. We already know that one-third of you do not have the right stuff—it only remains to find out who.

10 Furthermore, that was the way it turned out. At every level in one's progress up that staggeringly high pyramid, the world was once more divided into those men who had the right stuff to continue the climb and those who had to be *left behind* in the most obvious way. Some were eliminated in the course of the opening classroom work, as either not smart enough or not hardworking enough, and were left behind. Then came the basic flight instruction, in single-engine, propeller-driven trainers, and a few more—even though the military tried to make this stage easy—were washed out and left behind. Then came more demanding levels, one after the other, formation flying, instrument flying, jet training, all-weather flying, gunnery, and at each level more were washed out and left behind. By this point easily a third of the original candidates had been, indeed, eliminated . . . from the ranks of those who might prove to have the right stuff.

11 In the Navy, in addition to the stages that Air Force trainees went through, the neophyte always had waiting for him, out in the ocean, a certain grim gray slab; namely, the deck of an aircraft carrier; and with it perhaps the most difficult routine in military flying, carrier landings. He was shown films about it, he heard lectures about it, and he knew that carrier landings were hazardous. He first practiced touching down on the shape of a flight deck painted on an airfield. He was instructed to touch down and gun right off. This was safe enough—the shape didn't move, at least—but it could do terrible things to, let us say, the gyroscope of the soul. *That shape!—it's so damned small!* And more candidates were washed out and left behind. Then came the day, without warning, when those who remained were sent out over the ocean for the first of many days of reckoning with the slab. The first day was always a clear day with little wind and a calm sea. The carrier was so steady that it seemed, from up there in the air, to be resting on pilings, and the candidate usually made his first carrier landing successfully, with relief and even *élan.* Many young candidates looked like terrific aviators up to that very point—and it was not until they were actually standing on the carrier deck that they first began to wonder if they had the proper stuff, after all. In the training film the flight deck was a grand piece of gray geometry, perilous, to be sure, but an amazing abstract shape as one looks down upon it on the screen. And yet once the newcomer's two feet were on it . . . *Geometry*—my God, man, this is a . . . skillet! It *heaved,* it moved up and down underneath his feet, it pitched up, it pitched down, it rolled to port (this great beast *rolled!*) and it rolled to starboard, as the ship moved into the wind and, therefore, into the waves, and the wind kept sweeping across, sixty feet up in the air out in the open sea, and there were no railings whatsoever. This was a *skillet!*—a frying pan!—a short-order grill!—not gray but black, smeared with skid marks from one end to the other and glistening with pools of hydraulic fluid and the occasional jet-fuel slick, all of it still hot, sticky, greasy, runny, virulent from God knows what traumas—still ablaze!—consumed in detonations, explosions, flames, combustion, roars, shrieks, whines, blasts, horrible shudders, fracturing impacts, as little men in screaming red and yellow and purple and green shirts with black Mickey Mouse helmets over their ears skittered about on the surface as if for their very lives (you've said it now!), hooking fighter planes onto the catapult shuttles so that they can explode their afterburners and be slung off the deck in a red-mad fury with a *kaboom!* that pounds through the entire deck—a procedure that seems absolutely controlled, orderly, sublime, however, compared to what he is about to watch as aircraft return to the ship for what is known in the engineering stoicisms of the military as "recovery and arrest." To say that an F-4 was coming back onto this heaving barbecue from out of the sky at a speed of 135 knots . . . that might have been the truth in the training lecture, but it did not begin to get across the idea of what the newcomer saw from the deck itself, because it created the notion that perhaps the plane was gliding in. On the deck one knew differently! As the aircraft came closer and the carrier heaved on into the waves and the plane's speed did not diminish and the deck did not grow steady—indeed, it pitched up and down five or ten feet per greasy heave—one experienced a neural alarm that no lecture could have prepared him for: This is not an *airplane* coming toward me, it is a brick with some poor sonofabitch riding it *(someone much like myself!),* and it is not *gliding,* it is *falling,* a fifty-thousand-pound brick, headed not for a stripe on the deck but for *me*—and with

a horrible *smash!* it hits the skillet, and with a blur of momentum as big as a freight train's it hurtles toward the far end of the deck—another blinding storm!—another roar as the pilot pushes the throttle up to full military power and another smear of rubber screams out over the skillet—and this is nominal!—quite okay!—for a wire stretched across the deck has grabbed the hook on the end of the plane as it hit the deck tail down, and the smash was the rest of the fifteen-ton brute slamming onto the deck, as it tripped up, so that it is now straining against the wire at full throttle, in case it hadn't held and the plane had "boltered" off the end of the deck and had to struggle up into the air again. And already the Mickey Mouse helmets are running toward the fiery monster . . .

12 And the candidate, looking on, begins to *feel* that great heaving sun-blazing deathboard of a deck wallowing in his own vestibular system—and suddenly he finds himself backed up against his own limits. He ends up going to the flight surgeon with so-called conversion symptoms. Overnight he develops blurred vision or numbness in his hands and feet or sinusitis so severe that he cannot tolerate changes in altitude. On one level the symptom is real. He really cannot see too well or use his fingers or stand the pain. But somewhere in his subconscious he knows it is a plea and a beg-off; he shows not the slightest concern (the flight surgeon notes) that the condition might be permanent and affect him in whatever life awaits him outside the arena of the right stuff.

13 Those who remained, those who qualified for carrier duty—and even more so those who later on qualified for *night* carrier duty—began to feel a bit like Gideon's warriors. *So many have been left behind!* The young warriors were now treated to a deathly sweet and quite unmentionable sight. They could gaze at length upon the crushed and wilted pariahs who had washed out. They could inspect those who did not have that righteous stuff.

14 The military did not have very merciful instincts. Rather than packing up these poor souls and sending them home, the Navy, like the Air Force and the Marines, would try to make use of them in some other role, such as flight controller. So the washout has to keep taking classes with the rest of his group, even though he can no longer touch an airplane. He sits there in the classes staring at sheets of paper with cataracts of sheer human mortification over his eyes while the rest steal looks at him . . . this man reduced to an ant, this untouchable, this poor sonofabitch. And in what test had he been found wanting? Why, it seemed to be nothing less than *manhood* itself. Naturally, this was never mentioned, either. Yet there it was. *Manliness, manhood, manly courage . . .* there was something ancient, primordial, irresistible about the challenge of this stuff, no matter what a sophisticated and rational age one might think he lived in.

15 Perhaps because it could not be talked about, the subject began to take on superstitious and even mystical outlines. A man either had it or he didn't! There was no such thing as having *most* of it. Moreover, it could blow at any seam. One day a man would be ascending the pyramid at a terrific clip, and the next—bingo!—he would reach his own limits in the most unexpected way. Conrad and Schirra met an Air Force pilot who had had a great pal at Tyndall Air Force Base in Florida. This man had been the budding ace of the training class; he had flown the hottest fighter-style trainer, the T-38, like a dream; and then he began the routine step of

being checked out in the T-33. The T-33 was not nearly as hot an aircraft as the T-38; it was essentially the old P-80 jet fighter. It had an exceedingly small cockpit. The pilot could barely move his shoulders. It was the sort of airplane of which everybody said, "You don't get into it, you *wear* it." Once inside a T-33 cockpit this man, this budding ace, developed claustrophobia of the most paralyzing sort. He tried everything to overcome it. He even went to a psychiatrist, which was a serious mistake for a military officer if his superiors learned of it. But nothing worked. He was shifted over to flying jet transports, such as the C-135. Very demanding and necessary aircraft they were, too, and he was still spoken of as an excellent pilot. But as everyone knew—and, again, it was never explained in so many words—only those who were assigned to fighter squadrons, the "fighter jocks," as they called each other with a self-satisfied irony, remained in the true fraternity. Those assigned to transports were not humiliated like washouts—*somebody* had to fly those planes—nevertheless, they, too, had been *left behind* for lack of the right stuff.

16 Or a man could go for a routine physical one fine day, feeling like a million dollars, and be grounded for *fallen arches.* It happened!—just like that! (And try raising them.) Or for breaking his wrist and losing only *part* of its mobility. Or for a minor deterioration of eyesight, or for any of hundreds of reasons that would make no difference to a man in an ordinary occupation. As a result all fighter jocks began looking upon doctors as their natural enemies. Going to see a flight surgeon was a no-gain proposition; a pilot could only hold his own or lose in the doctor's office. To be grounded for a medical reason was no humiliation, looked at objectively. But it was a humiliation, nonetheless!—for it meant you no longer had that indefinable, unutterable, integral stuff. (It could blow at *any* seam.)

17 All the hot young fighter jocks began trying to test the limits themselves in a superstitious way. They were like believing Presbyterians of a century before who used to probe their own experience to see if they were truly among *the elect.* When a fighter pilot was in training, whether in the Navy or the Air Force, his superiors were continually spelling out strict rules for him, about the use of the aircraft and conduct in the sky. They repeatedly forbade so-called hot-dog stunts, such as outside loops, buzzing, flat-hatting, hedgehopping and flying under bridges. But somehow one got the message that the man who truly *had* it could ignore those rules—not that he should make a point of it, but that he *could*—and that after all there was only one way to find out—and that in some strange unofficial way, peeking through his fingers, his instructor halfway expected him to challenge all the limits. They would give a lecture about how a pilot should never fly without a good solid breakfast—eggs, bacon, toast, and so forth—because if he tried to fly with his blood-sugar level too low, it could impair his alertness. Naturally, the next day every hot dog in the unit would get up and have a breakfast consisting of one cup of black coffee and take off and go up into a vertical climb until the weight of the ship exactly canceled out the upward pull of the engine and his air speed was zero, and he would hang there for one thick adrenal instant—and then fall like a rock, until one of three things happened: he keeled over nose first and regained his aerodynamics and all was well, he went into a spin and fought his way out of it, or he went into a spin and had to eject or crunch it, which was always supremely possible.

18 Likewise, "hassling"—mock dogfighting—was strictly forbidden, and so natu-

rally young fighter jocks could hardly wait to go up in, say, a pair of F-100s and start the duel by making a pass at each other at 800 miles an hour, the winner being the pilot who could slip in behind the other one and get locked in on his tail ("wax his tail"), and it was not uncommon for some eager jock to try too tight an outside turn and have his engine flame out, whereupon, unable to restart it, he has to eject . . . and he shakes his fist at the victor as he floats down by parachute and his half-a-million-dollar aircraft goes *kaboom!* on the palmetto grass or the desert floor, and he starts thinking about how he can get together with the other guy back at the base in time for the two of them to get their stories straight before the investigation: "I don't know what happened, sir. I was pulling up after a target run, and it just flamed out on me." Hassling was forbidden, and hassling that led to the destruction of an aircraft was a serious court-martial offense, and the man's superiors knew that the engine hadn't *just flamed out,* but every unofficial impulse on the base seemed to be saying: "Hell, we wouldn't give you a nickel for a pilot who hasn't done some crazy rat-racing like that. It's all part of the right stuff."

19 The other side of this impulse showed up in the reluctance of the young jocks to admit it when they had maneuvered themselves into a bad corner they couldn't get out of. There were two reasons why a fighter pilot hated to declare an emergency. First, it triggered a complex and very public chain of events at the field: all other incoming flights were held up, including many of one's comrades who were probably low on fuel; the fire trucks came trundling out to the runway like yellow toys (as seen from way up there), the better to illustrate one's hapless state; and the bureaucracy began to crank up the paper monster for the investigation that always followed. And second, to declare an emergency, one first had to reach that conclusion in his own mind, which to the young pilot was the same as saying: "A minute ago I still *had* it—now I need your help!" To have a bunch of young fighter pilots up in the air thinking this way used to drive flight controllers crazy. They would see a ship beginning to drift off the radar, and they couldn't rouse the pilot on the microphone for anything other than a few meaningless mumbles, and they would know he was probably out there with engine failure at a low altitude, trying to reignite by lowering his auxiliary generator rig, which had a little propeller that was supposed to spin in the slipstream like a child's pinwheel.

20 "Whiskey Kilo Two Eight, do you want to declare an emergency?"

21 *This* would rouse him!—to say: "Negative, negative, Whiskey Kilo Two Eight is not declaring an emergency."

22 Kaboom. Believers in the right stuff would rather crash and burn.

23 One fine day, after he had joined a fighter squadron, it would dawn on the young pilot exactly how the losers in the great fraternal competition were now being left behind. Which is to say, not by instructors or other superiors or by failures at prescribed levels of competence, but by death. At this point the essence of the enterprise would begin to dawn on him. Slowly, step by step, the ante had been raised until he was now involved in what was surely the grimmest and grandest gamble of manhood. Being a fighter pilot—for that matter, simply taking off in a single-engine jet fighter of the Century series, such as an F-102, or any of the military's other marvelous bricks with fins on them—presented a man, on a perfectly sunny day, with more ways to get himself killed than his wife and children could

imagine in their wildest fears. If he was barreling down the runway at two hundred miles an hour, completing the takeoff run, and the board started lighting up red, should he (a) abort the takeoff (and try to wrestle with the monster, which was gorged with jet fuel, out in the sand beyond the end of the runway) or (b) eject (and hope that the goddamned human cannonball trick works at zero altitude and he doesn't shatter an elbow or a kneecap on the way out) or (c) continue the takeoff and deal with the problem aloft (knowing full well that the ship may be on fire and therefore seconds away from exploding)? He would have one second to sort out the options and act, and this kind of little workaday decision came up all the time. Occasionally a man would look coldly at the binary problem he was now confronting every day—Right Stuff/Death—and decide it wasn't worth it and voluntarily shift over to transports or reconnaissance or whatever. And his comrades would wonder, for a day or so, what evil virus had invaded his soul . . . as they left him behind. More often, however, the reverse would happen. Some college graduate would enter Navy aviation through the Reserves, simply as an alternative to the Army draft, fully intending to return to civilian life, to some waiting profession or family business; would become involved in the obsessive business of ascending the ziggurat pyramid of flying; and, at the end of his enlistment, would astound everyone back home and very likely himself as well by signing up for another one. What on earth got into him? He couldn't explain it. After all, the very words for it had been amputated. A Navy study showed that two-thirds of the fighter pilots who were rated in the top rungs of their groups—i.e., the hottest young pilots—reenlisted when the time came, and practically all were college graduates. By this point, a young fighter jock was like the preacher in *Moby Dick* who climbs up into the pulpit on a rope ladder and then pulls the ladder up behind him; except the pilot could not use the words necessary to express the vital lessons. Civilian life, and even home and hearth, now seemed not only far away but far *below*, back down many levels of the pyramid of the right stuff.

24 A fighter pilot soon found he wanted to associate only with other fighter pilots. Who else could understand the nature of the little proposition (right stuff/death) they were all dealing with? And what other subject could compare with it? It was riveting! To talk about it in so many words was forbidden, of course. The very words *death, danger, bravery, fear* were not to be uttered except in the occasional specific instance or for ironic effect. Nevertheless, the subject could be adumbrated in *code* or *by example.* Hence the endless evenings of pilots huddled together talking about flying. On these long and drunken evenings (the bane of their family life) certain theorems would be propounded and demonstrated—and all by *code* and *example.* One theorem was: There are no *accidents* and no fatal flaws in the machines; there are only pilots with the wrong stuff. (I.e., blind Fate can't kill me.) When Bud Jennings crashed and burned in the swamps at Jacksonville, the other pilots in Pete Conrad's squadron said: *How could he have been so stupid?* It turned out that Jennings had gone up in the SNJ with his cockpit canopy opened in a way that was expressly forbidden in the manual, and carbon monoxide had been sucked in from the exhaust, and he passed out and crashed. All agreed that Bud Jennings was a good guy and a good pilot, but his epitaph on the ziggurat was: *How could he have been so stupid?* This seemed shocking at first, but by the time Conrad had reached the

end of that bad string at Pax River, he was capable of his own corollary to the theorem: viz., no single factor ever killed a pilot; there was always a chain of mistakes. But what about Ted Whelan, who fell like a rock from 8,100 feet when his parachute failed? Well, the parachute was merely part of the chain: first, someone should have caught the structural defect that resulted in the hydraulic leak that triggered the emergency; second, Whelan did not check out his seat-parachute rig, and the drogue failed to separate the main parachute from the seat; but even after those two mistakes, Whelan had fifteen or twenty seconds, as he fell, to disengage himself from the seat and open the parachute manually. Why just stare at the scenery coming up to smack you in the face! And everyone nodded. (He failed—but I wouldn't have!) Once the theorem and the corollary were understood, the Navy's statistics about one in every four Navy aviators dying meant nothing. The figures were averages, and averages applied to those with average stuff.

25 A riveting subject, especially if it were one's own hide that was on the line. Every evening at bases all over America, there were military pilots huddled in officers clubs eagerly cutting the right stuff up in coded slices so they could talk about it. What more compelling topic of conversation was there in the world? In the Air Force there were even pilots who would ask the tower for priority landing clearance so that they could make the beer call on time, at 4 P.M. sharp, at the Officers Club. They would come right out and state the reason. The drunken rambles began at four and sometimes went on for ten or twelve hours. Such conversations! They diced that righteous stuff up into little bits, bowed ironically to it, stumbled blindfolded around it, groped, lurched, belched, staggered, bawled, sang, roared, and feinted at it with self-deprecating humor. Nevertheless!—they never mentioned it by name. No, they used the approved codes, such as: "Like a jerk I got myself into a hell of a corner today." They told of how they "lucked out of it." To get across the extreme peril of his exploit, one would use certain oblique cues. He would say, "I looked over at Robinson"—who would be known to the listeners as a non-com who sometimes rode backseat to read radar—"and he wasn't talking any more, he was just staring at the radar, like this, giving it that *zombie* look. Then I *knew* I was in trouble!" Beautiful! Just right! For it would also be known to the listeners that the non-coms advised one another: "*Never* fly with a lieutenant. *Avoid* captains and majors. Hell, man, do yourself a favor: don't fly with anybody below colonel." Which in turn said: "Those young bucks shoot dice with death!" And yet once in the air the non-com had his own standards. He was determined to remain as outwardly cool as the pilot, so that when the pilot did something that truly petrified him, he would say nothing; instead, he would turn silent, catatonic, like a zombie. Perfect! *Zombie.* There you had it, compressed into a single word all of the foregoing. I'm a hell of a pilot! I shoot dice with death! And now all you fellows know it! And I haven't spoken of that unspoken stuff even once!

26 The talking and drinking began at the beer call, and then the boys would break for dinner and come back afterward and get more wasted and more garrulous or else more quietly fried, drinking good cheap PX booze until 2 A.M. The night was young! Why not get the cars and go out for a little proficiency run? It seemed that every fighter jock thought himself an ace driver, and he would do anything to obtain a hot car, especially a sports car, and the drunker he was, the more convinced he would

be about his driving skills, as if the right stuff, being indivisible, carried over into any enterprise whatsoever, under any conditions. A little proficiency run, boys! (There's only one way to find out!) And they would roar off in close formation from, say, Nellis Air Force Base, down Route 15, into Las Vegas, barreling down the highway, rat-racing, sometimes four abreast, jockeying for position, piling into the most listless curve in the desert flats as if they were trying to root each other out of the groove at the Rebel 500—and then bursting into downtown Las Vegas with a rude fraternal roar like the Hell's Angels—and the natives chalked it up to youth and drink and the bad element that the Air Force attracted. They knew nothing about the right stuff, of course.

27 More fighter pilots died in automobiles than in airplanes. Fortunately, there was always some kindly soul up the chain to certify the papers "line of duty," so that the widow could get a better break on the insurance. That was okay and only proper because somehow the system itself had long ago said *Skol!* and *Quite right!* to the military cycle of Flying & Drinking and Drinking & Driving, as if there were no other way. Every young fighter jock knew the feeling of getting two or three hours' sleep and then waking up at 5:30 A.M. and having a few cups of coffee, a few cigarettes, and then carting his poor quivering liver out to the field for another day of flying. There were those who arrived not merely hungover but still drunk, slapping oxygen tank cones over their faces and trying to burn the alcohol out of their systems, and then going up, remarking later: "I don't *advise* it, you understand, but it *can* be done." (Provided you have the right stuff, you miserable pudknocker.)

28 Air Force and Navy airfields were usually on barren or marginal stretches of land and would have looked especially bleak and Low Rent to an ordinary individual in the chilly light of dawn. But to a young pilot there was an inexplicable bliss to coming out to the flight line while the sun was just beginning to cook up behind the rim of the horizon, so that the whole field was still in shadow and the ridges in the distance were in silhouette and the flight line was a monochrome of Exhaust Fume Blue, and every little red light on top of the water towers or power stanchions looked dull, shriveled, congealed, and the runway lights, which were still on, looked faded, and even the landing lights on a fighter that had just landed and was taxiing in were no longer dazzling, as they would be at night, and looked instead like shriveled gobs of candlepower out there—and yet it was beautiful, exhilarating!—for he was revved up with adrenalin, anxious to take off before the day broke, to burst up into the sunlight over the ridges before all those thousands of comatose souls down there, still dead to the world, snug in home and hearth, even came to their senses. To take off in an F-100F at dawn and cut on the afterburner and hurtle twenty-five thousand feet up into the sky in thirty seconds, so suddenly that you felt not like a bird but like a trajectory, yet with full control, full control of *four tons* of thrust, all of which flowed from your will and through your fingertips, with the huge engine right beneath you, so close that it was as if you were riding it bareback, until all at once you were supersonic, an event registered on earth by a tremendous cracking boom that shook windows, but up here only by the fact that you now felt utterly free of the earth—to describe it, even to wife, child, near ones and dear ones, seemed impossible. So the pilot kept it to himself, along with an even more inde-

scribable . . . an even more sinfully inconfessable . . . feeling of superiority, appropriate to him and to his kind, lone bearers of the right stuff.

29 From *up here* at dawn the pilot looked down upon poor hopeless Las Vegas (or Yuma, Corpus Christi, Meridian, San Bernardino, or Dayton) and began to wonder: How can all of them down there, those poor souls who will soon be waking up and trudging out of their minute rectangles and inching along their little noodle highways toward whatever slots and grooves make up their everyday lives—how could they live like that, with such earnestness, if they had the faintest idea of what it was like up here in this righteous zone?

30 But of course! Not only the washed-out, grounded, and dead pilots had been left behind—but also all of those millions of sleepwalking souls who never even attempted the great gamble. The entire world below . . . *left behind.* Only at this point can one begin to understand just how big, how titanic, the ego of the military pilot could be. The world was used to enormous egos in artists, actors, entertainers of all sorts, in politicians, sports figures, and even journalists, because they had such familiar and convenient ways to show them off. But that slim young man over there in uniform, with the enormous watch on his wrist and the withdrawn look on his face, that young officer who is so shy that he can't even open his mouth unless the subject is flying—that young pilot—well, my friends, his ego is even *bigger!*—so big, it's *breathtaking!* Even in the 1950's it was difficult for civilians to comprehend such a thing, but *all* military officers and many enlisted men tended to feel superior to civilians. It was really quite ironic, given the fact that for a good thirty years the rising business classes in the cities had been steering their sons away from the military, as if from a bad smell, and the officer corps had never been held in lower esteem. Well, career officers returned the contempt in trumps. They looked upon themselves as men who lived by higher standards of behavior than civilians, as men who were the bearers and protectors of the most important values of American life, who maintained a sense of discipline while civilians abandoned themselves to hedonism, who maintained a sense of honor while civilians lived by opportunism and greed. Opportunism and greed: there you had your much-vaunted corporate business world. Khrushchev was right about one thing: when it came time to hang the capitalist West, an American businessman would sell him the rope. When the showdown came—and the showdowns always came—not all the wealth in the world or all the sophisticated nuclear weapons and radar and missile systems it could buy would take the place of those who had the uncritical willingness to face danger, those who, in short, had the right stuff.

31 In fact, the feeling was so righteous, so exalted, it could become religious. Civilians seldom understood this, either. There was no one to teach them. It was no longer the fashion for serious writers to describe the glories of war. Instead, they dwelt upon its horrors, often with cynicism or disgust. It was left to the occasional pilot with a literary flair to provide a glimpse of the pilot's self-conception in its heavenly or spiritual aspect. When a pilot named Robert Scott flew his P-43 over Mount Everest, quite a feat at the time, he brought his hand up and snapped a salute to his fallen adversary. He thought he had *defeated* the mountain, surmounting all the forces of nature that had made it formidable. And why not? "God is my co-pilot," he said—that became the title of his book—and he meant it. So did the

most gifted of all the pilot authors, the Frenchman Antoine de Saint-Exupéry. As he gazed down upon the world . . . from up there . . . during transcontinental flights, the good Saint-Ex saw civilization as a series of tiny fragile patches clinging to the otherwise barren rock of Earth. He felt like a lonely sentinel, a protector of those vulnerable little oases, ready to lay down his life in their behalf, if necessary; a saint, in short, true to his name, flying up here at the right hand of God. The good Saint-Ex! And he was not the only one. He was merely the one who put it into words most beautifully and anointed himself before the altar of the right stuff.

(1979)

QUESTIONS

Thought and Structure

1. Wolfe said that he wrote "The Right Stuff" to explain what was going on with the pilots in "The Angels." If we look at those two chapters together, does it change our mind about those who have "the right stuff"?
2. What is "the right stuff"? What qualities and attributes are necessary for success as a military test-pilot? From your point of view, are all those qualities and attributes necessary or desirable?
3. What do you think Wolfe's overall assessment is of the "enclosing fraternity"?
4. In paragraphs 17 and 18 Wolfe shows us how those with the right stuff occasionally break the rules; he suggests that breaking the rules is an inherent part of the game these elected people play. Does he pass judgment on these unofficial acts that violate official policies?
5. In paragraphs 28–30 Wolfe gives us a sense of how those with the right stuff feel about those without it. Why does Wolfe take the pilots up above the sleeping cities so they can look down disdainfully on those below? Does the term "righteous" have a new ring to it at the beginning of paragraph 31? Why does Wolfe turn to "religious" imagery in this final paragraph of the essay? Is he passing judgment?
6. The overall structure of this essay breaks down this way: paragraphs 1–6; 7–10; 11; 12–16; 17–22; 23–27; 28–31. Explain what unifies each of these sections.
7. Paragraph 11 is a fascinating paragraph because of its length and because it deals with a very special subclass within the elite. Would we change the effect of this paragraph if we broke it up into smaller units?
8. Look at the way Wolfe uses repetition at the end of almost every paragraph in the essay. What does he gain from the refrain? How does he vary that refrain to achieve different effects?

Style and Strategy

9. Examine the special effects Wolfe uses in paragraph 11. He compares the slab—the aircraft carrier itself—to a skillet, a frying pan, a short-order grill. Are these comparisons effective? Why or why not? Why does he introduce the "Mickey Mouse helmets" near the middle of the paragraph and then end the paragraph with them? Why does Wolfe introduce the "gyroscope of the soul" in this paragraph?

10. What does Wolfe mean when he tells us that the members of the brotherhood were "like believing Presbyterians of a century before"? What does he imply that fighter pilots have decided about themselves as he goes on to tell us how they break the rules and get away with it (paragraph 17)?
11. What does Wolfe gain by using this encoded message of his own: (right stuff/death)? Has Wolfe appointed himself to talk about what can't be talked about? How do you suppose he managed to find out so much about the brotherhood if those with the right stuff can't talk about it?
12. In paragraph 24, Wolfe reuses material from "The Angels." How does he change those accounts of death? To what end?
13. Look at the very long sentence in paragraph 28 that begins "To take off in an F-100F at dawn. . . ." What is the purpose of that sentence? What is its effect on you?
14. Why does Wolfe include dialogue in paragraphs 18–21?
15. In the last sentence of paragraph 8 Wolfe stacks a series of parallel phrases:

    a dizzy progression of steps
    a ziggurat
    a pyramid

    and again

    that special few
    that elite
    the very Brotherhood

    What does he gain from these series? What would be the effect if he just told us once, without variation?

SUGGESTIONS FOR WRITING

A. Look at the institution where you go to school or where you work; try to see it as Wolfe would see it. Study too the techniques that Wolfe uses when he writes. Then write your own essay about some aspect of your institution that someone on the outside would not be likely to detect or understand. Give the outsiders the inside stuff, but remember that you must translate the sacred language of the insiders so that the outsiders can understand it.

B. Write a character sketch of someone you either know personally or have watched and studied from afar, someone who has "the right stuff."

C. Write a deft exposé of something in our culture that you do not like; try to write it the way you think Wolfe would write it.

Funky Chic

1 By October of 1969 Funky Chic was flying through London like an infected bat, which is to say, silently, blindly, insanely, and at night, fangs afoam . . . but with an infallible aim for the main vein . . . much like the Sideburns Fairy, who had been cruising about the city since 1966, visiting young groovies in their

sleep and causing them to awake with sideburns running down their jawbones. Funky Chic, as I say . . . So it happened that one night in a club called Arethusa, a favorite spot of the London *bon ton,* I witnessed the following: A man comes running into the Gents and squares off in front of a mirror, removes his tie and stuffs it into a pocket of his leather coat, jerks open the top four buttons of his shirt, shoves his fingers in under the hair on top of his head and starts thrashing and tousling it into a ferocious disarray, steps back and appraises the results, turns his head this way and that, pulls his shirt open a little wider to let the hair on his chest sprout out, and then, seeing that everything is just so, heads in toward the dining room for the main event. This dining room is a terrific place. It has just been done over in the white plaster arches and cylindrical lamps of the smart restaurant decor of that time known as Expense Chit Trattoria. In the grand salon only the waiters wear white shirts and black ties. The clientele sit there roaring and gurgling and flashing fireproof grins in a rout of leather jerkins, Hindu tunics, buckskin shirts, deerslayer boots, dueling shirts, bandannas knotted at the Adam's apple, love beads dangling to the belly, turtlenecks reaching up to meet the muttonchops at midjowl, Indian blouses worn thin and raggy to reveal the jutting nipples and crimson aureolae underneath . . . The place looks like some grand luxe dining room on the Mediterranean unaccountably overrun by mob-scene scruffs from out of *Northwest Passage, The Informer, Gunga Din,* and *Bitter Rice.* What I was gazing upon was in fact the full fashion splendor of London's *jeunesse dorée,* which by 1969, of course, included everyone under the age of sixty-seven with a taste for the high life.

2 Funky Chic came skipping and screaming into the United States the following year in the form of such marvelous figures as the Debutante in Blue Jeans. She was to be found on the fashion pages in every city of any size in the country. There she is in the photograph . . . wearing her blue jeans and her blue work shirt, open to the sternum, with her long pre-Raphaelite hair parted on top of the skull, uncoiffed but recently washed and blown dry with a Continental pro-style dryer (the word-of-mouth that year said the Continental gave her more "body") . . . and she is telling her interviewer:

3 "We're not having any 'coming-out balls' this year or any 'deb parties' or any of that. We're fed up with doing all the same old things, which are so useless, and seeing the same old faces and dancing to so-called society bands while a lot of old ladies in orange-juice-colored dresses stand around the edges talking to our parents. We're tired of cotillions and hunt cups and smart weekends. You want to know what I did last weekend? I spent last weekend at the day-care center, looking after the most beautiful black children . . . and *learning* from them!"

4 Or as a well-known, full-grown socialite, Amanda Burden, said at that time: "The sophistication of the baby blacks has made me rethink my attitudes." Whereupon she described herself as "anti-fashion."

5 Anti-fashion! Terrific. Right away anti-fashion itself became the most raving fashion imaginable . . . also known as Funky Chic. Everybody had sworn off fashion, but somehow nobody moved to Cincinnati to work among the poor. Instead, everyone stayed put and imported the poor to the fashion pages. That's the way it happened! For it was in that same year, 1970, that Funky Chic evolved into its most exquisite manifestation, namely, Radical Chic (if I may be forgiven for saying so)

. . . Socialites began to give parties for the Black Panthers (to name but one of many groups) at their homes, from Park Avenue to Croton-on-Hudson. Which is to say, they began to bring exotic revolutionaries into their living rooms and thereby achieved the ultimate in Funky Chic interior decoration: live black bodies.

6 It was at this point that fashion, on the one hand, and politics, ideology, and philosophy, on the other, began to interlock in a most puzzling way. The fashion of Radical Chic swept not only socialites but also intellectuals and cultivated persons of every sort in the years 1968–70. The situation began to contradict the conventional assumption of historians, which is that fashion is but the embroidery of history, if that. It is true that Radical Chic would have never become a fashion if certain political ideas and emotions had not already been in the air. But once Radical Chic became fashionable, it took on its own momentum. It had the power to create political change on its own—i.e., many influential people who had been generally apolitical began to express support for groups like the Panthers.

7 The conventional wisdom is that fashion is some sort of storefront that one chooses, honestly or deceptively, to place between the outside world and his "real self." But there is a counter notion: namely, that every person's "real self," his psyche, his soul, is largely the product of fashion and other outside influences on his status. Such has been the suggestion of the stray figure here and there; the German sociologist Rene Konig, for example, or the Spanish biologist Jose M. R. Delgado. This is not a notion that is likely to get a very charitable reception just now, among scholars or readers generally. If the Bourbon Louises may be said to have lived in the Age of Absolutism, we now live in the Age of Egalitarianism (with the emphasis on the *ism,* if one need edit). Even people who lend themselves to the fashion pages, the people whose faces run through *Vogue, Bazaar, Harper's Bazaar & Queen* and *Town & Country* like a bolt of crisp white-glazed chintz, are not going to be caught out today talking about fashion in terms of *being fashionable.* They talk instead of ease, comfort, convenience, practicality, simplicity, and, occasionally, fun and gaiety (for others to share). Right now I am looking at a page of photographs in *Bazaar* of a woman named Venetia Barker, a young English matron whose husband owns a stable of horses and a fleet of helicopters. She tells how two or three times a week she flies her own canary-yellow helicopter from their country home in Wiltshire to their townhouse in London in order to go antique hunting. Twice a week she flies it to Worcestershire to go horseback riding in the fox hunts. She speaks of the helicopter as a time-saving convenience, however, and of fox hunting in terms of mental hygiene: two days a week with horse & hound beats the psychiatrist any time in coping with the pressures of a busy modern life. "During the day," she says, "I wear what's most practical," items such as a Regency coachman's cape with three huge layers of flapping red overlaps about the shoulders plus leather pants by Foale and Tuffin of London. At night she changes "into something quite simple," which turns out to be outfits such as a black tunic gown by the good Madame Gres, slashed on the sides to reveal a floor-length scarlet slip and cross-laced black drawstrings, and surmounted at the bosom by a filigree diamond necklace with an emerald pendant the size of a Brazil nut. Convenience, health, practicality, simplicity . . . none of which means that the woman is being hypocritical or even cagy. She is merely observing a convention, a fashion taboo that is common to people at every level of income and status today.

8 The curious thing is that the same taboo makes fashion an even touchier subject for scholars. Louis Auchincloss once observed that academic writers seem to find the courage to write about society, in the sense of fashionable society, only from a great distance—either from across an ocean or across a gulf of a century or more in time, and preferably both. "Why can we find a hundred professors eager to explore the subtleties of the court of the Empress Theodora," he asks, "and not one to plumb the depths of a party given by Perle Mesta?" He also remarked, quite aptly, I would say, that nothing offers a more revealing insight into the character of the high tide of American capitalism than the social life of Newport in the 1890's—"a crazy patchwork of borrowed values financed on a scale that would have made the Sun King stare"—and to this day the one serious study of it is by a Frenchman (Paul Bourget).

9 Auchincloss is a novelist, of course, and ever since the time of Richardson and Fielding, some 230 years ago, novelists have been drawn to fashion as an essential ingredient of realistic narration. This was out of sheer instinct and not theory. Early in the game they seemed to sense that fashion is a code, a symbolic vocabulary that offers a subrational but instant and very brilliant illumination of the characters of individuals and even entire periods, especially periods of great turmoil. And yet novelists who have dwelled on fashion in just this way have usually been regarded in their own time as lightweights—"trivial" has been the going word—scarcely even literary artists, in fact; even those who eventually have been judged to be the literary giants of their eras. Dr. Johnson dismissed Fielding as a minor, trivial, unserious to the very end. He could not understand how any serious writer could wallow so contentedly in the manners and mores, the everyday habits, of so many rascals, high and low. Saint-Beuve continually compared Balzac to people like antique dealers, sellers of women's clothes, and—this was one of his favorites—the sort of down-at-the-heel petty bourgeois doctors who make house calls and become neighborhood gossips. Balzac was not regarded as a major writer until after his death; he was not even invited to join the French Academy.

10 In our own time I don't have the slightest doubt but that Evelyn Waugh will eventually stand as England's only major novelist of the twentieth century (oh, all right, him and Lawrence). But during the last decade of his life his stock sank very low; so low, in fact, that he seemed finally to downgrade himself, judging by the opening chapter of *The Ordeal of Gilbert Pinfold.* In his writing he immersed himself so deeply in the fashions of his times that many critics regarded him as a snob first and an artist second. (I recall one English reviewer who was furious because Waugh had the hero of his *Men at Arms* trilogy, Guy Crouchback, describe his father's funeral mainly in terms of how correctly everyone had dressed for the event despite the fact that it was wartime and the services were out in the country.) John O'Hara's reputation has undergone a similar deflation over the past fifteen years. As for Louis Auchincloss, more than once he has set in motion characters who pursue the lure of Wall Street & Wealth & Family & Men's Club in the most relentless manner—only to see critics complain that the character is not believable: People don't conduct their lives that way any more. Auchincloss notes with some annoyance that they are saying "don't" when what they mean is "shouldn't."

11 Auchincloss identifies the moral objection that underlies the taboo as follows. At the very core of fashionable society exists a monstrous vulgarity: "the habit of

judging human beings by standards having no necessary relation to their character." To be found dwelling upon this vulgarity, absorbed in it, is like being found watching a suck 'n' fuck movie. It is no use telling people you were merely there as a detached observer in the age of *Deep Throat;* in the case of fashion, too, the grubbiness rubs off all the same, upon scholars no less than novelists, socialites, and gossip columnists. Unlike a Balzac or a Gogol, the scholar seldom treats fashion as an essential ingredient of history. Instead, he treats it as comic relief, usually set apart from the narrative in an archly written chapter with a coy title such as "Bumpkins and Brummels: From Country Fair to Mayfair."

12 Today, in the age of Funky Chic Egalité, fashion is a much more devious, sly, and convoluted business than anything that was ever dreamed of at Versailles. At Versailles, where Louis XIV was installed in suites full of silver furniture (later melted down to finance a war), one could scarcely be *too* obvious. Versailles was above all the City of the Rich. Hundreds of well-to-do or upward-hustling families had quarters there. The only proper way to move about the place was in sedan chairs borne by hackmen with straining trapeziuses. Any time anyone of high social wattage gave a party, there would be a sedan-chair traffic jam of a half hour or more outside his entry way as the true and original *jeunesse dorée,* in actual golden threads and golden slippers, waited to make the proper drop-dead entrance.

13 One has only to compare such a scene with any involving the golden youth of our own day. I recommend to anyone interested in the subject the long block, or concourse, known as Broadway in New Haven, Connecticut, where Elm Street, York Street, Whalley and Dixwell Avenues come together. This is near the heart of Yale University. Twenty years ago, at Elm and York, there was a concentration of men's custom-tailoring shops that seemed to outnumber all the tailors on Fifth Avenue and Fifty-seventh Street put together. They were jammed in like pearls in a box. Yale was still the capital of collegiate smart dressing. Yale was, after all, the place where the *jeunesse dorée* of America were being groomed, in every sense of the word, to inherit the world; the world, of course, being Wall Street and Madison Avenue. Five out of every seven Yale undergraduates could tell whether the button-down Oxford cloth shirt you had on was from Fenn-Feinstein, J. Press, or Brooks Brothers from a single glance at your shirt front; Fenn-Feinstein: plain breast pocket; J. Press: breast pocket with buttoned flap; Brooks Brothers: no breast pocket at all. Today J. Press is still on the case, but others of the heavenly host are shipping out. Today a sane businessman would sooner open a souvlaki takeout counter at Elm and York than a tailor shop, for reasons any fool could see. On the other side of the grand concourse, lollygagging up against Brooks Health and Beauty Aids, Whitlock's, and the Yale Co-op, are the new Sons of Eli. They are from the same families as before, averaging about $37,500 gross income per annum among the non-scholarship students. But there is nobody out there checking breast pockets or jacket vents or any of the rest of it. The unvarying style at Yale today is best described as Late Army Surplus. Broadway Army & Navy enters heaven! Sons in Levi's, break through that line! that is the sign we hail! Visible at Elm and York are more olive-green ponchos, clodhoppers, and parachute boots, more leaky-dye blue turtlenecks, pea jackets, ski hats, long-distance trucker warms, sheepherder's coats, fisherman's slickers, down-

home tenant-farmer bib overalls, coal-stoker strap undershirts, fringed cowpoke jerkins, strike-hall blue workshirts, lumberjack plaids, forest-ranger mackinaws, Australian bushrider mackintoshes, Cong sandals, bike leathers, and more jeans, jeans, jeans, jeans, jeans, more prole gear of every description than you ever saw or read of in a hundred novels by Jack London, Jack Conroy, Maxim Gorky, Clara Weatherwax, and any who came before or after.

14 Of course, this happens to be precisely what America's most favored young men are wearing at every other major college in the country, so that you scarcely detect the significance of it all until you look down to the opposite end of the concourse, to the north, where Dixwell Avenue comes in. Dixwell Avenue is the main drag of one of New Haven's black slums. There, on any likely corner, one can see congregations of young men the same age as the Yales but . . . from the bottom end of the great greased pole of life, as it were, from families whose gross incomes no one but the eligibility worker ever bothered to tote up. All the young aces and dudes are out there lollygagging around the front of the Monterey Club, wearing their two-tone patent Pyramids with the five-inch heels that swell out at the bottom to match the Pierre Chareau Art Deco plaid bell-bottom baggies they have on with the three-inch-deep elephant cuffs tapering upward toward the "spray-can fit" in the seat, as it is known, and the peg-top waistband with self-covered buttons and the beagle-collar pattern-on-pattern Walt Frazier shirt, all of it surmounted by the midi-length leather piece with the welted waist seam and the Prince Albert pockets and the black Pimpmobile hat with the four-inch turn-down brim and the six-inch pop-up crown with the golden chain-belt hatband . . . and all of them, every ace, every dude, out there just *getting over* in the baddest possible way, come to play and dressed to slay . . . so that somehow the sons of the slums have become the Brummels and Gentlemen of Leisure, the true fashion plates of the 1970's, and the Sons of Eli dress like the working class of 1934 . . .

. . . a style note which I mention not merely for the sake of irony. Just as Radical Chic was a social fashion that ended up having a political impact—so did Funky Chic. Radical Chic helped various Left causes. Funky Chic hurt them. So far as I know, no one has ever recorded the disruption that Funky Chic caused within the New Left. (Remember the New Left?) In 1968, 1969, and 1970 the term "counterculture" actually meant something. In those wild spitting hot-bacon days on the campus "counterculture" referred to what seemed to be a fast-rising unity of spirit among all the youth of the nation, black and white, a new consciousness (to use a favorite word from that time) that was mobilizing half the country, the half that was now under twenty-five years old (to use a favorite statistic from that time), under the banner of revolution or something not far from it. Yet at that very moment the youth of the country were becoming bitterly divided along lines of class and status. The more the New Left tried to merge them in a united front, the more chaotic and out of the question the would-be coalition became.

15 Fashion was hardly one of the root causes of this division—that is another, longer story. But fashion was in many cases the cutting edge. Fashion brought out hopeless status conflict where there was no idealogical conflict whatsoever. In 1969 I went to San Francisco to do a story on the young militants who were beginning

to raise hell inside the supposedly shockproof compound of Chinatown. I had heard of a sensational public meeting held by a group called the Wah Ching, who were described as a supergang of young Chinese who had been born in Hong Kong, who immigrated to the United States with their parents in the mid-sixties, who couldn't speak English, couldn't get an education, couldn't get jobs, who were ready to explode. They held a public meeting and threatened to burn down Chinatown, Watts-style. So I came on into Chinatown, cold, looking for the Wah Ching. Right away, on the street corners, I see groups of really fierce-looking young men. They've got miles of long black hair, down to the shoulders, black berets, black T-shirts, black chinos, dirty Levi's, combat boots. These must be the dread Wah Ching, I figured. So I worked up my nerve and started talking to some of them and right away I found out they were not the Wah Ching at all. They were a group known as the Red Guard, affiliated at that time with the Black Panthers. Not only that, they were not lower-class Hong Kong-born Chinese at all but American-born. They spoke English just like any other Americans; and most of them, by Chinatown standards at least, were middle-class. But they said they were allied with the Wah Ching and told of various heavy battles the Wah Ching were going to help them out in.

16 It took me about two weeks, but I finally arranged a meeting with one of the main leaders of the Wah Ching themselves. We were going to meet in a restaurant, and I arrived first and was sitting there going over all the political points I wanted to cover. Finally the man walks in—and I take one look and forget every political question on the list. He has on a pair of blue slacks, a matching blue turtleneck jersey with a blue shirt over it and a jacket with a leather body and great fluffy flannel sleeves, kind of like a suburban bowling jacket. This man does not add up. But mainly it is his hair. After all the ferocious long black hair I have been seeing in Chinatown—his is chopped off down to what is almost a parody of the old Chinatown ricebowl haircut. So the first magnificent question I heard myself blurting out was: "What happened to your hair!"

17 There was no reason why he should, but he took the question seriously. He spoke a very broken English which I will not attempt to imitate, but the gist of what he said was this:

18 "We don't wear our hair like the hippies; we don't wear our hair like the Red Guards. We are not a part of the hippies; we are not a part of the Red Guards; we are not a part of anything. We are the Wah Ching. When we got to this country, those guys you were talking to out there, the ones who now call themselves the Red Guard, those same guys were calling us 'China Bugs' and beating up on us and pushing us around. But now we're unified, and we're the Wah Ching and nobody pushes us around. So now they come to us and tell us they are the Red Guard and they've got the message and Chairman Mao and the Red Book and all that. They'll give us the message and the direction, and we can be the muscle and the power on the street and together we will fight the Establishment.

19 "Well, the hell with that. We don't need any ideological benefactors. Look at these guys. Look at these outfits they're wearing. They come around us having a good time playing poor and saying, 'Hey, brother.' Look at those berets—they think they're Fidel Castro coming out of the mountains. Look at the Can't-Bust-'Em overalls they got on, with the hairy gorilla emblem on the back and the combat

boots and the olive-green socks on you buy two-for-29-cents at the Army-Navy Store. They're having a good time playing poor, but we are the ones who have to *be* poor. So the hell with that and the hell with them."

20 Here were two groups who were unified ideologically—who wanted to fight the old clan establishment of Chinatown as well as the white establishment of San Francisco—and yet they remained split along a sheerly dividing line, an instinctive status line, a line that might even be described by the accursed word itself, "fashion." This example could be multiplied endlessly, through every instance in which the New Left tried to enlist the youth of the working class or of the slums. There never was a "counterculture" in the sense of any broad unity among the young—and this curious, uncomfortable matter of fashion played a part over and over. I never talked to a group of black militants, or Latin militants, for that matter, who didn't eventually comment derisively about the poorboy outfits their middle-class white student allies insisted on wearing or the way they tried to use black street argot, all the *mans* and *cats* and *babies* and *brothers* and *baddests.* From the very first, fashion tipped them off to something that was not demonstrated on the level of logic until much later: namely, that most of the white New Lefters of the period 1968–70 were neither soldiers nor politicians but simply actors.

21 The tipoff was not the fact that the middle-class whites were dressing *down* in order to join their slum-bound brethren. The issue was not merely condescension. The tipoff was that when the whites dressed down, went Funky Chic, they did it *wrong!* They did it *lame!* They never bothered to look at what the brothers on the street were actually wearing! They needed to have their coats pulled! The New Left had a strictly old-fashioned conception of life on the street, a romantic and nostalgic one somehow derived from literary images of *proletarian* life from before World War II or even World War I. A lot of the white college boys, for example, would go for those checked lumberjack shirts that are so heavy and wooly that you can wear them like a jacket. It was as if all the little Lord Byrons had a hopeless nostalgia for the proletariat of about 1910, the Miners with Dirty Faces era, and never mind the realities—because the realities were that by 1968 the real hard-core street youth in the slums were not into lumberjack shirts, Can't Bust 'Ems, and Army surplus socks. They were into the James Brown look. They were into ruffled shirts and black-belted leather pieces and bell-cuff herringbones, all that stuff, macking around, getting over, looking sharp . . . heading toward the high-heeled Pimpmobile *got-to-get-over* look of Dixwell Avenue 1976. If you tried to put one of those lumpy mildew mothball lumberjack shirts on them—those aces . . . they'd *vomit.*

22 For years the sheerly dividing line was a single item of clothing that is practically synonymous with Funky Chic: blue jeans. Well-to-do Europeans appreciated the chic of jeans—that primitive rawness; that delicious grip on the gourd and the moist skinny slither up into all the cracks and folds and fissures!—long before Americans. Even in the early fifties such special styles as London S.W. 5 New Wave Habitat Bentwood Movie Producer Chic and South of France Young Jade Chic and Jardins du Luxembourg Post-Breathless Chic all had at their core: blue jeans. Cowboy Chic, involving blue jeans and walking around as if you have an aluminum beer keg between your thighs, has been popular among young Paris groovies for at least

fifteen years. Well-to-do whites in America began to discover the raw-vital reverse-spin funk thrill of jeans in the early sixties. But until recently any such appeal was utterly lost on black or any other colored street aces and scarlet creepers. Jeans were associated with funk in its miserable aspects, with Down-and-Out, bib overalls, Down Home, and I'm Gonna Send You Back to Georgia. Jeans have just begun to be incorporated in the Ace or Pimp look, thanks to certain dramatic changes in jeans couture: such as the addition of metal studwork, bias-cut two-tone swirl mosaic patterns, windowpane welt patterns, and the rising value of used denim fabric, now highly prized for its "velvet hand" (and highly priced, just as a used Tabriz rug is worth more than a new one). In other words, the aces will now tolerate jeans precisely because they have lost much of their funk.

23 Well-to-do white youths still associate jeans in any form and at any price with Funk, however, and Funky Chic still flies and bites the main vein and foams and reigns. The current talk of a Return to Elegance among the young immediately becomes a laugh and a half (or, more precisely, the latest clothing industry shuck) to anyone who sets foot on a mainly white American campus, whether Yale or the University of California at San Diego. A minor matter perhaps; but today, as always, the authentic language of fashion is worth listening to. For fashion, to put it most simply, is the code language of status. We are in an age when people will sooner confess their sexual secrets—much sooner, in many cases—than their status secrets, whether in the sense of longings and triumphs or humiliations and defeats. And yet we make broad status confessions every day in our response to fashion. No one—no one, that is, except the occasional fugitive or spy, such as Colonel Abel, who was willing to pose for years as a Low Rent photographer in a loft in Brooklyn—no one is able to resist that delicious itch to reveal his own picture of himself through fashion.

24 Goethe once noted that in the last year of his reign Louis XVI took to sleeping on the floor beside his enormous royal bed, because he had begun to feel that the monarchy was an abomination. Down here on the floor he felt closer to the people. How very . . . funky . . . Well, I won't attempt any broad analogies. Nevertheless, it demonstrates one thing. Even when so miserable a fashion as Funky Chic crops up . . . stay alert! use your bean!

(1976)

QUESTIONS

Thought and Structure

1. This essay claims to be about Funky Chic. Is that what it's really about? What is Wolfe's point? Do we know for sure before the ending (paragraphs 23–24)?
2. Why does Wolfe begin this essay with a scene in London? Why do you think he compares Funky Chic to "an infected bat"? And why do you think he brings that first paragraph to a close with a reference to "mob-scene scruffs" from the movies?
3. What is the relationship between politics and "anti-fashion" that Wolfe sets up in paragraph 5 and develops throughout the rest of the essay? What does paragraph 7 have

to do with that relationship? Is the "counter notion" Wolfe outlines in that paragraph the heart of this essay?

4. Paragraphs 8–11 constitute one section of the essay. What is the point of that section? What is Wolfe trying to tell us about a culture's ability to judge its own writers? Is Wolfe arguing indirectly about the importance of "fashion as an essential ingredient of history"?
5. What is Wolfe's point about the New Left's attempt to merge with their working class brothers? What did fashion have to do with the New Left's failure?

Style and Strategy

6. In paragraph 23 Wolfe finally tells us that fashion is the "code language of status." What does he mean by that phrase?
7. Occasionally Wolfe parodies the language of those he's writing about. What is the effect of those parodies?
8. What is Wolfe's tone in paragraphs 2–4 when he is writing about the new debutantes and the "full-grown socialite"? How can you detect Wolfe's attitude in his language?
9. In paragraph 9 Wolfe tells us that two eighteenth-century writers "seemed to sense that fashion is a code, a symbolic vocabulary that offers a subrational but instant and very brilliant illumination of the characters of individuals and even entire periods, especially periods of great turmoil." Given Wolfe's aim in this essay, is this a mildly self-serving assessment he attributes to other writers?
10. Among the many funny things in this essay are Wolfe's lists. Consider the one that closes paragraph 13. Does the list serve more than humor? Compare that list with the very different one in paragraph 14. Which is the more effective? Why?
11. Wolfe actually illustrated this essay with sketches. Do you need sketches to visualize the characters he creates, or does Wolfe paint effective word-pictures?

SUGGESTIONS FOR WRITING

A. Read Wolfe's essay "Radical Chic." Write a short account of how that essay helps you understand this essay. Pay particular attention to paragraphs 5–7 in "Funky Chic," but consider Wolfe's attitude in both essays about those who seem to pander to blacks in response to some fashionable ideal.

B. Identify some campus group that has its own fashion code. Write an essay about that group. Make a point by going beyond mere description to analysis and evaluation.

Honks and Wonks

1 "Dja do da chem-yet?"

2 *Dja do da chem-yet?*

3 —this being the voice of a freshman on the campus of C.C.N.Y. at 139 Street and Convent Avenue the other day asking the question: "Have you done the chemistry assignment yet?" The irony of it is that here is a boy who will probably

do da chem and God knows how many other assignments extremely well and score about a 3.5 academic average over four years and then go to law school at N.Y.U. and get his LL.B.—and then for some reason he can't quite figure out, he never does land the great glistening job he was thinking of at Sullivan & Cromwell or Cravath Swain & Moore. Instead, he ends up in . . . *the neighborhood,* on the south side of Northern Boulevard in Bayside, Queens, in an office he shares with a real-estate man, an old friend of his from here in Bayside—which some of the local wiseacres call Brayside, because of all the "Brooklyn" and "Bronx" accents you hear here in Queens now—

4 *Whaddya mean it's his voice?* He's upgraded the *da* with *the* by now, hasn't he? And hasn't he replaced the *r*'s he's been dropping all these years—well, a few of them, anyway: "This is the first house we evuh owned. We have a gahden an my wife is the gahd-*neh* . . ."

5 . . . here in Brayside . . .

6 The same day, in the little exotic knickknacks boutique on the ground floor of Henri Bendel, on Fifty-seventh Street just west of Fifth: a nice New York girl home from St. Timothy's, St. Tim's, the boarding school in Maryland. She and a girlfriend of hers are walking around town *checking boys,* among other things. It's true! They can tell just by looking at him whether a boy goes to an Eastern prep school or not. Not only that, they can tell *which prep school,* usually St. Paul's or Hotchkiss or Groton or Exeter or Andover, or whatever; just by checking his hair and his clothes. And *certainly* if they can get just one sentence out of him—

7 —like this gorgeous boy here, a tall milk-fed stud in a Brooks yellow shirt and tasseled loafers fumbling over a Cameroons egret-skin hassock with his tweedy-thatchy Prince Charles hanging over his brow and—He's Exeter, or possibly Andover. That is obvious immediately from the tie. His tie is tied properly at the throat, but the ends are slung over his left shoulder, after the fashion. And their eyes meet, and then his eyes shift to her shoes, naturally, and then he looks into her eyes again, into her soul, as it were, and says:

8 "Those are real Guccis, aren't they?"

9 Bliss! It's all there! Past, present, future! Certified! The Guccis, of course, being her loafers, bought at Gucci's, 699 Fifth Avenue, with the authentic Gucci gold chain across the tongue and not any of the countless imitations of the Gucci loafer. A shorthand! A very metonymy! For the whole Eastern boarding-school thing, but more than that—the *honk!* He has it, the Eastern boy's boarding-school *honk,* lifting every vowel—*Those are real Guccis, aren't they?*—up over the roof of his palate and sticking them into his nose and honking them out without moving his lower jaw. And there in one sentence he has said it all, announced that he belongs in the world of the New York *honks,* of the honks who rule and possess all and who every day sound the secret honk of New York wealth and position; the nasal knighthood of the Bobby Kennedys, the Robert Dowlings, Huntington Hartfords, Nelson Rockefellers, Thomas Hovings, Averell Harrimans—for in New York the world is sheerly but secretly divided into the *honks* and the wonks.*—*Dja do da*

---

*Honk is a term of Eastern prep-school derivation, connoting both the nasal quality of the upper-class voice and its presumably authoritative sound, commanding obedience, like the horn of a large

chem-yet?—and this fumbling milk-fed Exeter stud will carry a C-plus straight to Wall Street or mid-Manhattan, for he is *one of us,* you understand—

10 Very ironic—the way New Yorkers at every class level delighted for years in *My Fair Lady* on stage and screen. *My Fair Lady,* of course, is the musical version of Shaw's play *Pygmalion,* about a linguistics professor, Henry Higgins, turning a Cockney flower seller into a lady of Society by upgrading her accent. This silly, stuffy English class system!—whereupon we all settled back and just enjoyed the Cinderella love story. It was just as well. It is probably a good thing no Henry Higgins has come along to wake up New York to the phonetic truth about class and status in this city . . .

11 I have been talking to a man who could do it if he chose to, however—Professor Marshall D. Berger of C.C.N.Y. Berger is one of the country's leading geographical linguists, one of those extraordinary people, like Henry Lee Smith of the old radio days, who can listen to a man for thirty seconds and tell what part of what state he was raised in. Berger is a big husky man. He is fifty-five years old and has lived in New York since he was thirteen. His family moved from Buffalo to Liberty Avenue in the East New York section of Brooklyn, where the kids all thought it was odd to the point of *weird* that he said things like *core*-respondence instead of *cah*-respondence and referred to the well-known game of *go'f* as *gawlf.* He wrote an honors thesis at C.C.N.Y. in 1941 on "The Sources of New York Speech," and then a doctoral dissertation at Columbia on "American-English Pronunciations of Russian-born Immigrants." And so for the past three decades he has been doomed by his own specialty to listen, day in and day out, to New Yorkers unconsciously confessing their ancestry, their status, their social yearnings, every time they open their struggling lips.

12 "This is a very sensitive area you're asking me about," he tells me. "The first thing you'll notice is that people in New York always invent euphemisms when they get on the subject of speech. They don't want to talk about ethnic background or class. So they invent euphemisms. They talk about a 'Brooklyn' accent or a 'Bronx' accent, when what they're really talking about are working-class and lower-middle-class accents found all over the city. Years ago, when Brooklyn was still a big farm, they talked about the 'Bowery' accent."

13 Berger's own voice sounds to me like Radio Announcer Rugged, if you know that sound. In any case—

14 "Even the newspapers, at this late date, observe the taboo. I remember the *Post*'s biographical sketch of a local college president. 'His speech betrays his Bronx

---

1936 Packard. It is not to be confused with "honkie," the black slang word for "white man," which is apparently a variation on a still older slang word, "hunky," originally a term of opprobrium for Hungarian immigrants to the U.S. "Wonk" is an Eastern prep-school term referring to all those who do not have the "honk" voice, i.e., all who are non-aristocratic. There is some conjecture that the term is derived in the natural Anglophile bias of Eastern social life from the English adjective "wonky," meaning unsteady, shaky, feeble, awry, off. In current use, however, "wonk" is a vague, all-inclusive term, closely akin to the terms "wog" and "wop," which are sometimes used at Eastern prep schools to refer to all the rest of humanity.

origins,' they wrote. They were talking about 'lower class' and I suppose the readers get the point, but everyone observes the taboo.

15 "The same goes for 'New York accent.' Nothing pleases most New Yorkers more than to be told that they've 'lost their New York accent.' This is ironic, on the face of it, since New York is one of the great cosmopolitan centers of the world. But what they're thinking about, of course, is class. 'I've lost my lower-class accent,' they're thinking. Incidentally, people who tell you 'I've lost this or that accent' or 'I really don't have any accent any more' are almost invariably fooling themselves. What they've done in most cases is change a couple of obvious vowels or consonants—they may have changed their pronunciation of *example* from *ex-EHM-ple,* which is lower class or lower middle class, to ex-AM-ple, or something of the sort—but they've seldom changed their basic pattern. Even broadcasters."

16 The glorious New York accent!

17 *In 'is town deh's num-uhn doin at da foist of da week, so I was lookin at a likka avatisement an I bough a bah-uhl an relaxed.*

18 All this glorious dropping of *r*'s and *g*'s and *d*'s and muffing of the "voiceless linguadental fricative" (turning the *th* sound into *d*) and reducing vowels until they almost disappear—the usual explanation has been the waves of immigrants to New York in the 1890's and early 1900's. New York, of course, had had waves of immigrants before. But they were chiefly northern Europeans, Irish, German, Dutch, English, and they were middle as well as lower class. The new immigrants were chiefly from Eastern and Southern Europe, and they were lower class; Italians, Ukrainians, Poles, Russians, Greeks, Eastern European Jews, speaking Italian, Greek, Yiddish, Russian, and other Slavic tongues. Part of the "New York accent" that developed was a blend of the new speech patterns with English words.

19 For example, of the new tongues only Greek had the *th* sound. The result was millions of New Yorkers saying *wid* for *with* and *dis* for *this.* Or: in Yiddish a *t* in the middle of a word, like *winter,* was pronounced much more emphatically than it is in English. To this day, the New Yorker who says win-*ta* or fundamen-*t*al is usually someone from a home where Yiddish was spoken. Likewise, the heavily accented *g*, as in *sin-ga* for *singer* and *Lon Gy-land* for *Long Island.* Other innovations were in rhythm. Some of the most flamboyant came from Southern Italian and Sicilian lower-class speech, with the old . . . *So I says to my brudd'n'law, "Awriiide, so whaddya wan me to do, I says to him, whaddya* whaddya *or sump'm?"*

20 These were all foreign flavors coming into New York English, but many of the elements of the "New York accent" had been here for years before the 1890 wave of immigrants; notably, such things as *dis* for *this* and *foist* for *first.* Berger's theory hits on a far more subtle point. Namely, street masculinity. Here were millions of workingclass people massed into lower Manhattan, and their sons fell into the street life. On the street the big thing was physical competition, even if it was only stickball or, today, rock 'em games of basketball on a concrete slab shooting for a basket with a metal backboard and a rim with no net on it . . . In any case, the emphasis was always on the large muscles.

21 For a start, the street thing led to rapid speech in which words are swallowed

whole, *r*'s are dropped, vowels are reduced to the vanishing point, and even some hard consonants disappear. A three-syllable word like *memory* gets reduced to one and a half or less: *m'm'r. Bottle* becomes *bah-uhl, little* becomes *lih-uhl.* A pronunciation like *lih-uhl* is what is known as a glottal stop, in which the double *t* is replaced by what is in fact a miniature cough. It is common in New York City, although in England, among the lower classes, the glottal stop sometimes replaces *p*'s and *k*'s as well as *t*'s. Street masculinity has also led New Yorkers to carry their tongues low in their mouths like dockworker's forearms. The result is some heavy handling of many consonants: *t*'s and *d*'s get dropped or mushed around. Most people's speech patterns are set between the ages of five and fifteen, and they are not likely to revamp them in any thorough way after that without something on the order of dramatic training. Often not even that will do it. A boy growing up on the street may unconsciously scorn the kind of delicate muscle play an upper-class boy learns in articulating words. The fancy work with the tip of the tongue in pronouncing *portraiture,* for example, may strike him as effete, even girlish. It seems to me that when it comes to prep-school *honks* like Averell Harriman, or Thomas Hoving—well, it doesn't matter how many worlds they have conquered or how old they are. As soon as they open their mouths, a bell goes off in the brains of most local-bred New York males: *sissy.* Here are a coupla kids who woulda got *mashed* in the street life. John Lindsay (St. Paul's) suffered continually from this disability when he was mayor of New York; also Bobby Kennedy (Milton Academy). Kennedy took the edge off his Bugs Bunny delicacy with public displays of masculinity of various sorts.

22 Women generally try much harder than men in New York to escape from the rock-bottom working-class accents, but they are often unaware of where the true *honk-wonk* divide lies. They tug and pull on their accents, but often only get them into a form that the upper orders can laugh at in musical comedies. There is the musical-comedy working girl, for example, who is always saying,

23 Oh, Mr. Steiiiiiin, I had such a foiiiiin toiiiime, pronouncing the *i* as if she has wrapped it around a perfume bottle. In real life she is not a lower-class girl at all, but lower middle class.

24 The lower-middle-class girl who says *toiiiime* may also be aware, instinctively, that the muscle-bound tongue accounts for much of the lower-class sound. So she begins using her tongue in a vigorous way in pronouncing all sorts of things—only she overdoes it. She shoves her words all over the place but still doesn't hit them cleanly. This is the common phenomenon of the beautiful girl—"but she ruined it as soon as she opened her mouth." Here she is with her Twiggy eyes, Eve Nelson curly look, a wool jersey mini from Plymouth's, patent-leather pseudo-Guccis from A. S. Beck—and a huge rosy lingual blob rolling around between her orthodontic teeth.

25 The *oi* sound in *toiiiime,* by the way, is not to be confused with the so-called Brooklyn *oi* sound comedians always used to mimic: "Da oily boid gets da woim," "She read da New Yoik *Woild,*" "She lives on Toity-toid Street." These are all examples of dropping *r*'s and substituting *oi* for the *er* sound. Today you are only likely to hear it from older working-class people, such as some of the old cab drivers.

This is one lower-class sound that dates back well before 1890 and is not even a peculiarly New York pronunciation. The same sound—it is actually closer to *ui* than *oi,* more like *fuist* than *foist*—can be heard today in two Southern port cities, Charleston, S.C., and New Orleans, among both upper- and lower-class people. A century ago upper-class New Yorkers used the same pronunciation, only with a slightly flutier intonation. About half a century ago upper-class New Yorkers began changing their pronunciation of *first* from a fluty *fuist* to a Boston or English *fuhst.*

26 This is all *r*-dropping, as I say, and it is one of the most subtle and vital matters in phonetic social climbing in New York. This is where strivers get caught out. The New Yorker who has risen above *wid* and ex*ehm*ple and even *toiiiime* and aspires to true bourgeois status will next start to replace all the *r*'s he or his family have been dropping all his life.

27 The f*ir*st pahty I went to was in my senya yea*rr*—and so forth—not realizing that in the upper orders he envies everybody is busy dropping *r*'s like mad, in the ancient English mode.

28 Many New Yorkers have taken conscious pains to upgrade their accents socially and confidently believe that they now have the neutral accent of a "radio announcer." Three pronunciations almost invariably give them away: *owies* for *always* (lower-class *l*-dropping); *fo'ud* for *forward* (dropping the *r* and the *w*); frank*footer* for *frankfurter* and *footer moment* for *for the moment* (lower-class *r*-dropping).

29 "The fact is," Berger tells me, "that a person who tries to change one or two elements in his speech pattern may end up in worse shape than he thought he was in to begin with. His original pattern may not be prestigious, but it may be very good in terms of its internal arrangements, and he may succeed only in upsetting the equilibrium. Frankly, I like to hear people like Vito Battista and Jimmy Breslin talk. They have working-class accents and they don't care who knows it. They're very confident, that's the main thing. 'Dis is da way I tawk an dis is da way I'm *gonna* tawk, an you betta lissen.' A person's speech pattern is bound up with so many things, his personality, his role, his ambitions, that you can't deal with in isolation or simply in terms of some 'ideal.' "

30 Yes . . . but! . . . suppose your ideal is to get your daughter's picture on the first page of the Wedlock Section of the Sunday *Times,* and not in one of those scrimy little one-paragraphers at the bottom of the page, either—you know those little one-paragraphers, the ones hog-to-jowl up against the Arnold Constable ad with a little headlinette over the paragraph saying

Horlek–Klotkin

Suppose you're after the pole position, up at the top of the page, with a big three-column picture all downy silk with backlighting rising up behind her head like a choir of angels are back there singing and glowing, and a true headline proclaiming:

Satterthwaite–Klotkin
Betrothal Announced

31 One option is to do what Mrs. Bouvier did with her daughter Jacqueline. Namely, pack her off to a Virginia boarding school, whence she can return to New York bearing what the press chooses to call a "little girl voice" but which is known in the secret *honk* world as the "Southern 45-degree Upturn," in which your daughter turns her mouth up 45 degrees at either end, then her eyeballs, and says:

> Ah you rilly an ahkitect?
> Ah you rilly a docta?
> Ah you rilly a senata?

And travel *fuhst* class forever after.

32 The British broad *a* has no social cachet in New York. Quite the opposite, in fact. Unless it is being used by an Englishman, it is taken as a sign of striving for a naïve or Schrafft's Mid-afternoon gentility. The great hangout of the American broad *a* used to be a vast L-shaped Schrafft's restaurant that had entrances on both Madison Avenue and East Fifty-eighth Street. The most genteel-looking matrons imaginable, dressed up in outfits such as three-piece peach wool suits with fur trim at the collars and cuffs and hats with enormous puffed-up crowns of cream-colored velvet, over apricot-colored hair, used to gather in Schrafft's throughout the afternoon. Much of the conversation had to do with stock quotations. You would hear the ladies say to one another:

33 "Ackshewly, I think Automatex is rahther pahst its peak."

34 "Oh, I know. It opened higher this mawning, but ahfter hahlf an hour it was down by two."

35 Such a conversation indicated that they had spent the morning in the spectator seats of the midtown street-level offices of the brokerage houses, in the board rooms, as they are called. This does *not* indicate wealth and position. For one thing, the E.S.A. (Eastern Socially Attractive) way for a woman to refer to her investments (if at all) is to make them seem as if they are *way out there* somewhere and she hasn't the vaguest idea what happens to them. For another, the old parties who hang out in the spectator seats of the midtown brokerage houses are referred to by the brokerage house employees as "board-room bums."

36 For still another, Schrafft's was not exactly the most prestigious place for a woman to eat. But eating at Schrafft's did have a certain secret beauty to it: the much underestimated beauty of American Comfort. The ladies' typical meal at Schrafft's was a cheeseburger, coffee, and a sundae. But such sundaes! Sundaes with towers of ice cream and nuts and sauces and fudge and maraschino cherries of a quality and buttery beauty such as the outside world has never dreamed of! And the secret art of the mid-afternoon at Schrafft's was *pacing* and the *final shape.* It was not enough merely to consume the sundae. No, the idea was to pace one's consumption along with everyone else's at the table, so that one did not finish up more than thirty seconds ahead of anyone else and, furthermore, so that one's very last bite—*the final shape*—would be a *perfect miniature* of the original cheeseburger or of the original sundae, with precisely the same proportions of hamburger, cheese, and bread, or of ice cream, whipped cream, sauce, nuts, and fruit dressing, as the cheeseburger or the sundae had

at the outset when it was first served. And . . . they were *served so beautifully!* The waitresses at Schrafft's, who seemed to be women who had immigrated from Europe as adults, were perhaps the most considerate and sensitive waitresses in the history of America. They understood, tacitly, from long observation, about the final shape and its importance. If a woman had eaten two thirds of her cheeseburger but had eaten it incorrectly, so that the bread and the hamburger were left in the form of a perfect final shape, as if there were a perfect miniburger two inches in diameter on the plate, except that the cheese was all gone—she had only to ask for more cheese, and one of these waitresses, these angels, these nurses sent by Our Lady of Comfort, would take the cheeseburger, two thirds eaten, back to the kitchen and have a perfectly proportioned two-inch slab of cheese placed—but not merely *placed*—no!—*broiled!—broiled onto the remains!*—and they would bring it back with a smile, as if to say, "There! We understand, you and I!"

37 "Oh, I cahn't thank you enough, my dear!"

38 Now there, I submit, is Beauty. It is not, however, prestige.

39 The true social competitors among New York's older women gather earlier, about 1 P.M., for the Status Lunch, and the accents are quite different. The Status Lunch is a peculiarly New York institution in this country, although the same thing goes on in a less manic way in Paris and London. At the Status Lunch women who have reached the upper social orders gather during the week so that they may demonstrate and celebrate their position. They may be at the top through family background or marriage or other good fortune. In any case, they are mostly in their late thirties or in their forties or early fifties, starving themselves to near perfection in order to retain . . . *the look* . . . with just a few piano wires showing in their necks and forearms and the backs of their hands, owing to the deterioration of the body packing. Or perhaps they have begun to let themselves go into that glorious creamy Camembert look in which the flesh on the shoulders and the upper back and the backs of their arms looks like it could be shaped with a butter knife. They are Pucci'd and Gucci'd up to their temporal fossae, Pucci in the dress, Gucci in the shoes and handbag—the Pucci-Gucci girls!—yes. They start pulling into Status Lunch restaurants in the East and West Fifties, such as La Grenouille, Lutèce, Orsini's, about 1 P.M. and make a great point of calling the maître d' by his first name, which at La Grenouille is Paul, then peer into that ocher golden-mirrored gloom to case the important tables, which are along the walls in the front room, by way of weighing the social weight of today's gathering, as it were. Then they suck in their cheeks—near perfection!—and begin the entrance, looking straight ahead, as if they couldn't be more oblivious of who else is there, but waiting, hopefully, for the *voice*—

40 Dah-ling dah-ling dah-ling.

41 There it is!—the *dah-ling* voice, a languid weak baritone, not a man's voice, you understand, but a woman's. *The New York Social Baritone,* like that of a forty-eight-year-old male dwarf who just woke up after smoking three packs of Camels the day before, and then the social kisses, right out in the middle of the restaurant, with everybody locking heads, wincing slightly from the concentration on not actually pressing the lips, which would smudge the lipstick, or maybe even the powder covering the electrolysis lines above the lips, with the Social Baritone *dah-ling* voices beginning to bray softly in each other's ears, like an ensemble of

cellos—*we are all here!* This voice cannot be achieved without some ten or fifteen years of smoking cigarettes and drinking whiskey or gin, which literally smoke-cures and pickles the vocal cords and changes them from soprano to the golden richness of baritone. It takes, on the average, at least 13,000 cigarettes over a ten-year period. In pronunciation, the *dah-ling* voice seeks to set itself off from both the urgency (what's going to hit the fan next?) of the lower-class female voice and the usual efficiency (must pronounce everything *correctly*) of the middle-class female voice with a languor and a nasal *honk,* connoting ease, leisure, insouciance. Two techniques are the most vital: dropping *r*'s, as in *dahling,* and pronouncing most accented vowels with a sigh thrown in, particularly the *a*'s and *o*'s, as in—

42 Dahling, I caaaaan't [but not *cahnt*]. I just did the Mehhhht and, you know, the sets were stunnnnnning, Myron le Poove I think he is, but it was the most boooooring-sawt-of-thing—with the vowels coming out of the nose in gasps as if she is going to run out of gas at any moment.

43 And *yet!* She has worked on this voice for ten years, producing her deep rich pre-cancerous vocal cords, but it gives off the deadly odor: *parvenu.* The *dahling* voice, heard so often at Status Lunches and country weekends and dinner parties where two wineglasses are used, is almost invariably that of the striver who has come upon the upper-class *honk* voice too late in life. She has picked up a number of key principles: the nasality, the languor, the oiliness, the *r*-dropping. But she does not understand the underlying principle, which is historical. Her attention is fixed upon New York, and as a result her voice takes on a New York theatrical manner, a staginess, in the Tallulah Bankhead mode, which is show-business upper class, not *honk* upper class. The certified *honk* upper-class woman in New York has her attention fixed, phonetically although unconsciously, on Boston and the Richmond-Charleston social axis of the South.

44 The secret here, as among New York male *honks,* is the boarding school. The outstanding girls' boarding schools are oriented, socially, toward the nineteenth-century upper-class traditions of Boston and the South, which, until after World War I, had far more social clout than the upper-class world of New York. Miss Hall's, Miss Porter's, Westover, and Dana Hall are all girls' boarding schools where an old Boston upper-class tradition dominates, just as Foxcroft (Jackie Kennedy's school), Madeira, Chatham Hall, Garrison Forest, and St. Catherine's are still schools where the Richmond-Charleston tradition dominates. New York girls bring back the Boston or Southern sound in a somewhat crude form, but nevertheless it is not a New York sound. It is neither a street sound nor a theatrical sound nor an English sound. Its components are nasality, languor, oiliness, *r*-dropping—but with shorter, clearer, more open vowels than the *dahling* voice. If the girl has gone to a Southern school, like Jackie Kennedy, she will tend to have a soft, childish voice. If she has gone to a "Boston" school, the speech will be much brisker and yet still languid and oily, as if lubricated ball bearings were pouring out of both nostrils.

45 In the nineteenth century, the New York upper classes were much more directly influenced by Boston and the South. Boston overshadowed New York in many phases of business, finance, and law and was unquestionably New York's social superior in the area of Culture and the Arts. The New York upper classes had close ties with the Southern upper classes because of the shipping trade. Southern planters

came to New York continually for financing, and packet boats loaded with cotton came to New York on the way to England. About 1940, linguists at C.C.N.Y. made recordings of the voices of old New Yorkers, people in their seventies and eighties, most of them upper-middle-class, in order to get an idea of what speech patterns were like in New York in the nineteenth century. They tended to speak in a medley of Boston and Southern accents. One old party reminisced about an old structure on Twenty-third Street as "the old struk-cha on Twenty-thuid Street," with *struk-cha* a combination of the clipped Boston accent of *struk* and the Boston *r*-dropping of *cha;* and *Twenty-thuid* a case of Southern-style upper-class *r*-dropping, substituting a diphthong vowel sound, *ui,* for the standard *er* sound in *third.* Socially, New York was considered an exciting but crude town, and New York's upper classes felt the sense of inferiority and preferred to sound as if they came from some better spot. Even today some *honks* still use the Southern upper-class pronunciation of *thuid* for *third,* although most have shifted over the past half century to a more Bostonian *thuhd.* They still drop the *r* in any case.

46 Boys as well as girls, of course, learn the *honk* voice in prep school, and the same principle applies: the voice should suggest a languor that will separate one from the lower orders. The lower jaw is moved much less than in ordinary speech and the words are lifted up over the palate and secreted through the nose rather than merely blurted out of the mouth. The rigidity of the jaw may resemble an affliction to a person who has never watched someone speak this way before. In fact, the E.S.A. accent that is often heard on the north shore of Long Island in communities such as Huntington and Oyster Bay is known as Locust Valley Lockjaw. The same voice is known in Riverdale as Spotted Bostonian. Socially ambitious people in Riverdale may even try to keep their voices up by spending their summers in the select vacation communities of the Boston upper orders on the Maine shore.

47 *Honk* voices may fall anywhere in a range from Boston-Honk to New York-Honk. Leaning toward the Boston-Honk would be the late Bobby Kennedy (Milton Academy), Averell Harriman (Groton), the late Christian Herter (St. Paul's), and the late John F. Kennedy (Choate). The worst liabilities of the *honk* voice to a politician, quite aside from the class overtones, are the monotony and the delicacy and weakness brought about by this sort of voice's emphasis on languor and refinement. Bobby Kennedy, like his brother John, had great difficulty in conventional oratory from a rostrum. His voice was trained in delicacy rather than strength and tended to turn shrill at the very moment when the heavy chord should have been hit. He always sounded like a seventeen-year-old valedictorian with the goslings. In the case of Harriman and Herter, it was the nerve-gas monotony of the *honk* voice that caused them trouble as much as anything else.

48 The perfect New York *honk* voice is Huntington Hartford's (St. Paul's). Other notable New York *honks:* Nelson Rockefeller and the late Robert Dowling, the real-estate and investment tycoon. Their type of voice has the nasality of the *honk* voice without the delicacy of the same voice as practiced by Bobby Kennedy or even former New York Mayor John Lindsay (St. Paul's). The explanation, most likely, is that both Rockefeller and Dowling went to prep school in the city, Rockefeller at the Lincoln School and Dowling at Cutler. Rockefeller has gradually coarsened his voice for his public appearances. It is a kind of *honk* with a knish jammed in it, although he uses much more a conventional soft *honk* in private conversation. One

of the ironies of the 1962 race for governor was that Rockefeller's upper-class voice with a knish in it was so much more effective among Low Rent voters in New York than that of his upper-middle-class opponent, Robert Morgenthau. As a result of his time at Deerfield Academy, Morgenthau's voice had taken on a kind of *honk* subtlety and delicacy that made him, not Rockefeller, sound like the Fauntleroy in the plot.

49 Lindsay tried to come down off the *honk* accent somewhat by inserting *r*'s where they would ordinarily be dropped, making his speech sound almost middle-class at points. He also referred to St. Paul's as his "high school" from time to time, as if it were nothing more than a kind of Stuyvesant or DeWitt Clinton unaccountably set out in Concord, New Hampshire. This was a laugh and a half to all old "Paulies," who are generally fond of St. Paul's reputation as the most snobbish school in America.

50 Even Amy Vanderbilt tried to roughen up her female *honk* accent by adding middle-class *r*'s, perhaps in an unconscious rub-off from the various bourgeois commercial interests with which she was involved. In general, the public spotlight tends to make *honks* nervous about their voices, whether they are politicians or performers or merely celebrities. Very few have the self-assurance to just keep pouring it on, the way Roosevelt did:

51 *I hate wooouuggggggghawwwwwwwwwwwwgggggghhhhhhh*—meaning *war.*

52 Boys today at St. Paul's, Groton, Middlesex, Hotchkiss, Deerfield, St. Mark's, St. George's, Exeter, Andover, and the rest of them are strangely goosy about it themselves. They are apparently hung up on the masculinity thing, as they might put it, rather preferring to have both the social certification of the languid, delicate *honk* voice and the ruggedness and virility of various street voices. The upshot has been that they have kept the *honk* voice but picked up the dope argot of Greenwich Village, the Lower East Side, and other lower-middle-class bohemias, studding the most improbable conversations with the inarticulate litany of "like-I-mean-you-know-man" intoned in a kind of Bugs Bunny Bobby Kennedy *honk* spew of lubricated BB's:

53 Laiike, nyew nyeoow, man, ai mean, Fisha's Island is a groove and a gas compaaaiiihed to Deeah Island and, like, now, ai mean, Wildwood, Nyew Juhsey, is prackly a mindblowagggh . . .

54 And the whole *honk* world sinks, *wonking,* into a vast gummy Welt-smeared nostalgia for the mud.

(1976)

QUESTIONS

Thought and Structure

1. In the introduction (paragraphs 1–10), Wolfe presents two different groups of people—those from the New York boroughs and those from within the city, the Fifth-Avenue crowd. He devotes only a small section of that introduction to the first group. Why? Do you suppose he actually knows more about one group than the other?

2. At the end of paragraph 10, Wolfe says that it is a "good thing no Henry Higgins has come along to wake up New York to the phonetic truth about class and status in this city . . ." Is Wolfe playing Henry Higgins in this essay? If so, what is his point about class and status and language?
3. In paragraphs 11–15, Wolfe appeals to authority; he calls on Professor Marshall D. Berger of C.C.N.Y. to present evidence. Is this inclusion of Berger's testimony effective? Why? What if he had called on a linguistics professor at Berkeley, would that have been as effective? Is it important that Wolfe actually quotes Berger? (Notice the quotation marks.)
4. In paragraphs 18–19, Wolfe offers a partial explanation for the working-class accent. Is that explanation convincing? What about the explanation in paragraph 20 about masculinity? Is that more convincing?
5. Paragraphs 22–28 focus on women and on social climbing. Is Wolfe wise to yoke those two? Is he getting closer to the point of his essay in these paragraphs? Paragraph 29 shifts back to certain kinds of men. What is the point of that paragraph?
6. Do you see paragraph 30 as an important transitional paragraph from one social group to another? Explain.
7. What is Wolfe's point in paragraphs 32–38? Why does he turn away from language to other matters?
8. Still focusing on women in paragraphs 39–43, Wolfe turns to both manners (or customized behavior) and voice. What is the point of this section of the essay?
9. In paragraph 47 Wolfe focuses on well-bred politicians and the liabilities of the honk voice. Why does he do that? Do paragraphs 47–52 take us back to earlier paragraphs? Why and how?
10. Do paragraphs 53–54 constitute a typical conclusion, taking us back through the essay, summing things up? Or does Wolfe introduce a new but related idea? If we go back to examine the entire essay in light of the last two paragraphs, do we make new discoveries about meaning? Explain.

Style and Strategy

11. Throughout the essay Wolfe has to create accents with unorthodox spellings. How effective is he in creating different voices?
12. In this very technical argument about language, Wolfe manages to keep us interested. How does he do that? Does it have anything to do with Wolfe's own invented language: "the nasal knighthood of the Bobby Kennedys," "the kind of delicate muscle play an upper-class boy learns in articulating words," "phonetic social climbing," "glorious creamy Camembert look." Are those phrases particularly effective? Can you find others?
13. Look at *"the final shape"* sentence, the very long one, in paragraph 36. Does that sentence itself amuse you? Can you find other long sentences in the essay that are effective? What about the second sentence in paragraph 41?

SUGGESTIONS FOR WRITING

A. Look carefully at the way Wolfe uses clothing to create character in both "Funky Chic" and "Honks and Wonks." Write a short essay about your observations; convince your reader that Wolfe uses clothing in special ways to achieve special effects.

B. Create a scene that will pinpoint for your reader the way language and social status go hand-in-hand in your neighborhood. Make the scene dramatic and include dialogue so that we can get a sense of the way people talk.

C. In one paragraph, summarize "Honks and Wonks" using standard English.

D. Having read his essays in this anthology, write a two-page character sketch of Tom Wolfe based solely on those essays. Do no biographical research. Cite only evidence from the essays. Try to give us a sense of the man himself, his interests, his obsessions, his special way of seeing the world.

"Styrofoam Peanuts" from *The Bonfire of the Vanities*

1 Sherman turned over onto his left side, but soon his left knee developed an ache, as if the weight of his right leg were cutting off the circulation. His heart was beating a little fast. He turned over onto his right side. Somehow the heel of his right hand ended up under his right cheek. It felt as if he needed it to support his head, because the pillow wasn't enough, but that made no sense, and anyhow, how could he possibly get to sleep with his hand under his head? A little fast, that was all . . . It wasn't running away . . . He turned back onto his left side and then rolled over flat on his stomach, but that put a strain on the small of his back, and so he rolled back over on his right side. He usually slept on his right side. His heart was going faster now. But it was an even beat. He still had it under control.

2 He resisted the temptation to open his eyes and check out the intensity of the light under the Roman shades. The line gradually brightened toward dawn, so that you could always tell when it was getting on toward 5:30 or 6:00 at this time of year. Suppose it was brightening already! But that couldn't be. It couldn't be more than three o'clock, 3:30 at the worst. But maybe he had slept for an hour or so without knowing it!—and suppose the lines of light—

3 He could resist no longer. He opened his eyes. Thank God; still dim; so he was still safe.

4 With that—his heart bolted away from him. It began pounding at a terrific rate and with terrific force, trying to escape from his rib cage. It made his whole body shake. What did it matter whether he had a few more hours to lie here writhing on his bed or whether the heat of the dawn had already cooked up under the shades and the time had come—

5 *I'm going to jail.*

6 With his heart pounding and his eyes open, he was now terribly conscious of being alone in this vast bed. Billows of silk hung down from the ceiling at the four corners of the bed. More than $125 a yard the silk had cost. It was Judy's Decorator approximation of a royal bedchamber from the eighteenth century. *Royal!* What a mockery it was of himself, a throbbing lump of flesh and fear cowering in bed in the dead of the night!

7 *I'm going to jail.*

8 If Judy had been here next to him, if she hadn't gone to bed in the guest bedroom, he would have put his arms around her and held on for dear life. He wanted to embrace her, longed for it—

9 And with the next breath: *What good would that do?* None whatsoever. It would make him feel even weaker and more helpless. Was she asleep? What if he walked into the guest room? She often slept flat on her back, like a recumbent statue, like the statue of . . . He couldn't remember whose statue it was. He could see the slightly yellowish marble and the folds in the sheet that covered the body—someone famous, beloved and dead. Well, down the hall Campbell was asleep, for sure. He knew that much. He had looked in her room and watched her for a minute, as if this were the last time he would ever see her. She slept with her lips slightly parted and her body and soul utterly abandoned to the security and peace of her home and family. She had gone to sleep almost at once. Nothing that he had said to her was real . . . *arrest* . . . *newspapers* . . . "You'll be in history?" . . . If only he knew what she was thinking! Supposedly children picked up things in more ways than you knew, from the tone of your voice, the look on your face . . . But Campbell seemed to know only that something sad and exciting was about to happen, and her father was unhappy. Utterly insulated from the world . . . at the bosom of her family . . . her lips slightly parted . . . just down the hall . . . For her sake he had to pull himself together. And for the moment, anyway, he did. His heart slowed down. He began to take command of his body again. He would be strong for her, if for no one else on earth. *I am a man.* When he had to fight, he had fought. He had fought in the jungle, and he had won. The furious moment when he thrust the tire at the . . . brute . . . The brute was sprawled on the pavement . . . *Henry!* . . . If he had to, he would fight again. How bad could it be?

10 Last night, as long as he was talking to Killian, he had it worked out in his mind. It wasn't going to be so bad. Killian explained every step. It was a formality, not a pleasant formality, but not like really going to jail, either. It would not be like an ordinary arrest. Killian would see to that, Killian and his friend Fitzgibbon. A contract. Not like an ordinary arrest, not like an ordinary arrest; he clung to this phrase, "not like an ordinary arrest." Like what, then? He tried to picture how it was going to be, and before he knew it, his heart was racing, fleeing, panicked, amok with fear.

11 Killian had arranged it so that the two detectives, Martin and Goldberg, would drive by and pick him up about 7:30 on their way to work on the 8:00 A.M. shift in the Bronx. They both lived on Long Island, and they drove to the Bronx every day, and so they would make a detour and drive by and pick him up on Park Avenue. Killian would be here when they arrived, and he would ride up to the Bronx with him and be there when they *arrested* him—and this was *special treatment.*

12 Lying there in bed, with cascades of $125-a-yard silk at every corner, he closed his eyes and tried to think it through. He would get in the car with the two detectives, the small one and the fat one. Killian would be with him. They would go up the FDR Drive to the Bronx. The detectives would get him to Central Booking first thing, as the new shift began, and he would go through the process first, before the day's buildup of cases. Central Booking—but what was it? Last night

it had been a name Killian had used so matter-of-factly. But now, lying here, he realized he had no idea what it would look like. The process—what process? *Being arrested!* Despite everything Killian had tried to explain, it was unimaginable. He would be fingerprinted. *How?* And his fingerprints would be transmitted to Albany by a computer. Why? To make sure there were no warrants for his arrest already outstanding. But surely they knew better! Until the report from Albany came back, via the computer, he would have to wait in the detention pens. Pens! That was the word Killian kept using. *Pens!*—for what sort of animals! As if reading his mind, Killian had told him not to worry about the things you read about concerning jails. The unmentioned term was *homosexual rape.* The pens were temporary cells for people who had been arrested and were awaiting arraignment. Since arrests in the early daylight hours were rare, he might very well have the place to himself. After the report came back, he would go upstairs to appear before a judge. *Upstairs!* But what did that mean? Upstairs from what? He would plead not guilty and be released on $10,000 bail—tomorrow—in a few hours—when the dawn cooks up the light beneath the shade—

13 *I'm going to jail—as the man who ran down a black honor student and left him to die!*

14 His heart was beating violently now. His pajamas were wet with perspiration. He had to stop thinking. He had to close his eyes. He had to sleep. He tried to focus on an imaginary point between his eyes. Behind his eyelids . . . little movies . . . curling forms . . . a pair of puffy sleeves . . . They turned into a shirt, his own white shirt. Nothing too good, Killian said, because the holding pens might be filthy. But a suit and tie, of course, nonetheless, since this was not an ordinary arrest, not an ordinary arrest . . . The old blue-gray tweed suit, the one made in England . . . a white shirt, a solid navy tie or maybe the medium-blue tie with the pin dots . . . No, the navy tie, which would be dignified but not at all showy—*for going to jail in!*

15 He opened his eyes. The silk billowed down from the ceiling. "Get a grip on yourself!" He said it out loud. Surely this was not actually about to happen. *I'm going to jail.*

16 About 5:30, with the light turning yellow under the shade, Sherman gave up on the idea of sleep, or even rest, and got up. To his surprise, it made him feel a little better. His heartbeat was rapid, but he had the panic under control. It helped to be doing something, if only taking a shower and putting on the blue-gray tweed suit and the navy necktie . . . *my jail outfit.* The face he saw in the mirror didn't look as tired as he felt. The Yale chin; he *looked* strong.

17 He wanted to eat breakfast and be out of the apartment before Campbell got up. He wasn't sure he could be brave enough in front of her. He also didn't want to have to talk to Bonita. It would be too awkward. As for Judy, he didn't know what he wanted. He didn't want to see the look in her eye, which was the numb look of someone betrayed but also shocked and frightened. Yet he wanted *his wife* with him. In fact, he had scarcely had a glass of orange juice before Judy arrived in the kitchen, dressed and ready for the day. She hadn't had much more sleep than he had. A

moment later Bonita came in from the servants' wing and quietly began fixing them breakfast. Soon enough Sherman was glad Bonita was there. He didn't know what to say to Judy. With Bonita present he obviously wouldn't be able to say much. He could barely eat. He had three cups of coffee in hopes of clearing his head.

18 At 7:15 the doorman called up to say that Mr. Killian was downstairs. Judy walked with Sherman out into the entry gallery. He stopped and looked at her. She attempted a smile of encouragement, but it gave her face a look of terrible weariness. In a low but firm voice, she said: "Sherman, be brave. Remember who you are." She opened her mouth, as if she was about to say something more; but she didn't.

19 And that was it! That was the best she could do! I try to see more in you, Sherman, but all that's left is the shell, your dignity!

20 He nodded. He couldn't get a word out. He turned and went to the elevator.

21 Killian was standing under the marquee just outside the front door. He was wearing a chalk-striped gray suit, brown suede shoes, a brown fedora. (How dare he be so debonair on the day of my doom?) Park Avenue was an ashy gray. The sky was dark. It looked as if it was about to rain . . . Sherman shook hands with Killian, then moved down the sidewalk about twenty feet, to be out of earshot of the doorman.

22 "How do you feel?" asked Killian. He asked it the way you ask a sick person.

23 "Top-notch," said Sherman, with a morose smile.

24 "It's not gonna be so bad. I talked to Bernie Fitzgibbon again last night, after I talked to you. He's gonna get you through there as fast as possible. Fucking Abe Weiss, he's a wet finger in the wind. All this publicity has him terrified. Otherwise not even an idiot like him would do this."

25 Sherman just shook his head. He was far beyond speculation on the mentality of Abe Weiss. *I'm going to jail!*

26 Out of the corner of his eye, Sherman saw a car pull up alongside them, and then he saw the detective, Martin, at the wheel. The car was a two-door Oldsmobile Cutlass, reasonably new, and Martin had on a jacket and tie, and so perhaps the doorman would not figure it out. Oh, they would know soon enough, all the doormen and matrons and money managers and general partners and bond traders and CEO's and all their private-school children and nannies and governesses and housekeepers, all the inhabitants of this social fortress. But that anyone might see he was being *led away by the police* was more than he could bear.

27 The car had stopped just far enough away from the door of the building that the doorman didn't come out. Martin got out and opened the door and pulled the seat back forward, so that Sherman and Killian could get into the rear. Martin smiled at Sherman. *The smile of the tormentor!*

28 "Hey, Counselor!" Martin said to Killian. Very cheery about it, too. "Bill Martin," he said, and he held out his hand, and he and Killian shook hands. "Bernie Fitzgibbon tells me you guys worked together."

29 "Oh yeah," said Killian.

30 "Bernie's a pistol."

31 "Worse than that. I could tell ya some stories."

32 Martin chuckled, and Sherman experienced a small spurt of hope. Killian knew this man Fitzgibbon, who was the chief of the Homicide Bureau of the Bronx

District Attorney's Office, and Fitzgibbon knew Martin, and now Martin knew Killian . . . and Killian—Killian was his protector! . . . Just before Sherman bent down to get into the back seat, Martin said, "Watch your clothes back there. There're these fucking—'scuse my French—Styrofoam peanuts back there. My kid opened up a box, and all these white *pea*nuts they pack things in got all over the place, and they stick to your clothes and every other goddamned thing."

33 Once he bent down, Sherman saw the fat one with the mustache, Goldberg, sitting in the front passenger seat. He had a bigger smile on.

34 "Sherman." He said it the way you'd say hello or good morning. Most amiably. And the whole world froze, congealed. *My first name!* A servant . . . a slave . . . a prisoner . . . Sherman said nothing. Martin introduced Killian to Goldberg. More cheery lodge talk.

35 Sherman was sitting behind Goldberg. There were, indeed, white Styrofoam packing peanuts all over the place. Two had attached themselves to Sherman's pants leg. One was practically on top of his knee. He picked it off and then had trouble getting it off his finger. He could feel another one under his bottom and began fishing around for that.

36 They had barely started off, heading up Park Avenue toward Ninety-sixth Street and the entrance to the FDR Drive, when Goldberg turned around in his seat and said, "You know, I got a daughter in high school, and she loves to read, and she was reading this book, and this outfit you work for—Pierce & Pierce, right?—they were in it."

37 "Is that so?" Sherman managed to say. "What was the book?"

38 "I think it was *Murder Mania.* Something like that."

39 *Murder Mania?* The book was called *Merger Mania.* Was he trying to torment him with some hideous joke?

40 *"Murder Mania!"* said Martin. "F'r Chrissake, Goldberg, it's *Mer-ger Mania.*" Then over his shoulder to Killian and Sherman: "It's great to have a partner who's a intellectual." To his partner: "What shape's a book, Goldberg? A circle or a triangle?"

41 "I'll show you what shape," said Goldberg, extending the middle finger of his right hand. Then he twisted around toward Sherman again: "Anyway, she really liked that book, and she's only in high school. She says she wants to work on Wall Street when she finishes college. Or that's this week's plan, anyway."

42 This one, Goldberg, also! The same appalling malapert slave-master friendliness! Now he was supposed to *like* the two of them! Now that the game was over, and he had lost, and he belonged to them, he should hold nothing against them. He should admire them. They had their hooks in a Wall Street investment banker, and what was he now? Their catch! Their quarry! Their prize pet! In an Oldsmobile Cutlass! *The brutes* from the outer boroughs—the sort of people you saw heading on Fifty-eighth Street or Fifty-ninth Street toward the Queensboro Bridge—fat young men with drooping mustaches, like Goldberg . . . and now he belonged to them.

43 At Ninety-third Street, a doorman was helping an old woman out the door and onto the sidewalk. She wore a caracal overcoat. It was the sort of very formal black fur coat you never saw anymore. A long happy insulated life on Park Ave-

nue! Heartlessly, Park Avenue, *le tout New York,* would go on living its everyday life.

44 "All right," Killian said to Martin, "let's get it straight exactly what we're gonna do here. We're going in the 161st Street entrance, right? And then we go downstairs from there, and the Angel takes Sherman—Mr. McCoy—straight into fingerprinting. The Angel's still there?"

45 "Yeah," said Martin, "he's still there, but we gotta go in around the side, through the outside door to Central Booking."

46 "What for?"

47 "That's my orders. The zone captain's gonna be there, and the press is gonna be there."

48 "The *press!*"

49 "That's right. And we gotta have cuffs on him by the time we get there."

50 "Are you shitting me? I talked to Bernie last night. He gave me his word. There's gonna be no bullshit."

51 "I don't know about Bernie. This is Abe Weiss. This is the way Weiss wants it, and I got my orders straight from the zone captain. This arrest is supposed to be by the book. You're getting a break as it is. You know what they were talking about, don't you? They wanted to bring the fucking press to his apartment and cuff him there."

52 Killian glowered at Martin. "Who toldja to do this?"

53 "Captain, Crowther."

54 "When?"

55 "Last night. He called me at home. Listen, you know Weiss. What can I tell ya?"

56 "This . . . is . . . not . . . right," said Killian. "I had Bernie's word. This . . . is . . . very . . . wrong. You don't pull this kinda thing. This . . . is . . . not . . . right."

57 Both Martin and Goldberg turned around and looked at him.

58 "I'm not gonna forget this," said Killian, "and I'm not happy."

59 "Ayyyyy . . . whaddaya whaddaya," said Martin. "Don't blame it on us, because it's all the same to us one way or the other. Your beef is with Weiss."

60 They were now out on the FDR Drive, heading north toward the Bronx. It had begun to rain. The morning traffic was already backing up on the other side of the railing that divided the expressway, but there was nothing holding them back on this side of the road. They approached a footbridge that arched over the river from the Manhattan side to an island out in the middle. The trestle had been painted a hot heliotrope purple in a burst of euphoria in the 1970s. The false hopefulness of it depressed Sherman profoundly.

61 *I'm going to jail!*

62 Goldberg craned around again. "Look," he said, "I'm sorry, but I gotta put on the cuffs. I can't be fucking around with 'em when we get there."

63 "This is pure bullshit," said Killian. "I hope you know that."

64 "It's the lawwwr!" said Goldberg plaintively. He put an *r* on the end of *law.* "If you bring somebody in on a felony, you're supposed to put on the cuffs. I'll grant you there's times I ain't done that, but the fucking zone captain is gonna be there."

65 Goldberg held up his right hand. He held a pair of handcuffs. "Give me your wrists," he said to Sherman. "We can get this over with."

66 Sherman looked at Killian. The muscles in Killian's jaws were bunched up. "Yeah, go ahead!" he said to Sherman with the sort of high-pitched emphasis that insinuates, "Someone is gonna *pay* for this!"

67 Martin said, "I tell you what. Why don't you take your jacket off. He'll cuff you in front instead of in back, and you can hold the jacket over your wrists, and you won't even be able to see the fucking cuffs."

68 The way he said it, it was as if the four of them were friends, all pulling together against an unkind fate. For an instant, that made Sherman feel better. He struggled out of his tweed jacket. Then he leaned forward and put his hands through the gap between the two front seats.

69 They were crossing a bridge . . . perhaps the Willis Avenue Bridge . . . he didn't really know what bridge it was. All he knew was that it was a bridge, and it went across the Harlem River, away from Manhattan. Goldberg snapped the cuffs onto his wrists. Sherman sank back into the seat and looked down, and there he was, in manacles.

70 The rain was coming down harder. They reached the other end of the bridge. Well, here it was, the Bronx. It was like an old and decrepit part of Providence, Rhode Island. There were some massive but low buildings, grimy and moldering, and board weary black streets running up and down slopes. Martin drove down a ramp and onto another expressway.

71 Sherman reached around to his right to retrieve his jacket and put it over the handcuffs. When he realized that he had to move both hands in order to pick up the coat, and when the effort caused the manacles to cut into his wrists, a flood of humiliation . . . and *shame!* . . . swept over him. This was himself, the very self who existed in a unique and sacrosanct and impenetrable crucible at the center of his mind, who was now in manacles . . . in the Bronx . . . Surely this was a hallucination, a nightmare, a trick of the mind, and he would pull back a translucent layer . . . and . . . The rain came down harder, the windshield wipers were sweeping back and forth in front of the two policemen.

72 With the handcuffs on, he couldn't drape the jacket over his wrists. It kept balling up. So Killian helped him. There were three or four Styrofoam peanuts on the jacket. There were two more on his pants leg. He couldn't possibly get to them with his fingers. Perhaps Killian . . . But what did it matter?

73 Up ahead, to the right . . . Yankee Stadium! . . . An anchor! Something to hold on to! He had been to Yankee Stadium! For World Series games, nothing more . . . Nevertheless, he had been there! It was part of a sane and decent world! It was not this . . . Congo!

74 The car went down a ramp, leaving the expressway. The road went around the base of the huge bowl of the stadium. It wasn't forty feet away. There was a fat man with white hair wearing a New York Yankees warm-up jacket standing outside what looked like a little office door. Sherman had been to the World Series with Gordon Schoenburg, whose company had box seats for the season, and Gordon had served a picnic supper between the fifth and sixth innings from one of those wicker picnic baskets with all the compartments and stainless-steel utensils, and he

had served sourdough bread and pâté and caviar to everybody, which had infuriated some drunks, who saw it from the walkway behind and started saying some very abusive things and repeating a word they heard Gordon say. The word was *really*, which they repeated over and over as *rilly*. "Oh, rilly?" they said. "Oh, rilly?" It was the next thing to calling Gordon a faggot, and Sherman always remembered that, even though no one spoke about it afterward. The abuse! The pointless hostility! The resentment! Martin and Goldberg! They were all Martins and Goldbergs.

75 Then Martin turned onto a very wide street, and they went underneath some elevated subway tracks and headed up a hill. There were mostly dark faces on the sidewalk, hurrying along in the rain. They all looked so dark and sodden. A lot of gray decrepit little shops, like the decaying downtowns of cities all across America, like Chicago's, Akron's, Allentown's . . . The Daffyteria, the Snooker deli, Korn Luggage, the B. & G. Davidoff Travel & Cruise . . .

76 The windshield wipers swept aside sheets of rain. At the top of the hill there was an imposing limestone building that appeared to take up an entire block, the sort of monumental pile you see in the District of Columbia. Across the way, on the side of a low office building, was a prodigious sign reading, ANGELO COLON, U.S. CONGRESS. They went over the crest of the hill. What he saw down the slope on the other side shocked him. It was not merely decrepit and sodden but ruined, as though in some catastrophe. To the right an entire block was nothing but a great hole in the ground with cyclone fencing around it and raggedy catalpa trees sticking up here and there. At first it appeared to be a junkyard. Then he could see it was a parking lot, a vast pit for cars and trucks, apparently unpaved. Over to the left was a new building, modern in the cheap sense of the word, quite dreary-looking in the rain.

77 Martin stopped and waited for the traffic coming the other way, so he could turn left.

78 "What's that?" Sherman asked Killian, motioning toward the building with his head.

79 "The Criminal Courts Building."

80 "That's where we're going?"

81 Killian nodded yes and then stared straight ahead. He looked tense. Sherman could feel his heart going to town. It palpitated every now and then.

82 Instead of pulling up in front of the building, Martin drove down an incline to one side. There, near a mean little metal door, was a line of men and, behind them, a promiscuous huddle of people, thirty or forty of them, most of them white, all hunched over in the rain wrapped in ponchos, thermal jackets, dirty raincoats. A welfare office, thought Sherman. No, a soup kitchen. They looked like the people he had seen lined up for the soup-kitchen lunches at the church at Madison Avenue and Seventy-first Street. But then their desperate beaten eyes all turned, as if on a command, toward the car—toward *him*—and all at once he was aware of the cameras.

83 The mob seemed to shake itself, like a huge filthy sprawling dog, and came bounding toward the car. Some of them were running, and he could see television cameras jouncing up and down.

84 "Jesus Christ," Martin said to Goldberg. "Get out and get that door open or we'll never even get him out of the fucking car."

85 Goldberg jumped out. Immediately the shaggy sodden people were everywhere. Sherman could no longer see the building. He could only see the mob closing in on the car.

86 Killian said to Sherman, "Now listen. You don't say anything. You don't show any expression whatsoever. You don't cover your face, you don't hang your head. You don't even know they're there. You can't win with these assholes, so don't even try. Let me get out first."

87 Bango!—somehow Killian swung both feet over Sherman's knees and rolled over him, all in one motion. His elbows hit Sherman's crossed hands and drove the handcuffs into his lower abdomen. Sherman's tweed jacket was bunched up over his hands. There were five or six Styrofoam peanuts on the jacket, but there was nothing he could do about it. The door was open, and Killian was out of the car. Goldberg and Killian had their hands out toward him. Sherman swung his feet out. Killian, Goldberg, and Martin had created a pocket around the door with their bodies. The mob of reporters, photographers, and cameramen was on top of them. People were shouting. At first he thought it was a melee. They were trying to *get* him! Killian reached in under Sherman's coat and pulled him upright by the handcuffs. Someone stuck a camera over Killian's shoulder and into Sherman's face. He ducked. When he looked down, he could see that five, six, seven, Christ knew how many Styrofoam peanuts were stuck to his pants legs. They were all over his coat and his pants. The rain was streaming down his forehead and his cheeks. He started to wipe his face, but then he realized he would have to raise both hands and his jacket to do it, and he didn't want them to see his handcuffs. So the water just rolled down. He could feel it rolling down his shirt collar. Because of the handcuffs, his shoulders were slumped forward. He tried to throw his shoulders back, but all at once Goldberg yanked him forward by one elbow. He was trying to get him through the mob.

88 "Sherman!"

89 "Over here, Sherman!"

90 "Hey, Sherman!"

91 They were all yelling *Sherman!* His first name! He was *theirs,* too! The looks on their faces! Such pitiless intensity! They jammed their microphones toward him. Someone came barreling into Goldberg, knocking him back against Sherman. A camera appeared over Goldberg's shoulder. Goldberg swung his elbow and forearm forward with tremendous force, and there was a *thumpf,* and the camera fell to the ground. Goldberg still had his other arm hooked inside Sherman's elbow. The force of Goldberg's punch pulled Sherman off balance. Sherman stepped to the side, and his foot landed on the leg of a man who was writhing on the ground. He was a little man with dark curly hair. Goldberg stepped on his abdomen for good measure. The man went *Ooooohahhh.*

92 "Hey, Sherman! Hey, shitface!"

93 Startled, Sherman looked to the side. It was a photographer. His camera covered half his face. The other side had a piece of white paper stuck on it. *Toilet paper.* Sherman could see the man's lips moving. "That's it, shitface, look right here!"

94 Martin was a step in front of Sherman, trying to clear a path. "Coming through! Coming through! Get outta the way!"

95 Killian took Sherman's other elbow and tried to shield him from that side. But now both of his elbows were being pulled forward, and he was conscious of shambling forward, drenched, with his shoulders stooped. He couldn't keep his head up.

96 "Sherman!" A woman's voice. A microphone was in his face. "Have you ever been arrested before?"

97 "Hey, Sherman! How you gonna plead?"

98 "Sherman! Who's the brunette?"

99 "Sherman! Did you mean to hit him?"

100 They were sticking the microphones between Killian and Martin and between Martin and Goldberg. Sherman tried to keep his head up, but one of the microphones hit him in the chin. He kept flinching. Every time he looked down, he could see the white Styrofoam peanuts on his jacket and his pants.

101 "Hey, Sherman! Fuckhead! How you like this cocktail party!"

102 Such abuse! It was coming from photographers. Anything to try to make him look their way, but—such abuse! such filth! There was nothing too vile to abuse him with! He was now . . . theirs! Their creature! He had been thrown to them! They could do what they wanted! He hated them—but he felt so *ashamed.* The rain was running into his eyes. He couldn't do anything about it. His shirt was soaked. They were no longer moving forward as before. The little metal door was no more than twenty-five feet away. A line of men was jammed up in front of them. They weren't reporters or photographers or cameramen. Some of them were uniformed policemen. Some of them seemed to be Latins, young men mostly. Then there were some white . . . derelicts . . . winos . . . but, no, they wore badges. They were policemen. They were all standing in the rain. They were soaking wet. Martin and Goldberg were now pressing up against the Latinos and the policemen, with Killian and Sherman in close behind them. Goldberg and Killian still had Sherman's elbows. The reporters and cameramen were still coming at him from the sides and from behind.

103 "Sherman! Hey! Give us a statement!"

104 "Just one shot!"

105 "Hey, Sherman! Why'dja hit him?"

106 ". . . Park Avenue! . . ."

107 ". . . intentionally! . . ."

108 Martin turned and said to Goldberg, "Jesus Christ, they just busted that social club up on 167th. There's twelve fucking spaced-out carambas in line waiting to get into Central Booking!"

109 "Beautiful," said Goldberg.

110 "Look," said Killian, "you gotta get him inside a there. Talk to Crowther, if you have to, but get him in there."

111 Martin shoved his way out of the mob, and in no time he was back.

112 "No go," said Martin, with an apologetic shake of the head. "He says this one's gotta be by the book. He's gotta wait on line."

113 "This is very wrong," said Killian.

114 Martin arched his eyebrows. (I know, I know, but what can I do?)

115 "Sherman! How about a statement!"

116 "Sherman! Hey, cuntface!"

117 *"All right!"* It was Killian, yelling. "You want a statement? Mr. McCoy's not gonna make a statement. I'm his attorney, and I'm gonna make a statement."

118 More pushing and jostling. The microphones and cameras now converged on Killian.

119 Sherman stood just behind him. Killian let go of Sherman's elbow, but Goldberg still had the other one.

120 Somebody yelled, "What's your name?"

121 "Thomas Killian."

122 "Howdaya spell it?"

123 "K-I-L-L-I-A-N. Okay? This is a *circus arrest!* My client has been ready at all times to appear before a grand jury to confront the charges brought against him. Instead, this circus arrest has been staged in complete violation of an agreement between the district attorney and my client."

124 "What was he doing in the Bronx?"

125 "That's the statement, and that's the whole statement."

126 "Are you saying he's innocent?"

127 "Mr. McCoy denies these charges completely, and this outrageous circus arrest shoulda never been allowed."

128 The shoulders of Killian's suit were drenched. The rain had gone through Sherman's shirt, and he could feel the water on his skin.

129 "*¡Mira! ¡Mira!*" One of the Latins kept saying this word *¡Mira!*

130 Sherman stood there with his shoulders drenched and bowed. He could feel the sopping jacket weighing down on his wrists. Over Killian's shoulder he could see a thicket of microphones. He could hear the cameras whining away. The horrible fire in their faces! He wanted to die. He had never really wanted to die before, although, like many other souls, he had toyed with the feeling. Now he truly wanted God or Death to deliver him. That was how dreadful the feeling was, and that feeling was, in fact, a scalding shame.

131 "Sherman!"

132 "Fuckface!"

133 "*¡Mira! ¡Mira!*"

134 And then he was dead, so dead he couldn't even die. He didn't even possess the willpower to fall down. The reporters and cameramen and photographers—such vile abuse!—still here, not three feet away!—they were the maggots and the flies, and he was the dead beast they had found to crawl over and root into.

135 Killian's so-called statement had distracted them only for a moment. Killian!—who supposedly had his connections and was going to make sure it was not an ordinary arrest! It was *not* an ordinary arrest. It was *death.* Every bit of honor, respect, dignity, that he, a creature named Sherman McCoy, might ever have possessed had been removed, *just like that,* and it was his dead soul that now stood here in the rain, in handcuffs, in the Bronx, outside a mean little metal door, at the end of a line of a dozen other prisoners. The maggots called him *Sherman.* They were right on top of him.

136 "Hey, Sherman!"

137 "How you gonna plead, Sherman!"

138 Sherman looked straight ahead. Killian and the two detectives, Martin and Goldberg, continued to try to shield Sherman from the maggots. A television cameraman closed in, a fat one. The camera came over his shoulder like a grenade launcher.

139 Goldberg wheeled toward the man and yelled, "Get that fucking thing outta my face!"

140 The cameraman retreated. How odd! How completely hopeless! Goldberg was now his protector. He was Goldberg's creature, his animal. Goldberg and Martin had brought their animal in, and now they were determined to see that it was delivered.

141 Killian said to Martin, "This is not right. You guys gotta do something."

142 Martin shrugged. Then Killian said in all seriousness, "My shoes are getting fucking ruined."

143 "Mr. McCoy."

144 *Mr. McCoy.* Sherman turned his head. A tall pale man with long blond hair was at the forefront of a pack of reporters and cameramen.

145 "Peter Fallow of *The City Light,*" said the man. He had an English accent, an accent so blimpish it was like a parody of an English accent. Was he taunting him? "I've rung you up several times. I'd very much like to get your side of all this."

146 Sherman turned away . . . Fallow, his obsessive tormentor in *The City Light* . . . No compunctions at all about walking up and introducing himself . . . of course not . . . his quarry was dead . . . He should have hated him, and yet he couldn't, because he loathed himself so much more. He was dead even to himself.

147 Finally, all the prisoners arrested in the raid on the social club were inside the door, and Sherman, Killian, Martin, and Goldberg were just outside. "Okay, Counselor," Martin said to Killian, "we'll take it from here."

148 Sherman looked beseechingly at Killian. (Surely you're coming inside with me!) Killian said, "I'll be upstairs when they bring you up for arraignment. Don't worry about anything. Just remember, don't make any statements, don't talk about the case, not even to anybody in the pens, *especially* not to anybody in the pens."

149 *In the pens!* More shouting from beyond the door.

150 "How long will it take?" asked Sherman.

151 "I don't know exactly. They got these guys ahead a you." Then he said to Martin, "Look. Do the right thing. See if you can't get him through fingerprinting ahead a that bunch. I mean, f'r Chrissake."

152 "I'll try," said Martin, "but I already told you. For some reason they want this one step by step."

153 "Yeah, but you owe us," said Killian. "You owe us a lot—" He stopped. "Just do the right thing."

154 All at once Goldberg was pulling Sherman in by the elbow. Martin was right behind him. Sherman turned to keep Killian in sight. Killian's hat was so wet it looked black. His necktie and the shoulders of his suit were soaked.

155 "Don't worry," said Killian. "It's gonna be all right."

156 The way Killian said it, Sherman knew his own face must be a picture of pure despair. Then the door closed; no more Killian. Sherman was cut off from the world.

He had thought he had no fear left, only despair. But he was afraid all over again. His heart began to pound. The door had closed, and he had disappeared into the world of Martin and Goldberg in the Bronx.

157 He was in a large low room broken up by cubicles, some of which had plate-glass windows, like the interior windows of a broadcast studio. There were no outside windows. A bright electric haze filled the room. People in uniform were moving about, but they were not all wearing the same sort of uniform. Two men with their hands manacled behind their backs stood in front of a high desk. Two young men in rags were standing beside them. One of the prisoners looked over his shoulder and saw Sherman and nudged the other, and he turned around and looked at Sherman, and they both laughed. Off to the side, Sherman could hear the cry he had heard outside, a man screaming, "*¡Mira! ¡Mira!*" There were some cackles and then the loud flatulent sound of someone having a bowel movement. A deep voice said, "Yaggh. Filthy."

158 Another one said, "Okay, get 'em outta there. Hose it down."

159 The two men in rags were bending over behind the two prisoners. Behind the desk was a huge policeman with an absolutely bald head, a big nose, and a prognathous jaw. He appeared to be sixty years old at least. The men in rags were removing the handcuffs from the two prisoners. One of the young men in rags had on a thermal vest over a torn black T-shirt. He wore sneakers and dirty camouflage pants, tight at the ankles. There was a badge, a police shield, on the thermal vest. Then Sherman could see the other had a badge, too. Another old policeman came up to the desk and said, "Hey, Angel, Albany's down."

160 "Beautiful," said the man with the bald head. "We got this bunch, and the shift just started."

161 Goldberg looked at Martin and rolled his eyes and smiled and then looked at Sherman. He still held Sherman by the elbow. Sherman looked down. Styrofoam peanuts! The Styrofoam packing peanuts he had picked up in the back seat of Martin's car were all over the place. They were stuck to the wad of his jacket over his wrists. They were all over his tweed pants. His pants were wet, wrinkled, twisted shapelessly around his knees and his thighs, and the Styrofoam peanuts clung to them like vermin.

162 Goldberg said to Sherman, "You see that room in there?"

163 Sherman looked over into a room, through a large plate-glass window. There were filing cabinets and piles of paper. A big beige-and-gray apparatus took up the center of the room. Two policemen were staring at it.

164 "That's the Fax machine that sends the fingerprints to Albany," said Goldberg. He said it in a pleasant sort of singsong, the way you would say something to a child who is frightened and confused. The very tone terrified Sherman. "About ten years ago," said Goldberg, "some bright fellow got the idea—was it ten years ago, Marty?"

165 "I don't know," said Martin. "All I know is, it was a stupid fucking idea."

166 "Anyway, somebody got the idea a putting all the fingerprints, for the whole fucking State a New York, in this one office in Albany . . . see . . . and then every one a the Central Bookings, they're wired into Albany, and you send the prints to Albany on the computer, and you get back your report, and the suspect goes upstairs

and gets arraigned . . . see . . . Only it's a freakin' logjam in Albany, especially when the machine goes down, like right now."

167 Sherman couldn't take in a thing Goldberg was saying, except that something had gone wrong and Goldberg thought he was going out of his way to be nice and explain it.

168 "Yeah," Martin said to Sherman, "be thankful it's 8:30 in the morning and not 4:30 in the fucking afternoon. If this was the fucking afternoon, you'd probably have to spend the night at the Bronx House of Detention or even Rikers."

169 "Rikers Island?" asked Sherman. He was hoarse. He barely got the words out.

170 "Yeah," said Martin, "when Albany goes down in the afternoon, forgedaboud-it. You can't spend the night in this place, so they take you over to Rikers. I'm telling you, you're very fortunate."

171 He was telling him he was very fortunate. Sherman was supposed to like them now! Inside here, they were his only friends! Sherman felt intensely frightened.

172 Somebody yelled out, "Who *died* in here, f'r Chrissake!"

173 The smell reached the desk.

174 "Now *that's* disgusting," said the bald man called Angel. He looked around. "Hose it down!"

175 Sherman followed his eyes. Off to the side, down a corridor, he could make out two cells. White tiles and bars; they seemed to be constructed of white brick tiles, like a public bathroom. Two policemen stood in front of one of them.

176 One of them yelled through the bars, "Whatsa matter with you!"

177 Sherman could feel the pressure of Goldberg's huge hand on his elbow, steering him forward. He was in front of the desk, staring up at the Angel. Martin had a sheaf of papers in his hand.

178 The Angel said, "Name?"

179 Sherman tried to speak but couldn't. His mouth was utterly dry. His tongue seemed stuck to the roof of his mouth.

180 "Name?"

181 "Sherman McCoy." It was barely a whisper.

182 "Address?"

183 "816 Park Avenue. New York." He added "New York" in the interest of being modest and obedient. He didn't want to act as if he just assumed people here in the Bronx knew where Park Avenue was.

184 "Park Avenue, New York. Your age?"

185 "Thirty-eight."

186 "Ever been arrested before?"

187 "No."

188 "Hey, Angel," Martin said. "Mr. McCoy here's been very cooperative . . . and uh . . . whyn't you let him sit out here somewheres insteada putting him in there with that buncha bats? The fucking so-called press out there, they gave him a hard enough time."

189 A wave of profound, sentimental gratitude washed over Sherman. Even as he felt it, he knew it was irrational, but he felt it nonetheless.

190 The Angel puffed up his cheeks and stared off, as if ruminating. Then he said, "Can't do it, Marty." He closed his eyes and lifted his huge chin upward, as if to say, "The people upstairs."

191 "Whadda they worrying about? The fucking TV viruses got him standing out there in the rain for a fucking half an hour. Look at him. Looks like he crawled in here through a pipe."

192 Goldberg chuckled. Then, so as not to offend Sherman, he said to him, "You're not looking your best. You *know* that."

193 His only friends! Sherman wanted to cry, and all the more so because this horrible, pathetic feeling was genuine.

194 "Can't do it," said the Angel. "Gotta do the whole routine." He closed his eyes and lifted his chin again. "You can take the cuffs off."

195 Martin looked at Sherman and twisted his mouth to one side. (Well, friend, we tried.) Goldberg unlocked the handcuffs and took them off Sherman's wrists. There were white rings on his wrists where the metal had been. The veins on top of his hands were engorged with blood. *My blood pressure has gone through the roof.* There were Styrofoam peanuts all over his pants. Martin handed him his soggy jacket. Styrofoam peanuts all over the soggy jacket, too.

196 "Empty your pockets and hand me the contents," said the Angel.

197 On the advice of Killian, Sherman hadn't brought much with him. Four $5 bills, about a dollar in change, a key to the apartment, a handkerchief, a ballpoint pen, his driver's license—for some reason he thought he should have identification. As he handed over each item, the Angel described it aloud—"twenty dollars in bills," "one silver ballpoint pen"—and handed it to someone Sherman couldn't see.

198 Sherman said, "Can I . . . keep the handkerchief?"

199 "Let me see it."

200 Sherman held it up. His hand was shaking terribly.

201 "Yeah, you can keep it. But you gotta give me the watch."

202 "It's only—it's just a cheap watch," said Sherman. He held up his hand. The watch had a plastic case and a nylon band. "I don't care what happens to it."

203 "No can do."

204 Sherman undid the band and surrendered the little watch. A new spasm of panic went through him.

205 "Please," said Sherman. As soon as the word left his mouth, he knew he shouldn't have said it. He was begging. "How can I figure—can't I keep the watch?"

206 "You got an appointment or something?" The Angel attempted a smile to show he didn't mean it as much more than a pleasantry. But he didn't return the watch. Then he said, "Okay, and I need your belt and your shoestrings."

207 Sherman stared at him. He realized his mouth was open. He looked at Martin. Martin was looking at the Angel. Now Martin closed his eyes and lifted his chin, the way the Angel had, and said, "Oh boy." (They really *do* have it in for him.)

208 Sherman unbuckled the belt and pulled it out of the loops. As soon as he did, the pants fell down around his hips. He hadn't worn the tweed suit in a long time, and the waist was much too big. He pulled the pants up and stuffed his shirt back inside, and they fell down again. He had to hold them up in front. He squatted down to take off the shoelaces. Now he was an abject creature crouched at the feet of Martin and Goldberg. His face was close to the Styrofoam peanuts on his pants. He could see the crinkles on them. Some sort of horrible beetles or parasites! The heat of his body and the woolly funk of the pants gave off an unpleasant odor. He was aware of the humid smell of his armpits under the clammy shirt. A total mess. No

two ways about it. He had the feeling that one of them, Martin, Goldberg, the Angel, would just step on him, and, *pop,* that would be the end of that. He pulled out the shoestrings and stood up. Standing up from the crouch made him light-headed. For an instant he thought he might faint. His pants were falling down again. He pulled them up with one hand and handed the Angel the shoestrings with the other. They were like two little dried dead things.

209 The voice behind the desk said, "Two brown shoestrings."

210 "Okay, Angel," said Martin, "all yours."

211 "Right," said the Angel.

212 "Well, good luck, Sherman," said Goldberg, smiling in a kindly fashion.

213 "Thanks," said Sherman. It was horrible. He actually appreciated it.

214 He heard a cell door slide open. Down the little corridor stood three police officers herding a group of Latins out of one cell and into the one next to it. Sherman recognized several of the men who had been in line ahead of him outside.

215 "All right, knock it off, and get in there."

216 "*¡Mira! ¡Mira!*"

217 One man remained in the corridor. A policeman had him by the arm. He was tall, with a long neck, and his head lolled about. He seemed very drunk. He was muttering to himself. Then he threw his eyes to the heavens and screamed, "*¡Mira!*" He was holding up his pants the same way Sherman was.

218 "Hey, Angel, whadda I do with this one? It's all over his *pants!*" The policeman said "*pants*" with great disgust.

219 "Well, shit," said Angel. "Take the pants off him and *bury* 'em, and then wash him off, too, and give him some a those green fatigues."

220 "I don't even wanna touch him, Sarge. You got any a those things they take the cans off the shelf in the supermarket with?"

221 "Yeah, I got some," said the Angel, "and I'm gonna take your can off."

222 The policeman jerked the tall man back toward the first cell. The tall man's legs were like a marionette's.

223 The Angel said, "Whaddaya got all over *your* pants?"

224 Sherman looked down. "I don't know," he said. "They were on the back seat of the car."

225 "Whose car?"

226 "Detective Martin's car."

227 The Angel shook his head as if now he had seen everything. "Okay, Tanooch, take him over to Gabsie."

228 A young white officer took Sherman by the elbow. Sherman's hand was holding up his pants, and so the elbow came up like a bird's wing. His pants were damp even in the waistband. He carried his wet jacket over his other arm. He started walking. His right foot came out of his shoe, because the strings were gone. He stopped, but the policeman kept walking, jerking his elbow forward in an arc. Sherman put his foot back in the shoe, and the policeman motioned toward the little corridor. Sherman started shuffling, so that his feet wouldn't come out of the shoes. The shoes made a squishing sound because they were so wet.

229 Sherman was led toward the cubicle with the big windows. Now, just across the corridor, he could see inside the two cells. In one there appeared to be a dozen

figures, a dozen hulks of gray and black, up against the walls. The door to the other was open. There was only one person inside, the tall man, slumped on a ledge. There was a brown mess on the floor. The odor of excrement was overpowering.

230 The policeman steered Sherman into the cubicle with the windows. Inside was a huge freckled policeman with a wide face and blond wavy hair, who looked him up and down. The policeman called Tanooch said, "McCoy," and handed the big one a sheet of paper. The room seemed full of metal stands. One looked like the sort of metal-detection gate you see at airports. There was a camera on a tripod. There was something that looked like a music stand except that it had nothing at the top big enough to hold a page of music.

231 "Okay, McCoy," said the big policeman, "step through that gate there."

232 Squish, squish, squish . . . holding his pants up with one hand and holding his wet jacket in the other, Sherman shuffled through the gate. A loud whining beep came from the machine.

233 "Whoa, whoa," said the policeman. "Okay, give me your coat."

234 Sherman handed him the jacket. The man went through the pockets and then began kneading the jacket from top to bottom. He threw the jacket over the edge of a table.

235 "Okay, spread your feet and put your arms straight out to the side, like this."

236 The policeman put his arms out as if he were doing a swan dive. Sherman stared at the policeman's right hand. He was wearing a translucent rubber surgical glove. It came halfway up his forearm!

237 Sherman spread his feet. When he spread his arms, his pants fell way down. The man approached him and began patting down his arms, his chest, his ribs, his back and then his hips and his legs. The hand with the rubber glove created an unpleasant dry friction. A new wave of panic . . . He stared at the glove in terror. The man looked at him and grunted, apparently in amusement, and then held up his right hand. The hand and the wrist were enormous. The hideous rubber glove was right in front of Sherman's face.

238 "Don't worry about the glove," he said. "The thing is, I gotta do your prints, and I gotta pick your fingers up one by one and put 'em on the pad . . . You understand? . . ." His tone was conversational, neighborly, as if there were just the two of them, out by the alley, and he was explaining how the engine in his new Mazda worked. "I do this all day, and I get the ink on my hands, and my skin's rough to begin with, and sometimes I don't get the ink all off, and I go home, and my wife has the whole living room done in white, and I put my hand down on the sofa or someplace, and I get up and you can see three or four fingers on the sofa, and my wife throws a fit." Sherman stared at him. He didn't know what to say. This huge fierce-looking man wanted to be liked. It was all so very odd. Perhaps they all wanted to be liked.

239 "Okay, walk on back through the gate."

240 Sherman shuffled back through the gate, and the alarm went off again.

241 "Shit," said the man. "Try it again."

242 The alarm went off a third time.

243 "Beats the hell outta me," said the man. "Wait a minute. Come here. Open your mouth."

244 Sherman opened his mouth.

245 "Keep it open . . . Wait a minute, turn it this way. Can't get no light." He wanted to move Sherman's head to a strange angle. Sherman could smell the rubber of the glove. "Sonofabitch. You got a goddamn silver mine in there. I tell you what. Bend over at the waist like this. Try to get way down."

246 Sherman bent over, holding up his pants with one hand. *Surely he wouldn't—*

247 "Now back through the gate, but real slow."

248 Sherman started shuffling backward, bent over at an almost 90-degree angle.

249 "Okay, real slow, real slow, real slow—that's it . . . whoa!"

250 Sherman was now mostly through the gate. Only his shoulders and his head remained on the other side.

251 "Okay, back up . . . a little farther, a little farther, little farther, little farther . . ."

252 The alarm went off again.

253 "Whoa! Whoa! Right there! Stay right there!" The alarm remained on.

254 "Sonofabitch!" said the big man. He began pacing around and sighing. He slapped his legs with his hands. "I had one a these last year! Okay, you can stand up!"

255 Sherman stood up. He looked at the big man, bewildered. The man stuck his head out the door and yelled, "Hey, Tanooch! Come here! Look at this!"

256 Across the little corridor, a policeman was in the open cell with a hose, washing down the floor. The rush of the water echoed off the tile.

257 "Hey, Tanooch!"

258 The policeman who had brought Sherman into the room came from down the corridor.

259 "Look at this, Tanooch." Then he said to Sherman, "Okay, bend over and do that again. Back through the gate, real slow."

260 Sherman bent over and did as he was told.

261 "Okay, whoa, whoa, whoa . . . Now you see that, Tanooch? So far, nothing. Okay, now back up a little more, little more, little more . . ." The alarm went off. The big man was beside himself again. He paced about and sighed and put his hands together. "Dja see that, Tanooch! It's his *head!* Swear to Christ! . . . It's the fellow's head! . . . Okay, stand up. Open your mouth . . . That's it. No, turn it this way." He moved Sherman's head again, to get more light. "Look in there! You wanna see some metal?"

262 The one called Tanooch said not a word to Sherman. He looked in his mouth, like someone inspecting a crawl space in a cellar.

263 "Jesus Christ," said Tanooch. "You're right. Set a teeth look like a change maker." Then he said to Sherman, as if noticing him for the first time, "They ever let you on an airplane?"

264 The big one cracked up over this. "You're not the only one," he said. "I had one like you last year. Drove me outta my mind. I couldn't figure out . . . *what da fuck* . . . you know?" Suddenly it was the casual fellow-out-back-on-Saturday mode of conversation again. "This machine is very sensitive, but you do have a whole head fulla metal, I gotta tell you that."

265 Sherman was mortified, completely humiliated. But what could he do? Maybe

these two, if he played along with them, could keep him out of . . . *the pens!* With *those people!* Sherman just stood there, holding up his pants.

266 "What's that stuff all over your pants?" asked Tanooch.

267 "Styrofoam," said Sherman.

268 *"Styrofoam,"* said Tanooch, nodding his head, but in an uncomprehending fashion. He left the room.

269 Then the big man stood Sherman in front of a metal stand and took two pictures of him, one from the front and one from the side. It dawned on Sherman that this was what was known as a mug shot. This great huge bear had just taken his mug shot, while Sherman stood there holding up his pants. He led him over to a counter and took Sherman's fingers one by one and pressed them into an ink pad and then rolled them onto a printed form. It was a surprisingly rough operation. He gripped each of Sherman's fingers as if he were picking up a knife or a hammer and plunged it into the ink pad. Then he apologized.

270 "You have to do all the work yourself," he said to Sherman. "You can't expect nobody comes in here to lift a goddamned finger for you."

271 From across the corridor came the furious sound of someone retching. Three of the Latins were at the bars of the pen.

272 "Ayyyyyy!" yelled one of them. "The man puking! He puking plenty!"

273 Tanooch was the first policeman there.

274 "Oh, f'r Chrissake. Oh, beautiful. Hey, Angel! This guy's a one-man garbage barge. Whaddaya wanna do?"

275 "He the same one?" said Angel.

276 Then the smell of vomit began to spread.

277 "Ayyyyyyyy, whaddaya whaddaya," said Angel. "Hose it down and leave 'im in there."

278 They opened the bars, and two policemen stood by outside while a third went inside with the hose. The prisoners hopped this way and that, to keep from getting wet.

279 "Hey, Sarge," said the policeman. "Guy puked all over his pants."

280 "The fatigues?"

281 "Yeah."

282 "Fuck it. Hose 'em down. This ain't a laundry."

283 Sherman could see the tall man sitting on the ledge with his head down. His knees were covered in vomit, and his elbows were on his knees.

284 The big man was watching all this through the window of the fingerprint room. He was shaking his head. Sherman went up to him.

285 "Look, Officer, isn't there some other place I can wait? I can't go in there. I'm—I just can't do it."

286 The big man stuck his head out of the fingerprint room and yelled, "Hey, Angel, whaddaya wanna do with my man here, McCoy?"

287 Angel looked over from his desk and stared at Sherman and rubbed his hand over his bald head.

288 "Wellllll . . ." Then he motioned with his hand toward the cell. "That's it."

289 Tanooch came in and took Sherman by the arm again. Someone opened up

the bars. Tanooch steered Sherman inside, and he went shuffling onto the tile floor, holding up his pants. The bars shut behind him. Sherman stared at the Latins, who were sitting on the ledge. They stared back, all but the tall one, who still had his head down, rolling his elbows in the vomit on his knees.

290 The entire floor slanted in toward the drain in the middle. It was still wet. Sherman could feel the slant now that he was standing on it. A few driblets of water were still rolling down the drain. That was it. It was a drainpipe, where manhood sought its own level, and the meat spigot was on.

291 He heard the bars slide shut behind him, and he stood there in the cell holding his pants up with his right hand. He cradled his jacket with his left arm. He didn't know what to do or even where to look, and so he picked out an empty space on the wall and tried to take a look at . . . *them* . . . with peripheral vision. Their clothes were a blur of gray and black and brown, except for their sneakers, which created a pattern of stripes and swashes along the floor. He knew they were watching him. He glanced toward the bars. Not a single policeman! Would they even move a muscle if anything . . .

292 The Latinos had taken every seat on the ledge. He chose a spot about four feet from the end of the ledge and leaned his back up against the wall. The wall hurt his spine. He lifted his right foot, and his shoe fell off. He slipped his foot back into it as casually as he could. Looking down at his foot on the bright tile made him feel as if he was going to keel over with vertigo. The Styrofoam peanuts! They were still all over his pants legs.

293 He was seized with the terrible fear that they would take him to be a lunatic, the sort of hopeless case they could slaughter at their leisure. He was aware of the smell of vomit . . . vomit and cigarette smoke . . . He lowered his head, as if he were dozing, and cut his eyes toward them. They were staring at him! They were staring at him and smoking their cigarettes. The tall one, the one who had kept saying, "*¡Mira! ¡Mira!*" still sat on the ledge with his head down and his elbows on his knees, which were covered in vomit.

294 One of the Latinos was rising up from the ledge and walking toward him! He could see him out of the corner of his eye. Now it was starting! They weren't even waiting!

295 The man was settling up against the wall, right next to him, leaning back the same way Sherman was. He had thin curly hair, a mustache that curved down around his lips, a slightly yellowish complexion, narrow shoulders, a little potbelly, and a crazy look in his eyes. He must have been about thirty-five. He smiled, and that made him look crazier still.

296 "Hey, man, I see you outside."

297 *See me outside!*

298 "With the TV, man. Why you here?"

299 "Reckless endangerment," said Sherman. He felt as if he were croaking out his last words on this earth.

300 "Reckless endangerment?"

301 "That's . . . hitting somebody with your car."

302 "With you car? You hit somebody with you car, and the TV come here?"

303 Sherman shrugged. He didn't want to say anything more, but his fear of appearing aloof got the better of him.

304 "What are you here for?"

305 "Oh, man, 220, 265, 225." The fellow threw his hand out, as if to take in the entire world. "Drugs, handguns, gambling paraphernalia—ayyyyyy, every piece a bullshit, you know?"

306 The man seemed to take a certain pride in this calamity.

307 "You hit somebody with you car?" he asked once more. He apparently found this trivial and unmanly. Sherman raised his eyebrows and nodded wearily.

308 The man returned to the seating ledge, and Sherman could see him talking to three or four of his comrades, who looked at Sherman once more and then looked away, as if bored by the news. Sherman had the feeling that he had let them down. Very odd! And yet that was what he felt.

309 Sherman's fear was rapidly supplanted by tedium. The minutes crawled by. His left hip joint began to hurt. He shifted his weight to the right, and his back hurt. Then his right hip joint hurt. The floor was tile. The walls were tile. He rolled up his jacket to create a cushion. He put it on the floor, next to the wall, and sat down and leaned back. The jacket was damp, and so were his pants. His bladder was beginning to fill, and he could feel little knives of gas in his bowels.

310 The little man who had come over to talk to him, the little man who knew the numbers, walked to the bars. He had a cigarette in his mouth. He took the cigarette out, and he yelled, "Ayyyyyy! I need a light!" No response from the policeman beyond. "Ayyyyyy, I need a light!"

Finally, the one called Tanooch came up. "What's your problem?"

311 "Ayyy, I need a light." He held up his cigarette.

312 Tanooch dug a book of matches out of his pocket and lit one and held it about four feet away from the bars. The little man waited, then put the cigarette between his lips and pressed his face against the bars so that the cigarette protruded outside. Tanooch was motionless, holding the burning match. The match went out.

313 "Ayyyyyy!" said the little man.

314 Tanooch shrugged and let the match fall to the floor.

315 "Ayyyyyy!" The little man turned around toward his comrades and held the cigarette up in the air. (See what he did?) One of the men sitting on the ledge laughed. The little man made a face at this betrayal of sympathies. Then he looked at Sherman. Sherman didn't know whether to commiserate or look the other way. He ended up just staring. The man walked over and squatted down beside him. The unlit cigarette was hanging out of his mouth.

316 "Dja see that?" he asked.

317 "Yes," said Sherman.

318 "You wanna light, they suppose a give you a light. Son a mabitch. Ayyy . . . you got cigarettes?"

319 "No, they took everything away from me. Even my shoestrings."

320 "No shit?" He looked at Sherman's shoes. He himself still had on shoelaces, Sherman noticed.

321 Sherman could hear a woman's voice. She was angry about something. She appeared in the little corridor outside the cell. Tanooch was leading her. She was a tall thin woman with curly brown hair and dark tan skin, wearing black pants and an odd-looking jacket with very big shoulders. Tanooch was escorting her toward the fingerprint room. All at once she wheeled about and said to someone Sherman

couldn't see, "You big bag a . . ." She didn't complete the phrase. "Least I don't sit in 'is sewer here all day long, way you do! Think about it, fat boy!"

322 Much derisive laughter from the policemen in the background.

323 "Watch it or he'll flush you down, Mabel."

324 Tanooch prodded her on. "C'mon, Mabel."

325 She turned on Tanooch. "You talk to me, you call me by my right name! You don't call me Mabel!"

326 Tanooch said, "I'll call you worse'n that in a minute," and he kept pushing her on toward the fingerprint room.

327 "Two-twenty–thirty-one," said the little man. "Selling drugs."

328 "How do you know?" asked Sherman.

329 The little man just opened his eyes wide and put a knowing look on his face. (Some things go without saying.) Then he shook his head and said, "Focking bus come in."

330 "Bus?"

331 It seemed that ordinarily, when people were arrested, they were taken first to a precinct station house and locked up. Periodically a police van made the rounds of the precincts and transported the prisoners to Central Booking for fingerprinting and arraignment. So now a new lot had arrived. They would all end up in this pen, except for the women, who were taken to another pen, down the corridor and around a bend. And nothing was moving, because "Albany was down."

332 Three more women went by. They were younger than the first one.

333 "Two-thirty," said the little man. "Prostitutes."

334 The little man who knew the numbers was right. The bus had come in. The procession began, from the Angel's desk to the fingerprinting room to the cell. Sherman's pang of fear began to heat up all over again. One by one, three tall black youths with shaved heads, windbreakers, and big white sneakers came into the cell. All of the new arrivals were black or Latin. Most were young. Several appeared to be drunk. The little man who knew the numbers got up and went back to join his comrades and secure his place on the ledge. Sherman was determined not to move. He wanted to be invisible. Somehow . . . so long as he didn't move a muscle . . . they wouldn't see him.

335 Sherman stared at the floor and tried not to think about his aching bowels and bladder. One of the black lines between the tiles on the floor began to move. A cockroach! Then he saw another . . . and a third. Fascinating!—and horrible. Sherman glanced about to see if anyone else noticed. No one seemed to—but he caught the eye of one of the three black youths. All three were staring at him! Such thin hard malevolent faces! His heart immediately kicked into tachycardia. He could see his foot jerk with the force of his heartbeat pulse. He stared at the cockroaches to try to cool himself down. A cockroach had made its way over to the drunken Latino, who had slumped to the floor. The cockroach began ascending the heel of his shoe. It began walking up his leg. It disappeared up his pants leg. Then it reappeared. It climbed the cuff of his pants. It began climbing toward his knee. When it reached the knee, it settled in amid the cakes of vomit.

336 Sherman looked up. One of the black youths was heading toward him. He had a little smile on his face. He seemed tremendously tall. His eyes were set close

together. He wore black pants with stovepipe legs and big white sneakers that closed in front with Velcro straps rather than shoelaces. He stooped down in front of Sherman. His face had no expression at all. All the more terrifying! He looked right into Sherman's face.

337 "Hey, man, you got a cigarette?"

338 Sherman said, "No." But he didn't want him to think he was acting tough or even uncommunicative, and so he added, "Sorry. They took everything away from me."

339 As soon as he said it, he knew it was a mistake. It was an apology, a signal that he was weak.

340 "That's okay, man." The youth sounded halfway friendly. "What you in for?"

341 Sherman hesitated. "Manslaughter," he said. "Reckless endangerment" just wasn't enough.

342 "Yeah. That's *bad,*" said the youth in an approximation of a concerned voice. "What happened?"

343 "Nothing," said Sherman. "I don't know what they're talking about. What are you here for?"

344 "A 1-60-15," said the youth. Then he added, "Armed robbery."

345 The youth screwed up his lips. Sherman couldn't tell whether that was supposed to say, "Armed robbery is nothing special," or, "It's a bullshit charge."

346 The youth smiled at Sherman, still looking directly into his face. "Okay, Mr. Manslaughter," he said, and he stood up and turned about and walked back to the other side of the cell.

347 *Mr. Manslaughter! Immediately he knew he could treat me cavalierly!* What could they do? Surely they couldn't . . . There had been an incident—where?—in which some of the prisoners in a cell blocked the view through the bars with their bodies while the others . . . But would any of the others in here do such a thing for these three—would the Latinos?

348 Sherman's mouth was dry, absolutely parched. The urge to urinate was acute. His heart beat nervously, although not as rapidly as before. At that moment, the bars slid open. More policemen. One of them carried two cardboard trays, the sort delicatessens use. He set them down on the floor of the cell. On one was a mound of sandwiches; on the other, rows of paper cups.

349 He stood up and said, "Okay, chow time. Share and share alike, and I don't wanna hear any bullshit."

350 There was no rush toward the food. All the same, Sherman was glad he was not too far away from the two trays. He tucked his filthy jacket under his left arm and shuffled over and picked up a sandwich wrapped in Saran Wrap and a plastic cup containing a clear pinkish liquid. Then he sat down on his coat again and tried the drink. It had a weak sugary taste. He put the plastic cup on the floor beside him and pulled the wrap off the sandwich. He pulled the two pieces of bread apart and peeked inside. There was a slice of lunch meat. It was a sickly yellowish color. In the fluorescent light of the cell it looked almost chartreuse. It had a smooth clammy surface. He raised the sandwich toward his face and sniffed. A dead chemical smell came from the meat. He separated the two pieces of bread and pulled out the piece of meat and wrapped it up in the Saran Wrap and put the crumpled mess on the

floor. He would eat the bread by itself. But the bread gave off such an unpleasant smell from the meat he couldn't stand it. Laboriously, he unfolded the Saran Wrap and rolled up the bread into balls and wrapped up the whole mess, the meat and the bread. He was aware of someone standing in front of him. White sneakers with Velcro straps.

351 He looked up. The black youth was looking down at him with a curious little smile. He sank down on his haunches, until his head was only slightly above Sherman's.

352 "Hey, man," he said. "I'm kinda thirsty. Gimme your drink."

353 *Gimme your drink!* Sherman nodded toward the cardboard trays.

354 "Ain't none left, man. Gimme yours."

355 Sherman ransacked his mind for something to say. He shook his head.

356 "You heard the man. Share and share alike. Thought me and you's buddies."

357 Such a contemptuous tone of mock disappointment! Sherman knew it was time to draw a line, stop this . . . this . . . Quicker than Sherman's eye could follow it, the youth's arm shot out and seized the plastic cup on the floor beside Sherman. He stood up and threw back his head and ostentatiously drained the drink and held the cup over Sherman and said:

358 "I asked you politely . . . You understand? . . . In here, you gotta use your head and make *friends.*"

359 Then he opened his hand, let the cup fall down onto Sherman's lap, and walked away. Sherman was aware the entire room was watching. *I should—I should—* but he was paralyzed with fear and confusion. Across the way, a Latino was pulling the meat out of his sandwich and throwing it on the floor. There were slices of meat everywhere. Here and there were balled-up wads of Saran Wrap and entire sandwiches, unwrapped and thrown on the floor. The Latino had begun to eat the bread by itself—and his eyes were on Sherman. They were looking at him . . . in this human pen . . . yellow lunch meat, bread, Saran Wrap, paper cups . . . cockroaches! Here . . . over there . . . He looked toward the drunken Latino. He was still collapsed on the floor. There were three cockroaches rooting about in the folds of his left pants leg at the knee. All at once Sherman saw something moving at the mouth of the man's pants pocket. Another roach—no, much too big . . . gray . . . a mouse! . . . a mouse crawling out of the man's pocket . . . The mouse clung to the cloth for a moment, then scampered down to the tile floor and stopped again. Then it darted forward and reached a piece of yellow lunch meat. It stopped again, as if sizing up this bonanza . . .

360 "*¡Mira!*" One of the Latinos had seen the mouse.

361 A foot came flying out from the ledge. The mouse went skidding across the tile floor like a hockey puck. Another leg flew out. The mouse went flying back toward the ledge . . . A laugh, a cackle . . . "*¡Mira!*" . . . another foot . . . The mouse went skidding on its back, over a wad of lunch meat, which spun it upright again . . . Laughter, shouts . . . "*¡Mira! ¡Mira!*" . . . another kick . . . The mouse came spinning toward Sherman, on its back. It was just lying there, two or three inches from his foot, dazed, its legs jerking. Then it struggled to its feet, barely moving. The little rodent was out of it, finished. Not even fear was enough to get it moving. It lurched forward a couple of steps . . . More laughter . . . *Should I kick it as a sign of my solidarity with my cellmates?* . . . That was what he wondered . . . Without

thinking, he stood up. He reached down and picked up the mouse. He held it in his right hand and walked toward the bars. The cell grew silent. The mouse twitched feebly in his palm. He had almost reached the bars . . . *Sonofabitch!* . . . A tremendous pain in his index finger . . . The mouse had bitten him! . . . Sherman jumped and jerked his hand up. The mouse held on to his finger with its jaws. Sherman flailed his finger up and down as if he were shaking down a thermometer. The little beast wouldn't let go! . . . "*¡Mira! ¡Mira!*" . . . cackles, laughter . . . It was a terrific show! They were enjoying it immensely! Sherman banged the meaty side of his hand down on one of the crosspieces of the bars. The mouse went flying off . . . right in front of Tanooch, who had a sheaf of papers in his hand and was approaching the cell. Tanooch jumped back.

362 "Holy shit!" he said. Then he glowered at Sherman. "You gone off the platter?"

363 The mouse was lying on the floor. Tanooch stamped on it with the heel of his shoe. The animal lay flattened on the floor with its mouth open.

364 Sherman's hand hurt terribly, from where he had hit the bar. He cradled it with his other hand. *I've broken it!* He could see the teeth marks of the mouse on his index finger and a single tiny blob of blood. With his left hand, he reached around behind his back and pulled the handkerchief out of his right hip pocket. It required a tremendous contortion. They were all watching. Oh, yes . . . all watching. He swabbed the blood and wrapped the handkerchief around his hand. He heard Tanooch say to another policeman:

365 "The guy from Park Avenue. He threw *a mouse.*"

366 Sherman shuffled back toward where his jacket was balled up on the floor. He sat back down on the coat. His hand didn't hurt nearly so much any longer. *Maybe I haven't broken it. But my finger may be poisoned from the bite!* He pulled the handkerchief back far enough to look at the finger. It didn't look so bad. The blob of blood was gone.

367 The black youth was coming toward him again! Sherman looked up at him and then looked away. The fellow sat on his haunches in front of him, as before.

368 "Hey, man," he said, "you know something? I'm cold."

369 Sherman tried to ignore him. He turned his head. He was conscious of having a petulant look on his face. *The wrong expression! Weak!*

370 "Yo! Look at me when I'm talking to you!"

371 Sherman turned his head toward him. *Pure malevolence!*

372 "I ask you for a drink, and you wasn't nice, but I'm going to give you a chance to make up for that . . . see . . . I'm feeling cold, man. I want your coat. Gimme your coat."

373 *My coat! My clothes!*

374 Sherman's mind raced. He couldn't speak. He shook his head no.

375 "What'sa matter with you, man? You oughta try and be friendly, Mr. Manslaughter. My buddy, he say he know you. He saw you on TV. You wasted some ace, and you live on Park Avenue. That's nice, man. But this ain't Park Avenue. You understand? You best be making some friends, you understand? You been slicking me some kinda bad, bad, bad, but I'm gonna give you a chance to make up for it. Now gimme the fucking coat."

376 Sherman stopped thinking. His brain was on fire! He put his hands flat on the

floor and lifted his hips and then rocked forward until he was on one knee. Then he jumped up, clutching the jacket in his right hand. He did it so suddenly the black youth was startled.

377 "Shut up!" he heard himself saying. "You and I got nothing to talk about!"

378 The black youth stared at him blankly. Then he smiled. "Shut *up?*" he said. "Shut *up!*" He grinned and made a snorting noise. "*Shut* me up."

379 "Hey! You germs! Knock it off!" It was Tanooch at the bars. He was looking at the two of them. The black youth gave Sherman a big smile and stuck his tongue in his cheek. (Enjoy yourself! You're gonna own your mortal hide for about sixty seconds longer!) He walked back to the ledge and sat down, staring at Sherman the whole time.

380 Tanooch read from a sheet of paper: "Solinas! Gutiérrez! McCoy!"

381 *McCoy!* Sherman hurriedly put on the jacket, lest his nemesis rush forward and snatch it before he could leave the cell. The jacket was wet, greasy, fetid, completely shapeless. His pants fell down around his hips as he put it on. There were Styrofoam peanuts all over the coat and . . . *moving!* . . . two cockroaches had crawled into the folds. Frantically he swept them off onto the floor. He was still breathing rapidly and loudly.

382 As Sherman filed out of the cell behind the Latinos, Tanooch said to him in a low voice, "See? We didn't forget you. Your name's actually about six more down the list."

383 "Thank you," said Sherman. "I appreciate that."

384 Tanooch shrugged. "I'd rather walk you outta there than sweep you outta there."

385 The main room was now full of policemen and prisoners. At the desk, the Angel's desk, Sherman was turned over to a Department of Corrections officer, who manacled his hands behind his back and put him in a line with the Latinos. His pants now fell hopelessly around his hips. There was no way he could pull them up. He kept looking over his shoulder, fearful that the black youth might be right behind him. He was the last person in the little line. The Corrections officers led them up a narrow stairway. At the top of the stairs was another windowless room. More Corrections officers sat at some beat-up metal desks. Beyond the desk—*more cells!* They were smaller, grayer, dingier than the white-tile cells downstairs. Real jail cells, they were. On the first was a peeling sign that said, MEN ONLY—21 AND OVER—8 TO 10 CAP. The 21 AND OVER had been crossed out with some sort of marker. The entire line of prisoners was led into the cell. The handcuffs were left on. Sherman kept his eyes pinned on the doorway they had first entered. If the black youth came in and was put into this small cell with him—he—he—his fear made him crazy. He was sweating profusely. He had lost all track of time. He hung his head down to try to improve his circulation.

386 Presently they were led out of the cell and toward a door made of steel bars. On the other side of the door Sherman could see a line of prisoners sitting on the floor of a corridor. The corridor was scarcely thirty-six inches wide. One of the prisoners was a young white man with an enormous cast on his right leg. He wore shorts, so that the entire cast was visible. He was sitting on the floor. A pair of crutches leaned against the wall beside him. At the far end of the corridor was a

door. An officer stood beside it. He had a huge revolver on his hip. It occurred to Sherman that this was the first gun he had seen since he entered this place. As each prisoner left the detention area and went through the gate, his handcuffs were removed. Sherman slumped against the wall, like all the rest. The corridor was airless. There were no windows. It was filled with a fluorescent haze and the heat and stench of too many bodies. The meat spigot! The chute to the abattoir! Going . . . where?

387 The door at the end of the corridor opened, and a voice from the other side said, "Lantier." The Corrections officer inside the corridor said, "Okay, Lantier." The young man with the crutches struggled to his feet. The Latino next to him gave him a hand. He bounced on his good foot until he could get the crutches settled under his armpits. *What on earth could he have done in that condition?* The policeman opened the door for him, and Sherman could hear a voice on the other side calling out some numbers and then, "Herbert Lantier? . . . counsel representing Herbert Lantier?"

388 The courtroom! At the end of the chute was the courtroom!

389 By the time Sherman's turn came, he felt dazed, groggy, feverish. The voice from the other side said, "Sherman McCoy." The policeman inside said, "McCoy." Sherman shuffled through the door, holding his pants up, sliding his feet so as to keep his shoes on. He was aware of a bright modern room and a great many people going this way and that. The judge's bench, the desks, the seats, were all made of a cheap-looking blond wood. To one side people moved in waves around the judge's elevated blond-wood perch, and on the other side they moved in waves in what appeared to be a spectators' section. So many people . . . such a bright light . . . such confusion . . . such a commotion . . . Between the two sections was a fence, also of blond wood. And at the fence stood Killian . . . He was there! He looked very fresh and dapper in his fancy clothes. He was smiling. It was the reassuring smile you save for invalids. As Sherman shuffled toward him, he became acutely aware of what he himself must look like . . . the filthy sodden jacket and pants . . . the Styrofoam peanuts . . . the wrinkled shirt, the wet shoes with no strings . . . He could smell his own funk of filth, despair, and terror.

390 Someone was reading out some number, and then he heard his name, and then he heard Killian saying his own name, and the judge said, "How do you plead?" Killian said to Sherman, *sotto voce,* "Say, 'Not guilty.' " Sherman croaked out the words.

391 There seemed to be a great deal of commotion in the room. The press? How long had he been in this place? Then an argument broke out. There was an intense heavyset balding young man in front of the judge. He seemed to be from the District Attorney's Office. The judge said *buzz buzz buzz buzz Mr. Kramer.* Mr. Kramer.

392 To Sherman, the judge seemed very young. He was a chubby white man with receding curly hair and a set of robes that looked as if they had been rented for a graduation.

393 Sherman heard Killian mutter, "Sonofabitch."

394 Kramer was saying, "I realize, Your Honor, that our office agreed to bail of only $10,000 in this case. But subsequent developments, matters that have come

to our attention since that time, make it impossible for our office to agree to such a low bail. Your Honor, this case involves a serious injury, very possibly a fatal injury, and we have definite and specific knowledge that there was a witness in this case who has not come forward and that that witness was actually in the car driven by the defendant, Mr. McCoy, and we have every reason to believe that attempts have been or will be made to prevent that witness from coming forth, and we do not believe it will serve the interests of justice—"

395 Killian said, "Your Honor—"

396 "—to allow this defendant to go free on a token bail—"

397 A rumble, a growl, an immense angry mutter rose from the spectators' section, and a single deep voice shouted: "No bail!" Then a mighty mutterers' chorus: "No bail!" . . . "Lock 'im up!" . . . "Bang it shut!"

398 The judge rapped his gavel. The muttering died down.

399 Killian said, "Your Honor, Mr. Kramer knows very well—"

400 The rumble rose again.

401 Kramer plowed on, right over Killian's words: "Given the emotions in this community, quite justifiably aroused by this case, in which it has appeared that justice is a reed—"

402 Killian on the counterattack, shouting: "Your Honor, this is patent nonsense!"

403 A mighty rumble.

404 The rumble erupted into a roar; the muttering into a great raw yawp. "Awww, man!" . . . "Boooooo!" . . . "Yeggggh!" . . . "Shut your filthy mouth and let the man talk!"

405 The judge banged the gavel again. "Quiet!" The roar subsided. Then to Killian: "Let him finish his statement. You can respond."

406 "Thank you, Your Honor," said Kramer. "Your Honor, I would call the court's attention to the fact that this case, even in the arraignment stage, on very short notice, has brought out a heavy representation of the community and most specifically of the friends and neighbors of the victim in this case, Henry Lamb, who remains in extremely grave condition in the hospital."

407 Kramer turned and motioned toward the spectators' section. It was packed. There were people standing. Sherman noticed a group of black men in blue work shirts. One of them was very tall and wore a gold earring.

408 "I have a petition," said Kramer, and he lifted some sheets of paper and waved them over his head. "This document has been signed by more than a hundred members of the community and delivered to the Bronx District Attorney's Office with an appeal that our office be their representative, to see that justice is done in this case, and of course it is no more than our sworn duty to be their representative."

409 "Jesus H. Christ," muttered Killian.

410 "The neighborhood, the community, the people of the Bronx, intend to watch this case, diligently, every step of the judicial process."

411 *Right!* . . . *Yegggh!* . . . *Un-hunnnnh!* . . . *Tell 'im!* A terrific yammering started in the spectators' section.

412 The chubby judge rapped his gavel and called out, "Quiet! This is an arraignment. It's not a rally. Is that all, Mr. Kramer?"

413 Rumble rumble mutter mutter *booooo!*

414 "Your Honor," said Kramer, "I have been instructed by my office, by Mr. Weiss himself, to request bail in the amount of $250,000 in this case."

415 *Right! . . . Yegggh! . . . Tell 'im! . . .* Cheers, applause, stamping on the floor.

416 Sherman looked at Killian. *Tell me—tell me—tell me this can't possibly happen!* But Killian was straining toward the judge. He had his hand in the air. His lips were already moving. The judge was banging the gavel.

417 "Any more of this and I'll clear the room!"

418 "Your Honor," said Killian, as the din subsided, "Mr. Kramer is not content to violate an agreement between his office and my client. He wants a circus! This morning my client was subjected to a circus arrest, despite the fact that he has been ready at all times to testify voluntarily before a grand jury. And now Mr. Kramer manufactures a fictitious threat to an unnamed witness and asks the court to set a preposterous bail. My client is a homeowner of long standing in this city, he has a family and deep roots in his community, and a bail request has been agreed to, as even Mr. Kramer acknowledges, and nothing has occurred to alter the premise of that agreement."

419 "A lot has changed, Your Honor!" said Kramer.

420 "Yeah," said Killian, "the Office of the Bronx District Attorney is what's changed!"

421 "All right!" said the judge. "Mr. Kramer, if your office has information bearing upon the bail status of this case, I instruct you to gather that information and make a formal application to this court, and the matter will be reviewed at that time. Until then, the court is releasing the defendant, Sherman McCoy, under a bond in the amount of $10,000, pending presentation of this complaint to the grand jury."

422 Bellows and screams! *Boooo! . . . Yegggghh! . . . Noooooo! . . . Ged'im!* . . . And then a chant began: *"No bail—put 'im in jail!" . . . "No bail—put 'im in jail!"*

423 Killian was leading him away from the bench. To get out of the courtroom they would have to go straight through the spectators' section, straight through a mass of angry people who were now on their feet. Sherman could see fists in the air. Then he saw policemen coming toward him, half a dozen at least. They wore white shirts and bullet belts and colossal holsters with pistol handles showing. In fact, they were court officers. They closed in around him. *They're putting me back in the cell!* Then he realized they were forming a flying wedge to get him through the crowd. So many glowering faces, black and white! *Murderer! . . . Mother fucker! . . . You gonna get what Henry Lamb got! . . . Say your prayers, Park Avenue! . . . Tear you a new one! . . . McCoy, say—McDead, baby! . . .* He stumbled on, between his white-shirted protectors. He could hear them groaning and straining as they pushed back the crowd. "Coming through! Coming through!" . . . Here and there other faces popped up, lips moving . . . The tall Englishman with the blond hair . . . Fallow . . . The press . . . then more shouts . . . *You mine, Needlenose! Mine! . . . Count every breath, baby! . . . Geed'um! . . . Lights out, sucker! . . . Look at 'im—Park Avenue!*

424 Even in the midst of the storm, Sherman felt strangely unmoved by what was happening. His thoughts told him it was something dreadful, but he didn't feel it. *Since I'm already dead.*

425 The storm burst out of the courtroom and into a lobby. The lobby was full of people standing about. Sherman could see their expressions change from consternation to fear. They began scurrying to the sides, to make way for the rogue galaxy of bodies that had just burst out of the courtroom. Now Killian and the court officers were steering him onto an escalator. There was a hideous mural on the wall. The escalator was heading down. Pressure from behind—he pitched forward, landing on the back of a court officer on the step below. For a moment it seemed as if an avalanche of bodies—but the court officer caught himself on the rolling railings. Now the screaming galaxy burst through the front doors and out onto the main stairway on 161st Street. A wall of bodies was in the way. Television cameras, six or eight of them, microphones, fifteen or twenty of them, screaming white people—the press.

426 The two masses of humanity met, merged, froze. Killian rose up in front of Sherman. Microphones were in his face, and Killian was declaiming, most oratorically:

427 "I want you to show the whole city a New York"—*Yawk*—"what you just saw"—*sawwwwr*—"in there"—*in 'eh.* With the most curious detachment Sherman found himself aware of every street inflection of the fop's voice. "You saw a circus arrest, and then you saw a circus arraignment, and then you saw the District Attorney's Office prostituting itself and perverting the law"—*the lawwwr*—"for your cameras and for the approval of a partisan mob!"

428 *Booooo! . . . Yegggh! . . . Partisan you, you bent-nose bastard!* . . . Somewhere behind him, no more than twenty-four inches away, someone was keening in a singsong falsetto: *"Say your prayers, McCoy . . . Your day is done . . . Say your prayers, McCoy . . . Your day is done . . ."*

429 Killian said: "We reached an agreement with the district attorney yesterday . . ."

430 The singsong falsetto said: *"Say your prayers, McCoy . . . Count your breaths . . ."*

431 Sherman looked up at the sky. The rain had stopped. The sun had broken through. It was a lovely balmy day in June. There was a fluffy blue dome over the Bronx.

432 He looked at the sky and listened to the sounds, just the sounds, the orotund tropes and sententiae, the falsetto songs, the inquisitory shouts, the hippo mutterings, and he thought: I'm not going back in there, ever. I don't care what it takes to keep me out, even if I have to stick a shotgun in my mouth.

433 The only shotgun he had was, in fact, double-barreled. It was a big old thing. He stood on 161st Street, a block from the Grand Concourse, in the Bronx, and wondered if he could get both barrels in his mouth.

QUESTIONS

1. In the first fifteen paragraphs, the narrator gives us a sense of Sherman's feelings, a sense of his panic. Does he do that by rendering an objective report or does he seem to move "inside" Sherman's consciousness? What is the effect in these opening paragraphs of

repetition: repetition about Sherman's heart, about the curtains, about going to jail, about the "ordinary arrest"? How does Wolfe make use of these repetitions throughout the remainder of the chapter?

2. What is the "social fortress" the narrator mentions in paragraph 26? What is Sherman's place in that fortress? How do you know? How important is that fortress to this chapter?
3. What is the meaning of "cheery lodge talk" in paragraph 34? What is the effect of this lodge talk on Sherman? What do we learn about Sherman from his reaction to the talk? What "game" has Sherman lost to Goldberg, Martin, and Killian (paragraph 42)? How is it that Sherman thinks of these men as "His only friends!" (paragraph 193)?
4. Why do you suppose Goldberg snaps the cuffs on Sherman just as the car crosses the East River (paragraph 69)?
5. When the car arrives at the Criminal Courts Building in the Bronx, Sherman sees a mob of people waiting outside the building and thinks of them as people outside a "welfare office" or a "soup kitchen." The narrator refers to these people as "a huge, filthy sprawling dog." Why these similes to describe the press? Later, the same reporters are called "maggots" and "flies" (paragraph 134). What has Wolfe done to make you think they might deserve such names?
6. Why was the experience of going to the Criminal Courts Building "*death*" for Sherman? Why does Sherman feel like Goldberg's "creature"? His "animal" (paragraph 140)? The chapter closes with Sherman thinking about suicide. Given his frame of mind, and the social circumstances surrounding his disgrace, does Sherman face metaphorical death even if he is not convicted of manslaughter?
7. How many different social groups are represented in this chapter? Characterize each group's attitude toward Sherman.
8. What do you think about the language in this chapter? Select instances where you think Wolfe's use of slang is particularly appropriate. Explain. What would be lost if you were to change the slang to standard written English?
9. Why does Wolfe include in this chapter the young black with the Velcro straps on his tennis shoes (paragraph 336 ff.)?
10. Why does Sherman (or the narrator) refer to Killian as a "fop" (paragraph 427)? What does that tell us about Sherman's frame of mind at the arraignment?

SUGGESTIONS FOR WRITING

A. Look carefully at the car ride Sherman takes from Park Avenue to the Criminal Courts Building in the Bronx (paragraphs 18–87). See if you can isolate important phases of that ride. Write a short analysis of what Wolfe reveals to us about Sherman during this ride.

B. Make a list of the various scenes Wolfe creates to carry us from event to event in this chapter. Select one of those scenes (other than the car ride) and explain what the effects of the scene are on Sherman and on you as a reader. Think particularly about how the scene influences the way you feel about Sherman and about what Wolfe is trying to tell you about the interaction between social groups.

C. Write a short essay about the way Wolfe uses the title to give us a comic sense of Sherman's degenerating condition.

D. Assume that you are one of the newspaper reporters outside the Criminal Courts

Building. Write a brief account of Sherman's arraignment for your newspaper. How might that account differ from Wolfe's?

E. Consider Sherman's treatment by those connected with the law. Is it fair? Write a short essay about social inequality and the law. Could you write an interesting and persuasive essay using only the fictive evidence Wolfe presents in this chapter or would you have to do additional research? Explain. Begin by making a list of the points Wolfe makes about social inequality in this fictive account.

F. Write one or two paragraphs about what you think is Wolfe's attitude toward Sherman.

G. Look at the way Annie Dillard makes use of the weasel dangling from the naturalist's hand in the opening paragraph in "Living like Weasels" (page 9, paragraph 1). In a short report for your composition class, compare and contrast Dillard's use of the dangling weasel with Wolfe's use of the dangling mouse in paragraphs 359–361. Is Wolfe's use of the mouse purely comic, or does he get more from the mouse episode than laughs? Explain.

H. Compare and contrast the general ambience in a Hill Street Blues episode with the ambience at the Criminal Courts Building. To what extent do you think the two accounts are parodies of what you might find in a precinct setting? Does your evaluation involve making a judgment about which might be a more authentic, true-to-life account? Which is and why?

THIRTEEN

Joan Didion

(1934–   )

Didion begins one of her essays, "The White Album," with these words: "We tell ourselves stories in order to live." She ends her opening paragraph with an equally promising line that links storytelling, writing, living: "We live entirely, if we are writers, by the imposition of a narrative line upon disparate images, by the 'ideas' with which we have learned to freeze the shifting phantasmagoria which is our actual experience." But she begins the next paragraph with a stunning qualification: "Or at least we do for a while." She goes on in that essay to examine her own life at a moment when her personal center was not holding, when the world was showering her with praise, and when the pictures in her mind no longer made sense. She could no longer impose order by imposing a narrative line. Such are the swings of her mind and mood, and it is because of those swings and because of her willingness to record them and comment honestly on them that we come to trust her, come to look forward to hearing what she has to say about life, about self-respect, about morality, about writing, about Georgia O'Keeffe—about all those "places" in that turbulent, tough mind of hers.

Didion is a writer of great diversity. She has published four nonfiction works: *Slouching Toward Bethlehem* (1968), *The White Album* (1979), *Salvador* (1983), and *Miami* (1987); four novels: *Run River* (1963), *Play It As It Lays* (1970), *The Book of Common Prayer* (1977), and *Democracy* (1984); and sketches, reviews, and screen plays. But in this anthology, we are less interested in the range of her accomplishments than in her effort to make personal experience the legitimate stuff of persuasive nonfiction and of fiction. Like all of the other writers in this anthology, she writes the familiar (or some would say, the personal) essay, but unlike most of the others she writes theoretically about putting her self at the center. She experiments with and comments on that self in her latest novel *Democracy* (1984). And in both nonfiction and fiction, she writes about writing, exploring the relationships between fact and fiction, truth and lies, the author and the narrator, self and world. It is an intriguing exploration.

Educated at Berkeley, Didion came out of an era that predated student protests, antiwar demonstrations, and barricades. The Berkeley of the fifties was not quite as bent on idealist perfection as the Berkeley of the next decade, and Didion tells us that her generation was silent because "the exhilaration of social action seemed to many of us just one more way of escaping the personal, of masking for a while that dread of the meaninglessness which is man's fate." She also reminds us that the "mood was one of mild but chronic 'depression' " and that the images she recalls from those days "were personal, and the personal was all we expected to find." It is easy to read out of these comments and out of her later work much gloom and doom, but to do so is to pass over the implied messages, the insistence on our facing the world and constructing our own terms for dealing with it. In all of Didion's work, there is a subtle, understated longing for a less complex, more stable world, but there is no whining, no refusal to go forward. Neither is hers a solipsistic vision. Facing the personal, facing the self, is to face the world on the barest of terms: alone.

In "Georgia O'Keeffe" *(White Album),* we find Didion celebrating O'Keeffe's "hardness," turning that hardness into something more intriguing than fluttering eyelashes and submissiveness. O'Keeffe is tough minded just as Didion is, and her character is reflected in her style. While Didion suggests at the outset that "every brush stroke laid or not laid down—betrayed one's character," she writes less about the brush strokes than about the character behind the brush strokes, the woman herself, the woman who refused to listen to "the men" who wanted her to learn to paint on their terms. Two things seem most important about the essay's style, two things besides its unmistakable personal quality: the understated but powerful argument against "the men" that Didion wages with the help of O'Keeffe's words, and the repetitious use of words and phrases that create both hypnotic and rhetorical effects: " 'The men' believed it impossible to paint New York, so Georgia O'Keeffe painted New York. 'The men' didn't think much of her bright color, so she made it brighter." 'The men' didn't . . . so Georgia O'Keeffe did.

The same toughness we find in "O'Keeffe," we also find in "On Self-Respect" *(Slouching).* There too we find those informing hypnotic rhythms and her insistence that if we are to have self-respect, we must "eventually lie down alone in that notoriously uncomfortable bed, the one we make ourselves." But that is not all; we must also have "character—the willingness to accept responsibility for one's own life"; we must have "discipline, a habit of mind that can never be faked but can be developed, trained, coaxed forth"; and we must have ritual, a play of values in our lives gained from living with the smaller, daily disciplines.

So however vulnerable and sensitive this diminutive woman may seem to those who consider her only from the outside, there is more beneath the exterior: a tough mind, something durable. She is not just a woman who has headaches, as someone once suggested.

"Goodbye To All That" *(Slouching)* shows us the sensitivity and vulnerability as an older Didion reflects on the experience of a younger self. There is a lyrical quality to this essay, but there is nothing expansive and overly expressive. The prose is taut, the rhythms enticing, and the episodes largely the stuff of memories, interior reconstructions full of detail but free of other identifiable people. Others remain nameless; the focus is on Didion, or what Didion was experiencing during those golden years in New York. Almost as a voice-over, we get to witness the older Didion making sense of the experiences of the younger, commenting, drawing conclusions, extracting maxims. "Part of what I want to tell you is what it is like to be young in New York, how six months can become eight years with the deceptive ease of a film dissolve, for that is how those years appear to me now, in a long sequence of sentimental dissolves and old-fashioned trick shots." She gives us the dissolves and the trick shots, the freeze frames that allow her to make sense of the experience, but she gives us much more—the details, the sense of our own lives projected on a screen—our dreams, our naivete, our self-deceptions, but also our moments of elation, of satisfaction, of transitory freedom. She gives us our lives through hers.

Democracy is an experimental and provocative tour de force. It raises questions about writing, shows us new ways of developing characters, calls into the foreground relationships between the writer and her notebooks, between the writer and the narrator, between fact and fiction. It also raises questions about the extent to which a writer might feel free to bring fiction into nonfiction essays. Didion makes no direct comment about crossing boundary zones, but much of what she says begs that we consider seriously both the complications and the possibilities that arise when we mix fact and fiction.

No one in this anthology suggests more about writing; no one provides a more compelling argument for putting the self at the center of the essay. Like Eiseley, Didion knows how to make use of the image, how to gain clarity and emotional resonance from the picture. Above all else, she knows how to let selected details make her argument, showing us rather than telling us what is on her mind.

On Self-Respect

1 Once, in a dry season, I wrote in large letters across two pages of a notebook that innocence ends when one is stripped of the delusion that one likes oneself. Although now, some years later, I marvel that a mind on the outs with itself should have nonetheless made painstaking record of its every tremor, I recall with embarrassing clarity the flavor of those particular ashes. It was a matter of misplaced self-respect.

2 I had not been elected to Phi Beta Kappa. This failure could scarcely have been more predictable or less ambiguous (I simply did not have the grades), but I was unnerved by it; I had somehow thought myself a kind of academic Raskolnikov, curiously exempt from the cause-effect relationships which hampered others. Although even the humorless nineteen-year-old that I was must have recognized that the situation lacked real tragic stature, the day that I did not make Phi Beta Kappa nonetheless marked the end of something, and innocence may well be the word for it. I lost the conviction that lights would always turn green for me, the pleasant certainty that those rather passive virtues which had won me approval as a child automatically guaranteed me not only Phi Beta Kappa keys but happiness, honor, and the love of a good man; lost a certain touching faith in the totem power of good manners, clean hair, and proven competence on the Stanford-Binet scale. To such doubtful amulets had my self-respect been pinned, and I faced myself that day with the nonplused apprehension of someone who has come across a vampire and has no crucifix at hand.

3 Although to be driven back upon oneself is an uneasy affair at best, rather like trying to cross a border with borrowed credentials, it seems to me now the one condition necessary to the beginnings of real self-respect. Most of our platitudes notwithstanding, self-deception remains the most difficult deception. The tricks that work on others count for nothing in that very well-lit back alley where one keeps assignations with oneself: no winning smiles will do here, no prettily drawn lists of good intentions. One shuffles flashily but in vain through one's marked cards—the kindness done for the wrong reason, the apparent triumph which involved no real

effort, the seemingly heroic act into which one had been shamed. The dismal fact is that self-respect has nothing to do with the approval of others—who are, after all, deceived easily enough; has nothing to do with reputation, which, as Rhett Butler told Scarlett O'Hara, is something people with courage can do without.

4 To do without self-respect, on the other hand, is to be an unwilling audience of one to an interminable documentary that details one's failings, both real and imagined, with fresh footage spliced in for every screening. *There's the glass you broke in anger, there's the hurt on X's face; watch now, this next scene, the night Y came back from Houston, see how you muff this one.* To live without self-respect is to lie awake some night, beyond the reach of warm milk, phenobarbital, and the sleeping hand on the coverlet, counting up the sins of commission and omission, the trusts betrayed, the promises subtly broken, the gifts irrevocably wasted through sloth or cowardice or carelessness. However long we postpone it, we eventually lie down alone in that notoriously uncomfortable bed, the one we make ourselves. Whether or not we sleep in it depends, of course, on whether or not we respect ourselves.

5 To protest that some fairly improbable people, some people who *could not possibly respect themselves,* seem to sleep easily enough is to miss the point entirely, as surely as those people miss it who think that self-respect has necessarily to do with not having safety pins in one's underwear. There is a common superstition that "self-respect" is a kind of charm against snakes, something that keeps those who have it locked in some unblighted Eden, out of strange beds, ambivalent conversations, and trouble in general. It does not at all. It has nothing to do with the face of things, but concerns instead a separate peace, a private reconciliation. Although the careless, suicidal Julian English in *Appointment in Samarra* and the careless, incurably dishonest Jordan Baker in *The Great Gatsby* seem equally improbable candidates for self-respect, Jordan Baker had it, Julian English did not. With that genius for accommodation more often seen in women than in men, Jordan took her own measure, made her own peace, avoided threats to that peace: "I hate careless people," she told Nick Carraway. "It takes two to make an accident."

6 Like Jordan Baker, people with self-respect have the courage of their mistakes. They know the price of things. If they choose to commit adultery, they do not then go running, in an access of bad conscience, to receive absolution from the wronged parties; nor do they complain unduly of the unfairness, the undeserved embarrassment, of being named co-respondent. In brief, people with self-respect exhibit a certain toughness, a kind of moral nerve; they display what was once called *character,* a quality which, although approved in the abstract, sometimes loses ground to other, more instantly negotiable virtues. The measure of its slipping prestige is that one tends to think of it only in connection with homely children and United States senators who have been defeated, preferably in the primary, for reelection. Nonetheless, character—the willingness to accept responsibility for one's own life—is the source from which self-respect springs.

7 Self-respect is something that our grandparents, whether or not they had it, knew all about. They had instilled in them, young, a certain discipline, the sense that one lives by doing things one does not particularly want to do, by putting fears

and doubts to one side, by weighing immediate comforts against the possibility of larger, even intangible, comforts. It seemed to the nineteenth century admirable, but not remarkable, that Chinese Gordon put on a clean white suit and held Khartoum against the Mahdi; it did not seem unjust that the way to free land in California involved death and difficulty and dirt. In a diary kept during the winter of 1846, an emigrating twelve-year-old named Narcissa Cornwall noted coolly: "Father was busy reading and did not notice that the house was being filled with strange Indians until Mother spoke about it." Even lacking any clue as to what Mother said, one can scarcely fail to be impressed by the entire incident: the father reading, the Indians filing in, the mother choosing the words that would not alarm, the child duly recording the event and noting further than those particular Indians were not, "fortunately for us," hostile. Indians were simply part of the *donnée.*

8 In one guise or another, Indians always are. Again, it is a question of recognizing that anything worth having has its price. People who respect themselves are willing to accept the risk that the Indians will be hostile, that the venture will go bankrupt, that the liaison may not turn out to be one in which *every day is a holiday because you're married to me.* They are willing to invest something of themselves; they may not play at all, but when they do play, they know the odds.

9 That kind of self-respect is a discipline, a habit of mind that can never be faked but can be developed, trained, coaxed forth. It was once suggested to me that, as an antidote to crying, I put my head in a paper bag. As it happens, there is a sound physiological reason, something to do with oxygen, for doing exactly that, but the psychological effect alone is incalculable: it is difficult in the extreme to continue fancying oneself Cathy in *Wuthering Heights* with one's head in a Food Fair bag. There is a similar case for all the small disciplines, unimportant in themselves; imagine maintaining any kind of swoon, commiserative or carnal, in a cold shower.

10 But those small disciplines are valuable only insofar as they represent larger ones. To say that Waterloo was won on the playing fields of Eton is not to say that Napoleon might have been saved by a crash program in cricket; to give formal dinners in the rain forest would be pointless did not the candlelight flickering on the liana call forth deeper, stronger disciplines, values instilled long before. It is a kind of ritual, helping us to remember who and what we are. In order to remember it, one must have known it.

11 To have that sense of one's intrinsic worth which constitutes self-respect is potentially to have everything: the ability to discriminate, to love and to remain indifferent. To lack it is to be locked within oneself, paradoxically incapable of either love or indifference. If we do not respect ourselves, we are on the one hand forced to despise those who have so few resources as to consort with us, so little perception as to remain blind to our fatal weaknesses. On the other, we are peculiarly in thrall to everyone we see, curiously determined to live out—since our self-image is untenable—their false notions of us. We flatter ourselves by thinking this compulsion to please others an attractive trait: a gist for imaginative empathy, evidence of our willingness to give. *Of course* I will play Francesca to your Paolo, Helen Keller to anyone's Annie Sullivan: no expectation is too misplaced, no role too ludicrous. At the mercy of those we cannot but hold in contempt, we play roles doomed to failure

before they are begun, each defeat generating fresh despair at the urgency of divining and meeting the next demand made upon us.

12 It is the phenomenon sometimes called "alienation from self." In its advanced stages, we no longer answer the telephone, because someone might want something; that we could say *no* without drowning in self-reproach is an idea alien to this game. Every encounter demands too much, tears the nerves, drains the will, and the specter of something as small as an unanswered letter arouses such disproportionate guilt that answering it becomes out of the question. To assign unanswered letters their proper weight, to free us from the expectations of others, to give us back to ourselves—there lies the great, the singular power of self-respect. Without it, one eventually discovers the final turn of the screw: one runs away to find oneself, and finds no one at home.

(1961)

QUESTIONS

Thought and Structure

1. The title of this essay promises an exploration of the meaning of self-respect. Does Didion ever define the term? Can you boil her essay down to one good sentence? Are you satisfied with her exploration, or are there other considerations?
2. What aspect of self-respect does Didion develop in paragraphs 7–8?
3. What is the relationship between the "small disciplines" and the "larger ones" Didion mentions in paragraphs 9 and 10? Why does she refer to self-respect as a "kind of ritual"? What exactly does she mean by "ritual"?

Style and Strategy

4. If the first two paragraphs deal with "misplaced self-respect," and the next paragraph deals with the "beginnings of real self-respect," with what does paragraph 4 deal? What does Didion mean by each of these notions? Why does she have to get those notions established before beginning her more focused discussion of what self-respect is?
5. The first section of the essay ends with a ringing assertion about "character" (paragraph 6). What does Didion seem to mean by character, and why is it so important to self-respect?
6. Why do you suppose in paragraph 11 that Didion devotes one sentence to what it means to "have that sense of one's intrinsic worth" and devotes the rest of the paragraph (as well as paragraph 12) to what it means "to lack it"?
7. See if you can identify the essay's conclusion. Do paragraphs 9–12 constitute the conclusion, or do only the last two sentences of the essay?
8. Can you make an educated guess about Didion's audience? What are the clues within the text that form the basis for your guess?
9. Examine the following sentence (paragraph 4) that is so crucial to our understanding of what it means to live without self-respect:

To live without self-respect is to lie awake some night,

beyond the reach of warm milk,
phenobarbital, and
the sleeping hand on the coverlet,

counting up the sins of commission and omission,
the trusts betrayed,
the promises subtly broken,
the gifts irrevocably wasted through sloth or
cowardice or
carelessness.

Read this sentence aloud. Do you find it a compelling sentence? What effect do the series of three elements and four have on rhythm and meaning? Does the sentence actually read better if we read it in context within the paragraph? Why or why not?

SUGGESTIONS FOR WRITING

A. Identify a moment in your life when you were "stripped of the delusion that [you] like[d] [yourself]". Write a paragraph explaining how that moment did or did not have anything to do with your developing self-respect.

B. Select another abstract term such as success and write an essay in which you develop your sense of what the term means. Do not quote the dictionary. Use the term itself as few times as possible. Begin as Didion did with a personal anecdote, perhaps the one you developed in suggestion A.

C. In paragraph 3 Didion "shuffles flashily but in vain through [her] marked cards." Shuffle through yours, and create a sentence just like Didion's to show us what the cards reveal.

Goodbye to All That

How many miles to Babylon?
Three Score miles and ten—
Can I get there by candlelight?
Yes, and back again—
If your feet are nimble and light
You can get there by candlelight.

1 It is easy to see the beginnings of things, and harder to see the ends. I can remember now, with a clarity that makes the nerves in the back of my neck constrict, when New York began for me, but I cannot lay my finger upon the moment it ended, can never cut through the ambiguities and second starts and broken resolves to the exact place on the page where the heroine is no longer as optimistic as she once was. When I first saw New York I was twenty, and it was summertime, and I got off a DC-7 at the old Idlewild temporary terminal in a new dress which had seemed very smart in Sacramento but seemed less smart already,

even in the old Idlewild temporary terminal, and the warm air smelled of mildew and some instinct, programmed by all the movies I had ever seen and all the songs I had ever heard sung and all the stories I had ever read about New York, informed me that it would never be quite the same again. In fact it never was. Some time later there was a song on all the jukeboxes on the upper East Side that went "but where is the schoolgirl who used to be me," and if it was late enough at night I used to wonder that. I know now that almost everyone wonders something like that, sooner or later and no matter what he or she is doing, but one of the mixed blessings of being twenty and twenty-one and even twenty-three is the conviction that nothing like this, all evidence to the contrary notwithstanding, has ever happened to anyone before.

2 Of course it might have been some other city, had circumstances been different and the time been different and had I been different, might have been Paris or Chicago or even San Francisco, but because I am talking about myself I am talking here about New York. That first night I opened my window on the bus into town and watched for the skyline, but all I could see were the wastes of Queens and the big signs that said MIDTOWN TUNNEL THIS LANE and then a flood of summer rain (even that seemed remarkable and exotic, for I had come out of the West where there was no summer rain), and for the next three days I sat wrapped in blankets in a hotel room air-conditioned to 35° and tried to get over a bad cold and a high fever. It did not occur to me to call a doctor, because I knew none, and although it did occur to me to call the desk and ask that the air conditioner be turned off, I never called, because I did not know how much to tip whoever might come—was anyone ever so young? I am here to tell you that someone was. All I could do during those three days was talk long-distance to the boy I already knew I would never marry in the spring. I would stay in New York, I told him, just six months, and I could see the Brooklyn Bridge from my window. As it turned out the bridge was the Triborough, and I stayed eight years.

3 In retrospect it seems to me that those days before I knew the names of all the bridges were happier than the ones that came later, but perhaps you will see that as we go along. Part of what I want to tell you is what it is like to be young in New York, how six months can become eight years with the deceptive ease of a film dissolve, for that is how those years appear to me now, in a long sequence of sentimental dissolves and old-fashioned trick shots—the Seagram Building fountains dissolve into snowflakes, I enter a revolving door at twenty and come out a good deal older, and on a different street. But most particularly I want to explain to you, and in the process perhaps to myself, why I no longer live in New York. It is often said that New York is a city of only the very rich and the very poor. It is less often said that New York is also, at least for those of us who came there from somewhere else, a city for only the very young.

4 I remember once, one cold bright December evening in New York, suggesting to a friend who complained of having been around too long that he come with me to a party where there would be, I assured him with the bright resourcefulness of twenty-three, "new faces." He laughed literally until he choked, and I had to roll down the taxi window and hit him on the back. "New faces," he said finally, "don't

tell me about *new faces.*" It seems that the last time he had gone to a party where he had been promised "new faces," there had been fifteen people in the room, and he had already slept with five of the women and owed money to all but two of the men. I laughed with him, but the first snow had just begun to fall and the big Christmas trees glittered yellow and white as far as I could see up Park Avenue and I had a new dress and it would be a long while before I would come to understand the particular moral of the story.

5 It would be a long while because, quite simply, I was in love with New York. I do not mean "love" in any colloquial way, I mean that I was in love with the city, the way you love the first person who ever touches you and never love anyone quite that way again. I remember walking across Sixty-second Street one twilight that first spring, or the second spring, they were all alike for a while. I was late to meet someone but I stopped at Lexington Avenue and bought a peach and stood on the corner eating it and knew that I had come out of the West and reached the mirage. I could taste the peach and feel the soft air blowing from a subway grating on my legs and I could smell lilac and garbage and expensive perfume and I knew that it would cost something sooner or later—because I did not belong there, did not come from there—but when you are twenty-two or twenty-three, you figure that later you will have a high emotional balance, and be able to pay whatever it costs. I still believed in possibilities then, still had the sense, so peculiar to New York, that something extraordinary would happen any minute, any day, any month. I was making only $65 or $70 a week then ("Put yourself in Hattie Carnegie's hands," I was advised without the slightest trace of irony by an editor of the magazine for which I worked), so little money that some weeks I had to charge food at Bloomingdale's gourmet shop in order to eat, a fact which went unmentioned in the letters I wrote to California. I never told my father that I needed money because then he would have sent it, and I would never know if I could do it by myself. At that time making a living seemed a game to me, with arbitrary but quite inflexible rules. And except on a certain kind of winter evening—six-thirty in the Seventies, say, already dark and bitter with a wind off the river, when I would be walking very fast toward a bus and would look in the bright windows of brownstones and see cooks working in clean kitchens and imagine women lighting candles on the floor above and beautiful children being bathed on the floor above that—except on nights like those, I never felt poor; I had the feeling that if I needed money I could always get it. I could write a syndicated column for teenagers under the name "Debbi Lynn" or I could smuggle gold into India or I could become a $100 call girl, and none of it would matter.

6 Nothing was irrevocable; everything was within reach. Just around every corner lay something curious and interesting, something I had never before seen or done or known about. I could go to a party and meet someone who called himself Mr. Emotional Appeal and ran The Emotional Appeal Institute or Tina Onassis Blandford or a Florida cracker who was then a regular on what he called "the Big C," the Southampton—El Morocco circuit ("I'm well-connected on the Big C, honey," he would tell me over collard greens on his vast borrowed terrace), or the widow of the celery king of the Harlem market or a piano salesman from Bonne Terre, Missouri, or someone who had already made and lost two fortunes in Mid-

land, Texas. I could make promises to myself and to other people and there would be all the time in the world to keep them. I could stay up all night and make mistakes, and none of it would count.

7 You see I was in a curious position in New York: it never occurred to me that I was living a real life there. In my imagination I was always there for just another few months, just until Christmas or Easter or the first warm day in May. For that reason I was most comfortable in the company of Southerners. They seemed to be in New York as I was, on some indefinitely extended leave from wherever they belonged, disinclined to consider the future, temporary exiles who always knew when the flights left for New Orleans or Memphis or Richmond or, in my case, California. Someone who lives always with a plane schedule in the drawer lives on a slightly different calendar. Christmas, for example, was a difficult season. Other people could take it in stride, going to Stowe or going abroad or going for the day to their mothers' places in Connecticut; those of us who believed that we lived somewhere else would spend it making and canceling airline reservations, waiting for weatherbound flights as if for the last plane out of Lisbon in 1940, and finally comforting one another, those of us who were left, with the oranges and mementos and smoked-oyster stuffings of childhood, gathering close, colonials in a far country.

8 Which is precisely what we were. I am not sure that it is possible for anyone brought up in the East to appreciate entirely what New York, the idea of New York, means to those of us who came out of the West and the South. To an Eastern child, particularly a child who has always had an uncle on Wall Street and who has spent several hundred Saturdays first at F. A. O. Schwarz and being fitted for shoes at Best's and then waiting under the Biltmore clock and dancing to Lester Lanin, New York is just a city, albeit *the* city, a plausible place for people to live. But to those of us who came from places where no one had heard of Lester Lanin and Grand Central Station was a Saturday radio program, where Wall Street and Fifth Avenue and Madison Avenue were not places at all but abstractions ("Money," and "High Fashion," and "The Hucksters"), New York was no mere city. It was instead an infinitely romantic notion, the mysterious nexus of all love and money and power, the shining and perishable dream itself. To think of "living" there was to reduce the miraculous to the mundane; one does not "live" at Xanadu.

9 In fact it was difficult in the extreme for me to understand those young women for whom New York was not simply an ephemeral Estoril but a real place, girls who bought toasters and installed new cabinets in their apartments and committed themselves to some reasonable future. I never bought any furniture in New York. For a year or so I lived in other people's apartments; after that I lived in the Nineties in an apartment furnished entirely with things taken from storage by a friend whose wife had moved away. And when I left the apartment in the Nineties (that was when I was leaving everything, when it was all breaking up) I left everything in it, even my winter clothes and the map of Sacramento County I had hung on the bedroom wall to remind me who I was, and I moved into a monastic four-room floor-through on Seventy-fifth Street. "Monastic" is perhaps misleading here, implying some chic severity; until after I was married and my husband moved some furniture in, there was nothing at all in those four rooms except a cheap double mattress and box springs, ordered by telephone the day I decided to move, and two French garden

chairs lent me by a friend who imported them. (It strikes me now that the people I knew in New York all had curious and self-defeating sidelines. They imported garden chairs which did not sell very well at Hammacher Schlemmer or they tried to market hair straighteners in Harlem or they ghosted exposés of Murder Incorporated for Sunday supplements. I think that perhaps none of us was very serious, *engagé* only about our most private lives.)

10 All I ever did to that apartment was hang fifty yards of yellow theatrical silk across the bedroom windows, because I had some idea that the gold light would make me feel better, but I did not bother to weight the curtains correctly and all that summer the long panels of transparent gold silk would blow out the windows and get tangled and drenched in the afternoon thunderstorms. That was the year, my twenty-eighth, when I was discovering that not all of the promises would be kept, that some things are in fact irrevocable and that it had counted after all, every evasion and every procrastination, every mistake, every word, all of it.

11 That is what it was all about, wasn't it? Promises? Now when New York comes back to me it comes in hallucinatory flashes, so clinically detailed that I sometimes wish that memory would effect the distortion with which it is commonly credited. For a lot of the time I was in New York I used a perfume called *Fleurs de Rocaille,* and then *L'Air du Temps,* and now the slightest trace of either can short-circuit my connections for the rest of the day. Nor can I smell Henri Bendel jasmine soap without falling back into the past, or the particular mixture of spices used for boiling crabs. There were barrels of crab boil in a Czech place in the Eighties where I once shopped. Smells, of course, are notorious memory stimuli, but there are other things which affect me the same way. Blue-and-white striped sheets. Vermouth cassis. Some faded nightgowns which were new in 1959 or 1960, and some chiffon scarves I bought about the same time.

12 I suppose that a lot of us who have been young in New York have the same scenes on our home screens. I remember sitting in a lot of apartments with a slight headache about five o'clock in the morning. I had a friend who could not sleep, and he knew a few other people who had the same trouble, and we would watch the sky lighten and have a last drink with no ice and then go home in the early morning light, when the streets were clean and wet (had it rained in the night? we never knew) and the few cruising taxis still had their headlights on and the only color was the red and green of traffic signals. The White Rose bars opened very early in the morning; I recall waiting in one of them to watch an astronaut go into space, waiting so long that at the moment it actually happened I had my eyes not on the television screen but on a cockroach on the tile floor. I liked the bleak branches above Washington Square at dawn, and the monochromatic flatness of Second Avenue, and fire escapes and the grilled storefronts peculiar and empty in their perspective.

13 It is relatively hard to fight at six-thirty or seven in the morning without any sleep, which was perhaps one reason we stayed up all night, and it seemed to me a pleasant time of day. The windows were shuttered in that apartment in the Nineties and I could sleep a few hours and then go to work. I could work then on two or three hours' sleep and a container of coffee from Chock Full O' Nuts. I liked going to work, liked the soothing and satisfactory rhythm of getting out a magazine,

liked the orderly progression of four-color closings and two-color closings and black-and-white closings and then The Product, no abstraction but something which looked effortlessly glossy and could be picked up on a newsstand and weighed in the hand. I liked all the minutiae of proofs and layouts, liked working late on the nights the magazine went to press, sitting and reading *Variety* and waiting for the copy desk to call. From my office I could look across town to the weather signal on the Mutual of New York Building and the lights that alternately spelled out TIME and LIFE above Rockefeller Plaza; that pleased me obscurely, and so did walking uptown in the mauve eight o'clocks of early summer evenings and looking at things, Lowestoft tureens in Fifty-seventh Street windows, people in evening clothes trying to get taxis, the trees just coming into full leaf, the lambent air, all the sweet promises of money and summer.

14 Some years passed, but I still did not lose that sense of wonder about New York. I began to cherish the loneliness of it, the sense that at any given time no one need know where I was or what I was doing. I liked walking, from the East River over to the Hudson and back on brisk days, down around the Village on warm days. A friend would leave me the key to her apartment in the West Village when she was out of town, and sometimes I would just move down there, because by that time the telephone was beginning to bother me (the canker, you see, was already in the rose) and not many people had that number. I remember one day when someone who did have the West Village number came to pick me up for lunch there, and we both had hangovers, and I cut my finger opening him a beer and burst into tears, and we walked to a Spanish restaurant and drank Bloody Marys and *gazpacho* until we felt better. I was not then guilt-ridden about spending afternoons that way, because I still had all the afternoons in the world.

15 And even that late in the game I still liked going to parties, all parties, bad parties, Saturday-afternoon parties given by recently married couples who lived in Stuyvesant Town, West Side parties given by unpublished or failed writers who served cheap red wine and talked about going to Guadalajara, Village parties where all the guests worked for advertising agencies and voted for Reform Democrats, press parties at Sardi's, the worst kinds of parties. You will have perceived by now that I was not one to profit by the experience of others, that it was a very long time indeed before I stopped believing in new faces and began to understand the lesson in that story, which was that it is distinctly possible to stay too long at the Fair.

16 I could not tell you when I began to understand that. All I know is that it was very bad when I was twenty-eight. Everything that was said to me I seemed to have heard before, and I could no longer listen. I could no longer sit in little bars near Grand Central and listen to someone complaining of his wife's inability to cope with the help while he missed another train to Connecticut. I no longer had any interest in hearing about the advances other people had received from their publishers, about plays which were having second-act trouble in Philadelphia, or about people I would like very much if only I would come out to meet them. I had already met them, always. There were certain parts of the city which I had to avoid. I could not bear upper Madison Avenue on weekday mornings (this was a particularly inconvenient aversion, since I lived just fifty or sixty feet east of Madison), because I would see

women walking Yorkshire terriers and shopping at Gristede's, and some Veblenesque gorge would rise in my throat. I could not go to Times Square in the afternoon, or to the New York Public Library for any reason whatsoever. One day I could not go into a Schrafft's; the next day it would be Bonwit Teller.

17 I hurt the people I cared about, and insulted those I did not. I cut myself off from the one person who was closer to me than any other. I cried until I was not even aware when I was crying and when I was not, cried in elevators and in taxis and in Chinese laundries, and when I went to the doctor he said only that I seemed to be depressed, and should see a "specialist." He wrote down a psychiatrist's name and address for me, but I did not go.

18 Instead I got married, which as it turned out was a very good thing to do but badly timed, since I still could not walk on upper Madison Avenue in the mornings and still could not talk to people and still cried in Chinese laundries. I had never before understood what "despair" meant, and I am not sure that I understand now, but I understood that year. Of course I could not work. I could not even get dinner with any degree of certainty, and I would sit in the apartment on Seventy-fifth Street paralyzed until my husband would call from his office and say gently that I did not have to get dinner, that I could meet him at Michael's Pub or at Toots Shor's or at Sardi's East. And then one morning in April (we had been married in January) he called and told me that he wanted to get out of New York for a while, that he would take a six-month leave of absence, that we would go somewhere.

19 It was three years ago that he told me that, and we have lived in Los Angeles since. Many of the people we knew in New York think this a curious aberration, and in fact tell us so. There is no possible, no adequate answer to that, and so we give certain stock answers, the answers everyone gives. I talk about how difficult it would be for us to "afford" to live in New York right now, about how much "space" we need. All I mean is that I was very young in New York, and that at some point the golden rhythm was broken, and I am not that young any more. The last time I was in New York was in a cold January, and everyone was ill and tired. Many of the people I used to know there had moved to Dallas or had gone on Antabuse or had bought a farm in New Hampshire. We stayed ten days, and then we took an afternoon flight back to Los Angeles, and on the way home from the airport that night I could see the moon on the Pacific and smell jasmine all around and we both knew that there was no longer any point in keeping the apartment we still kept in New York. There were years when I called Los Angeles "the Coast," but they seem a long time ago.

(1967)

QUESTIONS

Thought and Structure

1. What does Didion suggest this essay's universal quality is in the first sentence of paragraph 2?

2. Why does Didion tell us first that she could see the Brooklyn Bridge from her window and then tell us the truth—that she could see the Triborough? Which of those claims is the "truth"? What special quality does she associate with the Brooklyn Bridge?
3. In paragraph 4 Didion mentions "the particular moral of the story." What is "the particular moral" of her story? Can you find one sentence in the essay that accounts for the moral and the essay?
4. What does Didion mean by "colonials in a far country" (paragraph 7)? By "Xanadu" (paragraph 8)? By the phrase "not all of the promises would be kept" (paragraph 10)? By the phrase "same scenes on our home screens" (paragraph 12)? By the recognition that "the canker . . . was already in the rose" (paragraph 14)? By her understanding "that it [was] distinctly possible to stay too long at the Fair" (paragraph 15)? By her clear sense "that at some point the golden rhythm was broken" (paragraph 19)? What does Didion get out of these metaphors: colonials, Xanadu, promises, rose, Fair, golden rhythm? Would it be better just to tell us straight out what is on her mind? Explain.

Style and Strategy

5. One of the sentences in paragraph 1 is interesting, but it seems to be slightly flawed. Let's look at the way it works, at its shape:

    When I first saw New York I was twenty,
  and
  it was summertime,
  and
  I got off a DC-7 at the old Idlewild temporary terminal in a new
    dress which had seemed very smart in Sacramento but seemed less
    smart already,
      even in the old Idlewild temporary terminal,
  and
  the warm air smelled of mildew
  and
  some instinct,
    programmed by all the movies I had ever seen and all the songs I
    had ever heard sung and all the stories I had ever read about New
    York,
          informed me that it would never be
            quite the same again.

   There are five independent clauses in this sentence joined by four coordinating conjunctions. Each of those conjunctions is preceeded by a comma except the last. Should it be? Why? What makes this an effective sentence? Can we infer the story of Didion's early life from this sentence? What is the effect of the much shorter sentence that follows: "In fact it never was"? Can we find the point of the essay embedded in these two sentences?
6. Didion seems to have a penchant for detail in this essay, some of it factual detail about New York, but most of it private detail about her life. Find examples of each and make some valuation of how well she uses that detail to enhance her essay.
7. Underline all of Didion's uses of the verb "liked" in paragraph 13. Read aloud the group of sentences that repeat the verb. What is the effect of the repetition? How does she vary your reading rhythm by the way she places the verb in the sentences? Is there any relationship between that rhythm and the "rhythm of getting out a magazine"?

SUGGESTIONS FOR WRITING

A. In one paragraph write down what you think Didion says about life in the first paragraph of her essay. See if you can extract what you think is her overview about life itself.

B. Look at paragraph 5 of Didion's essay and then consider these lines from T. S. Eliot's "The Love Song of J. Alfred Prufrock":

> I grow old . . . I grow old . . .
> I shall wear the bottoms of my trousers rolled.
>
> Shall I part my hair behind? Do I dare to eat a peach?
> I shall wear white flannel trousers, and walk upon the beach.
> I have heard the mermaids singing, each to each.
>
> I do not think that they will sing to me.

What can we learn about the stages of life by comparing Didion's essay and Eliot's poem? Write a short essay comparing and contrasting the states of mind of the young Didion and the older Prufrock.

C. Look carefully at the overall structure of the essay: paragraphs 1–2, 3–10, 11–15, and 16–19. Describe each of those sections with one word. Then write one sentence about each section, explaining its purpose. That purpose should account for the controlling idea in each section—if you can discern one.

D. Start with the base sentence "When I saw ____________ I was ____________. Add to that base sentence as Didion did to hers: "When I first saw New York I was twenty" (question 5, above). See if you too can, in one sentence, give us a sense of a particular moment in your life. Try, by adding detail and qualification (modifiers), to make that sentence taut even as it gets larger.

Why I Write

1 Of course I stole the title for this talk, from George Orwell. One reason I stole it was that I like the sound of the words: *Why I Write.* There you have three short unambiguous words that share a sound, and the sound they share is this:

I
I
I

2 In many ways writing is the act of saying *I,* of imposing oneself upon other people, of saying *listen to me, see it my way, change your mind.* It's an aggressive, even a hostile act. You can disguise its aggressiveness all you want with veils of subordinate clauses and qualifiers and tentative subjunctives, with ellipses and evasions—with the whole manner of intimating rather than claiming, of alluding rather than stating—but there's no getting around the fact that setting words on paper is the tactic of a secret bully, an invasion, an imposition of the writer's sensibility on the reader's most private space.

3 I stole the title not only because the words sounded right but because they seemed to sum up, in a no-nonsense way, all I have to tell you. Like many writers I have only this one "subject," this one "area": the act of writing. I can bring you no reports from any other front. I may have other interests: I am "interested," for example, in marine biology, but I don't flatter myself that you would come out to hear me talk about it. I am not a scholar. I am not in the least an intellectual, which is not to say that when I hear the word "intellectual" I reach for my gun, but only to say that I do not think in abstracts. During the years when I was an undergraduate at Berkeley I tried, with a kind of hopeless late-adolescent energy, to buy some temporary visa into the world of ideas, to forge for myself a mind that could deal with the abstract.

4 In short I tried to think. I failed. My attention veered inexorably back to the specific, to the tangible, to what was generally considered, by everyone I knew then and for that matter have known since, the peripheral. I would try to contemplate the Hegelian dialectic and would find myself concentrating instead on a flowering pear tree outside my window and the particular way the petals fell on my floor. I would try to read linguistic theory and would find myself wondering instead if the lights were on in the bevatron up the hill. When I say that I was wondering if the lights were on in the bevatron you might immediately suspect, if you deal in ideas at all, that I was registering the bevatron as a political symbol, thinking in shorthand about the military-industrial complex and its role in the university community, but you would be wrong. I was only wondering if the lights were on in the bevatron, and how they looked. A physical fact.

5 I had trouble graduating from Berkeley, not because of this inability to deal with ideas—I was majoring in English, and I could locate the house-and-garden imagery in "The Portrait of a Lady" as well as the next person, "imagery" being by definition the kind of specific that got my attention—but simply because I had neglected to take a course in Milton. For reasons which now sound baroque I needed a degree by the end of that summer, and the English department finally agreed, if I would come down from Sacramento every Friday and talk about the cosmology of "Paradise Lost," to certify me proficient in Milton. I did this. Some Fridays I took the Greyhound bus, other Fridays I caught the Southern Pacific's City of San Francisco on the last leg of its transcontinental trip. I can no longer tell you whether Milton put the sun or the earth at the center of his universe in "Paradise Lost," the central question of at least one century and a topic about which I wrote 10,000 words that summer, but I can still recall the exact rancidity of the butter in the City of San Francisco's dining car, and the way the tinted windows on the Greyhound bus cast the oil refineries around Carquinez Straits into a grayed and obscurely sinister light. In short my attention was always on the periphery, on what I could see and taste and touch, on the butter, and the Greyhound bus. During those years I was traveling on what I knew to be a very shaky passport, forged papers: I knew that I was no legitimate resident in any world of ideas. I knew I couldn't think. All I knew then was what I wasn't, and it took me some years to discover what I was.

6 Which was a writer.

7 By which I mean not a "good" writer or a "bad" writer but simply a writer, a person whose most absorbed and passionate hours are spent arranging words on

pieces of paper. Had my credentials been in order I would never have become a writer. Had I been blessed with even limited access to my own mind there would have been no reason to write. I write entirely to find out what I'm thinking, what I'm looking at, what I see and what it means. What I want and what I fear. Why did the oil refineries around Carquinez Straits seem sinister to me in the summer of 1956? Why have the night lights in the bevatron burned in my mind for twenty years? *What is going on in these pictures in my mind?*

8 When I talk about pictures in my mind I am talking, quite specifically, about images that shimmer around the edges. There used to be an illustration in every elementary psychology book showing a cat drawn by a patient in varying stages of schizophrenia. This cat had a shimmer around it. You could see the molecular structure breaking down at the very edges of the cat: the cat became the background and the background the cat, everything interacting, exchanging ions. People on hallucinogens describe the same perception of objects. I'm not a schizophrenic, nor do I take hallucinogens, but certain images do shimmer for me. Look hard enough, and you can't miss the shimmer. It's there. You can't think too much about these pictures that shimmer. You just lie low and let them develop. You stay quiet. You don't talk to many people and you keep your nervous system from shorting out and you try to locate the cat in the shimmer, the grammar in the picture.

9 Just as I meant "shimmer" literally I mean "grammar" literally. Grammar is a piano I play by ear, since I seem to have been out of school the year the rules were mentioned. All I know about grammar is its infinite power. To shift the structure of a sentence alters the meaning of that sentence, as definitely and inflexibly as the position of a camera alters the meaning of the object photographed. Many people know about camera angles now, but not so many know about sentences. The arrangement of the words matters, and the arrangement you want can be found in the picture in your mind. The picture dictates the arrangement. The picture dictates whether this will be a sentence with or without clauses, a sentence that ends hard or a dying-fall sentence, long or short, active or passive. The picture tells you how to arrange the words and the arrangement of the words tells you, or tells me, what's going on in the picture. *Nota bene:*

10 It tells you.

11 You don't tell it.

12 Let me show you what I mean by pictures in the mind. I began "Play It As It Lays" just as I have begun each of my novels, with no notion of "character" or "plot" or even "incident." I had only two pictures in my mind, more about which later, and a technical intention, which was to write a novel so elliptical and fast that it would be over before you noticed it, a novel so fast that it would scarcely exist on the page at all. About the pictures: the first was of white space. Empty space. This was clearly the picture that dictated the narrative intention of the book—a book in which anything that happened would happen off the page, a "white" book to which the reader would have to bring his or her own bad dreams—and yet this picture told me no "story," suggested no situation. The second picture did. This second picture was of something actually witnessed. A young woman with long hair and a short white halter dress walks through the casino at the Riviera in Las Vegas at one in the morning. She crosses the casino alone and picks up a house telephone.

I watch her because I have heard her paged, and recognize her name: she is a minor actress I see around Los Angeles from time to time, in places like Jax and once in a gynecologist's office in the Beverly Hills Clinic, but have never met. I know nothing about her. Who is paging her? Why is she here to be paged? How exactly did she come to this? It was precisely this moment in Las Vegas that made "Play It As It Lays" begin to tell itself to me, but the moment appears in the novel only obliquely, in a chapter which begins:

13 "Maria made a list of things she would never do. She would never: walk through the Sands or Caesar's alone after midnight. She would never: ball at a party, do S-M unless she wanted to, borrow furs from Abe Lipsey, deal. She would never: carry a Yorkshire in Beverly Hills."

14 That is the beginning of the chapter and that is also the end of the chapter, which may suggest what I meant by "white space."

15 I recall having a number of pictures in my mind when I began the novel I just finished, "A Book of Common Prayer." As a matter of fact one of these pictures was of that bevatron I mentioned, although I would be hard put to tell you a story in which nuclear energy figured. Another was a newspaper photograph of a hijacked 707 burning on the desert in the Middle East. Another was the night view from a room in which I once spent a week with paratyphoid, a hotel room on the Colombian coast. My husband and I seemed to be on the Colombian coast representing the United States of America at a film festival (I recall invoking the name "Jack Valenti" a lot, as if its reiteration could make me well), and it was a bad place to have fever, not only because my indisposition offended our hosts but because every night in this hotel the generator failed. The lights went out. The elevator stopped. My husband would go to the event of the evening and make excuses for me and I would stay alone in this hotel room, in the dark. I remember standing at the window trying to call Bogotá (the telephone seemed to work on the same principle as the generator) and watching the night wind come up and wondering what I was doing eleven degrees off the equator with a fever of 103. The view from that window definitely figures in "A Book of Common Prayer," as does the burning 707, and yet none of these pictures told me the story I needed.

16 The picture that did, the picture that shimmered and made these other images coalesce, was the Panama airport at 6 A.M. I was in this airport only once, on a plane to Bogotá that stopped for an hour to refuel, but the way it looked that morning remained superimposed on everything I saw until the day I finished "A Book of Common Prayer." I lived in that airport for several years. I can still feel the hot air when I step off the plane, can see the heat already rising off the tarmac at 6 A.M. I can feel my skirt damp and wrinkled on my legs. I can feel the asphalt stick to my sandals. I remember the big tail of a Pan American plane floating motionless down at the end of the tarmac. I remember the sound of a slot machine in the waiting room. I could tell you that I remember a particular woman in the airport, an American woman, a *norteamericana,* a thin *norteamericana* about 40 who wore a big square emerald in lieu of a wedding ring, but there was no such woman there.

17 I put this woman in the airport later. I made this woman up, just as I later made up a country to put the airport in, and a family to run the country. This woman in the airport is neither catching a plane nor meeting one. She is ordering tea in

the airport coffee shop. In fact she is not simply "ordering" tea but insisting that the water be boiled, in front of her, for twenty minutes. Why is this woman in this airport? Why is she going nowhere, where has she been? Where did she get that big emerald? What derangement, or disassociation, makes her believe that her will to see the water boiled can possibly prevail?

18 "She had been going to one airport or another for four months, one could see it, looking at the visas on her passport. All those airports where Charlotte Douglas's passport had been stamped would have looked alike. Sometimes the sign on the tower would say 'Bienvenidos' and sometimes the sign on the tower would say 'Bienvenue,' some places were wet and hot and others dry and hot, but at each of these airports the pastel concrete walls would rust and stain and the swamp off the runway would be littered with the fuselages of cannibalized Fairchild F-227's and the water would need boiling.

19 "I knew why Charlotte went to the airport even if Victor did not.

20 "I knew about airports."

21 These lines appear about halfway through "A Book of Common Prayer," but I wrote them during the second week I worked on the book, long before I had any idea where Charlotte Douglas had been or why she went to airports. Until I wrote these lines I had no character called "Victor" in mind: the necessity for mentioning a name, and the name "Victor," occurred to me as I wrote the sentence. *I knew why Charlotte went to the airport* sounded incomplete. *I knew why Charlotte went to the airport even if Victor did not* carried a little more narrative drive. Most important of all, until I wrote these lines I did not know who "I" was, who was telling the story. I had intended until that moment that the "I" be no more than the voice of the author, a 19th-century omniscient narrator. But there it was:

22 "I knew why Charlotte went to the airport even if Victor did not.

23 "I knew about airports."

24 This "I" was the voice of no author in my house. This "I" was someone who not only knew why Charlotte went to the airport but also knew someone called "Victor." Who was Victor? Who was this narrator? Why was this narrator telling me this story? Let me tell you one thing about why writers write: had I known the answer to any of these questions I would never have needed to write a novel.

(1976)

QUESTIONS

Thought and Structure

1. Didion says she "stole" her title from George Orwell. Under what circumstances is such literary "theft" legitimate? How far can any writer, including you, go with this kind of borrowing?
2. Didion links the word "abstracts" with the phrase "world of ideas," equating them in a sense (paragraph 3)? Are ideas necessarily abstract? What can you learn from paragraphs 3 and 4 that might help you in your own writing?

3. What do you think of Didion's definition of a writer: "a person whose most absorbed and passionate hours are spent arranging words on pieces of paper"? What about the words "absorbed and passionate"?
4. In paragraph 7 Didion claims that she writes "entirely to find out what [she's] thinking." The last sentence of the essay adds another dimension to this claim: "Let me tell you one thing about why writers write: had I known the answer to any of these questions [about the pictures in my mind] I would never have needed to write a novel." What about the word "needed"? What do you think it means in terms of what she has told us in the essay?
5. What does Didion mean when she says, "To shift the structure of a sentence alters the meaning of that sentence" (paragraph 9)? Alter one of Didion's sentences and see if the meaning changes. Write a sentence of your own, change it internally, and see if the meaning changes. Didion says that this shifting alters meaning much "as the position of a camera alters the meaning of the object photographed." What does she gain from that analogy? Does she help you see her point more clearly? Explain.
6. How does Didion begin writing? What does she start with? Are there advantages or disadvantages to the way she starts? Do you think her method might work for you?

Style and Strategy

7. In paragraph 1 Didion calls our attention to three interesting sounds: Why I Write: I I I. Look in paragraph 2 not for three sounds but for a number of different structural units of three. Consider the first sentence:

> In many ways writing is the act of saying *I*,
> of imposing oneself upon other people,
> of saying *listen to me,*
> *see it my way,*
> *change your mind.*

   Find other examples in the paragraph and consider what special effects Didion creates by such repetitions. In the third sentence of the paragraph, she changes from structural units of three to units of two. Can you find the point of change and trace its effect on the shape of that third and final sentence?
8. In paragraphs 7–11, Didion tells us about "shimmering pictures" in her mind; in the paragraphs that follow, she gives us examples of those pictures. Why does she spend so much time with these examples, and what kinds of things does she tell us as she goes along about the writing process, about the way she gets her writing done? To what extent does Didion seem to be in control of what she is doing as she composes? Do these paragraphs (7–24)—the way they work together, their order, their relationship to one another—suggest that something else goes on after the initial composing is finished?

SUGGESTIONS FOR WRITING

A. Select some abstract idea that you have copied in your notebook from another class. Start writing a paragraph about that idea, and see if you can move from the abstract to the specific. Which does your mind prefer? How do you think the two ways of thinking should work together in an essay, or even a paragraph such as the one you just wrote. Experiment with that paragraph, varying the amount of abstraction and the amount of specific detail. Bring two paragraphs to class—the one you like best from the experiment and another one explaining your preference.

B. Compare Didion's claim that she writes "entirely to find out what I'm thinking, what I'm looking at, what I see and what it means" and Dillard's claim that "seeing is . . . very much a matter of verbalization" ("Seeing," p. 553). As you develop your answer, provide evidence from your own writing experiences to illustrate what you think Dillard and Didion mean. Are they saying the same thing, and do you agree with them?

C. Look carefully at what Didion says about "shimmering pictures" and compare that with what Eiseley says in "Willy" about the pictures in the "artist's loft." Search your artist's loft for one of those pictures, preferably one that shimmers. Find words for what you see and write about the image so that we too can see it; it may be a dramatic moment, a fascinating object, or even a kind of moving-picture episode. Tell us about what you see so that we can see it.

D. As a continuation of the exercise you did for suggestion C, try to find an idea embedded in that picture you created. Write it down, or write them down. Look too to see if the picture did, as Didion claims, have its own "grammar". Did the picture "tell you" how to arrange the words? If not, who did? Can you account, in any rational way, for how the words actually got arranged?

E. In "On Keeping a Notebook" Didion says that she keeps a notebook not to have a record of what she's been doing but to keep in touch with who she was at different points in her life. Try for a month or so to keep some kind of notebook or journal of your responses to things you do, see, hear, encounter. Avoid making it either a diary so private you'd want no one to read it, or simply a record of trivial and uninteresting actions ("I got up; I brushed my teeth and went to work.") Make it a reacting notebook, a book of notes on your thoughts and feelings, your ideas and attitudes about any and every thing you find interesting. Include some word pictures of things you observed.

Georgia O'Keeffe

1 "Where I was born and where and how I have lived is unimportant," Georgia O'Keeffe told us in the book of paintings and words published in her ninetieth year on earth. She seemed to be advising us to forget the beautiful face in the Stieglitz photographs. She appeared to be dismissing the rather condescending romance that had attached to her by then, the romance of extreme good looks and advanced age and deliberate isolation. "It is what I have done with where I have been that should be of interest." I recall an August afternoon in Chicago in 1973 when I took my daughter, then seven, to see what Georgia O'Keeffe had done with where she had been. One of the vast O'Keeffe "Sky Above Clouds" canvases floated over the back stairs in the Chicago Art Institute that day, dominating what seemed to be several stories of empty light, and my daughter looked at it once, ran to the landing, and kept on looking. "Who drew it," she whispered after a while. I told her. "I need to talk to her," she said finally.

2 My daughter was making, that day in Chicago, an entirely unconscious but quite basic assumption about people and the work they do. She was assuming that the glory she saw in the work reflected a glory in its maker, that the painting was the painter as the poem is the poet, that every choice one made alone—every word chosen or rejected, every brush stroke laid or not laid down—betrayed one's character. *Style is character.* It seemed to me that afternoon that I had rarely seen so

instinctive an application of this familiar principle, and I recall being pleased not only that my daughter responded to style as character but that it was Georgia O'Keeffe's particular style to which she responded: this was a hard woman who had imposed her 192 square feet of clouds on Chicago.

3 "Hardness" has not been in our century a quality much admired in women, nor in the past twenty years has it even been in official favor for men. When hardness surfaces in the very old we tend to transform it into "crustiness" or eccentricity, some tonic pepperiness to be indulged at a distance. On the evidence of her work and what she has said about it, Georgia O'Keeffe is neither "crusty" nor eccentric. She is simply hard, a straight shooter, a woman clean of received wisdom and open to what she sees. This is a woman who could early on dismiss most of her contemporaries as "dreamy," and would later single out one she liked as "a very poor painter." (And then add, apparently by way of softening the judgment: "I guess he wasn't a painter at all. He had no courage and I believe that to create one's own world in any of the arts takes courage.") This is a woman who in 1939 could advise her admirers that they were missing her point, that their appreciation of her famous flowers was merely sentimental. "When I paint a red hill," she observed coolly in the catalogue for an exhibition that year, "you say it is too bad that I don't always paint flowers. A flower touches almost everyone's heart. A red hill doesn't touch everyone's heart." This is a woman who could describe the genesis of one of her most well-known paintings—the "Cow's Skull: Red, White and Blue" owned by the Metropolitan—as an act of quite deliberate and derisive orneriness. "I thought of the city men I had been seeing in the East," she wrote. "They talked so often of writing the Great American Novel—the Great American Play—the Great American Poetry. . . . So as I was painting my cow's head on blue I thought to myself, 'I'll make it an American painting. They will not think it great with the red stripes down the sides—Red, White and Blue—but they will notice it.' "

4 *The city men. The men. They.* The words crop up again and again as this astonishingly aggressive woman tells us what was on her mind when she was making her astonishingly aggressive paintings. It was those city men who stood accused of sentimentalizing her flowers: "I made you take time to look at what I saw and when you took time to really notice my flower you hung all your associations with flowers on my flower and you write about my flower as if I think and see what you think and see—and I don't." *And I don't.* Imagine those words spoken, and the sound you hear is *don't tread on me.* "The men" believed it impossible to paint New York, so Georgia O'Keeffe painted New York. "The men" didn't think much of her bright color, so she made it brighter. The men yearned toward Europe so she went to Texas, and then New Mexico. The men talked about Cézanne, "long involved remarks about the 'plastic quality' of his form and color," and took one another's long involved remarks, in the view of this angelic rattlesnake in their midst, altogether too seriously. "I can paint one of those dismal-colored paintings like the men," the woman who regarded herself always as an outsider remembers thinking one day in 1922, and she did: a painting of a shed "all low-toned and dreary with the tree beside the door." She called this act of rancor "The Shanty" and hung it in her next show. "The men seemed to approve of it," she reported fifty-four years later, her contempt

undimmed. "They seemed to think that maybe I was beginning to paint. That was my only low-toned dismal-colored painting."

5 Some women fight and others do not. Like so many successful guerrillas in the war between the sexes, Georgia O'Keeffe seems to have been equipped early with an immutable sense of who she was and a fairly clear understanding that she would be required to prove it. On the surface her upbringing was conventional. She was a child on the Wisconsin prairie who played with china dolls and painted watercolors with cloudy skies because sunlight was too hard to paint and, with her brother and sisters, listened every night to her mother read stories of the Wild West, of Texas, of Kit Carson and Billy the Kid. She told adults that she wanted to be an artist and was embarrassed when they asked what kind of artist she wanted to be: she had no idea "what kind." She had no idea what artists did. She had never seen a picture that interested her, other than a pen-and-ink Maid of Athens in one of her mother's books, some Mother Goose illustrations printed on cloth, a tablet cover that showed a little girl with pink roses, and the painting of Arabs on horseback that hung in her grandmother's parlor. At thirteen, in a Dominican convent, she was mortified when the sister corrected her drawing. At Chatham Episcopal Institute in Virginia she painted lilacs and sneaked time alone to walk out to where she could see the line of the Blue Ridge Mountains on the horizon. At the Art Institute in Chicago she was shocked by the presence of live models and wanted to abandon anatomy lessons. At the Art Students League in New York one of her fellow students advised her that, since he would be a great painter and she would end up teaching painting in a girls' school, any work of hers was less important than modeling for him. Another painted over her work to show her how the Impressionists did trees. She had not before heard how the Impressionists did trees and she did not much care.

6 At twenty-four she left all those opinions behind and went for the first time to live in Texas, where there were no trees to paint and no one to tell her how not to paint them. In Texas there was only the horizon she craved. In Texas she had her sister Claudia with her for a while, and in the late afternoons they would walk away from town and toward the horizon and watch the evening star come out. "That evening star fascinated me," she wrote. "It was in some way very exciting to me. My sister had a gun, and as we walked she would throw bottles into the air and shoot as many as she could before they hit the ground. I had nothing but to walk into nowhere and the wide sunset space with the star. Ten watercolors were made from that star." In a way one's interest is compelled as much by the sister Claudia with the gun as by the painter Georgia with the star, but only the painter left us this shining record. Ten watercolors were made from that star.

(1976)

QUESTIONS

Thought and Structure

1. Does Didion convince you that "Style is character"? What do you think she means by that notion? In what sense does Didion use the word "betrayed" in paragraph 2?

2. Find the main idea in paragraph 5, and relate it to the rest of the essay.
3. How does Didion manage to make "Hardness" appealing?

Style and Strategy

4. How effective do you find the anecdote that ends the first paragraph. Before Didion explains in paragraph 2 her daughter's remark, what is the specific effect of that remark on you as a reader? How does that remark work on your psyche? What do you make of the idea that Didion imposes on or reads out of her daughter's comment?
5. What is the effect of Didion's selective repetition of O'Keeffe's words at the beginning of paragraph 4? What about Didion's repetition of her own words "astonishingly aggressive" (woman), "astonishingly aggressive" (painting)? What extra benefit does she get by associating the nouns that the repeated words modify? Consider her earlier judgment: "Style is character." Examine the effect of other repetitions in paragraph 4.
6. Why do you think Didion chooses to include the anecdote about O'Keeffe's sister in the last paragraph? Does she broaden the appeal of the essay by doing so? Who do you think Didion's intended audience might be? Do you think the essay should appeal more to women or men? Why? What does your answer say about your own presuppositions?
7. Where are the quotations coming from that Didion uses throughout the essay? Would they be more effective if she identified them more formally, or do they do their job better the way Didion integrates them into her own text?

SUGGESTIONS FOR WRITING

A. Consider the way Didion defines "hardness" in paragraph 3. In what way does that paragraph recall Woolf's essay "Craftsmanship"? Watch the way meaning emerges in Didion's paragraph. See if you can jot down the various ways she makes meaning. Try to classify each as you work your way through the paragraph.

B. Make a list of the repetitions in paragraph 4. See if you can lay them out on a page so that we can see the effect and the movement throughout the paragraph. Do they fall into patterns within the paragraph? Do the patterns make points in their own special repetitive ways?

C. Select an artist (painter, novelist, essayist, musician) whom you very much admire. Write an essay about that artist that will give us a sense of one of the artist's very special qualities. Take lessons from Didion.

D. Go to the library and find a large book with quality reproductions of O'Keeffe's paintings. Select one, and write a paper explaining what you see in it. Use Didion's essay in any way you can.

Democracy Chapter 1

1 The light at dawn during those Pacific tests was something to see.

2 Something to behold.

3 Something that could almost make you think you saw God, he said.

4 He said to her.

5 Jack Lovett said to Inez Victor.

6 Inez Victor who was born Inez Christian.

7 He said: the sky was this pink no painter could approximate, one of the detonation theorists used to try, a pretty fair Sunday painter, he never got it. Just never captured it, never came close. The sky was this pink and the air was wet from the night rain, soft and wet and smelling like flowers, smelling like those flowers you used to pin in your hair when you drove out to Schofield, gardenias, the air in the morning smelled like gardenias, never mind there were not too many flowers around those shot islands.

8 They were just atolls, most of them.

9 Sand spits, actually.

10 Two Quonsets and one of those landing strips they roll down, you know, the matting, just roll it down like a goddamn bathmat.

11 It was kind of a Swiss Family Robinson deal down there, really. None of the observers would fly down until the technical guys had the shot set up, that's all I was, an observer. Along for the ride. There for the show. You know me. Sometimes we'd get down there and the weather could go off and we'd wait days, just sit around cracking coconuts, there was one particular event at Johnston where it took three weeks to satisfy the weather people.

12 Wonder Woman Two, that shot was.

13 I remember I told you I was in Manila.

14 I remember I brought you some little souvenir from Manila, actually I bought it on Johnston off a reconnaissance pilot who'd flown in from Clark.

15 Three weeks sitting around goddamn Johnston Island waiting for the weather and then no yield to speak of.

16 Meanwhile we lived in the water.

17 Caught lobsters and boiled them on the beach.

18 Played gin and slapped mosquitoes.

19 Couldn't walk. No place to walk. Couldn't write anything down, the point of the pen would go right through the paper, one thing you got to understand down there was why not much got written down on those islands.

20 What you could do was, you could talk. You got to hear everybody's personal life story down there, believe me, you're sitting on an island a mile and a half long and most of that is the landing strip.

21 Those technical guys, some of them had been down there three months.

22 Got pretty raunchy, believe me.

23 Then the weather people would give the go and bingo, no more stories. Everybody would climb on a transport around three A.M. and go out a few miles and watch for first light.

24 Watch for pink sky.

25 And then the shot, naturally.

26 Nevada, the Aleutians, those events were another situation altogether.

27 Nobody had very pleasurable feelings about Nevada, although some humorous things did happen there at Mercury, like the time a Livermore device fizzled and the Los Alamos photographers started snapping away at that Livermore tower—still standing, you understand, a two-meg gadget and the tower's still standing, which

was the humorous part—and laughing like hell. The Aleutians were just dog duty, ass end of the universe, they give the world an enema they stick it in at Amchitka. Those shots up there did a job because by then they were using computers instead of analog for the diagnostics, but you would never recall an Aleutian event with any nostalgia whatsoever, nothing even humorous, you got a lot of congressmen up there with believe it or not their wives and daughters, big deal for the civilians but zero interest, zip, none.

28 He said to her.

29 Jack Lovett said to Inez Victor (who was born Inez Christian) in the spring of 1975.

30 But those events in the Pacific, Jack Lovett said.

31 Those shots around 1952, 1953.

32 Christ they were sweet.

33 You were still a little kid in high school when I was going down there, you were pinning flowers in your hair and driving out to Schofield, crazy little girl with island fever, I should have been put in jail. I'm surprised your Uncle Dwight didn't show up out there with a warrant. I'm surprised the whole goddamn Christian Company wasn't turned out for the lynching.

34 Water under the bridge.

35 Long time ago.

36 You've been around the world a little bit since.

37 You did all right.

38 You filled your dance card, you saw the show.

39 Interesting times.

40 I told you when I saw you in Jakarta in 1969, you and I had the knack for interesting times.

41 Jesus Christ, Jakarta.

42 Ass end of the universe, southern tier.

43 But I'll tell you one thing about Jakarta in 1969, Jakarta in 1969 beat Bien Hoa in 1969.

44 "Listen, Inez, get it while you can," Jack Lovett said to Inez Victor in the spring of 1975.

45 "Listen, Inez, use it or lose it."

46 "Listen, Inez, *un regard d'adieu,* we used to say in Saigon, last look through the door."

47 "Oh shit, Inez," Jack Lovett said one night in the spring of 1975, one night outside Honolulu in the spring of 1975, one night in the spring of 1975 when the C-130s and the C-141s were already shuttling between Honolulu and Anderson and Clark and Saigon all night long, thirty-minute turnaround at Tan Son Nhut, touching down and loading and taxiing out on flight idle, bringing out the dependents, bringing out the dealers, bringing out the money, bringing out the pet dogs and the sponsored bar girls and the porcelain elephants: "Oh shit, Inez," Jack Lovett said to Inez Victor, "Harry Victor's wife."

48 Last look through more than one door.

49 This is a hard story to tell.

Democracy Chapter 2

1 Call me the author.

2 *Let the reader be introduced to Joan Didion, upon whose character and doings much will depend of whatever interest these pages may have, as she sits at her writing table in her own room in her own house on Welbeck Street.*

3 So Trollope might begin this novel.

4 I have no unequivocal way of beginning it, although I do have certain things in mind. I have for example these lines from a poem by Wallace Stevens:

> The palm at the end of the mind,
> Beyond the last thought, rises
> In the bronze distance,
> A gold-feathered bird
> Sings in the palm, without human meaning,
> Without human feeling, a foreign song.

5 Consider that.

6 I have: "Colors, moisture, heat, enough blue in the air," Inez Victor's fullest explanation of why she stayed on in Kuala Lumpur. Consider that too. I have those pink dawns of which Jack Lovett spoke. I have the dream, recurrent, in which my entire field of vision fills with rainbow, in which I open a door onto a growth of tropical green (I believe this to be a banana grove, the big glossy fronds heavy with rain, but since no bananas are seen on the palms symbolists may relax) and watch the spectrum separate into pure color. Consider any of these things long enough and you will see that they tend to deny the relevance not only of personality but of narrative, which makes them less than ideal images with which to begin a novel, but we go with what we have.

7 Cards on the table.

8 I began thinking about Inez Victor and Jack Lovett at a point in my life when I lacked certainty, lacked even that minimum level of ego which all writers recognize as essential to the writing of novels, lacked conviction, lacked patience with the past and interest in memory; lacked faith even in my own technique. A poignant (to me) assignment I came across recently in a textbook for students of composition: "*Didion begins with a rather ironic reference to her immediate reason to write this piece. Try using this ploy as the opening of an essay; you may want to copy the ironic-but-earnest tone of Didion, or you might try making your essay witty. Consider the broader question of the effect of setting: how does Didion use the scene as a rhetorical base? She returns again and again to different details of the scene: where and how and to what effect? Consider, too, Didion's own involvement in the setting: an atmosphere results. How?*"

9 Water under the bridge.

10 As Jack Lovett would say.

11 Water under the bridge and dynamite it behind you.

12 So I have no leper who comes to the door every morning at seven.

13 No Tropical Belt Coal Company, no unequivocal lone figure on the crest of the immutable hill.

14 In fact no immutable hill: as the granddaughter of a geologist I learned early to anticipate the absolute mutability of hills and waterfalls and even islands. When a hill slumps into the ocean I see the order in it. When a 5.2 on the Richter scale wrenches the writing table in my own room in my own house in my own particular Welbeck Street I keep on typing. A hill is a transitional accommodation to stress, and ego may be a similar accommodation. A waterfall is a self-correcting maladjustment of stream to structure, and so, for all I know, is technique. The very island to which Inez Victor returned in the spring of 1975—Oahu, an emergent post-erosional land mass along the Hawaiian Ridge—is a temporary feature, and every rainfall or tremor along the Pacific plates alters its shape and shortens its tenure as Crossroads of the Pacific. In this light it is difficult to maintain definite convictions about what happened down there in the spring of 1975, or before.

15 In fact I have already abandoned a great deal of what happened before.

16 Abandoned most of the stories that still dominate table talk down in that part of the world where Inez Victor was born and to which she returned in 1975.

17 Abandoned for example all stories about definite cases of typhoid contracted on sea voyages lasting the first ten months of 1856.

18 Abandoned all accounts of iridescence observed on the night sea off the Canaries, of guano rocks sighted southeast of the Falklands, of the billiards room at the old Hotel Estrella del Mar on the Chilean coast, of a particular boiled-beef lunch eaten on Tristan da Cunha in 1859; and of certain legendary poker games played on the Isthmus of Panama in 1860, with the losses and winnings (in gold) of every player.

19 Abandoned the bereaved widower who drowned himself at landfall.

20 Scuttled the festivities marking the completion of the first major irrigation ditch on the Nuannu ranch.

21 Jettisoned in fact those very stories with which most people I know in those islands confirm their place in the larger scheme, their foothold against the swell of the sea, the erosion of the reefs and the drowning of the valley systems and the glittering shallows left when islands vanish. Would it have been Inez Victor's grandmother Cissy or Cissy's best friend Tita Dowdell who wore the Highland Lassie costume to the Children's Ball at the palace in 1892? If Cissy went as the Highland Lassie and Tita Dowdell as the Spanish Dancer (Inez's grandfather definitely went as one of the Peasant Children of All Nationalities, that much was documented, that much Inez and her sister Janet knew from the photograph that hung on the landing of the house on Manoa Road), then how did the Highland Lassie costume end up with the Palace Restoration Committee on loan from Tita Dowdell's daughter-in-law? On the subject of Tita Dowdell's daughter-in-law, did her flat silver come to her through her father's and Inez and Janet's grandfather's mutual Aunt Tru? Was it likely that Aunt Tru's fire opal from the Great Barrier Reef (surrounded by diamond chips) would have been lost down a drain at the Outrigger Canoe Club if Janet or Inez or even their cousin Alice Campbell had been

wearing it instead of Tita Dowdell's daughter-in-law? Where were the calabashes Alice Campbell's father got from Judge Thayer? Who had Leilani Thayer's koa settee? When Inez and Janet's mother left Honolulu on the reconditioned *Lurline* and never came back, did she or did she not have the right to take Tru's yellow diamond? These are all important questions down there, suggestive details in the setting, but the setting is for another novel.

Democracy Chapter 3

1 "Imagine my mother dancing," that novel began, in the first person. The first person was Inez, and was later abandoned in favor of the third:

2 "Inez imagined her mother dancing.

3 "Inez remembered her mother dancing.

4 "Brown-and-white spectator shoes, very smart. High-heeled sandals made of white silk twine, very beautiful. White gardenias in her hair on the beach at Lanikai. A white silk blouse with silver sequins shaped like stars. Shaped like new moons. Shaped like snowflakes. The sentimental things of life as time went by. Dancing under the camouflage net on the lawn at Kaneohe. Blue moon on the Nuannu ranch. Saw her standing alone. She smiled as she danced.

5 "Inez remembered no such thing.

6 "Inez remembered the shoes and the sequins like snowflakes but she only imagined her mother dancing, to make clear to herself that the story was one of romantic outline. You will notice that the daughters in romantic stories always remember their mothers dancing, or about to leave for the dance: these dance-bound mothers materialize in the darkened nursery (never a bedroom in these stories, always a 'nursery,' on the English model) in a cloud of perfume, a burst of light off a diamond hair clip. They glance in the mirror. They smile. They do not linger, for this is one of those moments in which the interests of mothers are seen to diverge sharply from the wishes of daughters. These mothers get on with it. These mothers lean for a kiss and leave for the dance. Inez and Janet's mother left, but not for the dance. Inez and Janet's mother left for San Francisco, on the *Lurline,* reconditioned. I specify 'reconditioned' because that was how Carol Christian's departure was characterized for Inez and Janet, as a sudden but compelling opportunity to make the first postwar crossing on the reconditioned *Lurline.* 'Just slightly irresistible,' was the way Carol Christian put it exactly."

7 What I had there was a study in provincial manners, in the acute tyrannies of class and privilege by which people assert themselves against the tropics; Honolulu during World War Two, martial law, submariners and fliers and a certain investor from Hong Kong with whom Carol Christian was said to drink brandy and Coca-Cola, a local scandal. I was interested more in Carol Christian than in her daughters, interested in the stubborn loneliness she had perfected during her marriage to Paul Christian, interested in her position as an outsider in the islands and in her compen-

satory yearning to be "talented," not talented at anything in particular but just talented, a state of social grace denied her by the Christians. Carol Christian arrived in Honolulu as a bride in 1934. By 1946 she was sometimes moved so profoundly by the urge for company that she would keep Inez and Janet home from school on the pretext of teaching them how to do their nails. She read novels out loud to them on the beach at Lanikai, popular novels she checked out from the lending library at the drugstore in Kailua. " 'The random years were at an end,' " she would read, her voice rising to signal a dramatic effect, and then she would invent a flourish of her own: " 'Now, they could harvest them.' Look there, *random harvest,* that explains the title, very poetic, a happy ending, *n'est-ce pas?*"

8 She was attracted to French phrases but knew only the several she had memorized during the semester of junior college in Stockton, California, that constituted her higher education. She was also attracted to happy endings, and located them for Inez and Janet wherever she could: in the Coke float that followed the skinned knee, in the rainbow after the rain, in magazine stories about furlough weddings and fortuitously misdelivered Dear John letters and, not least, in her own romance, which she dated from the day she left Stockton and got a job modeling at I. Magnin in San Francisco. "Eighteen years old and dressed to kill in a Chanel suit, the real McCoy," she would say to Inez and Janet. Eighteen years old and dressed to kill in a Mainbocher evening pajama, the genuine article. Eighteen years old and dressed to kill in a Patou tea gown, white satin cut on the bias, talk about drop dead, bare to *here* in back. The bias-cut Patou tea gown figured large in Carol Christian's stories because this was the dress in which she had been sneaking a cigarette on the I. Magnin employees' floor when Paul Christian stepped off the elevator by mistake (another fortuitous misdelivery) and brushed the shadows away, brought her happiest day, one look at him and she had found a world completely new, the sole peculiarity being that the world was an island in the middle of the Pacific and Paul Christian was rarely there. "When a man stays away from a woman it means he wants to keep their love alive," Carol Christian advised Inez and Janet. She had an entire codex of these signals men and women supposedly sent to one another (when a woman blew smoke at a man it meant she was definitely interested, and when a man told a woman her dress was too revealing it meant he adored her), dreamy axioms she had heard or read or invented as a schoolgirl of romantic tendency and to which she clung in the face of considerable contrary evidence. That she had miscalculated when she married Paul Christian was a conclusion she seemed incapable of drawing. She made a love-knot of what she imagined to be her first gray hair and mailed it to him in Cuernavaca. "*Mon cher* Paul," she wrote on the card to which she pinned the love-knot. Inez watched her tie the hair but did not see the card for some years, loose in one of the boxes of shed belongings that Paul Christian would periodically ship express collect from wherever he was to Inez and Janet. "Who do you f--- to get off this island? (Just kidding of course) XXXX, C."

9 She left dark red lipstick marks on her cigarettes, smoked barely at all and then crushed out in coffee cups and Coke bottles and in the sand. She sat for hours at her dressing table, which was covered with the little paper parasols that came in drinks, yellow, turquoise, shocking pink, tissue parasols like a swarm of brittle butterflies. She sat at this dressing table and shaved her legs. She sat at this dressing

table and smoothed Vaseline into her eyebrows. She sat at this dressing table and instructed her daughters in what she construed to be the language of love, a course she had notably failed. For a year or two after Carol Christian left Honolulu Janet would sit on the beach at Lanikai and sift the sand looking for cigarettes stained with her mother's lipstick. She kept the few she found in a shoebox, along with the tissue parasols from Carol Christian's dressing table and the postcards from San Francisco and Carmel and Lake Tahoe.

10 Of the daughters I was at first more interested in Janet, who was the younger, than in Inez. I was interested in the mark the mother had left on Janet, in Janet's defensive veneer of provincial gentility, her startling and avid preoccupation with other people's sexual arrangements; in her mercantile approach to emotional transactions, and her condescension to anyone less marketable than she perceived herself to be. As an adolescent Janet had always condescended, for example, to Inez, and became bewildered and rather sulky when it worked out, in her view, so well for Inez and so disappointingly for herself. I was interested in how Janet's husband Dick Ziegler made a modest fortune in Hong Kong housing and lost it in the development of windward Oahu. I was interested in Inez and Janet's grandmother, the late Sybil "Cissy" Christian, a woman remembered in Honolulu for the vehement whims and irritations that passed in that part of the world as opinions, as well as for the dispatch with which she had divested herself of her daughter-in-law. *Aloha oe.* "I believe your mother wants to go to night clubs," Cissy Christian said to Inez and Janet by way of explaining Carol Christian's departure. "But she's coming back," Janet said. "Now and then," Cissy Christian said. This conversation took place at lunch at the Pacific Club, one hour after Inez and Janet and their uncle Dwight saw the reconditioned *Lurline* sail. Janet bolted from the table. "Happy now?" Dwight Christian asked his mother. "Somebody had to do it," Cissy Christian said. "Not necessarily before lunch," Dwight Christian said.

11 I saw it as a family in which the colonial impulse had marked every member. I was interested in Inez and Janet's father, Paul Christian, and in the way in which he had reinvented himself as a romantic outcast, a remittance man of the Pacific. "He's going to end up a goddamn cargo cult," Paul Christian's brother Dwight once said about him. I was interested not only in Paul but in Dwight Christian, in his construction contracts at Long Binh and Cam Ranh Bay, his claim to have played every Robert Trent Jones golf course in the world with the exception of the Royal in Rabat; the particular way in which he used Wendell Omura to squeeze Dick Ziegler out of windward Oahu and coincidentally out of the container business. "Let me give you a little piece of advice," Dwight Christian said when Paul Christian took up Dick Ziegler's side in this matter. " 'Life can only be understood backwards, but it must be lived forwards.' Kierkegaard." Dwight Christian had an actual file of such quotations, most of them torn from the "Thoughts on the Business of Life" page in *Forbes* and given to a secretary to be typed out on three-by-five index cards. The cards were his hedge against a profound shyness. "Recently I ran across a thought from Racine," he would say on those occasions when he was called upon to chair a stockholders' meeting or to keynote the Kickoff Dinner for Punahou School Annual Giving or to have his picture taken, wearing a silk suit tailored in

Hong Kong and an aluminum hard hat stencilled "D.C.," knee-deep in silica sand in the hold of a dry-bulk carrier.

12 That particular photograph appeared in *Business Week,* at the time Dwight Christian was trying (unsuccessfully, it turned out) to take over British Leyland.

13 I also had two photographs from *Fortune,* one showing Dwight Christian riding a crane over a cane field and the other showing him astride an eighteen-thousand-ton concrete dolos, with a Pan American Cargo Clipper overhead.

14 In fact I had a number of photographs of the Christians: in that prosperous and self-absorbed colony the Christians were sufficiently good-looking and sufficiently confident and, at least at the time Inez was growing up, sufficiently innocent not to mind getting their pictures in the paper. I had Cissy Christian smoking a cigarette in a white jade holder as she presented the Christian Prize in Sugar Chemistry at the University of Hawaii in 1938. I had Dwight and Ruthie Christian tea-dancing at the Alexander Young Hotel in 1940. I had Carol Christian second-from-the-left in a group of young Honolulu matrons who met every Tuesday in 1942 to drink daiquiris and eat chicken salad and roll bandages for the Red Cross. In this photograph Carol Christian is wearing a Red Cross uniform, but in fact she was invited to join this group only twice, both times by Ruthie Christian. "Spend time around that crowd and you see how the green comes out," she said when it became clear that she would not be included on a regular basis. "You see how the green comes out" was something Carol Christian said often. She said it whenever she divined a note of rejection or criticism or even suspended judgment in someone's response to her, or, by extension, to Inez or Janet. She seemed to believe herself the object of considerable "envy," a word Inez tried to avoid in later life, and perhaps she was.

15 "I detect just the slightest tinge of lime."

16 "Positively chartreuse."

17 "You find out fast enough who your friends are."

18 In fact it would have been hard to say who Carol Christian's friends were, since she had no friends at all who were not primarily Paul Christian's friends or Cissy Christian's friends or Dwight and Ruthie Christian's friends. "Seems like a nice enough gal," one of Paul Christian's cousins said about her when she had lived in Honolulu for ten years. "Of course I haven't known her that long."

19 I had, curiously, only two photographs of Paul Christian, and neither suggested the apparent confidence and innocence with which his mother and his brother and even his wife met the camera. The first showed Paul Christian playing backgammon with John Huston in Cuernavaca in 1948. Paul Christian was barefoot and dark from the sun in this snapshot, which would have been taken at roughly the time arrangements were being made for his wife to leave Honolulu on the reconditioned *Lurline.* The second photograph was taken as Paul Christian left the Honolulu YMCA in handcuffs on March 25, 1975, some hours after he fired the shots that resulted in the immediate death of Wendell Omura and the eventual death of Janet Christian Ziegler. In this photograph Paul Christian was again barefoot, and had his cuffed hands raised above his head in a posture of theatrical submission, even crucifixion; a posture so arresting, so peculiarly suggestive, that the photograph was carried in newspapers in parts of the world where there could have

been no interest in the Christians or in Wendell Omura or even in Harry Victor. In most parts of the United States there was of course an interest in Harry Victor. VICTOR FAMILY TOUCHED BY ISLAND TRAGEDY, the caption read in *The New York Times.*

20 You see the shards of the novel I am no longer writing, the island, the family, the situation. I lost patience with it. I lost nerve. Still: there is a certain hour between afternoon and evening when the sun strikes horizontally between the trees and that island and that situation are all I see. Some days at this time one aspect of the situation will seem to me to yield the point, other days another. I see Inez Christian Victor in the spring of 1975 walking on the narrow beach behind Janet's house, the last sun ahead of her, refracted in the spray off Black Point. I see Jack Lovett watching her, a man in his sixties in a custom-made seersucker suit, his tie loosened but his bearing correct, military, suggestive of disciplines practiced for the sake of discipline; a man who is now, as he watches Inez Victor steady herself on the rocks down where the water meets the sea wall, smoking one of the five cigarettes he allows himself daily. I see Inez turn and walk back toward him, the sun behind her now, the water washing the rough coral sand over her bare feet.

21 I see Jack Lovett waiting for her.

22 I have not told you much about Jack Lovett.

23 Most often these days I find that my notes are about Jack Lovett, about those custom-made seersucker suits he wore, about the wide range of his interests and acquaintances and of the people to whom he routinely spoke (embassy drivers, oil riggers, airline stewardesses, assistant professors of English literature traveling on Fulbright fellowships, tropical agronomists traveling under the auspices of the Rockefeller Foundation, desk clerks and ticket agents and salesmen of rice converters and coco dryers and Dutch pesticides and German pharmaceuticals) in Manila and in Jakarta and around the Malacca Strait.

24 About his view of information as an end in itself.

25 About his access to airplanes.

26 About the way he could put together an observation here and a conversation there and gauge when the time had come to lay hands on a 727 or a C-46.

27 About the way he waited for Inez.

28 I have been keeping notes for some time now about the way Jack Lovett waited for Inez Victor.

(1984)

QUESTIONS

Chapter 1

1. Much of what goes on in chapter 1 depends on our knowing in the first sentence of the novel, what those "Pacific tests" were. But if you have not kept up with the language of nuclear testing over the years, you have to wait some time for clarification. Look

through this chapter and the following ones for a similar pattern, a pattern in which the narrator offers information that keeps the reader at bay, followed later by a revelation through detail or through a clear explanation after the fact. Why would Didion rely on such a pattern? What as a writer of fiction does she gain by withholding temporarily information that we as readers need to know to make sense of what she is telling us? Is this a technique more suitable for fiction than for the essay? Why?

2. How much do we actually learn about Jack Lovett's character (see Didion's sense of the term in paragraphs 6ff., "On Self-Respect") from the things "Jack Lovett said to Inez Victor"? What do you suppose Jack Lovett does when he's not watching tests or taking one last look out the door in Saigon?
3. What do you suppose is the relationship between Inez Victor and Jack Lovett? How do we get a better sense of that relationship near the end of the chapter?
4. At the very end of the chapter, the narrator gives us an illuminating history of the fall of Saigon. What does that historical sketch tell us about Jack Lovett?

Chapter 2

5. Didion begins chapter 2 with an appeal: "Call me the author." What if she had said, "Call me the narrator"? Would it have changed the nature of all that we read in the chapter? Or would it make no difference at all? Why?
6. Didion seems to be trying to give us a sense of the writer writing. But she is not just playing metawriting games; she is trying to give us a sense of her relationship, her personal relationship with the material she's working with. Is that material imaginary, made up—or does it seem to be historical? What are your clues? Would there be reasons why Didion would want to keep us guessing about the line between fact and fiction?
7. The last section of this chapter begins with "In fact I have already abandoned a great deal of what happened before." Look first at the way she repeats and uses the word "abandoned" throughout that last section; look too at how it takes on new forms in the last two paragraphs: "Scuttled," and "Jettisoned." How does this repetition serve her? Does she in fact abandon all of that information, or is she using it despite her claims? How are we influenced by it? What does it tell us about the writer's problems? What does it tell us about the narrator? What does it tell us about the characters this novel set out to focus on: Victor and Inez?
8. Near the beginning of this chapter, the narrator quotes a textbook, showing us some other writer looking at Didion. Is Didion looking at her narrator in much the same way? Can we have Didion looking at "Didion"? To what end?

Chapter 3

9. Much of this chapter is ostensibly about a novel that did not get written, but it is nevertheless about the Christians; it is both directly and indirectly about Inez. What do we learn about her? What else do we learn about the narrator who is "Didion"? Look at the details she uses to give us a sense of three of the Christian women: Carol, Janet, and Inez. How do those details differ? Describe the three women in your own terms after reading chapter 3.
10. How does "Didion" mix fact and fiction when she develops Paul Christian?
11. Identify three sections where Didion uses rhetorical repetition. How do the various patterns associated with that repetition contribute to meaning? How do they entice the reader in perhaps a subconscious way?

SUGGESTIONS FOR WRITING

A. Go to the library and examine the first two or three chapters of Annie Dillard's book *Living by Fiction.* Prepare a brief report for a classroom presentation explaining how that text helps us understand what Didion is doing in chapter 2.

B. Go to the library and find a picture of René Magritte's *The Human Condition I* (1934). Look at the way the painting calls into question the relationship between the artist and the scene he is trying to paint. Look too at the number of frames one must look through to get to the reality outside the window. Can the artist ever get through to that reality? Write a short essay about the relationship between Magritte's painting and chapter 2. Write it in the language of everyday. Do not get mired down in the language of criticism. Write for those in your class. Write so they can understand what you have to say about the two "texts."

C. Write a short dialogue in which one of the characters is essentially a silent listener. Take lessons from chapter 1, but do not feel constrained by Didion's particular method of development. Remember that you are trying to reveal character through this dialogue.

D. Jot down a number of things that you have learned from these three chapters that might help you as an essay writer. What are the fictional techniques that you can use in nonfiction?

E. Consider the way each of these chapters ends. How do the endings differ from the endings that we use in essays? How are they the same?

FOURTEEN

Margaret Atwood

(1939–   )

Margaret Atwood is a Canadian writer who has published poetry, fiction, essays, film and television screenplays, and political cartoons. She was born in Ottawa, and she grew up in Ontario and Quebec. After graduating from the University of Toronto, she attended graduate school at Harvard University, where she specialized in Victorian literature. Her degrees include a B.A. from Toronto, an A.M. from Radcliffe, a Litt. D. from Trent University, and an LL.D. from Queen's University. She has traveled extensively, alternately teaching and writing in Canada, the United States, England, and Italy.

Like Katherine Anne Porter, Margaret Atwood began writing when she was a child and did not seriously consider becoming a writer until she was sixteen. Unlike Porter, Atwood began publishing her poetry and fiction in her late teens and her twenties. She had, by that time, accumulated a sizable body of work, including six novels, three short-story collections, nine volumes of poems, a book of essays, and a critical study of Canadian literature. One measure of her considerable versatility, talent, and popularity is that since 1973 she has been supporting herself with her writing.

Atwood's prose is characterized by precision, grace, and intelligence. Her work consistently reflects a stunning accuracy of detail and a striking imagistic suggestiveness. Consider, for example, this excerpt from the opening of her latest novel, *The Handmaid's Tale* (1986):

> We slept in what had once been the gymnasium. The floor was of varnished wood, with stripes and circles painted on it, for the games that were formerly played there; the hoops for the basketball nets were still in place, though the nets were gone. A balcony ran around the room, for the spectators, and I thought I could smell, faintly like an afterimage, the pungent scent of sweat, shot through with the sweet taint of chewing gum and perfume from the watching girls, felt-skirted as I knew from pictures, later in miniskirts, then pants, then in one earring, spiky green-streaked hair. Dances would have been held there; the music lingered, a palimpsest of unheard sound, style upon style, an undercurrent of drums, a forlorn wail, garlands made of tissue-paper flowers, cardboard devils, a revolving ball of mirrors, powdering the dancers with a snow of light.
>
> There was old sex in the room and loneliness, and expectation, of something without a shape or name. I remember that yearning, for something that was always about to happen and was never the same as the hands that were on us there and then,

in the small of the back, or out back, in the parking lot, or in the television room with the sound turned down . . .

Besides its precision of detail rendered in images of sight and sound, taste and smell and touch, the prose possesses an elusive quality. As we read we gradually infer what Atwood describes and refers to (or rather what her narrator is describing and referring to since this is a fictive account) yet we sense there is more to the experience we are hearing than we are understanding as we read. Something is held back that keeps us on edge mentally, on the alert for a telling word or phrase.

The language of the passage is both evocative and provocative. It evokes memories and provokes thought. Like the narrator we remember the feelings she describes. Or if we have not experienced them we imagine them. Perhaps that is what Atwood's prose does best: stimulate our imagination. This passage is particularly exemplary in that regard since it involves Atwood imagining a character who exists in the future, a character who both remembers and imagines the past.

Of the short works included here, the short story "Giving Birth" reveals what the experience can be like. Atwood focuses largely on the consciousness of her central character, concerned more with describing how she feels than with portraying external action. The essays devoted to Adrienne Rich and Tillie Olsen are reviews. In each essay Atwood assesses not only the specific book under review, but the writer's importance as well as significant issues, problems, and perspectives.

"On Being a 'Woman Writer,' " the longest selection, concerns the function and role of the writer. In this essay, Atwood reveals her feelings about being categorized as "woman writer." She discusses with honesty, wit, and shrewdness, the political and aesthetic dilemmas she confronts as a writer who also happens to be a woman.

Her comments about writing are thoroughly realistic: The writer's real struggle is her "daily battle with words." And: "Writing . . . tends to concentrate more on life, not as it ought to be, but as it is, as the writer feels it, experiences it." They also reflect her view of the writer's role in society: "Writers are eye-witnesses, I-witnesses." And again: "Writers are lenses, condensers of their society." And finally, they put the emphasis where it ought to be—on language and vision. For as Atwood says, "The aim of writing is to create a plausible and moving imaginative world, and to create it from words."

Taken together these remarks suggest something of Atwood's ambition and range as a writer. Moreover, they direct our attention to what, for her, are the things that matter.

Tillie Olsen: *Silences*

1 Tillie Olsen's is a unique voice. Few writers have gained such wide respect based on such a small body of published works: one book of short stories, *Tell Me A Riddle,* and the unfinished novel, *Yonnondio: From The Thirties.* Among women writers in the United States, "respect" is too pale a word: "reverence" is more like it. This is presumably because women writers, even more than their male counterparts, recognize what a heroic feat it is to have held down a job, raised four children, and still somehow managed to become and to remain a writer. The

exactions of this multiple identity cost Tillie Olsen twenty years of her writing life. The applause that greets her is not only for the quality of her artistic performance but, as at a gruelling obstacle race, for the near-miracle of her survival.

2 Tillie Olsen's third book, *Silences,* is about this obstacle course, this ordeal, not only as she herself experienced it but as many writers have experienced it, in many forms. It begins with an account, first drafted in 1962, of her own long circumstantially-enforced silence. She did not write for a very simple reason: a day has twenty-four hours. For twenty years she had no time, no energy and none of the money that would have bought both. It may be comforting to believe that garrets are good for geniuses, that artists are made in Heaven and God will take care of them; but if you believe, as Tillie Olsen does, that writers are nurtured on Earth and nobody necessarily takes care of them, society cannot be absolved from the responsibility for what it produces or fails to produce in the way of literature.

3 Though Tillie Olsen begins with her own experience, she rapidly proceeds to that of others. The second part of the book is a grab-bag of excerpts from the diaries, journals, letters, and concealed autobiographical work of a wide range of writers, past and present, male and female. They are used to demonstrate, first, the ideal conditions for creation as perceived by the writers themselves, and second, almost every imaginable impediment to that creation. The financial and cultural pressures that gagged Melville, the religious agonies of Hopkins, the bitterness of Thomas Hardy after the vicious reception of *Jude the Obscure,* Willa Cather's feeling of nullity in face of the suave eastern establishment; political, cultural, sexist and sexual censorship; the denial of a voice to a race, a class, a sex, by the denial of its access to literature; breakdowns, abdications, addictions; all are cited. Reading this section may be hazardous if you are actually writing a book. It's like walking along a sidewalk only to be shown suddenly that your sidewalk isn't a sidewalk but a tightrope over Niagara Falls. How have you managed to do it at all? "Chancy luck," Tillie Olsen replies, and in view of the evidence she musters, she's probably—for all writers not white, male, rich, and from a dominant culture—quite right.

4 Tillie Olsen's special concern is with how her general observations on silencings apply, more heavily and with additions, to women. Here, the obstacles may seem to be internal: the crippling effects of upbringing, the burdens of motherhood, the lack of confidence that may prevent women from writing at all; and, if they do write, their own male-determined view of women, the fear of competing, the fear of success. We've heard a lot of this before, but it's invigorating to see its first expressions by women coming new to the problems: Virginia Woolf worrying about her childlessness, Katherine Mansfield having to cope with all the domestic arrangements while John Middleton Murry nagged her about tea. And, in contrast, quotations from men whose wives dedicated their lives to sharpening pencils and filling the inkwell for them. As Tillie Olsen points out, almost all of the women in the nineteenth century who wrote were childless and/or had servants. Her study of Rebecca Harding Davies, author of the remarkable *Life In The Iron Mills,* is a telling example of what happened to one writer who made the switch from solitude to biological fecundity.

5 In construction, *Silences* is a scrapbook, a patchwork quilt: bits and pieces joined to form a powerful whole. And, despite the condensed and fragmentary

quality of this book, the whole is powerful. Even the stylistic breathlessness—the elliptical prose, the footnotes blooming on every page as if the author, reading her own manuscript, belatedly thought of a dozen other things too important to leave out—is reminiscent of a Biblical messenger, sole survivor of a relentless and obliterating catastrophe, a witness: "I only am escaped alone to tell thee." The tone is right: the catastrophes do occur, daily, though they may not be seen as such. What Tillie Olsen has to say about them is of primary importance both to those who want to understand how art is generated or subverted and to those trying to create it themselves.

6 The true measure of a book's success, for the reader, is the number of people she wants to give it to. My own list is already long.

(1978)

QUESTIONS

Thought and Structure

1. Atwood remarks toward the end of this piece that she intends to give Olsen's *Silences* to many people. Why?
2. Given what you know about Margaret Atwood from reading the headnote and her other selections in this book, why do you think Tillie Olsen's life and writing are important to her?
3. This essay is clearly a book review written within the typical limitations and constraints of that literary genre. How well, in this brief space, do you think Atwood has succeeded in conveying a sense of *Silences?*
4. Consider this rearrangement of Atwood's six paragraphs: 2, 4, 5, 3, 1, and 6. How does that structure compare to Atwood's?
5. Of the six paragraphs in this essay, the first and last could conceivably be omitted. What would be gained or lost with the omission of each?

Style and Strategy

6. The opening and closing sentences are brief. Comment on the effect of each.
7. Explain the significance of the following images from the first paragraph: heroic feat, multiple identity, obstacle race.
8. Explain the distinction Atwood implies between "respect" and "reverence" (1).
9. Consider the sentences that use a colon in paragraphs 1, 2, 4, and 5. Explain the purpose and effect of the colons. Consider also the effectiveness of the dash sentences in paragraphs 3 and 5.

SUGGESTIONS FOR WRITING

A. Write a review of a book you admire. Try to give your readers a sense of the book's central concerns and an explanation of its importance to you.

B. Read *Silences* and write your own review of it. Or write an essay accepting or disputing Atwood's claims for the book.

Adrienne Rich: *Of Woman Born*

1 Adrienne Rich is not just one of America's best feminist poets or one of America's best woman poets, she is one of America's best poets. Her most exemplary poems are read not because they are supposed to be good for us, but because they are good, and in some cases (which is all any poet can ask for) they are very good. This is not to deny the feminist content of her poems, or their sometimes overtly polemical intent. At her best, Rich pulls off what few poets with the courage of their convictions can ever manage: she is eloquent, she convinces and inspires. She is a serious writer and an important one, and her prose book on the institution of motherhood is a serious and important book.

2 "Motherhood?" The very word evokes the trivial. "It's a motherhood issue," we say, meaning that no one could be against it. "American as Mom and apple pie," we say, meaning banal, but comforting, permanent, healthy, a *given.* But it's the unexamined assumptions behind phrases like this that Rich is writing about. Such assumptions, she says, are unwarranted; in fact, *all* assumptions about "motherhood" are unwarranted, because it is something we really know very little about. Science would back her up: even among young primates, such as baboons, "mothering" is not an instinct. It is a learned process, and female primates isolated in youth from models of "mothering" reject their offspring. What then do we learn about mothering, what are we taught? The sum of these things and their hidden rationales constitute motherhood as an "institution;" the way they shape how women live their lives, and the conflicts between what women are taught they should be feeling and doing and what they actually feel and do, constitute motherhood as "experience."

3 Rich is writing about pernicious myths. One of the most pernicious, of course, is that mothering is an instinct, that it simply wells up in all "real" women who give birth to children (and according to the same myth, a woman who does not give birth to children is not a "real" woman; she is a cipher). Once a biological mother, you will automatically become a Madonna, a virtuous model of self-sacrifice and devotion. This myth is pernicious because it leaves many women feeling inadequate, baffled or even evil if the promised happiness and fulfillment fail to materialize. It also means that few wish to teach motherhood or even discuss it: why teach an "instinct?" The very suggestion that mothering is not an instinct opens up a number of worm-cans that not only most men but most women prefer to keep tightly closed. To question the institution at all—that set of beliefs which requires mothers to be at once both superhuman and sub-human—is to evoke the most primal and deeply threatening fears going around, fear of rejection by one's own mother. Yet, as Rich says, we all have mothers; every adult in this society was raised by a person who was expected to be a "mother," to take primary and largely single responsibility for her children, who felt thwarted by this and projected her resentment onto her children to a greater or lesser degree. Many did not choose motherhood; it was thrust upon

them by a society unwilling to provide either contraception or recognized and dignified opportunities for any other occupation but "housewife." If we learn mothering from our mothers, would it not be better to replace the present institution with one with less built-in resentment?

4 This seems to me the question at the core of the book, though Rich touches ground elsewhere. There are interesting chapters on historical motherhood, bits of information on such diverse but pertinent subjects as the development of obstetrical forceps, the takeover of midwifery by male doctors, puerperal fever (often caused because the attending physician had come straight from the dissection of corpses without washing his hands), the rise of the factory system and its effects on home life, the segregation of women and children from fathers by the institutions of "work" and "the home." There are reflections on the paucity of female-centered mythologies, with the Core-Persephone myth cited as a meaningful exception. Rich is most moving on the subject of her own life as a mother. It would be nice to be able to say that her experiences of the fifties—the drugged childbirths, the hostile hospitals, the incredible pressures from relatives, the isolation, the consequent guilt and rage—are things of the past, but notwithstanding the advent of more human obstetrical practices and definitions of "motherhood" that allow more freedom, her experiences are probably still typical for a large part of the female population.

5 This is an important book, but it is not flawless. One could quibble about many points. Some will question the historical and anthropological material, others the theoretical underpinnings. Some are bound to find the book too harsh on men: if women are objecting to being lumped together as Woman, cannot men be given credit for their individualities too? Aren't there any *nice* men? Don't some men love their children, too? I myself would question the rather sensationalistic last chapter, which takes off from the case of a woman who chopped up her two youngest children on the front lawn of her suburban house and goes on to suggest that such emotions and such actions are possible for all mothers under "the system." The work of Mary Van Stolk on battered children indicates that this is simply not so, any more than child-battering is a possibility for everyone. (It isn't, says Van Stolk; only for those who have learned it, often by being battered themselves. But the axioms of our society encourage it, just as they encourage rage in mothers.)

6 This is a book that can be quarreled with, but it cannot be ignored, or dismissed because of this or that fine point, this or that emphasis. To write a flawless book on this subject would be impossible; to write a popular one would be equally impossible, because Rich is saying a number of things many would rather not hear. However, it was not Rich's intention to write a flawless book or a popular one; rather, she wished to open a dialogue, a dialogue which must be pursued. There is really nothing less at stake than the future of the human race. If "mothering" is learned, then ways of mothering can be changed; if "mothering" is learned, so is "fathering." And so are violence, cruelty, aggression, punishment, and war. These things are learned by children, absorbed by them before school age; under the current system, young children are "taught" almost exclusively by isolated, guilty, squashed, trapped, tired, bored and thwarted women, who are taught to believe that they themselves are second-rate failures and children are at once their punishment, their vindication and their fate. How much better if children could be *chosen,* and loved for what

they are, not viewed as an inadequate substitute for a "career" or some kind of parasitic burden?

(1976)

QUESTIONS

Thought and Structure

1. What is Atwood's overall evaluation of Rich's *Of Woman Born?* What does she object to? Why? What does she approve? Why?
2. What ideas about motherhood and mothering emerge in Atwood's discussion? Do you agree, for example, with what Atwood suggests in paragraphs 2 and 3? Why or why not?
3. Does Atwood's discussion of Rich's book convince you that it is indeed a serious and important work worth your consideration? Why or why not?
4. Comment on the advisability of altering Atwood's essay to begin with paragraph 2. What would be gained or lost with such a revision? What adjustments to paragraph 2 would be necessary if it were placed first? If paragraph 1 were omitted?
5. Divide the review into two or three parts and comment on the reason for your division.

Style and Strategy

6. A number of Atwood's sentences are framed as questions. Comment on the effectiveness of those in paragraphs 2, 3, 5, and 6.
7. Atwood uses parentheses in a few sentences. Explain the purposes and effects of the parenthetical sentences in paragraphs 1, 3, 4, and 5.
8. The following words are italicized: *given* (2), *all* (2), *nice* (5), *chosen* (6). Why?
9. These words appear in quotation marks: "motherhood" (2), "mothering" (2), "institution" (2), "experience" (2), "real" (3), "instinct" (3), "mother" (3), "housewife" (3), "work" (4), "the home" (4), "the system" (5), "mothering" (6), "fathering" (6), "taught" (6), and "career" (6). Does Atwood need these quotation marks? What function do they serve?
10. The first and last sentences of Atwood's opening paragraph include repeated words within each sentence: "America's best" and "serious and important." What is gained by such repetition?
11. Consider the function of Atwood's repetitions between sentences in paragraphs 3 and 6.
12. Comment on the purpose and effect of the strings of words—the mini-accumulations in the following sentences:

    a. And so are violence, cruelty, aggression, punishment, and war.
    b. . . . children are "taught" almost exclusively by isolated, guilty, squashed, trapped, tired, bored and thwarted women.

SUGGESTIONS FOR WRITING

A. Write imitations of the sentences noted in questions 11 and 12.

B. Write an imitation of paragraph 1 or 5 or 6.

C. Write your own essay on the concept of motherhood—or fatherhood.
D. Read Rich's *Of Woman Born* and write an essay discussing your ideas about motherhood in relation to hers and/or to Atwood's.

On Being a "Woman Writer": Paradoxes and Dilemmas

1 I approach this article with a good deal of reluctance. Once having promised to do it, in fact, I've been procrastinating to such an extent that my own aversion is probably the first subject I should attempt to deal with. Some of my reservations have to do with the questionable value of writers, male or female, becoming directly involved in political movements of any sort: their involvement may be good for the movement, but it has yet to be demonstrated that it's good for the writer. The rest concern my sense of the enormous complexity not only of the relationships between Man and Woman, but also of those between those other abstract intangibles, Art and Life, Form and Content, Writer and Critic, etcetera.

2 Judging from conversations I've had with many other woman writers in this country, my qualms are not unique. I can think of only one writer I know who has any formal connection with any of the diverse organizations usually lumped together under the titles of Women's Liberation or the Women's Movement. There are several who have gone out of their way to disavow even any fellow-feeling; but the usual attitude is one of grudging admiration, tempered with envy: the younger generation, they feel, has it a hell of a lot better than they did. Most writers old enough to have a career of any length behind them grew up when it was still assumed that a woman's place was in the home and nowhere else, and that anyone who took time off for an individual selfish activity like writing was either neurotic or wicked or both, derelict in her duties to a man, child, aged relatives or whoever else was supposed to justify her existence on earth. I've heard stories of writers so consumed by guilt over what they had been taught to feel was their abnormality that they did their writing at night, secretly, so no one would accuse them of failing as housewives, as "women." These writers accomplished what they did by themselves, often at great personal expense; in order to write at all, they had to defy other women's as well as men's ideas of what was proper, and it's not finally all that comforting to have a phalanx of women—some younger and relatively unscathed, others from their own generation, the bunch that was collecting china, changing diapers and sneering at any female with intellectual pretensions twenty or even ten years ago—come breezing up now to tell them they were right all along. It's like being judged innocent after you've been hanged: the satisfaction, if any, is grim. There's a great temptation to say to Women's Lib, "Where were you when I really needed you?" or "It's too late for me now." And you can see, too, that it would be fairly galling for these writers, if they have any respect for historical accuracy, which most do, to be hailed as products, spokeswomen, or advocates of the Women's Movement. When they were undergoing their often drastic formative years there *was* no Women's Move-

ment. No matter that a lot of what they say can be taken by the theorists of the Movement as supporting evidence, useful analysis, and so forth: their own inspiration was not theoretical, it came from wherever all writing comes from. Call it experience and imagination. These writers, if they are honest, don't want to be wrongly identified as the children of a movement that did not give birth to them. Being adopted is not the same as being born.

3 A third area of reservation is undoubtedly a fear of the development of a one-dimensional Feminist Criticism, a way of approaching literature produced by women that would award points according to conformity or non-conformity to an ideological position. A feminist criticism is, in fact, already emerging. I've read at least one review, and I'm sure there have been and will be more, in which a novelist was criticized for not having made her heroine's life different, even though that life was more typical of the average woman's life in this society than the reviewer's "liberated" version would have been. Perhaps Women's Lib reviewers will start demanding that heroines resolve their difficulties with husband, kids, or themselves by stomping out to join a consciousness raising group, which will be no more satisfactory from the point of view of literature than the legendary Socialist Realist romance with one's tractor. However, a feminist criticism need not necessarily be one-dimensional. And—small comfort—no matter how narrow, purblind and stupid such a criticism in its lowest manifestations may be, it cannot possibly be *more* narrow, purblind and stupid than some of the non-feminist critical attitudes and styles that have preceded it.

4 There's a fourth possible factor, a less noble one: the often observed phenomenon of the member of a despised social group who manages to transcend the limitations imposed on the group, at least enough to become "successful." For such a person the impulse—whether obeyed or not—is to disassociate him/herself from the group and to side with its implicit opponents. Thus the Black millionaire who deplores the Panthers, the rich *Québecois* who is anti-Separatist, the North American immigrant who changes his name to an "English" one; thus, alas, the Canadian writer who makes it, sort of, in New York, and spends many magazine pages decrying provincial dull Canadian writers; and thus the women with successful careers who say "*I've* never had any problems, I don't know what they're talking about." Such a woman tends to regard herself, and to be treated by her male colleagues, as a sort of honorary man. It's the rest of them who are inept, brainless, tearful, self-defeating: not her. "You think like a man," she is told, with admiration and unconscious put-down. For both men and women, it's just too much of a strain to fit together the traditionally incompatible notions of "woman" and "good at something." And if you *are* good at something, why carry with you the stigma attached to that dismal category you've gone to such lengths to escape from? The only reason for rocking the boat is if you're still chained to the oars. Not everyone reacts like this, but this factor may explain some of the more hysterical opposition to Women's Lib on the part of a few woman writers, even though they may have benefitted from the Movement in the form of increased sales and more serious attention.

5 A couple of ironies remain; perhaps they are even paradoxes. One is that, in the development of modern Western civilization, writing was the first of the arts, before painting, music, composing, and sculpting, which it was possible for women

to practice; and it was the fourth of the job categories, after prostitution, domestic service and the stage, and before wide-scale factory work, nursing, secretarial work, telephone operating and school teaching, at which it was possible for them to make any money. The reason for both is the same: writing as a physical activity is private. You do it by yourself, on your own time; no teachers or employers are involved, you don't have to apprentice in a studio or work with musicians. Your only business arrangements are with your publisher, and these can be conducted through the mails; your real "employers" can be deceived, if you choose, by the adoption of an assumed (male) name; witness the Brontës and George Eliot. But the private and individual nature of writing may also account for the low incidence of direct involvement by woman writers in the Movement now. If you are a writer, prejudice against women will affect you *as a writer* not directly but indirectly. You won't suffer from wage discrimination, because you aren't paid any wages; you won't be hired last and fired first, because you aren't hired or fired anyway. You have relatively little to complain of, and, absorbed in your own work as you are likely to be, you will find it quite easy to shut your eyes to what goes on at the spool factory, or even at the university. *Paradox:* reason for involvement then equals reason for non-involvement now.

6 Another paradox goes like this. As writers, woman writers are like other writers. They have the same professional concerns, they have to deal with the same contracts and publishing procedures, they have the same need for solitude to work and the same concern that their work be accurately evaluated by reviewers. There is nothing "male" or "female" about these conditions; they are just attributes of the activity known as writing. As biological specimens and as citizens, however, women are like other women: subject to the same discriminatory laws, encountering the same demeaning attitudes, burdened with the same good reasons for not walking through the park alone after dark. They too have bodies, the capacity to bear children; they eat, sleep and bleed, just like everyone else. In bookstores and publishers' offices and among groups of other writers, a woman writer may get the impression that she is "special;" but in the eyes of the law, in the loan office or bank, in the hospital and on the street she's just another woman. She doesn't get to wear a sign to the grocery store saying "Respect me, I'm a Woman Writer." No matter how good she may feel about herself, strangers who aren't aware of her shelf-full of nifty volumes with cover blurbs saying how gifted she is will still regard her as a nit.

7 We all have ways of filtering out aspects of our experience we would rather not think about. Woman writers can keep as much as possible to the "writing" end of their life, avoiding the less desirable aspects of the "woman" end. Or they can divide themselves in two, thinking of themselves as two different people: a "writer" and a "woman." Time after time, I've had interviewers talk to me about my writing for a while, then ask me, "As a woman, what do you think about—for instance—the Women's Movement," as if I could think two sets of thoughts about the same thing, one set as a writer or person, the other as a woman. But no one comes apart this easily; categories like Woman, White, Canadian, Writer are only ways of looking at a thing, and the thing itself is whole, entire and indivisible. *Paradox:* Woman and Writer are separate categories; but in any individual woman writer, they are inseparable.

8 One of the results of the paradox is that there are certain attitudes, some overt, some concealed, which women writers encounter *as* writers, but *because* they are women. I shall try to deal with a few of these, as objectively as I can. After that, I'll attempt a limited personal statement.

A. Reviewing and the Absence of an Adequate Critical Vocabulary

9 Cynthia Ozick, in the American magazine *Ms.,* says, "For many years, I had noticed that no book of poetry by a woman was ever reviewed without reference to the poet's sex. The curious thing was that, in the two decades of my scrutiny, there were *no* exceptions whatever. It did not matter whether the reviewer was a man or a woman; in every case, the question of the 'feminine sensibility' of the poet was at the centre of the reviewer's response. The maleness of male poets, on the other hand, hardly ever seemed to matter."

10 Things aren't this bad in Canada, possibly because we were never fully indoctrinated with the Holy Gospel according to the distorters of Freud. Many reviewers manage to get through a review without displaying the kind of bias Ozick is talking about. But that it does occur was demonstrated to me by a project I was involved with at York University in 1971–72.

11 One of my groups was attempting to study what we called "sexual bias in reviewing," by which we meant not unfavourable reviews, but points being added or subtracted by the reviewer on the basis of the author's sex and supposedly associated characteristics rather than on the basis of the work itself. Our study fell into two parts: i) a survey of writers, half male, half female, conducted by letter: had they ever experienced sexual bias directed against them in a review? ii) the reading of a large number of reviews from a wide range of periodicals and newspapers.

12 The results of the writers' survey were perhaps predictable. Of the men, none said Yes, a quarter said Maybe, and three quarters said No. Half of the women said Yes, a quarter said Maybe and a quarter said No. The women replying Yes often wrote long, detailed letters, giving instances and discussing their own attitudes. All the men's letters were short.

13 This proved only that women were more likely to *feel* they had been discriminated against on the basis of sex. When we got around to the reviews, we discovered that they were sometimes justified. Here are the kinds of things we found.

I) ASSIGNMENT OF REVIEWS

14 Several of our letter writers mentioned this. Some felt books by women tended to be passed over by book-page editors assigning books for review; others that books by women tended to get assigned to women reviewers. When we started totting up reviews we found that most books in this society are written by men, and so are most reviews. Disproportionately often, books by women were assigned to women reviewers, indicating that books by women fell in the minds of those dishing out the reviews

into some kind of "special" category. Likewise, woman reviewers tended to be reviewing books by women rather than by men (though because of the preponderance of male reviewers, there were quite a few male-written reviews of books by women).

II) THE QUILLER-COUCH SYNDROME

15 The heading of this one refers to the turn-of-the-century essay by Quiller-Couch, defining "masculine" and "feminine" styles in writing. The "masculine" style is, of course, bold, forceful, clear, vigorous, etc.; the "feminine" style is vague, weak, tremulous, pastel, etc. In the list of pairs you can include "objective" and "subjective," "universal" or "accurate depiction of society" versus "confessional," "personal," or even "narcissistic" and "neurotic." It's roughly seventy years since Quiller-Couch's essay, but the "masculine" group of adjectives is still much more likely to be applied to the work of male writers; female writers are much more likely to get hit with some version of "the feminine style" or "feminine sensibility," whether their work merits it or not.

III) THE LADY PAINTER, OR SHE WRITES LIKE A MAN

16 This is a pattern in which good equals male, and bad equals female. I call it the Lady Painter Syndrome because of a conversation I had about female painters with a male painter in 1960. "When she's good," he said, "we call her a painter; when she's bad, we call her a lady painter." "She writes like a man" is part of the same pattern; it's usually used by a male reviewer who is impressed by a female writer. It's meant as a compliment. See also "She thinks like a man," which means the author thinks, unlike most women, who are held to be incapable of objective thought (their province is "feeling"). Adjectives which often have similar connotations are ones such as "strong," "gutsy," "hard," "mean," etc. A hard-hitting piece of writing by a man is liable to be thought of as merely realistic; an equivalent piece by a woman is much more likely to be labelled "cruel" or "tough." The assumption is that women are by nature soft, weak and not very good, and that if a woman writer happens to be good, she should be deprived of her identity as a female and provided with higher (male) status. Thus the woman writer has, in the minds of such reviewers, two choices. She can be bad but female, a carrier of the "feminine sensibility" virus; or she can be "good" in male-adjective terms, but sexless. Badness seems to be ascribed then to a surplus of female hormones, whereas badness in a male writer is usually ascribed to nothing but badness (though a "bad" male writer is sometimes held, by adjectives implying sterility or impotence, to be deficient in maleness). "Maleness" is exemplified by the "good" male writer; "femaleness," since it is seen by such reviewers as a handicap or deficiency, is held to be transcended or discarded by the "good" female one. In other words, there is no critical vocabulary for expressing the concept "good/female." Work by a male writer is often spoken of by critics admiring it as having "balls;" ever hear anyone speak admiringly of work by a woman as having "tits?" *Possible antidotes:* Development of a "good/female"

vocabulary ("Wow, has that ever got Womb . . ."); or, preferably, the development of a vocabulary that can treat structures made of words as though they are exactly that, not biological entities possessed of sexual organs.

IV) DOMESTICITY

17 One of our writers noted a (usually male) habit of concentrating on domestic themes in the work of a female writer, ignoring any other topic she might have dealt with, then patronizing her for an excessive interest in domestic themes. We found several instances of reviewers identifying an author as a "housewife" and consequently dismissing anything she has produced (since, in our society, a "housewife" is viewed as a relatively brainless and talentless creature). We even found one instance in which the author was called a "housewife" and put down for writing like one when in fact she was no such thing.

18 For such reviewers, when a man writes about things like doing the dishes, it's realism; when a woman does, it's an unfortunate feminine genetic limitation.

V) SEXUAL COMPLIMENT-PUT-DOWN

19 This syndrome can be summed up as follows;

SHE: "How do you like my (design for an airplane/mathematical formula/medical miracle)?"
HE: "You sure have a nice ass."

In reviewing it usually takes the form of commenting on the cute picture of the (female) author on the cover, coupled with dismissal of her as a writer.

VI) PANIC REACTION

20 When something the author writes hits too close to home, panic reaction may set in. One of our correspondents noticed this phenomenon in connection with one of her books: she felt that the content of the book threatened male reviewers, who gave it much worse reviews than did any female reviewer. Their reaction seemed to be that if a character such as she'd depicted did exist, they didn't want to know about it. In panic reaction, a reviewer is reacting to content, not to technique or craftsmanship or a book's internal coherence or faithfulness to its own assumptions. (Panic reaction can be touched off in any area, not just male-female relationships.)

B. Interviewers and Media Stereotypes

21 Associated with the reviewing problem, but distinct from it, is the problem of the interview. Reviewers are supposed to concentrate on books, interviewers on

the writer as a person, human being, or, in the case of women, woman. This means that an interviewer is ostensibly trying to find out what sort of person you are. In reality, he or she may merely be trying to match you up with a stereotype of "Woman Author" that pre-exists in her/his mind; doing it that way is both easier for the interviewer, since it limits the range and slant of questions, and shorter, since the interview can be practically written in advance. It isn't just women who get this treatment: all writers get it. But the range for male authors is somewhat wider, and usually comes from the literary tradition itself, whereas stereotypes for female authors are often borrowed from other media, since the ones provided by the tradition are limited in number.

22 In a bourgeois, industrial society, so the theory goes, the creative artist is supposed to act out suppressed desires and prohibited activities for the audience; thus we get certain Post-romantic male-author stereotypes, such as Potted Poe, Bleeding Byron, Doomed Dylan, Lustful Layton, Crucified Cohen, etc. Until recently the only personality stereotype of this kind was Elusive Emily, otherwise known as Recluse Rossetti: the woman writer as aberration, neurotically denying herself the delights of sex, kiddies and other fun. The Twentieth Century has added Suicidal Sylvia, a somewhat more dire version of the same thing. The point about these stereotypes is that attention is focused not on the actual achievements of the authors, but on their lives, which are distorted and romanticized; their work is then interpreted in the light of the distorted version. Stereotypes like these, even when the author becomes a cult object, do no service to anyone or anything, least of all the author's work. Behind all of them is the notion that authors must be more special, peculiar or weird than other people, and that their lives are more interesting than their work.

23 The following examples are taken from personal experience (mine, of interviewers); they indicate the range of possibilities. There are a few others, such as Earth Mother, but for those you have to be older.

I) HAPPY HOUSEWIFE

24 This one is almost obsolete: it used to be for Woman's Page or programme. Questions were about what you liked to fix for dinner; attitude was, "Gosh, all the housework and you're a writer too!" Writing was viewed as a hobby, like knitting, one did in one's spare time.

II) OPHELIA

25 The writer as crazy freak. Female version of Doomed Dylan, with more than a little hope on the part of the interviewer that you'll turn into Suicidal Sylvia and give them something to *really* write about. Questions like "Do you think you're in danger of going insane?" or "Are writers closer to insanity than other people?" No need to point out that most mental institutions are crammed with people who have never written a word in their life. "Say something interesting," one interviewer said to me. "Say you write all your poems on drugs."

III) MISS MARTYR; OR, MOVIE MAG

26 Read any movie mag on Liz Taylor and translate into writing terms and you've got the picture. The writer as someone who *suffers* more than others. Why does the writer suffer more? Because she's successful, and you all know Success Must Be Paid For. In blood and tears, if possible. If you say you're happy and enjoy your life and work, you'll be ignored.

IV) MISS MESSAGE

27 Interviewer incapable of treating your work as what it is, i.e. poetry and/or fiction. Great attempt to get you to say something about an Issue and then make you into an exponent, spokeswoman or theorist. (The two Messages I'm most frequently saddled with are Women's Lib and Canadian Nationalism, though I belong to no formal organization devoted to either.) Interviewer unable to see that putting, for instance, a nationalist into a novel doesn't make it a nationalistic novel, any more than putting in a preacher makes it a religious novel. Interviewer incapable of handling more than one dimension at a time.

28 *What is Hard to Find* is an interviewer who regards writing as a respectable profession, not as some kind of magic, madness, trickery or evasive disguise for a Message; and who regards an author as someone engaged in a professional activity.

C. Other Writers and Rivalry

29 Regarding yourself as an "exception," part of an unspoken quota system, can have interesting results. If there are only so many available slots for your minority in the medical school/law school/literary world, of course you will feel rivalry, not only with members of the majority for whom no quota operates, but especially for members of your minority who are competing with you for the few coveted places. And you will have to be better than the average Majority member to get in at all. But we're familiar with that.

30 Woman-woman rivalry does occur, though it is surprisingly less severe than you'd expect; it's likely to take the form of *wanting* another woman writer to be better than she is, expecting more of her than you would of a male writer, and being exasperated with certain kinds of traditional "female" writing. One of our correspondents discussed these biases and expectations very thoroughly and with great intelligence: her letter didn't solve any problems but it did emphasize the complexities of the situation. Male-male rivalry is more extreme; we've all been treated to media-exploited examples of it.

31 What a woman writer is often unprepared for is the unexpected personal attack on her by a jealous male writer. The motivation is envy and competitiveness, but the form is often sexual put-down. "You may be a good writer," one older man said to a young woman writer who had just had a publishing success, "but I wouldn't

want to fuck you." Another version goes more like the compliment-put-down noted under Reviewing. In either case, the ploy diverts attention from the woman's achievement as a writer—the area where the man feels threatened—to her sexuality, where either way he can score a verbal point.

PERSONAL STATEMENT

32 I've been trying to give you a picture of the arena, or that part of it where being a "woman" and "writer," as concepts, overlap. But, of course, the arena I've been talking about has to do largely with externals: reviewing, the media, relationships with other writers. This, for the writer, may affect the tangibles of her career: how she is received, how viewed, how much money she makes. But in relationship to the writing itself, this is a false arena. The real one is in her head, her real struggle the daily battle with words, the language itself. The false arena becomes valid for writing itself only insofar as it becomes part of her material and is transformed into one of the verbal and imaginative structures she is constantly engaged in making. Writers, as writers, are not propagandists or examples of social trends or preachers or politicians. They are makers of books, and unless they can make books well they will be bad writers, no matter what the social validity of their views.

33 At the beginning of this article, I suggested a few reasons for the infrequent participation in the Movement of woman writers. Maybe these reasons were the wrong ones, and this is the real one: no good writer wants to be merely a transmitter of someone else's ideology, no matter how fine that ideology may be. The aim of propaganda is to convince, and to spur people to action; the aim of writing is to create a plausible and moving imaginative world, and to create it from words. Or, to put it another way, the aim of a political movement is to improve the quality of people's lives on all levels, spiritual and imaginative as well as material (and any political movement that doesn't have this aim is worth nothing). Writing, however, tends to concentrate more on life, not as it ought to be, but as it is, as the writer feels it, experiences it. Writers are eye-witnesses, I-witnesses. Political movements, once successful, have historically been intolerant of writers, even those writers who initially aided them; in any revolution, writers have been among the first to be lined up against the wall, perhaps for their intransigence, their insistence on saying what they perceive, not what, according to the ideology, ought to exist. Politicians, even revolutionary politicians, have traditionally had no more respect for writing as an activity valuable in itself, quite apart from any message or content, than has the rest of the society. And writers, even revolutionary writers, have traditionally been suspicious of anyone who tells them what they ought to write.

34 The woman writer, then, exists in a society that, though it may turn certain individual writers into revered cult objects, has little respect for writing as a profession, and not much respect for women either. If there were more of both, articles like this would be obsolete. I hope they become so. In the meantime, it seems to me that the proper path for a woman writer is not an all-out manning (or womaning)

of the barricades, however much she may agree with the aims of the Movement. The proper path is to become better as a writer. Insofar as writers are lenses, condensers of their society, her work may include the Movement, since it is so palpably among the things that exist. The picture that she gives of it is altogether another thing, and will depend, at least partly, on the course of the Movement itself.

(1976)

QUESTIONS

Thought and Structure

1. What is the source of Atwood's trepidation in writing this essay? Is her anxiety justified? Why or why not?
2. What is her attitude toward "the Women's Movement"? Toward feminism? Why?
3. How are women writers exempt, as writers, from some of the forms of discrimination leveled against women in other professions? Why and in what ways are women writers, however good and talented, not exempt, as women, from such discrimination?
4. Atwood divides her essay with heads and subheads in a quasi-outline format. Did you find this a help or a hindrance? Why?
5. What is Atwood's objection to the depiction of "masculine" and "feminine" literary styles described by Sir Arthur Quiller-Couch? Does she object to his terminology? To his categories? To something else? Is she right?
6. Atwood quotes those who praise a woman because she can "think like a man." What is she talking about? Can a woman "think like a man"? Can a man "think like a woman"? How helpful are such characterizations? Why?

Style and Strategy

7. How would you characterize the tone of this essay? Is it angry? Bitter? Belligerent? Tolerant? Or what?
8. The essay is primarily argumentative in approach and purpose. What strategies does Atwood use to discredit opposing viewpoints? How successfully does she accomplish this discrediting?
9. Atwood's language, on occasion, becomes "physical." She talks about "balls," "Wombs" and "tits," for example. Why does she do this? To what effect?
10. Identify an additional feature of Atwood's language you find striking or startling, amusing, or engaging, and explain why.

SUGGESTIONS FOR WRITING

A. Write an essay supporting Atwood's views, modifying them, or attacking them.

B. Write your own essay "On Being a Male or Female X." Consider issues of sexual stereotyping and gender roles as they apply to your topic.

Giving Birth

1 But who gives it? And to whom is it given? Certainly it doesn't feel like giving, which implies a flow, a gentle handing over, no coercion. But there is scant gentleness here; it's too strenuous, the belly like a knotted fist, squeezing, the heavy trudge of the heart, every muscle in the body tight and moving, as in a slow-motion shot of a high-jump, the faceless body sailing up, turning, hanging for a moment in the air, and then—back to real time again—the plunge, the rush down, the result. Maybe the phrase was made by someone viewing the result only: in this case, the rows of babies to whom birth has occurred, lying like neat packages in their expertly wrapped blankets, pink or blue, with their labels Scotch Taped to their clear plastic cots, behind the plate-glass window.

2 No one ever says *giving death,* although they are in some ways the same, events, not things. And *delivering,* that act the doctor is generally believed to perform: who delivers what? Is it the mother who is delivered, like a prisoner being released? Surely not; nor is the child delivered to the mother like a letter through a slot. How can you be both the sender and the receiver at once? Was someone in bondage, is someone made free? Thus language, muttering in its archaic tongues of something, yet one more thing, that needs to be re-named.

It won't be by me, though. These are the only words I have, I'm stuck with them, stuck in them. (That image of the tar sands, old tableau in the Royal Ontario Museum, second floor north, how persistent it is. Will I break free, or will I be sucked down, fossilized, a sabre-toothed tiger or lumbering brontosaurus who ventured out too far? Words ripple at my feet, black, sluggish, lethal. Let me try once more, before the sun gets me, before I starve or drown, while I can. It's only a tableau after all, it's only a metaphor. See, I can speak, I am not trapped, and you on your part can understand. So we will go ahead as if there were no problem about language.)

3 This story about giving birth is not about me. In order to convince you of that I should tell you what I did this morning, before I sat down at this desk—a door on top of two filing cabinets, radio to the left, calendar to the right, these devices by which I place myself in time. I got up at twenty-to-seven, and, halfway down the stairs, met my daughter, who was ascending, autonomously she thought, actually in the arms of her father. We greeted each other with hugs and smiles; we then played with the alarm clock and the hot water bottle, a ritual we go through only on the days her father has to leave the house early to drive into the city. This ritual exists to give me the illusion that I am sleeping in. When she finally decided it was time for me to get up, she began pulling my hair. I got dressed while she explored the bathroom scales and the mysterious white altar of the toilet. I took her downstairs and we had the usual struggle over her clothes. Already she is wearing miniature jeans, miniature T-shirts. After this she fed herself: orange, banana, muffin, porridge.

4 We then went out to the sun porch, where we recognized anew, and by their names, the dog, the cats and the birds, blue jays and goldfinches at this time of year, which is winter. She puts her fingers on my lips as I pronounce these words; she

hasn't yet learned the secret of making them. I am waiting for her first word: surely it will be miraculous, something that has never yet been said. But if so, perhaps she's already said it and I, in my entrapment, my addiction to the usual, have not heard it.

5 In her playpen I discovered the first alarming thing of the day. It was a small naked woman, made of that soft plastic from which jiggly spiders and lizards and the other things people hang in their car windows are also made. She was given to my daughter by a friend, a woman who does props for movies, she was supposed to have been a prop but she wasn't used. The baby loved her and would crawl around the floor holding her in her mouth like a dog carrying a bone, with the head sticking out one side and the feet out the other. She seemed chewy and harmless, but the other day I noticed that the baby had managed to make a tear in the body with her new teeth. I put the woman into the cardboard box I use for toy storage.

6 But this morning she was back in the playpen and the feet were gone. The baby must have eaten them, and I worried about whether or not the plastic would dissolve in her stomach, whether it was toxic. Sooner or later, in the contents of her diaper, which I examine with the usual amount of maternal brooding, I knew I would find two small pink plastic feet. I removed the doll and later, while she was still singing to the dog outside the window, dropped it into the garbage. I am not up to finding tiny female arms, breasts, a head, in my daughter's disposable diapers, partially covered by undigested carrots and the husks of raisins, like the relics of some gruesome and demented murder.

7 Now she's having her nap and I am writing this story. From what I have said, you can see that my life (despite these occasional surprises, reminders of another world) is calm and orderly, suffused with that warm, reddish light, those well-placed blue highlights and reflecting surfaces (mirrors, plates, oblong window-panes) you think of as belonging to Dutch genre paintings; and like them it is realistic in detail and slightly sentimental. Or at least it has an aura of sentiment. (Already I'm having moments of muted grief over those of my daughter's baby clothes which are too small for her to wear any more. I will be a keeper of hair, I will store things in trunks, I will weep over photos.) But above all it's solid, everything here has solidity. No more of those washes of light, those shifts, nebulous effects of cloud, Turner sunsets, vague fears, the impalpables Jeanie used to concern herself with.

8 I call this woman Jeanie after the song. I can't remember any more of the song, only the title. The point (for in language there are always these "points," these reflections; this is what makes it so rich and sticky, this is why so many have disappeared beneath its dark and shining surface, why you should never try to see your own reflection in it; you will lean over too far, a strand of your hair will fall in and come out gold, and, thinking it is gold all the way down, you yourself will follow, sliding into those outstretched arms, towards the mouth you think is opening to pronounce your name but instead, just before your ears fill with pure sound, will form a word you have never heard before. . . .)

9 The point, for me, is in the hair. My own hair is not light brown, but Jeanie's was. This is one difference between us. The other point is the dreaming; for Jeanie isn't real in the same way that I am real. But by now, and I mean your time, both of us will have the same degree of reality, we will be equal: wraiths, echoes, reverbera-

tions in your own brain. At the moment though Jeanie is to me as I will someday be to you. So she is real enough.

10 Jeanie is on her way to the hospital, to give birth, to be delivered. She is not quibbling over these terms. She's sitting in the back seat of the car, with her eyes closed and her coat spread over her like a blanket. She is doing her breathing exercises and timing her contractions with a stopwatch. She has been up since two-thirty in the morning, when she took a bath and ate some lime Jell-O, and it's now almost ten. She has learned to count, during the slow breathing, in numbers (from one to ten while breathing in, from ten to one while breathing out) which she can actually see while she is silently pronouncing them. Each number is a different colour and, if she's concentrating very hard, a different typeface. They range from plain roman to ornamented circus numbers, red with gold filigree and dots. This is a refinement not mentioned in any of the numerous books she's read on the subject. Jeanie is a devotee of handbooks. She has at least two shelves of books that cover everything from building kitchen cabinets to auto repairs to smoking your own hams. She doesn't do many of these things, but she does some of them, and in her suitcase, along with a washcloth, a package of lemon Life Savers, a pair of glasses, a hot water bottle, some talcum powder and a paper bag, is the book that suggested she take along all of these things.

11 (By this time you may be thinking that I've invented Jeanie in order to distance myself from these experiences. Nothing could be further from the truth. I am, in fact, trying to bring myself closer to something that time has already made distant. As for Jeanie, my intention is simple: I am bringing her back to life.)

12 There are two other people in the car with Jeanie. One is a man, whom I will call A., for convenience. A. is driving. When Jeanie opens her eyes, at the end of every contraction, she can see the back of his slightly balding head and his reassuring shoulders. A. drives well and not too quickly. From time to time he asks her how she is, and she tells him how long the contractions are lasting and how long there is between them. When they stop for gas he buys them each a Styrofoam container of coffee. For months he has helped her with the breathing exercises, pressing on her knee as recommended by the book, and he will be present at the delivery. (Perhaps it's to him that the birth will be given, in the same sense that one gives a performance.) Together they have toured the hospital maternity ward, in company with a small group of other pairs like them: one thin solicitous person, one slow bulbous person. They have been shown the rooms, shared and private, the sitz-baths, the delivery room itself, which gave the impression of being white. The nurse was light-brown, with limber hips and elbows; she laughed a lot as she answered questions.

13 "First they'll give you an enema. You know what it is? They take a tube of water and put it up your behind. Now, the gentlemen must put on this—and these, over your shoes. And these hats, this one for those with long hair, this for those with short hair."

14 "What about those with no hair?" says A.

15 The nurse looks up at his head and laughs. "Oh, you still have some," she says. "If you have a question, do not be afraid to ask."

16 They have also seen the film made by the hospital, a full-colour film of a

woman giving birth to, can it be a baby? "Not all babies will be this large at birth," the Australian nurse who introduces the movie says. Still, the audience, half of which is pregnant, doesn't look very relaxed when the lights go on. ("If you don't like the visuals," a friend of Jeanie's has told her, "you can always close your eyes.") It isn't the blood so much as the brownish-red disinfectant that bothers her. "I've decided to call this whole thing off," she says to A., smiling to show it's a joke. He gives her a hug and says, "Everything's going to be fine."

17 And she knows it is. Everything will be fine. But there is another woman in the car. She's sitting in the front seat, and she hasn't turned or acknowledged Jeanie in any way. She, like Jeanie, is going to the hospital. She too is pregnant. She is not going to the hospital to give birth, however, because the words, the words, are too alien to her experience, the experience she is about to have, to be used about it at all. She's wearing a cloth coat with checks in maroon and brown, and she has a kerchief tied over her hair. Jeanie has seen her before, but she knows little about her except that she is a woman who did not wish to become pregnant, who did not choose to divide herself like this, who did not choose any of these ordeals, these initiations. It would be no use telling her that everything is going to be fine. The word in English for unwanted intercourse is rape. But there is no word in the language for what is about to happen to this woman.

18 Jeanie has seen this woman from time to time throughout her pregnancy, always in the same coat, always with the same kerchief. Naturally, being pregnant herself has made her more aware of other pregnant women, and she has watched them, examined them covertly, every time she has seen one. But not every other pregnant woman is this woman. She did not, for instance, attend Jeanie's pre-natal classes at the hospital, where the women were all young, younger than Jeanie.

19 "How many will be breast-feeding?" asks the Australian nurse with the hefty shoulders.

20 All hands but one shoot up. A modern group, the new generation, and the one lone bottle-feeder, who might have (who knows?) something wrong with her breasts, is ashamed of herself. The others look politely away from her. What they want most to discuss, it seems, are the differences between one kind of disposable diaper and another. Sometimes they lie on mats and squeeze each other's hands, simulating contractions and counting breaths. It's all very hopeful. The Australian nurse tells them not to get in and out of the bathtub by themselves. At the end of an hour they are each given a glass of apple juice.

21 There is only one woman in the class who has already given birth. She's there, she says, to make sure they give her a shot this time. They delayed it last time and she went through hell. The others look at her with mild disapproval. *They* are not clamouring for shots, they do not intend to go through hell. Hell comes from the wrong attitude, they feel. The books talk about *discomfort.*

22 "It's not discomfort, it's pain, baby," the woman says.

23 The others smile uneasily and the conversation slides back to disposable diapers.

24 Vitaminized, conscientious, well-read Jeanie, who has managed to avoid morning sickness, varicose veins, stretch marks, toxemia and depression, who has had no aberrations of appetite, no blurrings of vision—why is she followed, then, by this

other? At first it was only a glimpse now and then, at the infants' clothing section in Simpson's Basement, in the supermarket lineup, on street corners as she herself slid by in A.'s car: the haggard face, the bloated torso, the kerchief holding back the too-sparse hair. In any case, it was Jeanie who saw her, not the other way around. If she knew she was following Jeanie she gave no sign.

25 As Jeanie has come closer and closer to this day, the unknown day on which she will give birth, as time has thickened around her so that it has become something she must propel herself through, a kind of slush, wet earth underfoot, she has seen this woman more and more often, though always from a distance. Depending on the light, she has appeared by turns as a young girl of perhaps twenty to an older woman of forty or forty-five, but there was never any doubt in Jeanie's mind that it was the same woman. In fact it did not occur to her that the woman was not real in the usual sense (and perhaps she was, originally, on the first or second sighting, as the voice that causes an echo is real), until A. stopped for a red light during this drive to the hospital and the woman, who had been standing on the corner with a brown paper bag in her arms, simply opened the front door of the car and got in. A. didn't react, and Jeanie knows better than to say anything to him. She is aware that the woman is not really there: Jeanie is not crazy. She could even make the woman disappear by opening her eyes wider, by staring, but it is only the shape that would go away, not the feeling. Jeanie isn't exactly afraid of this woman. She is afraid for her.

26 When they reach the hospital, the woman gets out of the car and is through the door by the time A. has come around to help Jeanie out of the back seat. In the lobby she is nowhere to be seen. Jeanie goes through Admission in the usual way, unshadowed.

27 There has been an epidemic of babies during the night and the maternity ward is overcrowded. Jeanie waits for her room behind a dividing screen. Nearby someone is screaming, screaming and mumbling between screams in what sounds like a foreign language. Portuguese, Jeanie thinks. She tells herself that for them it is different, you're supposed to scream, you're regarded as queer if you don't scream, it's a required part of giving birth. Nevertheless she knows that the woman screaming is the other woman and she is screaming from pain. Jeanie listens to the other voice, also a woman's, comforting, reassuring: her mother? A nurse?

28 A. arrives and they sit uneasily, listening to the screams. Finally Jeanie is sent for and she goes for her prep. Prep school, she thinks. She takes off her clothes—when will she see them again?—and puts on the hospital gown. She is examined, labelled around the wrist and given an enema. She tells the nurse she can't take Demerol because she's allergic to it, and the nurse writes this down. Jeanie doesn't know whether this is true or not but she doesn't want Demerol, she has read the books. She intends to put up a struggle over her pubic hair—surely she will lose her strength if it is all shaved off—but it turns out the nurse doesn't have very strong feelings about it. She is told her contractions are not far enough along to be taken seriously, she can even have lunch. She puts on her dressing gown and rejoins A., in the freshly vacated room, eats some tomato soup and a veal cutlet, and decides to take a nap while A. goes out for supplies.

29 Jeanie wakes up when A. comes back. He has brought a paper, some detective

novels for Jeanie and a bottle of Scotch for himself. A. reads the paper and drinks Scotch, and Jeanie reads *Poirot's Early Cases.* There is no connection between Poirot and her labour, which is now intensifying, unless it is the egg-shape of Poirot's head and the vegetable marrows he is known to cultivate with strands of wet wool (placentae? umbilical cords?). She is glad the stories are short; she is walking around the room now, between contractions. Lunch was definitely a mistake.

30 "I think I have back labour," she says to A. They get out the handbook and look up the instructions for this. It's useful that everything has a name. Jeanie kneels on the bed and rests her forehead on her arms while A. rubs her back. A. pours himself another Scotch, in the hospital glass. The nurse, in pink, comes, looks, asks about the timing, and goes away again. Jeanie is beginning to sweat. She can only manage half a page or so of Poirot before she has to clamber back up on the bed again and begin breathing and running through the coloured numbers.

31 When the nurse comes back, she has a wheelchair. It's time to go down to the labour room, she says. Jeanie feels stupid sitting in the wheelchair. She tells herself about peasant women having babies in the fields, Indian women having them on portages with hardly a second thought. She feels effete. But the hospital wants her to ride, and considering the fact that the nurse is tiny, perhaps it's just as well. What if Jeanie were to collapse, after all? After all her courageous talk. An image of the tiny pink nurse, antlike, trundling large Jeanie through the corridors, rolling her along like a heavy beach ball.

32 As they go by the check-in desk a woman is wheeled past on a table, covered by a sheet. Her eyes are closed and there's a bottle feeding into her arm through a tube. Something is wrong. Jeanie looks back—she thinks it was the other woman—but the sheet table is hidden now behind the counter.

33 In the dim labour room Jeanie takes off her dressing gown and is helped up onto the bed by the nurse. A. brings her suitcase, which is not a suitcase actually but a small flight bag, the significance of this has not been lost on Jeanie, and in fact she now has some of the apprehensive feelings she associates with planes, including the fear of a crash. She takes out her Life Savers, her glasses, her washcloth and the other things she thinks she will need. She removes her contact lenses and places them in their case, reminding A. that they must not be lost. Now she is purblind.

34 There is something else in her bag that she doesn't remove. It's a talisman, given to her several years ago as a souvenir by a travelling friend of hers. It's a rounded oblong of opaque blue glass, with four yellow-and-white eye shapes on it. In Turkey, her friend has told her, they hang them on mules to protect against the Evil Eye. Jeanie knows this talisman probably won't work for her, she is not Turkish and she isn't a mule, but it makes her feel safe to have it in the room with her. She had planned to hold it in her hand during the most difficult part of labour but somehow there is no longer any time for carrying out plans like this.

35 An old woman, a fat old woman dressed all in green, comes into the room and sits beside Jeanie. She says to A., who is sitting on the other side of Jeanie, "That is a good watch. They don't make watches like that any more." She is referring to his gold pocket watch, one of his few extravagances, which is on the night table. Then she places her hand on Jeanie's belly to feel the contraction. "This is good,"

she says, her accent is Swedish or German. "This, I call a contraction. Before, it was nothing." Jeanie can no longer remember having seen her before. "Good. Good."

36 "When will I have it?" Jeanie asks, when she can talk, when she is no longer counting.

37 The old woman laughs. Surely that laugh, those tribal hands, have presided over a thousand beds, a thousand kitchen tables . . . "A long time yet," she says. "Eight, ten hours."

38 "But I've been *doing* this for twelve hours already," Jeanie says.

39 "Not hard labour," the woman says. "Not good, like this."

40 Jeanie settles into herself for the long wait. At the moment she can't remember why she wanted to have a baby in the first place. That decision was made by someone else, whose motives are now unclear. She remembers the way women who had babies used to smile at one another, mysteriously, as if there was something they knew that she didn't, the way they would casually exclude her from their frame of reference. What was the knowledge, the mystery, or was having a baby really no more inexplicable than having a car accident or an orgasm? (But these too were indescribable, events of the body, all of them; why should the mind distress itself trying to find a language for them?) She has sworn she will never do that to any woman without children, engage in those passwords and exclusions. She's old enough, she's been put through enough years of it to find it tiresome and cruel.

41 But—and this is the part of Jeanie that goes with the talisman hidden in her bag, not with the part that longs to build kitchen cabinets and smoke hams—she is, secretly, hoping for a mystery. Something more than this, something else, a vision. After all she is risking her life, though it's not too likely she will die. Still, some women do. Internal bleeding, shock, heart failure, a mistake on the part of someone, a nurse, a doctor. She deserves a vision, she deserves to be allowed to bring something back with her from this dark place into which she is now rapidly descending.

42 She thinks momentarily about the other woman. Her motives, too, are unclear. Why doesn't she want to have a baby? Has she been raped, does she have ten other children, is she starving? Why hasn't she had an abortion? Jeanie doesn't know, and in fact it no longer matters why. *Uncross your fingers,* Jeanie thinks to her. Her face, distorted with pain and terror, floats briefly behind Jeanie's eyes before it too drifts away.

43 Jeanie tries to reach down to the baby, as she has many times before, sending waves of love, colour, music, down through her arteries to it, but she finds she can no longer do this. She can no longer feel the baby as a baby, its arms and legs poking, kicking, turning. It has collected itself together, it's a hard sphere, it does not have time right now to listen to her. She's grateful for this because she isn't sure anyway how good the message would be. She no longer has control of the numbers either, she can no longer see them, although she continues mechanically to count. She realizes she has practised for the wrong thing, A. squeezing her knee was nothing, she should have practised for this, whatever it is.

44 "Slow down," A. says. She's on her side now, he's holding her hand. "Slow it right down."

45 "I can't, I can't do it, I can't do this."

46 "Yes, you can."

47 "Will I sound like that?"

48 "Like what?" A. says. Perhaps he can't hear it: it's the other woman, in the room next door or the room next door to that. She's screaming and crying, screaming and crying. While she cries she is saying, over and over, "It hurts. It hurts."

49 "No, you won't," he says. So there is someone, after all.

50 A doctor comes in, not her own doctor. They want her to turn over on her back.

51 "I can't," she says. "I don't like it that way." Sounds have receded, she has trouble hearing them. She turns over and the doctor gropes with her rubber-gloved hand. Something wet and hot flows over her thighs.

52 "It was just ready to break," the doctor says. "All I had to do was touch it. Four centimeters," she says to A.

53 "Only *four?*" Jeanie says. She feels cheated; they must be wrong. The doctor says her own doctor will be called in time. Jeanie is outraged at them. They have not understood, but it's too late to say this and she slips back into the dark place, which is not hell, which is more like being inside, trying to get out. *Out,* she says or thinks. Then she is floating, the numbers are gone, if anyone told her to get up, go out of the room, stand on her head, she would do it. From minute to minute she comes up again, grabs for air.

54 "You're hyperventilating," A. says. "Slow it down." He is rubbing her back now, hard, and she takes his hand and shoves it viciously further down, to the right place, which is not the right place as soon as his hand is there. She remembers a story she read once, about the Nazis tying the legs of Jewish women together during labour. She never really understood before how that could kill you.

55 A nurse appears with a needle. "I don't want it," Jeanie says.

56 "Don't be hard on yourself," the nurse says. "You don't have to go through pain like that." What pain? Jeanie thinks. When there is no pain she feels nothing, when there is pain, she feels nothing because there is no *she.* This, finally, is the disappearance of language. *You don't remember afterwards,* she has been told by almost everyone.

57 Jeanie comes out of a contraction, gropes for control. "Will it hurt the baby?" she says.

58 "It's a mild analgesic," the doctor says. "We wouldn't allow anything that would hurt the baby." Jeanie doesn't believe this. Nevertheless she is jabbed, and the doctor is right, it is very mild, because it doesn't seem to do a thing for Jeanie, though A. later tells her she has slept briefly between contractions.

59 Suddenly she sits bolt upright. She is wide awake and lucid. "You have to ring that bell right now," she says. "This baby is being born."

60 A. clearly doesn't believe her. "I can feel it, I can feel the head," she says. A. pushes the button for the call bell. A nurse appears and checks, and now everything is happening too soon, nobody is ready. They set off down the hall, the nurse wheeling Jeanie feels fine. She watches the corridors, the edges of everything shadowy because she doesn't have her glasses on. She hopes A. will remember to bring them. They pass another doctor.

61 "Need me?" she asks.

62 "Oh no," the nurse answers breezily. "Natural childbirth."

63 Jeanie realizes that this woman must have been the anaesthetist. "What?" she says, but it's too late now, they are in the room itself, all those glossy surfaces, tubular strange apparatus like a science-fiction movie, and the nurse is telling her to get onto the delivery table. No one else is in the room.

64 "You must be crazy," Jeanie says.

65 "Don't push," the nurse says.

66 "What do you mean?" Jeanie says. This is absurd. Why should she wait, why should the baby wait for them because they're late?

67 "Breathe through your mouth," the nurse says. "Pant," and Jeanie finally remembers how. When the contraction is over she uses the nurse's arm as a lever and hauls herself across onto the table.

68 From somewhere her own doctor materializes, in her doctor suit already, looking even more like Mary Poppins than usual, and Jeanie says, "Bet you weren't expecting to see me so soon!" The baby is being born when Jeanie said it would, though just three days ago the doctor said it would be at least another week, and this makes Jeanie feel jubilant and smug. Not that she knew, she'd believed the doctor.

69 She's being covered with a green tablecloth, they are taking far too long, she feels like pushing the baby out now, before they are ready. A. is there by her head, swathed in robes, hats, masks. He has forgotten her glasses. "Push now," the doctor says. Jeanie grips with her hands, grits her teeth, face, her whole body together, a snarl, a fierce smile, the baby is enormous, a stone, a boulder, her bones unlock, and, once, twice, the third time, she opens like a birdcage turning slowly inside out.

70 A pause; a wet kitten slithers between her legs. "Why don't you look?" says the doctor, but Jeanie still has her eyes closed. No glasses, she couldn't have seen a thing anyway. "Why don't you look?" the doctor says again.

71 Jeanie opens her eyes. She can see the baby, who has been wheeled up beside her and is fading already from the alarming birth purple. A good baby, she thinks, meaning it as the old woman did: *a good watch,* well-made, substantial. The baby isn't crying; she squints in the new light. Birth isn't something that has been given to her, nor has she taken it. It was just something that has happened so they could greet each other like this. The nurse is stringing beads for her name. When the baby is bundled and tucked beside Jeanie, she goes to sleep.

72 As for the vision, there wasn't one. Jeanie is conscious of no special knowledge; already she's forgetting what it was like. She's tired and very cold; she is shaking, and asks for another blanket. A. comes back to the room with her; her clothes are still there. Everything is quiet, the other woman is no longer screaming. Something has happened to her, Jeanie knows. Is she dead? Is the baby dead? Perhaps she is one of those casualties (and how can Jeanie herself be sure, yet, that she will not be among them) who will go into postpartum depression and never come out. "You see, there was nothing to be afraid of," A. says before he leaves, but he was wrong.

73 The next morning Jeanie wakes up when it's light. She's been warned about getting out of bed the first time without the help of a nurse, but she decides to do it anyway (peasant in the field! Indian on the portage!). She's still running adrenaline, she's also weaker than she thought, but she wants very much to look out the window. She feels she's been inside too long, she wants to see the sun come up. Being

awake this early always makes her feel a little unreal, a little insubstantial, as if she's partly transparent, partly dead.

74 (It was to me, after all, that the birth was given, Jeanie gave it, I am the result. What would she make of me? Would she be pleased?)

75 The window is two panes with a venetian blind sandwiched between them; it turns by a knob at the side. Jeanie has never seen a window like this before. She closes and opens the blind several times. Then she leaves it open and looks out.

76 All she can see from the window is a building. It's an old stone building, heavy and Victorian, with a copper roof oxidized to green. It's solid, hard, darkened by soot, dour, leaden. But as she looks at this building, so old and seemingly immutable, she sees that it's made of water. Water, and some tenuous jelly-like substance. Light flows through it from behind (the sun is coming up), the building is so thin, so fragile, that it quivers in the slight dawn wind. Jeanie sees that if the building is this way (a touch could destroy it, a ripple of the earth, why has no one noticed, guarded it against accidents?) then the rest of the world must be like this too, the entire earth, the rocks, people, trees, everything needs to be protected, cared for, tended. The enormity of this task defeats her; she will never be up to it, and what will happen then?

77 Jeanie hears footsteps in the hall outside her door. She thinks it must be the other woman, in her brown-and-maroon-checked coat, carrying her paper bag, leaving the hospital now that her job is done. She has seen Jeanie safely through, she must go now to hunt through the streets of the city for her next case. But the door opens, it's a nurse, who is just in time to catch Jeanie as she sinks to the floor, holding on to the edge of the air-conditioning unit. The nurse scolds her for getting up too soon.

78 After that the baby is carried in, solid, substantial, packed together like an apple, Jeanie examines her, she is complete, and in the days that follow Jeanie herself becomes drifted over with new words, her hair slowly darkens, she ceases to be what she was and is replaced, gradually, by someone else.

(1977)

QUESTIONS

1. What ideas and feelings about giving birth emerge from the narrator's opening reflections about the meaning(s) of the words used to name the act?
2. Identify the images Atwood employs in the opening paragraph and comment on their significance and effects.
3. In paragraph 3 the narrator asserts that language can be found to describe the experience of giving birth (and indeed presumably of any experience). Atwood thus seems to set for herself in the story the challenging task of explaining what it is like to give birth, even to those who have never or can never do so. How well do you think she succeeds? Why?
4. What part do the narrator's descriptions of her one-year-old daughter play in the story?
5. What is the point of the discussion of Jeanie's and the narrator's "reality" in paragraph 10?

6. What is the purpose of the first parenthetical paragraph (11)? How would the story and your response differ if it were omitted?
7. Why is the story narrated in the present tense? Rewrite one paragraph changing the verbs to the past tense. What happens?
8. Explain the point of the last sentence of the story.

SUGGESTIONS FOR WRITING

A. Analyze the character of the narrator. Describe your perception of her. Explain how you size her up and why.

B. Write an essay in which you describe what it is like to undergo a particular kind of experience. Try to give your readers a sense of what the experience is like by finding images and other comparisons that will serve to communicate your sense of the experience.

FIFTEEN

Alice Walker

(1944–   )

Born in Georgia in 1944, Alice Walker is the youngest of eight children of black sharecroppers. She attended Spelman College and Sarah Lawrence, from which she graduated with a B.A. During her college years she became deeply involved in the civil rights movement and worked with a variety of social programs, including voter registration, welfare rights, and Head Start. She has also taught at a number of colleges and universities, including Jackson State, Wellesley, Brandeis, and the University of California at Berkeley.

Walker's prose has been highly acclaimed for its passion, its honesty, and its beauty. Walker is perhaps best known for her fiction, which includes two collections of short stories and three novels, the most recent of which, *The Color Purple,* won both the Pulitzer Prize and the American Book Award. Her essays, from which all but one of the selections that follow were taken, are collected in her 1983 volume, *In Search of Our Mothers' Gardens.*

Throughout her works, both fictional and factual, in poetry and prose, Walker ranges over subjects such as family relations, race relations, and the relations between the sexes. Walker explores family relationships, which, in another context she has described as "sacred." For Walker believes that "love, cohesion, and support" are crucial for the survival of any family, but especially for the black American family.

This deep concern for family matters manifests itself in each of the works included in this book. In "The Black Writer and the Southern Experience," Walker launches her argument with a family story about her mother. Later in the essay, she focuses on the "neighborly kindness" and "sustaining love" she believes are essential for the health of both the family and the individual self. Walker's family figures more prominently in "Beauty: When the Other Dancer Is the Self," in which she discusses her concern about growing up "pretty" and physically unblemished. Not lucky enough to remain unblemished, Walker suffered a disfiguring injury to her eye, which also damaged her vision. She learned, however, to live with her changed physical self, and she learned to see things differently, not least of all family things.

"In Search of Our Mothers' Gardens" pays strongest tribute to Walker's own mother and to the mothers of other modern black American women. This important essay invites us to consider how so many poor black women without an opportunity for education and with no formal avenues of self-expression, nonetheless found outlets for their considerable artistic talent. Walker's own mother found her creative outlet in gardening, particularly in planting, nurturing, and growing flowers. Others found it in sewing and handicrafts; still others in music and song. Walker's essay is a powerful testimony to the creative spirit and a moving tribute to her mother. It is also an indictment of a society that allows the creative energies of talented women to languish.

These and other concerns are evident in Walker's short story, "Everyday Use." In this work, however, Walker complicates matters by providing a series of contrasts and counterperspectives on family relationships, family history, and racial heritage. The values upheld in the story strongly connect with those displayed in the essays, especially "In Search of Our Mothers' Gardens."

Walker's writing is consistently polemical: she has a position to argue from and a case to advance. Writing as a black feminist, she reveals the tremendous suffering, frustration, and waste in the lives of the poor black women she considers to be "among America's greatest heroes." Yet, while Walker makes the lives of such women her most frequent subject, she occasionally transcends those lives to explore questions about our common humanity. On such occasions the impact of her writing is felt across boundaries of race, sex, and social class, largely because Walker offers us a vision of survival. One of her reviewers has argued that her work exemplifies the capacity of human beings "to live in spiritual health and beauty" in such a way that "their inner selves can blossom." It is that blossoming of the self that Walker's work so eloquently celebrates.

The Black Writer and the Southern Experience

1 My mother tells of an incident that happened to her in the thirties during the Depression. She and my father lived in a small Georgia town and had half a dozen children. They were sharecroppers, and food, especially flour, was almost impossible to obtain. To get flour, which was distributed by the Red Cross, one had to submit vouchers signed by a local official. On the day my mother was to go into town for flour she received a large box of clothes from one of my aunts who was living in the North. The clothes were in good condition, though well worn, and my mother needed a dress, so she immediately put on one of those from the box and wore it into town. When she reached the distribution center and presented her voucher she was confronted by a white woman who looked her up and down with marked anger and envy.

2 "What'd you come up here for?" the woman asked.

3 "For some flour," said my mother, presenting her voucher.

4 "Humph," said the woman, looking at her more closely and with unconcealed fury. "Anybody dressed up as good as you don't need to come here *begging* for food."

5 "I ain't begging," said my mother; "the government is giving away flour to those that need it, and I need it. I wouldn't be here if I didn't. And these clothes I'm wearing was given to me." But the woman had already turned to the next person in line, saying over her shoulder to the white man who was behind the counter with

her, "The *gall* of niggers coming in here dressed better than me!" This thought seemed to make her angrier still, and my mother, pulling three of her small children behind her and crying from humiliation, walked sadly back into the street.

6 "What did you and Daddy do for flour that winter?" I asked my mother.

7 "Well," she said, "Aunt Mandy Aikens lived down the road from us and she got plenty of flour. We had a good stand of corn so we had plenty of meal. Aunt Mandy would swap me a bucket of flour for a bucket of meal. We got by all right."

8 Then she added thoughtfully, "And that old woman that turned me off so short got down so bad in the end that she was walking on *two* sticks." And I knew she was thinking, though she never said it: Here I am today, my eight children healthy and grown and three of them in college and me with hardly a sick day for years. Ain't Jesus wonderful?

9 In this small story is revealed the condition and strength of a people. Outcasts to be used and humiliated by the larger society, the Southern black sharecropper and poor farmer clung to his own kind and to a religion that had been given to pacify him as a slave but which he soon transformed into an antidote against bitterness. Depending on one another, because they had nothing and no one else, the sharecroppers often managed to come through "all right." And when I listen to my mother tell and retell this story I find that the white woman's vindictiveness is less important than Aunt Mandy's resourceful generosity or my mother's ready stand of corn. For their lives were not about that pitiful example of Southern womanhood, but about themselves.

10 What the black Southern writer inherits as a natural right is a sense of *community*. Something simple but surprisingly hard, especially these days, to come by. My mother, who is a walking history of our community, tells me that when each of her children was born the midwife accepted as payment such home-grown or homemade items as a pig, a quilt, jars of canned fruits and vegetables. But there was never any question that the midwife would come when she was needed, whatever the eventual payment for her services. I consider this each time I hear of a hospital that refuses to admit a woman in labor unless she can hand over a substantial sum of money, cash.

11 Nor am I nostalgic, as a French philosopher once wrote, for lost poverty. I am nostalgic for the solidarity and sharing a modest existence can sometimes bring. We knew, I suppose, that we were poor. Somebody knew; perhaps the landowner who grudgingly paid my father three hundred dollars a year for twelve months' labor. But we never considered ourselves to be poor, unless, of course, we were deliberately humiliated. And because we never believed we were poor, and therefore worthless, we could depend on one another without shame. And always there were the Burial Societies, the Sick-and-Shut-in Societies, that sprang up out of spontaneous need. And no one seemed terribly upset that black sharecroppers were ignored by white insurance companies. It went without saying, in my mother's day, that birth and death required assistance from the community, and that the magnitude of these events was lost on outsiders.

12 As a college student I came to reject the Christianity of my parents, and it took me years to realize that though they had been force-fed a white man's palliative, in the form of religion, they had made it into something at once simple and noble.

True, even today, they can never successfully picture a God who is not white, and that is a major cruelty, but their lives testify to a greater comprehension of the teachings of Jesus than the lives of people who sincerely believe a God *must* have a color and that there can be such a phenomenon as a "white" church.

13 The richness of the black writer's experience in the South can be remarkable, though some people might not think so. Once, while in college, I told a white middle-aged Northerner that I hoped to be a poet. In the nicest possible language, which still made me as mad as I've ever been, he suggested that a "farmer's daughter" might not be the stuff of which poets are made. On one level, of course, he had a point. A shack with only a dozen or so books is an unlikely place to discover a young Keats. But it is narrow thinking, indeed, to believe that a Keats is the only kind of poet one would want to grow up to be. One wants to write poetry that is understood by one's people, not by the Queen of England. Of course, should she be able to profit by it too, so much the better, but since that is not likely, catering to her tastes would be a waste of time.

14 For the black Southern writer, coming straight out of the country, as Wright did—Natchez and Jackson are still not as citified as they like to think they are—there is the world of comparisons; between town and country, between the ugly crowding and griminess of the cities and the spacious cleanliness (which actually seems impossible to dirty) of the country. A country person finds the city confining, like a too tight dress. And always, in one's memory, there remain all the rituals of one's growing up: the warmth and vividness of Sunday worship (never mind that you never quite believed) in a little church hidden from the road, and houses set so far back into the woods that at night it is impossible for strangers to find them. The daily dramas that evolve in such a private world are pure gold. But this view of a strictly private and hidden existence, with its triumphs, failures, grotesqueries, is not nearly as valuable to the socially conscious black Southern writer as his double vision is. For not only is he in a position to see his own world, and its close community ("Homecomings" on First Sundays, barbecues to raise money to send to Africa—one of the smaller ironies—the simplicity and eerie calm of a black funeral, where the beloved one is buried way in the middle of a wood with nothing to mark the spot but perhaps a wooden cross already coming apart), but also he is capable of knowing, with remarkably silent accuracy, the people who make up the larger world that surrounds and suppresses his own.

15 It is a credit to a writer like Ernest J. Gaines, a black writer who writes mainly about the people he grew up with in rural Louisiana, that he can write about whites and blacks exactly as he sees them and *knows* them, instead of writing of one group as a vast malignant lump and of the other as a conglomerate of perfect virtues.

16 In large measure, black Southern writers owe their clarity of vision to parents who refused to diminish themselves as human beings by succumbing to racism. Our parents seemed to know that an extreme negative emotion held against other human beings for reasons they do not control can be blinding. Blindness about other human beings, especially for a writer, is equivalent to death. Because of this blindness, which is, above all, racial, the works of many Southern writers have died. Much that we read today is fast expiring.

17 My own slight attachment to William Faulkner was rudely broken by realiz-

ing, after reading statements he made in *Faulkner in the University,* that he believed whites superior morally to blacks; that whites had a duty (which at their convenience they would assume) to "bring blacks along" politically, since blacks, in Faulkner's opinion, were "not ready" yet to function properly in a democratic society. He also thought that a black man's intelligence is directly related to the amount of white blood he has.

18 For the black person coming of age in the sixties, where Martin Luther King stands against the murderers of Goodman, Chaney, and Schwerner, there appears no basis for such assumptions. Nor was there any in Garvey's day, or in Du Bois's or in Douglass's or in Nat Turner's. Nor at any other period in our history, from the very founding of the country; for it was hardly incumbent upon slaves to be slaves and saints too. Unlike Tolstoy, Faulkner was not prepared to struggle to change the structure of the society he was born in. One might concede that in his fiction he did seek to examine the reasons for its decay, but unfortunately, as I have learned while trying to teach Faulkner to black students, it is not possible, from so short a range, to separate the man from his works.

19 One reads Faulkner knowing that his "colored" people had to come through "Mr. William's" back door, and one feels uneasy, and finally enraged that Faulkner did not burn the whole house down. When the provincial mind starts out *and continues* on a narrow and unprotesting course, "genius" itself must run on a track.

20 Flannery O'Connor at least had the conviction that "reality" is at best superficial and that the puzzle of humanity is less easy to solve than that of race. But Miss O'Connor was not so much of Georgia, as in it. The majority of Southern writers have been too confined by prevailing social customs to probe deeply into mysteries that the Citizens Councils insist must never be revealed.

21 Perhaps my Northern brothers will not believe me when I say there is a great deal of positive material I can draw from my "underprivileged" background. But they have never lived, as I have, at the end of a long road in a house that was faced by the edge of the world on one side and nobody for miles on the other. They have never experienced the magnificent quiet of a summer day when the heat is intense and one is so very thirsty, as one moves across the dusty cotton fields, that one learns forever that water is the essence of all life. In the cities it cannot be so clear to one that he is a creature of the earth, feeling the soil between the toes, smelling the dust thrown up by the rain, loving the earth so much that one longs to taste it and sometimes does.

22 Nor do I intend to romanticize the Southern black country life. I can recall that I hated it, generally. The hard work in the fields, the shabby houses, the evil greedy men who worked my father to death and almost broke the courage of that strong woman, my mother. No, I am simply saying that Southern black writers, like most writers, have a heritage of love and hate, but that they also have enormous richness and beauty to draw from. And, having been placed, as Camus says, "halfway between misery and the sun," they, too, know that "though all is not well under the sun, history is not everything."

23 No one could wish for a more advantageous heritage than that bequeathed to the black writer in the South: a compassion for the earth, a trust in humanity beyond our knowledge of evil, and an abiding love of justice. We inherit a great responsi-

bility as well, for we must give voice to centuries not only of silent bitterness and hate but also of neighborly kindness and sustaining love.

(1970)

QUESTIONS

Thought and Structure

1. What is Walker's main point and where does she make it most forcefully?
2. Is Walker's argument applicable beyond her twin subjects of blackness and southern experience? Is what she says relevant to white writers? To writers born and raised in other regions of the country?
3. What point does Walker make about racism in paragraphs 16–19?
4. How and where does Walker handle possible objections to her ideas about her southern racial heritage?
5. Why does Walker begin the essay with an anecdote? How is it related to what follows?
6. Divide the essay into three or four parts. Provide a heading for each. Explain the relationship among the sections you designate.

Style and Strategy

7. Notice how Walker employs repetition in the sentences of paragraphs 10 and 11. Listen for how she achieves emphasis, coherence, and continuity by repeating words and phrases, especially "community," "payment," "nostalgic," and "poor."
8. What does Walker gain or lose by including the last word of paragraph 10: "cash"? Should it be cut? Why or why not?
9. Explain why Walker has placed quotation marks around the following: "all right" (9), "white" (12), "farmer's daughter" (13), "bring blacks along" (17), "not ready" (17), "colored" (19), "genius" (19), and "underprivileged" (21).
10. Explain why Walker has italicized the following words: *begging* (4), *gall* (5), *community* (10), *knows* (15), *and continues* (19).
11. Walker's diction offers a combination of formal and informal language. "As mad as I've ever been" (13) and "a waste of time" (13) sit alongside "advantageous" and "bequeathed" (23). Find other examples and comment on their effects.
12. Identify and explain the point and effect of four of Walker's comparisons. Here are two to get you started:

    "My mother, who is a walking history of our community . . ." (10)
    "an antidote against bitterness . . ." (9)

SUGGESTIONS FOR WRITING

A. Discuss the idea that a writer's background—his or her social status, economic circumstances, childhood environment—provide a rich storehouse of material for writing.

B. Write imitations of the sentences referred to in question 7.

C. Compare Walker's discussion of racism in this essay with Baldwin's in either "Fifth Avenue Uptown" or "Notes of a Native Son."

Beauty: When the Other Dancer Is the Self

1 It is a bright summer day in 1947. My father, a fat, funny man with beautiful eyes and a subversive wit, is trying to decide which of his eight children he will take with him to the county fair. My mother, of course, will not go. She is knocked out from getting most of us ready: I hold my neck stiff against the pressure of her knuckles as she hastily completes the braiding and then beribboning of my hair.

2 My father is the driver for the rich old white lady up the road. Her name is Miss Mey. She owns all the land for miles around, as well as the house in which we live. All I remember about her is that she once offered to pay my mother thirty-five cents for cleaning her house, raking up piles of her magnolia leaves, and washing her family's clothes, and that my mother—she of no money, eight children, and a chronic earache—refused it. But I do not think of this in 1947. I am two and a half years old. I want to go everywhere my daddy goes. I am excited at the prospect of riding in a car. Someone has told me fairs are fun. That there is room in the car for only three of us doesn't faze me at all. Whirling happily in my starchy frock, showing off my biscuit-polished patent-leather shoes and lavender socks, tossing my head in a way that makes my ribbons bounce, I stand, hands on hips, before my father. "Take me, Daddy," I say with assurance; "I'm the prettiest!"

3 Later, it does not surprise me to find myself in Miss Mey's shiny black car, sharing the back seat with the other lucky ones. Does not surprise me that I thoroughly enjoy the fair. At home that night I tell the unlucky ones all I can remember about the merry-go-round, the man who eats live chickens, and the teddy bears, until they say: that's enough, baby Alice. Shut up now, and go to sleep.

4 It is Easter Sunday, 1950. I am dressed in a green, flocked, scalloped-hem dress (handmade by my adoring sister, Ruth) that has its own smooth satin petticoat and tiny hot-pink roses tucked into each scallop. My shoes, new T-strap patent leather, again highly biscuit-polished. I am six years old and have learned one of the longest Easter speeches to be heard that day, totally unlike the speech I said when I was two: "Easter lilies / pure and white / blossom in / the morning light." When I rise to give my speech I do so on a great wave of love and pride and expectation. People in the church stop rustling their new crinolines. They seem to hold their breath. I can tell they admire my dress, but it is my spirit, bordering on sassiness (womanishness), they secretly applaud.

5 "That girl's a little *mess,*" they whisper to each other, pleased.

6 Naturally I say my speech without stammer or pause, unlike those who stutter, stammer, or, worst of all, forget. This is before the word "beautiful" exists in people's

vocabulary, but "Oh, isn't she the *cutest* thing!" frequently floats my way. "And got so much sense!" they gratefully add . . . for which thoughtful addition I thank them to this day.

7 *It was great fun being cute. But then, one day, it ended.*

8 I am eight years old and a tomboy. I have a cowboy hat, cowboy boots, checkered shirt and pants, all red. My playmates are my brothers, two and four years older than I. Their colors are black and green, the only difference in the way we are dressed. On Saturday nights we all go to the picture show, even my mother; Westerns are her favorite kind of movie. Back home, "on the ranch," we pretend we are Tom Mix, Hopalong Cassidy, Lash LaRue (we've even named one of our dogs Lash LaRue); we chase each other for hours rustling cattle, being outlaws, delivering damsels from distress. Then my parents decide to buy my brothers guns. These are not "real" guns. They shoot "BBs," copper pellets my brothers say will kill birds. Because I am a girl, I do not get a gun. Instantly I am relegated to the position of Indian. Now there appears a great distance between us. They shoot and shoot at everything with their new guns. I try to keep up with my bow and arrows.

9 One day while I am standing on top of our makeshift "garage"—pieces of tin nailed across some poles—holding my bow and arrow and looking out towards the fields, I feel an incredible blow in my right eye. I look down just in time to see my brother lower his gun.

10 Both brothers rush to my side. My eye stings, and I cover it with my hand. "If you tell," they say, "we will get a whipping. You don't want that to happen, do you?" I do not. "Here is a piece of wire," says the older brother, picking it up from the roof; "say you stepped on one end of it and the other flew up and hit you." The pain is beginning to start. "Yes," I say. "Yes, I will say that is what happened." If I do not say this is what happened, I know my brothers will find ways to make me wish I had. But now I will say anything that gets me to my mother.

11 Confronted by our parents we stick to the lie agreed upon. They place me on a bench on the porch and I close my left eye while they examine the right. There is a tree growing from underneath the porch that climbs past the railing to the roof. It is the last thing my right eye sees. I watch as its trunk, its branches, and then its leaves are blotted out by the rising blood.

12 I am in shock. First there is intense fever, which my father tries to break using lily leaves bound around my head. Then there are chills: my mother tries to get me to eat soup. Eventually, I do not know how, my parents learn what has happened. A week after the "accident" they take me to see a doctor. "Why did you wait so long to come?" he asks, looking into my eye and shaking his head. "Eyes are sympathetic," he says. "If one is blind, the other will likely become blind too."

13 This comment of the doctor's terrifies me. But it is really how I look that bothers me most. Where the BB pellet struck there is a glob of whitish scar tissue, a hideous cataract, on my eye. Now when I stare at people—a favorite pastime, up to now—they will stare back. Not at the "cute" little girl, but at her scar. For six years I do not stare at anyone, because I do not raise my head.

14 Years later, in the throes of a mid-life crisis, I ask my mother and sister whether I changed after the "accident." "No," they say, puzzled. "What do you mean?"

15 *What do I mean?*

16 I am eight, and, for the first time, doing poorly in school, where I have been something of a whiz since I was four. We have just moved to the place where the "accident" occurred. We do not know any of the people around us because this is a different county. The only time I see the friends I knew is when we go back to our old church. The new school is the former state penitentiary. It is a large stone building, cold and drafty, crammed to overflowing with boisterous, ill-disciplined children. On the third floor there is a huge circular imprint of some partition that has been torn out.

17 "What used to be here?" I ask a sullen girl next to me on our way past it to lunch.

18 "The electric chair," says she.

19 At night I have nightmares about the electric chair, and about all the people reputedly "fried" in it. I am afraid of the school, where all the students seem to be budding criminals.

20 "What's the matter with your eye?" they ask, critically.

21 When I don't answer (I cannot decide whether it was an "accident" or not), they shove me, insist on a fight.

22 My brother, the one who created the story about the wire, comes to my rescue. But then brags so much about "protecting" me, I become sick.

23 After months of torture at the school, my parents decide to send me back to our old community, to my old school. I live with my grandparents and the teacher they board. But there is no room for Phoebe, my cat. By the time my grandparents decide there *is* room, and I ask for my cat, she cannot be found. Miss Yarborough, the boarding teacher, takes me under her wing, and begins to teach me to play the piano. But soon she marries an African—a "prince," she says—and is whisked away to his continent.

24 At my old school there is at least one teacher who loves me. She is the teacher who "knew me before I was born" and bought my first baby clothes. It is she who makes life bearable. It is her presence that finally helps me turn on the one child at the school who continually calls me "one-eyed bitch." One day I simply grab him by his coat and beat him until I am satisfied. It is my teacher who tells me my mother is ill.

25 My mother is lying in bed in the middle of the day, something I have never seen. She is in too much pain to speak. She has an abscess in her ear. I stand looking down on her, knowing that if she dies, I cannot live. She is being treated with warm oils and hot bricks held against her cheek. Finally a doctor comes. But I must go back to my grandparents' house. The weeks pass but I am hardly aware of it. All I know is that my mother might die, my father is not so jolly, my brothers still have their guns, and I am the one sent away from home.

26 "You did not change," they say.

27 *Did I imagine the anguish of never looking up?*

28 I am twelve. When relatives come to visit I hide in my room. My cousin Brenda, just my age, whose father works in the post office and whose mother is a nurse, comes to find me. "Hello," she says. And then she asks, looking at my recent school picture, which I did not want taken, and on which the "glob," as I think of it, is clearly visible, "You still can't see out of that eye?"

29 "No," I say, and flop back on the bed over my book.

30 That night, as I do almost every night, I abuse my eye. I rant and rave at it, in front of the mirror. I plead with it to clear up before morning. I tell it I hate and despise it. I do not pray for sight. I pray for beauty.

31 "You did not change," they say.

32 I am fourteen and baby-sitting for my brother Bill, who lives in Boston. He is my favorite brother and there is a strong bond between us. Understanding my feelings of shame and ugliness he and his wife take me to a local hospital, where the "glob" is removed by a doctor named O. Henry. There is still a small bluish crater where the scar tissue was, but the ugly white stuff is gone. Almost immediately I become a different person from the girl who does not raise her head. Or so I think. Now that I've raised my head I win the boyfriend of my dreams. Now that I've raised my head I have plenty of friends. Now that I've raised my head classwork comes from my lips as faultlessly as Easter speeches did, and I leave high school as valedictorian, most popular student, and *queen,* hardly believing my luck. Ironically, the girl who was voted most beautiful in our class (and was) was later shot twice through the chest by a male companion, using a "real" gun, while she was pregnant. But that's another story in itself. Or is it?

33 "You did not change," they say.

34 It is now thirty years since the "accident." A beautiful journalist comes to visit and to interview me. She is going to write a cover story for her magazine that focuses on my latest book. "Decide how you want to look on the cover," she says. "Glamorous, or whatever."

35 Never mind "glamorous," it is the "whatever" that I hear. Suddenly all I can think of is whether I will get enough sleep the night before the photography session: if I don't, my eye will be tired and wander, as blind eyes will.

36 At night in bed with my lover I think up reasons why I should not appear on the cover of a magazine. "My meanest critics will say I've sold out," I say. "My family will now realize I write scandalous books."

37 "But what's the real reason you don't want to do this?" he asks.

38 "Because in all probability," I say in a rush, "my eye won't be straight."

39 "It will be straight enough," he says. Then, "Besides, I thought you'd made your peace with that."

40 And I suddenly remember that I have.

41 *I remember:*

42 I am talking to my brother Jimmy, asking if he remembers anything unusual about the day I was shot. He does not know I consider that day the last time my father, with his sweet home remedy of cool lily leaves, chose me, and that I suffered and raged inside because of this. "Well," he says, "all I remember is standing by the side of the highway with Daddy, trying to flag down a car. A white man stopped,

but when Daddy said he needed somebody to take his little girl to the doctor, he drove off."

43 *I remember:*

44 I am in the desert for the first time. I fall totally in love with it. I am so overwhelmed by its beauty, I confront for the first time, consciously, the meaning of the doctor's words years ago: "Eyes are sympathetic. If one is blind, the other will likely become blind too." I realize I have dashed about the world madly, looking at this, looking at that, storing up images against the fading of the light. *But I might have missed seeing the desert!* The shock of that possibility—and gratitude for over twenty-five years of sight—sends me literally to my knees. Poem after poem comes—which is perhaps how poets pray.

ON SIGHT

I am so thankful I have seen
The Desert
And the creatures in the desert
And the desert Itself.

The desert has its own moon
Which I have seen
With my own eye.

There is no flag on it.

Trees of the desert have arms
All of which are always up
That is because the moon is up
The sun is up
Also the sky
The stars
Clouds
None with flags.

If there *were* flags, I doubt
the trees would point.
Would you?

45 *But mostly, I remember this:*

46 I am twenty-seven, and my baby daughter is almost three. Since her birth I have worried about her discovery that her mother's eyes are different from other people's. Will she be embarrassed? I think. What will she say? Every day she watches a television program called "Big Blue Marble." It begins with a picture of the earth as it appears from the moon. It is bluish, a little battered-looking, but full of light, with whitish clouds swirling around it. Every time I see it I weep with love, as if it is a picture of Grandma's house. One day when I am putting Rebecca down for her nap, she suddenly focuses on my eye. Something inside me cringes, gets ready to try to protect myself. All children are cruel about physical differences, I know from experience, and that they don't always mean to be is another matter. I assume Rebecca will be the same.

47 But no-o-o-o. She studies my face intently as we stand, her inside and me

outside her crib. She even holds my face maternally between her dimpled little hands. Then, looking every bit as serious and lawyerlike as her father, she says, as if it may just possibly have slipped my attention: "Mommy, there's a *world* in your eye." (As in, "Don't be alarmed, or do anything crazy.") And then, gently, but with great interest: "Mommy, where did you *get* that world in your eye?"

48 For the most part, the pain left then. (So what, if my brothers grew up to buy even more powerful pellet guns for their sons and to carry real guns themselves. So what, if a young "Morehouse man" once nearly fell off the steps of Trevor Arnett Library because he thought my eyes were blue.) Crying and laughing I ran to the bathroom, while Rebecca mumbled and sang herself off to sleep. Yes indeed, I realized, looking into the mirror. There *was* a world in my eye. And I saw that it was possible to love it: that in fact, for all it had taught me of shame and anger and inner vision, I *did* love it. Even to see it drifting out of orbit in boredom, or rolling up out of fatigue, not to mention floating back at attention in excitement (bearing witness, a friend has called it), deeply suitable to my personality, and even characteristic of me.

49 That night I dream I am dancing to Stevie Wonder's song "Always" (the name of the song is really "As," but I hear it as "Always"). As I dance, whirling and joyous, happier than I've ever been in my life, another bright-faced dancer joins me. We dance and kiss each other and hold each other through the night. The other dancer has obviously come through all right, as I have done. She is beautiful, whole and free. And she is also me.

(1983)

QUESTIONS

Thought and Structure

1. In what ways does the young Alice Walker change after the injury to her eye? What effect has the injury had on her as an adult.
2. Discuss whether Walker has overreacted to her injury. Consider how an injury can alter our perception of ourselves or our sense of how others perceive and respond to us.
3. How is the essay organized? How does Walker signal her changes of focus and emphasis? What ties the various sections of the essay together?
4. Cite at least one example of a repeated sentence, and comment on its effects.

Style and Strategy

5. Consider the effect in paragraph 32 of the use of a repeated sentence pattern: "Now that I've . . ." In the same paragraph, comment on the effect of these two short sentences: "Or so I think. . . . Or is it?"
6. Explain the effect of the double dashes in the following sentence:

> But soon she marries an African—a "prince," she says—and is whisked away to his continent. (23)

> The shock of that possibility—and gratitude for over twenty-five years of sight—sends me literally to my knees. (44)

Consider the differences in tone that would result if the dashes were replaced either with parentheses or with commas.

7. Cite three uses of dialogue you think effective and explain what makes them so.
8. At the end of the essay Walker invokes the image of a dancer—another dancer who joins her in a dance. She also makes reference to a world in her eye. What do you think is the point and purpose of each of these images?

SUGGESTIONS FOR WRITING

A. Describe a time when an accident or other turn of events damaged your self-image, made you feel insecure or unhappy with yourself. Explain how you came to terms with your situation and what the consequences for your later life have been—or might be.

B. Compare Walker's discussion of her injury and its effects with Richard Selzer's story "Minor Surgery."

In Search of Our Mothers' Gardens

MOTHEROOT

Creation often
needs two hearts
one to root
and one to flower
One to sustain
in time of drouth
and hold fast
against winds of pain
the fragile bloom
that in the glory
of its hour
affirms a heart
unsung, unseen.

—Marilou Awiakta,
ABIDING APPALACHIA

I described her own nature and temperament. Told how they needed a larger life for their expression. . . . I pointed out that in lieu of proper channels, her emotions had overflowed into paths that dissipated them. I talked, beautifully I thought, about an art that would be born, an art that would open the way for women the likes of her. I asked her to hope, and build up an inner life against the coming of that day. . . . I sang, with a strange quiver in my voice, a promise song.

—*Jean Toomer, "Avey,"*
CANE

The poet speaking to a prostitute who falls asleep while he's talking—

1 When the poet Jean Toomer walked through the South in the early twenties, he discovered a curious thing: black women whose spirituality was so intense, so deep, so *unconscious,* that they were themselves unaware of the richness they held. They stumbled blindly through their lives: creatures so abused and mutilated in body, so dimmed and confused by pain, that they considered themselves unworthy even of hope. In the selfless abstractions their bodies became to the men who used them, they became more than "sexual objects," more even than mere women: they became "Saints." Instead of being perceived as whole persons, their bodies became shrines: what was thought to be their minds became temples suitable for worship. These crazy Saints stared out at the world, wildly, like lunatics—or quietly, like suicides; and the "God" that was in their gaze was as mute as a great stone.

2 Who were these Saints? These crazy, loony, pitiful women?

3 Some of them, without a doubt, were our mothers and grandmothers.

4 In the still heat of the post-Reconstruction South, this is how they seemed to Jean Toomer: exquisite butterflies trapped in an evil honey, toiling away their lives in an era, a century, that did not acknowledge them, except as "the *mule* of the world." They dreamed dreams that no one knew—not even themselves, in any coherent fashion—and saw visions no one could understand. They wandered or sat about the countryside crooning lullabies to ghosts, and drawing the mother of Christ in charcoal on courthouse walls.

5 They forced their minds to desert their bodies and their striving spirits sought to rise, like frail whirlwinds from the hard red clay. And when those frail whirlwinds fell, in scattered particles, upon the ground, no one mourned. Instead, men lit candles to celebrate the emptiness that remained, as people do who enter a beautiful but vacant space to resurrect a God.

6 Our mothers and grandmothers, some of them: moving to music not yet written. And they waited.

7 They waited for a day when the unknown thing that was in them would be made known; but guessed, somehow in their darkness, that on the day of their revelation they would be long dead. Therefore to Toomer they walked, and even ran, in slow motion. For they were going nowhere immediate, and the future was not yet within their grasp. And men took our mothers and grandmothers, "but got no pleasure from it." So complex was their passion and their calm.

8 To Toomer, they lay vacant and fallow as autumn fields, with harvest time never in sight: and he saw them enter loveless marriages, without joy; and become prostitutes, without resistance; and become mothers of children, without fulfillment.

9 For these grandmothers and mothers of ours were not Saints, but Artists; driven to a numb and bleeding madness by the springs of creativity in them for which there was no release. They were Creators, who lived lives of spiritual waste, because they were so rich in spirituality—which is the basis of Art—that the strain of enduring their unused and unwanted talent drove them insane. Throwing away this spirituality was their pathetic attempt to lighten the soul to a weight their work-worn, sexually abused bodies could bear.

10 What did it mean for a black woman to be an artist in our grandmothers' time? In our great-grandmothers' day? It is a question with an answer cruel enough to stop the blood.

11 Did you have a genius of a great-great-grandmother who died under some ignorant and depraved white overseer's lash? Or was she required to bake biscuits for a lazy backwater tramp, when she cried out in her soul to paint watercolors of sunsets, or the rain falling on the green and peaceful pasturelands? Or was her body broken and forced to bear children (who were more often than not sold away from her)—eight, ten, fifteen, twenty children—when her one joy was the thought of modeling heroic figures of rebellion, in stone or clay?

12 How was the creativity of the black woman kept alive, year after year and century after century, when for most of the years black people have been in America, it was a punishable crime for a black person to read or write? And the freedom to paint, to sculpt, to expand the mind with action did not exist. Consider, if you can bear to imagine it, what might have been the result if singing, too, had been forbidden by law. Listen to the voices of Bessie Smith, Billie Holiday, Nina Simone, Roberta Flack, and Aretha Franklin, among others, and imagine those voices muzzled for life. Then you may begin to comprehend the lives of our "crazy," "Sainted" mothers and grandmothers. The agony of the lives of women who might have been Poets, Novelists, Essayists, and Short-Story Writers (over a period of centuries), who died with their real gifts stifled within them.

13 And, if this were the end of the story, we would have cause to cry out in my paraphrase of Okot p'Bitek's great poem:

> O, my clanswomen
> Let us all cry together!
> Come,
> Let us mourn the death of our mother,
> The death of a Queen
> The ash that was produced
> By a great fire!
> O, this homestead is utterly dead
> Close the gates
> With *lacari* thorns,
> For our mother
> The creator of the Stool is lost!
> And all the young women
> Have perished in the wilderness!

14 But this is not the end of the story, for all the young women—our mothers and grandmothers, *ourselves*—have not perished in the wilderness. And if we ask ourselves why, and search for and find the answer, we will know beyond all efforts to erase it from our minds, just exactly who, and of what, we black American women are.

15 One example, perhaps the most pathetic, most misunderstood one, can provide a backdrop for our mothers' work: Phillis Wheatley, a slave in the 1700s.

16 Virginia Woolf, in her book *A Room of One's Own,* wrote that in order for

a woman to write fiction she must have two things, certainly: a room of her own (with key and lock) and enough money to support herself.

17 What then are we to make of Phillis Wheatley, a slave, who owned not even herself? This sickly, frail black girl who required a servant of her own at times—her health was so precarious—and who, had she been white, would have been easily considered the intellectual superior of all the women and most of the men in the society of her day.

18 Virginia Woolf wrote further, speaking of course not of our Phillis, that "any woman born with a great gift in the sixteenth century [insert "eighteenth century," insert "black woman," insert "born or made a slave"] would certainly have gone crazed, shot herself, or ended her days in some lonely cottage outside the village, half witch, half wizard [insert "Saint"], feared and mocked at. For it needs little skill and psychology to be sure that a highly gifted girl who had tried to use her gift for poetry would have been so thwarted and hindered by contrary instincts [add "chains, guns, the lash, the ownership of one's body by someone else, submission to an alien religion"], that she must have lost her health and sanity to a certainty."

19 The key words, as they relate to Phillis, are "contrary instincts." For when we read the poetry of Phillis Wheatley—as when we read the novels of Nella Larsen or the oddly false-sounding autobiography of that freest of all black women writers, Zora Hurston—evidence of "contrary instincts" is everywhere. Her loyalties were completely divided, as was, without question, her mind.

20 But how could this be otherwise? Captured at seven, a slave of wealthy, doting whites who instilled in her the "savagery" of the Africa they "rescued" her from . . . one wonders if she was even able to remember her homeland as she had known it, or as it really was.

21 Yet, because she did try to use her gift for poetry in a world that made her a slave, she was "so thwarted and hindered by . . . contrary instincts, that she . . . lost her health. . . ." In the last years of her brief life, burdened not only with the need to express her gift but also with a penniless, friendless "freedom" and several small children for whom she was forced to do strenuous work to feed, she lost her health, certainly. Suffering from malnutrition and neglect and who knows what mental agonies, Phillis Wheatley died.

22 So torn by "contrary instincts" was black, kidnapped, enslaved Phillis that her description of "the Goddess"—as she poetically called the Liberty she did not have—is ironically, cruelly humorous. And, in fact, has held Phillis up to ridicule for more than a century. It is usually read prior to hanging Phillis's memory as that of a fool. She wrote:

> The Goddess comes, she moves divinely fair,
> Olive and laurel binds her *golden* hair.
> Wherever shines this native of the skies,
> Unnumber'd charms and recent graces rise. [My italics]

23 It is obvious that Phillis, the slave, combed the "Goddess's" hair every morning; prior, perhaps, to bringing in the milk, or fixing her mistress's lunch. She took her imagery from the one thing she saw elevated above all others.

24 With the benefit of hindsight we ask, "How could she?"

25 But at last, Phillis, we understand. No more snickering when your stiff, struggling, ambivalent lines are forced on us. We know now that you were not an idiot or a traitor; only a sickly little black girl, snatched from your home and country and made a slave; a woman who still struggled to sing the song that was your gift, although in a land of barbarians who praised you for your bewildered tongue. It is not so much what you sang, as that you kept alive, in so many of our ancestors, *the notion of song.*

26 Black women are called, in the folklore that so aptly identifies one's status in society, "the *mule* of the world," because we have been handed the burdens that everyone else—*everyone* else—refused to carry. We have also been called "Matriarchs," "Superwomen," and "Mean and Evil Bitches." Not to mention "Castraters" and "Sapphire's Mama." When we have pleaded for understanding, our character has been distorted; when we have asked for simple caring, we have been handed empty inspirational appellations, then stuck in the farthest corner. When we have asked for love, we have been given children. In short, even our plainer gifts, our labors of fidelity and love, have been knocked down our throats. To be an artist and a black woman, even today, lowers our status in many respects, rather than raises it: and yet, artists we will be.

27 Therefore we must fearlessly pull out of ourselves and look at and identify with our lives the living creativity some of our great-grandmothers were not allowed to know. I stress *some* of them because it is well known that the majority of our great-grandmothers knew, even without "knowing" it, the reality of their spirituality, even if they didn't recognize it beyond what happened in the singing at church—and they never had any intention of giving it up.

28 How they did it—those millions of black women who were not Phillis Wheatley, or Lucy Terry or Frances Harper or Zora Hurston or Nella Larsen or Bessie Smith; or Elizabeth Catlett, or Katherine Dunham, either—brings me to the title of this essay, "In Search of Our Mothers' Gardens," which is a personal account that is yet shared, in its theme and its meaning, by all of us. I found, while thinking about the far-reaching world of the creative black woman, that often the truest answer to a question that really matters can be found very close.

29 In the late 1920s my mother ran away from home to marry my father. Marriage, if not running away, was expected of seventeen-year-old girls. By the time she was twenty, she had two children and was pregnant with a third. Five children later, I was born. And this is how I came to know my mother: she seemed a large, soft, loving-eyed woman who was rarely impatient in our home. Her quick, violent temper was on view only a few times a year, when she battled with the white landlord who had the misfortune to suggest to her that her children did not need to go to school.

30 She made all the clothes we wore, even my brothers' overalls. She made all the towels and sheets we used. She spent the summers canning vegetables and fruits. She spent the winter evenings making quilts enough to cover all our beds.

31 During the "working" day, she labored beside—not behind—my father in the fields. Her day began before sunup, and did not end until late at night. There was never a moment for her to sit down, undisturbed, to unravel her own private thoughts; never a time free from interruption—by work or the noisy inquiries of her many children. And yet, it is to my mother—and all our mothers who were not famous—that I went in search of the secret of what has fed that muzzled and often mutilated, but vibrant, creative spirit that the black woman has inherited, and that pops out in wild and unlikely places to this day.

32 But when, you will ask, did my overworked mother have time to know or care about feeding the creative spirit?

33 The answer is so simple that many of us have spent years discovering it. We have constantly looked high, when we should have looked high—and low.

34 For example: in the Smithsonian Institution in Washington, D.C., there hangs a quilt unlike any other in the world. In fanciful, inspired, and yet simple and identifiable figures, it portrays the story of the Crucifixion. It is considered rare, beyond price. Though it follows no known pattern of quilt-making, and though it is made of bits and pieces of worthless rags, it is obviously the work of a person of powerful imagination and deep spiritual feeling. Below this quilt I saw a note that says it was made by "an anonymous Black woman in Alabama, a hundred years ago."

35 If we could locate this "anonymous" black woman from Alabama, she would turn out to be one of our grandmothers—an artist who left her mark in the only materials she could afford, and in the only medium her position in society allowed her to use.

36 As Virginia Woolf wrote further, in *A Room of One's Own:*

> Yet genius of a sort must have existed among women as it must have existed among the working class. [Change this to "slaves" and "the wives and daughters of sharecroppers."] Now and again an Emily Brontë or a Robert Burns [change this to "a Zora Hurston or a Richard Wright"] blazes out and proves its presence. But certainly it never got itself on to paper. When, however, one reads of a witch being ducked, of a woman possessed by devils [or "Sainthood"], of a wise woman selling herbs [our root workers], or even a very remarkable man who had a mother, then I think we are on the track of a lost novelist, a suppressed poet, of some mute and inglorious Jane Austen. . . . Indeed, I would venture to guess that Anon, who wrote so many poems without signing them, was often a woman. . . .

37 And so our mothers and grandmothers have, more often than not anonymously, handed on the creative spark, the seed of the flower they themselves never hoped to see: or like a sealed letter they could not plainly read.

38 And so it is, certainly, with my own mother. Unlike "Ma" Rainey's songs, which retained their creator's name even while blasting forth from Bessie Smith's mouth, no song or poem will bear my mother's name. Yet so many of the stories that I write, that we all write, are my mother's stories. Only recently did I fully realize this: that through years of listening to my mother's stories of her life, I have absorbed not only the stories themselves, but something of the manner in which she spoke, something of the urgency that involves the knowledge that her stories—like

her life—must be recorded. It is probably for this reason that so much of what I have written is about characters whose counterparts in real life are so much older than I am.

39 But the telling of these stories, which came from my mother's lips as naturally as breathing, was not the only way my mother showed herself as an artist. For stories, too, were subject to being distracted, to dying without conclusion. Dinners must be started, and cotton must be gathered before the big rains. The artist that was and *is* my mother showed itself to me only after many years. This is what I finally noticed:

40 Like Mem, a character in *The Third Life of Grange Copeland,* my mother adorned with flowers whatever shabby house we were forced to live in. And not just your typical straggly country stand of zinnias, either. She planted ambitious gardens—and still does—with over fifty different varieties of plants that bloom profusely from early March until late November. Before she left home for the fields, she watered her flowers, chopped up the grass, and laid out new beds. When she returned from the fields she might divide clumps of bulbs, dig a cold pit, uproot and replant roses, or prune branches from her taller bushes or trees—until night came and it was too dark to see.

41 Whatever she planted grew as if by magic, and her fame as a grower of flowers spread over three counties. Because of her creativity with her flowers, even my memories of poverty are seen through a screen of blooms—sunflowers, petunias, roses, dahlias, forsythia, spirea, delphiniums, verbena . . . and on and on.

42 And I remember people coming to my mother's yard to be given cuttings from her flowers; I hear again the praise showered on her because whatever rocky soil she landed on, she turned into a garden. A garden so brilliant with colors, so original in its design, so magnificent with life and creativity, that to this day people drive by our house in Georgia—perfect strangers and imperfect strangers—and ask to stand or walk among my mother's art.

43 I notice that it is only when my mother is working in her flowers that she is radiant, almost to the point of being invisible—except as Creator: hand and eye. She is involved in work her soul must have. Ordering the universe in the image of her personal conception of Beauty.

44 Her face, as she prepares the Art that is her gift, is a legacy of respect she leaves to me, for all that illuminates and cherishes life. She has handed down respect for the possibilities—and the will to grasp them.

45 For her, so hindered and intruded upon in so many ways, being an artist has still been a daily part of her life. This ability to hold on, even in very simple ways, is work black women have done for a very long time.

46 This poem is not enough, but it is something, for the woman who literally covered the holes in our walls with sunflowers:

They were women then
My mama's generation
Husky of voice—Stout of
Step
With fists as well as

Hands
How they battered down
Doors
And ironed
Starched white
Shirts
How they led
Armies
Headragged Generals
Across mined
Fields
Booby-trapped
Kitchens
To discover books
Desks
A place for us
How they knew what we
Must know
Without knowing a page
Of it
Themselves.

47 Guided by my heritage of a love of beauty and a respect for strength—in search of my mother's garden, I found my own.

48 And perhaps in Africa over two hundred years ago, there was just such a mother; perhaps she painted vivid and daring decorations in oranges and yellows and greens on the walls of her hut; perhaps she sang—in a voice like Roberta Flack's—*sweetly* over the compounds of her village; perhaps she wove the most stunning mats or told the most ingenious stories of all the village storytellers. Perhaps she was herself a poet—though only her daughter's name is signed to the poems that we know.

49 Perhaps Phillis Wheatley's mother was also an artist.

50 Perhaps in more than Phillis Wheatley's biological life is her mother's signature made clear.

(1974)

QUESTIONS

Thought and Structure

1. What does Walker propose as an answer to the question she asks in paragraph 10: "What did it mean for a black woman to be an artist in our grandmothers' time?" How about the question she asks in paragraph 12: "How was the creativity of the black woman kept alive . . . century after century?"
2. Explain the relationships Walker postulates between sainthood, madness, and artistic creation.

3. Define in your own words the main point and purpose of this piece.
4. If the introductory portion of this essay comprises paragraphs 1–13, what constitutes its body and its conclusion?
5. What function do the paragraphs about Phyllis Wheatley serve: What would be lost if they were to be omitted? Would anything be gained?

Style and Strategy

6. Single out for analysis and study two sentences that strike you as arresting or beautiful. Account for their power.
7. What are the function and effect of the interrogative sentences in paragraphs 10, 11, 12, and 17?
8. What is the point of the description of southern black women as saints?
9. What are the force and effect of the comparisons Walker alludes to in paragraph 26?
10. Explain the function and effect of the garden and flower images in paragraphs 40–44.

SUGGESTIONS FOR WRITING

A. Write an essay recording your debt to someone or something in your past. Explain how the person or event has helped you become who and what you are. If a tribute seems in order, pay tribute—as Walker does.

B. Write an essay analyzing Walker's piece. Consider its main ideas; its structure, purpose, and tone; its language and imagery.

Everyday Use

For your grandmama

1 I will wait for her in the yard that Maggie and I made so clean and wavy yesterday afternoon. A yard like this is more comfortable than most people know. It is not just a yard. It is like an extended living room. When the hard clay is swept clean as a floor and the fine sand around the edges lined with tiny, irregular grooves anyone can come and sit and look up into the elm tree and wait for the breezes that never come inside the house.

2 Maggie will be nervous until after her sister goes: she will stand hopelessly in corners homely and ashamed of the burn scars down her arms and legs, eyeing her sister with a mixture of envy and awe. She thinks her sister has held life always in the palm of one hand, that "no" is a word the world never learned to say to her.

3 You've no doubt seen those TV shows where the child who has "made it" is confronted, as a surprise, by her own mother and father, tottering in weakly from backstage. (A pleasant surprise, of course: What would they do if parent and child came on the show only to curse out and insult each other?) On TV mother and child embrace and smile into each other's faces. Sometimes the mother and father weep,

the child wraps them in her arms and leans across the table to tell how she would not have made it without their help. I have seen these programs.

4 Sometimes I dream a dream in which Dee and I are suddenly brought together on a TV program of this sort. Out of a dark and soft-seated limousine I am ushered into a bright room filled with many people. There I meet a smiling, gray, sporty man like Johnny Carson who shakes my hand and tells me what a fine girl I have. Then we are on the stage and Dee is embracing me with tears in her eyes. She pins on my dress a large orchid, even though she has told me once that she thinks orchids are tacky flowers.

5 In real life I am a large, big-boned woman with rough, man-working hands. In the winter I wear flannel nightgowns to bed and overalls during the day. I can kill and clean a hog as mercilessly as a man. My fat keeps me hot in zero weather. I can work outside all day, breaking ice to get water for washing. I can eat pork liver cooked over the open fire minutes after it comes steaming from the hog. One winter I knocked a bull calf straight in the brain between the eyes with a sledge hammer and had the meat hung up to chill before nightfall. But of course all this does not show on television. I am the way my daughter would want me to be: a hundred pounds lighter, my skin like an uncooked barley pancake. My hair glistens in the hot bright lights. Johnny Carson has much to do to keep up with my quick and witty tongue.

6 But that is a mistake. I know even before I wake up. Who ever knew a Johnson with a quick tongue? Who can even imagine me looking a strange white man in the eye? It seems to me I have talked to them always with one foot raised in flight, with my head turned in whichever way is farthest from them. Dee, though. She would always look anyone in the eye. Hesitation was no part of her nature.

7 "How do I look, Mama?" Maggie says, showing just enough of her thin body enveloped in pink skirt and red blouse for me to know she's there, almost hidden by the door.

8 "Come out into the yard," I say.

9 Have you ever seen a lame animal, perhaps a dog run over by some careless person rich enough to own a car, sidle up to someone who is ignorant enough to be kind to him? That is the way my Maggie walks. She has been like this, chin on chest, eyes on ground, feet in shuffle, ever since the fire that burned the other house to the ground.

10 Dee is lighter than Maggie, with nicer hair and a fuller figure. She's a woman now, though sometimes I forget. How long ago was it that the other house burned? Ten, twelve years? Sometimes I can still hear the flames and feel Maggie's arms sticking to me, her hair smoking and her dress falling off her in little black papery flakes. Her eyes seemed stretched open, blazed open by the flames reflected in them. And Dee. I see her standing off under the sweet gum tree she used to dig gum out of; a look of concentration on her face as she watched the last dingy gray board of the house fall in toward the red-hot brick chimney. Why don't you do a dance around the ashes? I'd wanted to ask her. She had hated the house that much.

11 I used to think she hated Maggie, too. But that was before we raised the money, the church and me, to send her to Augusta to school. She used to read to us without pity; forcing words, lies, other folks' habits, whole lives upon us two,

sitting trapped and ignorant underneath her voice. She washed us in a river of make-believe, burned us with a lot of knowledge we didn't necessarily need to know. Pressed us to her with the serious way she read, to shove us away at just the moment, like dimwits, we seemed about to understand.

12 Dee wanted nice things. A yellow organdy dress to wear to her graduation from high school; black pumps to match a green suit she'd made from an old suit somebody gave me. She was determined to stare down any disaster in her efforts. Her eyelids would not flicker for minutes at a time. Often I fought off the temptation to shake her. At sixteen she had a style of her own: and knew what style was.

13 I never had an education myself. After second grade the school was closed down. Don't ask me why: in 1927 coloreds asked fewer questions than they do now. Sometimes Maggie reads to me. She stumbles along good-naturedly but can't see well. She knows she is not bright. Like good looks and money, quickness passed her by. She will marry John Thomas (who has mossy teeth in an earnest face) and then I'll be free to sit here and I guess just sing church songs to myself. Although I never was a good singer. Never could carry a tune. I was always better at a man's job. I used to love to milk till I was hoofed in the side in '49. Cows are soothing and slow and don't bother you, unless you try to milk them the wrong way.

14 I have deliberately turned my back on the house. It is three rooms, just like the one that burned, except the roof is tin; they don't make shingle roofs any more. There are no real windows, just some holes cut in the sides, like the portholes in a ship, but not round and not square, with rawhide holding the shutters up on the outside. This house is in a pasture, too, like the other one. No doubt when Dee sees it she will want to tear it down. She wrote me once that no matter where we "choose" to live, she will manage to come see us. But she will never bring her friends. Maggie and I thought about this and Maggie asked me, "Mama, when did Dee ever *have* any friends?"

15 She had a few. Furtive boys in pink shirts hanging about on washday after school. Nervous girls who never laughed. Impressed with her they worshiped the well-turned phrase, the cute shape, the scalding humor that erupted like bubbles in lye. She read to them.

16 When she was courting Jimmy T she didn't have much time to pay to us, but turned all her faultfinding power on him. He *flew* to marry a cheap gal from a family of ignorant flashy people. She hardly had time to recompose herself.

17 When she comes I will meet—but there they are!

18 Maggie attempts to make a dash for the house, in her shuffling way, but I stay her with my hand. "Come back here," I say. And she stops and tries to dig a well in the sand with her toe.

19 It is hard to see them clearly through the strong sun. But even the first glimpse of leg out of the car tells me it is Dee. Her feet were always neat-looking, as if God himself had shaped them with a certain style. From the other side of the car comes a short, stocky man. Hair is all over his head a foot long and hanging from his chin like a kinky mule tail. I hear Maggie suck in her breath. "Uhnnnh," is what it sounds

like. Like when you see the wriggling end of a snake just in front of your foot on the road. "Uhnnnh."

20 Dee next. A dress down to the ground, in this hot weather. A dress so loud it hurts my eyes. There are yellows and oranges enough to throw back the light of the sun. I feel my whole face warming from the heat waves it throws out. Earrings, too, gold and hanging down to her shoulders. Bracelets dangling and making noises when she moves her arm up to shake the folds of the dress out of her armpits. The dress is loose and flows, and as she walks closer, I like it. I hear Maggie go "Uhnnnh" again. It is her sister's hair. It stands straight up like the wool on a sheep. It is black as night and around the edges are two long pigtails that rope about like small lizards disappearing behind her ears.

21 "Wa-su-zo-Tean-o!" she says, coming on in that gliding way the dress makes her move. The short stocky fellow with the hair to his navel is all grinning and he follows up with "Asalamalakim, my mother and sister!" He moves to hug Maggie but she falls back, right up against the back of my chair. I feel her trembling there and when I look up I see the perspiration falling off her chin.

22 "Don't get up," says Dee. Since I am stout it takes something of a push. You can see me trying to move a second or two before I make it. She turns, showing white heels through her sandals, and goes back to the car. Out she peeks next with a Polaroid. She stoops down quickly and lines up picture after picture of me sitting there in front of the house with Maggie cowering behind me. She never takes a shot without making sure the house is included. When a cow comes nibbling around the edge of the yard she snaps it and me and Maggie *and* the house. Then she puts the Polaroid in the back seat of the car, and comes up and kisses me on the forehead.

23 Meanwhile Asalamalakim is going through the motions with Maggie's hand. Maggie's hand is as limp as a fish, and probably as cold, despite the sweat, and she keeps trying to pull it back. It looks like Asalamalakim wants to shake hands but wants to do it fancy. Or maybe he don't know how people shake hands. Anyhow, he soon gives up on Maggie.

24 "Well," I say. "Dee."

25 "No, Mama," she says. "Not 'Dee,' Wangero Leewanika Kemanjo!"

26 "What happened to 'Dee'?" I wanted to know.

27 "She's dead," Wangero said. "I couldn't bear it any longer being named after the people who oppress me."

28 "You know as well as me you was named after your aunt Dicie," I said. Dicie is my sister. She named Dee. We called her "Big Dee" after Dee was born.

29 "But who was *she* named after?" asked Wangero.

30 "I guess after Grandma Dee," I said.

31 "And who was she named after?" asked Wangero.

32 "Her mother," I said, and saw Wangero was getting tired. "That's about as far back as I can trace it," I said. Though, in fact, I probably could have carried it back beyond the Civil War through the branches.

33 "Well," said Asalamalakim, "there you are."

34 "Uhnnnh," I heard Maggie say.

35 "There I was not," I said, "before 'Dicie' cropped up in our family, so why should I try to trace it that far back?"

36 He just stood there grinning, looking down on me like somebody inspecting a Model A car. Every once in a while he and Wangero sent eye signals over my head.

37 "How do you pronounce this name?" I asked.

38 "You don't have to call me by it if you don't want to," said Wangero.

39 "Why shouldn't I?" I asked. "If that's what you want us to call you, we'll call you."

40 "I know it might sound awkward at first," said Wangero.

41 "I'll get used to it," I said. "Ream it out again."

42 Well, soon we got the name out of the way. Asalamalakim had a name twice as long and three times as hard. After I tripped over it two or three times he told me to just call him Hakim-a-barber. I wanted to ask him was he a barber, but I didn't really think he was, so I didn't ask.

43 "You must belong to those beef-cattle peoples down the road," I said. They said "Asalamalakim" when they met you, too, but they didn't shake hands. Always too busy: feeding the cattle, fixing the fences, putting up salt-lick shelters, throwing down hay. When the white folks poisoned some of the herd the men stayed up all night with rifles in their hands. I walked a mile and a half just to see the sight.

44 Hakim-a-barber said, "I accept some of their doctrines, but farming and raising cattle is not my style." (They didn't tell me, and I didn't ask, whether Wangero [Dee] had really gone and married him.)

45 We sat down to eat and right away he said he didn't eat collards and pork was unclean. Wangero, though, went on through the chitlins and corn bread, the greens and everything else. She talked a blue streak over the sweet potatoes. Everything delighted her. Even the fact that we still used the benches her daddy made for the table when we couldn't afford to buy chairs.

46 "Oh, Mama!" she cried. Then turned to Hakim-a-barber. "I never knew how lovely these benches are. You can feel the rump prints," she said, running her hands underneath her and along the bench. Then she gave a sigh and her hand closed over Grandma Dee's butter dish. "That's it!" she said. "I knew there was something I wanted to ask you if I could have." She jumped up from the table and went over in the corner where the churn stood, the milk in it clabber by now. She looked at the churn and looked at it.

47 "This churn top is what I need," she said. "Didn't Uncle Buddy whittle it out of a tree you all used to have?"

48 "Yes," I said.

49 "Uh huh," she said happily. "And I want the dasher, too."

50 "Uncle Buddy whittle that, too?" asked the barber.

51 Dee (Wangero) looked up at me.

52 "Aunt Dee's first husband whittled the dash," said Maggie so low you almost couldn't hear her. "His name was Henry, but they called him Stash."

53 "Maggie's brain is like an elephant's," Wangero said, laughing. "I can use the churn top as a centerpiece for the alcove table," she said, sliding a plate over the churn, "and I'll think of something artistic to do with the dasher."

54 When she finished wrapping the dasher the handle stuck out. I took it for a moment in my hands. You didn't even have to look close to see where hands pushing the dasher up and down to make butter had left a kind of sink in the wood. In fact,

there were a lot of small sinks; you could see where thumbs and fingers had sunk into the wood. It was beautiful light yellow wood, from a tree that grew in the yard where Big Dee and Stash had lived.

55 After dinner Dee (Wangero) went to the trunk at the foot of my bed and started rifling through it. Maggie hung back in the kitchen over the dishpan. Out came Wangero with two quilts. They had been pieced by Grandma Dee and then Big Dee and me had hung them on the quilt frames on the front porch and quilted them. One was in the Lone Star pattern. The other was Walk Around the Mountain. In both of them were scraps of dresses Grandma Dee had worn fifty and more years ago. Bits and pieces of Grandpa Jarrell's paisley shirts. And one teeny faded blue piece, about the piece of a penny matchbox, that was from Great Grandpa Ezra's uniform that he wore in the Civil War.

56 "Mama," Wangero said sweet as a bird. "Can I have these old quilts?"

57 I heard something fall in the kitchen, and a minute later the kitchen door slammed.

58 "Why don't you take one or two of the others?" I asked. "These old things was just done by me and Big Dee from some tops your grandma pieced before she died."

59 "No," said Wangero. "I don't want those. They are stitched around the borders by machine."

60 "That's make them last better," I said.

61 "That's not the point," said Wangero. "These are all pieces of dresses Grandma used to wear. She did all this stitching by hand. Imagine!" She held the quilts securely in her arms, stroking them.

62 "Some of the pieces, like those lavender ones, come from old clothes her mother handed down to her," I said, moving up to touch the quilts. Dee (Wangero) moved back just enough so that I couldn't reach the quilts. They already belonged to her.

63 "Imagine!" she breathed again, clutching them closely to her bosom.

64 "The truth is," I said, "I promised to give them quilts to Maggie, for when she marries John Thomas."

65 She gasped like a bee had stung her.

66 "Maggie can't appreciate these quilts!" she said. "She'd probably be backward enough to put them to everyday use."

67 "I reckon she would," I said. "God knows I been saving 'em for long enough with nobody using 'em. I hope she will!" I didn't want to bring up how I had offered Dee (Wangero) a quilt when she went away to college. Then she had told me they were old-fashioned, out of style.

68 "But they're *priceless!*" she was saying now, furiously; for she has a temper. "Maggie would put them on the bed and in five years they'd be in rags. Less than that!"

69 "She can always make some more," I said. "Maggie knows how to quilt."

70 Dee (Wangero) looked at me with hatred. "You just will not understand. The point is these quilts, *these* quilts!"

71 "Well," I said, stumped. "What would *you* do with them?"

72 "Hang them," she said. As if that was the only thing you *could* do with quilts.

73 Maggie by now was standing in the door. I could almost hear the sound her feet made as they scraped over each other.

74 "She can have them, Mama," she said, like somebody used to never winning anything, or having anything reserved for her. "I can 'member Grandma Dee without the quilts."

75 I looked at her hard. She had filled her bottom lip with checkerberry snuff and it gave her face a kind of dopey, hangdog look. It was Grandma Dee and Big Dee who taught her how to quilt herself. She stood there with her scarred hands hidden in the folds of her skirt. She looked at her sister with something like fear but she wasn't mad at her. This was Maggie's portion. This was the way she knew God to work.

76 When I looked at her like that something hit me in the top of my head and ran down to the soles of my feet. Just like when I'm in church and the spirit of God touches me and I get happy and shout. I did something I never had done before: hugged Maggie to me, then dragged her on into the room, snatched the quilts out of Miss Wangero's hands and dumped them into Maggie's lap. Maggie just sat there on my bed with her mouth open.

77 "Take one or two of the others," I said to Dee.

78 But she turned without a word and went out to Hakim-a-barber.

79 "You just don't understand," she said, as Maggie and I came out to the car.

80 "What don't I understand?" I wanted to know.

81 "Your heritage," she said. And then she turned to Maggie, kissed her, and said, "You ought to try to make something of yourself, too, Maggie. It's really a new day for us. But from the way you and Mama still live you'd never know it."

82 She put on some sunglasses that hid everything above the tip of her nose and her chin.

83 Maggie smiled; maybe at the sunglasses. But a real smile, not scared. After we watched the car dust settle I asked Maggie to bring me a dip of snuff. And then the two of us sat there just enjoying, until it was time to go in the house and go to bed.

(1973)

QUESTIONS

1. What is the central conflict of the story? What subsidiary conflicts exist? Are they resolved at the end? Why or why not?
2. What is the significance of Wangero's name change? Of her mother's reluctance to use her daughter's new name?
3. Divide the story into scenes, title each, and comment on the purpose of each.
4. What is Asalamalakim's role in the story? How important is he? Explain.
5. Explain the importance of the quilts. What do they represent?
6. How is Wangero's mother like Walker's? See "In Search of Our Mothers' Gardens."

SUGGESTIONS FOR WRITING

A. Compare Wangero to the narrator of Baldwin's "Sonny's Blues." Focus on their respective attitudes toward their past, particularly toward their family relationships and cultural heritage.

B. Compare the two sisters in this story. Consider their lives, their environments, and their probable futures.

SIXTEEN

Annie Dillard

(1945–)

Annie Dillard's is a fascinating and expansive imagination that takes wings from the natural world around us. She sees what we cannot see, or will not see, and by hook and by crook, she pulls us out into the open, into nature where she instructs us about seeing not only with our eyes but also with our senses. And by a process she calls "internal verbalization," she gives us glimpses of what she sees during visionary moments. Like Eiseley, she is never content to narrate or record. A meditative observer, Dillard tells us what she sees around her as well as in her mind's eye; she lets us in on her most secret moments, moments when she's trying to see beyond pain and cruelty to an unfathomable God, moments when she's squinting, trying to catch sight of the wind, moments when she's rocking with pain or reeling with joy.

The range of her imagination is matched by the range of her writing: a collection of poems, *Tickets for a Prayer Wheel* (1974); works of philosophical speculation, *Holy the Firm* (1977); and of literary theory, *Living by Fiction* (1979); and most recently, a collection of essays, *Teaching a Stone to Talk* (1982) and an autobiography, *An American Childhood* (1987). Her first book, *Pilgrim at Tinker Creek* (1974), was a best-seller and won a Pulitzer Prize. Nowhere is the range of her prose more evident than in that book where meditative, expansive passages become taut and poetic, where incantatory rhythms draw us spellbound beneath the roots of sycamore trees, and where different rhythms entice us to join the dance of the universe. But she doesn't just make meaning through rhythm. She also creates wonderful internal rhymes and other sounds that play over our minds as she takes us behind nature's closed doors. "Seeing," a chapter from *Tinker Creek* that is a self-contained essay, shows us the more positive, upbeat side of Dillard's imagination.

Two additional selections reveal Dillard's darker side and give us a fuller sense of her mind's play. "The Deer at Providencia," from *Stone,* gives us an unusual chance to see Dillard describing dispassionately the slow painful death of a deer, an event that would seem to demand sympathy and compassion. In clear and transparent prose, she renders a report of her encounter with the deer and with the others who also witness the death. As she does so, she plays off traditional and perhaps wrongheaded notions of woman against her own reaction to the event taking place before her eyes and before ours. We get to observe her observing the deer; we also get glimpses of the men who are watching her on the scene. Just as we think we have sized up this Dillard, she reverses the terms of the argument, offers a different view of the same woman from another room. She ends on a note of philosophical and theological speculation, shocking us with her piercing insight and her implied questions about God's mercy.

"God's Tooth," a meditative, philosophical piece from *Holy the Firm,* is a companion piece for "Deer," but the presentation is centered more directly on the inquiry into the nature of God. It explores the meaning of suffering, particularly the seemingly senseless suffering of children. The essay is casual in structure, angry in tone, and passionate in its agonized quest for meaning in the face of a tragic, chance event.

"Sojourner" from *Stone* gives us a glimpse of the two sides of Dillard in one essay, and it affords an excellent opportunity to see her developing and extending a controlling metaphor. In the face of a cosmic disaster, our planet hurtling through space to an unknown destination, she encourages us to turn "drift to dance." She encourages us to look straight into the abyss and envision unsentimental possibilities—to be heroically pessimistic, to dance on the rim of disaster.

Dillard has described herself as "an explorer" and "a stalker"—both of the natural world and of the meanings locked within it. As a naturalist and symbolist, she searches in and through nature for transcendent truths, and her intense scrutiny of nature is fueled by a passion for meaning. The risks she takes in describing the marvelous, steep her writing in wonder and give us insight into our own lives. To go with Dillard to Tinker Creek or to any of her other haunts is to go on a journey into the heartland. But it is also to go beyond the heartland into uncharted regions of the mind and the spirit. We find in the heartland and in those uncharted regions both terror and ecstasy.

Seeing

1 When I was six or seven years old, growing up in Pittsburgh, I used to take a precious penny of my own and hide it for someone else to find. It was a curious compulsion; sadly, I've never been seized by it since. For some reason I always "hid" the penny along the same stretch of sidewalk up the street. I would cradle it at the roots of a sycamore, say, or in a hole left by a chipped-off piece of sidewalk. Then I would take a piece of chalk, and, starting at either end of the block, draw huge arrows leading up to the penny from both directions. After I learned to write I labeled the arrows: SURPRISE AHEAD or MONEY THIS WAY. I was greatly excited, during all this arrow-drawing, at the thought of the first lucky passer-by who would receive in this way, regardless of merit, a free gift from the universe. But I never lurked about. I would go straight home and not give the matter another thought, until, some months later, I would be gripped again by the impulse to hide another penny.

2 It is still the first week in January, and I've got great plans. I've been thinking about seeing. There are lots of things to see, unwrapped gifts and free surprises. The world is fairly studded and strewn with pennies cast broadside from a generous hand. But—and this is the point—who gets excited by a mere penny? If you follow one arrow, if you crouch motionless on a bank to watch a tremulous ripple thrill on the

water and are rewarded by the sight of a muskrat kit paddling from its den, will you count that sight a chip of copper only, and go your rueful way? It is dire poverty indeed when a man is so malnourished and fatigued that he won't stoop to pick up a penny. But if you cultivate a healthy poverty and simplicity, so that finding a penny will literally make your day, then, since the world is in fact planted in pennies, you have with your poverty bought a lifetime of days. It is that simple. What you see is what you get.

3 I used to be able to see flying insects in the air. I'd look ahead and see, not the row of hemlocks across the road, but the air in front of it. My eyes would focus along that column of air, picking out flying insects. But I lost interest, I guess, for I dropped the habit. Now I can see birds. Probably some people can look at the grass at their feet and discover all the crawling creatures. I would like to know grasses and sedges—and care. Then my least journey into the world would be a field trip, a series of happy recognitions. Thoreau, in an expansive mood, exulted, "What a rich book might be made about buds, including, perhaps, sprouts!" It would be nice to think so. I cherish mental images I have of three perfectly happy people. One collects stones. Another—an Englishman, say—watches clouds. The third lives on a coast and collects drops of seawater which he examines microscopically and mounts. But I don't see what the specialist sees, and so I cut myself off, not only from the total picture, but from the various forms of happiness.

4 Unfortunately, nature is very much a now-you-see-it, now-you-don't affair. A fish flashes, then dissolves in the water before my eyes like so much salt. Deer apparently ascend bodily into heaven; the brightest oriole fades into leaves. These disappearances stun me into stillness and concentration; they say of nature that it conceals with a grand nonchalance, and they say of vision that it is a deliberate gift, the revelation of a dancer who for my eyes only flings away her seven veils. For nature does reveal as well as conceal: now-you-don't-see-it, now-you-do. For a week last September migrating red-winged blackbirds were feeding heavily down by the creek at the back of the house. One day I went out to investigate the racket; I walked up to a tree, an Osage orange, and a hundred birds flew away. They simply materialized out of the tree. I saw a tree, then a whisk of color, then a tree again. I walked closer and another hundred blackbirds took flight. Not a branch, not a twig budged: the birds were apparently weightless as well as invisible. Or, it was as if the leaves of the Osage orange had been freed from a spell in the form of red-winged blackbirds; they flew from the tree, caught my eye in the sky, and vanished. When I looked again at the tree the leaves had reassembled as if nothing had happened. Finally I walked directly to the trunk of the tree and a final hundred, the real diehards, appeared, spread, and vanished. How could so many hide in the tree without my seeing them? The Osage orange, unruffled, looked just as it had looked from the house, when three hundred red-winged blackbirds cried from its crown. I looked downstream where they flew, and they were gone. Searching, I couldn't spot one. I wandered downstream to force them to play their hand, but they'd crossed the creek and scattered. One show to a customer. These appearances catch at my throat; they are the free gifts, the bright coppers at the roots of trees.

5 It's all a matter of keeping my eyes open. Nature is like one of those line drawings of a tree that are puzzles for children: Can you find hidden in the leaves

a duck, a house, a boy, a bucket, a zebra, and a boot? Specialists can find the most incredibly well-hidden things. A book I read when I was young recommended an easy way to find caterpillars to rear: you simply find some fresh caterpillar droppings, look up, and there's your caterpillar. More recently an author advised me to set my mind at ease about those piles of cut stems on the ground in grassy fields. Field mice make them; they cut the grass down by degrees to reach the seeds at the head. It seems that when the grass is tightly packed, as in a field of ripe grain, the blade won't topple at a single cut through the stem; instead, the cut stem simply drops vertically, held in the crush of grain. The mouse severs the bottom again and again, the stem keeps dropping an inch at a time, and finally the head is low enough for the mouse to reach the seeds. Meanwhile, the mouse is positively littering the field with its little piles of cut stems into which, presumably, the author of the book is constantly stumbling.

6 If I can't see these minutiae, I still try to keep my eyes open. I'm always on the lookout for antlion traps in sandy soil, monarch pupae near milkweed, skipper larvae in locust leaves. These things are utterly common, and I've not seen one. I bang on hollow trees near water, but so far no flying squirrels have appeared. In flat country I watch every sunset in hopes of seeing the green ray. The green ray is a seldom-seen streak of light that rises from the sun like a spurting fountain at the moment of sunset; it throbs into the sky for two seconds and disappears. One more reason to keep my eyes open. A photography professor at the University of Florida just happened to see a bird die in midflight; it jerked, died, dropped, and smashed on the ground. I squint at the wind because I read Stewart Edward White: "I have always maintained that if you looked closely enough you could *see* the wind—the dim, hardly-made-out, fine debris fleeing high in the air." White was an excellent observer, and devoted an entire chapter of *The Mountains* to the subject of seeing deer: "As soon as you can forget the naturally obvious and construct an artificial obvious, then you too will see deer."

7 But the artificial obvious is hard to see. My eyes account for less than one percent of the weight of my head; I'm bony and dense; I see what I expect. I once spent a full three minutes looking at a bullfrog that was so unexpectedly large I couldn't see it even though a dozen enthusiastic campers were shouting directions. Finally I asked, "What color am I looking for?" and a fellow said, "Green." When at last I picked out the frog, I saw what painters are up against: the thing wasn't green at all, but the color of wet hickory bark.

8 The lover can see, and the knowledgeable. I visited an aunt and uncle at a quarter-horse ranch in Cody, Wyoming. I couldn't do much of anything useful, but I could, I thought, draw. So, as we all sat around the kitchen table after supper, I produced a sheet of paper and drew a horse. "That's one lame horse," my aunt volunteered. The rest of the family joined in: "Only place to saddle that one is his neck"; "Looks like we better shoot the poor thing, on account of those terrible growths." Meekly, I slid the pencil and paper down the table. Everyone in that family, including my three young cousins, could draw a horse. Beautifully. When the paper came back it looked as though five shining, real quarter horses had been corraled by mistake with a papier-mâché moose; the real horses seemed to gaze at the monster with a steady, puzzled air. I stay away from horses now, but I can do

a creditable goldfish. The point is that I just don't know what the lover knows; I just can't see the artificial obvious that those in the know construct. The herpetologist asks the native, "Are there snakes in that ravine?" "Nosir." And the herpetologist comes home with, yessir, three bags full. Are there butterflies on that mountain? Are the bluets in bloom, are there arrowheads here, or fossil shells in the shale?

9 Peeping through my keyhole I see within the range of only about thirty percent of the light that comes from the sun; the rest is infrared and some little ultraviolet, perfectly apparent to many animals, but invisible to me. A nightmare network of ganglia, charged and firing without my knowledge, cuts and splices what I do see, editing it for my brain. Donald E. Carr points out that the sense impressions of one-celled animals are *not* edited for the brain: "This is philosophically interesting in a rather mournful way, since it means that only the simplest animals perceive the universe as it is."

10 A fog that won't burn away drifts and flows across my field of vision. When you see fog move against a backdrop of deep pines, you don't see the fog itself, but streaks of clearness floating across the air in dark shreds. So I see only tatters of clearness through a pervading obscurity. I can't distinguish the fog from the overcast sky; I can't be sure if the light is direct or reflected. Everywhere darkness and the presence of the unseen appalls. We estimate now that only one atom dances alone in every cubic meter of intergalactic space. I blink and squint. What planet or power yanks Halley's Comet out of orbit? We haven't seen that force yet; it's a question of distance, density, and the pallor of reflected light. We rock, cradled in the swaddling band of darkness. Even the simple darkness of night whispers suggestions to the mind. Last summer, in August, I stayed at the creek too late.

11 Where Tinker Creek flows under the sycamore log bridge to the tear-shaped island, it is slow and shallow, fringed thinly in cattail marsh. At this spot an astonishing bloom of life supports vast breeding populations of insects, fish, reptiles, birds, and mammals. On windless summer evenings I stalk along the creek bank or straddle the sycamore log in absolute stillness, watching for muskrats. The night I stayed too late I was hunched on the log staring spellbound at spreading, reflected stains of lilac on the water. A cloud in the sky suddenly lighted as if turned on by a switch; its reflection just as suddenly materialized on the water upstream, flat and floating, so that I couldn't see the creek bottom, or life in the water under the cloud. Downstream, away from the cloud on the water, water turtles smooth as beans were gliding down with the current in a series of easy, weightless push-offs, as men bound on the moon. I didn't know whether to trace the progress of one turtle I was sure of, risking sticking my face in one of the bridge's spider webs made invisible by the gathering dark, or take a chance on seeing the carp, or scan the mudbank in hope of seeing a muskrat, or follow the last of the swallows who caught at my heart and trailed it after them like streamers as they appeared from directly below, under the log, flying upstream with their tails forked, so fast.

12 But shadows spread, and deepened, and stayed. After thousands of years we're still strangers to darkness, fearful aliens in an enemy camp with our arms crossed over our chests. I stirred. A land turtle on the bank, startled, hissed the air from its lungs and withdrew into its shell. An uneasy pink here, an unfathomable blue there,

gave great suggestion of lurking beings. Things were going on. I couldn't see whether that sere rustle I heard was a distant rattlesnake, slit-eyed, or a nearby sparrow kicking in the dry flood debris slung at the foot of a willow. Tremendous action roiled the water everywhere I looked, big action, inexplicable. A tremor welled up beside a gaping muskrat burrow in the bank and I caught my breath, but no muskrat appeared. The ripples continued to fan upstream with a steady, powerful thrust. Night was knitting over my face an eyeless mask, and I still sat transfixed. A distant airplane, a delta wing out of nightmare, made a gliding shadow on the creek's bottom that looked like a stingray cruising upstream. At once a black fin slit the pink cloud on the water, shearing it in two. The two halves merged together and seemed to dissolve before my eyes. Darkness pooled in the cleft of the creek and rose, as water collects in a well. Untamed, dreaming lights flickered over the sky. I saw hints of hulking underwater shadows, two pale splashes out of the water, and round ripples rolling close together from a blackened center.

13 At last I stared upstream where only the deepest violet remained of the cloud, a cloud so high its underbelly still glowed feeble color reflected from a hidden sky lighted in turn by a sun halfway to China. And out of that violet, a sudden enormous black body arced over the water. I saw only a cylindrical sleekness. Head and tail, if there was a head and tail, were both submerged in cloud. I saw only one ebony fling, a headlong dive to darkness; then the waters closed, and the lights went out.

14 I walked home in a shivering daze, up hill and down. Later I lay open-mouthed in bed, my arms flung wide at my sides to steady the whirling darkness. At this latitude I'm spinning 836 miles an hour round the earth's axis; I often fancy I feel my sweeping fall as a breakneck arc like the dive of dolphins, and the hollow rushing of wind raises hair on my neck and the side of my face. In orbit around the sun I'm moving 64,800 miles an hour. The solar system as a whole, like a merry-go-round unhinged, spins, bobs, and blinks at the speed of 43,200 miles an hour along a course set east of Hercules. Someone has piped, and we are dancing a tarantella until the sweat pours. I open my eyes and I see dark, muscled forms curl out of water, with flapping gills and flattened eyes. I close my eyes and I see stars, deep stars giving way to deeper stars, deeper stars bowing to deepest stars at the crown of an infinite cone.

15 "Still," wrote van Gogh in a letter, "a great deal of light falls on everything." If we are blinded by darkness, we are also blinded by light. When too much light falls on everything, a special terror results. Peter Freuchen describes the notorious kayak sickness to which Greenland Eskimos are prone. "The Greenland fjords are peculiar for the spells of completely quiet weather, when there is not enough wind to blow out a match and the water is like a sheet of glass. The kayak hunter must sit in his boat without stirring a finger so as not to scare the shy seals away. . . . The sun, low in the sky, sends a glare into his eyes, and the landscape around moves into the realm of the unreal. The reflex from the mirrorlike water hypnotizes him, he seems to be unable to move, and all of a sudden it is as if he were floating in a bottomless void, sinking, sinking, and sinking. . . . Horror-stricken, he tries to stir, to cry out, but he cannot, he is completely paralyzed, he just falls and falls." Some hunters are especially cursed with this panic, and bring ruin and sometimes starvation to their families.

16 Sometimes here in Virginia at sunset low clouds on the southern or northern horizon are completely invisible in the lighted sky. I only know one is there because I can see its reflection in still water. The first time I discovered this mystery I looked from cloud to no-cloud in bewilderment, checking my bearings over and over, thinking maybe the ark of the covenant was just passing by south of Dead Man Mountain. Only much later did I read the explanation: polarized light from the sky is very much weakened by reflection, but the light in clouds isn't polarized. So invisible clouds pass among visible clouds, till all slide over the mountains; so a greater light extinguishes a lesser as though it didn't exist.

17 In the great meteor shower of August, the Perseid, I wail all day for the shooting stars I miss. They're out there showering down, committing hara-kiri in a flame of fatal attraction, and hissing perhaps at last into the ocean. But at dawn what looks like a blue dome clamps down over me like a lid on a pot. The stars and planets could smash and I'd never know. Only a piece of ashen moon occasionally climbs up or down the inside of the dome, and our local star without surcease explodes on our heads. We have really only that one light, one source for all power, and yet we must turn away from it by universal decree. Nobody here on the planet seems aware of this strange, powerful taboo, that we all walk about carefully averting our faces, this way and that, lest our eyes be blasted forever.

18 Darkness appalls and light dazzles; the scrap of visible light that doesn't hurt my eyes hurts my brain. What I see sets me swaying. Size and distance and the sudden swelling of meanings confuse me, bowl me over. I straddle the sycamore log bridge over Tinker Creek in the summer. I look at the lighted creek bottom: snail tracks tunnel the mud in quavering curves. A crayfish jerks, but by the time I absorb what has happened, he's gone in a billowing smokescreen of silt. I look at the water: minnows and shiners. If I'm thinking minnows, a carp will fill my brain till I scream. I look at the water's surface: skaters, bubbles, and leaves sliding down. Suddenly, my own face, reflected, startles me witless. Those snails have been tracking my face! Finally, with a shuddering wrench of the will, I see clouds, cirrus clouds. I'm dizzy, I fall in. This looking business is risky.

19 Once I stood on a humped rock on nearby Purgatory Mountain, watching through binoculars the great autumn hawk migration below, until I discovered that I was in danger of joining the hawks on a vertical migration of my own. I was used to binoculars, but not, apparently, to balancing on humped rocks while looking through them. I staggered. Everything advanced and receded by turns; the world was full of unexplained foreshortenings and depths. A distant huge tan object, a hawk the size of an elephant, turned out to be the browned bough of a nearby loblolly pine. I followed a sharp-shinned hawk against a featureless sky, rotating my head unawares as it flew, and when I lowered the glass a glimpse of my own looming shoulder sent me staggering. What prevents the men on Palomar from falling, voiceless and blinded, from their tiny, vaulted chairs?

20 I reel in confusion; I don't understand what I see. With the naked eye I can see two million light-years to the Andromeda galaxy. Often I slop some creek water in a jar and when I get home I dump it in a white china bowl. After the silt settles I return and see tracings of minute snails on the bottom, a planarian or two winding round the rim of water, roundworms shimmying frantically, and finally, when my

eyes have adjusted to these dimensions, amoebae. At first the amoebae look like muscae volitantes, those curled moving spots you seem to see in your eyes when you stare at a distant wall. Then I see the amoebae as drops of water congealed, bluish, translucent, like chips of sky in the bowl. At length I choose one individual and give myself over to its idea of an evening. I see it dribble a grainy foot before it on its wet, unfathomable way. Do its unedited sense impressions include the fierce focus of my eyes? Shall I take it outside and show it Andromeda, and blow its little endoplasm? I stir the water with a finger, in case it's running out of oxygen. Maybe I should get a tropical aquarium with motorized bubblers and lights, and keep this one for a pet. Yes, it would tell its fissioned descendants, the universe is two feet by five, and if you listen closely you can hear the buzzing music of the spheres.

21 Oh, it's mysterious lamplit evenings, here in the galaxy, one after the other. It's one of those nights when I wander from window to window, looking for a sign. But I can't see. Terror and a beauty insoluble are a ribband of blue woven into the fringes of garments of things both great and small. No culture explains, no bivouac offers real haven or rest. But it could be that we are not seeing something. Galileo thought comets were an optical illusion. This is fertile ground: since we are certain that they're not, we can look at what our scientists have been saying with fresh hope. What if there are *really* gleaming, castellated cities hung upsidedown over the desert sand? What limpid lakes and cool date palms have our caravans always passed untried? Until, one by one, by the blindest of leaps, we light on the road to these places, we must stumble in darkness and hunger. I turn from the window. I'm blind as a bat, sensing only from every direction the echo of my own thin cries.

22 I chanced on a wonderful book by Marius von Senden, called *Space and Sight.* When Western surgeons discovered how to perform safe cataract operations, they ranged across Europe and America operating on dozens of men and women of all ages who had been blinded by cataracts since birth. Von Senden collected accounts of such cases; the histories are fascinating. Many doctors had tested their patients' sense perceptions and ideas of space both before and after the operations. The vast majority of patients, of both sexes and all ages, had, in von Senden's opinion, no idea of space whatsoever. Form, distance, and size were so many meaningless syllables. A patient "had no idea of depth, confusing it with roundness." Before the operation a doctor would give a blind patient a cube and a sphere; the patient would tongue it or feel it with his hands, and name it correctly. After the operation the doctor would show the same objects to the patient without letting him touch them; now he had no clue whatsoever what he was seeing. One patient called lemonade "square" because it pricked on his tongue as a square shape pricked on the touch of his hands. Of another postoperative patient, the doctor writes, "I have found in her no notion of size, for example, not even within the narrow limits which she might have encompassed with the aid of touch. Thus when I asked her to show me how big her mother was, she did not stretch out her hands, but set her two index-fingers a few inches apart." Other doctors reported their patients' own statements to similar effect. "The room he was in . . . he knew to be but part of the house, yet he could not conceive that the whole house could look bigger"; "Those who are blind from birth . . . have no real conception of height or distance. A house that

is a mile away is thought of as nearby, but requiring the taking of a lot of steps. . . . The elevator that whizzes him up and down gives no more sense of vertical distance than does the train of horizontal."

23 For the newly sighted, vision is pure sensation unencumbered by meaning: "The girl went through the experience that we all go through and forget, the moment we are born. She saw, but it did not mean anything but a lot of different kinds of brightness." Again, "I asked the patient what he could see; he answered that he saw an extensive field of light, in which everything appeared dull, confused, and in motion. He could not distinguish objects." Another patient saw "nothing but a confusion of forms and colours." When a newly sighted girl saw photographs and paintings, she asked, "Why do they put those dark marks all over them?' 'Those aren't dark marks,' her mother explained, 'those are shadows. That is one of the ways the eye knows that things have shape. If it were not for shadows many things would look flat.' 'Well, that's how things do look,' Joan answered. 'Everything looks flat with dark patches.' "

24 But it is the patients' concepts of space that are most revealing. One patient, according to his doctor, "practiced his vision in a strange fashion; thus he takes off one of his boots, throws it some way off in front of him, and then attempts to gauge the distance at which it lies; he takes a few steps towards the boot and tries to grasp it; on failing to reach it, he moves on a step or two and gropes for the boot until he finally gets hold of it." "But even at this stage, after three weeks' experience of seeing," von Senden goes on, " 'space,' as he conceives it, ends with visual space, i.e. with colour-patches that happen to bound his view. He does not yet have the notion that a larger object (a chair) can mask a smaller one (a dog), or that the latter can still be present even though it is not directly seen."

25 In general the newly sighted see the world as a dazzle of color-patches. They are pleased by the sensation of color, and learn quickly to name the colors, but the rest of seeing is tormentingly difficult. Soon after his operation a patient "generally bumps into one of these colour-patches and observes them to be substantial, since they resist him as tactual objects do. In walking about it also strikes him—or can if he pays attention—that he is continually passing in between the colours he sees, that he can go past a visual object, that a part of it then steadily disappears from view; and that in spite of this, however he twists and turns—whether entering the room from the door, for example, or returning back to it—he always has a visual space in front of him. Thus he gradually comes to realize that there is also a space behind him, which he does not see."

26 The mental effort involved in these reasonings proves overwhelming for many patients. It oppresses them to realize, if they ever do at all, the tremendous size of the world, which they had previously conceived of as something touchingly manageable. It oppresses them to realize that they have been visible to people all along, perhaps unattractively so, without their knowledge or consent. A disheartening number of them refuse to use their new vision, continuing to go over objects with their tongues, and lapsing into apathy and despair. "The child can see, but will not make use of his sight. Only when pressed can he with difficulty be brought to look at objects in his neighbourhood; but more than a foot away it is impossible to bestir him to the necessary effort." Of a twenty-one-year-old girl, the doctor relates, "Her

unfortunate father, who had hoped for so much from this operation, wrote that his daughter carefully shuts her eyes whenever she wishes to go about the house, especially when she comes to a staircase, and that she is never happier or more at ease than when, by closing her eyelids, she relapses into her former state of total blindness." A fifteen-year-old boy, who was also in love with a girl at the asylum for the blind, finally blurted out, "No, really, I can't stand it any more; I want to be sent back to the asylum again. If things aren't altered, I'll tear my eyes out."

27 Some do learn to see, especially the young ones. But it changes their lives. One doctor comments on "the rapid and complete loss of that striking and wonderful serenity which is characteristic only of those who have never yet seen." A blind man who learns to see is ashamed of his old habits. He dresses up, grooms himself, and tries to make a good impression. While he was blind he was indifferent to objects unless they were edible; now, "a sifting of values sets in . . . his thoughts and wishes are mightily stirred and some few of the patients are thereby led into dissimulation, envy, theft and fraud."

28 On the other hand, many newly sighted people speak well of the world, and teach us how dull is our own vision. To one patient, a human hand, unrecognized, is "something bright and then holes." Shown a bunch of grapes, a boy calls out, "It is dark, blue and shiny. . . . It isn't smooth, it has bumps and hollows." A little girl visits a garden. "She is greatly astonished, and can scarcely be persuaded to answer, stands speechless in front of the tree, which she only names on taking hold of it, and then as 'the tree with the lights in it.' " Some delight in their sight and give themselves over to the visual world. Of a patient just after her bandages were removed, her doctor writes, "The first things to attract her attention were her own hands; she looked at them very closely, moved them repeatedly to and fro, bent and stretched the fingers, and seemed greatly astonished at the sight." One girl was eager to tell her blind friend that "men do not really look like trees at all," and astounded to discover that her every visitor had an utterly different face. Finally, a twenty-two-year-old girl was dazzled by the world's brightness and kept her eyes shut for two weeks. When at the end of that time she opened her eyes again, she did not recognize any objects, but, "the more she now directed her gaze upon everything about her, the more it could be seen how an expression of gratification and astonishment overspread her features; she repeatedly exclaimed: 'Oh God! How beautiful!' "

29 I saw color-patches for weeks after I read this wonderful book. It was summer; the peaches were ripe in the valley orchards. When I woke in the morning, color-patches wrapped round my eyes, intricately, leaving not one unfilled spot. All day long I walked among shifting color-patches that parted before me like the Red Sea and closed again in silence, transfigured, wherever I looked back. Some patches swelled and loomed, while others vanished utterly, and dark marks flitted at random over the whole dazzling sweep. But I couldn't sustain the illusion of flatness. I've been around for too long. Form is condemned to an eternal danse macabre with meaning: I couldn't unpeach the peaches. Nor can I remember ever having seen without understanding; the color-patches of infancy are lost. My brain then must have been smooth as any balloon. I'm told I reached for the moon; many babies do. But the color-patches of infancy swelled as meaning filled them; they arrayed

themselves in solemn ranks down distance which unrolled and stretched before me like a plain. The moon rocketed away. I live now in a world of shadows that shape and distance color, a world where space makes a kind of terrible sense. What gnosticism is this, and what physics? The fluttering patch I saw in my nursery window—silver and green and shape-shifting blue—is gone; a row of Lombardy poplars takes its place, mute, across the distant lawn. That humming oblong creature pale as light that stole along the walls of my room at night, stretching exhilaratingly around the corners, is gone, too, gone the night I ate of the bittersweet fruit, put two and two together and puckered forever my brain. Martin Buber tells this tale: "Rabbi Mendel once boasted to his teacher Rabbi Elimelekh that evenings he saw the angel who rolls away the light before the darkness, and mornings the angel who rolls away the darkness before the light. 'Yes,' said Rabbi Elimelekh, 'in my youth I saw that too. Later on you don't see these things any more.' "

30 Why didn't someone hand those newly sighted people paints and brushes from the start, when they still didn't know what anything was? Then maybe we all could see color-patches too, the world unraveled from reason, Eden before Adam gave names. The scales would drop from my eyes; I'd see trees like men walking; I'd run down the road against all orders, hallooing and leaping.

31 Seeing is of course very much a matter of verbalization. Unless I call my attention to what passes before my eyes, I simply won't see it. It is, as Ruskin says, "not merely unnoticed, but in the full, clear sense of the word, unseen." My eyes alone can't solve analogy tests using figures, the ones which show, with increasing elaborations, a big square, then a small square in a big square, then a big triangle, and expect me to find a small triangle in a big triangle. I have to say the words, describe what I'm seeing. If Tinker Mountain erupted, I'd be likely to notice. But if I want to notice the lesser cataclysms of valley life, I have to maintain in my head a running description of the present. It's not that I'm observant; it's just that I talk too much. Otherwise, especially in a strange place, I'll never know what's happening. Like a blind man at the ball game, I need a radio.

32 When I see this way I analyze and pry. I hurl over logs and roll away stones; I study the bank a square foot at a time, probing and tilting my head. Some days when a mist covers the mountains, when the muskrats won't show and the microscope's mirror shatters, I want to climb up the blank blue dome as a man would storm the inside of a circus tent, wildly, dangling, and with a steel knife claw a rent in the top, peep, and, if I must, fall.

33 But there is another kind of seeing that involves a letting go. When I see this way I sway transfixed and emptied. The difference between the two ways of seeing is the difference between walking with and without a camera. When I walk with a camera I walk from shot to shot, reading the light on a calibrated meter. When I walk without a camera, my own shutter opens, and the moment's light prints on my own silver gut. When I see this second way I am above all an unscrupulous observer.

34 It was sunny one evening last summer at Tinker Creek; the sun was low in the sky, upstream. I was sitting on the sycamore log bridge with the sunset at my

back, watching the shiners the size of minnows who were feeding over the muddy sand in skittery schools. Again and again, one fish, then another, turned for a split second across the current and flash! the sun shot out from its silver side. I couldn't watch for it. It was always just happening somewhere else, and it drew my vision just as it disappeared: flash, like a sudden dazzle of the thinnest blade, a sparking over a dun and olive ground at chance intervals from every direction. Then I noticed white specks, some sort of pale petals, small, floating from under my feet on the creek's surface, very slow and steady. So I blurred my eyes and gazed towards the brim of my hat and saw a new world. I saw the pale white circles roll up, roll up, like the world's turning, mute and perfect, and I saw the linear flashes, gleaming silver, like stars being born at random down a rolling scroll of time. Something broke and something opened. I filled up like a new wineskin. I breathed an air like light; I saw a light like water. I was the lip of a fountain the creek filled forever; I was ether, the leaf in the zephyr; I was flesh-flake, feather, bone.

35 When I see this way I see truly. As Thoreau says, I return to my senses. I am the man who watches the baseball game in silence in an empty stadium. I see the game purely; I'm abstracted and dazed. When it's all over and the white-suited players lope off the green field to their shadowed dugouts, I leap to my feet; I cheer and cheer.

36 But I can't go out and try to see this way. I'll fail, I'll go mad. All I can do is try to gag the commentator, to hush the noise of useless interior babble that keeps me from seeing just as surely as a newspaper dangled before my eyes. The effort is really a discipline requiring a lifetime of dedicated struggle; it marks the literature of saints and monks of every order East and West, under every rule and no rule, discalced and shod. The world's spiritual geniuses seem to discover universally that the mind's muddy river, this ceaseless flow of trivia and trash, cannot be dammed, and that trying to dam it is a waste of effort that might lead to madness. Instead you must allow the muddy river to flow unheeded in the dim channels of consciousness; you raise your sights; you look along it, mildly, acknowledging its presence without interest and gazing beyond it into the realm of the real where subjects and objects act and rest purely, without utterance. "Launch into the deep," says Jacques Ellul, "and you shall see."

37 The secret of seeing is, then, the pearl of great price. If I thought he could teach me to find it and keep it forever I would stagger barefoot across a hundred deserts after any lunatic at all. But although the pearl may be found, it may not be sought. The literature of illumination reveals this above all: although it comes to those who wait for it, it is always, even to the most practiced and adept, a gift and a total surprise. I return from one walk knowing where the killdeer nests in the field by the creek and the hour the laurel blooms. I return from the same walk a day later scarcely knowing my own name. Litanies hum in my ears; my tongue flaps in my mouth Ailinon, alleluia! I cannot cause light; the most I can do is try to put myself in the path of its beam. It is possible, in deep space, to sail on solar wind. Light, be it particle or wave, has force: you rig a giant sail and go. The secret of seeing is to sail on solar wind. Hone and spread your spirit till you yourself are a sail, whetted, translucent, broadside to the merest puff.

38 When her doctor took her bandages off and led her into the garden, the girl who was no longer blind saw "the tree with the lights in it." It was for this tree I searched through the peach orchards of summer, in the forests of fall and down winter and spring for years. Then one day I was walking along Tinker Creek thinking of nothing at all and I saw the tree with the lights in it. I saw the backyard cedar where the mourning doves roost charged and transfigured, each cell buzzing with flame. I stood on the grass with the lights in it, grass that was wholly fire, utterly focused and utterly dreamed. It was less like seeing than like being for the first time seen, knocked breathless by a powerful glance. The flood of fire abated, but I'm still spending the power. Gradually the lights went out in the cedar, the colors died, the cells unflamed and disappeared. I was still ringing. I had been my whole life a bell, and never knew it until at that moment I was lifted and struck. I have since only very rarely seen the tree with the lights in it. The vision comes and goes, mostly goes, but I live for it, for the moment when the mountains open and a new light roars in spate through the crack, and the mountains slam.

(1974)

QUESTIONS

Thought and Structure

1. Would it make any difference if we deleted paragraph 1? Why?
2. How important is the phrase "unwrapped gifts and free surprises" (paragraph 2)? Are there other phrases scattered throughout the essay that serve as reminders of this notion? If so, how do they bind the essay together?
3. Does Dillard make any money, so to speak, with her economic metaphors in paragraph 2?
4. What does Dillard mean when she says that "nature is very much a now-you-see-it, now-you-don't affair" (paragraph 4)? What is necessary for us to see as the knowledgeable and the lover see?
5. What do you think of the wish Dillard seems to be making in paragraph 30?
6. What is it like being "an unscrupulous observer" (paragraphs 33–37)? How does one become such an observer?

Style and Strategy

7. What is the effect of this sentence at the end of paragraph 4: "These appearances catch at my throat; they are the free gifts, the bright coppers at the roots of trees"? Does it make us think about something we have already read? What are "coppers"?
8. Why do you suppose Dillard mentions the "photography professor" and Stewart Edward White in paragraph 6?
9. Look carefully at paragraphs 11–30; see if you can tell what Dillard's purpose is in this section of the essay. What is she trying to tell us, and how does she make use of darkness, shadow, and color to get her point across? How effectively does she use the information from *Space and Sight* (paragraphs 22–30 and 38)? Would the essay be just as good without those paragraphs? Why?

10. Paragraph 14 is obviously a transitional paragraph between a section of the essay dealing with darkness and a section dealing with light. What does Dillard accomplish in this paragraph by mixing her personal reaction to experienced events with technical information about the solar system? What is a "tarantella"? How effective is the notion of a tarantella as a summarizing metaphor for the paragraph?
11. What do you think of the effectiveness of the sail metaphor in paragraph 37? Does it help you understand the mystery Dillard is trying to reveal?
12. Relate the phrase "spending the power" (paragraph 38) to the essay's first two paragraphs. What is the point?

SUGGESTIONS FOR WRITING

A. Test, if you will, Dillard's theory that seeing is "all a matter of keeping my eyes open." Go outside, or find a window onto the outside world, and practice keeping your eyes open. Repeat the exercise several times. Keep a record of what you see over time and then try to write a paragraph very much like the fourth paragraph in Dillard's essay. See if you can create out of your experience something as spectacular in its written form as the "Osage orange." Try to make what you have seen accessible to your readers.

B. In one short paragraph summarize Dillard's main points about the two ways of seeing identified in her essay. Try to answer these questions in your paragraph without simply creating a list: How do the two ways differ? What are their respective rewards? What can we do to be able to see both ways? Would our preparation for one way differ from our preparation for the other?

C. Think of something you are knowledgeable about—something that you really love. You might be an expert camper, skater, sailor, dancer, athlete, guitarist, coin collector, model builder. Write an interesting essay revealing your knowledge. Try to let your reader see and understand as you do. Remember as you shape your draft into an essay that you should make a point; merely reporting information is not sufficient.

The Deer at Providencia

1 There were four of us North Americans in the jungle, in the Ecuadorian jungle on the banks of the Napo River in the Amazon watershed. The other three North Americans were metropolitan men. We stayed in tents in one riverside village, and visited others. At the village called Providencia we saw a sight which moved us, and which shocked the men.

2 The first thing we saw when we climbed the riverbank to the village of Providencia was the deer. It was roped to a tree on the grass clearing near the thatch shelter where we would eat lunch.

3 The deer was small, about the size of a whitetail fawn, but apparently full-grown. It had a rope around its neck and three feet caught in the rope. Someone said that the dogs had caught it that morning and the villagers were going to cook and eat it that night.

4 This clearing lay at the edge of the little thatched-hut village. We could see the villagers going about their business, scattering feed corn for hens about their houses, and wandering down paths to the river to bathe. The village headman was our host; he stood beside us as we watched the deer struggle. Several village boys were interested in the deer; they formed part of the circle we made around it in the clearing. So also did four businessmen from Quito who were attempting to guide us around the jungle. Few of the very different people standing in this circle had a common language. We watched the deer, and no one said much.

5 The deer lay on its side at the rope's very end, so the rope lacked slack to let it rest its head in the dust. It was "pretty," delicate of bone like all deer, and thin-skinned for the tropics. Its skin looked virtually hairless, in fact, and almost translucent, like a membrane. Its neck was no thicker than my wrist; it was rubbed open on the rope, and gashed. Trying to paw itself free of the rope, the deer had scratched its own neck with its hooves. The raw underside of its neck showed red stripes and some bruises bleeding inside the muscles. Now three of its feet were hooked in the rope under its jaw. It could not stand, of course, on one leg, so it could not move to slacken the rope and ease the pull on its throat and enable it to rest its head.

6 Repeatedly the deer paused, motionless, its eyes veiled, with only its rib cage in motion, and its breaths the only sound. Then, after I would think, "It has given up; now it will die," it would heave. The rope twanged; the tree leaves clattered; the deer's free foot beat the ground. We stepped back and held our breaths. It thrashed, kicking, but only one leg moved; the other three legs tightened inside the rope's loop. Its hip jerked; its spine shook. Its eyes rolled; its tongue, thick with spittle, pushed in and out. Then it would rest again. We watched this for fifteen minutes.

7 Once three young native boys charged in, released its trapped legs, and jumped back to the circle of people. But instantly the deer scratched up its neck with its hooves and snared its forelegs in the rope again. It was easy to imagine a third and then a fourth leg soon stuck, like Brer Rabbit and the Tar Baby.

8 We watched the deer from the circle, and then we drifted on to lunch. Our palm-roofed shelter stood on a grassy promontory from which we could see the deer tied to the tree, pigs and hens walking under village houses, and black-and-white cattle standing in the river. There was even a breeze.

9 Lunch, which was the second and better lunch we had that day, was hot and fried. There was a big fish called *doncella,* a kind of catfish, dipped whole in corn flour and beaten egg, then deep fried. With our fingers we pulled soft fragments of it from its sides to our plates, and ate; it was delicate fish-flesh, fresh and mild. Someone found the roe, and I ate of that too—it was fat and stronger, like egg yolk, naturally enough, and warm.

10 There was also a stew of meat in shreds with rice and pale brown gravy. I had asked what kind of deer it was tied to the tree; Pepe had answered in Spanish, "*Gama.*" Now they told us this was *gama* too, stewed. I suspect the word means

merely game or venison. At any rate, I heard that the village dogs had cornered another deer just yesterday, and it was this deer which we were now eating in full sight of the whole article. It was good. I was surprised at its tenderness. But it is a fact that high levels of lactic acid, which builds up in muscle tissues during exertion, tenderizes.

11 After the fish and meat we ate bananas fried in chunks and served on a tray; they were sweet and full of flavor. I felt terrific. My shirt was wet and cool from swimming; I had had a night's sleep, two decent walks, three meals, and a swim—everything tasted good. From time to time each one of us, separately, would look beyond our shaded roof to the sunny spot where the deer was still convulsing in the dust. Our meal completed, we walked around the deer and back to the boats.

12 That night I learned that while we were watching the deer, the others were watching me.

13 We four North Americans grew close in the jungle in a way that was not the usual artificial intimacy of travelers. We liked each other. We stayed up all that night talking, murmuring, as though we rocked on hammocks slung above time. The others were from big cities: New York, Washington, Boston. They all said that I had no expression on my face when I was watching the deer—or at any rate, not the expression they expected.

14 They had looked to see how I, the only woman, and the youngest, was taking the sight of the deer's struggles. I looked detached, apparently, or hard, or calm, or focused, still. I don't know. I was thinking. I remember feeling very old and energetic. I could say like Thoreau that I have traveled widely in Roanoke, Virginia. I have thought a great deal about carnivorousness; I eat meat. These things are not issues; they are mysteries.

15 Gentlemen of the city, what surprises you? That there is suffering here, or that I know it?

16 We lay in the tent and talked. "If it had been my wife," one man said with special vigor, amazed, "she wouldn't have cared *what* was going on; she would have dropped *everything* right at that moment and gone in the village from here to there to there, she would not have *stopped* until that animal was out of its suffering one way or another. She couldn't *bear* to see a creature in agony like that."

17 I nodded.

18 Now I am home. When I wake I comb my hair before the mirror above my dresser. Every morning for the past two years I have seen in that mirror, beside my sleep-softened face, the blackened face of a burnt man. It is a wire-service photograph clipped from a newspaper and taped to my mirror. The caption reads: "Alan McDonald in Miami hospital bed." All you can see in the photograph is a smudged triangle of face from his eyelids to his lower lip; the rest is bandages. You cannot see the expression in his eyes; the bandages shade them.

19 The story, headed MAN BURNED FOR SECOND TIME, begins:

> "Why does God hate me?" Alan McDonald asked from his hospital bed.
>
> "When the gunpowder went off, I couldn't believe it," he said. "I just couldn't believe it. I said, 'No, God couldn't do this to me again.' "

He was in a burn ward in Miami, in serious condition. I do not even know if he lived. I wrote him a letter at the time, cringing.

20 He had been burned before, thirteen years previously, by flaming gasoline. For years he had been having his body restored and his face remade in dozens of operations. He had been a boy, and then a burnt boy. He had already been stunned by what could happen, by how life could veer.

21 Once I read that people who survive bad burns tend to go crazy; they have a very high suicide rate. Medicine cannot ease their pain; drugs just leak away, soaking the sheets, because there is no skin to hold them in. The people just lie there and weep. Later they kill themselves. They had not known, before they were burned, that the world included such suffering, that life could permit them personally such pain.

22 This time a bowl of gunpowder had exploded on McDonald.

> "I didn't realize what had happened at first," he recounted. "And then I heard that sound from 13 years ago. I was burning. I rolled to put the fire out and I thought, 'Oh God, not again.'
>
> "If my friend hadn't been there, I would have jumped into a canal with a rock around my neck."

His wife concludes the piece, "Man, it just isn't fair."

23 I read the whole clipping again every morning. This is the Big Time here, every minute of it. Will someone please explain to Alan McDonald in his dignity, to the deer at Providencia in his dignity, what is going on? And mail me the carbon.

When we walked by the deer at Providencia for the last time, I said to Pepe, with a pitying glance at the deer, "*Pobrecito*"—"poor little thing." But I was trying out Spanish. I knew at the time it was a ridiculous thing to say.

(1982)

QUESTIONS

Thought and Structure

1. Why do you suppose Dillard sets herself up in paragraphs 15–16 as a woman different from other women—at least different from the other woman she reveals through the comments of one man in the essay?
2. What do you think this essay is about? Is it about Dillard, or is it about God, or is it about both? What other things might we say it is about? What is the main, controlling point of the essay? What is our final assessment of Dillard as observer and participant?

How does our assessment begin to change in paragraph 18? How does she give us a different sense of the detached, unemotional woman we have been observing? Does she change our sense again in the last sentence of the final paragraph?

3. Is it ironic that the incident of the deer's struggle takes place in "Providencia"?

Style and Strategy

4. In the first paragraph, what is the effect of these two phrases: "metropolitan men" and "shocked the men"? What is Dillard's strategy? Does she call attention to herself without actually appearing in the paragraph? Do we get a better sense of her strategy by looking forward to paragraphs 12–14?
5. In paragraphs 2–4, Dillard's language is that of a detached observer, but there are a few words that play on our feelings. What are they? In paragraph 5, she starts to let out all the stops, to play more openly the hymn of pain. How does she do it? Is an idea emerging by this time? Does it turn out to be the controlling idea of the essay?
6. By the time you get to paragraph 8, what do you think of the observers? What do you think about their going to "lunch"?
7. Why does Dillard go into such elaborate detail about the lunch? What do you make of this sentence in paragraph 10: "But it is a fact that high levels of lactic acid, which builds up in muscle tissues during exertion, tenderizes"? Why does Dillard tell us this fact at this particular point in the narration—before we even get to the dessert? Why does she keep looking out the window and telling us what she sees?

SUGGESTIONS FOR WRITING

A. Have you ever killed an animal or watched one die or looked at the carcass hanging on a rack in the backyard while listening to the tales of the hunt? If so write an essay about your experience. Make sure that you are in the essay as observer or as participant. Let your readers know how you felt as you experienced that event. Let them know, too, what you have made of it after the fact, perhaps even after the fact of writing your drafts. In other words, your final version of the essay ought to make a point. Perhaps that point will be your judgment about the experience itself. Perhaps the essay and the judgment, like Dillard's, will extend beyond the immediate boundaries of the experience.

B. Consider Dillard's "The Deer," and Richard Wilbur's poem "The Pardon":

> My dog lay dead five days without a grave
> In the thick of summer, hid in a clump of pine
> And a jungle of grass and honeysuckle-vine.
> I who had loved him while he kept alive
>
> Went only close enough to where he was
> To sniff the heavy honeysuckle-smell
> Twined with another odor heavier still
> And hear the flies' intolerable buzz.
>
> Well, I was ten and very much afraid.
> In my kind world the dead were out of range
> And I could not forgive the sad or strange
> In beast or man. My father took the spade

And buried him. Last night I saw the grass
Slowly divide (it was the same scene
But now it glowed a fierce and mortal green)
And saw the dog emerging. I confess

I felt afraid again, but still he came
In the carnal sun, clothed in a hymn of flies,
And death was breeding in his lively eyes.
I started in to cry and call his name,

Asking forgiveness of his tongueless head.
. . . I dreamt the past was never past redeeming:
But whether this was false or honest dreaming
I beg death's pardon now. And mourn the dead.

Think about the relationship between the essayist and her text and the poet and his text. Is this really Dillard in the essay or is this a fictional "Dillard"? How about Wilbur? We usually talk about the persona of a poem (the actor acting out the part, or a character the poet has created) to distinguish that person from the poet. Should we make such distinctions when we consider the "I" in the essay, or should we just assume that the "I" is in fact the essayist, pure and simple and unadorned? Think about this question and write a few paragraphs in which you work out your own opinion. Think about whether Dillard is creating a special "Dillard" in the essay. If she is, does it change the way we react to her ideas and to her? Compare that "Dillard" with the "Dillard" in one of her other essays.

C. Refer to "The Pardon" in suggestion B. Compare and contrast the way Dillard in her essay and the "I" in the poem deal with death.

D. Compare Dillard's account of death and pain with Orwell's account of shooting an elephant. If you did not know who wrote the essays, could you tell that one was written by a man and one by a woman? As you develop your explanation, look beyond the most obvious indications in the text. Look at nuances and images and attitudes. Consider strategies, the way the writer's mind plays over the material and leads the reader to a conclusion. Does woman write woman and man write man as one critic suggests, or is writing and thinking independent of gender? Test your conclusion against one or two other essays in this anthology. Make notes as you read, and be prepared to debate the topic when you come to class.

Sojourner

1 If survival is an art, then mangroves are artists of the beautiful: not only that they exist at all—smooth-barked, glossy-leaved, thickets of lapped mystery—but that they can and do exist as floating islands, as trees upright and loose, alive and homeless on the water.

2 I have seen mangroves, always on tropical ocean shores, in Florida and in the Galápagos. There is the red mangrove, the yellow, the button, and the black. They are all short, messy trees, waxy-leaved, laced all over with aerial roots, woody arching buttresses, and weird leathery berry pods. All this tangles from a black muck soil,

a black muck matted like a mud-sopped rag, a muck without any other plants, shaded, cold to the touch, tracked at the water's edge by herons and nosed by sharks.

3 It is these shoreline trees which, by a fairly common accident, can become floating islands. A hurricane flood or a riptide can wrest a tree from the shore, or from the mouth of a tidal river, and hurl it into the ocean. It floats. It is a mangrove island, blown.

4 There are floating islands on the planet; it amazes me. Credulous Pliny described some islands thought to be mangrove islands floating on a river. The people called these river islands *the dancers,* "because in any consort of musicians singing, they stir and move at the stroke of the feet, keeping time and measure."

5 Trees floating on rivers are less amazing than trees floating on the poisonous sea. A tree cannot live in salt. Mangrove trees exude salt from their leaves; you can see it, even on shoreline black mangroves, as a thin white crust. Lick a leaf and your tongue curls and coils; your mouth's a heap of salt.

6 Nor can a tree live without soil. A hurricane-born mangrove island may bring its own soil to the sea. But other mangrove trees make their own soil—and their own islands—from scratch. These are the ones which interest me. The seeds germinate in the fruit on the tree. The germinated embryo can drop anywhere—say, onto a dab of floating muck. The heavy root end sinks; a leafy plumule unfurls. The tiny seedling, afloat, is on its way. Soon aerial roots shooting out in all directions trap debris. The sapling's networks twine, the interstices narrow, and water calms in the lee. Bacteria thrive on organic broth; amphipods swarm. These creatures grow and die at the trees' wet feet. The soil thickens, accumulating rainwater, leaf rot, seashells, and guano; the island spreads.

7 More seeds and more muck yield more trees on the new island. A society grows, interlocked in a tangle of dependencies. The island rocks less in the swells. Fish throng to the backwaters stilled in snarled roots. Soon, Asian mudskippers—little four-inch fish—clamber up the mangrove roots into the air and peer about from periscope eyes on stalks, like snails. Oysters clamp to submersed roots, as do starfish, dog whelk, and the creatures that live among tangled kelp. Shrimp seek shelter there, limpets a holdfast, pelagic birds a rest.

8 And the mangrove island wanders on, afloat and adrift. It walks teetering and wanton before the wind. Its fate and direction are random. It may bob across an ocean and catch on another mainland's shores. It may starve or dry while it is still a sapling. It may topple in a storm, or pitchpole. By the rarest of chances, it may stave into another mangrove island in a crash of clacking roots, and mesh. What it is most likely to do is drift anywhere in the alien ocean, feeding on death and growing, netting a makeshift soil as it goes, shrimp in its toes and terns in its hair.

9 We could do worse.

10 I alternate between thinking of the planet as home—dear and familiar stone hearth and garden—and as a hard land of exile in which we are all sojourners. Today I favor the latter view. The word "sojourner" occurs often in the English Old Testament. It invokes a nomadic people's sense of vagrancy, a praying people's knowledge of estrangement, a thinking people's intuition of sharp loss: "For we are

strangers before thee, and sojourners, as were all our fathers: our days on the earth are as a shadow, and there is none abiding."

11 We don't know where we belong, but in times of sorrow it doesn't seem to be here, here with these silly pansies and witless mountains, here with sponges and hard-eyed birds. In times of sorrow the innocence of the other creatures—from whom and with whom we evolved—seems a mockery. Their ways are not our ways. We seem set among them as among lifelike props for a tragedy—or a broad lampoon—on a thrust rock stage.

12 It doesn't seem to be here that we belong, here where space is curved, the earth is round, we're all going to die, and it seems as wise to stay in bed as budge. It is strange here, not quite warm enough, or too warm, too leafy, or inedible, or windy, or dead. It is not, frankly, the sort of home for people one would have thought of—although I lack the fancy to imagine another.

13 The planet itself is a sojourner in airless space, a wet ball flung across nowhere. The few objects in the universe scatter. The coherence of matter dwindles and crumbles toward stillness. I have read, and repeated, that our solar system as a whole is careering through space toward a point east of Hercules. Now I wonder: what could that possibly mean, east of Hercules? Isn't space curved? When we get "there," how will our course change, and why? Will we slide down the universe's inside arc like mud slung at a wall? Or what sort of welcoming shore is this east of Hercules? Surely we don't anchor there, and disembark, and sweep in to dinner with our host. Does someone cry, "Last stop, last stop"? At any rate, east of Hercules, like east of Eden, isn't a place to call home. It is a course without direction; it is "out." And we are cast.

14 These are enervating thoughts, the thoughts of despair. They crowd back, unbidden, when human life as it unrolls goes ill, when we lose control of our lives or the illusion of control, and it seems that we are not moving toward any end but merely blown. Our life seems cursed to be a wiggle merely, and a wandering without end. Even nature is hostile and poisonous, as though it were impossible for our vulnerability to survive on these acrid stones.

15 Whether these thoughts are true or not I find less interesting than the possibilities for beauty they may hold. We are down here in time, where beauty grows. Even if things are as bad as they could possibly be, and as meaningless, then matters of truth are themselves indifferent; we may as well please our sensibilities and, with as much spirit as we can muster, go out with a buck and wing.

16 The planet is less like an enclosed spaceship—spaceship earth—than it is like an exposed mangrove island beautiful and loose. We the people started small and have since accumulated a great and solacing muck of soil, of human culture. We are rooted in it; we are bearing it with us across nowhere. The word "nowhere" is our cue: the consort of musicians strikes up, and we in the chorus stir and move and start twirling our hats. A mangrove island turns drift to dance. It creates its own soil as it goes, rocking over the salt sea at random, rocking day and night and round the sun, rocking round the sun and out toward east of Hercules.

(1982)

QUESTIONS

Thought and Structure

1. In what sense do you think the point of the essay is implied in this initial phrase: "If survival is an art"? If we remove the condition—survival is an art—and track that notion through the essay, does it take on new meaning? Look at it especially in light of the final paragraph.
2. In the first eight paragraphs Dillard tells us in great detail about "mangrove islands." What she gives us in those paragraphs is a miniprocess essay in which we find out how mangrove islands form themselves. But while she is giving us the details and the process of formation, she is doing something else. She is preparing us for the section of the essay that follows. Here are some of the clues: "There are floating islands on the planet"; "A society grows, interlocked in a tangle of dependencies"; "And the mangrove island wanders on, afloat and adrift." How do these clues foreshadow what follows?
3. How many senses of the word "sojourner" can you find in the essay?
4. What is the main idea of paragraphs 10–12? Paragraphs 13–14 present what Dillard calls "enervating thoughts." What does that mean? How does she counter those thoughts and change her rhetorical direction in the last two paragraphs of the essay?

Style and Strategy

5. What is the effect of her one-sentence paragraph (9)? How does it play on our minds as we read the rest of the essay?
6. This essay relies primarily on metaphorical thinking and analogy. What is the primary metaphor, and how does Dillard develop it?
7. Look at the last sentence of the essay with its three repetitive elements:

   It creates its own soil as it goes,
   rocking over the salt sea at random,
   rocking day and night and round the sun,
   rocking round the sun and out toward east of Hercules.

   Notice how Dillard repeats a phrase from the third element into the fourth. What is the immediate effect of the repetition? Read the sentence aloud before you answer that question. Does the form, the repetition in this case, have anything to do with the content or the idea she is developing in that last paragraph? Before you answer that question consider this sentence and its relationship to the one about rocking: "A mangrove island turns drift to dance." Dance?

SUGGESTIONS FOR WRITING

A. For starters, see if you can create a metaphor. Start with a simple one of your own, something like "So far my life is a dizzying journey." Go from that simple beginning to an elaboration or an extension of the metaphorical idea. Remember that metaphors are not signs; they do not point directly to something we know; they point beyond themselves to something we cannot account for absolutely.

B. Consider Didion's metaphor in "Goodbye to All That": "You will have perceived by now that I was not one to profit by the experience of others, that it was a very long time indeed before I stopped believing in new faces and began to understand the lesson in that story, which was that it is distinctly possible to stay too long at the Fair." Fair. That's it. How does Didion's use of her metaphor differ from the way Dillard uses hers? Record your answer to that fairly tough question by writing down in your journal the play of your mind as it considers the question. Do not try to write anything formal; just let your mind play with the question, but let it play through your pen or through your fingers at the keyboard.

God's Tooth

1 Into this world falls a plane.

2 The earth is a mineral speckle planted in trees. The plane snagged its wing on a tree, fluttered in a tiny arc, and struggled down.

3 I heard it go. The cat looked up. There was no reason: the plane's engine simply stilled after takeoff, and the light plane failed to clear the firs. It fell easily; one wing snagged on a fir top; the metal fell down the air and smashed in the thin woods where cattle browse; the fuel exploded; and Julie Norwich seven years old burnt off her face.

4 Little Julie mute in some room at St. Joe's now, drugs dissolving into the sheets. Little Julie with her eyes naked and spherical, baffled. Can you scream without lips? Yes. But do children in long pain scream?

5 It is November 19 and no wind, and no hope of heaven, and no wish for heaven, since the meanest of people show more mercy than hounding and terrorist gods.

6 The airstrip, a cleared washboard affair on the flat crest of a low hill, is a few long fields distant from my house—up the road and through the woods, or across the sheep pasture and through the woods. A flight instructor told me once that when his students get cocky, when they think they know how to fly a plane, he takes them out here and makes them land on that field. You go over the wires and down, and along the strip and up before the trees, or vice versa, vice versa, depending on the wind. But the airstrip is not unsafe. Jesse's engine failed. The FAA will cart the wreckage away, bit by bit, picking it out of the tree trunk, and try to discover just why that engine failed. In the meantime, the emergency siren has sounded, causing everyone who didn't see the plane go down to halt—Patty at her weaving, Jonathan slicing apples, Jan washing her baby's face—to halt, in pity and terror, wondering which among us got hit, by what bad accident, and why. The volunteer firemen have mustered; the fire trucks have come—stampeding Shuller's sheep—and gone, bearing burnt Julie and Jesse her father to the emergency room in town, leaving the rest of us to gossip, fight grass fires on the airstrip, and pray, or wander from window to window, fierce.

7 So she is burnt on her face and neck, Julie Norwich. The one whose teeth are short in a row, Jesse and Ann's oldest, red-kneed, green-socked, carrying cats.

8 I saw her only once. It was two weeks ago, under an English hawthorn tree, at the farm.

9 There are many farms in this neck of the woods, but only one we call "the farm"—the old Corcoran place, where Gus grows hay and raises calves: the farm, whose abandoned frame chicken coops ply the fields like longboats, like floating war canoes; whose clay driveway and grass footpaths are a tangle of orange calendula blossoms, ropes, equipment, and seeding grasses; the farm, whose canny heifers and bull calves figure the fences, run amok to the garden, and plant themselves suddenly black and white, up to their necks in green peas.

10 Between the gray farmhouse and the barn is the green grass farmyard, suitable for all projects. That day, sixteen of us were making cider. It was cold. There were piles of apples everywhere. We had filled our trucks that morning, climbing trees and shaking their boughs, dragging tarps heavy with apples, hauling bushels and boxes and buckets of apples, and loading them all back to the farm. Jesse and Ann, who are in their thirties, with Julie and the baby, whose name I forget, had driven down from the mountains that morning with a truckload of apples, loose, to make cider with us, fill their jugs, and drive back. I had not met them before. We all drank coffee on the farmhouse porch to warm us; we hosed jugs in the yard. Now we were throwing apples into a shredder and wringing the mash through pillowcases, staining our palms and freezing our fingers, and decanting the pails into seventy one-gallon jugs. And all this long day, Julie Norwich chased my cat Small around the farmyard and played with her, manhandled her, next to the porch under the hawthorn tree.

11 She was a thin child, pointy-chinned, yellow bangs and braids. She squinted, and when you looked at her she sometimes started laughing, as if you had surprised her at using some power she wasn't yet ready to show. I kept my eye on her, wondering if she was cold with her sweater unbuttoned and bony knees bare.

12 She would hum up a little noise for half-hour stretches. In the intervals, for maybe five minutes each, she was trying, very quietly, to learn to whistle. I think. Or she was practicing a certain concentrated face. But I think she was trying to learn to whistle, because sometimes she would squeak a little falsetto note through an imitation whistle hole in her lips, as if that could fool anyone. And all day she was dressing and undressing the yellow cat, sticking it into a black dress, a black dress long and full as a nun's.

13 I was amazed at that dress. It must have been some sort of doll clothing she had dragged with her in the truck; I've never seen its kind before or since. A white collar bibbed the yoke of it like a guimpe. It had great black sleeves like wings. Julie scooped up the cat and rammed her into the cloth. I knew how she felt, exasperated, breaking her heart on a finger curl's width of skinny cat arm. I knew the many feelings she had sticking those furry arms through the sleeves. Small is not large: her limbs feel like bird bones strung in a sock. When Julie had the cat dressed in its curious habit, she would rock it like a baby doll. The cat blinked, upside down.

14 Once she whistled at it, or tried, blowing in its face; the cat poured from her arms and ran. It leapt across the driveway, lightfoot in its sleeves; its black dress pulled this way and that, dragging dust, bent up in back by its yellow tail. I was squeezing one end of a twisted pillowcase full of apple mash and looking over my

shoulder. I watched the cat hurdle the driveway and vanish under the potting shed, cringing; I watched Julie dash after it without hesitation, seize it, hit its face, and drag it back to the tree, carrying it caught fast by either forepaw, so its body hung straight from its arms.

15 She saw me watching her and we exchanged a look, a very conscious and self-conscious look—because we look a bit alike and we both knew it; because she was still short and I grown; because I was stuck kneeling before the cider pail, looking at her sidewise over my shoulder; because she was carrying the cat so oddly, so that she had to walk with her long legs parted; because it was my cat, and she'd dressed it, and it looked like a nun; and because she knew I'd been watching her, and how fondly, all along. We were laughing.

16 We *looked* a bit alike. Her face is slaughtered now, and I don't remember mine. It is the best joke there is, that we are here, and fools—that we are sown into time like so much corn, that we are souls sprinkled at random like salt into time and dissolved here, spread into matter, connected by cells right down to our feet, and those feet likely to fell us over a tree root or jam us on a stone. The joke part is that we forget it. Give the mind two seconds alone and it thinks it's Pythagoras. We wake up a hundred times a day and laugh.

17 The joke of the world is less like a banana peel than a rake, the old rake in the grass, the one you step on, foot to forehead. It all comes together. In a twinkling. You have to admire the gag for its symmetry, accomplishing all with one right angle, the same right angle which accomplishes all philosophy. One step on the rake and it's mind under matter once again. You wake up with a piece of tree in your skull. You wake up with fruit on your hands. You wake up in a clearing and see yourself, ashamed. You see your own face and it's seven years old and there's no knowing why, or where you've been since. We're tossed broadcast into time like so much grass, some ravening god's sweet hay. You wake up and a plane falls out of the sky.

18 That day was a god, too, the day we made cider and Julie played under the hawthorn tree. He must have been a heyday sort of god, a husbandman. He was spread under gardens, sleeping in time, an innocent old man scratching his head, thinking of pruning the orchard, in love with families.

19 Has he no power? Can the other gods carry time and its loves upside down like a doll in their blundering arms? As though we the people were playing house—when we are serious and do love—and not the gods? No, that day's god has no power. No gods have power to save. There are only days. The one great god abandoned us to days, to time's tumult of occasions, abandoned us to the gods of days each brute and amok in his hugeness and idiocy.

20 Jesse her father had grabbed her clear of the plane this morning, and was hauling her off when the fuel blew. A glob of flung ignited vapor hit her face, or something flaming from the plane or fir tree hit her face. No one else was burned, or hurt in any way.

21 So this is where we are. Ashes, ashes, all fall down. How could I have forgotten? Didn't I see the heavens wiped shut just yesterday, on the road walking? Didn't I fall from the dark of the stars to these senselit and noisome days? The great ridged

granite millstone of time is illusion, for only the good is real; the great ridged granite millstone of space is illusion, for God is spirit and worlds his flimsiest dreams: but the illusions are almost perfect, are apparently perfect for generations on end, and the pain is also, and undeniably, real. The pain within the millstones' pitiless turning is real, for our love for each other—for world and all the products of extension—is real, vaulting, insofar as it is love, beyond the plane of the stones' sickening churn and arcing to the realm of spirit bare. And you can get caught holding one end of a love, when your father drops, and your mother; when a land is lost, or a time, and your friend blotted out, gone, your brother's body spoiled, and cold, your infant dead, and you dying: you reel out love's long line alone, stripped like a live wire loosing its sparks to a cloud, like a live wire loosed in space to longing and grief everlasting.

22 I sit at the window. It is a fool's lot, this sitting always at windows spoiling little blowy slips of paper and myself in the process. Shall I be old? Here comes Small, old sparrow-mouth, wanting my lap. Done. Do you have any earthly idea how young I am? Where's your dress, kitty? I suppose I'll outlive this wretched cat. Get another. Leave it my silver spoons, like old ladies you hear about. I prefer dogs.

23 So I read. Angels, I read, belong to nine different orders. Seraphs are the highest; they are aflame with love for God, and stand closer to him than the others. Seraphs love God; cherubs, who are second, possess perfect knowledge of him. So love is greater than knowledge; how could I have forgotten? The seraphs are born of a stream of fire issuing from under God's throne. They are, according to Dionysius the Areopagite, "all wings," having, as Isaiah noted, six wings apiece, two of which they fold over their eyes. Moving perpetually toward God, they perpetually praise him, crying Holy, Holy, Holy. . . . But, according to some rabbinic writings, they can sing only the first "Holy" before the intensity of their love ignites them again and dissolves them again, perpetually, into flames. "Abandon everything," Dionysius told his disciple. "God despises ideas."

24 God despises everything, apparently. If he abandoned us, slashing creation loose at its base from any roots in the real; and if we in turn abandon everything—all these illusions of time and space and lives—in order to love only the real: then where are we? Thought itself is impossible, for subject can have no guaranteed connection with object, nor any object with God. Knowledge is impossible. We are precisely nowhere, sinking on an entirely imaginary ice floe, into entirely imaginary seas themselves adrift. Then we reel out love's long line alone toward a God less lovable than a grasshead, who treats us less well than we treat our lawns.

25 Of faith I have nothing, only of truth: that this one God is a brute and traitor, abandoning us to time, to necessity and the engines of matter unhinged. This is no leap; this is evidence of things seen: one Julie, one sorrow, one sensation bewildering the heart, and enraging the mind, and causing me to look at the world stuff appalled, at the blithering rock of trees in a random wind, at my hand like some gibberish sprouted, my fist opening and closing, so that I think, Have I once turned my hand in this circus, have I ever called it home?

26 Faith would be that God is self-limited utterly by his creation—a contraction

of the scope of his will; that he bound himself to time and its hazards and haps as a man would lash himself to a tree for love. That God's works are as good as we make them. That God is helpless, our baby to bear, self-abandoned on the doorstep of time, wondered at by cattle and oxen. Faith would be that God moved and moves once and for all and "down," so to speak, like a diver, like a man who eternally gathers himself for a dive and eternally is diving, and eternally splitting the spread of the water, and eternally drowned.

27 Faith would be, in short, that God has any willful connection with time whatsoever, and with us. For I know it as given that God is all good. And I take it also as given that whatever he touches has meaning, if only in his mysterious terms, the which I readily grant. The question is, then, whether God touches anything. Is anything firm, or is time on the loose? Did Christ descend once and for all to no purpose, in a kind of divine and kenotic suicide, or ascend once and for all, pulling his cross up after him like a rope ladder home? Is there—even if Christ holds the tip of things fast and stretches eternity clear to the dim souls of men—is there no link at the base of things, some kernel or air deep in the matrix of matter from which universe furls like a ribbon twined into time?

28 Has God a hand in this? Then it is a good hand. But has he a hand at all? Or is he a holy fire burning self-contained for power's sake alone? Then he knows himself blissfully as flame unconsuming, as all brilliance and beauty and power, and the rest of us can go hang. Then the accidental universe spins mute, obedient only to its own gross terms, meaningless, out of mind, and alone. The universe is neither contingent upon nor participant in the holy, in being itself, the real, the power play of fire. The universe is illusion merely, not one speck of it real, and we are not only its victims, falling always into or smashed by a planet slung by its sun—but also its captives, bound by the mineral-made ropes of our senses.

29 But how do we know—how could we know—that the real is there? By what freak chance does the skin of illusion ever split, and reveal to us the real, which seems to know us by name, and by what freak chance and why did the capacity to prehend it evolve?

30 I sit at the window, chewing the bones in my wrist. Pray for them: for Julie, for Jesse her father, for Ann her mother, pray. Who will teach us to pray? The god of today is a glacier. We live in his shifting crevasses, unheard. The god of today is delinquent, a barn-burner, a punk with a pittance of power in a match. It is late, a late time to be living. Now it is afternoon; the sky is appallingly clear. Everything in the landscape points to sea, and the sea is nothing; it is snipped from the real as a stuff without form, rising up the sides of islands and falling, mineral to mineral, salt.

31 Everything I see—the water, the log-wrecked beach, the farm on the hill, the bluff, the white church in the trees—looks overly distinct and shining. (What is the relationship of color to this sun, of sun to anything else?) It all looks staged. It all looks brittle and unreal, a skin of colors painted on glass, which if you prodded it with a finger would powder and fall. A blank sky, perfectly blended with all other sky, has sealed over the crack in the world where the plane fell, and the air has hushed the matter up.

32 If days are gods, then gods are dead, and artists pyrotechnic fools. Time is a hurdy-gurdy, a lampoon, and death's a bawd. We're beheaded by the nick of time. We're logrolling on a falling world, on time released from meaning and rolling loose, like one of Atalanta's golden apples, a bauble flung and forgotten, lapsed, and the gods on the lam.

33 And now outside the window, deep on the horizon, a new thing appears, as if we needed a new thing. It is a new land blue beyond islands, hitherto hidden by haze and now revealed, and as dumb as the rest. I check my chart, my amateur penciled sketch of the skyline. Yes, this land is new, this spread blue spark beyond yesterday's new wrinkled line, beyond the blue veil a sailor said was Salt Spring Island. How long can this go on? But let us by all means extend the scope of our charts.

34 I draw it as I seem to see it, a blue chunk fitted just so beyond islands, a wag of graphite rising just here above another anonymous line, and here meeting the slope of Salt Spring: though whether this be headland I see or heartland, or the distance-blurred bluffs of a hundred bays, I have no way of knowing, or if it be island or main. I call it Thule, O Julialand, Time's Bad News; I name it Terror, the Farthest Limb of the Day, God's Tooth.

(1977)

QUESTIONS

Thought and Structure

1. The most basic question about this essay has a very complex answer. This is the question: What point or points is Dillard trying to make in this essay? Read carefully as you try to come to terms with the complex answer. Is Dillard angry, understanding, puzzled, baffled, reverent?
2. What caused the plane crash? Does it matter in terms of Dillard's inquiry?
3. At the beginning of section five (paragraphs 18–20), Dillard says, "That day was a god, too, the day we made cider and Julie played under the hawthorn tree." What does she mean by "That day was a god"? What especially does she mean by "too"? How does the "glob of flung ignited vapor" (paragraph 20) temper our judgment about the god who was in charge on that other day?
4. What do you make of Dillard's meditation in paragraphs 21–22? Why does she shift the focus from Julie to herself? What about love and pain? What seems to be their relationship in Dillard's mind? Where does God fit into this scheme of things?
5. In your own words, explain the meaning of "God's Tooth"—both the image and the essay.

Style and Strategy

6. Look carefully at the opening section of the essay. What is the tone of the first three paragraphs? When does the tone shift, and what is the effect on the next two para-

graphs? What does this shift in tone have to do with the point Dillard is trying to make in this essay? Why do you think Dillard refers to Julie Norwich as "Little Julie"? Why does Dillard introduce "the cat" in this opening section?

7. What are the effects of these two lists in paragraph 6: the first—"Patty at her weaving, Jonathan slicing apples, Jan washing her baby's face"—and the second—"bearing burnt Julie and Jesse her father to the emergency room in town, leaving the rest of us to gossip, fight grass fires on the airstrip, and pray, or wander from window to window, fierce"? Note particularly in that final series where Dillard shifts from "bearing" and "leaving" (verbals) to the explicit and implied infinitives: "to gossip, [to] fight . . . and [to] pray, or [to] wander . . . fierce." What do you think of the effectiveness of that shift?
8. Examine Dillard's mind in operation in section three (paragraphs 8–10) and in section four (paragraphs 11–17). What is the point of section three? How does the focus shift at the beginning of section four? Trace all of the shifts; write them down. Note the way Dillard establishes in our minds her relationship with Julie. Why does she concentrate so intently on the cat's clothing (its habit) and Julie's relationship with the cat? How does Julie actually treat the cat? Does Dillard, the owner of the cat, approve? What does Dillard's attitude have to do with the point she's trying to make in the essay? Why in this section does Dillard want us to imagine Julie's trying to whistle?
9. List and explain the comparisons in paragraphs 16 and 17. What do the comparisons have in common, and what point does Dillard make in using them? What is their purpose? To describe? To amuse? To explain? To persuade?
10. Look at paragraphs 19 and 21, 28 and 29, and also at paragraph 4—in that order. Why does Dillard ask so many questions in these paragraphs? Are the kinds of questions similar or different in each set of paragraphs? Explain.
11. What is the tone of paragraphs 24 and 25? Which words in particular convey that tone? In these paragraphs, what is Dillard's attitude toward God? Does her attitude seem to differ elsewhere in the essay?
12. In paragraphs 26 and 27 Dillard uses words and phrases that we have all heard before; she repeats those words and phrases at the beginning of her sentences. What advantage is there to such a procedure?

SUGGESTIONS FOR WRITING

A. Write an essay about an event that disturbed you, an event that you had (or still have) trouble understanding. Try to incorporate into your essay the process you underwent in trying to understand the experience.

B. Write an essay describing how you came to lose a belief you once held or how you came to believe something you formerly didn't believe. Why did you hold or not hold the belief in the first place? What prompted the change?

C. Rewrite paragraph 2, combining the short statements into longer, smoother sentences. Compare your version with that of another student, then with Dillard's version. What differences in tone and effect do you notice?

D. Write a paragraph exclusively, or almost exclusively, of questions (like paragraphs 27, 28, or 29).

E. Write a paragraph imitating the repetition of word and phrase at the beginnings of sentences that Dillard employs in paragraphs 26 and 27.

F. In this essay Dillard says that we are "precisely nowhere, sinking on an entirely imaginary ice floe, into entirely imaginary seas themselves adrift." In "Sojourner" she asks us to imagine that our planet is an island adrift, veering to the right of Hercules, out to an indeterminate point. Examine the two essays and write a few paragraphs comparing and contrasting Dillard's attitude to these similar fates. Try to account for any differences you see. Do those differences have anything to do with the requirements of her writing, of these two essays? Or can you think of other explanations for the differences?

SEVENTEEN

Gretel Ehrlich

(1946–   )

Gretel Ehrlich and her husband are ranchers in Wyoming. Born in California, educated at Bennington, the UCLA Film School, and the New School for Social Research, she went to Wyoming in 1976 to film a documentary on sheep herders. The spirit of place captured her, and after a brief stint of wandering following the loss of a loved one, she returned to stay. The essays in this anthology, taken from Ehrlich's first book *The Solace of Open Spaces* (1985), give us a sense of why she is there, as does the short story taken from *City Tales, Wyoming Stories* (1986), a collection she did with Edward Hoagland. Ehrlich has also published two volumes of poetry, and she is completing a novel *(Heart Mountain)* as well as a second collection of essays *Islands, Universe, and Home* (1988).

Ehrlich claims that when she went to Wyoming to make the documentary film, she "had the experience of waking up not knowing where I was, whether I was a man or a woman, or which toothbrush was mine." In the face of a personal tragedy, she says she "*had* lost (at least for a while) . . . my appetite for the life I had left: city surroundings, old friends, familiar comforts." She made her way through that fairly desperate stage, somehow getting round the road blocks: "The detour, of course, became the actual path; the digressions in my writing, the narrative." That writing began as "raw journal entries" shared with a friend, and those entries eventually became *Solace,* a collection of essays so astonishing that we believe Ehrlich got what she called the "truest art":

> The truest art I would strive for in any work would be to give the page the same qualities as earth: weather would land on it harshly; light would elucidate the most difficult truths; wind would sweep away obtuse padding. Finally, the lessons of impermanence taught me this: loss constitutes an odd kind of fullness; despair empties out into an unquenchable appetite for life.

Ehrlich shows us that she, like the earth, is acted upon by the storms, by the light, by the wind. It is not that the earth becomes personified but that she takes on the qualities of the earth. She becomes earth—at once full, barren, contradictory, acted upon, changed, and charged. When she finds beauty and sadness in the changing seasons we know why. She makes us feel and see and understand the reacting natural forces that bring about such changes on the earth and in the body. Hers is a sensuous delight mingled with sadness, and in such essays as "The Smooth Skull of Winter," and "A Storm, the Cornfield, and Elk," she puts us inside the envelop of change, awakening in us untapped yearnings.

Ehrlich's prose can be as spare and undecorated as a Wyoming plain in the glaring sun, but it can also be as magical as the clouds that blow by from nowhere, changing a hot day into thunder and cloud and snow. To pass those changes off as "fancy pants prose" as one reporter did is to fail to see how apt are the changes, how broad the range of her prose performance. An essay like "Skull" develops almost entirely through images of natural beauty where another, such as "About Men," depends on dozens of small stories about the cowboys Ehrlich knows, the men she rubs working shoulders with, and admires for their rough tenderness. Occasionally both image and explanation come together in delightful ways: "Twenty or thirty below makes the breath we exchange visible: all of mine for all of yours. It is the tacit way we express the intimacy no one talks about." She has a fine ear for the western voice and for the local sayings that capture character; she has an even finer sense of how to use such local color to make her points and enliven her essays. Listen, for example to Frank Hinckley, in "On Water." His business is to spread scarce water when it comes down the mountains with the spring thaws: "Irrigating is a contemptible damned job. I've been fighting water all my life. Mother Nature is a bitter old bitch, isn't she? But we have to have that challenge. We crave it and I'll be goddamned if I know why." Frank goes on to show why he does: "I love the fragrances—grass growing, wild rose on the ditch bank—and hearing the damned old birds twittering away. How can we live without that?" Ehrlich asks the same question over and over, but in different and more revealing ways.

Ehrlich sees Mother Nature as plainly as Frank Hinckley. When she writes about Her, she does so not in the cowboy's idiom, but in the language of a woman who both sees and feels the natural life. Less bookish and less overtly metaphysical than Annie Dillard, Ehrlich gives us a sense not of the theological mysteries behind Nature's veil but of the female mysteries, the ones we've almost forgotten to think about, reminded of them by the myths we occasionally read. Nature is more than a mere idea in Ehrlich's mind. She suggests that we are living the myths. Life acts on us; we in turn enact the myths.

Her stories as well as her essays remind us how much she cares about people. Each story is a study not just of a simple life but of lives interacting, moving beyond themselves. Little people become larger than the lives they live, and all of them are, in her eyes, as "eccentric as they are ordinary." McKay's life is lived out at the hands of what seems a merciless fate, but the story of that life moves us, calls on us to see larger possibilities in our own lives. McKay and the characters in the other stories all live in a small Wyoming town near Heart Mountain Relocation Camp, a holding area for Japanese-Americans during World War II. Ehrlich shows us in these stories how town and camp interact. "McKay" shows us most clearly how loneliness dogs the human spirit. It also shows us that Ehrlich learned much from the masters she cites in her "Foreword" to the collection: V. S. Pritchett, Faulkner, D. H. Lawrence, Hemingway, and Chekhov. She knows about the human heart in conflict with itself, about the vitality of animal life, about spareness and economy, about the relationship between the land and its people. But she also knows much that she did not learn from anyone else. In both the stories and the essays, we sense the emerging vision of a writer who cares not only about her words but also about her land, her characters, and our lives.

About Men

1 When I'm in New York but feeling lonely for Wyoming I look for the Marlboro ads in the subway. What I'm aching to see is horseflesh, the glint of a spur, a line of distant mountains, brimming creeks, and a reminder of the ranchers and cowboys I've ridden with for the last eight years. But the men I see in those posters with their stern, humorless looks remind me of no one I know here. In our hellbent earnestness to romanticize the cowboy we've ironically disesteemed his true character. If he's "strong and silent" it's because there's probably no one to talk to. If he "rides away into the sunset" it's because he's been on horseback since four in the morning moving cattle and he's trying, fifteen hours later, to get home to his family. If he's "a rugged individualist" he's also part of a team: ranch work is teamwork and even the glorified open-range cowboys of the 1880s rode up and down the Chisholm Trail in the company of twenty or thirty other riders. Instead of the macho, trigger-happy man our culture has perversely wanted him to be, the cowboy is more apt to be convivial, quirky, and softhearted. To be "tough" on a ranch has nothing to do with conquests and displays of power. More often than not, circumstances—like the colt he's riding or an unexpected blizzard—are overpowering him. It's not toughness but "toughing it out" that counts. In other words, this macho, cultural artifact the cowboy has become is simply a man who possesses resilience, patience, and an instinct for survival. "Cowboys are just like a pile of rocks—everything happens to them. They get climbed on, kicked, rained and snowed on, scuffed up by wind. Their job is 'just to take it,' " one old-timer told me.

2 A cowboy is someone who loves his work. Since the hours are long—ten to fifteen hours a day—and the pay is $30 he has to. What's required of him is an odd mixture of physical vigor and maternalism. His part of the beef-raising industry is to birth and nurture calves and take care of their mothers. For the most part his work is done on horseback and in a lifetime he sees and comes to know more animals than people. The iconic myth surrounding him is built on American notions of heroism: the index of a man's value as measured in physical courage. Such ideas have perverted manliness into a self-absorbed race for cheap thrills. In a rancher's world, courage has less to do with facing danger than with acting spontaneously—usually on behalf of an animal or another rider. If a cow is stuck in a boghole he throws a loop around her neck, takes his dally (a half hitch around the saddle horn), and pulls her out with horsepower. If a calf is born sick, he may take her home, warm her in front of the kitchen fire, and massage her legs until dawn. One friend, whose favorite horse was trying to swim a lake with hobbles on, dove under water and cut her legs loose with a knife, then swam her to shore, his arm around her neck lifeguard-style, and saved her from drowning. Because these incidents are usually linked to someone or something outside himself, the westerner's courage is selfless, a form of compassion.

3 The physical punishment that goes with cowboying is greatly underplayed. Once fear is dispensed with, the threshold of pain rises to meet the demands of the job. When Jane Fonda asked Robert Redford (in the film *Electric Horseman*) if he

was sick as he struggled to his feet one morning, he replied, "No, just bent." For once the movies had it right. The cowboys I was sitting with laughed in agreement. Cowboys are rarely complainers; they show their stoicism by laughing at themselves.

4 If a rancher or cowboy has been thought of as a "man's man"—laconic, hard-drinking, inscrutable—there's almost no place in which the balancing act between male and female, manliness and femininity, can be more natural. If he's gruff, handsome, and physically fit on the outside, he's androgynous at the core. Ranchers are midwives, hunters, nurturers, providers, and conservationists all at once. What we've interpreted as toughness—weathered skin, calloused hands, a squint in the eye and a growl in the voice—only masks the tenderness inside. "Now don't go telling me these lambs are cute," one rancher warned me the first day I walked into the football-field-sized lambing sheds. The next thing I knew he was holding a black lamb. "Ain't this little rat good-lookin'?"

5 So many of the men who came to the West were southerners—men looking for work and a new life after the Civil War—that chivalrousness and strict codes of honor were soon thought of as western traits. There were very few women in Wyoming during territorial days, so when they did arrive (some as mail-order brides from places like Philadelphia) there was a stand-offishness between the sexes and a formality that persists now. Ranchers still tip their hats and say, "Howdy, ma'am" instead of shaking hands with me.

6 Even young cowboys are often evasive with women. It's not that they're Jekyll and Hyde creatures—gentle with animals and rough on women—but rather, that they don't know how to bring their tenderness into the house and lack the vocabulary to express the complexity of what they feel. Dancing wildly all night becomes a metaphor for the explosive emotions pent up inside, and when these are, on occasion, released, they're so battery-charged and potent that one caress of the face or one "I love you" will peal for a long while.

7 The geographical vastness and the social isolation here make emotional evolution seem impossible. Those contradictions of the heart between respectability, logic, and convention on the one hand, and impulse, passion, and intuition on the other, played out wordlessly against the paradisical beauty of the West, give cowboys a wide-eyed but drawn look. Their lips pucker up, not with kisses but with immutability. They may want to break out, staying up all night with a lover just to talk, but they don't know how and can't imagine what the consequences will be. Those rare occasions when they do bare themselves result in confusion. "I feel as if I'd sprained my heart," one friend told me a month after such a meeting.

8 My friend Ted Hoagland wrote, "No one is as fragile as a woman but no one is as fragile as a man." For all the women here who use "fragileness" to avoid work or as a sexual ploy, there are men who try to hide theirs, all the while clinging to an adolescent dependency on women to cook their meals, wash their clothes, and keep the ranch house warm in winter. But there is true vulnerability in evidence here. Because these men work with animals, not machines or numbers, because they live outside in landscapes of torrential beauty, because they are confined to a place and a routine embellished with awesome variables, because calves die in the arms that pulled others into life, because they go to the mountains as if on a pilgrimage

to find out what makes a herd of elk tick, their strength is also a softness, their toughness, a rare delicacy.

(1985)

QUESTIONS

Thought and Structure

1. What does Ehrlich mean when she says that the cowboy must have an "odd mixture of physical vigor and maternalism"? In what ways does she try to convince you that this notion is sound?
2. In paragraph 4 Ehrlich claims that under certain circumstances, a rancher or cowboy is "androgynous at the core." What is she suggesting?
3. What does Ehrlich mean by the underlined phrase in this sentence from paragraph 7: "Their lips pucker up, not with kisses but with immutability"?
4. There are only eight short paragraphs in this essay. Identify the main idea for each paragraph, and see if you can find logical connections, common threads that tie this rhetorical package together.

Style and Strategy

5. Think, if you will, in traditional rhetorical terms. Consider this essay a *definition.* Jot down the various ways Ehrlich develops her definition of a cowboy, ways that convince you she knows what she is talking about. Consider the different kinds of evidence she uses.
6. Look at Ehrlich's very first sentence. Try to think of what she accomplishes in just that sentence. She gives you, among other things, an image and a mood. What are they? In that paragraph, she also has a number of expressions in quotation marks. What do those expressions represent? How does she make use of them? How do they differ from the final quotation in the paragraph?
7. Why do you think Ehrlich chose the word "peal" in the last sentence of paragraph 6: "one 'I love you' will peal for a long while"?
8. What are the distinguishing features of the last sentence of Ehrlich's essay? Do you find the sentence effective? Is it, in and of itself, an adequate conclusion for the essay? Explain. Can you think of any reason why Ehrlich might have set this sentence apart in a separate, final paragraph?

SUGGESTIONS FOR WRITING

A. Write an essay of your own that demonstrates the truth of Ehrlich's claim: "It's not toughness but 'toughing it out' that counts." Your essay, of course, need not be about cowboys. Call on your own experience for evidence. Or you might argue for a counter-proposal such as this:

> Gretel Ehrlich, trying to revise our notions about cowboys, makes this general assertion about the men she rides with and lives around in Wyoming: "It's not toughness but

'toughing it out' that counts." Ehrlich may be right about cowboys, but I've found that you have to be very tough to tough it out. This is a dog-eat-dog world we live in, and toughing it out with tenderness just won't always get the job done.

B. Write an essay that poses an answer to this question: To what extent is it still true in the community where you live that "the index of a man's value [is] measured in physical courage"? Consider Ehrlich's argument in paragraph 2 as you develop your own.

C. Throughout this essay Ehrlich makes use of *examples.* Find one paragraph where you think her examples are particularly effective. Explain why they work. Find another paragraph were they do not work. Explain why.

D. Develop a character sketch of a man or woman you know who doesn't "know how to bring . . . tenderness into the house and lack[s] the vocabulary to express the complexity of what [he or she] feel[s]."

E. Read all of Ehrlich's essays in this anthology to get a full sense of what she thinks about cowboys and ranchers. Think too about her writing and the way she "treats" her subjects. Assume that you are Gretel Ehrlich and write a letter to Larry King about his essay "Playing Cowboy." The idea is not to attack King, but to try to initiate a dialogue with him that might focus on two subjects: cowboys and writing.

F. When this essay appeared in *Harper's,* it was titled "Revisionist Cowboy." Write a couple of paragraphs defending one title or the other. Select your evidence from within the essay.

The Smooth Skull of Winter

1 Winter looks like a fictional place, an elaborate simplicity, a Nabokovian invention of rarefied detail. Winds howl all night and day, pushing litters of storm fronts from the Beartooth to the Big Horn Mountains. When it lets up, the mountains disappear. The hayfield that runs east from my house ends in a curl of clouds that have fallen like sails luffing from sky to ground. Snow returns across the field to me, and the cows, dusted with white, look like snowcapped continents drifting.

2 The poet Seamus Heaney said that landscape is sacramental, to be read as text. Earth is instinct: perfect, irrational, semiotic. If I read winter right, it is a scroll—the white growing wider and wider like the sweep of an arm—and from it we gain a peripheral vision, a capacity for what Nabokov calls "those asides of spirit, those footnotes in the volume of life by which we know life and find it to be good."

3 Not unlike emotional transitions—the loss of a friend or the beginning of new work—the passage of seasons is often so belabored and quixotic as to deserve separate names so the year might be divided eight ways instead of four.

4 This fall ducks flew across the sky in great "V"s as if that one letter were defecting from the alphabet, and when the songbirds climbed to the memorized pathways that route them to winter quarters, they lifted off in a confusion, like paper scraps blown from my writing room.

5 A Wyoming winter laminates the earth with white, then hardens the lacquer work with wind. Storms come announced by what old-timers call "mare's tails"—long wisps that lash out from a snow cloud's body. Jack Davis, a packer who used to trail his mules all the way from Wyoming to southern Arizona when the first snows came, said, "The first snowball that hits you is God's fault; the second one is yours."

6 Every three days or so white pastures glide overhead and drop themselves like skeins of hair to earth. The Chinese call snow that has drifted "white jade mountains," but winter looks oceanic to me. Snow swells, drops back, and hits the hulls of our lives with a course-bending sound. Tides of white are overtaken by tides of blue, and the logs in the woodstove, like sister ships, tick toward oblivion.

7 On the winter solstice it is thirty-four degrees below zero and there is very little in the way of daylight. The deep ache of this audacious Arctic air is also the ache in our lives made physical. Patches of frostbite show up on our noses, toes, and ears. Skin blisters as if cold were a kind of radiation to which we've been exposed. It strips what is ornamental in us. Part of the ache we feel is also a softness growing. Our connections with neighbors—whether strong or tenuous, as lovers or friends—become too urgent to disregard. We rub the frozen toes of a stranger whose pickup has veered off the road; we open water gaps with a tamping bar and an ax; we splice a friend's frozen water pipe; we take mittens and blankets to the men who herd sheep. Twenty or thirty below makes the breath we exchange visible: all of mine for all of yours. It is the tacit way we express the intimacy no one talks about.

8 One of our recent winters is sure to make the history books because of not the depth of snow but, rather, the depth of cold. For a month the mercury never rose above zero and at night it was fifty below. Cows and sheep froze in place and an oil field worker who tried taking a shortcut home was found next spring two hundred yards from his back door. To say you were snowed in didn't express the problem. You were either "froze in," "froze up," or "froze out," depending on where your pickup or legs stopped working. The day I helped tend sheep camp we drove through a five-mile tunnel of snow. The herder had marked his location for us by deliberately cutting his finger and writing a big "X" on the ice with his blood.

9 When it's fifty below, the mercury bottoms out and jiggles there as if laughing at those of us still above ground. Once I caught myself on tiptoes, peering down into the thermometer as if there were an extension inside inscribed with higher and higher declarations of physical misery: ninety below to the power of ten and so on.

10 Winter sets up curious oppositions in us. Where a wall of snow can seem threatening, it also protects our staggering psyches. All this cold has an anesthetizing effect: the pulse lowers and blankets of snow induce sleep. Though the rancher's workload is lightened in winter because of the short days, the work that does need to be done requires an exhausting patience. And while earth's sudden frigidity can seem to dispossess us, the teamwork on cold nights during calving, for instance, creates a profound camaraderie—one that's laced with dark humor, an effervescent lunacy, and unexpected fits of anger and tears. To offset Wyoming's Arctic seascape, a nightly flush of Northern Lights dances above the Big Horns, irradiating winter's pallor and reminding us that even though at this time of year we veer toward our

various nests and seclusions, nature expresses itself as a bright fuse, irrepressible and orgasmic.

11 Winter is smooth-skulled, and all our skids on black ice are cerebral. When we begin to feel cabin-feverish, the brain pistons thump against bone and mind irrupts—literally invading itself—unable to get fresh air. With the songbirds gone only scavengers are left: magpies, crows, eagles. As they pick on road-killed deer we humans are apt to practice the small cruelties on each other.

12 We suffer from snow blindness, selecting what we see and feel while our pain whites itself out. But where there is suffocation and self-imposed ignorance, there is also refreshment—snow on flushed cheeks and a pristine kind of thinking. All winter we skate the small ponds—places that in summer are water holes for cattle and sheep—and here a reflection of mind appears, sharp, vigilant, precise. Thoughts, bright as frostfall, skate through our brains. In winter, consciousness looks like an etching.

(1985)

QUESTIONS

Thought and Structure

1. Ehrlich paraphrases Seamus Heaney in the second paragraph and then immediately offers her own version of landscape: "Earth is instinct: perfect, irrational, semiotic." What does this statement mean? Might it be taken as the point of the essay, or is it too broad? How important is Nabokov's phrase "asides of spirit" to the meaning of this essay?
2. How does a threatening "wall of snow" protect their "staggering psyches" during those Wyoming winters (paragraph 10)? Does Ehrlich substantiate her claim that "teamwork on cold nights . . . creates a profound camaraderie"? Why do you suppose Ehrlich claims that "nature expresses itself as a bright fuse, irrepressible and orgasmic"? What does she mean?
3. Ehrlich closes her essay with an image: "In winter, consciousness looks like an etching." What does that suggest to you? Is that image an adequate one to account for the entire essay, or is there more to "The Smooth Skull of Winter"? Explain.

Style and Strategy

4. How, in the first sentence of the essay, does Ehrlich make it unnecessary for you to know anything about Nabokov to understand her allusion to him? Why do you suppose she alludes to him, turning him into an adjective, Nabokovian? In the second paragraph, Ehrlich refers more directly to another writer, Seamus Heaney, and then refers again to Nabokov, more directly this time. What is her strategy? Is she making obvious good use of these writers, and is she also doing more than meets the eye, creating mood, perhaps? Explain.
5. In the first paragraph Ehrlich relies very much on images. List them and see if they tell you anything about the meaning of this essay. Pay particular attention to the opening clause: "Winter looks like a fictional place. . . ." Does this essay turn out to make other claims, or does Ehrlich simply develop that idea in interesting, elaborate ways? Explain.

6. In paragraph 6, Ehrlich moves very subtly from snow and clouds to something human: "Snow swells, drops back, and hits the hulls of our lives with a course-bending sound." Can you see more clearly in paragraph 7 why she makes this transition? Explain. Find the complementary sentence in paragraph 7, and look at the evidence Ehrlich accumulates to illustrate her point.
7. In paragraph 8 we get a chance to compare the way Ehrlich accounts for Wyoming winters and the way the less articulate natives account for them (" 'froze in,' 'froze up,' or 'froze out' "). Which way do you prefer? Why? How effectively does Ehrlich combine the two ways of speaking in that paragraph? Explain.

SUGGESTIONS FOR WRITING

A. Go to the Library and read Dillard's essay "Untying the Knot," from her book *Pilgrim at Tinker Creek.* Write a paragraph, speculating about Dillard's reaction to Ehrlich's claim that "the passage of seasons is often so belabored and quixotic as to deserve separate names so the year might be divided eight ways instead of four."

B. Write a short essay about one of the seasons, relying as Ehrlich does almost entirely on the images you can create. As you do your prewriting, concentrate primarily on developing the images, relying on memory or your observations as you walk around trying to see more clearly. If you have no mental pictures to recall from memory, read Dillard's essay "Seeing" before you go out to look around. After you have done your preliminary work—observing, taking notes, recalling, developing your images—look at your collection of pictures; see if they contain a hidden idea or two. Consider those ideas as you look for the point you want your essay to make. After you find the idea, let it guide you as you reshape your preliminary work, creating an essay.

On Water

1 Frank Hinckley, a neighboring rancher in his seventies, would rather irrigate than ride a horse. He started spreading water on his father's hay- and grainfields when he was nine, and his long-term enthusiasm for what's thought of disdainfully by cowboys as "farmers' work" is an example of how a discipline—a daily chore—can grow into a fidelity. When I saw Frank in May he was standing in a dry irrigation ditch looking toward the mountains. The orange tarp dams, hung like curtains from ten-foot-long poles, fluttered in the wind like prayer flags. In Wyoming we are supplicants, waiting all spring for the water to come down, for the snow pack to melt and fill the creeks from which we irrigate. Fall and spring rains amount to less than eight inches a year, while above our ranches, the mountains hold their snows like a secret: no one knows when they will melt or how fast. When the water does come, it floods through the state as if the peaks were silver pitchers tipped forward by mistake. When I looked in, the ditch water had begun dripping over Frank's feet. Then we heard a sound that might have been wind in a steep patch of pines. "Jumpin' Jesus, here it comes," he said, as a head of water, brown and

foamy as beer, snaked toward us. He set five dams, digging the bright edges of plastic into silt. Water filled them the way wind fattens a sail, and from three notches cut in the ditch above each dam, water coursed out over a hundred acres of hayfield. When he finished, and the beadwork wetness had spread through the grass, he lowered himself to the ditch and rubbed his face with water.

2 A season of irrigating here lasts four months. Twenty, thirty, or as many as two hundred dams are changed every twelve hours, ditches are repaired and head gates adjusted to match the inconsistencies of water flow. By September it's over: all but the major Wyoming rivers dry up. Running water is so seasonal it's thought of as a mark on the calendar—a vague wet spot—rather than a geographical site. In May, June, July, and August, water is the sacristy at which we kneel; it equates time going by too fast.

3 Waiting for water is just one of the ways Wyoming ranchers find themselves at the mercy of weather. The hay they irrigate, for example, has to be cut when it's dry but baled with a little dew on it to preserve the leaf. Three days after Frank's water came down, a storm dumped three feet of snow on his alfalfa and the creeks froze up again. His wife, "Mike," who grew up in the arid Powder River country, and I rode to the headwaters of our creeks. The elk we startled had been licking ice in a draw. A snow squall rose up from behind a bare ridge and engulfed us. We built a twig fire behind a rock to warm ourselves, then rode home. The creeks didn't thaw completely until June.

4 Despite the freak snow, April was the second driest in a century; in the lower elevations there had been no precipitation at all. Brisk winds forwarded thunderclouds into local skies—commuters from other states—but the streamers of rain they let down evaporated before touching us. All month farmers and ranchers burned their irrigation ditches to clear them of obstacles and weeds—optimistic that water would soon come. Shell Valley resembled a battlefield: lines of blue smoke banded every horizon and the cottonwoods that had caught fire by mistake, their outstretched branches blazing, looked human. April, the cruelest month, the month of dry storms.

5 Six years ago, when I lived on a large sheep ranch, a drought threatened. Every water hole on 100,000 acres of grazing land went dry. We hauled water in clumsy beet-harvest trucks forty miles to spring range, and when we emptied them into a circle of stock tanks, the sheep ran toward us. They pushed to get at the water, trampling lambs in the process, then drank it all in one collective gulp. Other Aprils have brought too much moisture in the form of deadly storms. When a ground blizzard hit one friend's herd in the flatter, eastern part of the state, he knew he had to keep his cattle drifting. If they hit a fence line and had to face the storm, snow would blow into their noses and they'd drown. "We cut wire all the way to Nebraska," he told me. During the same storm another cowboy found his cattle too late: they were buried in a draw under a fifteen-foot drift.

6 High water comes in June when the runoff peaks, and it's another bugaboo for the ranchers. The otherwise amiable thirty-foot-wide creeks swell and change courses so that when we cross them with livestock, the water is belly-deep or more. Cowboys in the 1800s who rode with the trail herds from Texas often worked in

the big rivers on horseback for a week just to cross a thousand head of longhorn steers, losing half of them in the process. On a less-grand scale we have drownings and near drownings here each spring. When we crossed a creek this year the swift current toppled a horse and carried the rider under a log. A cowboy who happened to look back saw her head go under, dove in from horseback, and saved her. At Trapper Creek, where Owen Wister spent several summers in the 1920s and entertained Mr. Hemingway, a cloudburst slapped down on us like a black eye. Scraps of rainbow moved in vertical sweeps of rain that broke apart and disappeared behind a ridge. The creek flooded, taking out a house and a field of corn. We saw one resident walking in a flattened alfalfa field where the river had flowed briefly. "Want to go fishing?" he yelled to us as we rode by. The fish he was throwing into a white bucket were trout that had been "beached" by the flood.

7 Westerners are ambivalent about water because they've never seen what it can create except havoc and mud. They've never walked through a forest of wild orchids or witnessed the unfurling of five-foot-high ferns. "The only way I like my water is if there's whiskey in it," one rancher told me as we weaned calves in a driving rainstorm. That day we spent twelve hours on horseback in the rain. Despite protective layers of clothing: wool union suits, chaps, ankle-length yellow slickers, neck scarves and hats, we were drenched. Water drips off hat brims into your crotch; boots and gloves soak through. But to stay home out of the storm is deemed by some as a worse fate: "Hell, my wife had me cannin' beans for a week," one cowboy complained. "I'd rather drown like a muskrat out there."

8 Dryness is the common denominator in Wyoming. We're drenched more often in dust than in water; it is the scalpel and the suit of armor that make westerners what they are. Dry air presses a stockman's insides outward. The secret, inner self is worn not on the sleeve but in the skin. It's an unlubricated condition: there's not enough moisture in the air to keep the whole emotional machinery oiled and working. "What you see is what you get, but you have to learn to look to see all that's there," one young rancher told me. He was physically reckless when coming to see me or leaving. That was his way of saying he had and would miss me, and in the clean, broad sweeps of passion between us, there was no heaviness, no muddy residue. Cowboys have learned not to waste words from not having wasted water, as if verbosity would create a thirst too extreme to bear. If voices are raspy, it's because vocal cords are coated with dust. When I helped ship seven thousand head of steers one fall, the dust in the big, roomy sorting corrals churned as deeply and sensually as water. We wore scarves over our noses and mouths; the rest of our faces blackened with dirt so we looked like raccoons or coal miners. The westerner's face is stiff and dark red as jerky. It gives no clues beyond the discerning look that says, "You've been observed." Perhaps the too-early lines of aging that pull across these ranchers' necks are really cracks in a wall through which we might see the contradictory signs of their character: a complacency, a restlessness, a shy, boyish pride.

9 I knew a sheepherder who had the words "hard luck" tattooed across his knuckles. "That's for all the times I've been dry," he explained. "And when you've been as thirsty as I've been, you don't forget how something tastes." That's how he mapped out the big ranch he worked for: from thirst to thirst, whiskey to whiskey.

To follow the water courses in Wyoming—seven rivers and a network of good-sized creeks—is to trace the history of settlement here. After a few bad winters the early ranchers quickly discovered the necessity of raising feed for livestock. Long strips of land on both sides of the creeks and rivers were grabbed up in the 1870s and '80s before Wyoming was a state. Land was cheap and relatively easy to accumulate, but control of water was crucial. The early ranches such as the Swan Land & Cattle Company, the Budd Ranch, the M-L, the Bug Ranch, and the Pitchfork took up land along the Chugwater, Green, Greybull, Big Horn, and Shoshone rivers. It was not long before feuds over water began. The old law of "full and undiminished flow" to those who owned land along a creek was changed to one that adjudicated and allocated water by the acre foot to specified pieces of land. By 1890 residents had to file claims for the right to use the water that flowed through their ranches. These rights were, and still are, awarded according to the date a ranch was established regardless of ownership changes. This solved the increasing problem of upstream-downstream disputes, enabling the first ranch established on a creek to maintain the first water right, regardless of how many newer settlements occurred upstream.

10 Land through which no water flowed posed another problem. Frank's father was one of the Mormon colonists sent by Brigham Young to settle and put under cultivation the arid Big Horn Basin. The twenty thousand acres they claimed were barren and waterless. To remedy this problem they dug a canal thirty-seven miles long, twenty-seven feet across, and sixteen feet deep by hand. The project took four years to complete. Along the way a huge boulder gave the canal diggers trouble: it couldn't be moved. As a last resort the Mormon men held hands around the rock and prayed. The next morning the boulder rolled out of the way.

11 Piousness was not always the rule. Feuds over water became venomous as the population of the state grew. Ditch riders—so called because they monitored on horseback the flow and use of water—often found themselves on the wrong end of an irrigating shovel. Frank remembers when the ditch rider in his district was hit over the head so hard by the rancher whose water he was turning off that he fell unconscious into the canal, floating on his back until he bumped into the next head gate.

12 With the completion of the canal, the Mormons built churches, schools, and houses communally, working in unison as if taking their cue from the water that snaked by them. "It was a socialistic sonofabitch from the beginning," Frank recalls, "a beautiful damned thing. These 'western individualists' forget how things got done around here and not so damned many years ago at that."

13 Frank is the opposite of the strapping, conservative western man. Sturdy, but small-boned, he has an awkward, knock-kneed gait that adds to his chronic amiability. Though he's made his life close to home, he has a natural, panoramic vision as if he had upped-periscope through the Basin's dust clouds and had a good look around. Frank's generosity runs like water: it follows the path of least resistance and, tumbling downhill, takes on a fullness so replete and indiscriminate as to sometimes appear absurd. "You can't cheat an honest man," he'll tell you and laugh at the paradox implied. His wide face and forehead indicate the breadth of his unruly fair-mindedness—one that includes not just local affections but the whole human community.

14 When Frank started irrigating there were no tarp dams. "We plugged up those ditches with any old thing we had—rags, bones, car parts, sod." Though he could afford to hire an irrigator now he prefers to do the work himself, and when I'm away he turns my water as well, then mows my lawn. "Irrigating is a contemptible damned job. I've been fighting water all my life. Mother Nature is a bitter old bitch, isn't she? But we have to have that challenge. We crave it and I'll be goddamned if I know why. I feel sorry for these damned rich ranchers with their pumps and sprinkler systems and gated pipe because they're missing out on something. When I go to change my water at dawn and just before dark, it's peaceful out there, away from everybody. I love the fragrances—grass growing, wild rose on the ditch bank—and hearing the damned old birds twittering away. How can we live without that?"

15 Two thousand years before the Sidon Canal was built in Wyoming, the Hohokam, a people who lived in what became Arizona, used digging sticks to channel water from the Salt and Gila rivers to dry land. Theirs was the most extensive irrigation system in aboriginal North America. Water was brought thirty miles to spread over fields of corn, beans, and pumpkins—crops inherited from tribes in South and Central America. "It's a primitive damned thing," Frank said about the business of using water. "The change from a digging stick to a shovel isn't much of an evolution. Playing with water is something all kids have done, whether it's in creeks or in front of fire hydrants. Maybe that's how agriculture got started in the first place."

16 Romans applied their insoluble cement to waterways as if it could arrest the flux and impermanence they knew water to signify. Of the fourteen aqueducts that brought water from mountains and lakes to Rome, several are still in use today. On a Roman latifundium—their equivalent of a ranch—they grew alfalfa, a hot-weather crop introduced by way of Persia and Greece around the fifth century B.C., and fed it to their horses as we do here. Feuds over water were common: Nero was reprimanded for bathing in the canal that carried the city's drinking water, the brothels tapped aqueducts on the sly until once the whole city went dry. The Empire's staying power began to collapse when the waterways fell into disrepair. Crops dried up and the water that had carried life to the great cities stagnated and became breeding grounds for mosquitoes until malaria, not water, flowed into the heart of Rome.

17 There is nothing in nature that can't be taken as a sign of both mortality and invigoration. Cascading water equates loss followed by loss, a momentum of things falling in the direction of death, then life. In Conrad's *Heart of Darkness,* the river is a redundancy flowing through rain forest, a channel of solitude, a solid thing, a trap. Hemingway's Big Two-Hearted River is the opposite: it's an accepting, restorative place. Water can stand for what is unconscious, instinctive, and sexual in us, for the creative swill in which we fish for ideas. It carries, weightlessly, the imponderable things in our lives: death and creation. We can drown in it or else stay buoyant, quench our thirst, stay alive.

18 In Navajo mythology, rain is the sun's sperm coming down. A Crow woman I met on a plane told me that. She wore a flowered dress, a man's wool jacket with

a package of Vantages stuck in one pocket, and calf-high moccasins held together with two paper clips. "Traditional Crow think water is medicinal," she said as we flew over the Yellowstone River which runs through the tribal land where she lives. "The old tribal crier used to call out every morning for our people to drink all they could, to make water touch their bodies. 'Water is your body,' they used to say." Looking down on the seared landscape below, it wasn't difficult to understand the real and imagined potency of water. "All that would be a big death yard," she said with a sweep of her arm. That's how the drought would come: one sweep and all moisture would be banished. Bluebunch and June grass would wither. Elk and deer would trample sidehills into sand. Draws would fill up with dead horses and cows. Tucked under ledges of shale, dens of rattlesnakes would grow into city-states of snakes. The roots of trees would rise to the surface and flail through dust in search of water.

19 Everything in nature invites us constantly to be what we are. We are often like rivers: careless and forceful, timid and dangerous, lucid and muddied, eddying, gleaming, still. Lovers, farmers, and artists have one thing in common, at least—a fear of "dry spells," dormant periods in which we do no blooming, internal droughts only the waters of imagination and psychic release can civilize. All such matters are delicate of course. But a good irrigator knows this: too little water brings on the weeds while too much degrades the soil the way too much easy money can trivialize a person's initiative. In his journal Thoreau wrote, "A man's life should be as fresh as a river. It should be the same channel but a new water every instant."

20 This morning I walked the length of a narrow, dry wash. Slabs of stone, broken off in great squares, lay propped against the banks like blank mirrors. A sage brush had drilled a hole through one of these rocks. The roots fanned out and down like hooked noses. Farther up, a quarry of red rock bore the fossilized marks of rippling water. Just yesterday, a cloudburst sent a skinny stream beneath these frozen undulations. Its passage carved the same kind of watery ridges into the sand at my feet. Even in this dry country, where internal and external droughts always threaten, water is self-registering no matter how ancient, recent, or brief.

(1985)

QUESTIONS

Thought and Structure

1. Ehrlich's first paragraph is like a mini-essay. Make a list of her accomplishments in that paragraph. Is this paragraph just a character sketch of Frank Hinckley or is it more? Explain.
2. In paragraph 3, Ehrlich says, "Waiting for water is just one of the ways Wyoming ranchers find themselves at the mercy of weather." What are some other ways?

3. Frank says that the "rich ranchers with their pumps and sprinkler systems and gated pipe" miss out on something. What do they miss? What does Frank mean?
4. Paragraphs 9–16 might be considered a subsection of this essay. What would you title this subsection? What is the point of this rhetorical unit? Paragraphs 17–18 constitute another unit. What is the point of that unit? Finally, judging from the beginning and the ending (the last paragraph), what do you think is the essay's main point? How do the two subsections you've just considered help Ehrlich develop that main point?

Style and Strategy

5. What does Ehrlich suggest in the first paragraph with these words and phrases: "fidelity," "fluttered in the wind like prayer flags," "supplicants," "mountains hold their snows like a secret," "silver pitchers," "Jumpin' Jesus," "rubbed his face with water"? Does Ehrlich carry this interesting dimension into the rest of the essay? Explain.
6. Recall the first lines of "The General Prologue" of Chaucer's *The Canterbury Tales:*

    Whan that April with his* showres soote* — its/sweet
    The droughte of March hath perced to the roote
    And bathed every veine in swich* licour*, — such/liquid
    Of which vertu engendred is the flowr;

    Recall too the opening lines of Eliot's *The Waste Land:*

    April is the cruellest month, breeding
    Lilacs out of the dead land, mixing
    Memory and desire, stirring
    Dull roots with spring rain.

    How does Ehrlich give new meaning to these words? Does she gain anything by recalling the literary tradition?
7. Throughout the essay Ehrlich includes one, two, or three lines of dialogue within her paragraphs. Why does she do this? Do you think what she does is effective? Explain.
8. In paragraph 13, Ehrlich lets us know how she really feels about Frank Hinckley as a person. How does she do that? Identify the various ways she uses language to create feeling.

SUGGESTIONS FOR WRITING

A. Frank Hinckley says, "Mother Nature is a bitter old bitch." Write an essay confirming or refuting Hinckley's view. Use your own experience and research to make your case.

B. Write an essay either about a dry spell or dormant period in your life when you did no "blooming" or about a civilizing period in your life when the "waters of imagination" were running and there was "psychic release."

C. Write a one-paragraph mini-essay like the first one in this essay. Focus on an unforgettable character like Frank Hinckley, but let us see that character as a representative man or woman, someone larger than the single life under examination. Take lessons from Ehrlich.

D. Write an essay on either air, earth, sky, wind, or fire. Take one of these rather expansive topics, and make it accessible to us. Build your essay out of your actual experiences rather than out of your fantasies. As you begin to record detail and to recount your experiences, see what idea your evidence is generating. Make that idea the point of your essay. Shape and order your evidence so that it supports the idea. In short, turn your notes and ruminations into an essay.

A Storm, the Cornfield, and Elk

1 Last week a bank of clouds lowered itself down summer's green ladder and let loose with a storm. A heavy snow can act like fists: trees are pummeled, hay- and grainfields are flattened, splayed out like deer beds; field corn, jackknifed and bleached blond by the freeze, is bedraggled by the brawl. All night we heard groans and crashes of cottonwood trunks snapping. "I slept under the damned kitchen table," one rancher told me. "I've already had one of them trees come through my roof." Along the highway electric lines were looped to the ground like dropped reins.

2 As the storm blows east toward the Dakotas, the blue of the sky intensifies. It inks dry washes and broad grasslands with quiet. In their most complete gesture of restraint, cottonwoods, willows, and wild rose engorge themselves with every hue of ruddiness—russet, puce, umber, gold, musteline—whose spectral repletion we know also to be an agony, riding oncoming waves of cold.

3 The French call the autumn leaf *feuille morte.* When the leaves are finally corrupted by frost they rain down into themselves until the tree, disowning itself, goes bald.

4 All through autumn we hear a double voice: one says everything is ripe; the other says everything is dying. The paradox is exquisite. We feel what the Japanese call "aware"—an almost untranslatable word meaning something like "beauty tinged with sadness." Some days we have to shoulder against a marauding melancholy. Dreams have a hallucinatory effect: in one, a man who is dying watches from inside a huge cocoon while stud colts run through deep mud, their balls bursting open, their seed spilling onto the black ground. My reading brings me this thought from the mad Zen priest Ikkyu: "Remember that under the skin you fondle lie the bones, waiting to reveal themselves." But another day, I ride in the mountains. Against rimrock, tall aspens have the graceful bearing of giraffes, and another small grove, not yet turned, gives off a virginal limelight that transpierces everything heavy.

5 Fall is the end of a rancher's year. Third and fourth cuttings of hay are stacked; cattle and sheep are gathered, weaned, and shipped; yearling bulls and horse colts are sold. "We always like this time of year, but it's a lot more fun when the cattle prices are up!" a third-generation rancher tells me.

6 This week I help round up their cows and calves on the Big Horns. The storm system that brought three feet of snow at the beginning of the month now brings intense and continual rain. Riding for cows resembles a wild game of touch football played on skis: cows and cowboys bang into each other, or else, as the calves run

back, the horse just slides. Twice today my buckskin falls with me, crushing my leg against a steep sidehill, but the mud and snow, now trampled into a gruel, is so deep it's almost impossible to get bruised.

7 When the cattle are finally gathered, we wean the calves from the cows in portable corrals by the road. Here, black mud reaches our shins. The stock dogs have to swim in order to move. Once, while trying to dodge a cow, my feet stuck, and losing both boots in the effort to get out of the way, I had to climb the fence barefooted. Weaning is noisy; cows don't hide their grief. As calves are loaded into semis and stock trucks, their mothers—five or six hundred of them at a time—crowd around the sorting alleys with outstretched necks, their squared-off faces all opened in a collective bellowing.

8 On the way home a neighboring rancher who trails his steers down the mountain highway loses one as they ride through town. There's a high-speed chase across lawns and flower beds, around the general store and the fire station. Going at a full lope, the steer ducks behind the fire truck just as Mike tries to rope him. "Missing something?" a friend yells out her window as the second loop sails like a burning hoop to the ground.

9 "That's nothing," one onlooker remarks. "When we brought our cattle through Kaycee one year, the minister opened the church door to see what all the noise was about and one old cow just ran in past him. He had a hell of a time getting her out."

10 In the valley, harvest is on but it's soggy. The pinto bean crops are sprouting, and the sugar beets are balled up with mud so that one is indistinguishable from the other. Now I can only think of mud as being sweet. At night the moon makes a brief appearance between storms and laces mud with a confectionary light. Farmers whose last cutting of hay is still on the ground turn windrows to dry as if they were limp, bedridden bodies. The hay that has already been baled is damp, and after four inches of rain (in a county where there's never more than eight inches a year) mold eats its way to the top again.

11 The morning sky looks like cheese. Its cobalt wheel has been cut down and all the richness of the season is at our feet. The quick-blanch of frost stings autumn's rouge into a skin that is tawny. At dawn, mowed hay meadows are the color of pumpkins, and the willows, leafless now, are pink and silver batons conducting inaudible river music. When I dress for the day, my body, white and suddenly numb, looks like dead coral.

12 After breakfast there are autumn chores to finish. We grease head gates on irrigation ditches, roll up tarp dams, pull horseshoes, and truck horses to their winter pasture. The harvest moon gives way to the hunter's moon. Elk, deer, and moose hunters repopulate the mountains now that the livestock is gone. One young hunting guide has already been hurt. While he was alone at camp, his horse kicked him in the spleen. Immobilized, he scratched an SOS with the sharp point of a bullet on a piece of leather he cut from his chaps. "Hurt bad. In pain. Bring doctor with painkiller," it read. Then he tied the note to the horse's halter and threw rocks at the horse until it trotted out of camp. When the horse wandered into a ranch yard

down the mountain, the note was quickly discovered and a doctor was helicoptered to camp. Amid orgiastic gunfire, sometimes lives are saved.

13 October lifts over our heads whatever river noise is left. Long carrier waves of clouds seem to emanate from hidden reefs. There's a logjam of them around the mountains, and the horizon appears to drop seven thousand feet. Though the rain has stopped, the road ruts are filled to the brim. I saw a frog jump cheerfully into one of them. Once in a while the mist clears and we can see the dark edge of a canyon or an island of vertical rimrock in the white bulk of snow. Up there, bull elk have been fighting all fall over harems. They charge with antlered heads, scraping the last of the life-giving velvet off, until one bull wins and trots into the private timber to mount his prize, standing almost humanly erect on hind legs while holding a cow elk's hips with his hooves.

14 In the fall, my life, too, is timbered, an unaccountably libidinous place: damp, overripe, and fading. The sky's congestion allows the eye's iris to open wider. The cornfield in front of me is torn parchment paper, as brittle as bougainvillea leaves whose tropical color has somehow climbed these northern stalks. I zigzag through the rows as if they were city streets. Now I want to lie down in the muddy furrows, under the frictional sawing of stalks, under corncobs which look like erections, and out of whose loose husks sprays of bronze silk dangle down.

15 Autumn teaches us that fruition is also death; that ripeness is a form of decay. The willows, having stood for so long near water, begin to rust. Leaves are verbs that conjugate the seasons.

16 Today the sky is a wafer. Placed on my tongue, it is a wholeness that has already disintegrated; placed under the tongue, it makes my heart beat strongly enough to stretch myself over the winter brilliances to come. Now I feel the tenderness to which this season rots. Its defenselessness can no longer be corrupted. Death is its purity, its sweet mud. The string of storms that came across Wyoming like elephants tied tail to trunk falters now and bleeds into a stillness.

17 There is neither sun, nor wind, nor snow falling. The hunters are gone; snow geese waddle in grainfields. Already, the elk have started moving out of the mountains toward sheltered feed-grounds. Their great antlers will soon fall off like chandeliers shaken from ballroom ceilings. With them the light of these autumn days, bathed in what Tennyson called "a mockery of sunshine," will go completely out.

(1985)

QUESTIONS

Thought and Structure

1. In the introductory section of the essay, Ehrlich writes about a "paradox" that is "exquisite." What is that paradox? Why is it exquisite?

2. What does Fall mean to the rancher?
3. What do you find most unusual about paragraph 11 in a section of the essay that sets out to deal with the "harvest"? Do we still find both "sadness" and "beauty" in the third section of the essay (paragraphs 10–12)? Explain.
4. What is the most distinguishing feature of the essay's conclusion (paragraphs 15–17)? Is it language? Is it the idea of Ehrlich's personal association with the season's fruition? Is it simply the way she manages to say afresh what she's already said throughout the essay? Or is there a new quality in these last three paragraphs, something made possible through the development of the essay's four preceding sections? Explain your choice of answers.

Style and Strategy

5. Pick out the words and phrases in the introductory section of the essay that capture both the "beauty" and the "sadness" that Ehrlich associates with Autumn and the first storm. Be especially mindful of the phrases that capture both simultaneously. Are those phrases poetic? Explain. Do you like them better than the other language in these first four paragraphs? Explain.
6. The second section of the essay deals with the problems ranchers have with their various animals in the Fall. How does Ehrlich continue to capture both sadness and beauty in this section? How does the nature of beauty change in this section? How sadness? Note the overall change from the general in section one to the specific in section two. What is the effect of this change?
7. Look carefully at paragraphs 13 and 14 in the final section of the essay's body. How do those paragraphs work together? What is Ehrlich's main purpose in telling us about the Elk? Account for the poetic shift in the language in paragraph 14. Why does Ehrlich use such ripe language? Do we still have sadness and beauty?

SUGGESTIONS FOR WRITING

A. Write a short report about whether or not you think a man could have written this essay. Is there something distinctly female about this presentation? Support your answer by citing evidence from the text of the essay.

B. Write a few paragraphs about your favorite season. Make one of those paragraphs general; make two very specific as you accumulate details to capture the season's mood. Do not make things up. Recall your own experiences and observations. If you like the season you're in, make notes for a few days about your observations. Try to make your language match the season when you finally begin to write.

C. Go to the library and do a little mythological research. See what you can find out about Demeter and Persephone. Prepare a short report for the class relating your research to Ehrlich's essay, especially the part that deals with her own personal response to the autumnal pull of the season. If your library has the journal *Antaeus,* look in Volume 57 (Autumn 86) for Ehrlich's essay "Spring." How does that essay complement this one? Do either of the essays make the myth of Demeter and Persephone more meaningful or does the myth make the two essays by Ehrlich more meaningful? Explain in your report.

McKay

"The weather spirit is blowing the storm out,
the weather spirit is driving the weeping snow away over the earth, and the helpless storm-child Narsuk shakes the lungs of the air with his weeping."

—*COOPER ESKIMO*

1 When McKay woke there was a dead rooster on the floor. He sat up with a start because he was in the wrong bedroom. He picked up the bird. At first he didn't know how it had landed there, then he remembered the cockfight the night before. The rooster was light in his hands. Its scarlet comb had been clipped short and at the back of each yellow foot a sharpened spur protruded, white as a woman's fingernail.

2 McKay stood and the room went black. There was no heat in that part of the house and he pulled on his long underwear quickly. As he straightened the bed he caught sight of himself in the mirror: the one side of his face looked old, the eye twitched and the soft flesh under the eye was gray as if ash had been smeared there; the other side, the bright side, looked childlike, the way one corner of the mouth was pulled down, and the split face was topped by one insouciant tumble of blond hair.

3 He called for Bobby, the cook, but no one answered. It was the third day of a savage, unseasonal storm. During the night a cloud shaped like an appendix had burst, dropping its white cargo like poison, and wind had violated the one tree. Its green topknot exploded and dropped branches into the arms of lower limbs like bodies being carried home from war.

4 The house had never seemed so quiet. When McKay looked down into the living room from the balcony he saw that everything was covered with snow. In front of each window and door were duncecaps of white. Some had toppled sideways. Wind had sprayed snow over furniture, into the black corners of the fireplace, and across the Navajo rugs on the floor.

5 McKay hobbled down the stairs. Today was the thirteenth anniversary of his parents' death. They had drowned when their car rolled into an irrigation canal. He picked up their silver-framed photograph taken the day they died. His mother was bundled in a fur coat. Her gray eyes sparkled and she was smiling at McKay's father whose black hair stood on end. It had been windy. He had the hurt, far-off look of someone who only finds happiness elsewhere.

6 McKay went to the kitchen and stoked the cookstove. Outside wind had swept the ground almost free of snow. Only the buildings and fencelines were drifted. He pulled a stool up and turned the radio on. Each morning McKay braced himself for bad news, expecting to hear his brothers' names on the casualty list. Instead, there was no news at all.

7 After his brothers left to go to war the rooms of the house felt too big and the huge pasture McKay rode to check cows looked like the moon. The sky went gray as if the planet had turned from the sun, averting its face. Sometimes McKay

imagined one of the bombs had gone astray and floated alongside him. His loneliness took on a metallic glare—metal flying fast. The snowdrifts at the doors pressed at him and the ungodly stillness roared.

8 The morning of the cockfight McKay rode out through the west gate towards sheep camp where he was to meet his neighbor, Madeleine. It was shipping day. The ranchers had gathered their cattle and trailed them to sorting corrals where they would be shipped by rail to Omaha. On the way McKay saw seven cow elk on the flank of Heart Mountain. A young bull bugled, his low whistle ascending sharply until air caught at the entrance to his throat, then he gave out three seal-like, grunting cries. The bull approached a cow. He thrust a knee between her back legs and horned her, tilting his branching antlers into her rump. She jumped and ran. He pursued her, lifting his nose in the air to inhale the full brunt of her sexual fragrance.

9 McKay dropped down the slope to a creekbed and entered a canyon. It narrowed quickly. The straight-up red walls hemmed him in. Far above, thin pine trees swan-necked out from cracks in the rock, then grew straight towards the sky. Occasionally, three foot long icicles dropped, taking the air like harpoons. One arched past the horse's nose then broke like crystal stemware across the trail. McKay watched the tracks in front of his horse: deer, elk, rabbit, bird, and bobcat. They looked like music to him, a skating, hopping, notational scrawl left behind by players who had gone elsewhere.

10 At the far end the canyon widened and McKay rode to Raoul's camp. Madeleine wasn't there. He warmed himself by the tiny cookstove inside the wagon. On the bed was a Bible and a loaded rifle. He remembered the night he and Raoul had been snowed in together. They shared the high, built-in bed across the back of the wagon. The old sheepherder lit a candle and their shadows blossomed on the rounded ceiling. That was the night he told McKay about the hurricane.

11 "The *tormenta*—that is what we called the hurricane in Mexico. She comes on so fast, see . . . sand blowing so hard I can't see nothing. Then it grows dark and it rains. Our village is on a hill and all of us are crowding together praying. We hear a big roar, like God himself talking, and we run out to see what has happened. It is the hill falling. It is water running everywhere. This woman, she is standing next to me, holding her baby. The water comes and sweeps that baby right out of her arms . . . then she goes too. Just like that—all that creation—pufff. Then I *knew* it was God talking. In the morning I see the whole village is gone. Well then, what am I to do? So I walk all the way to La Paz. Three days I am walking. When I get there I meet others just like me—who have come from nothing, who have nothing. But pretty soon we find jobs. And the man whose wife was washed away, he meets another woman and starts his life all over again. In no time he is happy. You think is crazy? But life is like that. *La vida es muy historica, no?*"

12 Then Raoul blew out the candle and McKay rolled onto his side, away from the old man, and pretended to sleep.

13 McKay rode on following two sets of horsetracks across a ridge, down into a coulee. Two eagles circled. He saw Madeleine and Raoul digging sheep out of a

snowdrift that had curled back at the top like an upper lip sneering. McKay stepped off his horse.

14 "I guess they just gave up and suffocated," Madeleine said, handing McKay the back legs of two bloated ewes. When they dragged the last of seven dead sheep from the drift it collapsed into a white ruin like the cities of Europe that had been destroyed.

15 Raoul emerged from the timber with five crosses made from pine twigs tied at the center with bits of string. He kneeled in front of the dead sheep and planted the crosses in the snow.

16 Afterwards Madeleine and McKay rode towards town. They had been childhood friends, then lovers. By the time she surrendered her virginity to him and his to her in a dry irrigation ditch wrapped in a canvas dam that smelled of mildew, they had already worked cattle, roped, and ridden colts together and continued to do so. They had been born on the same day in the same hospital, McKay in the delivery room and Madeleine in the labor room, there being only one of each in the small country hospital, and when she came home after four years of college with a husband on her arm McKay felt as welcoming to the man as he did betrayed.

17 They rode for a time without talking. McKay liked the way she sat a horse: she took a deep seat and kept a light hand. A fresh set of clouds billowed and leapfrogged across the face of Heart Mountain. They stopped for lunch though McKay wasn't hungry. He'd finally understood the arbitrariness of life since the War had begun: it was vicarious shell-shock—black dreams, trembling, an absence of the small lusts.

18 He unrolled his yellow slicker and laid it across an outcropping of rock. From their perch he and Madeleine could see a corner of the Relocation Camp. McKay uncorked his flask and offered it to Madeleine. She took a swallow and wiped her mouth. It had been a week since she had heard her husband, Henry, had been taken prisoner of war in Japan.

19 McKay unwrapped a sandwich for her. She watched as he fed his to his dog.

20 "What are you thinking about?" she asked. She always asked the questions she wanted someone to ask her.

21 "Henry," McKay said.

22 "Are you thinking well of him?"

23 "That's a mean thing to say," McKay said and looked at her.

24 "Maybe he's dead, anyway," she said bitterly.

25 Down at the Camp they heard roosters crowing and the lines of a baseball diamond showed through melting snow. McKay leaned back on the rock and closed his eyes.

26 "Are you sure you want to ride to Omaha with the cattle?" he asked sleepily.

27 "Are you worried about me?"

28 "Hell no. It just means I'll be short-handed for a week."

29 "Thanks," she said and mussed his hair playfully. He looked at her. The gray light made her eyes turn violet.

30 "I'll miss you," she said almost inaudibly.

31 He turned towards her. Under the hat her long hair was tucked behind an ear

whose bony convolutions shone, inviting him to fall in there. A tumbling rock startled them. McKay smiled his crooked, mischievious smile.

32 "I think you were the first person I saw when I was born," he said.

33 The shipping corrals loomed back against the sky and everywhere there was great commotion. Weaned calves bawled for their mothers, yardmen snapped bull-whips over the backs of steers, cowboys on horseback pushed a pen-full of heifers down a wide alley to a loading chute. Waiting boxcars thumped forward as each was loaded.

34 For the rest of the day McKay and Madeleine worked the chute. They pushed steers up the slippery ramp, sometimes hoisting them bodily. Some fell and had to be righted, others turned so they were facing backwards in the chute. Madeleine and McKay were kicked and tromped, their pantlegs green with manure. Falling snow piled up in their hatbrims as they worked.

35 When the door of the last cattle car rolled shut, Madeleine unsaddled her horse and let him drink and roll in an empty pen. The windows of the cafe across the road had steamed up and the lights looked like an ornament against so much desolate land. She grabbed McKay's arm and drew him towards her. Just then the yardlights came on and shadows from the sorting corrals made bars across her face.

36 McKay remembered the night the telegram about Henry had come. He had urged Madeleine to stay the night at the ranch. Bobby made a bed in an upstairs room and led her the length of the balcony with a kerosene lamp. Once again their twin lives were stacked like a double entendre. He felt her presence in the house that night as some kind of tenderness swelling. It filled him and somehow he was lifted up through the ceiling to her bed.

37 Now her teeth chattered. Snow blew in a crossfire between them. McKay closed his eyes. It seemed they were naked and he was moving in and out of her like a furred animal, long and warm and sweet, standing on his hind legs. To be inside her he had to hitch his whole body up and when he came or thought he had come, water rushed by the narrow bones in his face and he heard sheets of ice cracking. Then he was cold as if he had been without clothes all winter. The air was dry. The dryness crackled between them and a spark popped when he finally touched her arm.

38 Now McKay clasped Madeleine's arm so tightly his knuckles turned white. He didn't know if he was shaking her or if the cold in her body was shaking him, or if, in stopping her embrace he had intended to pull her against him. Her amethyst eyes shone.

39 "I'm sorry," she said, and the flush on her cheeks travelled sideways to her ears.

40 McKay carried his dog into the cafe. It was hot inside and the floor was greasy with melted snow and mud. He swung onto a stool at the long counter. The dog curled up at his feet and began snoring. The room was full with men. Those who weren't eating stood behind those who were and each time the door swung open the noise inside the cafe redoubled with the sound of bawling calves.

41 "McKay?" Carol Lyman stood in front of the young rancher, a coffee pot

suspended in air. He nodded. She poured, then turned, catching a glimpse of herself in the mirror, and primped her brittle hair.

42 "And I'll have a piece of that pie," McKay said.

43 She slid a plate towards him.

44 "And the little shit probably wants a hamburger," he said indicating the dog on the floor.

45 "With everything?"

46 "No onions," he said and winked at her.

47 More bodies crowded in behind McKay, men he had known all his life, men his father's age, bundled in long wool coats and tall boots.

48 "I'll have a whiskey and ditch of some of that pie," one of them shouted.

49 "Which kind?"

50 "I don't care. Just one of them round ones," he said and broke into laughter.

51 Two old cowboys shouldered in behind McKay and set their cups on the counter to be refilled.

52 ". . . Hell no, I was tied hard and fast and when that ol' bull hit the end of the rope he whipped around . . ."

53 Carol Lyman returned with the pie.

54 "Where's my whiskey?" the man asked.

55 "It's too damned early for you to be starting on that stuff," she said curtly and poured the coffee for the cowboys.

56 ". . . And my horse backed up so fast the saddle rode up on his neck. Hell I was sittin' plumb between his ears. . . ."

57 "Well it's been a crazy goddamned storm. Those guys over in Sheridan really got it bad. Lost forty-five percent of their lamb crop, I heard . . ."

58 ". . . And she went out in the morning and they was just dead cows and horses everywhere. Then her hired man come up froze to death. Christ, things is bad enough with this war going on without a mess like that. Poor woman."

59 Carol Lyman brought the dog's hamburger and refilled McKay's cup. "No onions."

60 "No onions," he replied.

61 One of the yardmen talked to someone behind him. "Hey, did you hear about Fred's boy and Henry? They was taken prisoner of war by them dirty Japs."

62 "I think I could stand anything but that," a voice behind McKay said.

63 "Carol, where's my whiskey at?"

64 "You eat that pie first."

65 "Well when was you hired on to be my mother?"

66 Carol snorted and turned on her heel. Steam from the coffee pot flew over her shoulder like a feather boa.

67 "Shutup everyone . . . excuse me, Ma'm . . . I think the news is coming on," one of the ranchers said.

68 The seat next to McKay emptied and filled up again.

69 "How'd you fare, McKay? Get those ornery old cows of yours loaded up?"

70 "Yep. I guess we did."

71 Carol Lyman removed the empty pie plate from in front of McKay and wiped the counter clean. Her quick movements reminded McKay of his mother. That's

how his memory of her worked: nothing whole came to him, just parts of her in motion—a turbulence he could feel as she passed from room to room, a fragrance ballooning out from her.

72 McKay looked out the window. Someone had wiped the panes clean. The sorting pens were full again with another man's cattle and through the slats of the cars he could see the bulge of a rump and protruding horns.

73 "There goes more Japs," someone yelled excitedly.

74 A passenger train slid behind the cattle cars on another track. The shades were all drawn.

75 "I don't see how they could get any more in that camp."

76 "They say there's going to be ten thousand of them."

77 "Hell, I ain't even seen that many cattle in one bunch before."

78 Instead of the news, music came on the radio. An old cowboy with a hat shaped like a volcano and no front teeth grabbed Carol Lyman's hand and tugged at her until she came out from behind the counter. The crowd made a space for the couple in the center of the cafe and they waltzed.

79 McKay thought about the day his parents' car had been pulled from the canal. Something across the road had caught his eye: a woman standing in the doorway of the beauty parlor. As she watched the rescue crew, a curler dropped from her head—like an antler, McKay thought—and bounced on the floor. The woman was Carol Lyman.

80 "I heard Madeleine's gonna ride with them cows," the man next to McKay said.

81 "Yep. She sure is."

82 "I wonder what poor old Henry would think of that."

83 McKay warmed his hands around his coffee cup and said nothing.

84 The blacksmith took Carol Lyman's place behind the counter and started pouring coffee. He stopped in front of McKay.

85 "I've been thinking about your Ma and Pa this morning," he said quietly.

86 "Well thank you, Fred," McKay said.

87 "I guess you must be having a time out there . . . kinda lonely on that ranch, isn't it? Kinda lonely for a young man . . ."

88 McKay looked down, then out the window. His face had reddened. When Madeleine entered, every man in the cafe turned to look at her.

89 It was dark when the "all-aboard" sounded. Snow blew across the tall yard-lights like black gravel. Madeleine boarded the train. She wore a long yellow slicker over her chaps and her hat was pulled down low against the wind.

90 "Call when you get to Omaha," McKay yelled up to her. "And watch for that shipping fever. I had Bobby pack the medicine kit. And if you need help that kid from the Two Dot ranch is on board somewhere."

91 "Yes, McKay," she said and winked.

92 "And be careful. . . ."

93 The train lurched once and stopped. They could hear cattle scramble for footing, then the train lurched again.

94 "McKay, I'm sorry."

95 "For what?"

96 Madeleine shrugged. Then the train moved and she slid away from him.

97 McKay went to the cockfight before going home. He slid down the hill to the gravel wash under the flume. The two old men, Mañuel and Tony, were weighing their roosters on an old packer's scale. Then they dropped the birds onto the frozen ground swept clean of rock and lit uncertainly by three hissing Coleman lanterns.

98 The brown rooster had a speckled neck and red tail feathers. The other had black wings flecked with iridescent green. Parts of its body had been plucked and the bare skin looked blue. Bronze feathers streamed down the bird's neck. They stood on end when the birds went at each other, forming a ruffled collar.

99 At first the birds pecked timidly, and nuzzled neck to neck—like lovers, McKay thought. Then the brown bird jumped straight up, lashing out with his sharpened spurs as he came down. The black bird ducked, leapt and gashed back. They used their beaks and feet, pecking at each other's heads until blood came. They jumped again and when they came down this time, the brown rooster's spur stuck into the black bird's neck and blood from the jugular flowed onto the ground.

100 A bottle of tequila was passed. Mañuel dropped to his hands and knees over the dead rooster and when he stood again the front of his shirt was stained red. A man passed the tequila to McKay with a wild grin on his face. McKay raised the bottle in honor of the dead cock and tilted his head back until a line of stars—Orion's belt—rushed through his head. The gold liquid tasted like mineral and something overripe and very green. When they took the bottle from him he knelt down and stroked the dead rooster. "Bird of paradise," he thought, and imagined the feathers were really a woman's hair. He clutched the bird to his chest, rolled over and smiled.

101 McKay took the shortcut home in the dark. His horse climbed through the breaks. Snow from juniper branches spilled down his neck as he brushed by. His companion, the errant bomb, made a little wind just above his head. When the horse climbed to the top of the bench McKay could see the train, at a great distance now, shooting in a straight line east across the Basin.

102 He didn't know how long he rode with his eyes closed. Blasts of snow scratched his face like crushed oyster shells and the electric needle of hard cold punctured each toe. A dead rooster tied with two saddle strings, hung behind his rolled slicker. When he opened his eyes McKay knew he had reached the lower end of the ranch.

103 He passed the gate and climbed the knob towards the family graveyard. When he reached the top he stepped off his horse. Snow from the ground blew up in his face, then plummeted mixing with new snow. McKay could see nothing but white. He leaned towards the ground and pawed the air: no gravestone. A noise startled the horse and the reins pulled out of McKay's numb hands.

104 "Shit." He kicked at snow. His foot hit something hard. He crouched down and brushed snow away but it was a rock, not his parents' headstone. Something—either the tequila or blowing snow—made his eyes close again.

105 McKay woke with a start and whistled. His dog came to him. He began a blindman's search for his horse. He walked back and forth, circling one way, then the other. He tripped and his hands slid across polished rock.

106 "Hello, Pa," he said and threw an arm around the gravestone.

107 "Just this once tell me where my damned horse is, will you?" he said, cupping his hands to the grave. His nose was running and tufts of blond hair stuck out from under his hat. Suddenly he stood and walked towards a tree. A dark form appeared behind the trunk.

108 "Well you dumb sonofabitch," he said and planted a kiss on the horse's jaw.

109 Snow had drifted against the tree and the horse was buried up to his shoulder. McKay began digging, working his hands the way dogs do, while the horse looked on quizzically. Blocks of snow fell away, exposing a foreleg, and shoulder, then a shuddering flank.

110 McKay thought about his parents, how they had been extracted from their car and pulled dead from the canal, up through a thin layer of ice that broke over his mother's head in long translucent staves; how her gray hair had come unbraided and floated like seagrass. He remembered his father's wounded, wistful eyes—how they had still been open and when he went to close them with his own hand he couldn't; how the lariat, always kept on the front seat of his parents' car in strict coils had opened across his father's chest as if to spell out one last cry of dismay: ooooooo.

111 Snow fell from the horse's back and knees. The whites of his eyes shone and he worked his ears. McKay grabbed the rein and led the horse from the collapsed drift. He sighed deeply, then his head fell into his blue hands and he cried.

112 When McKay reached the ranch no lights were on. He lit an oil lamp and wandered through the house. The snow in the living room had been mopped up—Bobby must be home. The photograph of McKay's parents had been set on the mantle over the stone fireplace and three sticks of incense were still burning.

113 McKay went upstairs. The old pine staircase creaked. He opened the door of the bedroom where Madeleine had slept the week before and set the lamp on a small table. For a long time he stared at the unmade bed. Then he took off all his clothes, pulled the blankets back and rubbed his aching, lonely body on the sheets where she had been.

(1986)

QUESTIONS

1. What kind of expectations does Ehrlich create in the first paragraph? What kind of informed guesses can you make about McKay? Why is the last phrase, "white as a woman's fingernail" associated with the rooster? How long do you have to wait in the story to find out the answer to the latter question?
2. Ehrlich's narrator describes the two sides of McKay's face. Does that early bit of description give us a clue about McKay's character?
3. How does the last paragraph of the first section of the story alter our perception of McKay's predicament?
4. In the second section of the story, the narrator begins moving back in time; at the end

of that section, there is yet another flashback. What does Ehrlich manage to do by going back? What is the general tone of this second section. The first section ended on a note of war and loneliness. The second section ends with McKay's remembrance of Raoul's story about the *tormenta.* Is there any connection?

5. In paragraph 14 of section three of the story there is an interesting simile: "the drift . . . collapsed into a white ruin like the cities of Europe that had been destroyed." What is the effect of that simile?
6. Why is Madeleine so important to McKay? What is a "Relocation Camp," and why do you suppose Ehrlich introduces it in section three of the story, instead of somewhere else? In terms of the story itself—McKay's story—why do you suppose Madeleine *has* to be going to Omaha? Is her having to go part of a larger pattern? Does it have anything to do with their "twin lives"? Explain.
7. Why, inside the cafe, do we continue to hear "the sound of bawling calves"? What two roles does Carol Lyman seem to be performing for the men in the cafe? Why is she so important to McKay? Why does Ehrlich introduce the "Japs" again in this section of the essay? What does she gain by doing so at this particular time in the narrative?
8. In section six of the story, Madeleine says again to McKay, "McKay, I'm sorry" (paragraph 94). What do you think she is sorry for? Why does she keep apologizing?
9. In the seventh section of the story, McKay goes to the cockfight, and we find that by going backward in time, we've actually made it back almost to the beginning. What kinds of things does Ehrlich do in this section that are particularly effective in bringing the story of McKay's life together?
10. Section eight does takes us back to the story's beginning. Do you find that closing section confusing in terms of time? Has Ehrlich made a mistake? Do you find the last scene of the essay redundant, or do you find it haunting? Explain.
11. What is significant about the day on which the story begins and ends?

SUGGESTIONS FOR WRITING

A. Write a short account of the importance of animals in this story. Account particularly for McKay's dog, the calves, and the dead rooster.

B. Compare and contrast Ehrlich's use of images in this story and in "The Smooth Skull of Winter." What can an essay writer learn from such a comparison?

C. How does Ehrlich show us the impact of war on the lives of the characters in this story? Jot down the allusions as well as the direct references. Write a couple of paragraphs about the extent to which you think the war is a significant part of this story.

D. Write a short report for class about the way this story differs from one of Ehrlich's essays. Do not try to make a point-by-point comparison. Rather, try to trace general differences. You might start by considering in your own mind how they are alike.

E. In one well-developed paragraph explain how the epigraph at the beginning of the story gives us some sense of what the story is about.

APPENDIX

1. THEMATIC TABLE OF CONTENTS

History and Politics

The Natural World

Personal Values

Science and Technology

Work and Play

Race, Culture, and Society

Relationships

Writing, Art, Language

People

Places

2. RHETORICAL TABLE OF CONTENTS

Description

Narration

All the Short Stories and selections from longer fiction.

Fiction

The American Redneck, p. 358 / *The Bonfire of the Vanities,* p. 419 / *Giving Birth,* p. 504 / *Everyday Use,* p. 535 / *McKay,* p. 592 / *The Point of It,* p. 38 / *Kew Gardens,* p. 75 / *The Horse Dealer's Daughter,* p. 100 / *Rope,* p. 133 / *The Grave,* p. 138 / *1984,* p. 200 / *Democracy,* p. 474 / *Minor Surgery,* p. 328 / *Sonny's Blues,* p. 283 / *The Door,* p. 164 / *The Dance of the Frogs,* p. 241

Exposition

Seeing (Illustration), p. 544 / *Sojourner* (Analogy), p. 561 / *God's Tooth* (Cause/Effect), p. 565 / *On Being a 'Woman Writer'* (Cause/Effect), p. 494 / *The Right Stuff* (Definition), p. 386 / *The Angels* (Illustration), p. 375 / *Funky Chic* (Definition/Illustration), p. 398 / *Honks and Wonks* (Definition/Illustration), p. 407 / *Goodbye to All That* (Comparison/Contrast), p. 457 / *Why I Write* (Cause/Effect), p. 465 / *On Self-Respect* (Definition/Illustration), p. 453 / *Georgia O'Keeffe* (Analysis), p. 471 / *Cocksure Women and Hensure Men* (Analogy), p. 88 / *The Masked Marvel's Last Toehold* (Comparison/Contrast), p. 309 / *Playing Cowboy* (Comparison/Contrast), p. 332 / *The American Redneck* (Definition/Illustration), p. 358 / *The Black Writer and the Southern Experience* (Cause/Effect), p. 516 / *In Search of Our Mothers' Gardens* (Cause/Effect), p. 527 / *Beauty: When the Other Dancer Is the Self* (Illustration), p. 521 / *Fifth Avenue, Uptown: A Letter from Harlem* (Cause/Effect), p. 259 / *Adrienne Rich* (Illustration), p. 491 / *Virginia Woolf* (Illustration), p. 116 / *Tillie Olsen* (Cause/Effect), p. 488 / *About Men* (Definition), p. 575 / *On Water* (Process), p. 581 / *English Prose Between 1918 and 1938* (Division/Classification), p. 29

Persuasion

Notes of a Native Son, p. 267 / *The Right Stuff,* p. 386 / *Living Like Weasels,* p. 11 / *In Search of Our Mothers' Gardens,* p. 527 / *What I Believe,* p. 18 / *Not Looking at Pictures,* p. 26 / *English Prose Between 1918 and 1938,* p. 29 / *Women and Fiction,* p. 52 / *Old Mrs. Grey,* p. 69 / *Craftsmanship,* p. 69 / *Benjamin Franklin,* p. 91 / *Politics and the English Language,* p. 177 / *Cocksure Women and Hensure Men,* p. 88 / *Marrakech,* p. 194 / *The Illusion of the Two Cultures,* p. 231 / *The Hidden Teacher,* p. 221 / *The Dance of the Frogs,* p. 241 / *Fifth Avenue, Uptown: A Letter from Harlem,* p. 259 / *Stranger in the Village,* p. 250 / *On Being a 'Woman Writer',* p. 494 / *St. Augustine and the Bullfight,* p. 120 / *The Necessary Enemy,* p. 128 / *A Hanging,* p. 171 / *Virginia Woolf,* p. 116 / *Tillie Olsen,* p. 488 / *Adrienne Rich,* p. 491 / *About Men,* p. 575 / *A Storm, the Cornfield, and Elk,* p. 588 / *On Water,* p. 581 / *The Smooth Skull of Winter,* p. 578

COPYRIGHT ACKNOWLEDGMENTS

"What I Believe" from *Two Cheers for Democracy* by E. M. Forster. Copyright 1939, 1967 by E. M. Forster. Reprinted from his volume *Two Cheers for Democracy* by permission of Harcourt Brace Jovanovich, Inc.

"Forster and 'Bloomsbury' Prose" by P. N. Furbank in *E. M. Forster: A Human Exploration,* edited by G. K. Das and John Beer (New York: New York University Press, 1979).

"Not Looking at Pictures" from *Two Cheers for Democracy* by E. M. Forster. Copyright 1939, 1967 by E. M. Forster. Reprinted from his volume *Two Cheers for Democracy* by permission of Harcourt Brace Jovanovich, Inc.

"English Prose Between 1918 and 1939" from *Two Cheers for Democracy* by E. M. Forster. Copyright 1939, 1967 by E. M. Forster. Reprinted from his volume *Two Cheers for Democracy* by permission of Harcourt Brace Jovanovich, Inc.

"The Point of It" from *The Eternal Moment* by E. M. Forster, copyright 1928 by Harcourt Brace Jovanovich, Inc.; renewed 1956 by E. M. Forster. Reprinted by permission of the publisher.

"Women and Fiction" from *Granite and Rainbow* by Virginia Woolf, copyright © 1958 by Leonard Woolf; renewed 1986 by Marjorie T. Parons. First appeared in *The Forum,* March 1929. Reprinted by permission of Harcourt Brace Jovanovich, Inc. and the Estate of Virginia Woolf and The Hogarth Press, Ltd.

"Montaigne" from *The Common Reader,* First Series, by Virginia Woolf, copyright 1925 by Harcourt Brace Jovanovich, Inc.; renewed 1953 by Leonard Woolf. Reprinted by permission of the publisher and the Estate of Virginia Woolf and The Hogarth Press, Ltd.

"Montaigne: Of Smells" reprinted from *The Complete Essays of Montaigne* translated by Donald M. Frame with the permission of the publisher, Stanford University Press. © 1958 by the Board of Trustees of the Leland Stanford Junior University.

"Old Mrs. Grey" from *The Death of the Moth and Other Essays* by Virginia Woolf, copyright 1942 by Harcourt Brace Jovanovich, Inc.; renewed 1970 by Marjorie T. Parons, Executrix. Reprinted by permission of the publisher and the Estate of Virginia Woolf and The Hogarth Press, Ltd.

"Craftsmanship" from *The Death of the Moth and Other Essays* by Virginia Woolf, copyright 1942 by Harcourt Brace Jovanovich, Inc.; renewed 1970 by Marjorie T. Parsons, Executrix. Reprinted by permission of the publisher and the Estate of Virginia Woolf and The Hogarth Press, Ltd.

"Kew Gardens" from *A Haunted House and Other Stories* by Virginia Woolf, copyright 1944, 1972 by Harcourt Brace Jovanovich, Inc. Reprinted by permission of the publisher and the Estate of Virginia Woolf and The Hogarth Press, Ltd.

"Adolf," from *Phoenix: The Posthumous Papers of D. H. Lawrence,* edited by Edward MacDonald. Copyright 1936 by Frieda Lawrence. Copyright renewed © 1964 by the Estate of Frieda Lawrence. All rights reserved. Reprinted by permission of Viking Penguin Inc.

"Cocksure Women and Hensure Men," from *Phoenix II, More Uncollected Writings,* edited by Warren Roberts and Harry T. Moore. Copyright © 1959, 1963, 1968 by the Estate of Frieda Lawrence Ravagli. All rights reserved. Reprinted by permission of Viking Penguin Inc.

"Benjamin Franklin," from *Studies in Classic American Literature* by D. H. Lawrence. Copyright 1923 by Thomas Seltzer, Inc., renewed 1950 by Frieda Lawrence. All rights reserved. Reprinted by permission of Viking Penguin Inc.

"The Horse Dealer's Daughter," from *The Complete Short Stories of D. H. Lawrence, Vol. II* by D. H. Lawrence. Copyright 1933 by the Estate of D. H. Lawrence. Copyright renewed © 1961 by Angelo Ravagli and C. M. Weekley, Executors of the Estate of Frieda Lawrence Ravagli. All rights reserved. Reprinted by permission of Viking Penguin Inc.

"Virginia Woolf" from *The Collected Essays and Occasional Writings of Katherine Anne Porter.* Copyright © 1950 by Katherine Anne Porter. First published in *The New York Times/The Days Before.* Reprinted by permission of Delacorte Press/Seymour Lawrence.

"St. Augustine and the Bullfight" from *The Collected Essays and Occasional Writings of Katherine Anne Porter.* Copyright © 1955 by Katherine Anne Porter. Originally published in *Mademoiselle.* Reprinted by permission of Delacorte Press/Seymour Lawrence.

"The Necessary Enemy" from *The Collected Essays and Occasional Writings of Katherine Anne Porter.* Copyright © 1948 by Katherine Anne Porter. Originally published in *Mademoiselle* as "Love and Hate." Reprinted by permission of Delacorte Press/Seymour Lawrence.

"Symptoms of Love" by Robert Graves taken from *Collected Poems 1975.* Reprinted by permission of A. P. Watt Ltd. on behalf of the Executors of the Estate of Robert Graves.

"Rope" from *Flowering Judas and Other Stories* by Katherine Ann Porter. Copyright 1930, 1958 by Katherine Anne Porter. Reprinted from her volume *Flowering Judas and Other Stories* by permission of Harcourt Brace Jovanovich, Inc.

"The Grave" from *The Leaning Tower and Other Stories* by Katherine Anne Porter. Copyright 1934 by Katherine Anne Porter. Reprinted from her volume *The Leaning Tower and Other Stories* by permission of Harcourt Brace Jovanovich, Inc.

"The Geese" from *Essays of E. B. White.* Copyright © 1971 by E. B. White. Reprinted by permission of Harper & Row, Publishers, Inc.

"The Ring of Time" from *Essays of E. B. White.* Copyright © 1956 by E. B. White. Reprinted by permission of Harper & Row, Publishers, Inc.

"Up in the Gallery" from *The Complete Stories* by Franz Kafka. Copyright © 1946–49, 1954, 1958, 1971 by Shocken Books, Inc. Reprinted by permission of Shocken Books Inc.

"Once More to the Lake" from *Essays of E. B. White.* Copyright 1941 by E. B. White. Reprinted by permission of Harper & Row, Publishers, Inc.

"Men at Forty" from *Night Light* by Donald Justice. Copyright © 1966 by Donald Justice. Reprinted from *Night Light* by permission of Wesleyan University Press.

"The Door" from *The Second Tree from the Corner* by E. B. White. Copyright 1939 by E. B. White. Reprinted by permission of Harper & Row, Publishers, Inc.

"A Hanging" from *Shooting An Elephant and Other Essays* by George Orwell, copyright 1950 by Sonia Brownell Orwell; renewed 1978 by Sonia Pitt-Rivers. Reprinted by permission of Harcourt Brace Jovanovich, Inc. and the Estate of the late Sonia Brownell Orwell and Secker & Warburg Limited.

"People" from *Selected Poems* by Yevgeny Yevtushenko, translated by Robin Milner-Gulland and Peter Levi, S. J. (Penguin Modern European Poets, 1962), copyright © Robin Milner-Gulland and Peter Levi, 1962.

"Michael Lake Describes What the Executioner Actually Faces," by Michael Lake in *Guardian,* April 19, 1973. Reprinted by permission of the author.

"Politics and the English Language" from *Shooting An Elephant and Other Essays* by George Orwell, copyright 1946 by Sonia Brownell Orwell; renewed 1974 by Sonia Orwell.

Reprinted by permission of Harcourt Brace Jovanovich, Inc., and the Estate of the Late Sonia Brownell Orwell and Secker & Warburg Limited.

"Shooting An Elephant" from *Shooting An Elephant and Other Essays* by George Orwell, copyright 1950 by Sonia Brownell Orwell; renewed 1978 by Sonia Pitt-Rivers. Reprinted by permission of Harcourt Brace Jovanovich, Inc. and the Estate of the late Sonia Brownell Orwell and Secker & Warburg Limited.

"Marrakech" from *Such, Such Were the Joys* by George Orwell, copyright 1953 by Sonia Brownell Orwell; renewed 1981 by Mrs. George K. Perutz, Mrs. Miriam Gross, Dr. Michael Dickson, Executors of the Estate of Sonia Brownell Orwell. Reprinted by permission of Harcourt Brace Jovanovich, Inc. and the Estate of the late Sonia Brownell Orwell and Secker & Warburg Limited.

Excerpt from Chapter 1 from *Nineteen Eighty-Four* by George Orwell, copyright 1949 by Harcourt Brace Jovanovich, Inc.; renewed 1977 by Sonia Brownell Orwell. Reprinted by permission of the publisher, the Estate of the late Sonia Brownell Orwell and Secker and Warburg Limited.

"Willy" from *All the Strange Hours* by Loren Eiseley. Copyright © 1975 Loren Eiseley. Reprinted with the permission of Charles Scribner's Sons, a division of Macmillan, Inc.

"The Hidden Teacher" from *The Unexpected Universe* by Loren Eiseley, copyright © 1964, 1969 by Loren Eiseley. Reprinted by permission of Harcourt Brace Jovanovich, Inc.

"Mind" from *Things of this world* by Richard Wilbur, copyright © 1956, 1984 by Richard Wilbur. Reprinted by permission of Harcourt Brace Jovanovich, Inc.

"The Illusion of the Two Cultures" from *The Star Thrower* by Loren Eiseley. Copyright © 1978 The Estate of Loren C. Eiseley, Mabel L. Eiseley, Executrix. Reprinted by permission of Times Books, a Division of Random House, Inc.

"The Dance of the Frogs" from *The Star Thrower* by Loren Eiseley. Copyright © 1978 The Estate of Loren C. Eiseley, Mabel L. Eiseley, Executrix. Reprinted by permission of Times Books, a Division of Random House, Inc.

"Stranger in the Village" from *Nobody Knows My Name,* by James Baldwin. Copyright © 1954, 1956, 1958, 1959, 1960, 1961 by James Baldwin. Reprinted by permission of Doubleday Publishing Group.

"Fifth Avenue, Uptown: A Letter from Harlem" from *Nobody Knows My Name* by James Baldwin. Copyright © 1954, 1956, 1958, 1959, 1960, 1961 by James Baldwin. Reprinted by permission of Doubleday Publishing Group.

"Notes of a Native Son" from *Notes of a Native Son* by James Baldwin. Copyright © 1955, renewed 1983, by James Baldwin. Reprinted by permission of Beacon Press.

"Sonny's Blues" from *Going to Meet the Man* by James Baldwin. Copyright © 1948, 1951, 1957, 1958, 1960, 1965 by James Baldwin. Reprinted by permission of Doubleday Publishing Group.

"The Masked Marvel's Last Toehold" from *Confessions of a Knife* by Richard Selzer. Copyright © 1979 David Goldman and Janet Selzer, Trustees. By permission of William Morrow & Co.

"Four Appointments with the Discus Thrower" from *Confessions of a Knife* by Richard Selzer. Copyright © 1979 David Goldman and Janet Selzer, Trustees. By permission of William Morrow & Co.

"Imelda" from *Letters to a Young Doctor* by Richard Selzer. Copyright © 1982 by David Goldman and Janet Selzer, Trustees. Reprinted by permission of Simon & Schuster, Inc.

"Minor Surgery" from *Rituals of Surgery* by Richard Selzer. Copyright © 1974 by Richard Selzer. By permission of William Morrow & Co.

"Playing Cowboy" from *Outlaws, Con Men, Whores, Politicians, & Other Artists* by Larry L. King. Copyright © 1974 by Larry L. King. All rights reserved. Reprinted by permission of Viking Penguin Inc.

"Shoot-out with Amarillo Slim" from *Outlaws, Con Men, Whores, Politicians, & Other Artists* by Larry L. King. Copyright © 1974 by Larry L. King. All rights reserved. Reprinted by permission of Viking Penguin Inc.

"Remembering the Hard Times" from *Outlaws, Con Men, Whores, Politicians, & Other Artists* by Larry L. King. Copyright © 1974 by Larry L. King. All rights reserved. Reprinted by permission of Viking Penguin Inc.

"The American Redneck" from *Outlaws, Con Men, Whores, Politicians, & Other Artists* by Larry L. King. Copyright © 1974 by Larry L. King. All rights reserved. Reprinted by permission of Viking Penguin Inc.

"The Angels" from *The Right Stuff* by Tom Wolfe. Copyright © 1979 by Tom Wolfe. Reprinted by permission of Farrar, Straus and Giroux, Inc.

"The Right Stuff" from *The Right Stuff* by Tom Wolfe. Copyright © 1979 by Tom Wolfe. Reprinted by permission of Farrar, Straus and Giroux, Inc.

"Funky Chic" from *Mauve Gloves & Madmen, Clutter & Vine* by Tom Wolfe. Copyright © 1968, 1976 by Tom Wolfe. Reprinted by permission of Farrar, Straus and Giroux, Inc.

"Honks and Wonks" from *Mauve Gloves & Madmen, Clutter & Vine,* by Tom Wolfe. Copyright © 1968, 1973, 1976 by Tom Wolfe. Reprinted by permission of Farrar, Straus and Giroux, Inc.

"Styrofoam Peanuts" from *The Bonfire of the Vanities* by Tom Wolfe. Copyright © 1987 by Tom Wolfe. Reprinted by permission of Farrar, Straus and Giroux, Inc.

"On Self-Respect" from *Slouching Towards Bethlehem* by Joan Didion. Copyright © 1961, 1968 by Joan Didion. Reprinted by permission of Farrar, Straus and Giroux, Inc.

"Goodbye to All That" from *Slouching Towards Bethlehem* by Joan Didion. Copyright © 1961, 1967, 1968 by Joan Didion. Reprinted by permission of Farrar, Straus and Giroux, Inc.

"Why I Write" by Joan Didion. Reprinted by permission of Wallace & Sheil Agency, Inc. Copyright © 1976 by Joan Didion. First published in the New York Times Book Review.

"Georgia O'Keeffe" from *The White Album* by Joan Didion. Copyright © 1979 by Joan Didion. Reprinted by permission of Simon & Schuster, Inc.

Chapters 1, 2, and 3 from *Democracy* by Joan Didion. Copyright © 1984 by Joan Didion. Reprinted by permission of Simon & Schuster, Inc.

"Tillie Olsen: Silences" from *Second Words: Selected Critical Prose* by Margaret Atwood. Copyright © 1982 by O. W. Toad Limited (Toronto: House of Anansi Press). First published in the United States by Beacon Press, 1984. Reprinted by permission of Beacon Press and House of Anansi Press.

"Adrienne Rich: Of Woman Born" from *Second Words: Selected Critical Prose* by Margaret Atwood. Copyright © 1982 by O. W. Toad Limited (Toronto: House of Anansi Press). First published in the United States by Beacon Press, 1984. Reprinted by permission of Beacon Press and House of Anansi Press.

"On Being a Woman Writer: Paradoxes and Dilemmas" from *Second Words: Selected Critical Prose* by Margaret Atwood. Copyright © 1982 by O. W. Toad Limited (Toronto: House of Anansi Press). First published in the United States by Beacon Press, 1984. Reprinted by permission of Beacon Press and House of Anansi Press.

"Giving Birth" from *Dancing Girls* by Margaret Atwood. Copyright © 1977, 1982 by O. W. Toad, Ltd. Reprinted by permission of Simon & Schuster, Inc. and the Canadian Publishers, McClelland and Stewart, Toronto.

"The Black Writer and the Southern Experience" from *In Search of Our Mothers' Gardens* by Alice Walker. Copyright © 1983 by Alice Walker. Reprinted from her volume *In Search of Our Mothers' Gardens* by permission of Harcourt Brace Jovanovich, Inc.

"Beauty: When the Other Dancer Is the Self" from *In Search of Our Mothers' Gardens* by Alice Walker. Copyright © 1983 by Alice Walker. Reprinted from her volume *In Search of Our Mothers' Gardens* by permission of Harcourt Brace Jovanovich, Inc.

"Motheroot" from *Abiding Appalachia* by Marilou Awiakta. Copyright © 1978. Reprinted by permission of St. Lukes Press.

"In Search of Our Mothers' Gardens" from *In Search of Our Mothers' Gardens* by Alice Walker. Copyright © 1974 by Alice Walker. Reprinted from her volume *In Search of Our Mothers' Gardens* by permission of Harcourt Brace Jovanovich, Inc.

"Everyday Use" from *In Love & Trouble* by Alice Walker. Copyright © 1973 by Alice Walker. Reprinted from her volume *In Love & Trouble* by permission of Harcourt Brace Jovanovich, Inc.

"Seeing" from *Pilgrim at Tinker Creek* by Annie Dillard. Copyright © 1974 by Annie Dillard. Reprinted by permission of Harper & Row, Publishers, Inc.

"The Pardon" from *Ceremony and Other Poems* by Richard Wilbur, copyright 1950, 1978 by Richard Wilbur. Reprinted by permission of Harcourt Brace Jovanovich, Inc.

"Living Like Weasels" from *Teaching A Stone to Talk* by Annie Dillard. Copyright © 1982 by Annie Dillard. Reprinted by permission of Harper & Row, Publishers, Inc.

"The Deer at Providencia" from *Teaching A Stone to Talk* by Annie Dillard. Copyright © 1982 by Annie Dillard. Reprinted by permission of Harper & Row, Publishers, Inc.

"Sojourner" from *Teaching A Stone to Talk* by Annie Dillard. Copyright © 1982 by Annie Dillard. Reprinted by permission of Harper & Row, Publishers, Inc.

"God's Tooth" from *Holy the Firm* by Annie Dillard. Copyright © 1977 by Annie Dillard. Reprinted by permission of Harper & Row, Publishers, Inc.

Portions of the biographical essay on Gretel Ehrlich on pages 573 to 574 appear in a critical piece by Pat C. Hoy II in the Winter 1987 issue of *The Sewanee Review.*

"About Men" from *The Solace of Open Spaces* by Gretel Ehrlich. Copyright © 1985 by Gretel Ehrlich. All rights reserved. Reprinted by permission of Viking Penguin Inc.

"The Smooth Skull of Winter" from *The Solace of Open Spaces* by Gretel Ehrlich. Copyright © 1985 by Gretel Ehrlich. All rights reserved. Reprinted by permission of Viking Penguin Inc.

"On Water" from *The Solace of Open Spaces* by Gretel Ehrlich. Copyright © 1985 by Gretel Ehrlich. All rights reserved. Reprinted by permission of Viking Penguin Inc.

"A Storm, the Cornfield, and Elk" from *The Solace of Open Spaces* by Gretel Ehrlich. Copyright © 1985 by Gretel Ehrlich. All rights reserved. Reprinted by permission of Viking Penguin Inc.

"McKay" from *Wyoming Stories/City Tales,* by Gretel Ehrlich, from Vol. VI, Capra Back-to-Back Series, © 1986 by Gretel Ehrlich. Reprinted by permission of Capra Press, Santa Barbara.

"The Mother" by Gwendolyn Brooks. Reprinted by permission of Gwendolyn Brooks (The David Company).

ABOUT THE EDITORS

Pat C. Hoy II is a Professor of English at the U. S. Military Academy where he directs the freshman writing program and teaches British and American Literature and Composition. He has also taught writing courses at Bergen Community College. He received his B.A. from the Military Academy and his Ph.D. from the University of Pennsylvania.

He is especially interested in pedagogical notions that link the modern essay with writing theory. His interest in the literary aspects of nonfiction draws sustenance from the courses he teaches on Conrad, Woolf, Lawrence, and Forster. His publications include articles and reviews in *South Atlantic Review, Twentieth Century Literature,* and *The Sewanee Review.* A recent essay on images and ideas will be included in *Literary Nonfiction: Theory, Criticism, Pedagogy* (Southern Illinois University Press, 1989). *Women's Voices* (with Esther Schor and Robert DiYanni) is forthcoming from Random House. He is also at work on *Writing Essays: A Persuasive Art* (McGraw-Hill, 1989).

Robert DiYanni is Professor of English at Pace University, Pleasantville, New York where he teaches courses in Literature, Music, and Composition. He is also Director of Interdisciplinary Studies.

Professor DiYanni received his B.A. from Rutgers and his Ph.D. from the City University of New York. He has published articles and reviews on various aspects of literature and pedagogy. Among his publications are a number of textbooks including *Connections* (Boynton/Cook, 1985); *Literature* (Random House, 1986); *Modern American Prose* (with John Clifford, Random House, 1986); *The Art of Reading* (with Eric Gould and William Smith, Random House, 1987); *Reading Fiction* (Random House, 1988); and *Like Season'd Timber: The Work of George Herbert* (with Edmund Miller for Peter Lang, 1988). He is currently co-editing a book of essays by women writers *(Women's Voices)* and is collaborating on a Humanities textbook.